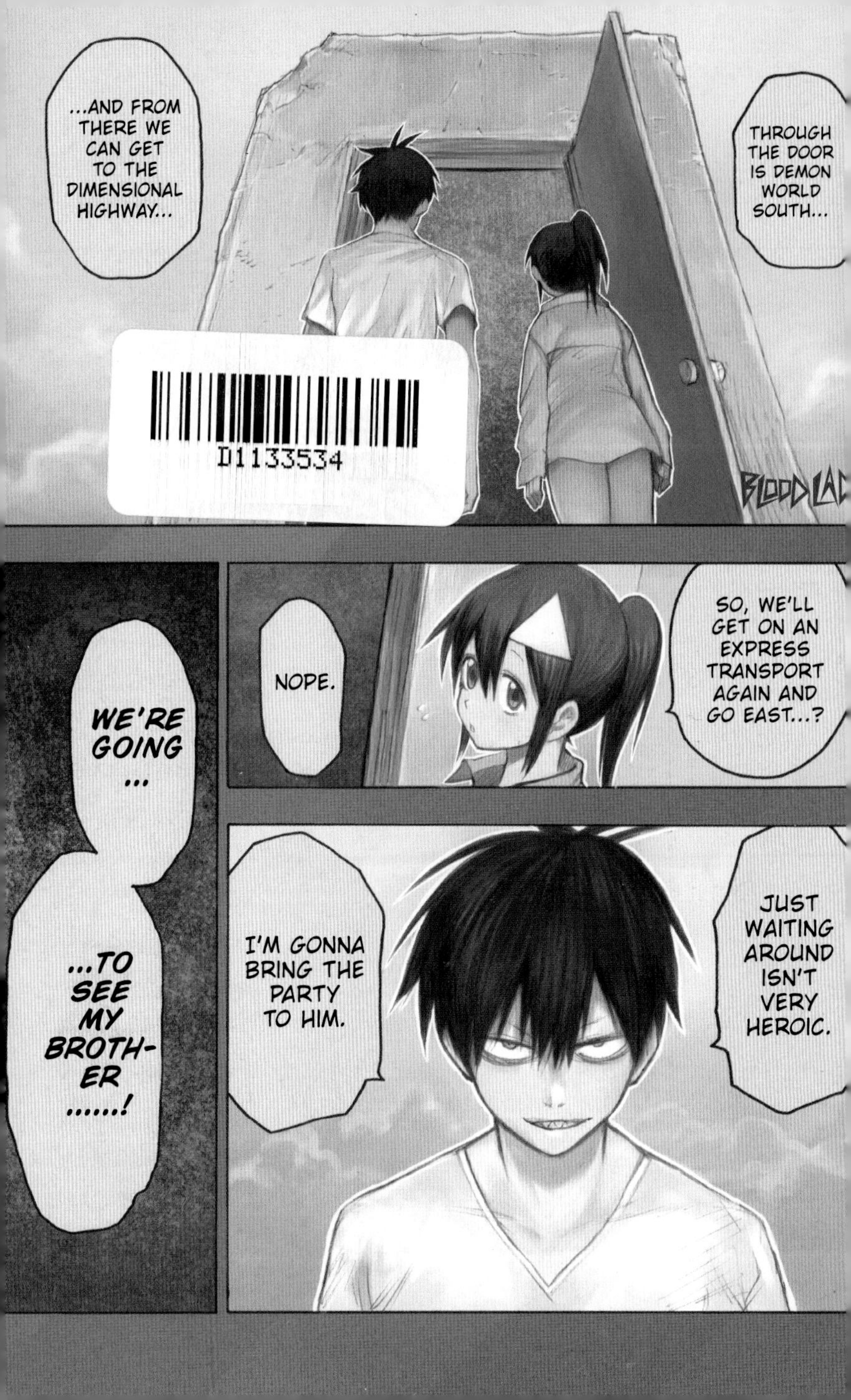
THROUGH THE DOOR IS DEMON WORLD SOUTH...
...AND FROM THERE WE CAN GET TO THE DIMENSIONAL HIGHWAY...
SO, WE'LL GET ON AN EXPRESS TRANSPORT AGAIN AND GO EAST...?
NOPE.
JUST WAITING AROUND ISN'T VERY HEROIC.
I'M GONNA BRING THE PARTY TO HIM.
WE'RE GOING...
...TO SEE MY BROTHER......!

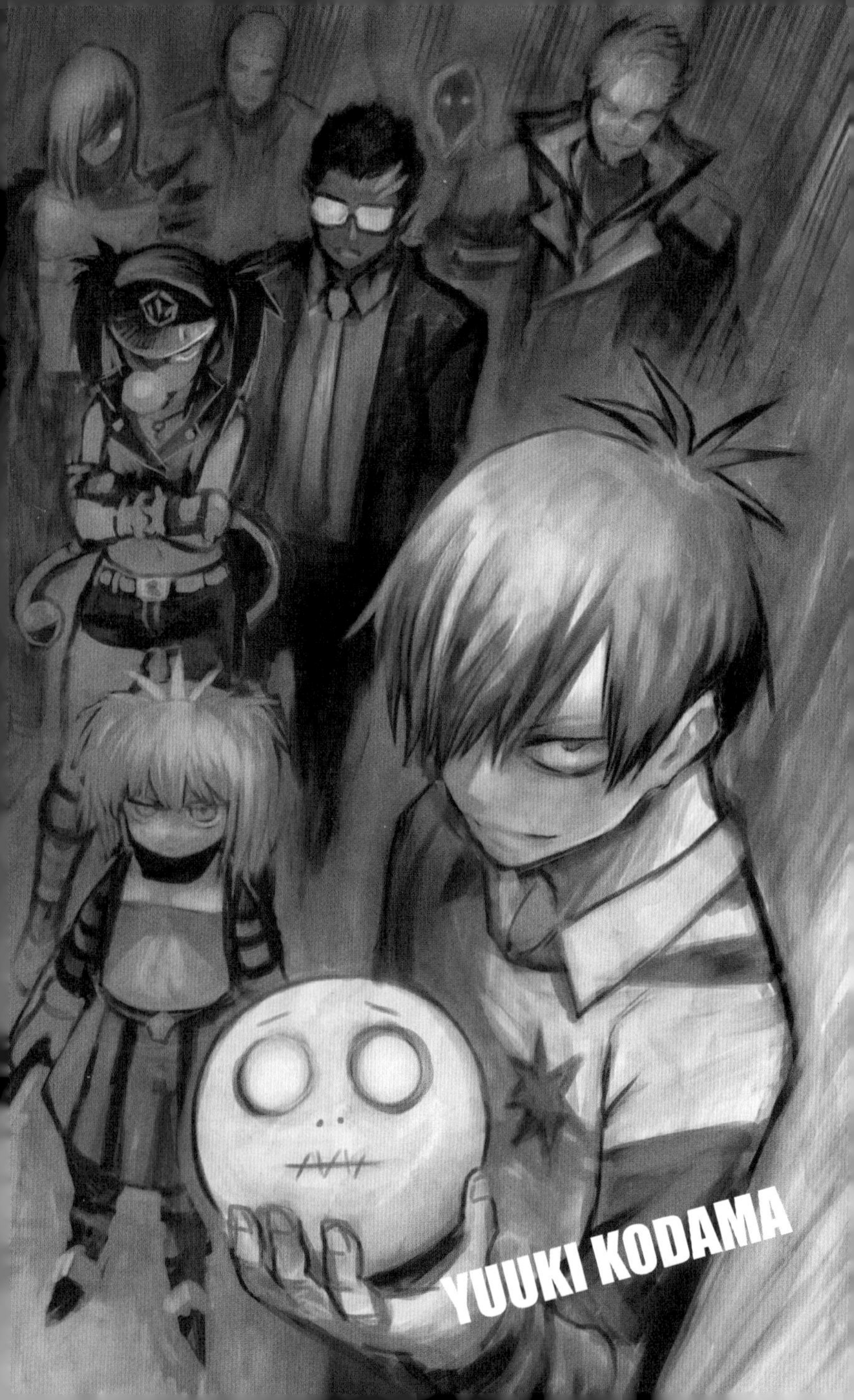
YUUKI KODAMA

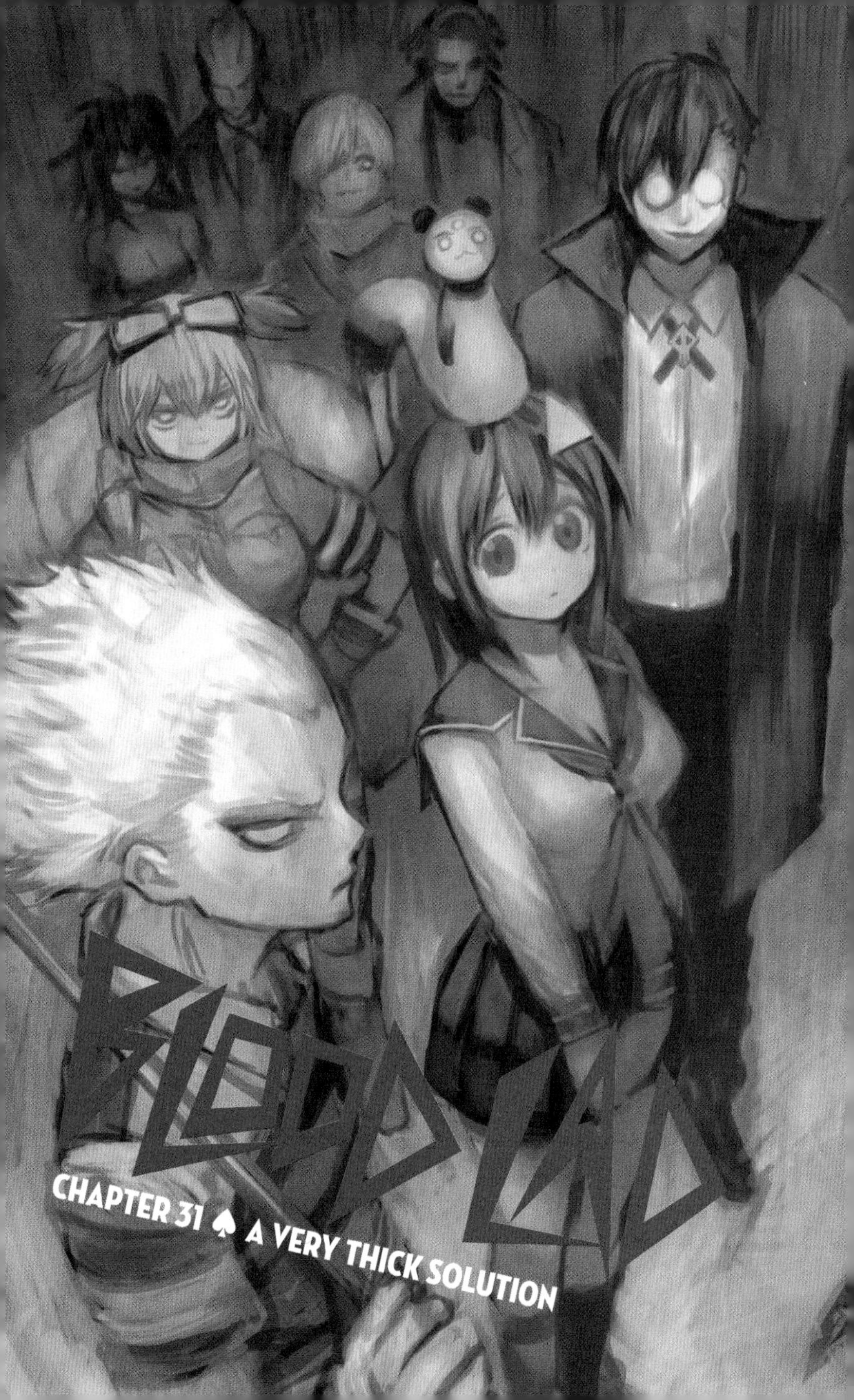
BLOOD LAD
CHAPTER 31 ♠ A VERY THICK SOLUTION

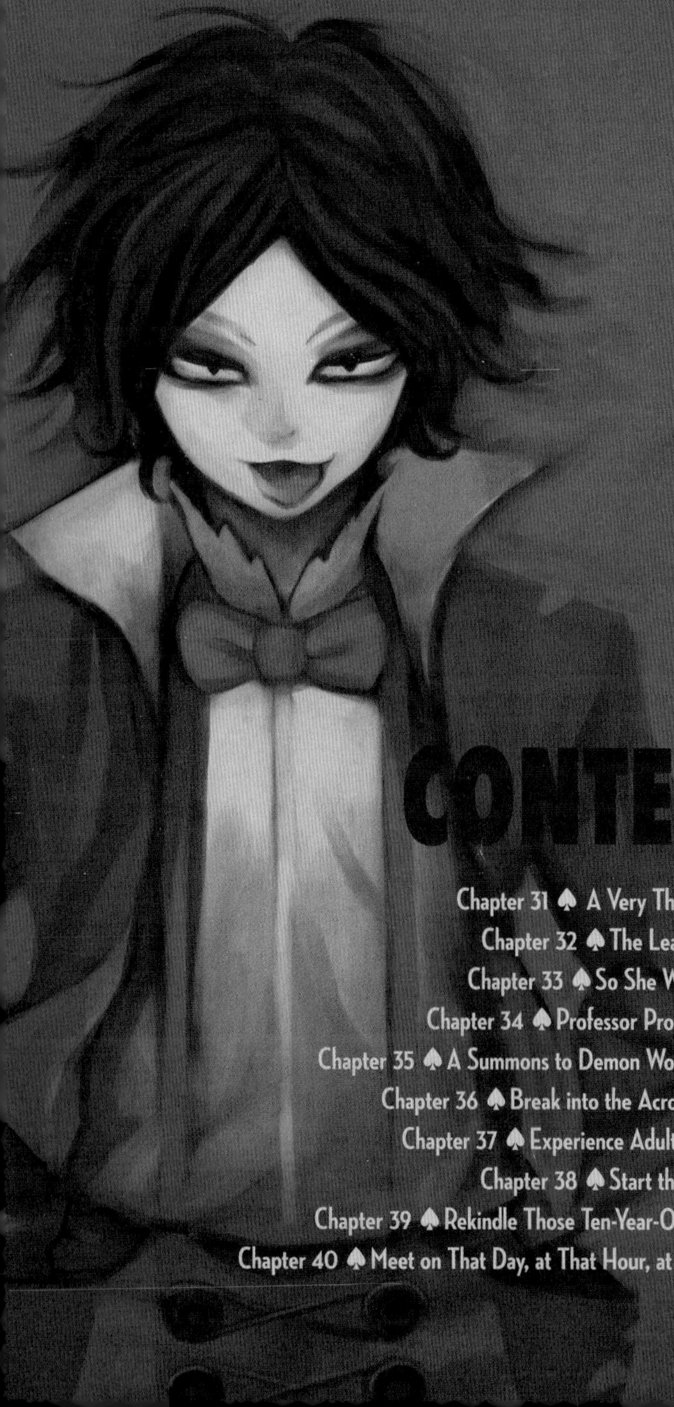

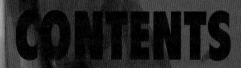

CONTENTS

BLOOD LAD 8

These images appeared under the jacket of the original edition of *Blood Lad*!

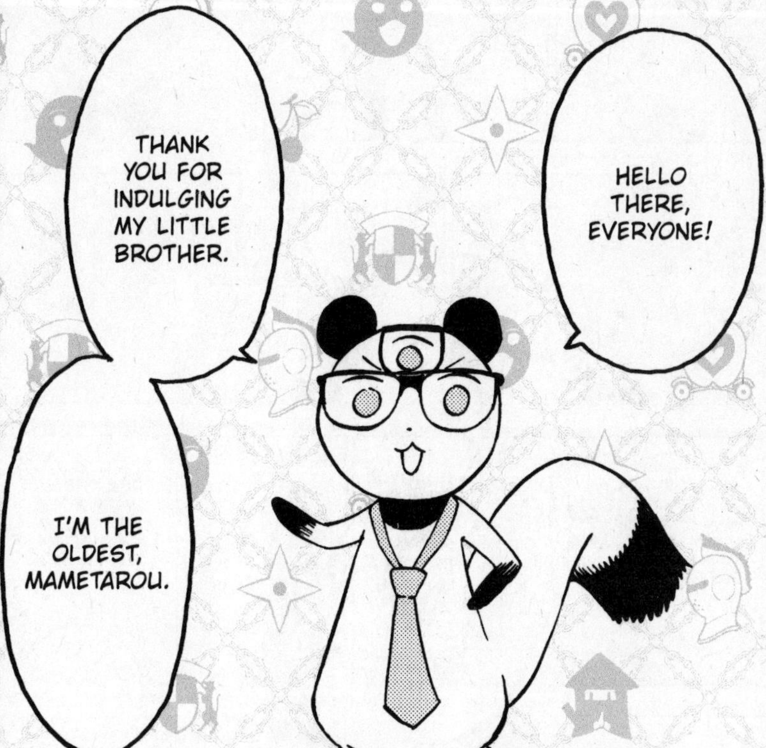
HELLO THERE, EVERYONE!
THANK YOU FOR INDULGING MY LITTLE BROTHER.
I'M THE OLDEST, MAMETAROU.

NOTE: "TAROU" IS A TRADITIONAL NAME ENDING FOR THE FIRST SON IN A FAMILY.

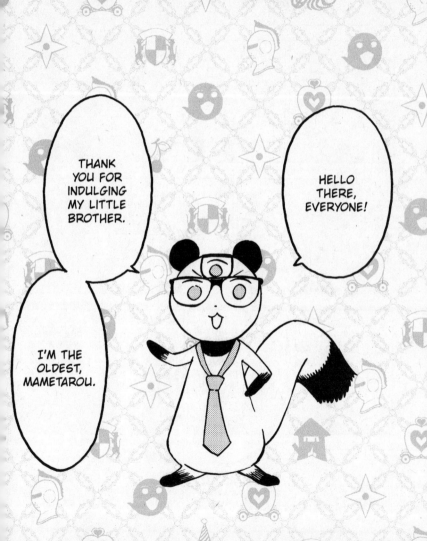

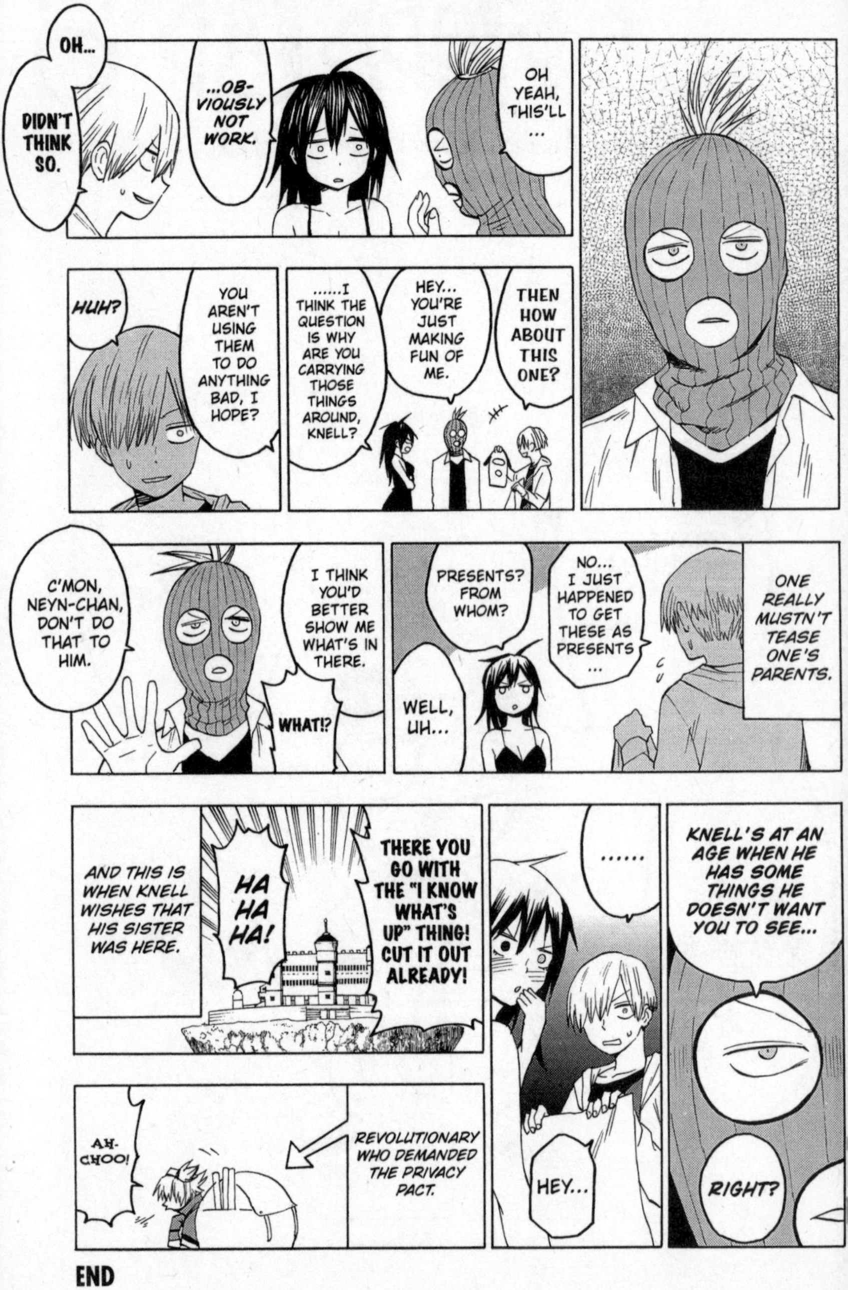
OH YEAH, THIS'LL ...
...OB-VIOUSLY NOT WORK.
OH...
DIDN'T THINK SO.
THEN HOW ABOUT THIS ONE?
HEY... YOU'RE JUST MAKING FUN OF ME.
......I THINK THE QUESTION IS WHY ARE YOU CARRYING THOSE THINGS AROUND, KNELL?
YOU AREN'T USING THEM TO DO ANYTHING BAD, I HOPE?
HUH?
ONE REALLY MUSTN'T TEASE ONE'S PARENTS.
NO... I JUST HAPPENED TO GET THESE AS PRESENTS ...
PRESENTS? FROM WHOM?
WELL, UH...
I THINK YOU'D BETTER SHOW ME WHAT'S IN THERE.
WHAT!?
C'MON, NEYN-CHAN, DON'T DO THAT TO HIM.
KNELL'S AT AN AGE WHEN HE HAS SOME THINGS HE DOESN'T WANT YOU TO SEE...
RIGHT?
......
HEY...
THERE YOU GO WITH THE "I KNOW WHAT'S UP" THING! CUT IT OUT ALREADY!
HA HA HA!
AND THIS IS WHEN KNELL WISHES THAT HIS SISTER WAS HERE.
REVOLUTIONARY WHO DEMANDED THE PRIVACY PACT.
AH-CHOO!

END

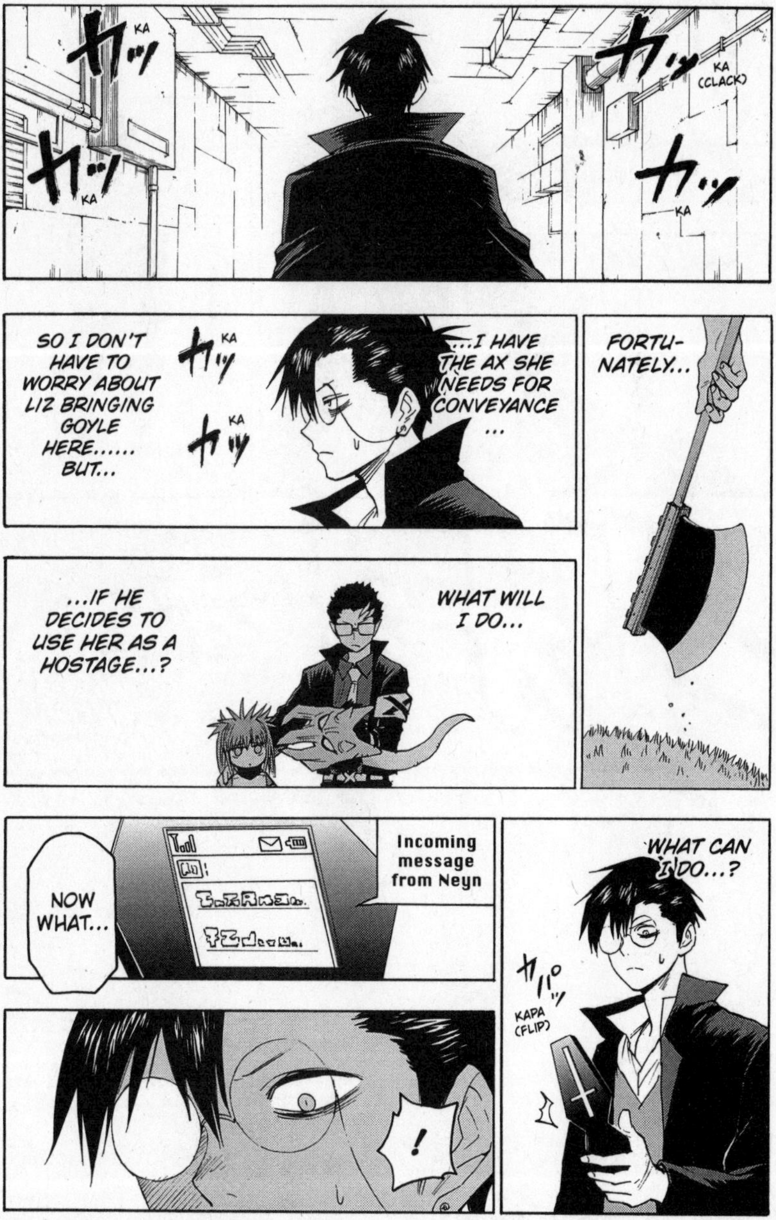

カッ
KA
(CLACK)
カッ
KA
カッ
KA
カッ
KA
FORTUNATELY...
...I HAVE THE AX SHE NEEDS FOR CONVEYANCE ...
カッ
KA
カッ
KA
SO I DON'T HAVE TO WORRY ABOUT LIZ BRINGING GOYLE HERE...... BUT...
WHAT WILL I DO...
...IF HE DECIDES TO USE HER AS A HOSTAGE...?
WHAT CAN I DO...?
カパッ
KAPA
(FLIP)
Incoming message from Neyn
NOW WHAT...
!

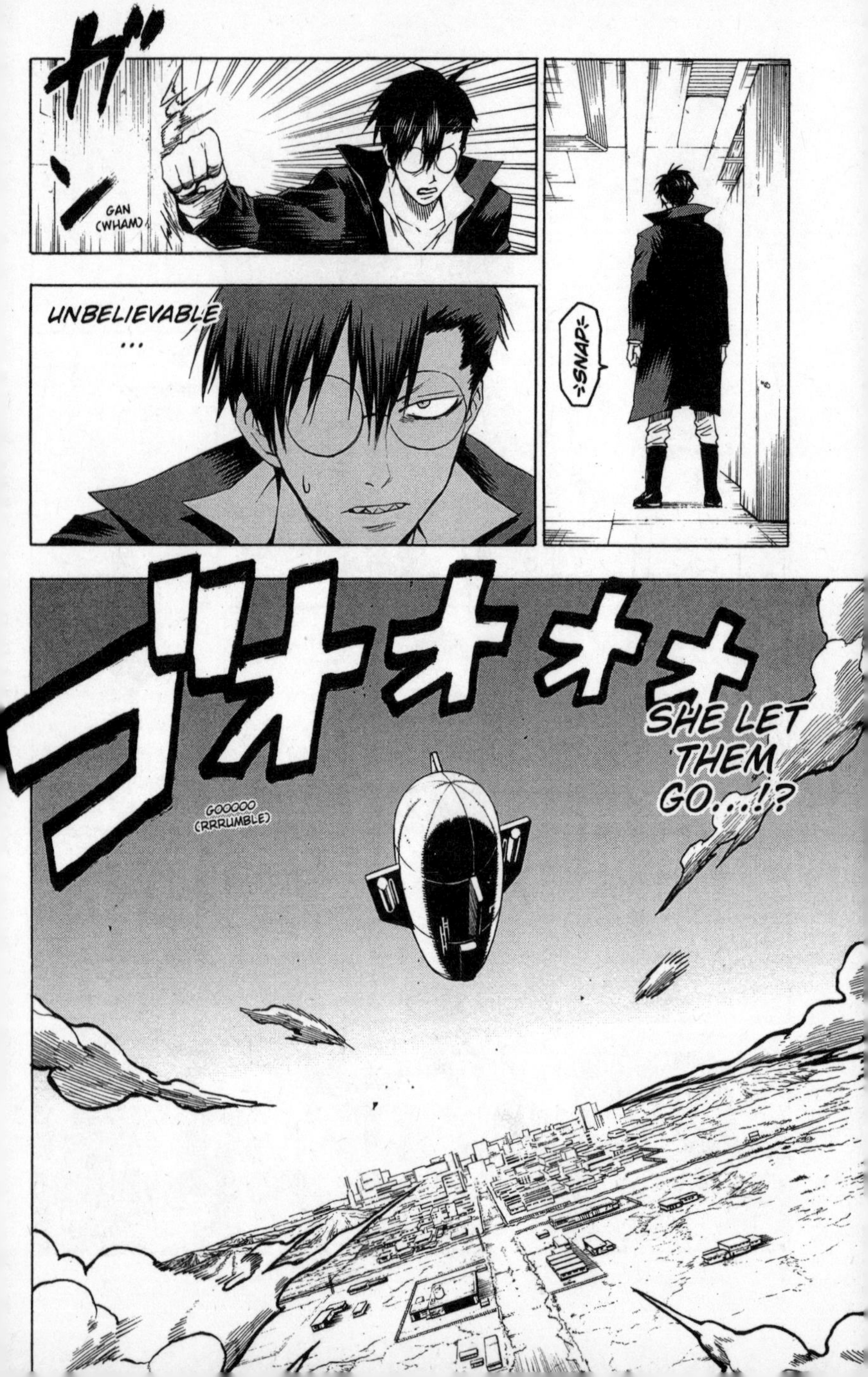

SNAP
ガン
GAN (WHAM)
UNBELIEVABLE...
ゴオオオ
SHE LET THEM GO...!?
GOOOOO (RRRUMBLE)

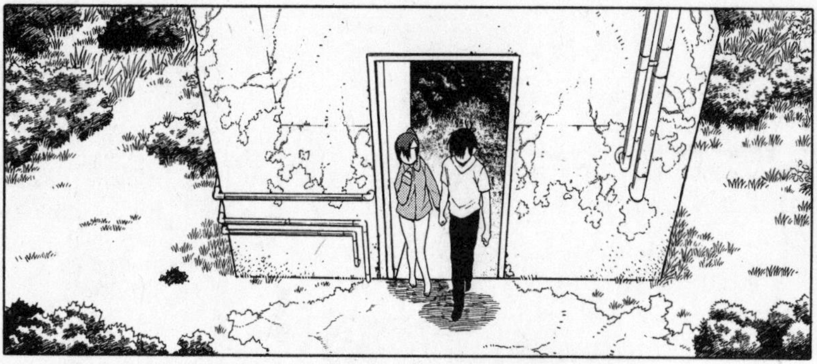

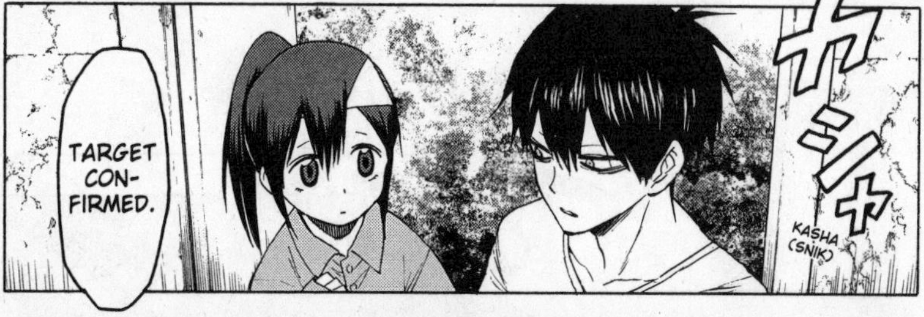
カシャ
KASHA (SNIK)
TARGET CON-FIRMED.

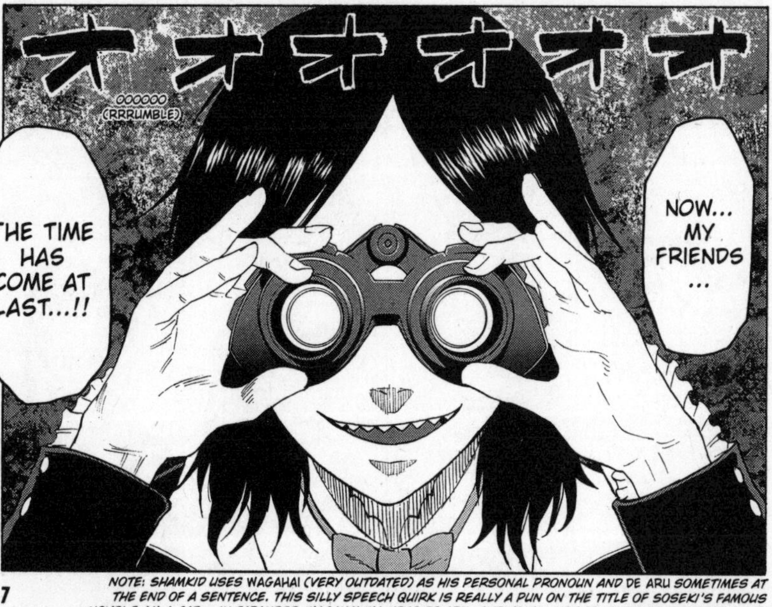
オオオオオオ
OOOOOO (RRRUMBLE)
NOW... MY FRIENDS ...
THE TIME HAS COME AT LAST...!!

NOTE: SHAMKID USES WAGAHAI (VERY OUTDATED) AS HIS PERSONAL PRONOUN AND DE ARU SOMETIMES AT THE END OF A SENTENCE. THIS SILLY SPEECH QUIRK IS REALLY A PUN ON THE TITLE OF SOSEKI'S FAMOUS NOVEL I AM A CAT—IN JAPANESE, WAGAHAI WA NEKO DE ARU. AND YOU'LL NOTICE, SHAMKID IS INDEED A CAT.

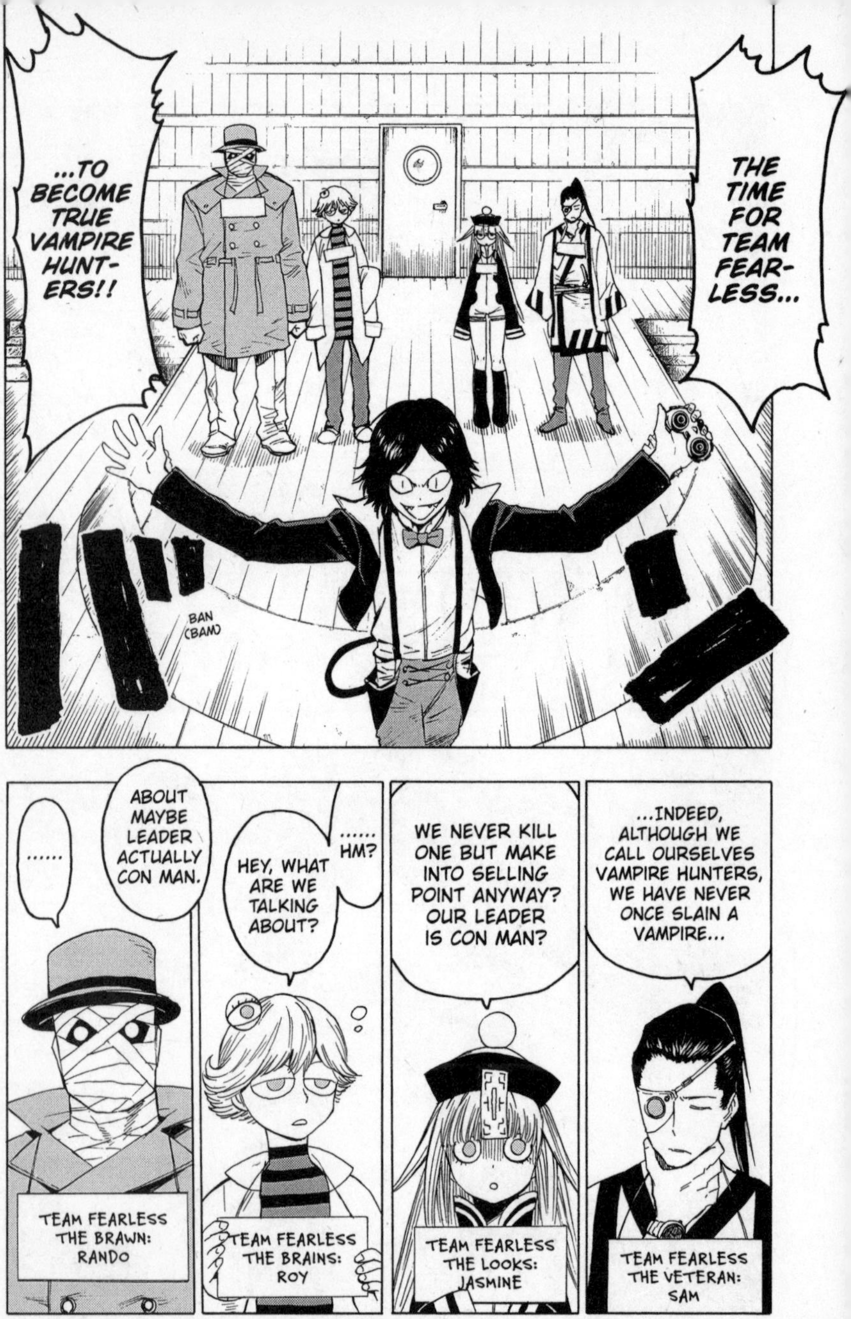
THE TIME FOR TEAM FEARLESS...
...TO BECOME TRUE VAMPIRE HUNTERS!!
BAN (BAM)
...INDEED, ALTHOUGH WE CALL OURSELVES VAMPIRE HUNTERS, WE HAVE NEVER ONCE SLAIN A VAMPIRE...
TEAM FEARLESS THE VETERAN: SAM
WE NEVER KILL ONE BUT MAKE INTO SELLING POINT ANYWAY? OUR LEADER IS CON MAN?
TEAM FEARLESS THE LOOKS: JASMINE
......HM?
HEY, WHAT ARE WE TALKING ABOUT?
TEAM FEARLESS THE BRAINS: ROY
ABOUT MAYBE LEADER ACTUALLY CON MAN.
......
TEAM FEARLESS THE BRAWN: RANDO

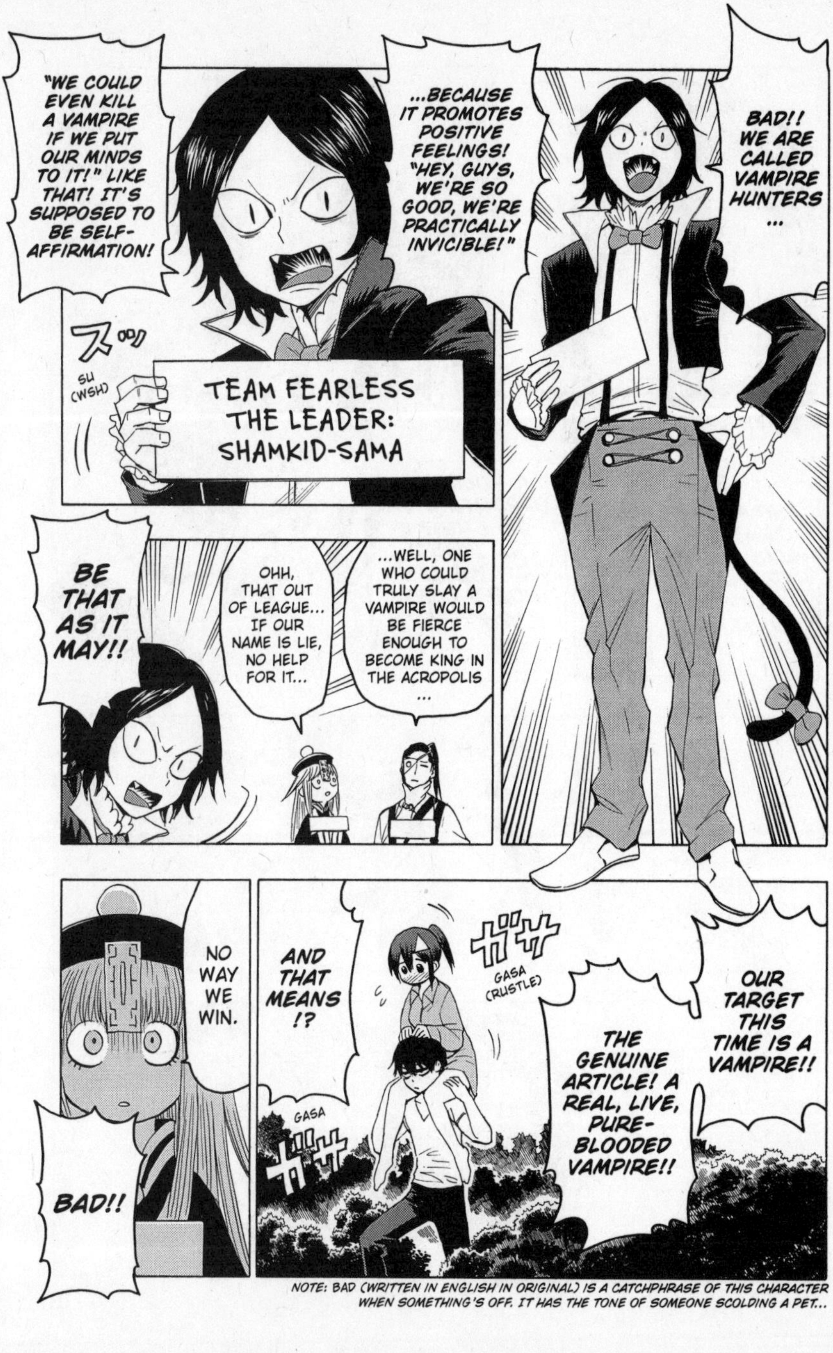
BAD!! WE ARE CALLED VAMPIRE HUNTERS ...
...BECAUSE IT PROMOTES POSITIVE FEELINGS! "HEY, GUYS, WE'RE SO GOOD, WE'RE PRACTICALLY INVICIBLE!"
"WE COULD EVEN KILL A VAMPIRE IF WE PUT OUR MINDS TO IT!" LIKE THAT! IT'S SUPPOSED TO BE SELF-AFFIRMATION!
SU (WSH)
TEAM FEARLESS THE LEADER: SHAMKID-SAMA
...WELL, ONE WHO COULD TRULY SLAY A VAMPIRE WOULD BE FIERCE ENOUGH TO BECOME KING IN THE ACROPOLIS ...
OHH, THAT OUT OF LEAGUE... IF OUR NAME IS LIE, NO HELP FOR IT...
BE THAT AS IT MAY!!
OUR TARGET THIS TIME IS A VAMPIRE!!
THE GENUINE ARTICLE! A REAL, LIVE, PURE-BLOODED VAMPIRE!!
GASA (RUSTLE)
AND THAT MEANS !?
GASA
NO WAY WE WIN.
BAD!!

NOTE: BAD (WRITTEN IN ENGLISH IN ORIGINAL) IS A CATCHPHRASE OF THIS CHARACTER WHEN SOMETHING'S OFF. IT HAS THE TONE OF SOMEONE SCOLDING A PET...

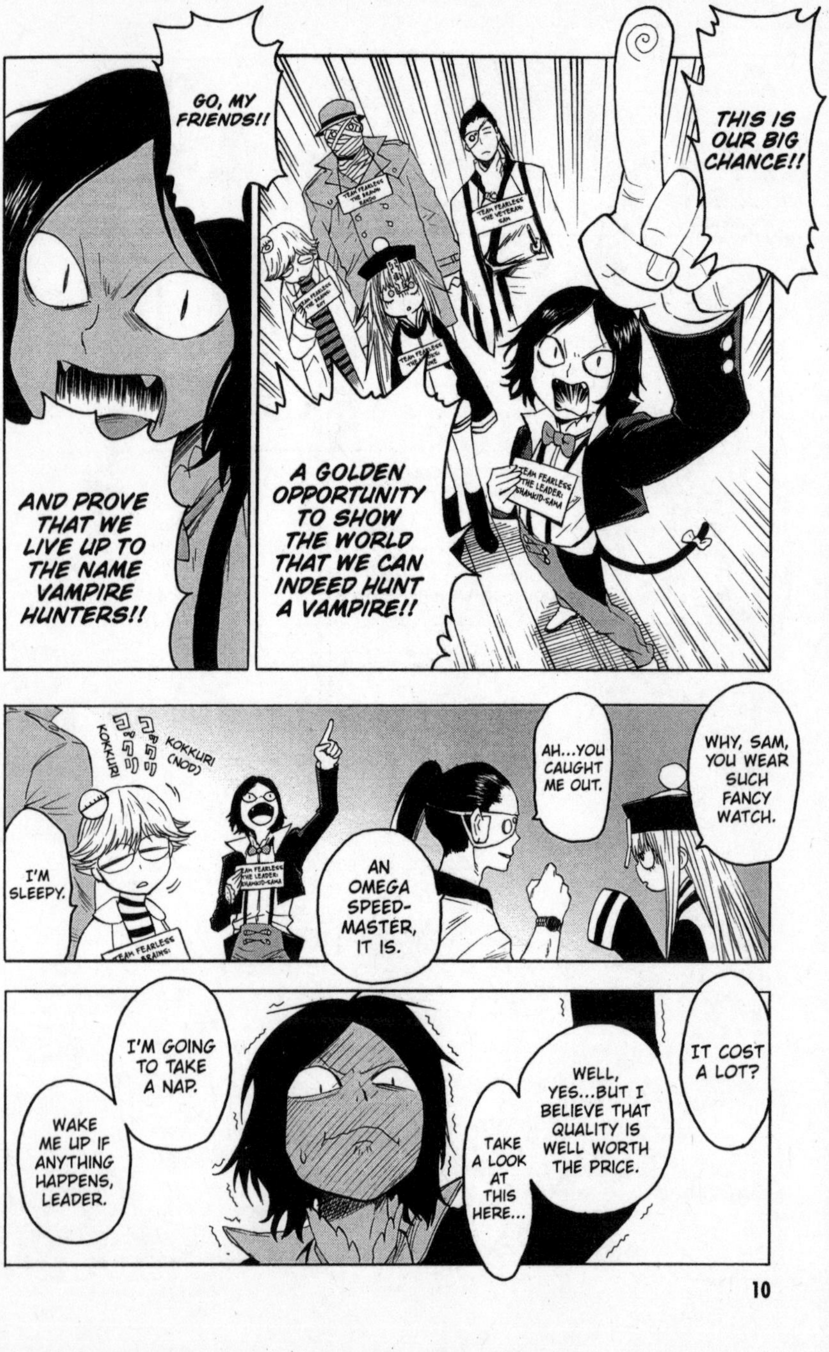
THIS IS OUR BIG CHANCE!!
A GOLDEN OPPORTUNITY TO SHOW THE WORLD THAT WE CAN INDEED HUNT A VAMPIRE!!
GO, MY FRIENDS!!
AND PROVE THAT WE LIVE UP TO THE NAME VAMPIRE HUNTERS!!
TEAM FEARLESS THE LEADER: SHAMKID-SAMA
WHY, SAM, YOU WEAR SUCH FANCY WATCH.
AH...YOU CAUGHT ME OUT.
AN OMEGA SPEED-MASTER, IT IS.
KOKKURI (NOD)
I'M SLEEPY.
IT COST A LOT?
WELL, YES...BUT I BELIEVE THAT QUALITY IS WELL WORTH THE PRICE.
TAKE A LOOK AT THIS HERE...
I'M GOING TO TAKE A NAP.
WAKE ME UP IF ANYTHING HAPPENS, LEADER.

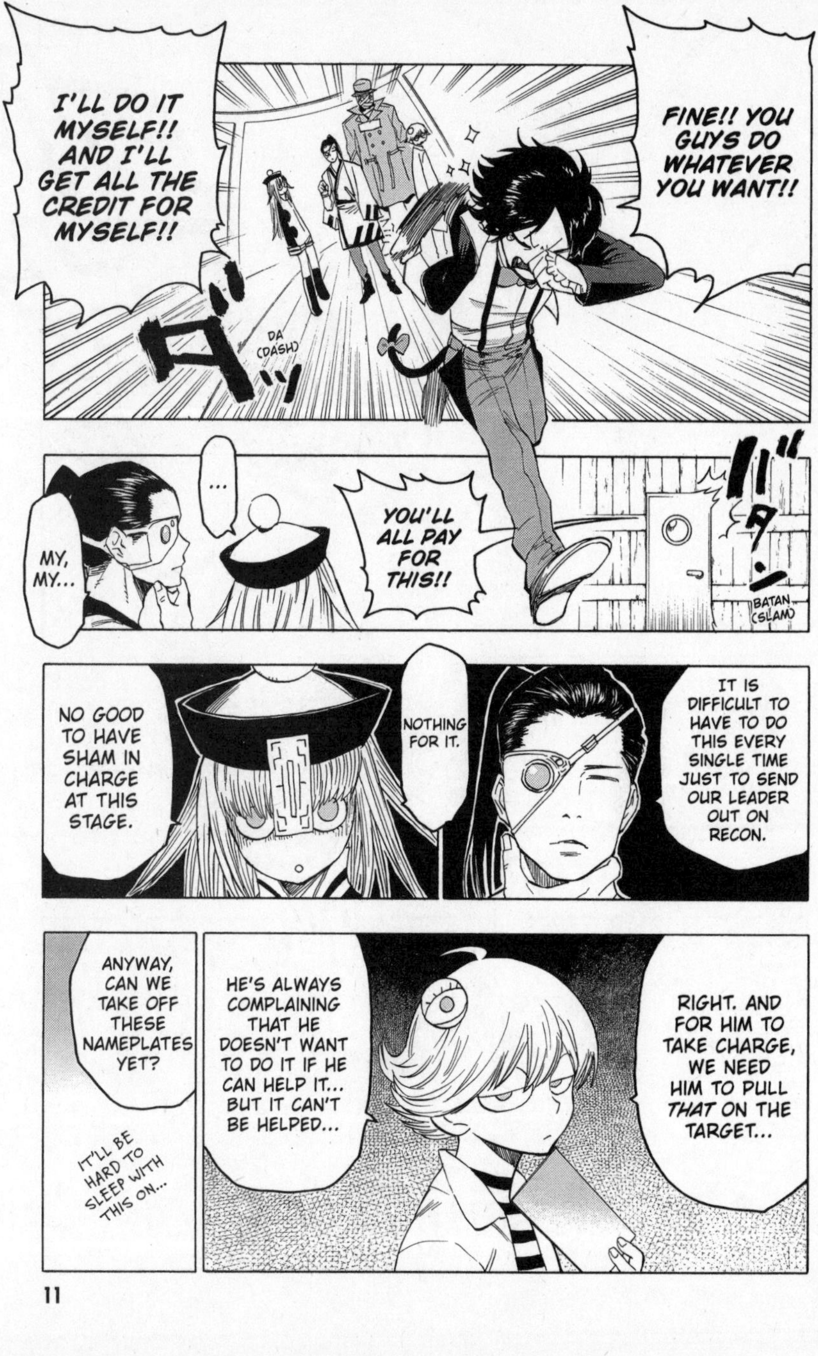
FINE!! YOU GUYS DO WHATEVER YOU WANT!!
I'LL DO IT MYSELF!! AND I'LL GET ALL THE CREDIT FOR MYSELF!!
DA (DASH)
BATAN (SLAM)
YOU'LL ALL PAY FOR THIS!!
...
MY, MY...
IT IS DIFFICULT TO HAVE TO DO THIS EVERY SINGLE TIME JUST TO SEND OUR LEADER OUT ON RECON.
NOTHING FOR IT.
NO GOOD TO HAVE SHAM IN CHARGE AT THIS STAGE.
RIGHT. AND FOR HIM TO TAKE CHARGE, WE NEED HIM TO PULL THAT ON THE TARGET...
HE'S ALWAYS COMPLAINING THAT HE DOESN'T WANT TO DO IT IF HE CAN HELP IT... BUT IT CAN'T BE HELPED...
ANYWAY, CAN WE TAKE OFF THESE NAMEPLATES YET?
IT'LL BE HARD TO SLEEP WITH THIS ON...

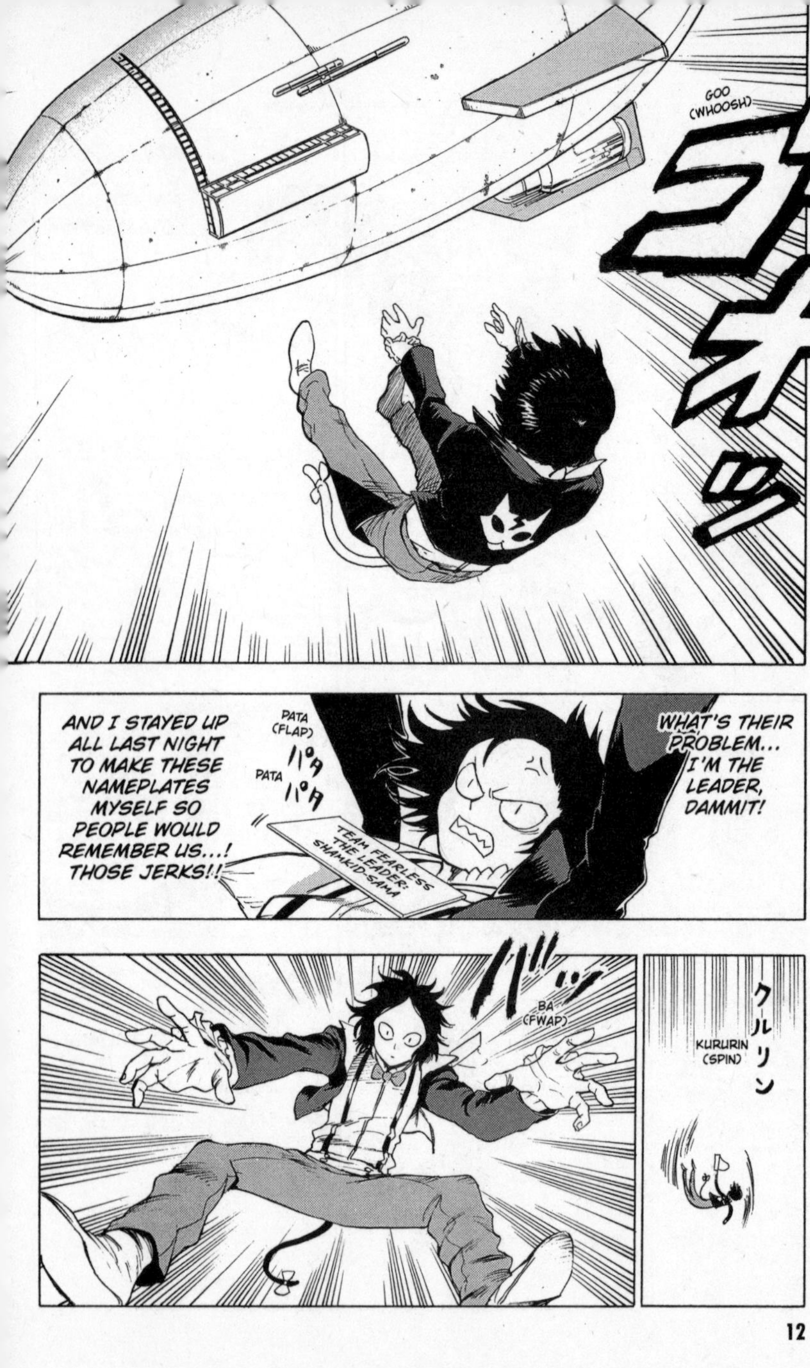
GOO (WHOOSH)
WHAT'S THEIR PROBLEM... I'M THE LEADER, DAMMIT!
パタ
PATA (FLAP)
パタ
PATA
AND I STAYED UP ALL LAST NIGHT TO MAKE THESE NAMEPLATES MYSELF SO PEOPLE WOULD REMEMBER US...! THOSE JERKS!!
TEAM FEARLESS THE LEADER: SHAMKID-SAMA
クルリン
KURURIN (SPIN)
バッ
BA (FWAP)

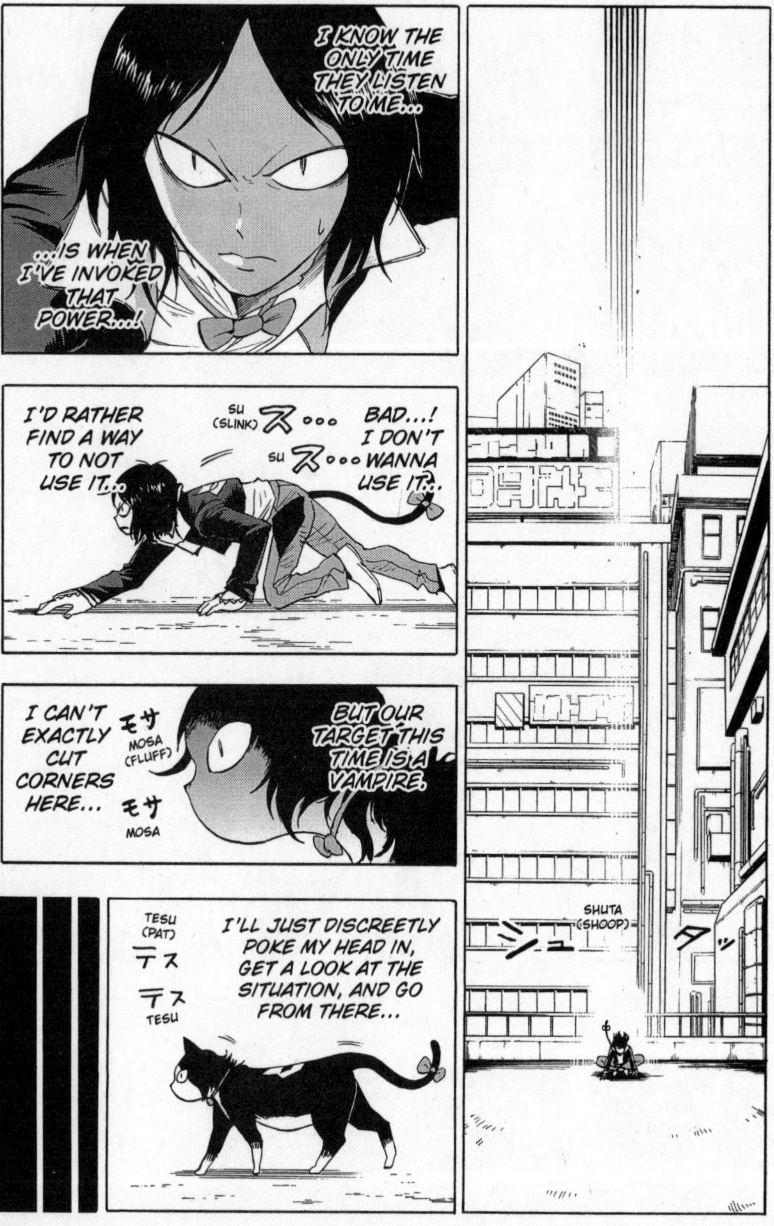

シュ
SHUTA (SHOOP)
タッ
I KNOW THE ONLY TIME THEY LISTEN TO ME...
...IS WHEN I'VE INVOKED THAT POWER...!
BAD...! I DON'T WANNA USE IT...
ス...
SU (SLINK)
ス...
SU
I'D RATHER FIND A WAY TO NOT USE IT...
BUT OUR TARGET THIS TIME IS A VAMPIRE.
モサ
MOSA (FLUFF)
モサ
MOSA
I CAN'T EXACTLY CUT CORNERS HERE...
I'LL JUST DISCREETLY POKE MY HEAD IN, GET A LOOK AT THE SITUATION, AND GO FROM THERE...
テス
TESU (PAT)
テス
TESU

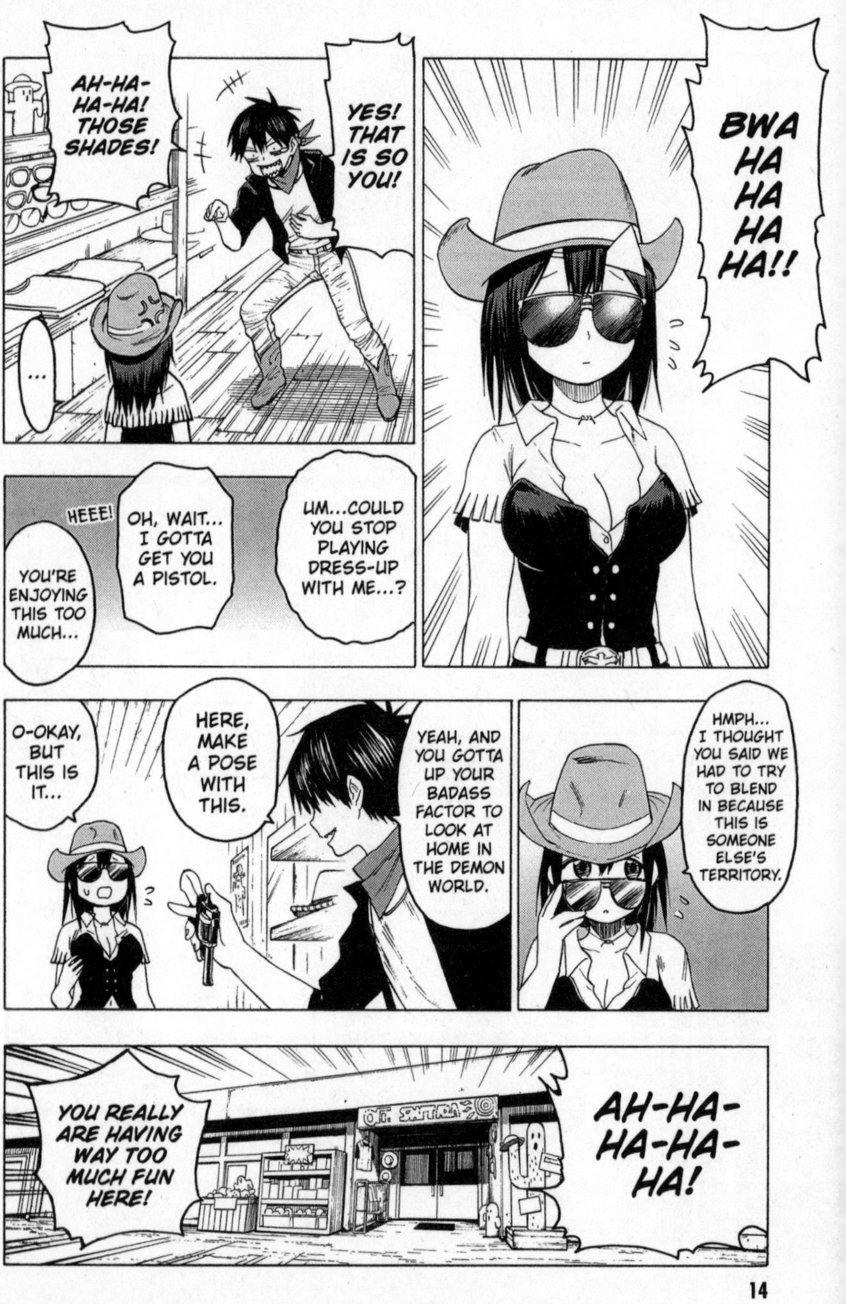
BWA HA HA HA HA!!
YES! THAT IS SO YOU!
AH-HA-HA-HA! THOSE SHADES!
...
UM...COULD YOU STOP PLAYING DRESS-UP WITH ME...?
OH, WAIT... I GOTTA GET YOU A PISTOL.
HEEE!
YOU'RE ENJOYING THIS TOO MUCH...
HMPH... I THOUGHT YOU SAID WE HAD TO TRY TO BLEND IN BECAUSE THIS IS SOMEONE ELSE'S TERRITORY.
YEAH, AND YOU GOTTA UP YOUR BADASS FACTOR TO LOOK AT HOME IN THE DEMON WORLD.
HERE, MAKE A POSE WITH THIS.
O-OKAY, BUT THIS IS IT...
AH-HA-HA-HA-HA!
YOU REALLY ARE HAVING WAY TOO MUCH FUN HERE!

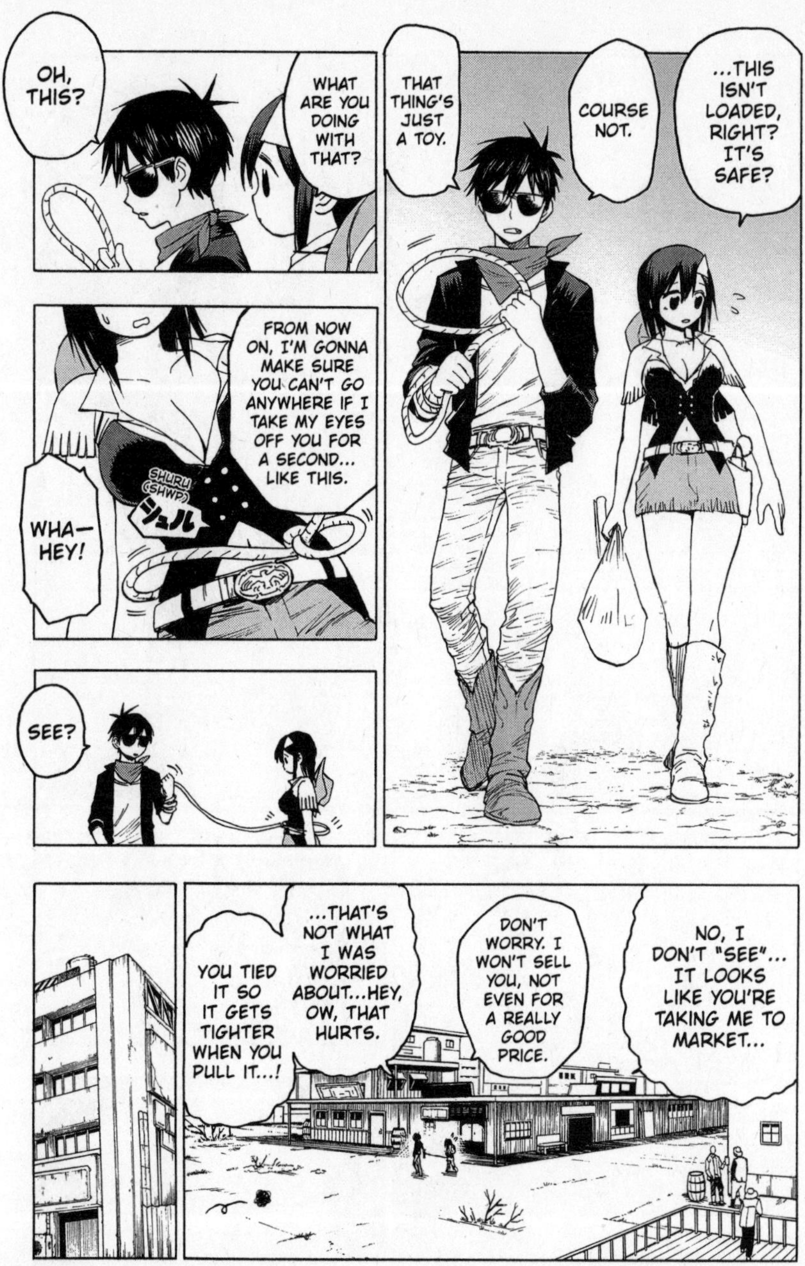
...THIS ISN'T LOADED, RIGHT? IT'S SAFE?
COURSE NOT.
THAT THING'S JUST A TOY.
WHAT ARE YOU DOING WITH THAT?
OH, THIS?
FROM NOW ON, I'M GONNA MAKE SURE YOU CAN'T GO ANYWHERE IF I TAKE MY EYES OFF YOU FOR A SECOND... LIKE THIS.
SHURU (SHWP)
シュル
WHA—HEY!
SEE?
NO, I DON'T "SEE"... IT LOOKS LIKE YOU'RE TAKING ME TO MARKET...
DON'T WORRY. I WON'T SELL YOU, NOT EVEN FOR A REALLY GOOD PRICE.
...THAT'S NOT WHAT I WAS WORRIED ABOUT...HEY, OW, THAT HURTS.
YOU TIED IT SO IT GETS TIGHTER WHEN YOU PULL IT...!

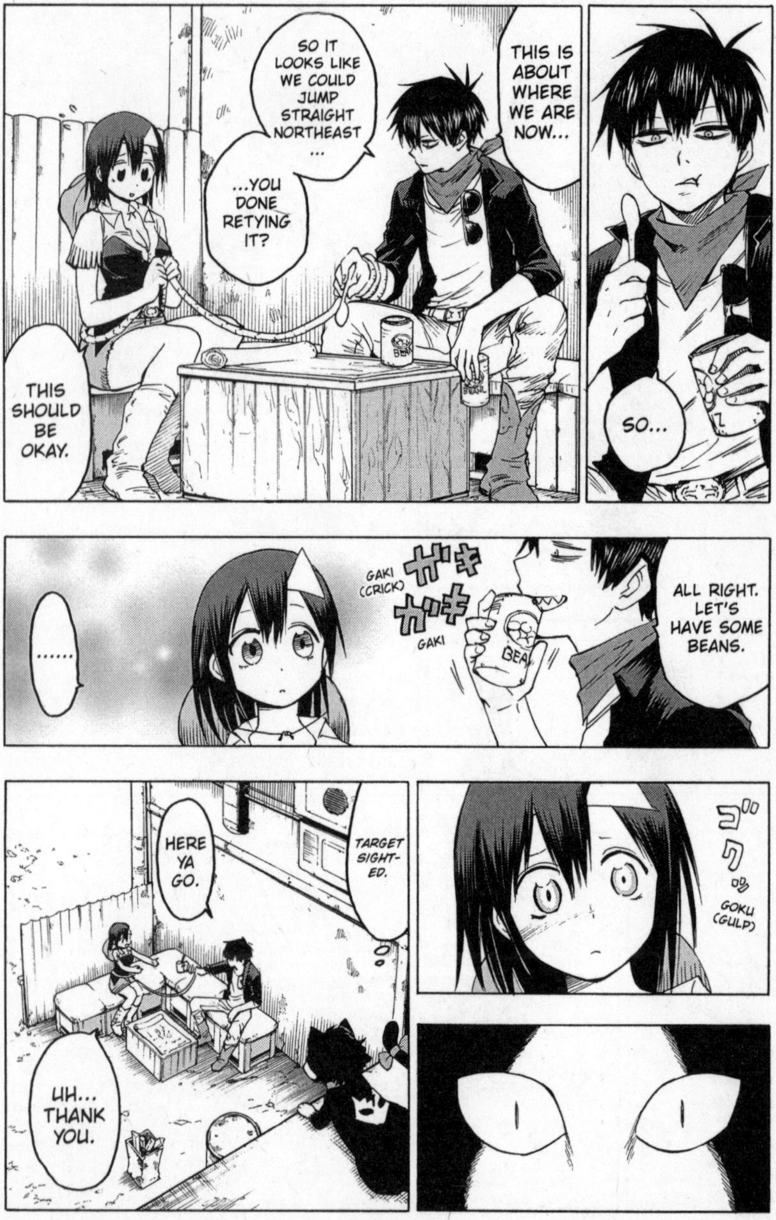
SO...
THIS IS ABOUT WHERE WE ARE NOW...
SO IT LOOKS LIKE WE COULD JUMP STRAIGHT NORTHEAST...
...YOU DONE RETYING IT?
THIS SHOULD BE OKAY.
ALL RIGHT. LET'S HAVE SOME BEANS.
ガキ
GAKI (CRICK)
ガキ
GAKI
......
ゴクッ
GOKU (GULP)
TARGET SIGHTED.
HERE YA GO.
UH... THANK YOU.

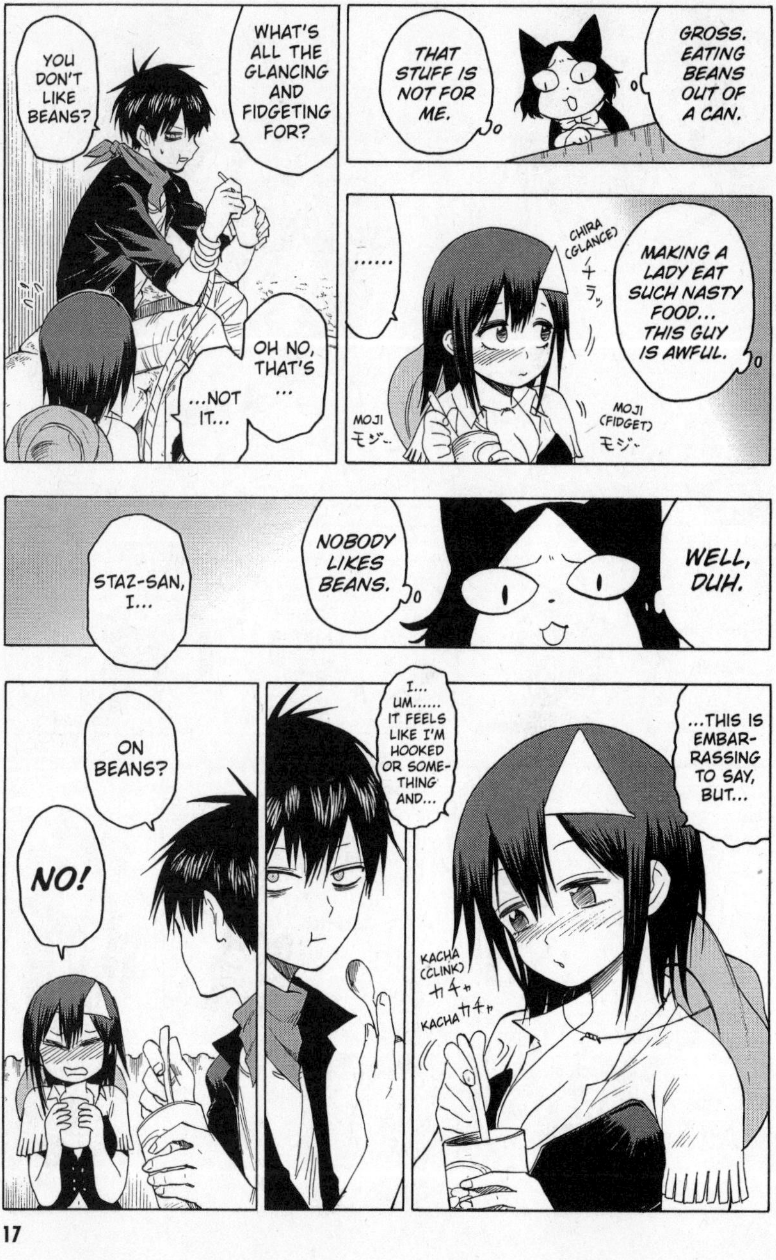
GROSS. EATING BEANS OUT OF A CAN.
THAT STUFF IS NOT FOR ME.
MAKING A LADY EAT SUCH NASTY FOOD... THIS GUY IS AWFUL.
CHIRA (GLANCE)
チラッ
......
MOJI (FIDGET)
モジ
MOJI
モジ
WHAT'S ALL THE GLANCING AND FIDGETING FOR?
YOU DON'T LIKE BEANS?
OH NO, THAT'S ...
...NOT IT...
WELL, DUH.
NOBODY LIKES BEANS.
STAZ-SAN, I...
...THIS IS EMBAR-RASSING TO SAY, BUT...
I... UM...... IT FEELS LIKE I'M HOOKED OR SOME-THING AND...
KACHA (CLINK)
カチャ
KACHA
カチャ
ON BEANS?
NO!

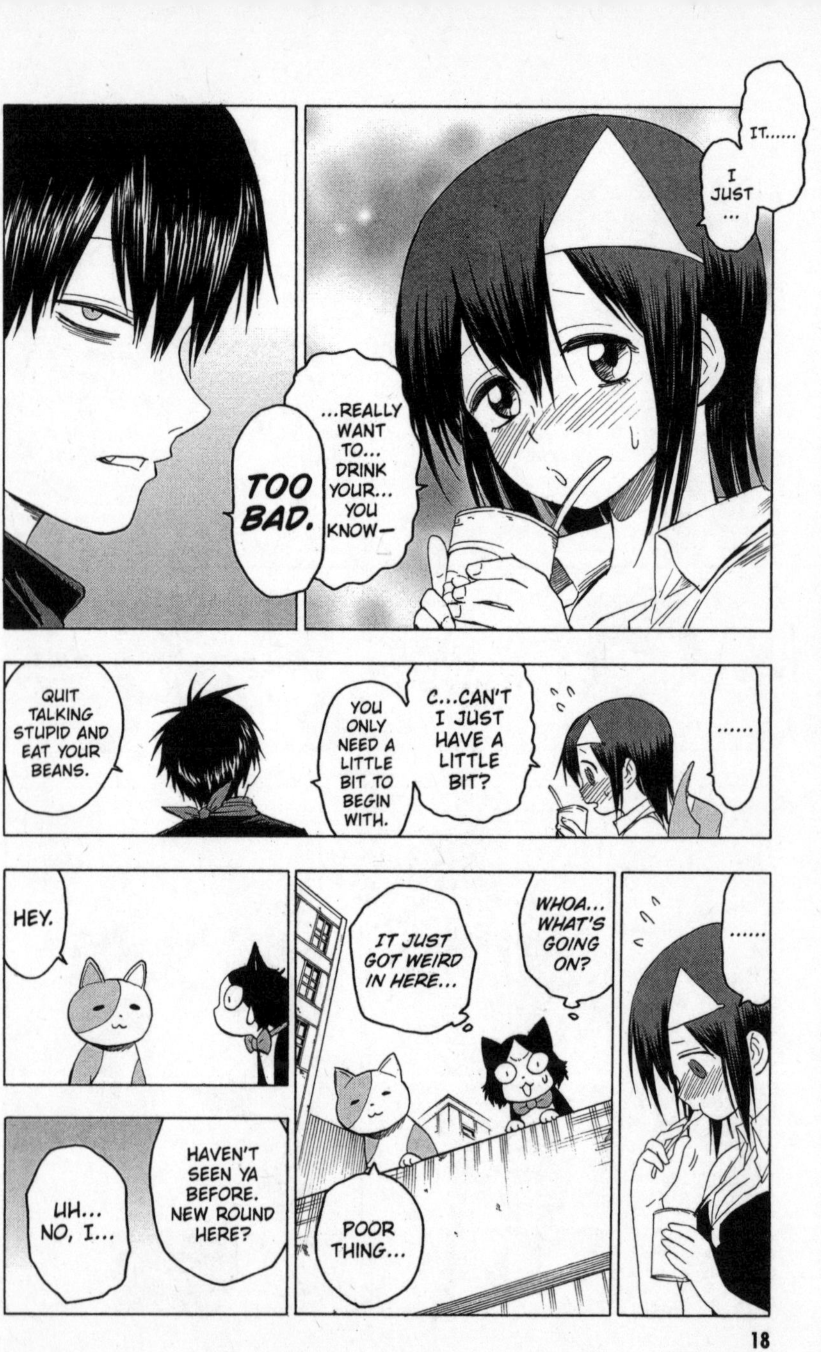
IT......
I JUST ...
...REALLY WANT TO... DRINK YOUR... YOU KNOW—
TOO BAD.
......
C...CAN'T I JUST HAVE A LITTLE BIT?
YOU ONLY NEED A LITTLE BIT TO BEGIN WITH.
QUIT TALKING STUPID AND EAT YOUR BEANS.
......
WHOA... WHAT'S GOING ON?
IT JUST GOT WEIRD IN HERE...
POOR THING...
HEY.
HAVEN'T SEEN YA BEFORE. NEW ROUND HERE?
UH... NO, I...

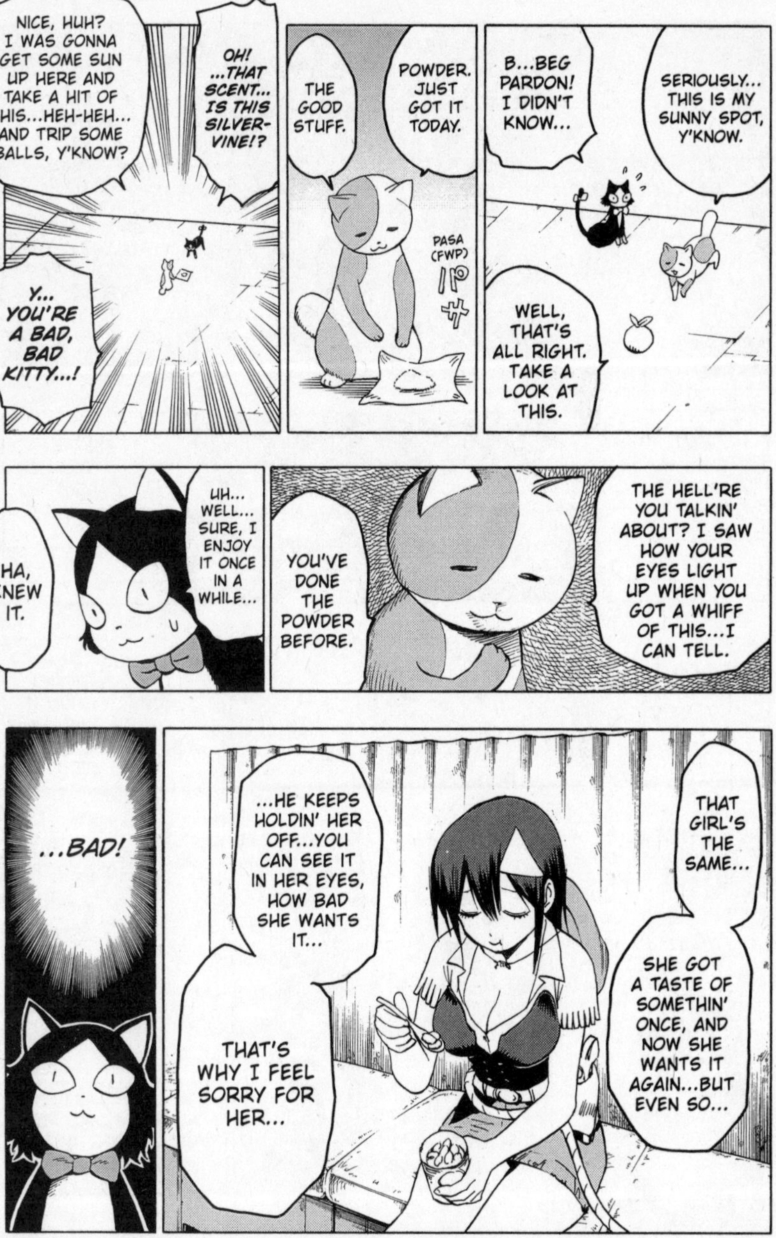
SERIOUSLY... THIS IS MY SUNNY SPOT, Y'KNOW.
B...BEG PARDON! I DIDN'T KNOW...
WELL, THAT'S ALL RIGHT. TAKE A LOOK AT THIS.
POWDER. JUST GOT IT TODAY.
THE GOOD STUFF.
PASA (FWP)
パサ
OH! ...THAT SCENT... IS THIS SILVER-VINE!?
NICE, HUH? I WAS GONNA GET SOME SUN UP HERE AND TAKE A HIT OF THIS...HEH-HEH... AND TRIP SOME BALLS, Y'KNOW?
Y... YOU'RE A BAD, BAD KITTY...!
THE HELL'RE YOU TALKIN' ABOUT? I SAW HOW YOUR EYES LIGHT UP WHEN YOU GOT A WHIFF OF THIS...I CAN TELL.
YOU'VE DONE THE POWDER BEFORE.
UH... WELL... SURE, I ENJOY IT ONCE IN A WHILE...
HA, KNEW IT.
THAT GIRL'S THE SAME...
...HE KEEPS HOLDIN' HER OFF...YOU CAN SEE IT IN HER EYES, HOW BAD SHE WANTS IT...
SHE GOT A TASTE OF SOMETHIN' ONCE, AND NOW SHE WANTS IT AGAIN...BUT EVEN SO...
THAT'S WHY I FEEL SORRY FOR HER...
...BAD!

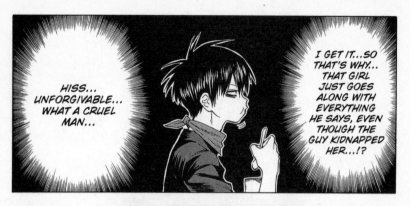

I GET IT...SO THAT'S WHY... THAT GIRL JUST GOES ALONG WITH EVERYTHING HE SAYS, EVEN THOUGH THE GUY KIDNAPPED HER...!?
HISS... UNFORGIVABLE... WHAT A CRUEL MAN...
INDEED, IT SEEMS I HAVE NO CHOICE...
...BUT TO USE MY POWER...!!
HEH-HEH-HEH... WON'T GIVE HIM A QUICK DEATH...
IT'LL BE...SO SLOW AND PAINFUL...
GORON (ROLL)
GORON
HUH? I SURE DO FEEL NICE...WOO! WOO-HOO! WOO-HOO-HOO-HOO!
WELL...
WELL, THAT WAS LUNCH, LET'S GET GOING.
GUI (YANK)
C'MON, STAND UP.
OH... MY LEGS ARE GONE. I CAN'T STAND.

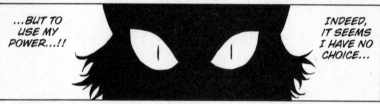

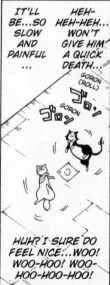

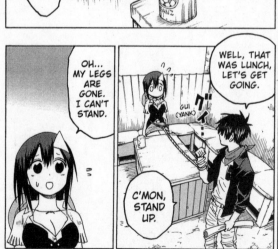

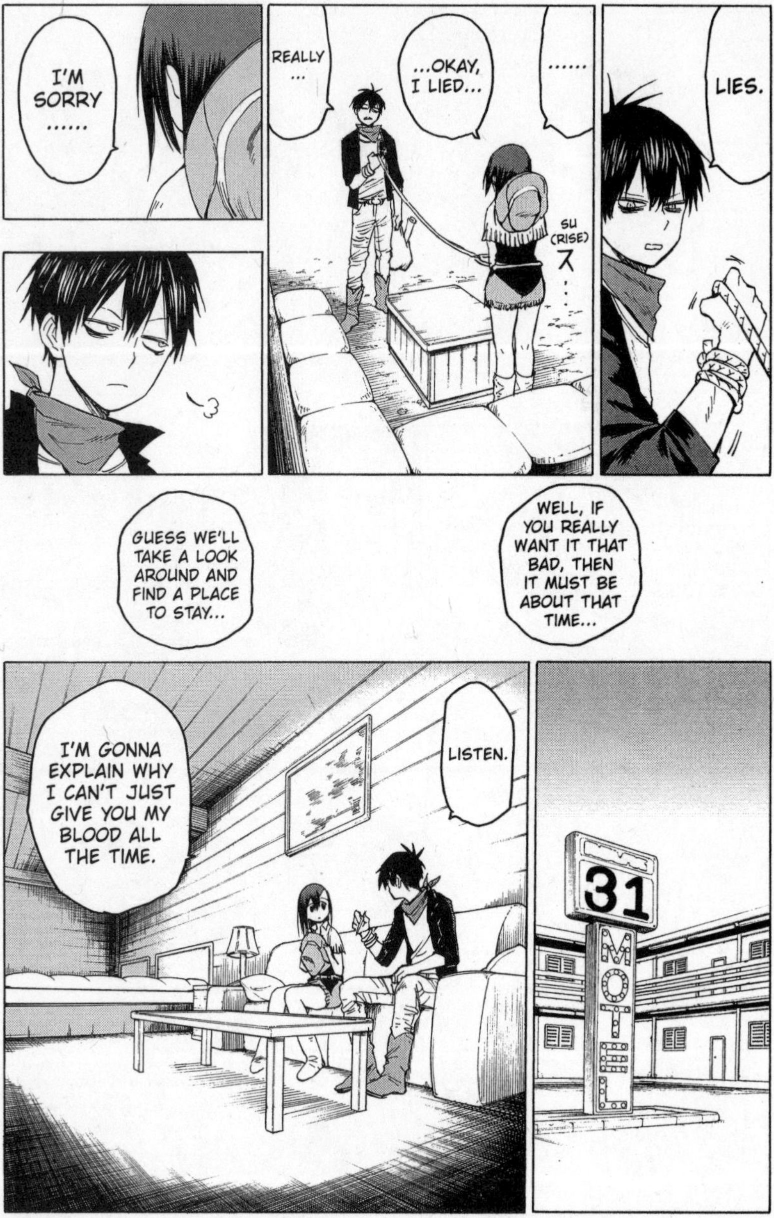
LIES.
......
...OKAY, I LIED...
REALLY ...
SU (RISE)
ス...
I'M SORRY ......
WELL, IF YOU REALLY WANT IT THAT BAD, THEN IT MUST BE ABOUT THAT TIME...
GUESS WE'LL TAKE A LOOK AROUND AND FIND A PLACE TO STAY...
31
MOTEL
LISTEN.
I'M GONNA EXPLAIN WHY I CAN'T JUST GIVE YOU MY BLOOD ALL THE TIME.

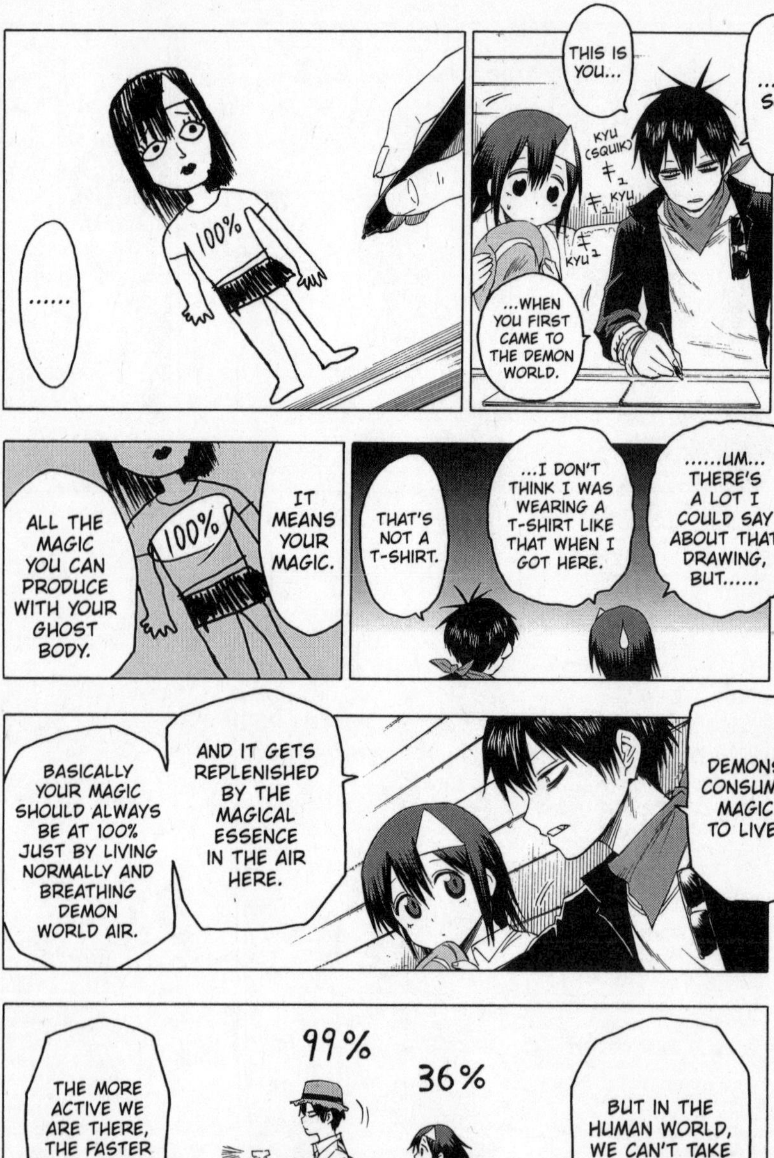

......SO.
THIS IS YOU...
KYU (SQUIK) KYU KYU
...WHEN YOU FIRST CAME TO THE DEMON WORLD.
......
......UM... THERE'S A LOT I COULD SAY ABOUT THAT DRAWING, BUT......
...I DON'T THINK I WAS WEARING A T-SHIRT LIKE THAT WHEN I GOT HERE.
THAT'S NOT A T-SHIRT.
IT MEANS YOUR MAGIC.
ALL THE MAGIC YOU CAN PRODUCE WITH YOUR GHOST BODY.
DEMONS CONSUME MAGIC TO LIVE.
AND IT GETS REPLENISHED BY THE MAGICAL ESSENCE IN THE AIR HERE.
BASICALLY YOUR MAGIC SHOULD ALWAYS BE AT 100% JUST BY LIVING NORMALLY AND BREATHING DEMON WORLD AIR.
BUT IN THE HUMAN WORLD, WE CAN'T TAKE IN ANY MAGICAL ESSENCE.
36%
99%
THE MORE ACTIVE WE ARE THERE, THE FASTER OUR MAGIC IS DEPLETED.

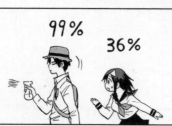

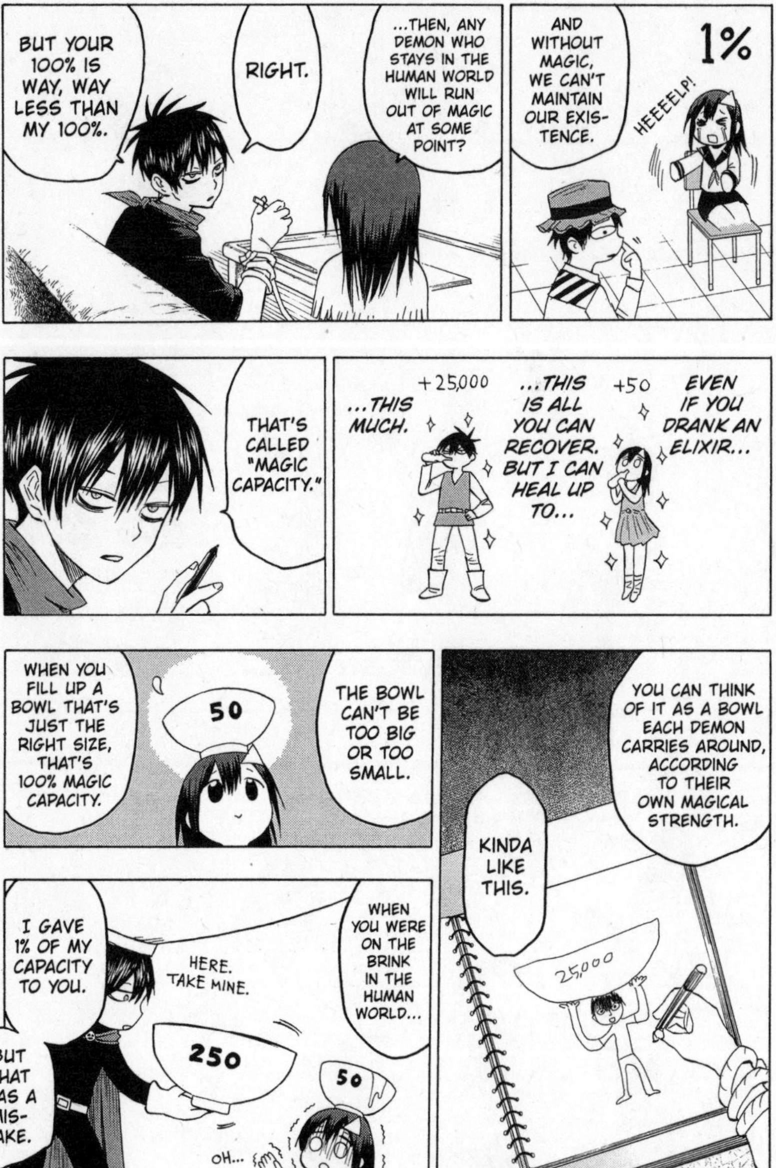

AND WITHOUT MAGIC, WE CAN'T MAINTAIN OUR EXISTENCE.
1%
HEEEELP!
...THEN, ANY DEMON WHO STAYS IN THE HUMAN WORLD WILL RUN OUT OF MAGIC AT SOME POINT?
RIGHT.
BUT YOUR 100% IS WAY, WAY LESS THAN MY 100%.
EVEN IF YOU DRANK AN ELIXIR...
+50
...THIS IS ALL YOU CAN RECOVER. BUT I CAN HEAL UP TO...
+25,000
...THIS MUCH.
THAT'S CALLED "MAGIC CAPACITY."
YOU CAN THINK OF IT AS A BOWL EACH DEMON CARRIES AROUND, ACCORDING TO THEIR OWN MAGICAL STRENGTH.
KINDA LIKE THIS.
25,000
THE BOWL CAN'T BE TOO BIG OR TOO SMALL.
50
WHEN YOU FILL UP A BOWL THAT'S JUST THE RIGHT SIZE, THAT'S 100% MAGIC CAPACITY.
WHEN YOU WERE ON THE BRINK IN THE HUMAN WORLD...
HERE. TAKE MINE.
50
I GAVE 1% OF MY CAPACITY TO YOU.
250
BUT THAT WAS A MISTAKE.
OH...
OH...

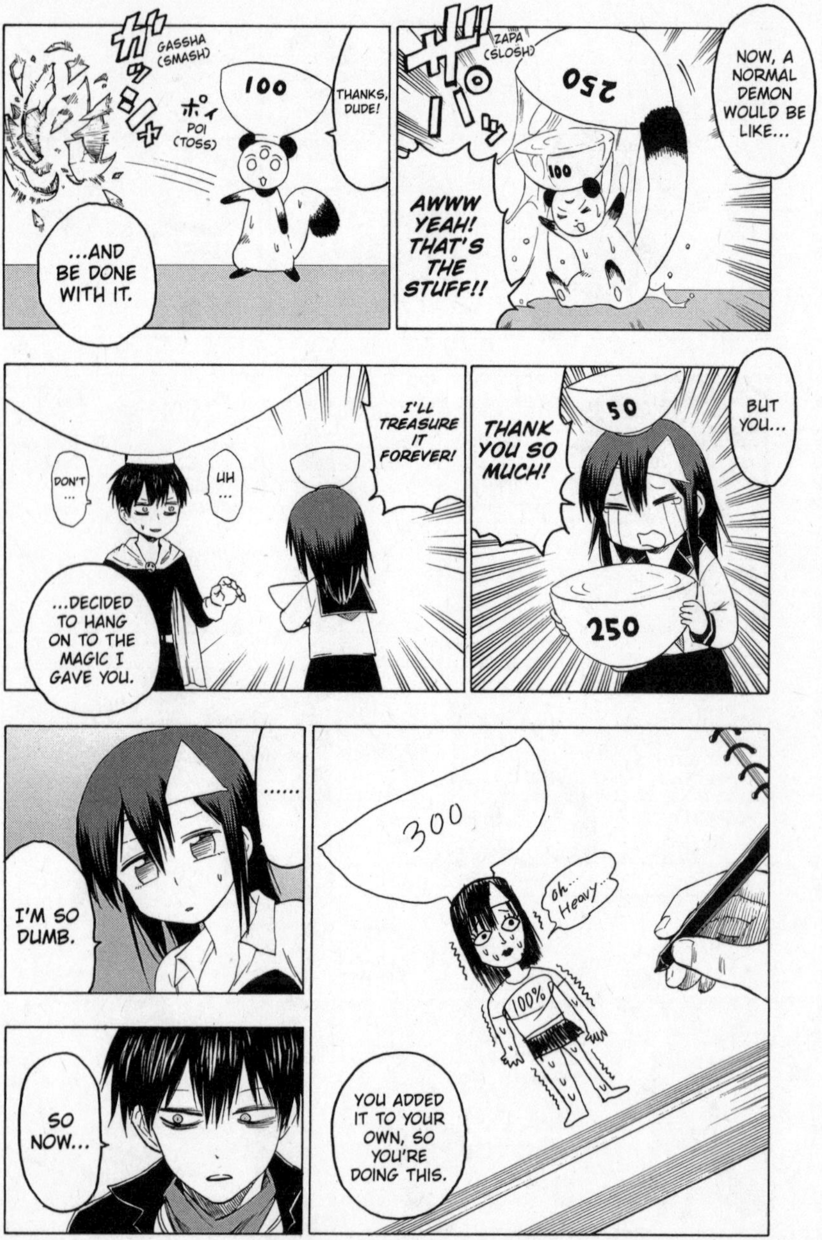
NOW, A NORMAL DEMON WOULD BE LIKE...
ZAPA (SLOSH)
250
100
AWWW YEAH! THAT'S THE STUFF!!
THANKS, DUDE!
100
GASSHA (SMASH)
ポイ
POI (TOSS)
...AND BE DONE WITH IT.
BUT YOU...
50
THANK YOU SO MUCH!
250
I'LL TREASURE IT FOREVER!
UH...
DON'T...
...DECIDED TO HANG ON TO THE MAGIC I GAVE YOU.
300
Oh... Heavy...
100%
YOU ADDED IT TO YOUR OWN, SO YOU'RE DOING THIS.
......
I'M SO DUMB.
SO NOW...

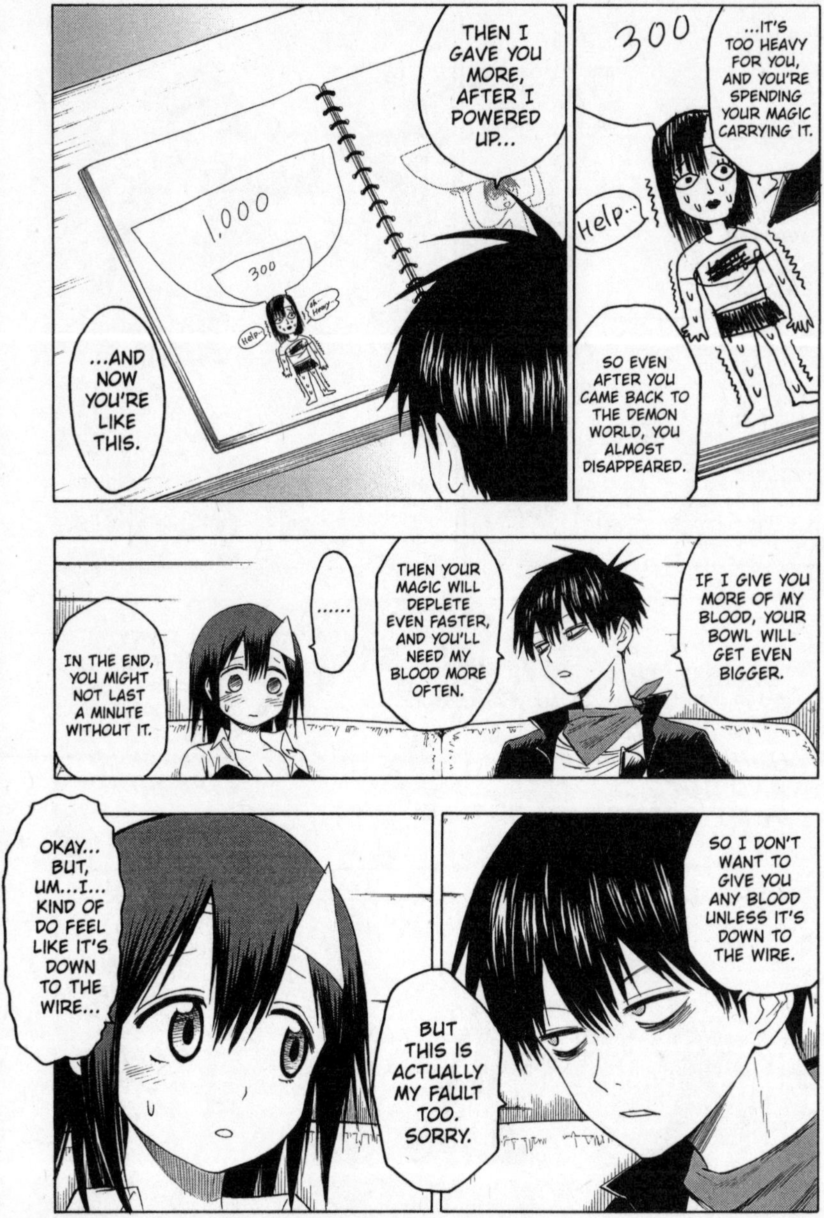
300
...IT'S TOO HEAVY FOR YOU, AND YOU'RE SPENDING YOUR MAGIC CARRYING IT.
Help...
SO EVEN AFTER YOU CAME BACK TO THE DEMON WORLD, YOU ALMOST DISAPPEARED.
THEN I GAVE YOU MORE, AFTER I POWERED UP...
1,000
300
Help...
...AND NOW YOU'RE LIKE THIS.
IF I GIVE YOU MORE OF MY BLOOD, YOUR BOWL WILL GET EVEN BIGGER.
THEN YOUR MAGIC WILL DEPLETE EVEN FASTER, AND YOU'LL NEED MY BLOOD MORE OFTEN.
......
IN THE END, YOU MIGHT NOT LAST A MINUTE WITHOUT IT.
SO I DON'T WANT TO GIVE YOU ANY BLOOD UNLESS IT'S DOWN TO THE WIRE.
OKAY... BUT, UM...I... KIND OF DO FEEL LIKE IT'S DOWN TO THE WIRE...
BUT THIS IS ACTUALLY MY FAULT TOO. SORRY.

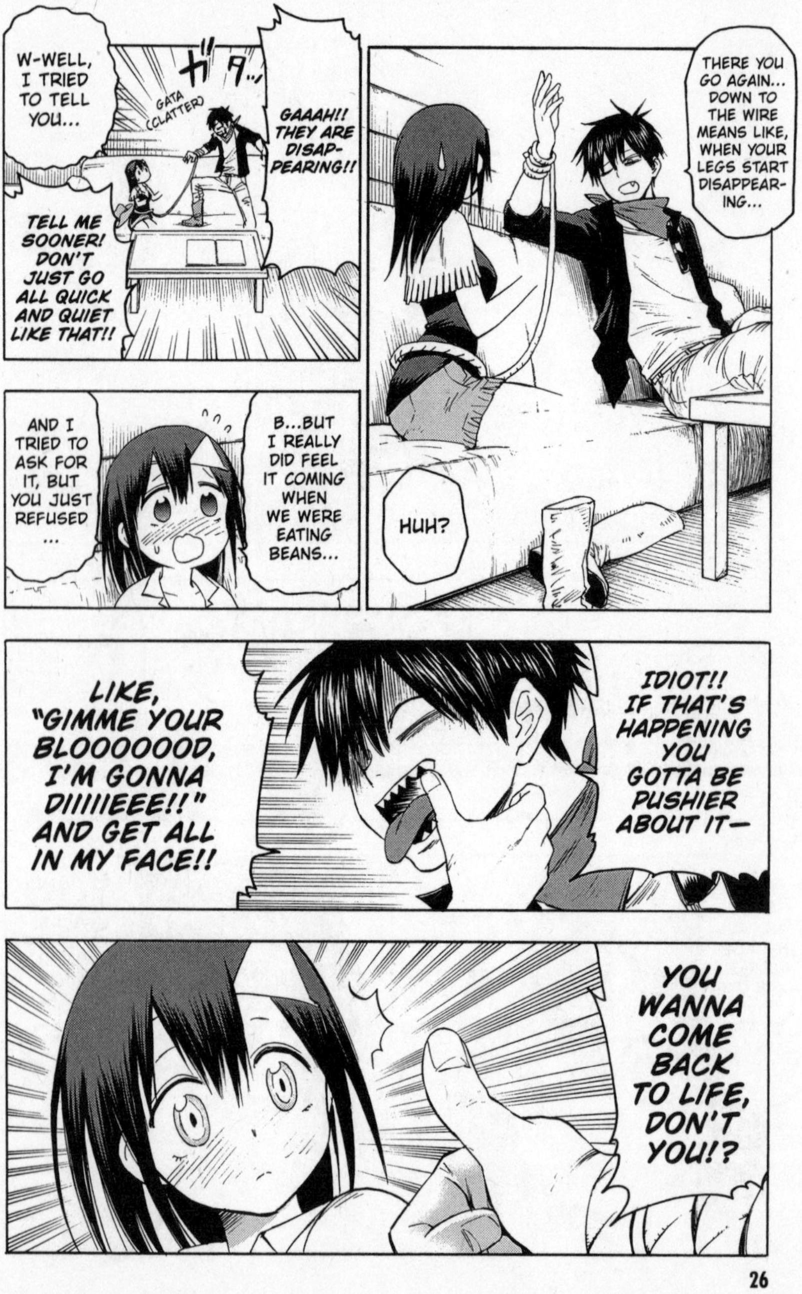
THERE YOU GO AGAIN... DOWN TO THE WIRE MEANS LIKE, WHEN YOUR LEGS START DISAPPEARING...
HUH?
GAAAH!! THEY ARE DISAPPEARING!!
ガタ..
GATA (CLATTER)
W-WELL, I TRIED TO TELL YOU...
TELL ME SOONER! DON'T JUST GO ALL QUICK AND QUIET LIKE THAT!!
B...BUT I REALLY DID FEEL IT COMING WHEN WE WERE EATING BEANS...
AND I TRIED TO ASK FOR IT, BUT YOU JUST REFUSED ...
IDIOT!! IF THAT'S HAPPENING YOU GOTTA BE PUSHIER ABOUT IT—
LIKE, "GIMME YOUR BLOOOOOOD, I'M GONNA DIIIIIEEE!!" AND GET ALL IN MY FACE!!
YOU WANNA COME BACK TO LIFE, DON'T YOU!?

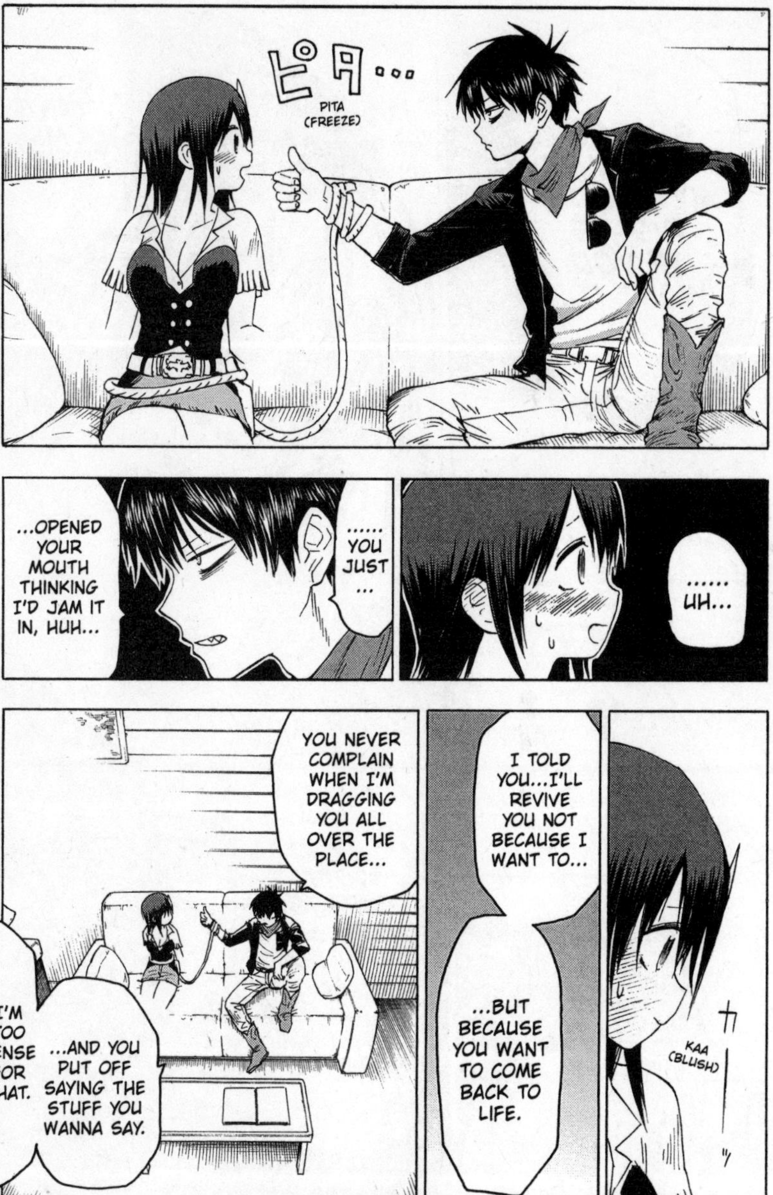
ピタ...
PITA (FREEZE)
......UH...
......YOU JUST...
...OPENED YOUR MOUTH THINKING I'D JAM IT IN, HUH...
カーッ
KAA (BLUSH)
I TOLD YOU...I'LL REVIVE YOU NOT BECAUSE I WANT TO...
...BUT BECAUSE YOU WANT TO COME BACK TO LIFE.
YOU NEVER COMPLAIN WHEN I'M DRAGGING YOU ALL OVER THE PLACE...
...AND YOU PUT OFF SAYING THE STUFF YOU WANNA SAY.
I'M TOO DENSE FOR THAT.

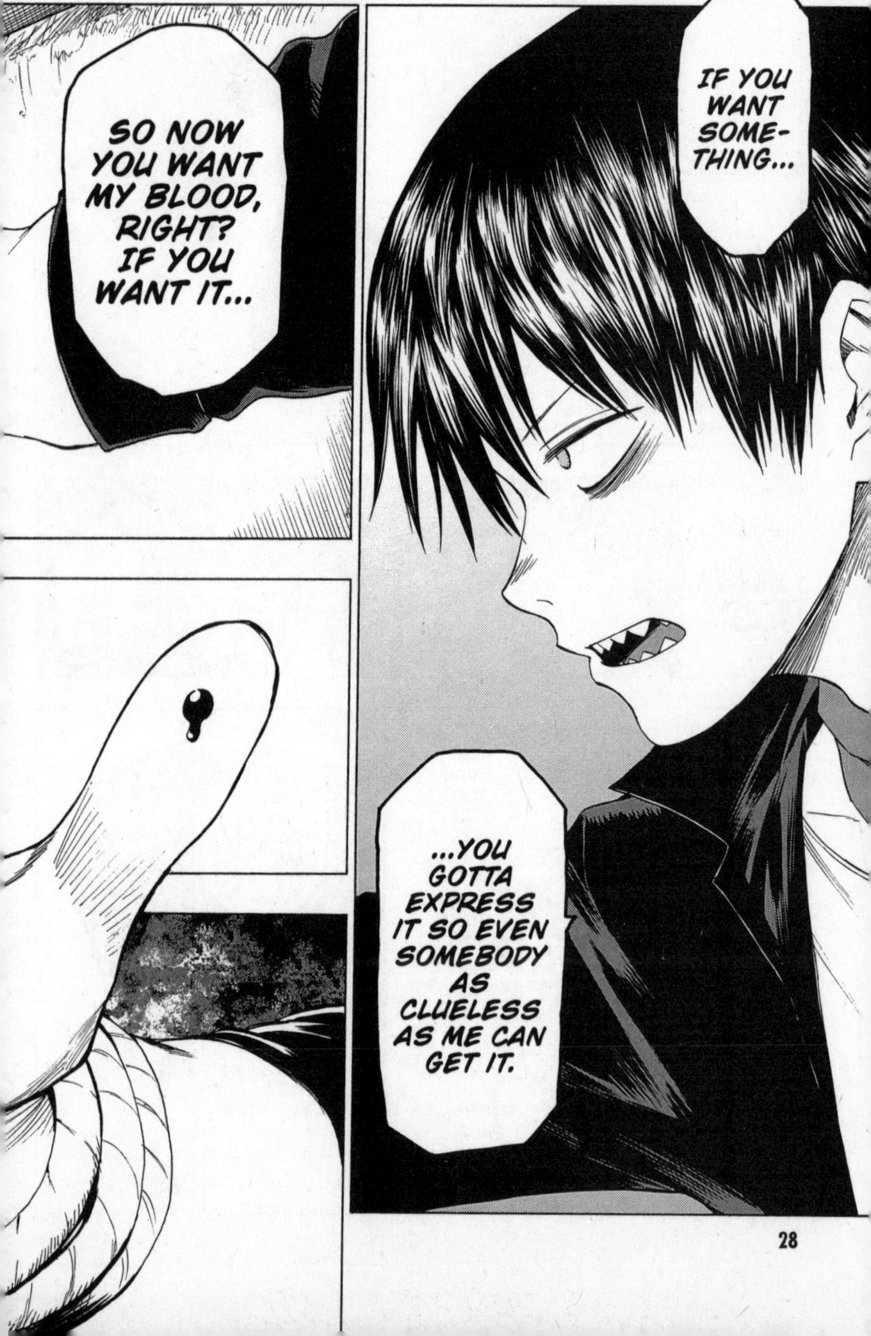
IF YOU WANT SOME-THING...
...YOU GOTTA EXPRESS IT SO EVEN SOMEBODY AS CLUELESS AS ME CAN GET IT.
SO NOW YOU WANT MY BLOOD, RIGHT? IF YOU WANT IT...

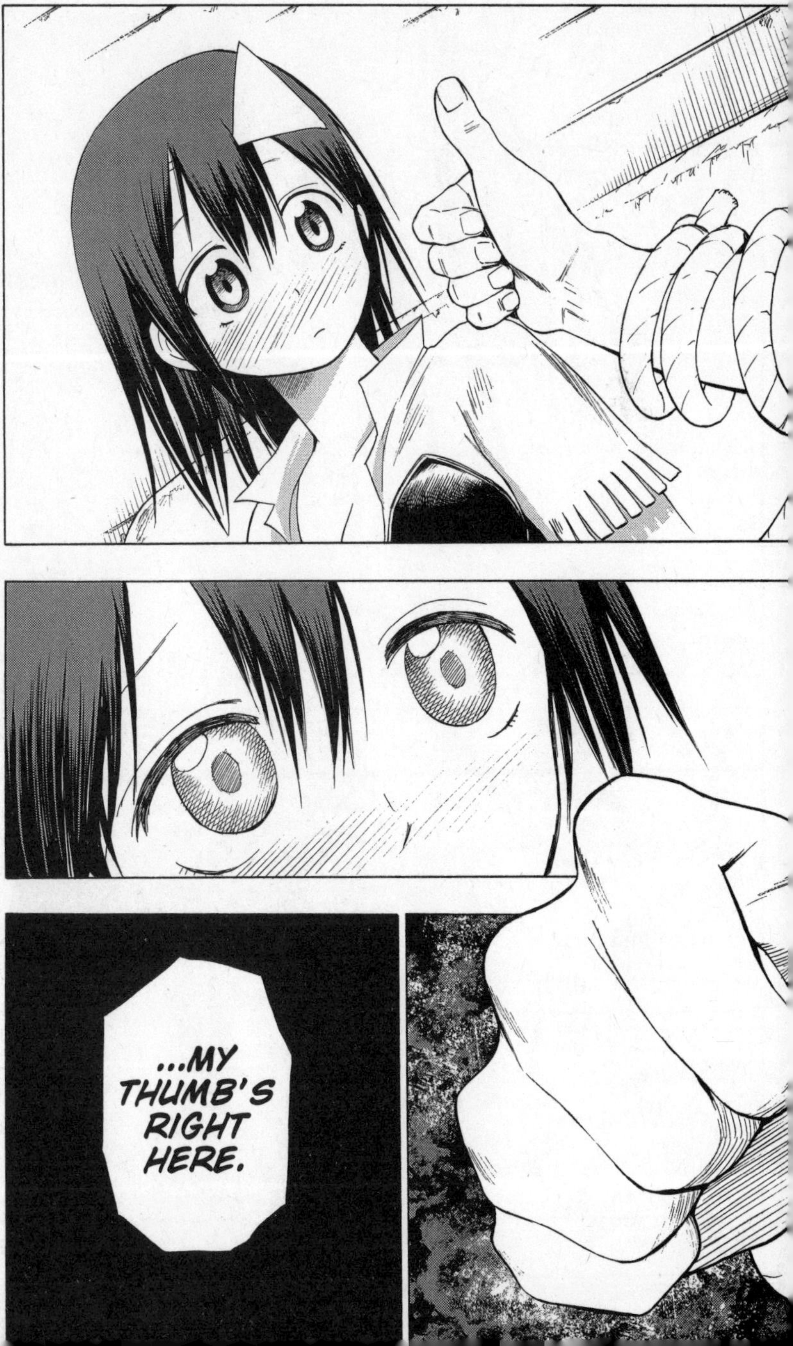
...MY THUMB'S RIGHT HERE.

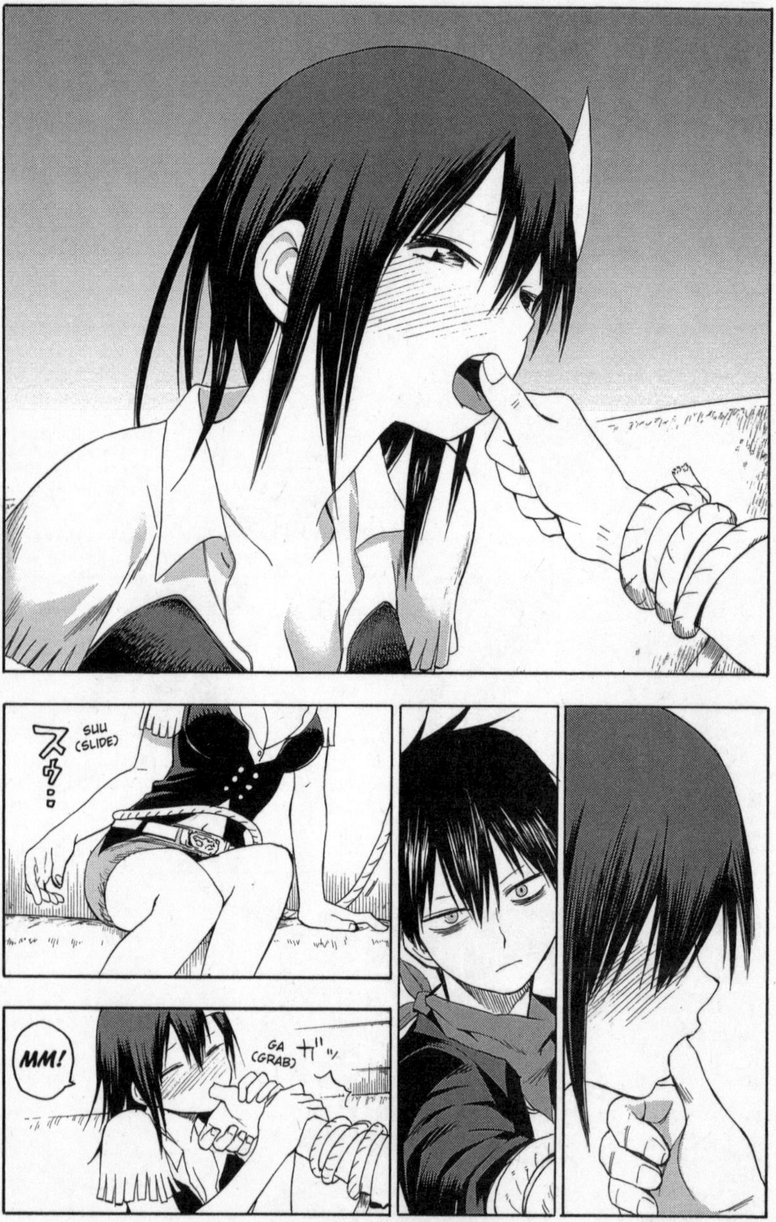
SUU (SLIDE)
スゥ..
GA (GRAB)
ガッ
MM!

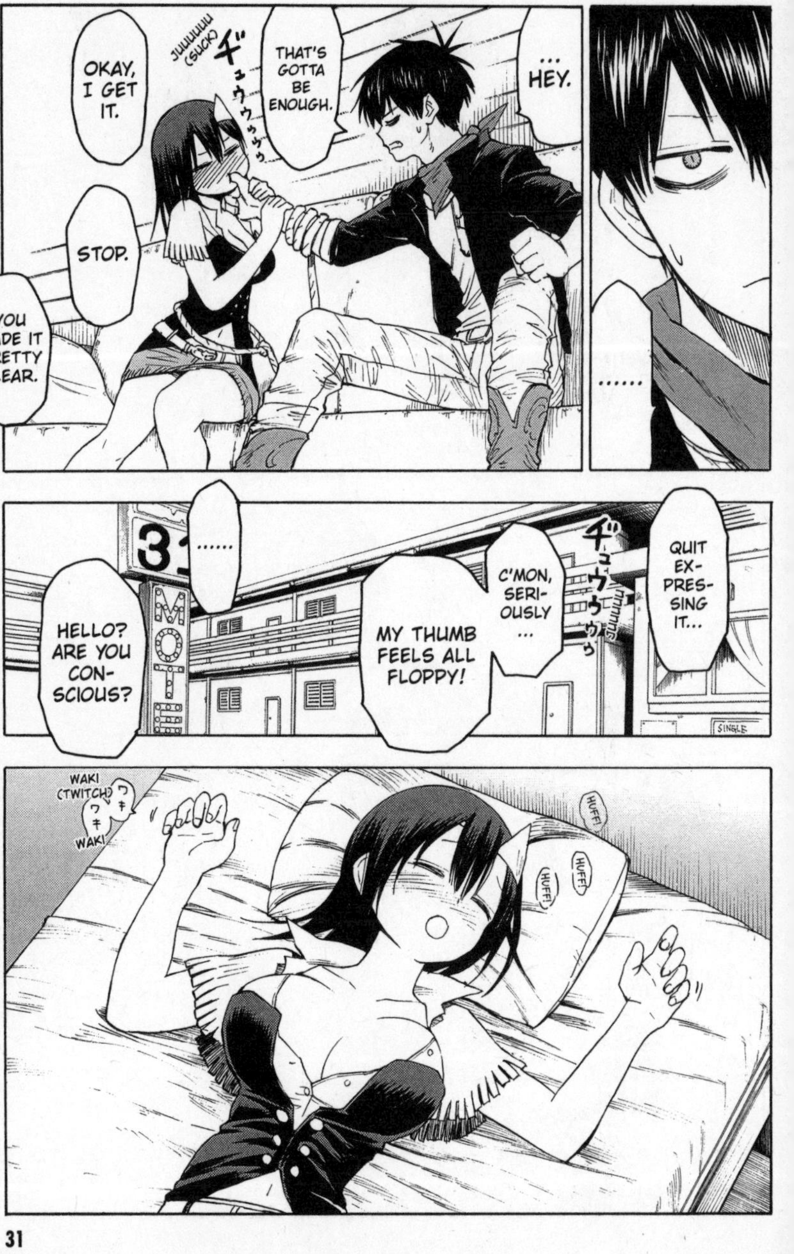
......
... HEY.
THAT'S GOTTA BE ENOUGH.
ギュウウゥゥゥ
JUUUUUUU (SUCK)
OKAY, I GET IT.
STOP.
YOU MADE IT PRETTY CLEAR.
QUIT EX-PRES-SING IT...
ギュウウゥゥ
JUUUUUU
C'MON, SERI-OUSLY ...
MY THUMB FEELS ALL FLOPPY!
......
HELLO? ARE YOU CON-SCIOUS?
SINGLE
HUFF!
HUFF!
HUFF!
ワキ
WAKI (TWITCH)
ワキ
WAKI

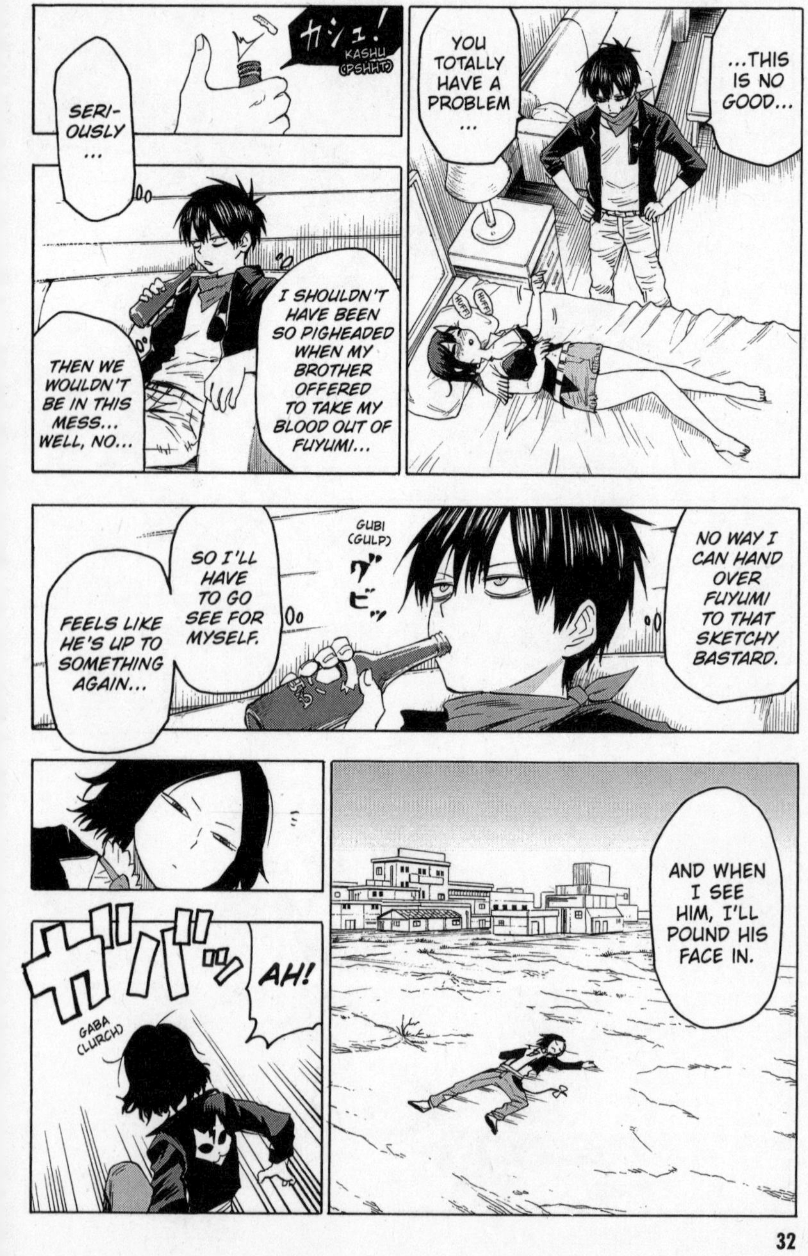
...THIS IS NO GOOD...
YOU TOTALLY HAVE A PROBLEM...
HUFF
HUFF
カシュ!
KASHU (PSHHT)
SERI-OUSLY...
I SHOULDN'T HAVE BEEN SO PIGHEADED WHEN MY BROTHER OFFERED TO TAKE MY BLOOD OUT OF FUYUMI...
THEN WE WOULDN'T BE IN THIS MESS... WELL, NO...
NO WAY I CAN HAND OVER FUYUMI TO THAT SKETCHY BASTARD.
ゴビッ
GUBI (GULP)
SO I'LL HAVE TO GO SEE FOR MYSELF.
FEELS LIKE HE'S UP TO SOMETHING AGAIN...
AND WHEN I SEE HIM, I'LL POUND HIS FACE IN.
AH!
ガバッ
GABA (LURCH)

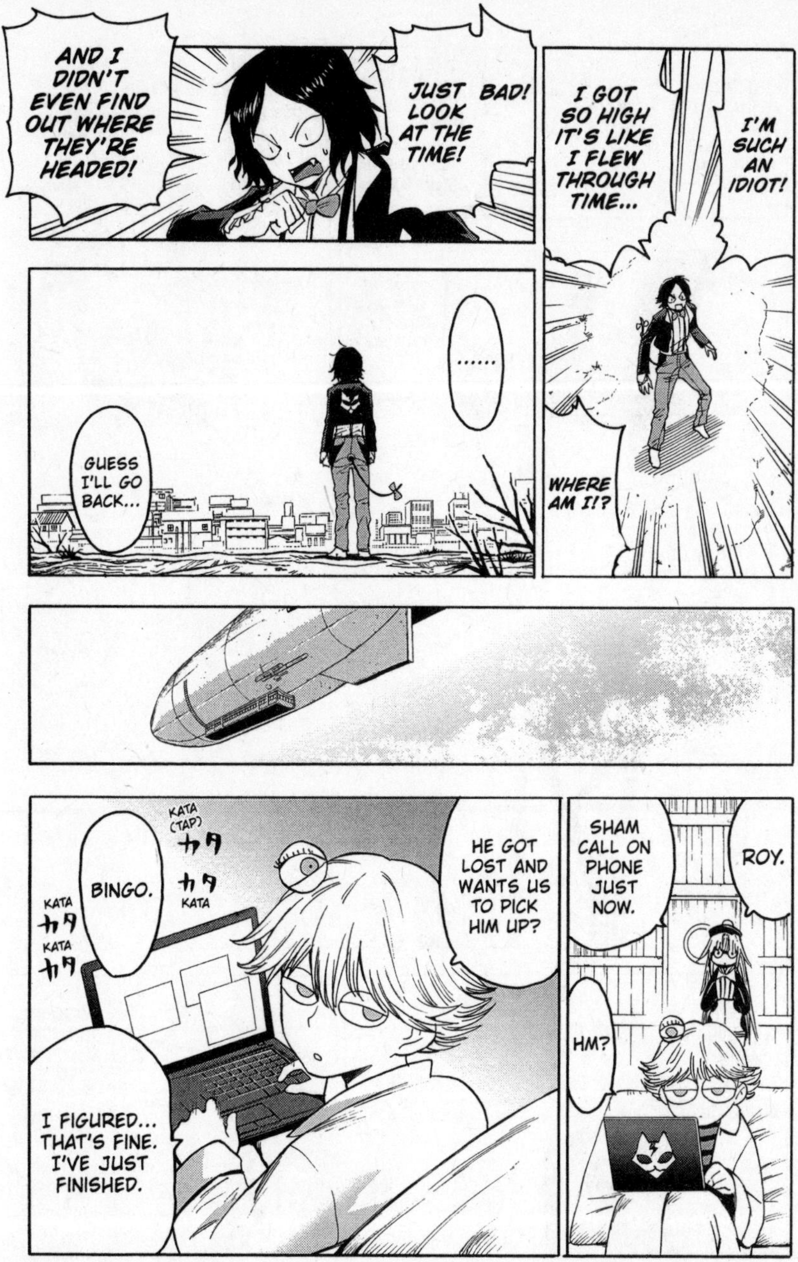
I'M SUCH AN IDIOT!
I GOT SO HIGH IT'S LIKE I FLEW THROUGH TIME...
WHERE AM I!?
BAD!
JUST LOOK AT THE TIME!
AND I DIDN'T EVEN FIND OUT WHERE THEY'RE HEADED!
......
GUESS I'LL GO BACK...
ROY.
SHAM CALL ON PHONE JUST NOW.
HM?
HE GOT LOST AND WANTS US TO PICK HIM UP?
KATA (TAP) カタ
カタ KATA
KATA カタ
KATA カタ
BINGO.
I FIGURED... THAT'S FINE. I'VE JUST FINISHED.

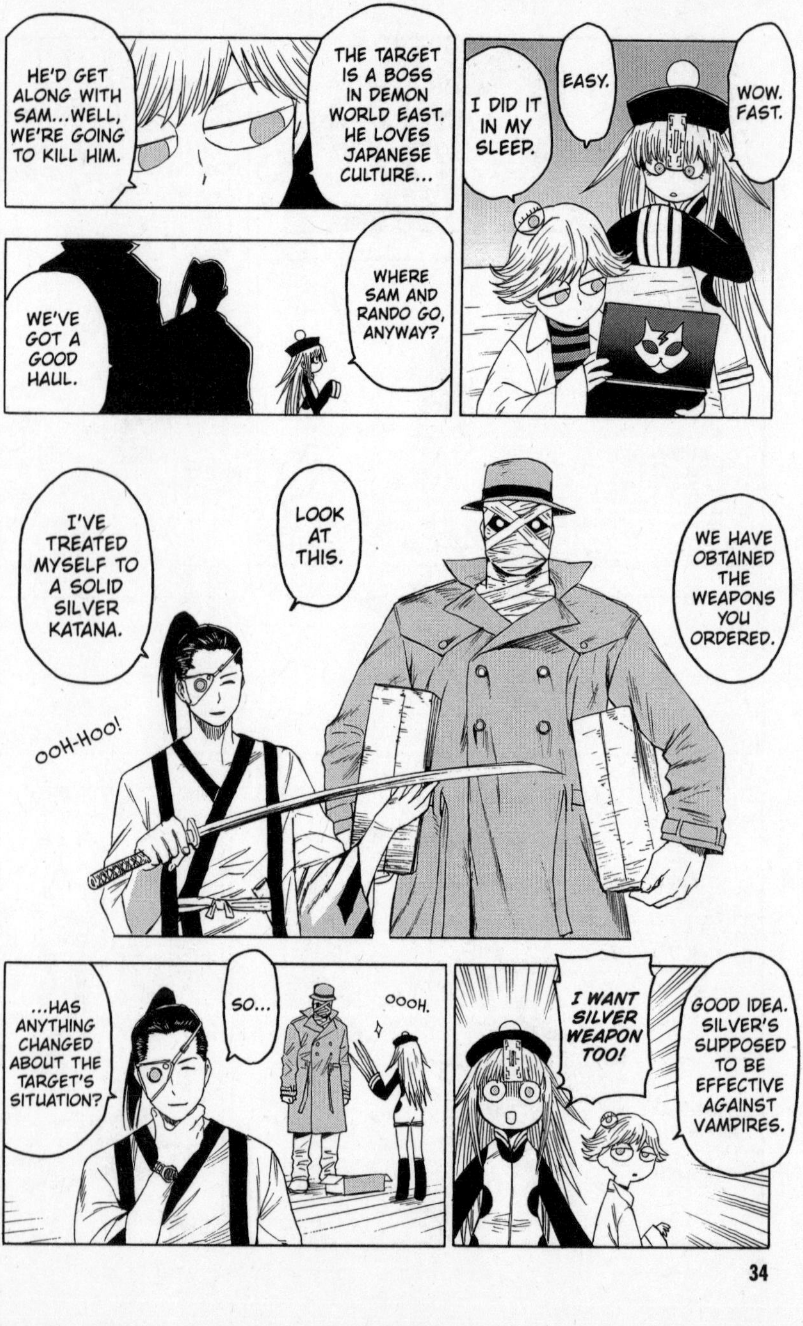

WOW. FAST.
EASY.
I DID IT IN MY SLEEP.
THE TARGET IS A BOSS IN DEMON WORLD EAST. HE LOVES JAPANESE CULTURE...
HE'D GET ALONG WITH SAM...WELL, WE'RE GOING TO KILL HIM.
WHERE SAM AND RANDO GO, ANYWAY?
WE'VE GOT A GOOD HAUL.
WE HAVE OBTAINED THE WEAPONS YOU ORDERED.
LOOK AT THIS.
I'VE TREATED MYSELF TO A SOLID SILVER KATANA.
OOH-HOO!
I WANT SILVER WEAPON TOO!
GOOD IDEA. SILVER'S SUPPOSED TO BE EFFECTIVE AGAINST VAMPIRES.
OOOH.
SO...
...HAS ANYTHING CHANGED ABOUT THE TARGET'S SITUATION?

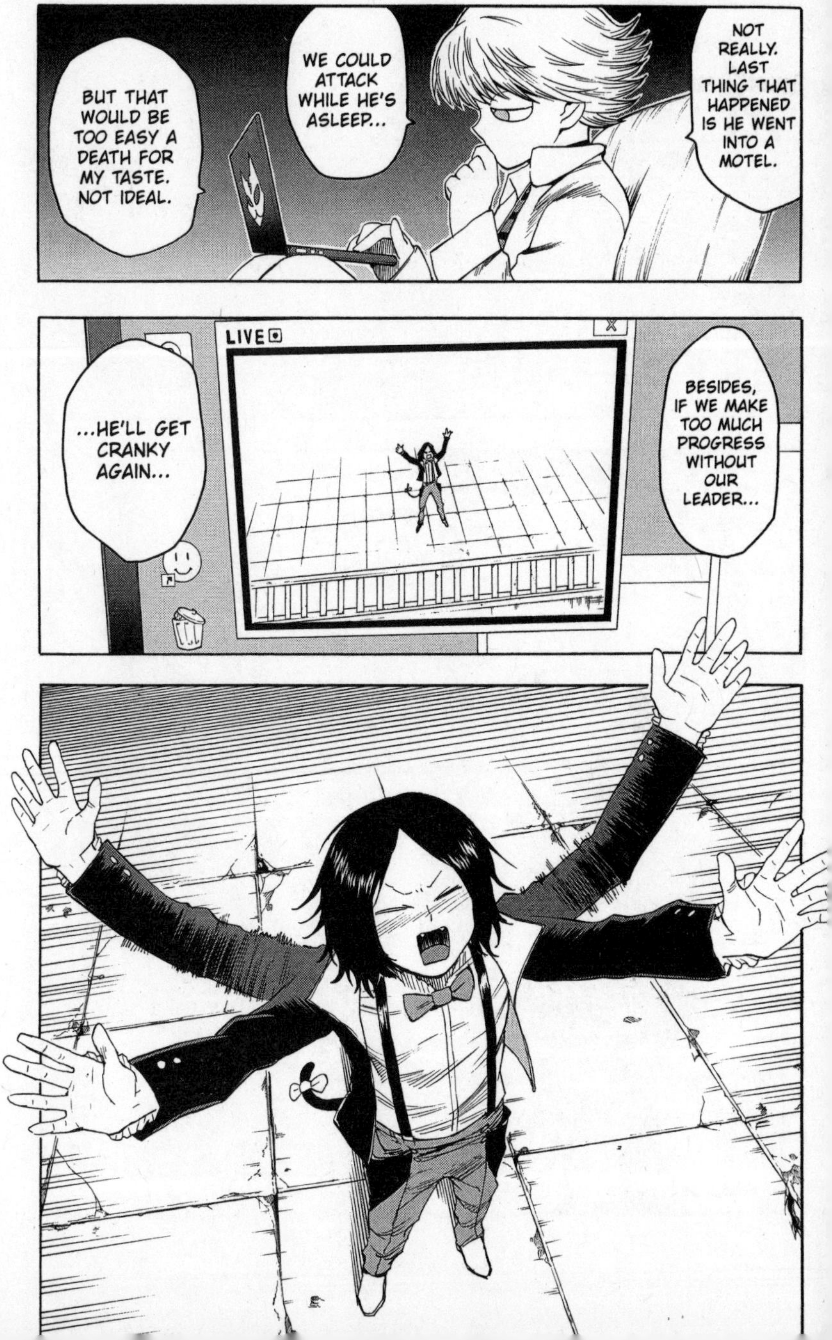
NOT REALLY. LAST THING THAT HAPPENED IS HE WENT INTO A MOTEL.
WE COULD ATTACK WHILE HE'S ASLEEP...
BUT THAT WOULD BE TOO EASY A DEATH FOR MY TASTE. NOT IDEAL.
LIVE
BESIDES, IF WE MAKE TOO MUCH PROGRESS WITHOUT OUR LEADER...
...HE'LL GET CRANKY AGAIN...

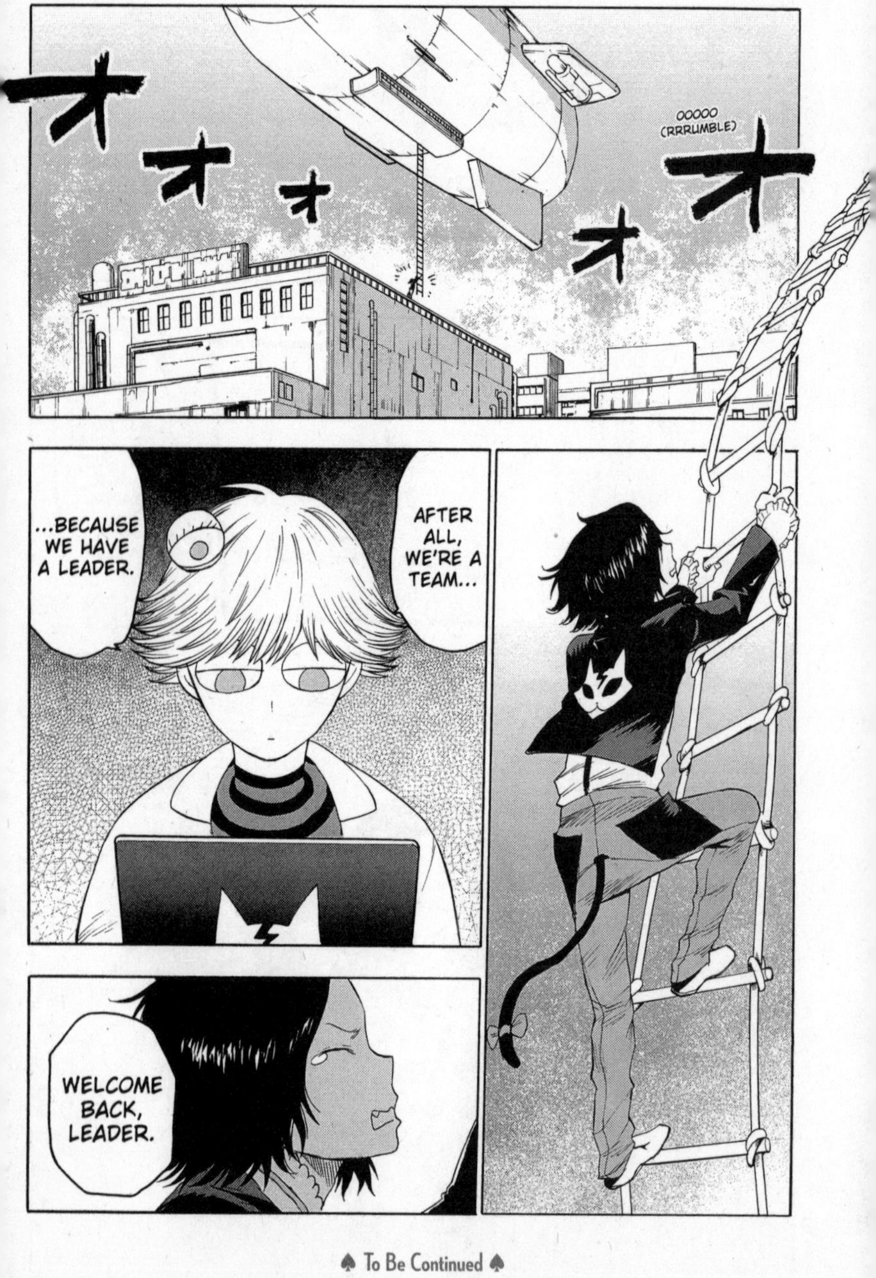
OOOOO (RRRUMBLE)
AFTER ALL, WE'RE A TEAM...
...BECAUSE WE HAVE A LEADER.
WELCOME BACK, LEADER.

♠ To Be Continued ♠

BLOOD LAD

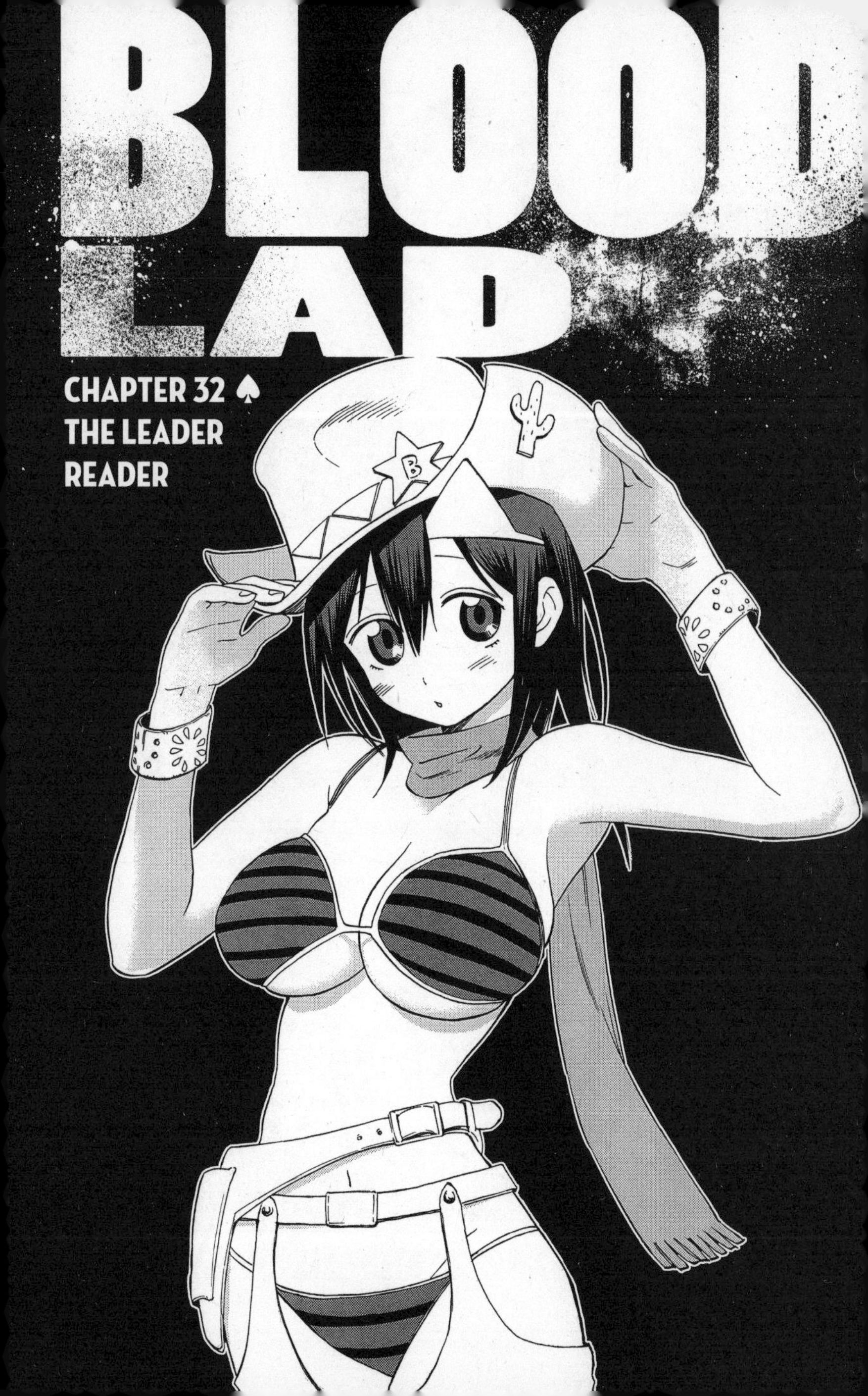
BLOOD LAD
CHAPTER 32 ♠
THE LEADER READER

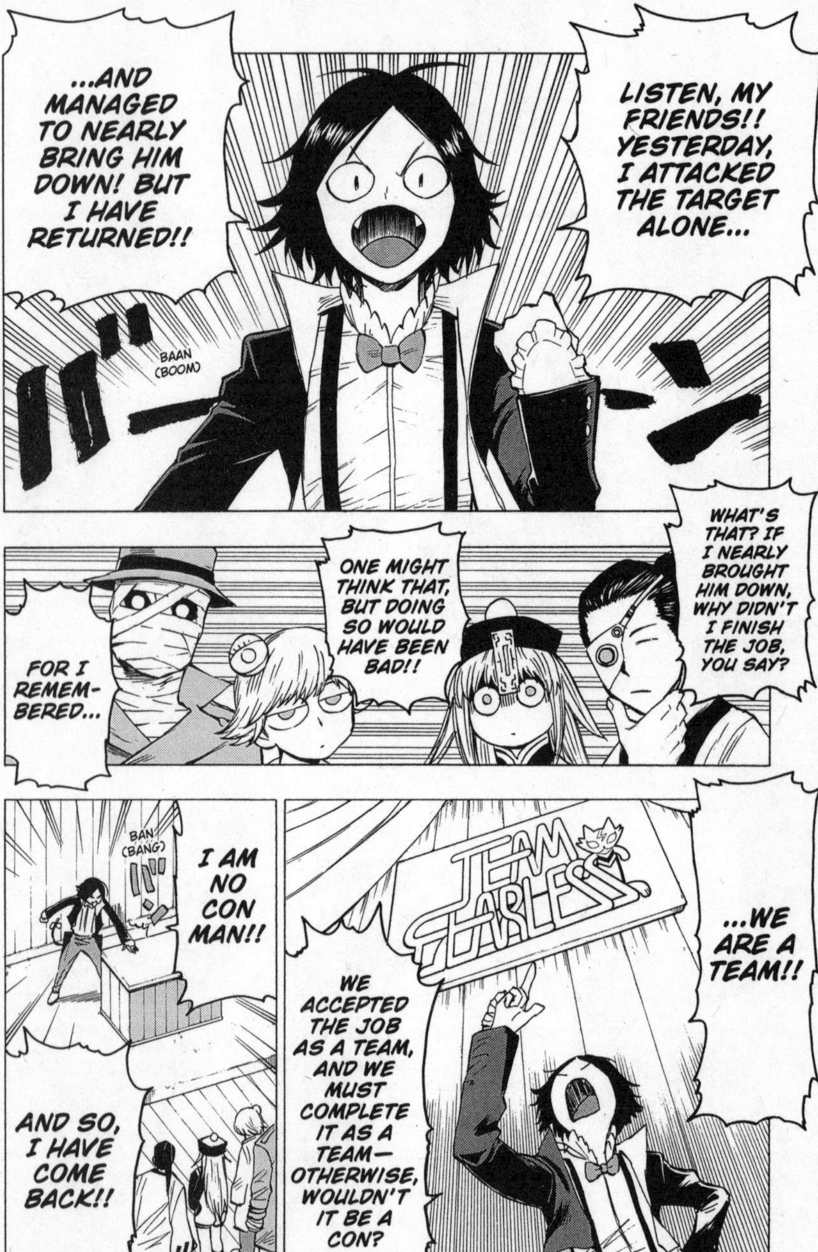
LISTEN, MY FRIENDS!! YESTERDAY, I ATTACKED THE TARGET ALONE...
...AND MANAGED TO NEARLY BRING HIM DOWN! BUT I HAVE RETURNED!!
BAAN (BOOM)
WHAT'S THAT? IF I NEARLY BROUGHT HIM DOWN, WHY DIDN'T I FINISH THE JOB, YOU SAY?
ONE MIGHT THINK THAT, BUT DOING SO WOULD HAVE BEEN BAD!!
FOR I REMEMBERED...
...WE ARE A TEAM!!
TEAM FEARLESS
WE ACCEPTED THE JOB AS A TEAM, AND WE MUST COMPLETE IT AS A TEAM—OTHERWISE, WOULDN'T IT BE A CON?
BAN (BANG)
I AM NO CON MAN!!
AND SO, I HAVE COME BACK!!

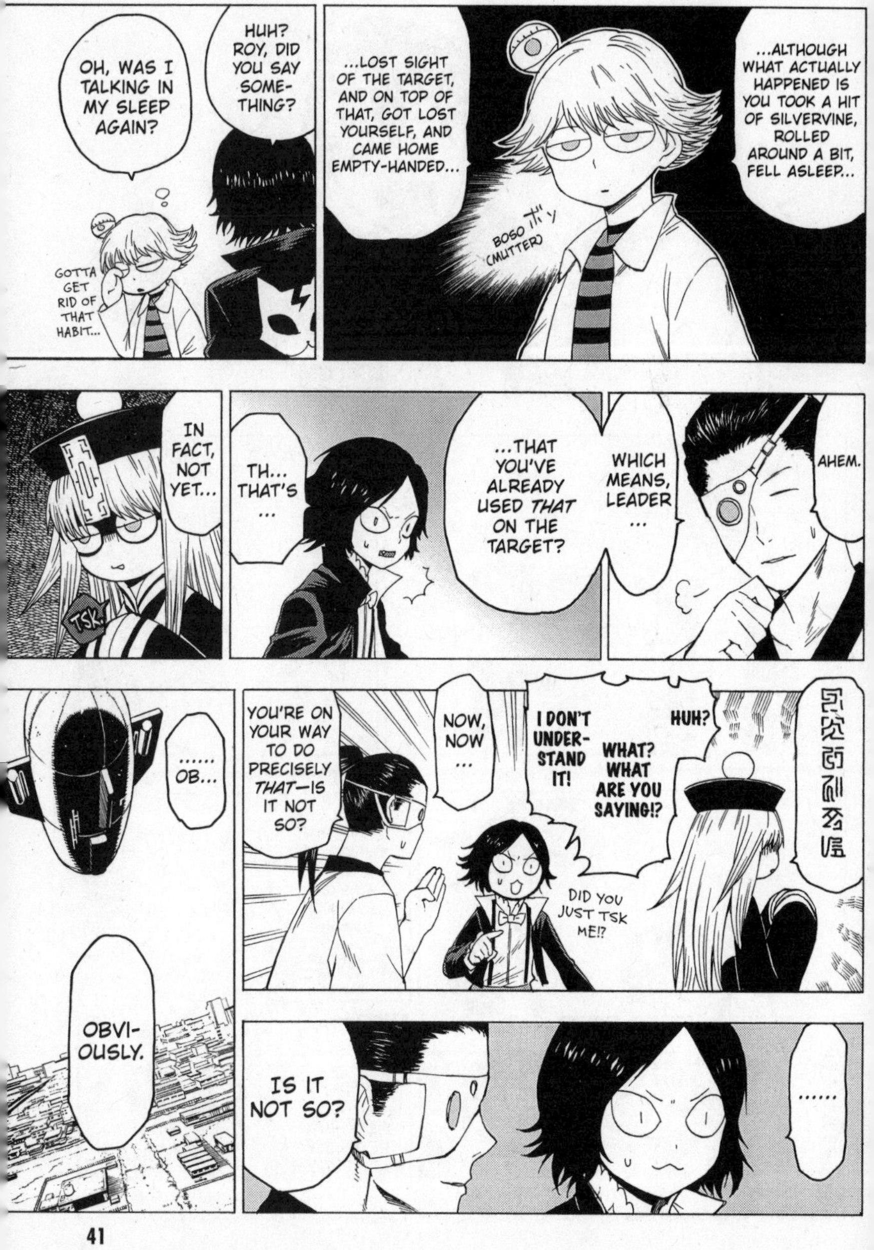
...ALTHOUGH WHAT ACTUALLY HAPPENED IS YOU TOOK A HIT OF SILVERVINE, ROLLED AROUND A BIT, FELL ASLEEP...
...LOST SIGHT OF THE TARGET, AND ON TOP OF THAT, GOT LOST YOURSELF, AND CAME HOME EMPTY-HANDED...
BOSO ボソ (MUTTER)
HUH? ROY, DID YOU SAY SOME-THING?
OH, WAS I TALKING IN MY SLEEP AGAIN?
GOTTA GET RID OF THAT HABIT...
AHEM.
WHICH MEANS, LEADER...
...THAT YOU'VE ALREADY USED *THAT* ON THE TARGET?
TH... THAT'S ...
IN FACT, NOT YET...
TSK.
HUH?
I DON'T UNDERSTAND IT!
WHAT? WHAT ARE YOU SAYING!?
DID YOU JUST TSK ME!?
NOW, NOW ...
YOU'RE ON YOUR WAY TO DO PRECISELY *THAT*—IS IT NOT SO?
......
IS IT NOT SO?
...... OB...
OBVI-OUSLY.

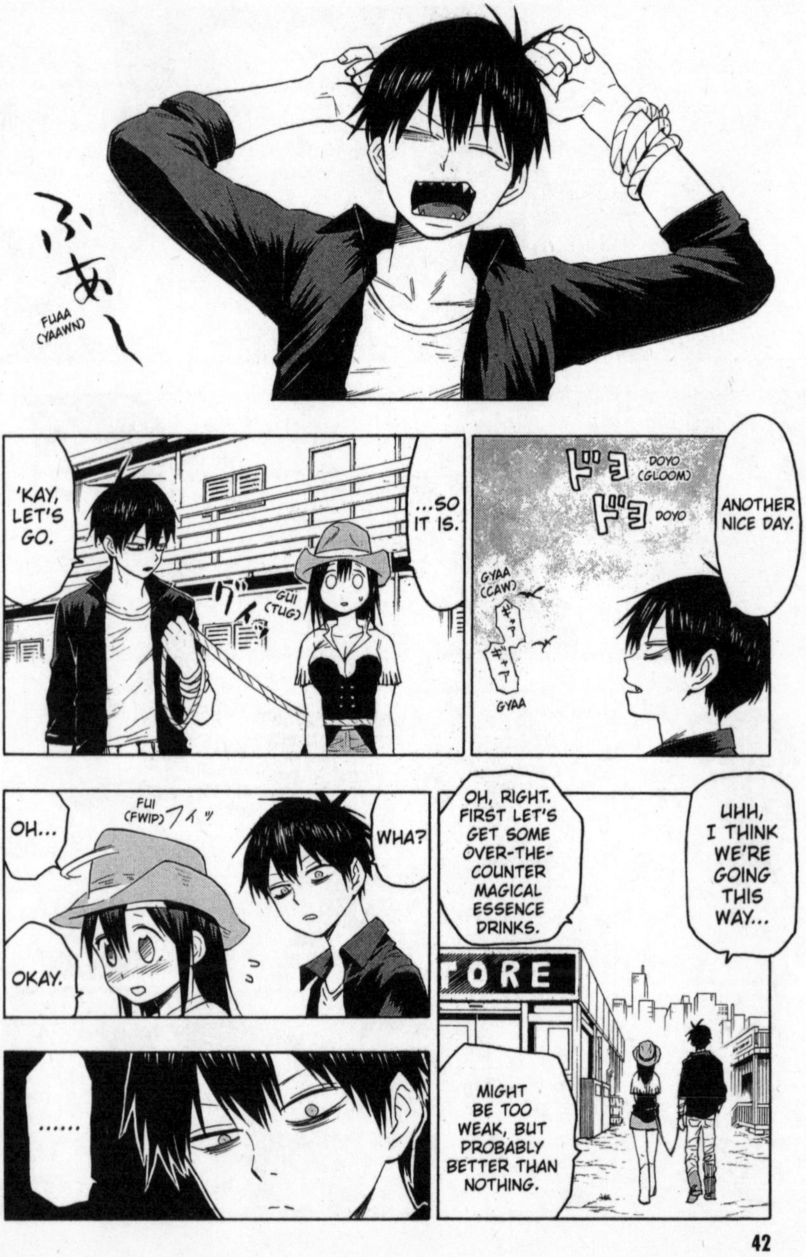
ふあ～
FUAA (YAAWN)
ANOTHER NICE DAY.
ドヨ
DOYO (GLOOM)
ドヨ
DOYO
GYAA (CAW)
ギャア
ギャア
GYAA
...SO IT IS.
'KAY, LET'S GO.
グイ
GUI (TUG)
UHH, I THINK WE'RE GOING THIS WAY...
OH, RIGHT. FIRST LET'S GET SOME OVER-THE-COUNTER MAGICAL ESSENCE DRINKS.
TORE
MIGHT BE TOO WEAK, BUT PROBABLY BETTER THAN NOTHING.
WHA?
FUI (FWIP) フイッ
OH...
OKAY.
......

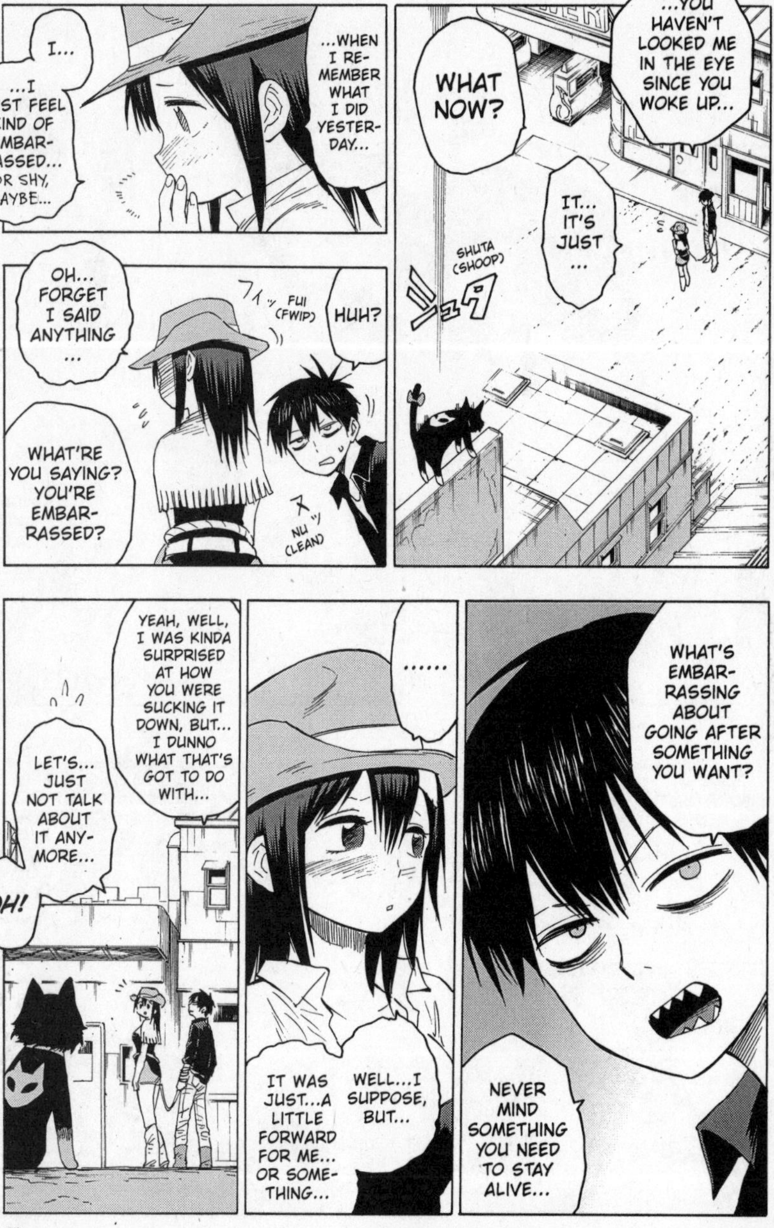
...YOU HAVEN'T LOOKED ME IN THE EYE SINCE YOU WOKE UP...
WHAT NOW?
IT... IT'S JUST ...
シュタ SHUTA (SHOOP)
...WHEN I REMEMBER WHAT I DID YESTERDAY...
I...
...I JUST FEEL KIND OF EMBARRASSED... OR SHY, MAYBE...
HUH?
フィッ FUI (FWIP)
OH... FORGET I SAID ANYTHING...
WHAT'RE YOU SAYING? YOU'RE EMBARRASSED?
ヌッ NU (LEAN)
WHAT'S EMBARRASSING ABOUT GOING AFTER SOMETHING YOU WANT?
NEVER MIND SOMETHING YOU NEED TO STAY ALIVE...
......
WELL...I SUPPOSE, BUT...
IT WAS JUST...A LITTLE FORWARD FOR ME... OR SOMETHING...
YEAH, WELL, I WAS KINDA SURPRISED AT HOW YOU WERE SUCKING IT DOWN, BUT... I DUNNO WHAT THAT'S GOT TO DO WITH...
LET'S... JUST NOT TALK ABOUT IT ANYMORE...
OH!

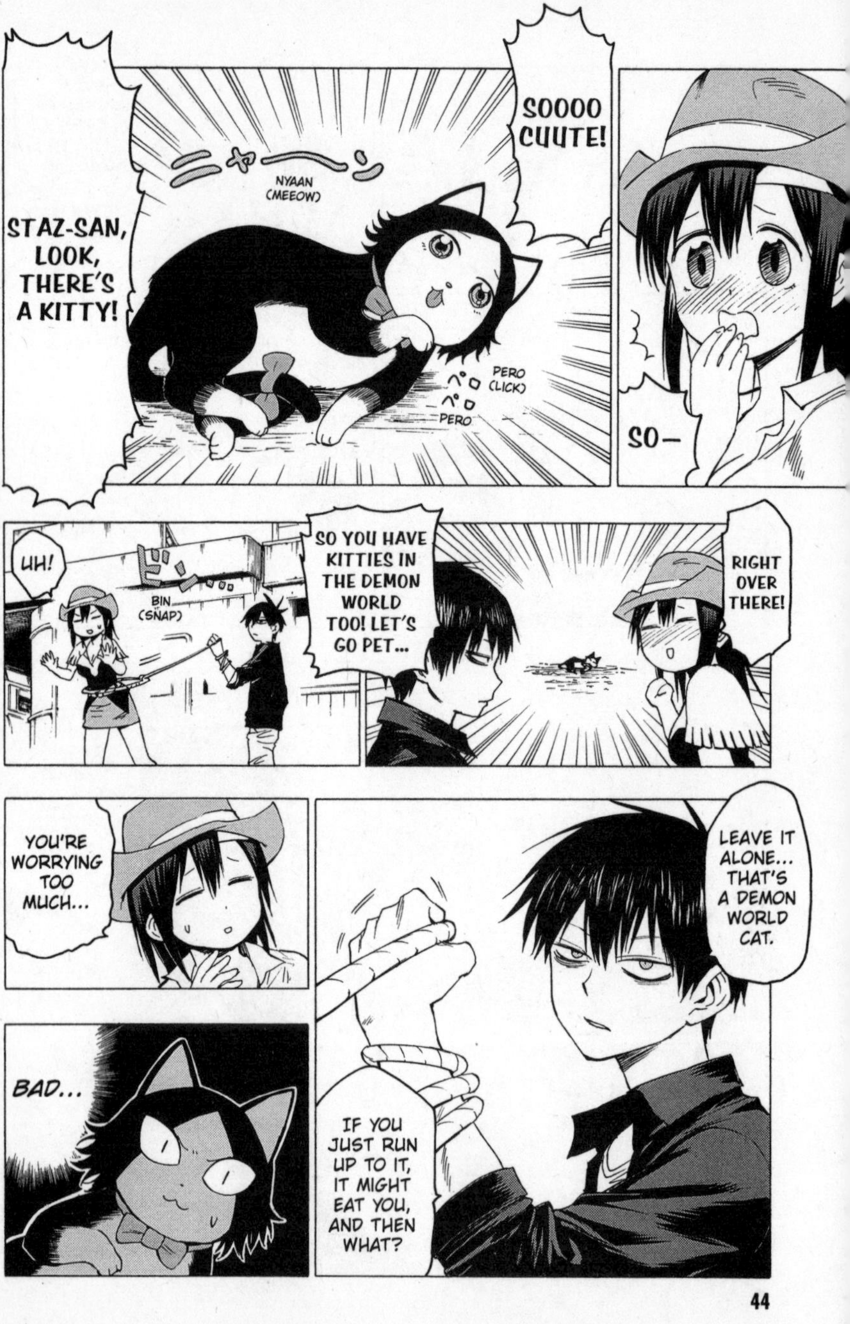
SO–
SOOOO CUUTE!
ニャ〜〜ン
NYAAN (MEEOW)
STAZ-SAN, LOOK, THERE'S A KITTY!
ペロ ペロ
PERO (LICK) PERO
RIGHT OVER THERE!
SO YOU HAVE KITTIES IN THE DEMON WORLD TOO! LET'S GO PET...
ビン
BIN (SNAP)
UH!
LEAVE IT ALONE... THAT'S A DEMON WORLD CAT.
IF YOU JUST RUN UP TO IT, IT MIGHT EAT YOU, AND THEN WHAT?
YOU'RE WORRYING TOO MUCH...
BAD...

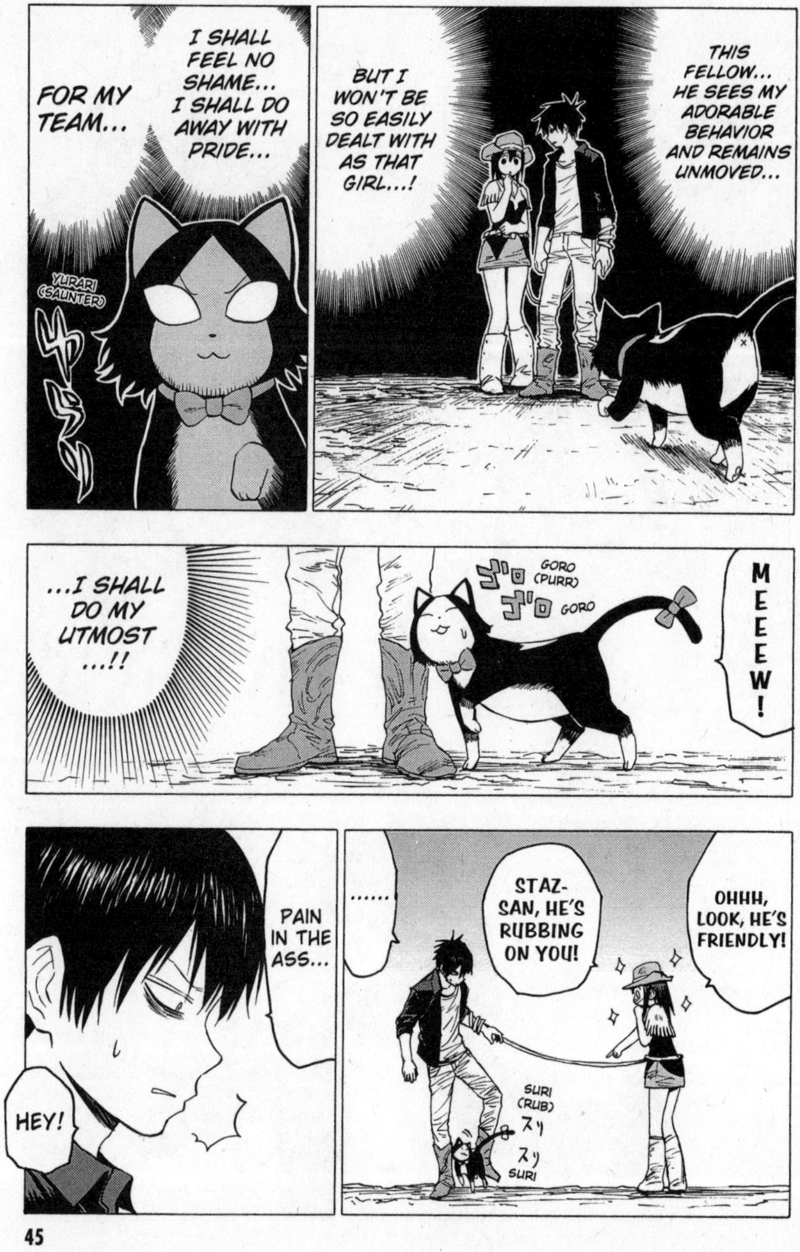

THIS FELLOW... HE SEES MY ADORABLE BEHAVIOR AND REMAINS UNMOVED...
BUT I WON'T BE SO EASILY DEALT WITH AS THAT GIRL...!
I SHALL FEEL NO SHAME... I SHALL DO AWAY WITH PRIDE...
FOR MY TEAM...
YURARI (SAUNTER)
MEEEW!
GORO (PURR) GORO
...I SHALL DO MY UTMOST...!!
OHHH, LOOK, HE'S FRIENDLY!
STAZ-SAN, HE'S RUBBING ON YOU!
......
SURI (RUB) SURI
PAIN IN THE ASS...
HEY!

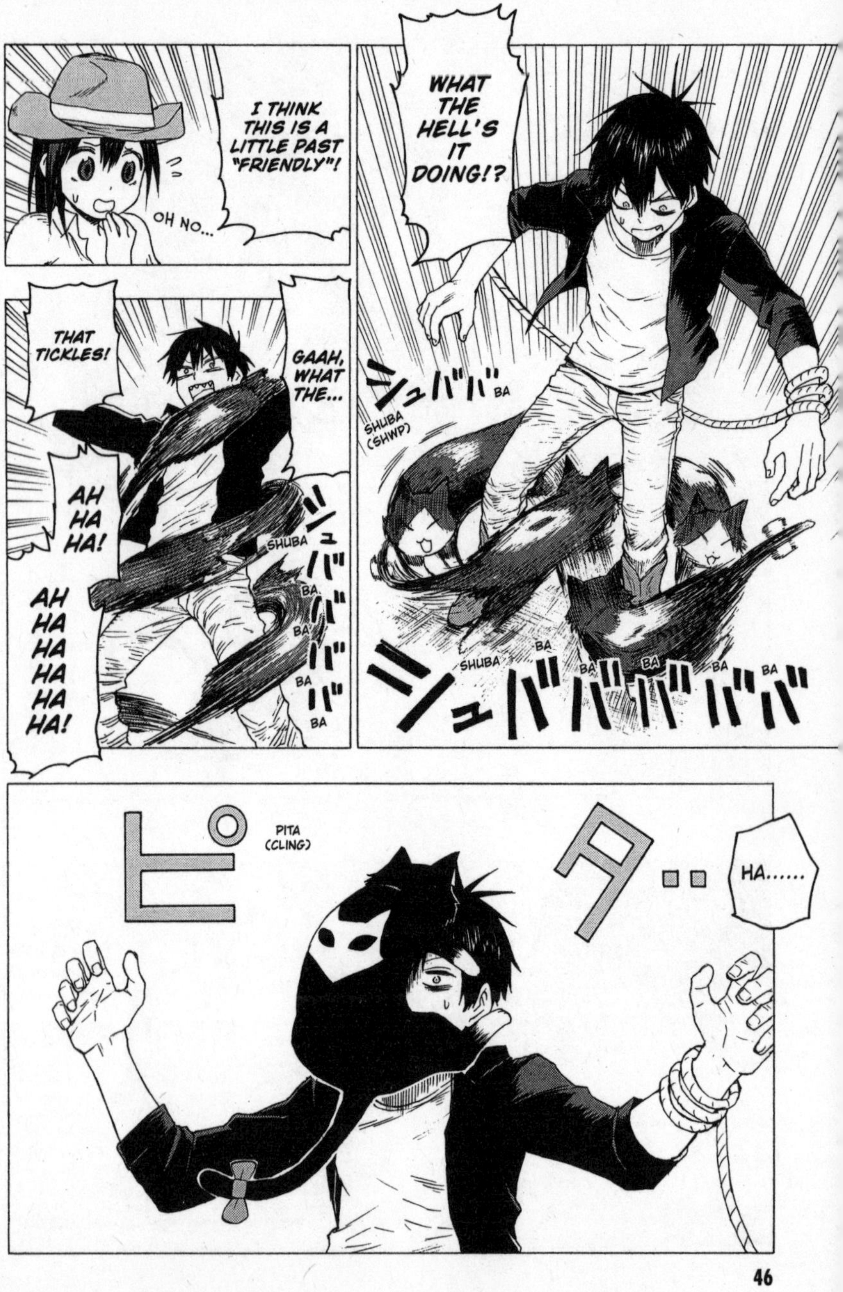
WHAT THE HELL'S IT DOING!?
シュババ BA
SHUBA (SHWP)
シュババババ
SHUBA BA BA BA BA BA
I THINK THIS IS A LITTLE PAST "FRIENDLY"!
OH NO...
GAAH, WHAT THE...
THAT TICKLES!
シュババババ
SHUBA BA BA BA BA
AH HA HA!
AH HA HA HA HA HA HA!
ピタ‥
PITA (CLING)
HA......

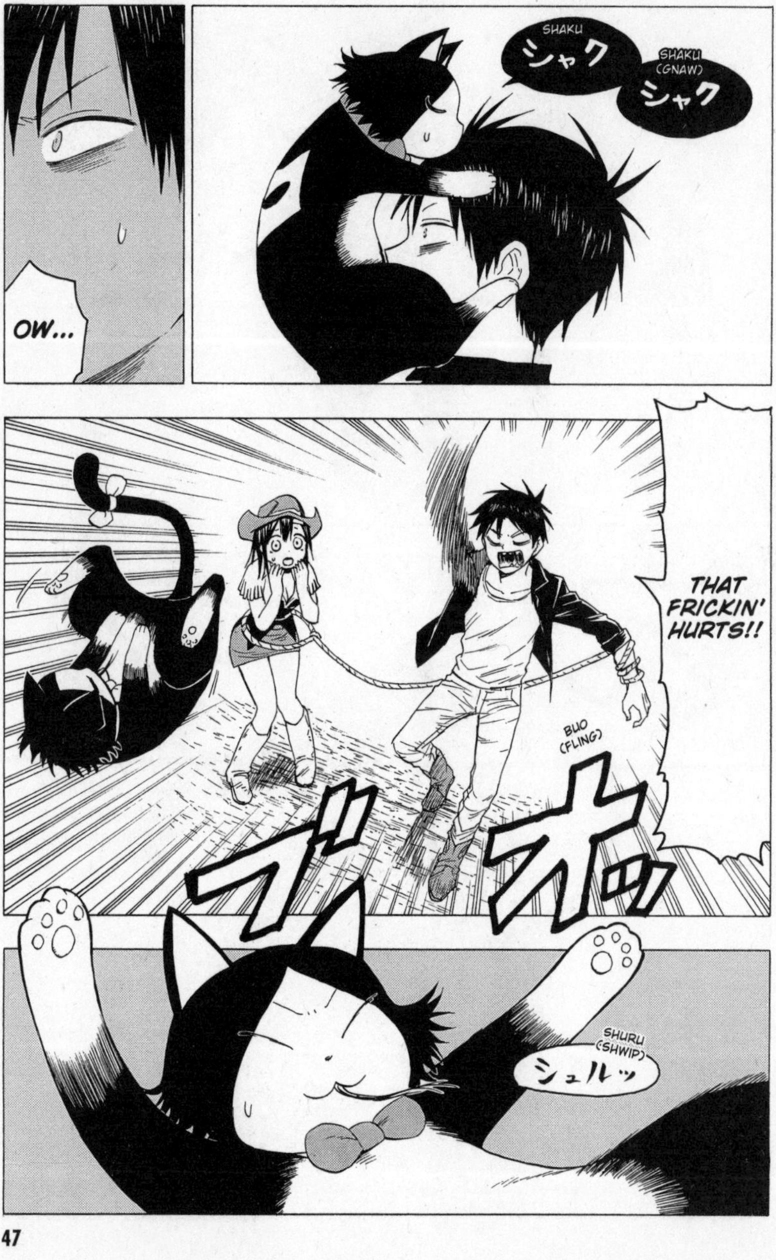
SHAKU
シャク
SHAKU (GNAW)
シャク
OW...
THAT FRICKIN' HURTS!!
BUO (FLING)
ブオッ
SHURU (SHWIP)
シュルッ

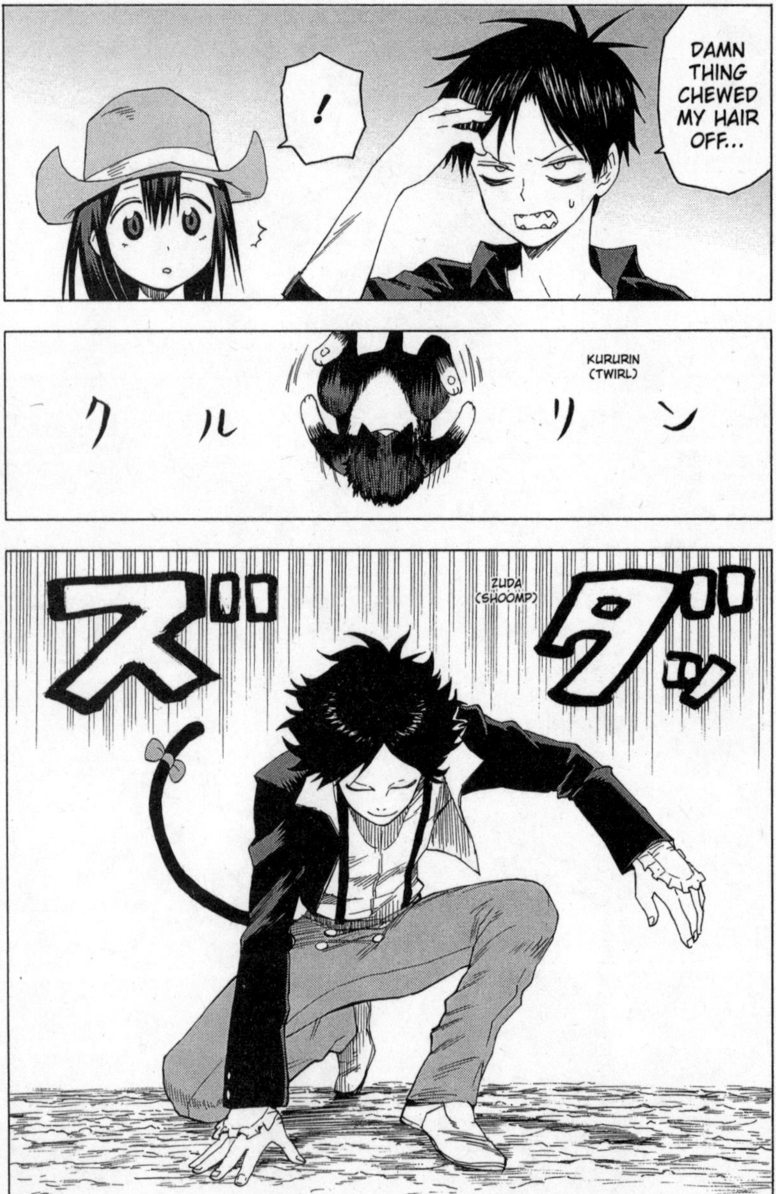
DAMN THING CHEWED MY HAIR OFF...
!
KURURIN (TWIRL)
クルリン
ZUDA (SHOOMP)
ズダッ

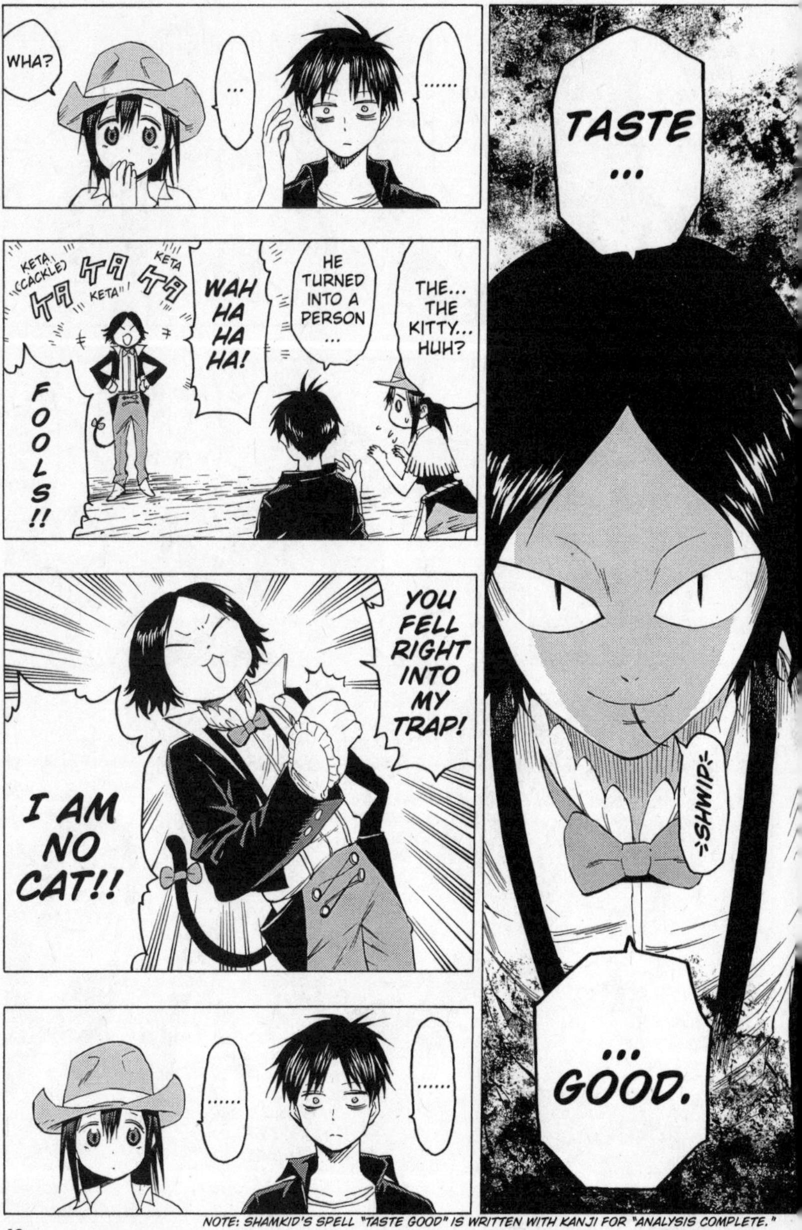
TASTE ...
SHWIP
... GOOD.
......
...
WHA?
THE... THE KITTY... HUH?
HE TURNED INTO A PERSON ...
WAH HA HA HA!
KETA KETA KETA (CACKLE)
FOOLS!!
YOU FELL RIGHT INTO MY TRAP!
I AM NO CAT!!
......
......

NOTE: SHAMKID'S SPELL "TASTE GOOD" IS WRITTEN WITH KANJI FOR "ANALYSIS COMPLETE."

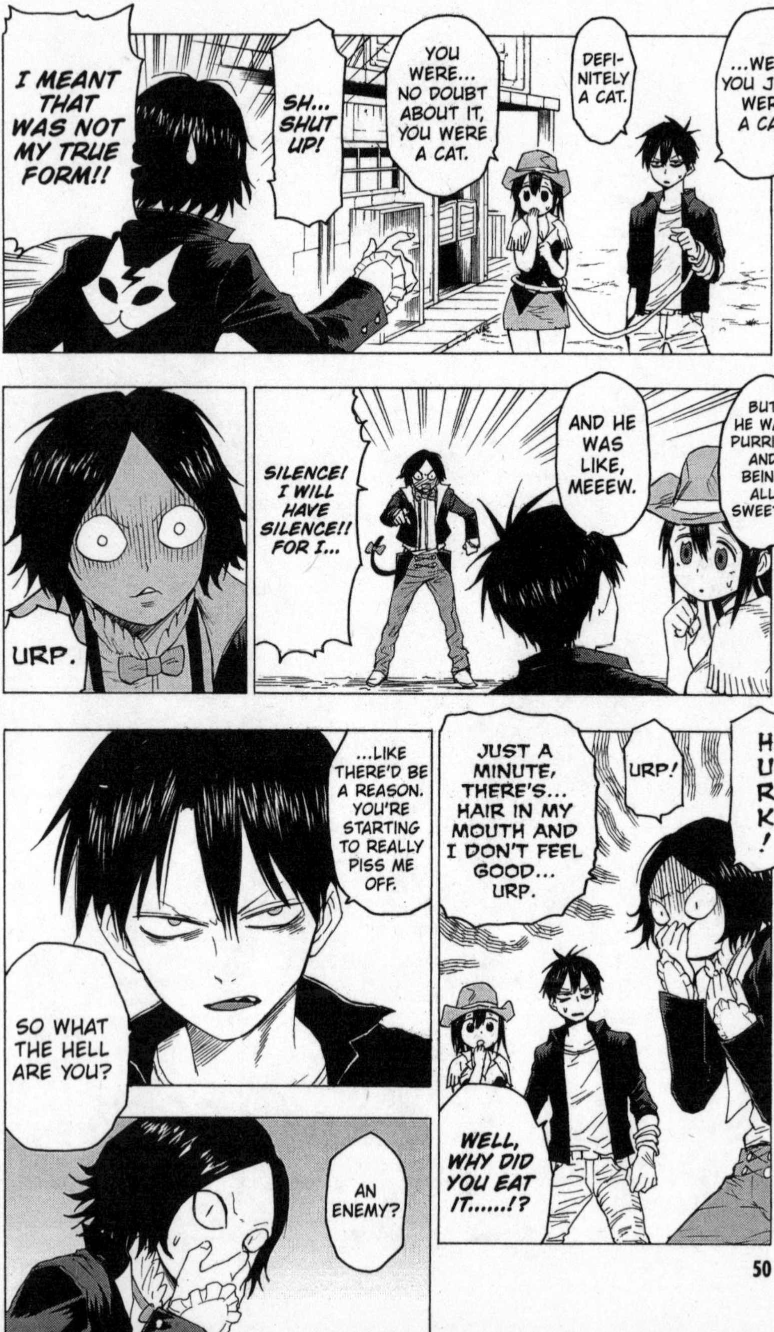
...WELL, YOU JUST WERE A CAT.
DEFI-NITELY A CAT.
YOU WERE... NO DOUBT ABOUT IT, YOU WERE A CAT.
SH... SHUT UP!
I MEANT THAT WAS NOT MY TRUE FORM!!
BUT HE WAS PURRING AND BEING ALL SWEET...
AND HE WAS LIKE, MEEEW.
SILENCE! I WILL HAVE SILENCE!! FOR I...
URP.
HURK!
URP!
JUST A MINUTE, THERE'S... HAIR IN MY MOUTH AND I DON'T FEEL GOOD... URP.
WELL, WHY DID YOU EAT IT......!?
...LIKE THERE'D BE A REASON. YOU'RE STARTING TO REALLY PISS ME OFF.
SO WHAT THE HELL ARE YOU?
AN ENEMY?

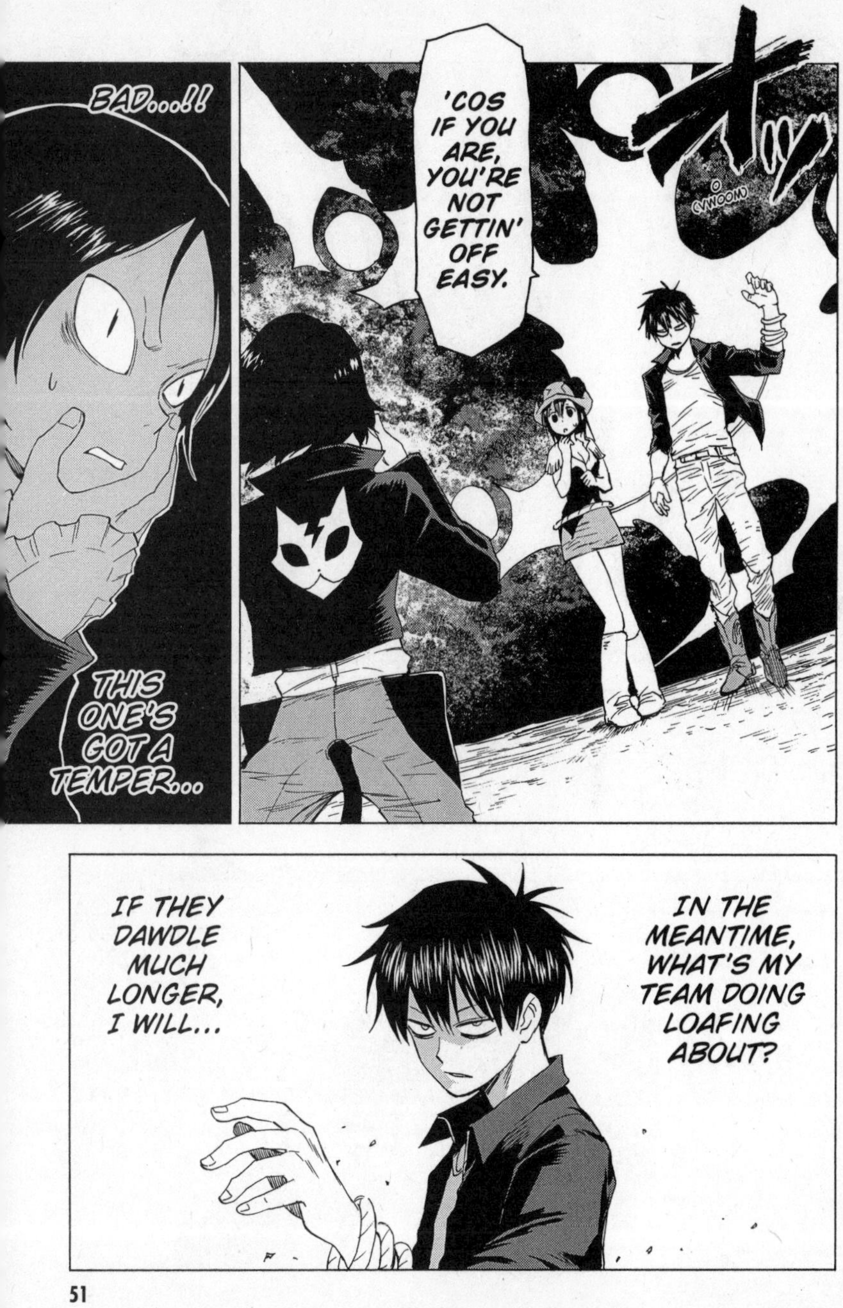
(VWOOM)
'COS IF YOU ARE, YOU'RE NOT GETTIN' OFF EASY.
BAD...!!
THIS ONE'S GOT A TEMPER...
IN THE MEANTIME, WHAT'S MY TEAM DOING LOAFING ABOUT?
IF THEY DAWDLE MUCH LONGER, I WILL...

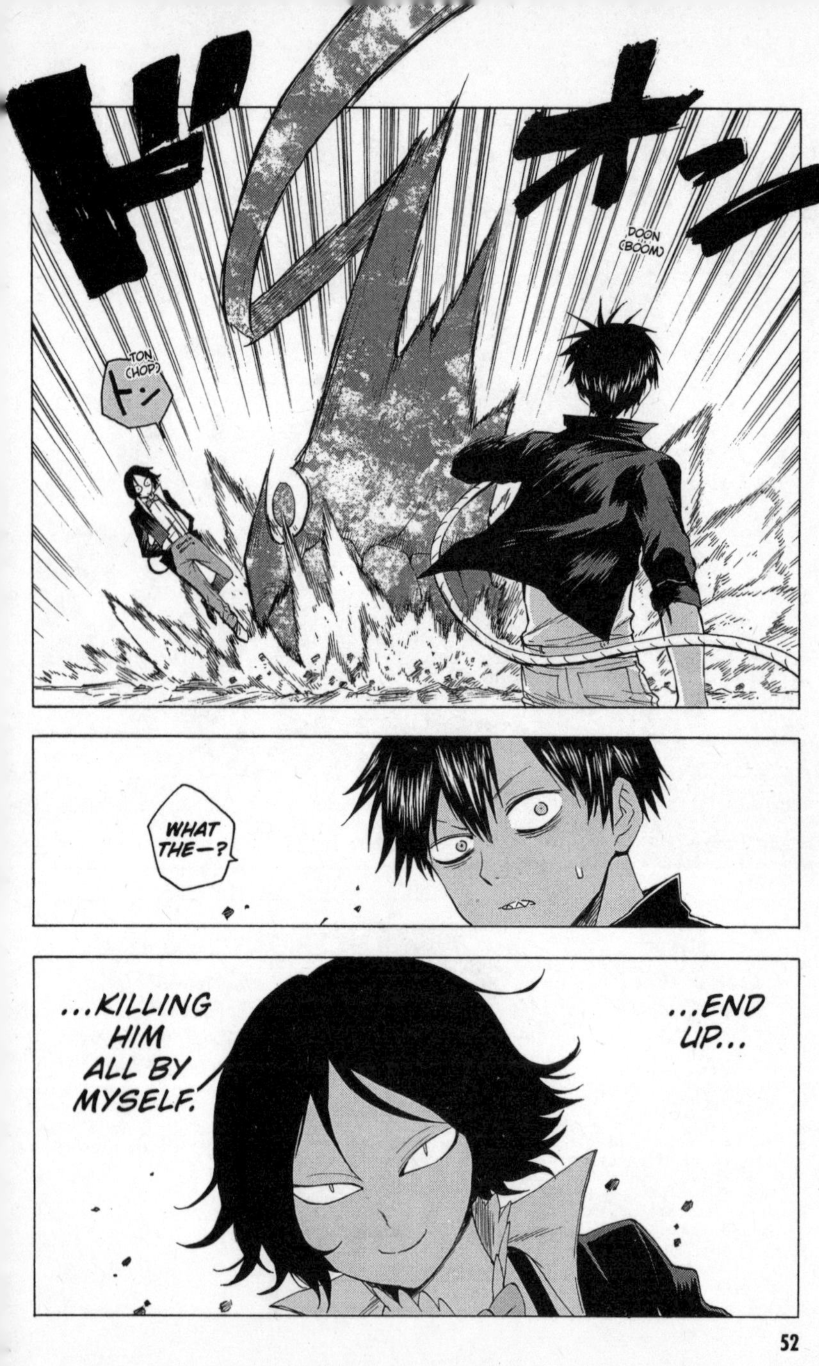

DOON (BOOM)
TON (HOP)
トン
WHAT THE—?
...END UP...
...KILLING HIM ALL BY MYSELF.

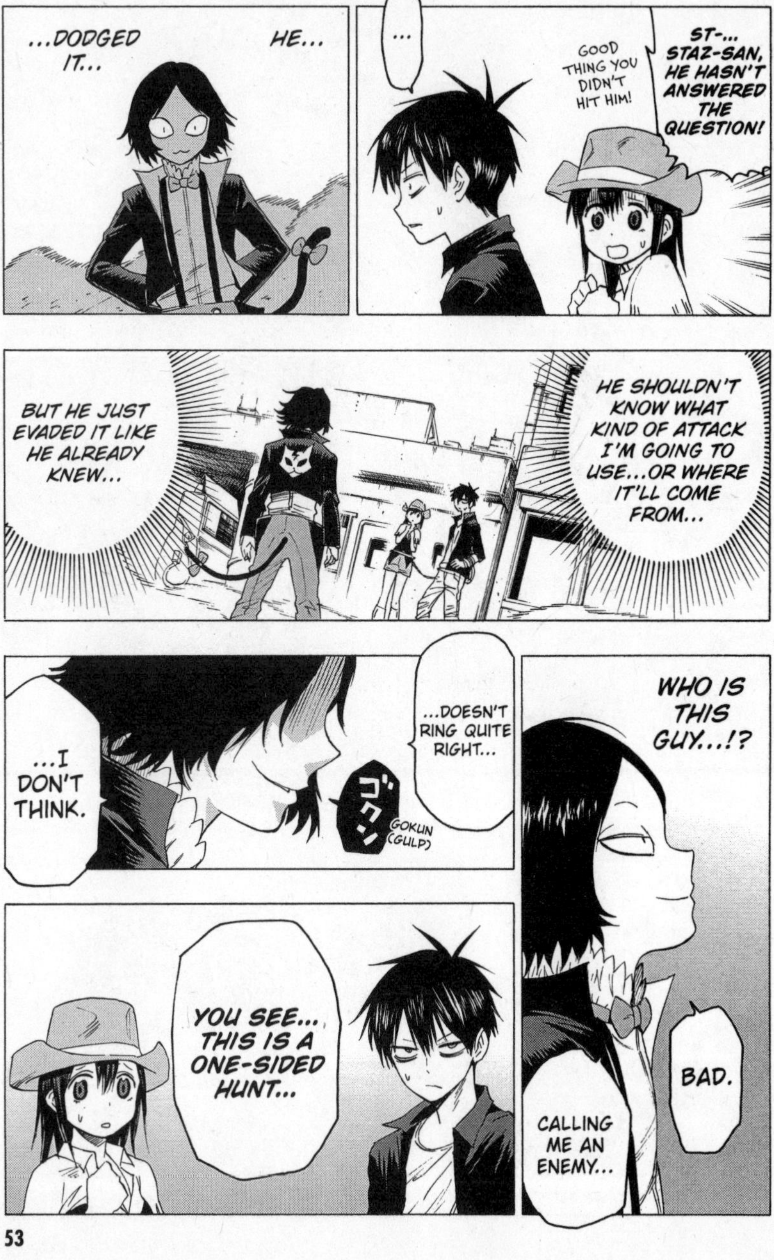

ST-... STAZ-SAN, HE HASN'T ANSWERED THE QUESTION!
GOOD THING YOU DIDN'T HIT HIM!
...
HE...
...DODGED IT...
HE SHOULDN'T KNOW WHAT KIND OF ATTACK I'M GOING TO USE...OR WHERE IT'LL COME FROM...
BUT HE JUST EVADED IT LIKE HE ALREADY KNEW...
WHO IS THIS GUY...!?
BAD.
CALLING ME AN ENEMY...
...DOESN'T RING QUITE RIGHT...
ゴクン
GOKUN (GULP)
...I DON'T THINK.
YOU SEE... THIS IS A ONE-SIDED HUNT...

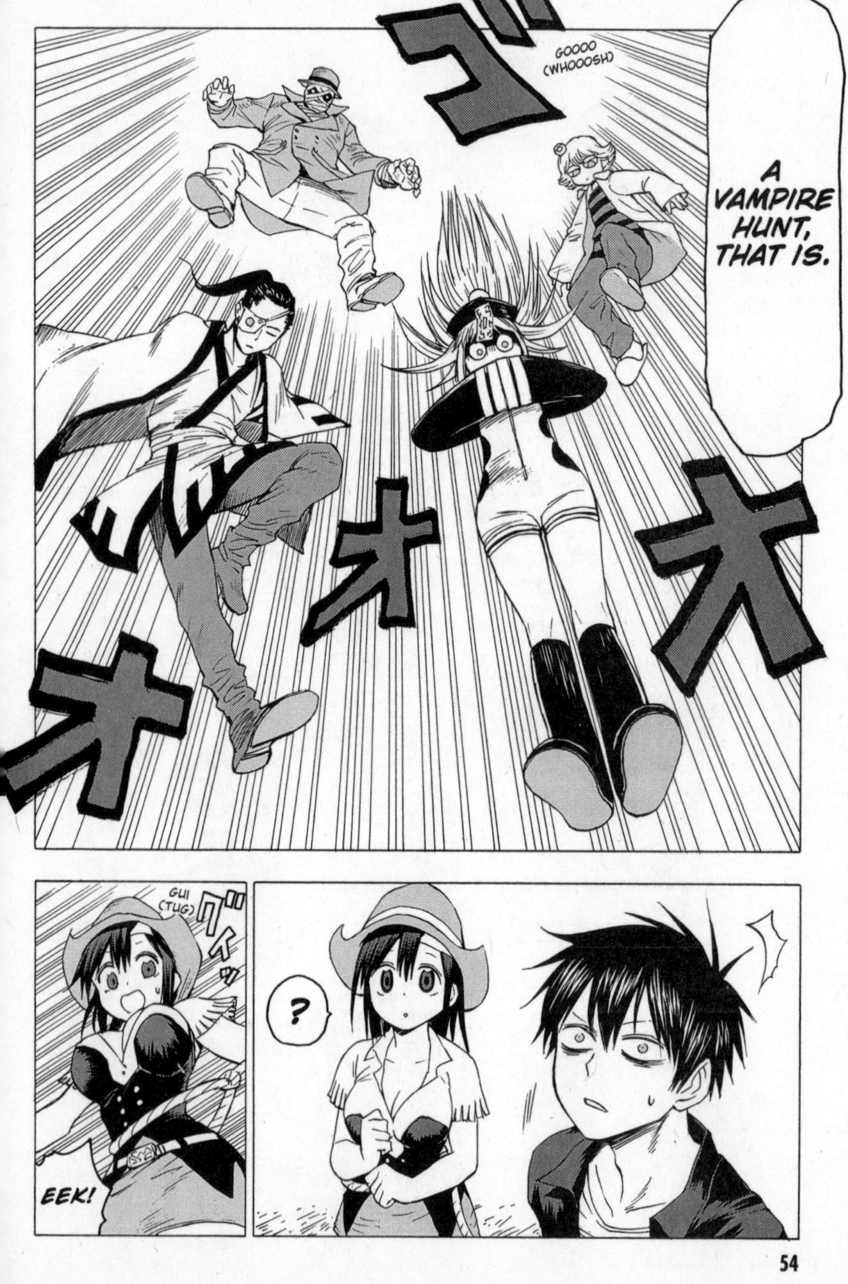
A VAMPIRE HUNT, THAT IS.
GOOOO (WHOOOSH)
!
?
GUI (TUG)
EEK!

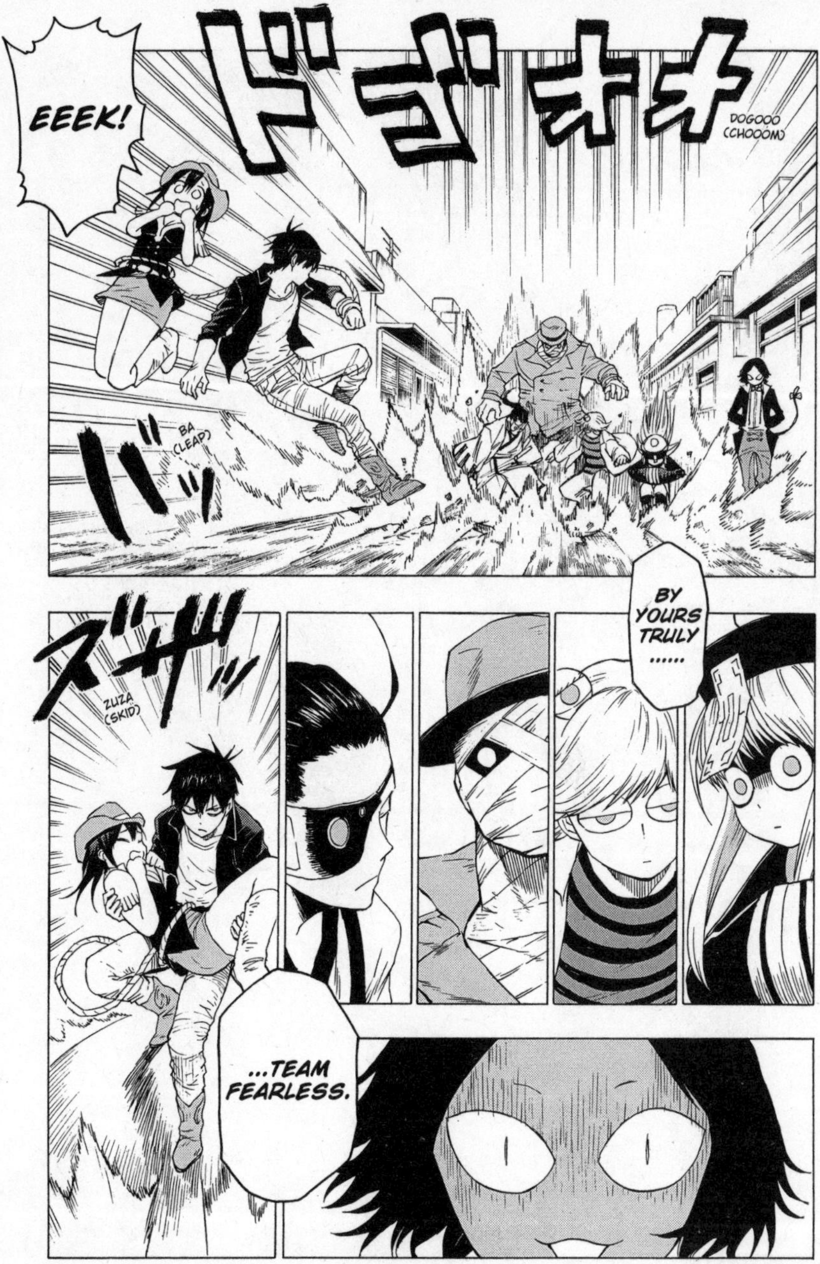
ドゴオオ
DOGOOO (CHOOOM)
EEEK!
バッ
BA (LEAP)
BY YOURS TRULY ......
...TEAM FEARLESS.
ズザッ
ZUZA (SKID)

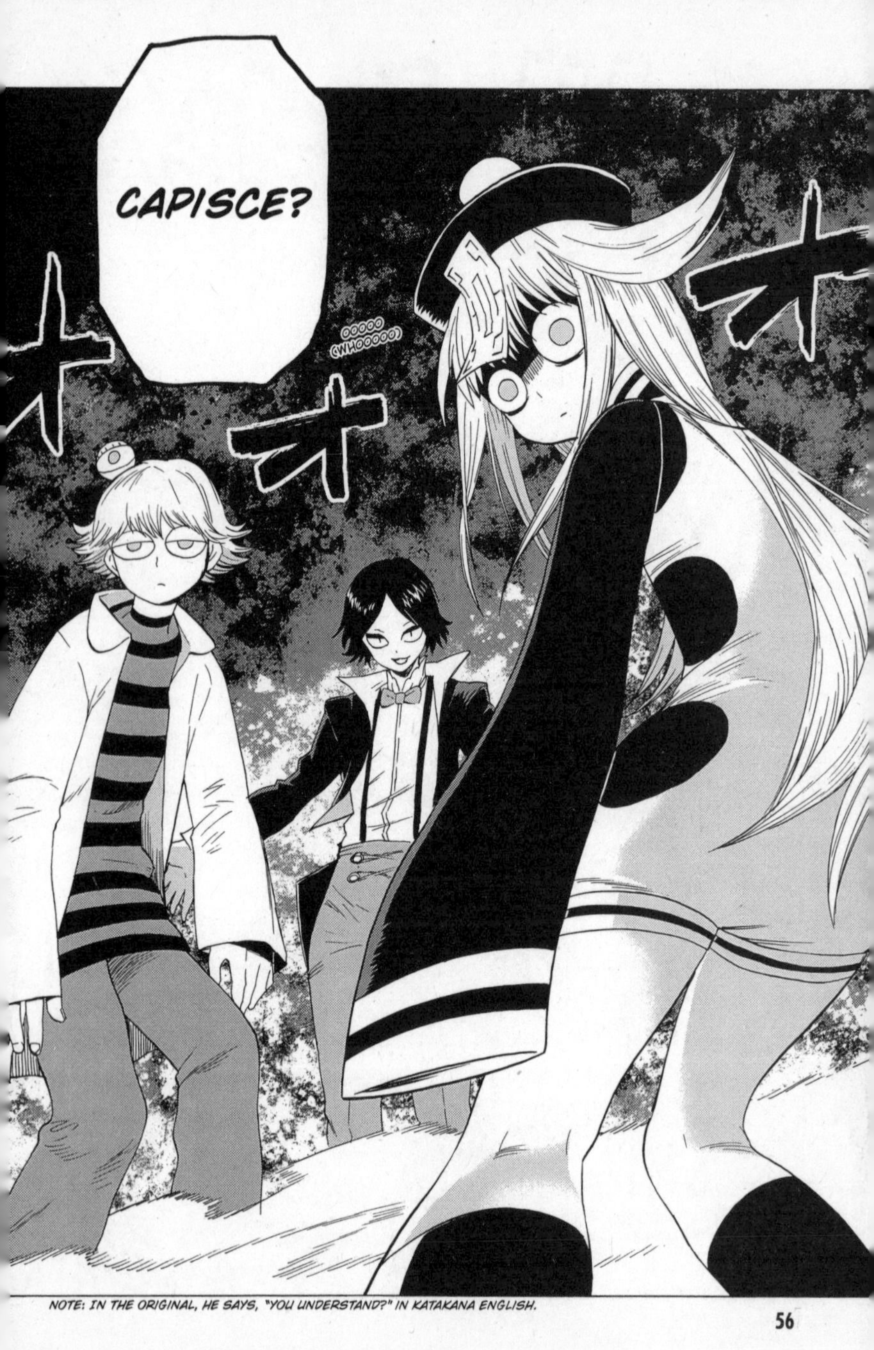
CAPISCE?
OOOOO (WHOOOOO)

NOTE: IN THE ORIGINAL, HE SAYS, "YOU UNDERSTAND?" IN KATAKANA ENGLISH.

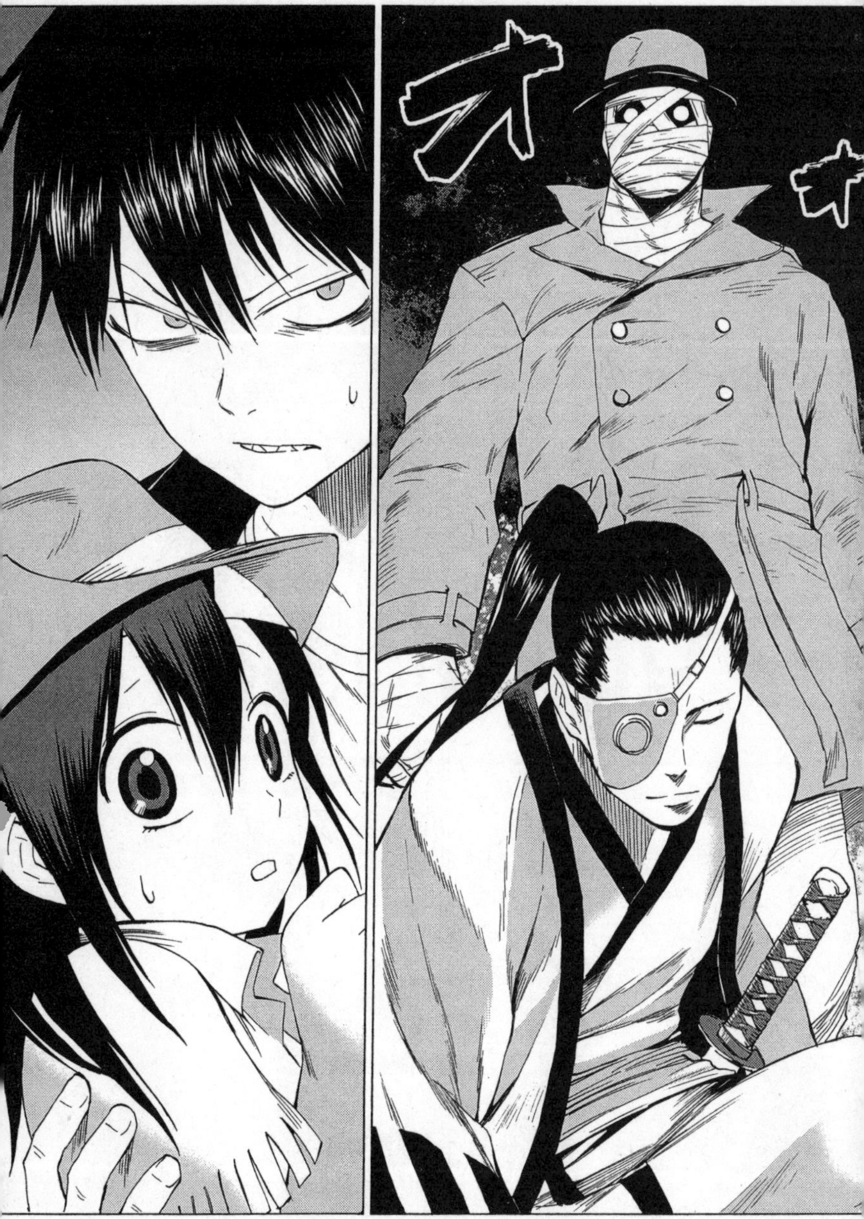
オ
オ

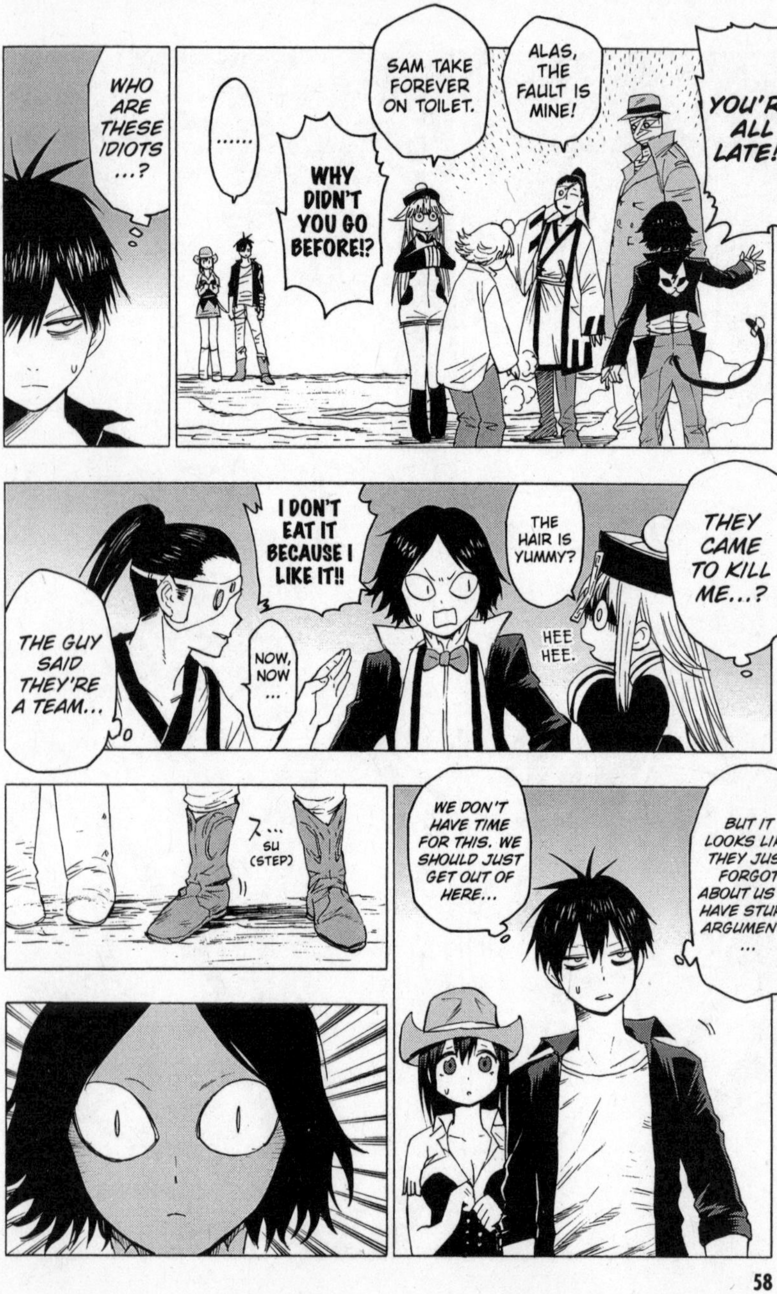
YOU'RE ALL LATE!!
ALAS, THE FAULT IS MINE!
SAM TAKE FOREVER ON TOILET.
WHY DIDN'T YOU GO BEFORE!?
......
WHO ARE THESE IDIOTS ...?
THEY CAME TO KILL ME...?
THE HAIR IS YUMMY?
HEE HEE.
I DON'T EAT IT BECAUSE I LIKE IT!!
NOW, NOW ...
THE GUY SAID THEY'RE A TEAM...
BUT IT LOOKS LIKE THEY JUST FORGOT ABOUT US TO HAVE STUPID ARGUMENTS ...
WE DON'T HAVE TIME FOR THIS. WE SHOULD JUST GET OUT OF HERE...
ス... SU (STEP)

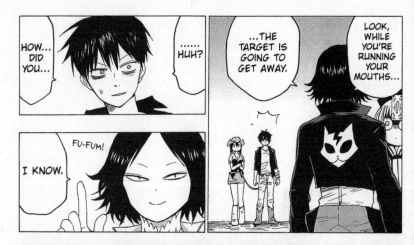

LOOK, WHILE YOU'RE RUNNING YOUR MOUTHS...
...THE TARGET IS GOING TO GET AWAY.
...... HUH?
HOW... DID YOU...
FU-FUM!
I KNOW.
I'M THE LEADER, BUT MY POWER MAKES ME THE READER ......
WHILE I HAVE A PIECE OF A TARGET'S BODY WITHIN ME...
...I CAN FORETELL THEIR ACTIONS...
ZU (ZMMM)
ZU

NOTE: SHAMKID'S TITLE HAS A DOUBLE MEANING, WITH NO DIFFERENTIATION BETWEEN THE R AND L SOUNDS IN JAPANESE. "LEADER" AND "READER" ARE SPELLED EXACTLY THE SAME IN KATAKANA.

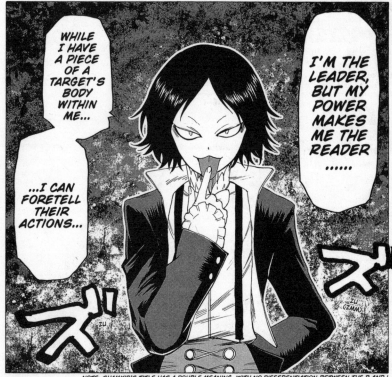

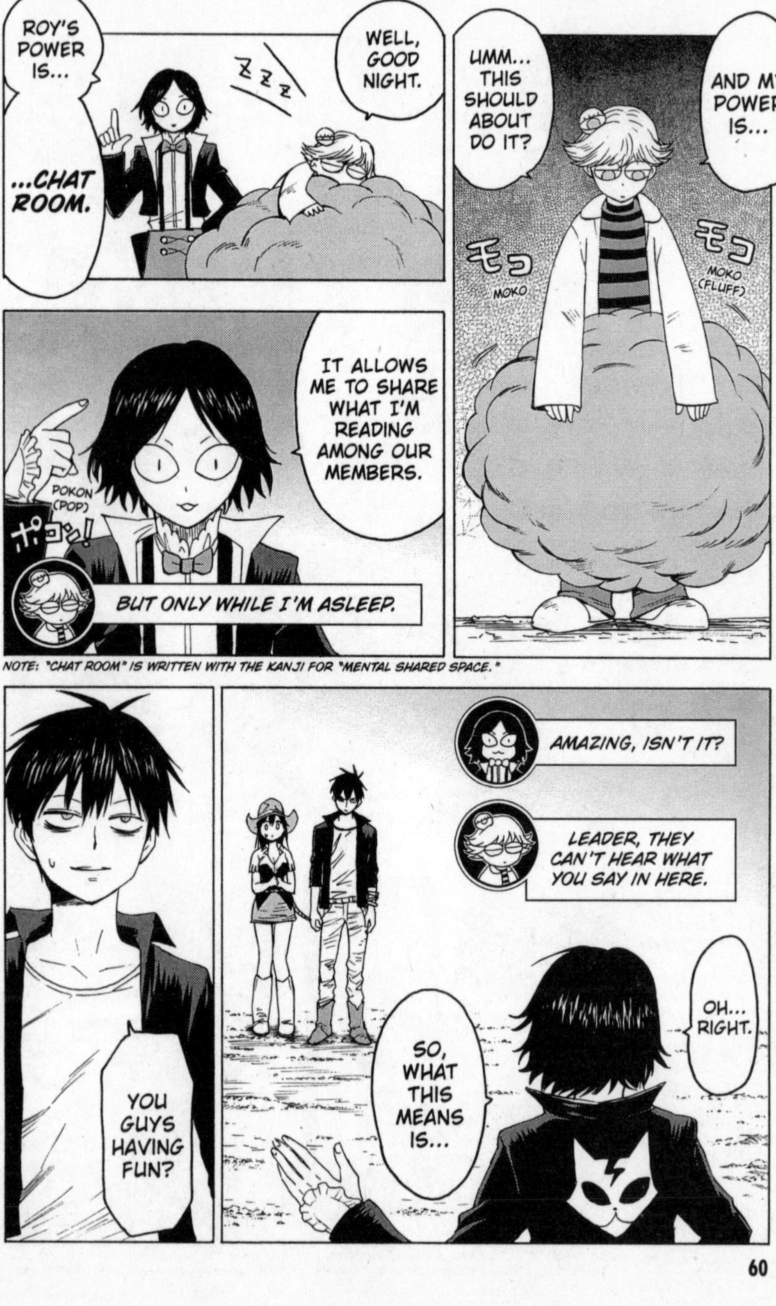
AND MY POWER IS...
UMM... THIS SHOULD ABOUT DO IT?
モコ
MOKO (FLUFF)
モコ
MOKO
WELL, GOOD NIGHT.
Z Z Z
ROY'S POWER IS...
...CHAT ROOM.
IT ALLOWS ME TO SHARE WHAT I'M READING AMONG OUR MEMBERS.
POKON (POP)
BUT ONLY WHILE I'M ASLEEP.
AMAZING, ISN'T IT?
LEADER, THEY CAN'T HEAR WHAT YOU SAY IN HERE.
OH... RIGHT.
SO, WHAT THIS MEANS IS...
YOU GUYS HAVING FUN?

NOTE: "CHAT ROOM" IS WRITTEN WITH THE KANJI FOR "MENTAL SHARED SPACE."

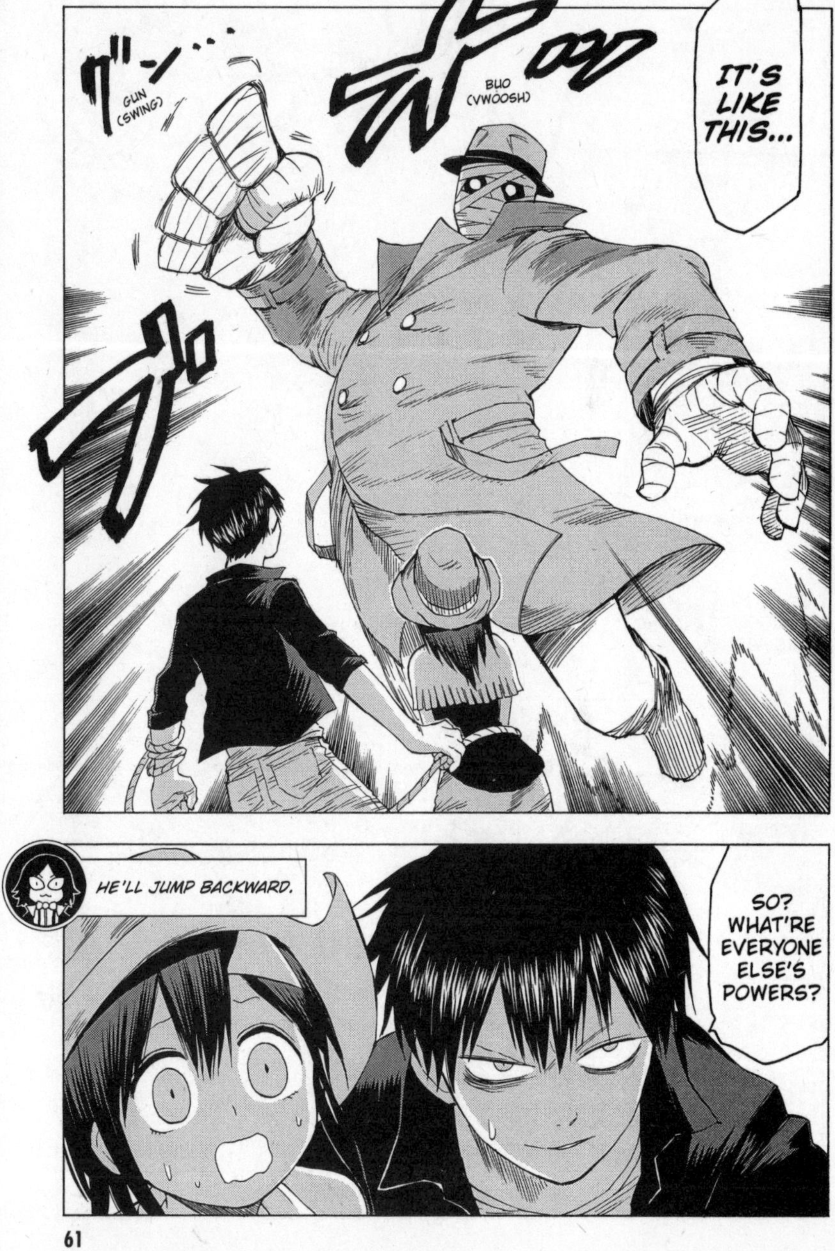

IT'S LIKE THIS...
BUO (VWOOSH)
GUN (SWING)
SO? WHAT'RE EVERYONE ELSE'S POWERS?
HE'LL JUMP BACKWARD.

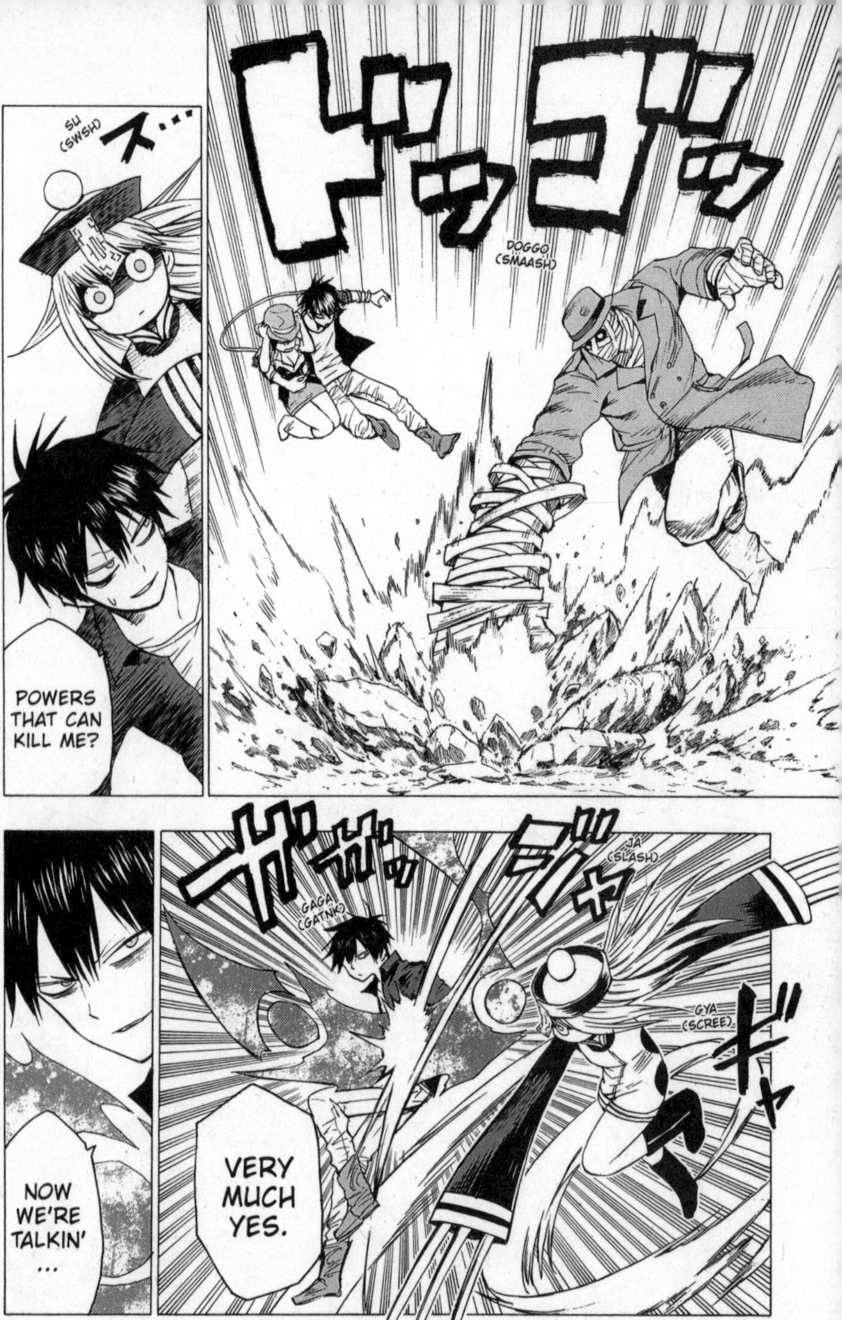
DOGGO
(SMAASH)
SU
(SWSH)
POWERS THAT CAN KILL ME?
JA
(SLASH)
GAGA
(GATNK)
GYA
(SCREE)
VERY MUCH YES.
NOW WE'RE TALKIN'...

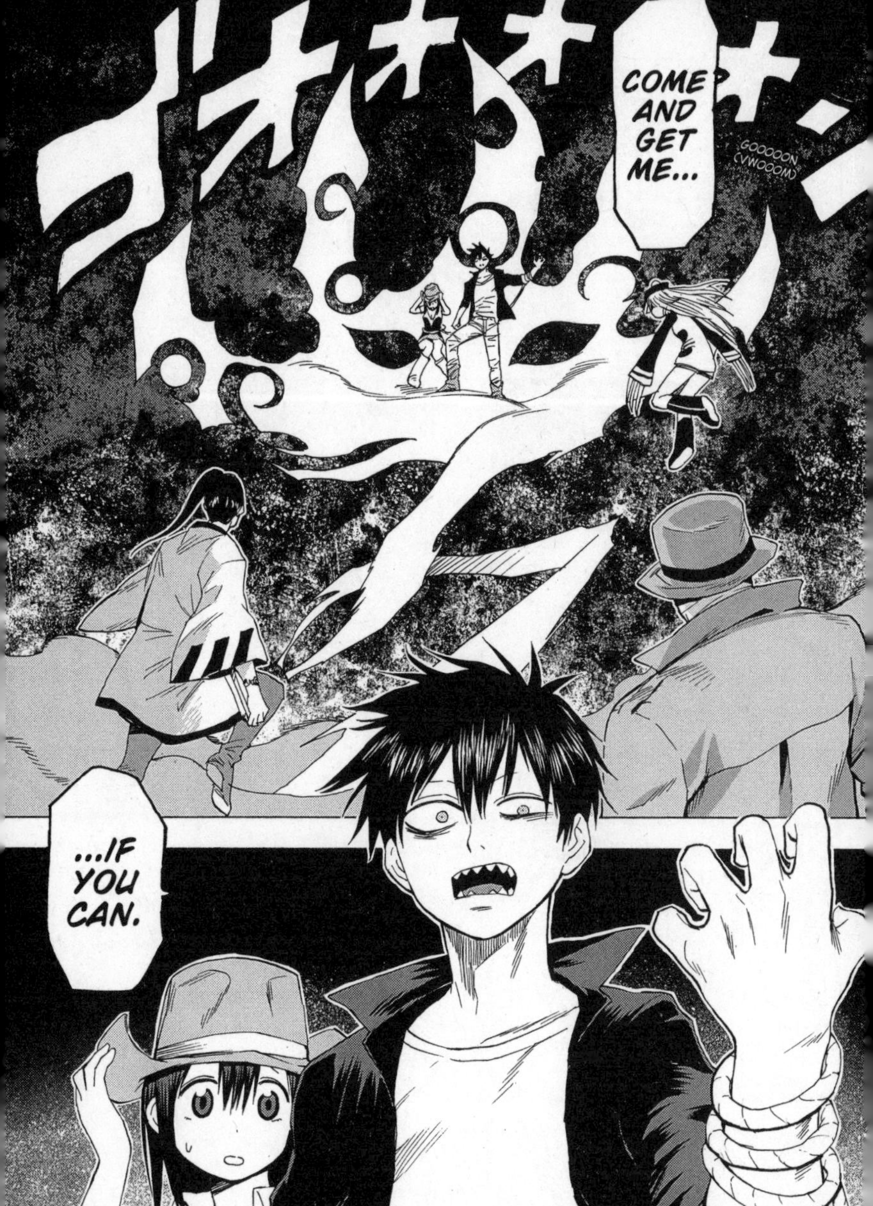
COME AND GET ME...
GOOOOON (VWOOOM)
...IF YOU CAN.

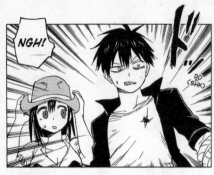

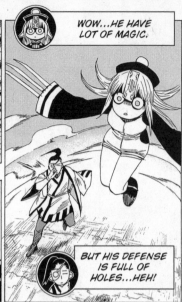

WOW...HE HAVE LOT OF MAGIC.
BUT HIS DEFENSE IS FULL OF HOLES...HEH!
NGH!
ド!!
DO (SHK)
A BLOW DART, IT IS.
...THE HELL'S THIS?
HEY, C'MON...
YOU GUYS SERIOUSLY THINK YOU CAN KILL ME WITH CHEAP-ASS ATTACKS LIKE THAT...?
GET REAL...
HE GET MAD?
IT SEEMS TO HAVE HAD THE DESIRED EFFECT.
NOW FOR THE ATTACK FORMATION WE DISCUSSED...

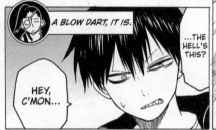

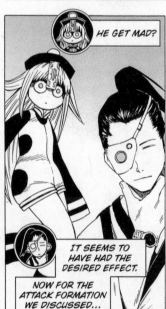

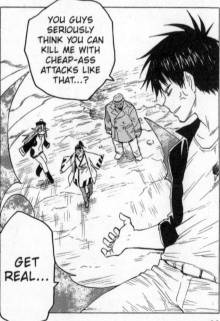

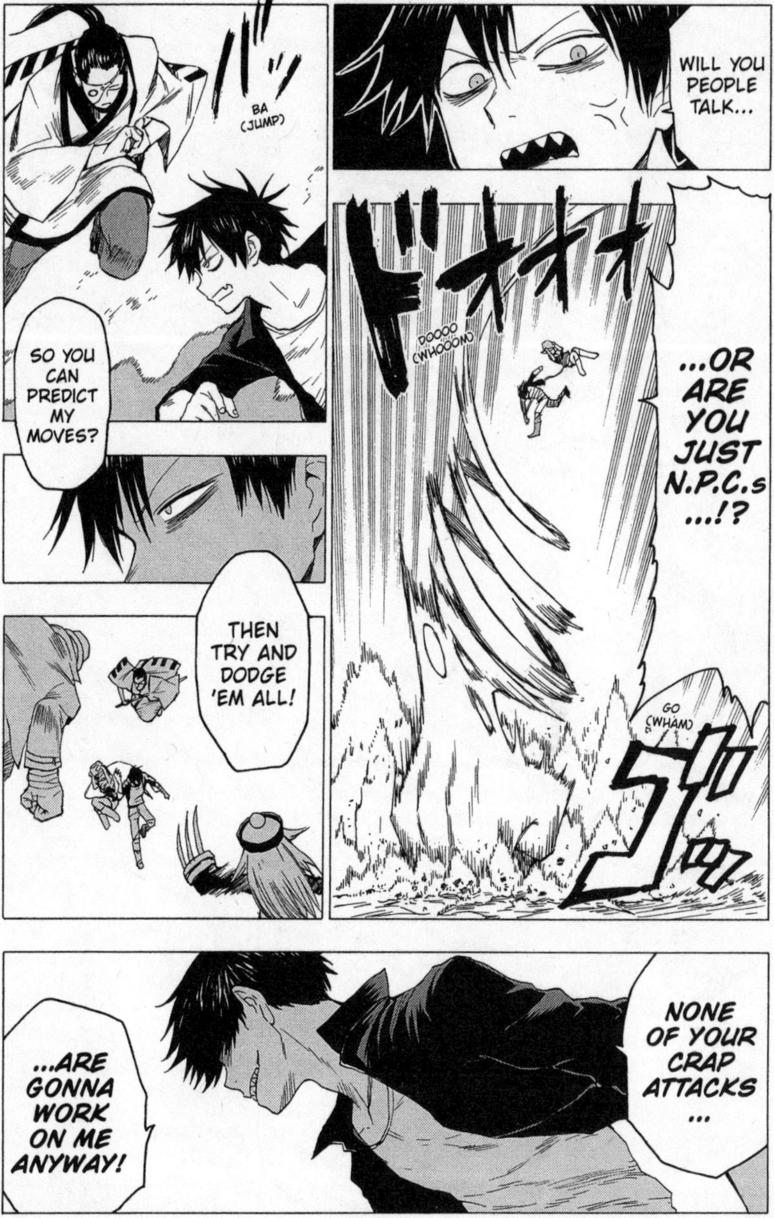
WILL YOU PEOPLE TALK...
ドオオオ
DOOOO (WHOOOM)
...OR ARE YOU JUST N.P.C.s ...!?
GO (WHAM)
ゴッ
バッ
BA (JUMP)
SO YOU CAN PREDICT MY MOVES?
THEN TRY AND DODGE 'EM ALL!
NONE OF YOUR CRAP ATTACKS ...
...ARE GONNA WORK ON ME ANYWAY!

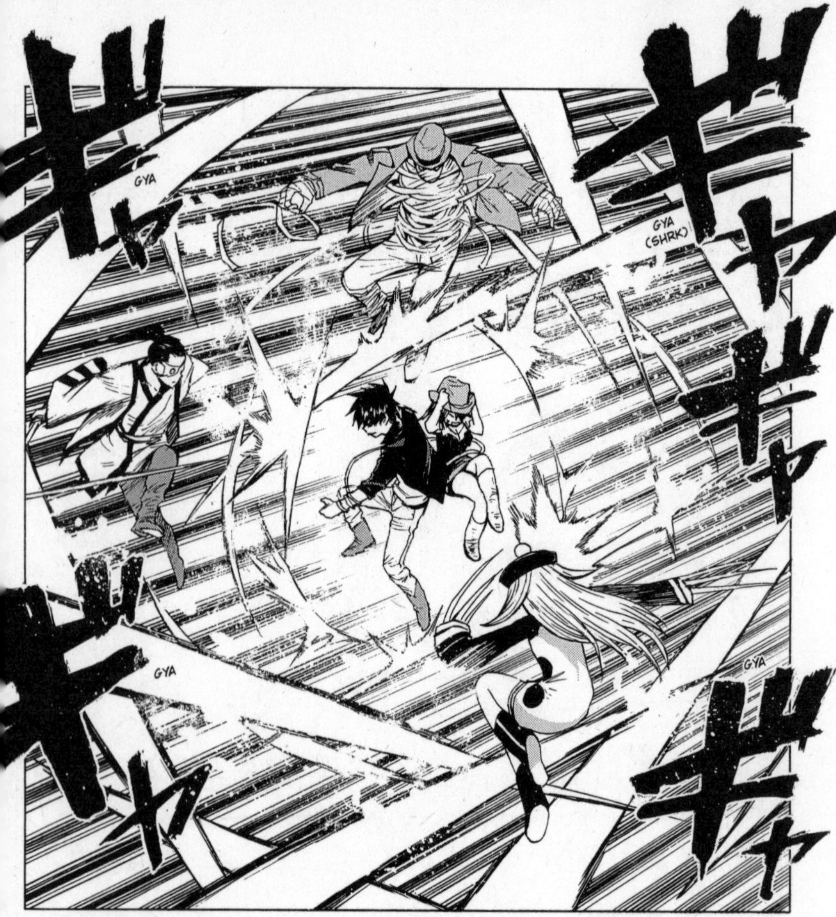
ギャギャギャ
GYA
(SHRK)
ギャ
GYA
ギャ
GYA
ギャ
GYA

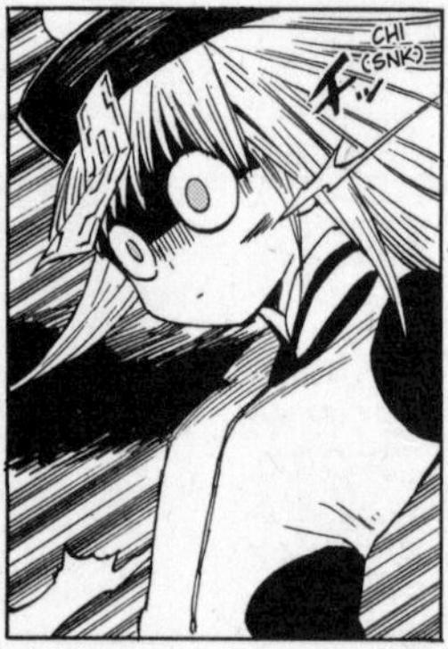
チッ
CHI
(SNK)

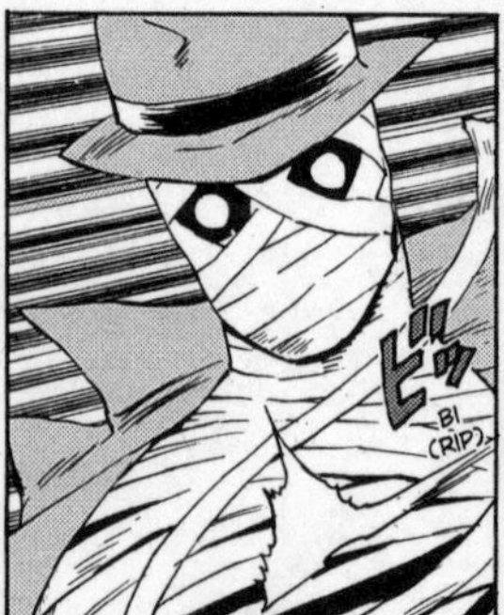
ビッ
BI
(RIP)

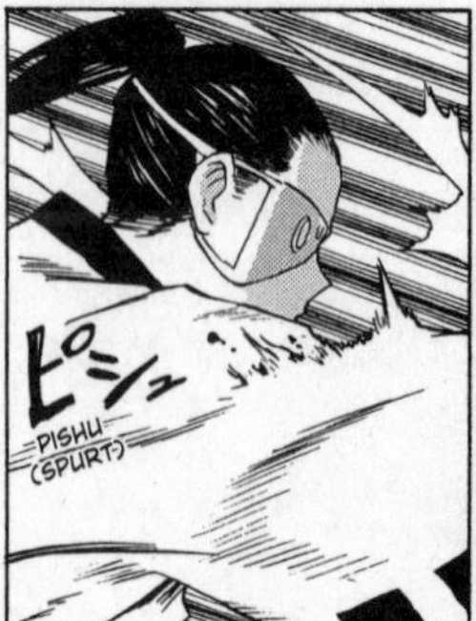
ピシュ
PISHU
(SPURT)

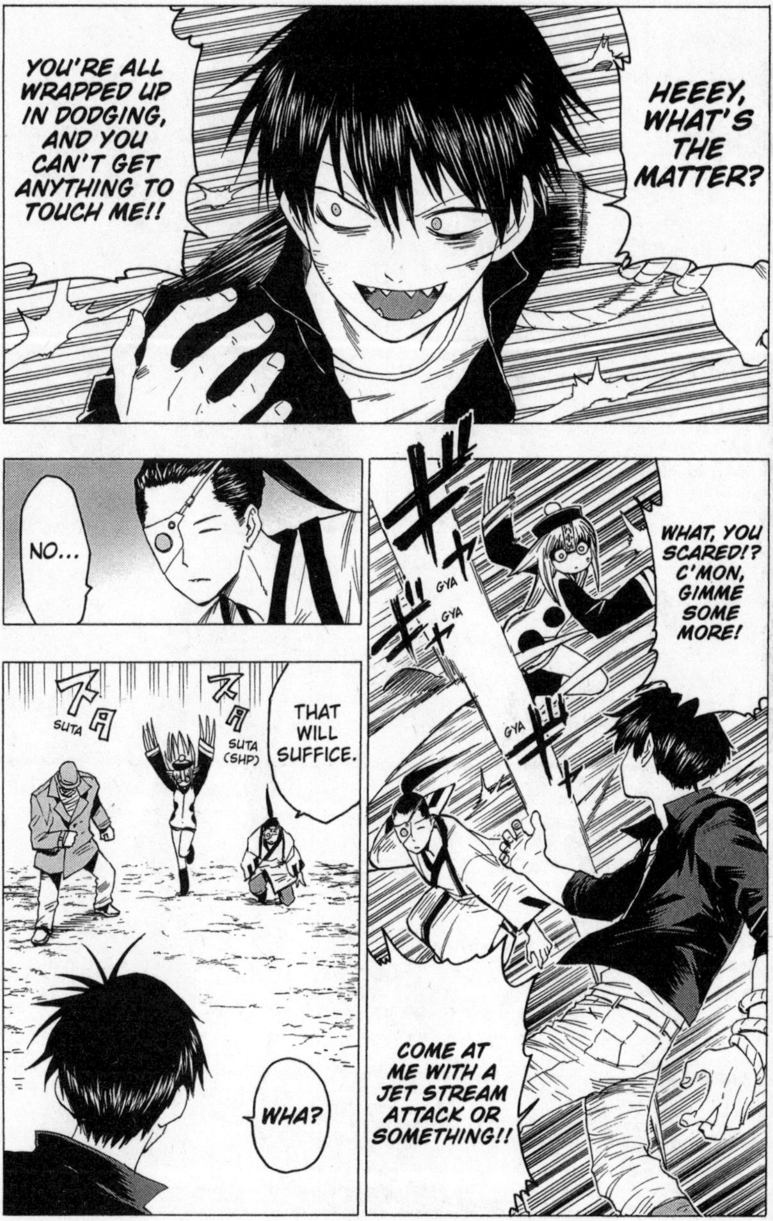
HEEEY, WHAT'S THE MATTER?
YOU'RE ALL WRAPPED UP IN DODGING, AND YOU CAN'T GET ANYTHING TO TOUCH ME!!
WHAT, YOU SCARED!? C'MON, GIMME SOME MORE!
GYA
GYA
GYA
COME AT ME WITH A JET STREAM ATTACK OR SOMETHING!!
NO...
THAT WILL SUFFICE.
SUTA (SHP)
SUTA
WHA?

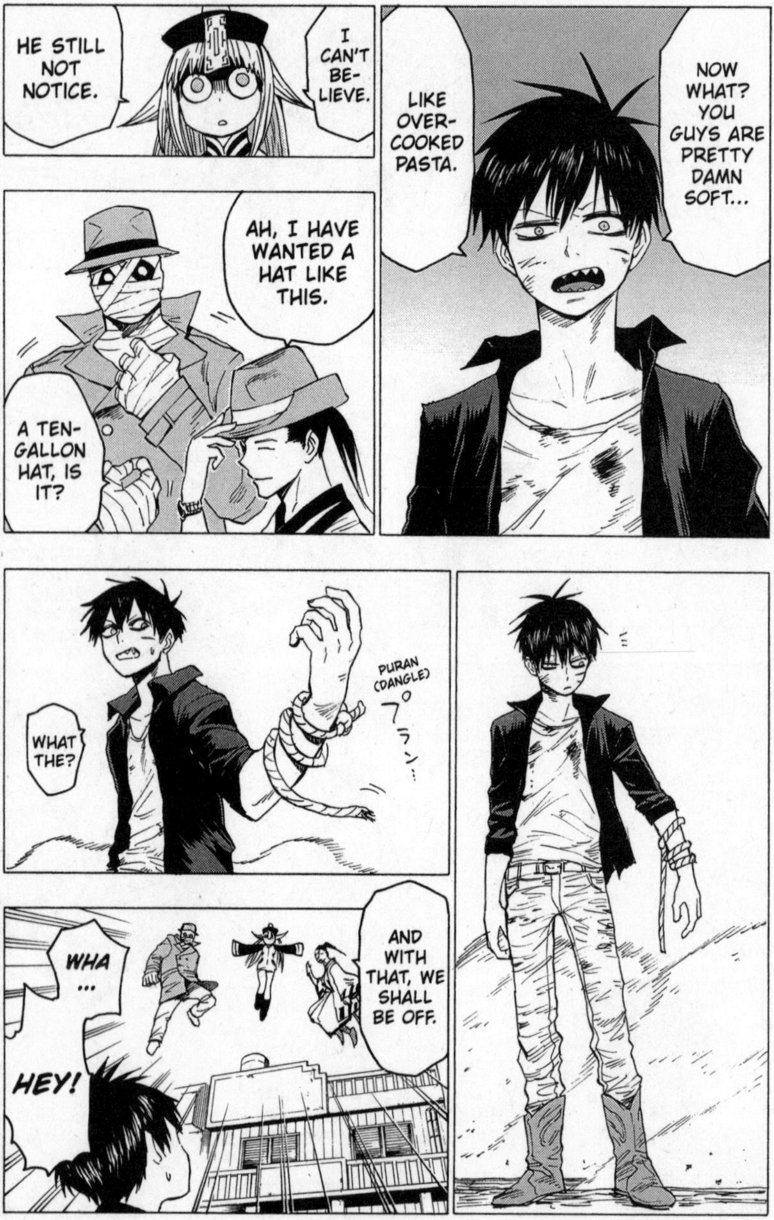
NOW WHAT? YOU GUYS ARE PRETTY DAMN SOFT...
LIKE OVER-COOKED PASTA.
I CAN'T BE-LIEVE.
HE STILL NOT NOTICE.
AH, I HAVE WANTED A HAT LIKE THIS.
A TEN-GALLON HAT, IS IT?
PURAN (DANGLE)
プラン‥
WHAT THE?
AND WITH THAT, WE SHALL BE OFF.
WHA ...
HEY!

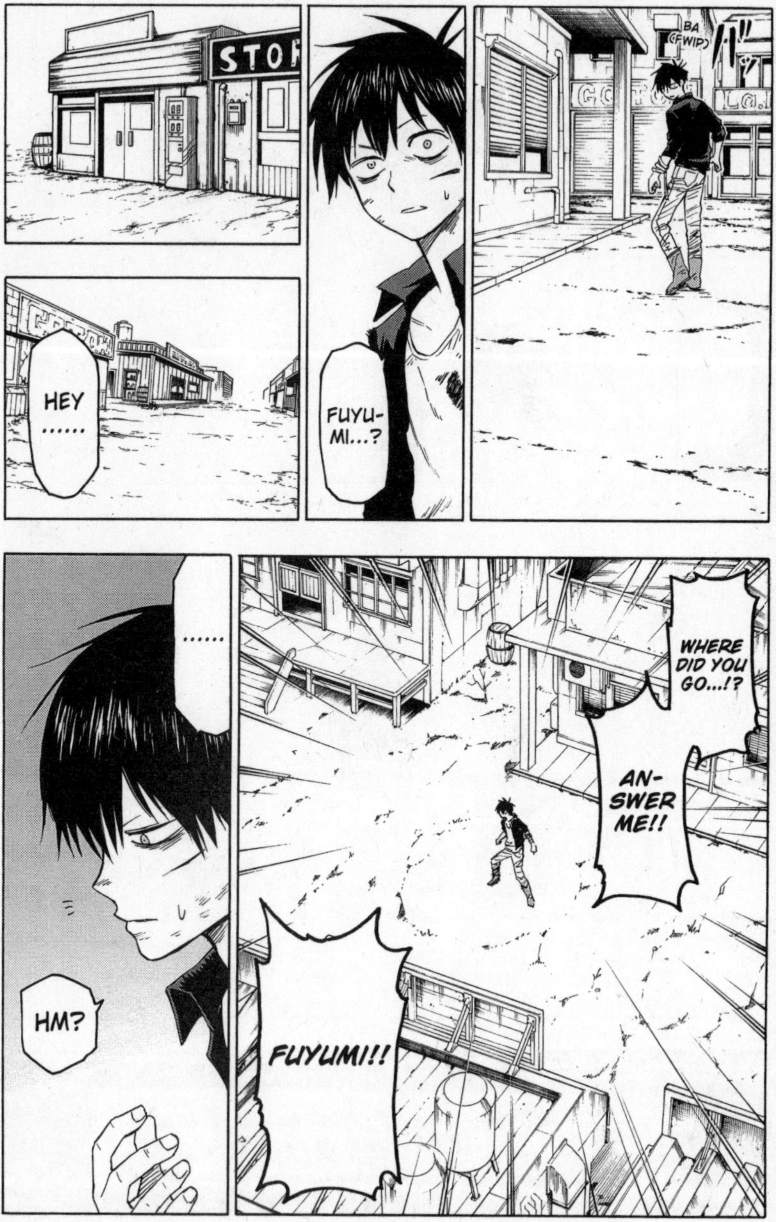
BA (FWIP)
FUYU-MI...?
HEY ......
WHERE DID YOU GO...!?
ANSWER ME!!
FUYUMI!!
......
HM?

... HURTS ......

THIS CAN'T BE RIGHT...

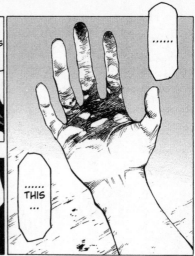

......

....

I'M HURT ......

JIWA (SEEP)

I'M NOT HEALING ...

ピコン
PIKON (POP)

ALL RIGHT, WE'VE CLEARED PHASE ONE...
GOOD WORK, EVERYONE.

♠ To Be Continued ♠

BLOOD LAD

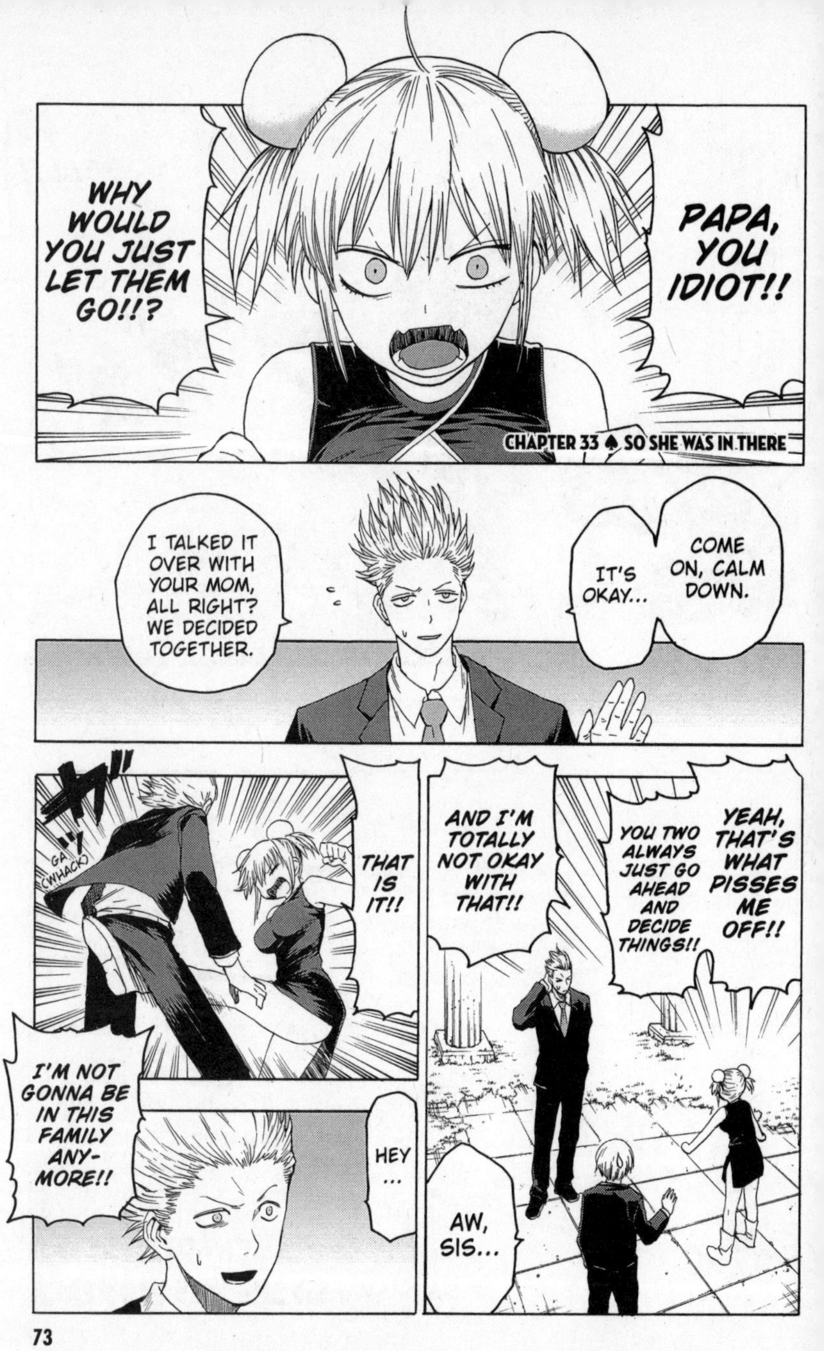
PAPA, YOU IDIOT!!
WHY WOULD YOU JUST LET THEM GO!!?
CHAPTER 33 ♠ SO SHE WAS IN THERE
COME ON, CALM DOWN.
IT'S OKAY...
I TALKED IT OVER WITH YOUR MOM, ALL RIGHT? WE DECIDED TOGETHER.
YEAH, THAT'S WHAT PISSES ME OFF!!
YOU TWO ALWAYS JUST GO AHEAD AND DECIDE THINGS!!
AND I'M TOTALLY NOT OKAY WITH THAT!!
AW, SIS...
THAT IS IT!!
GA (WHACK)
HEY...
I'M NOT GONNA BE IN THIS FAMILY ANY-MORE!!

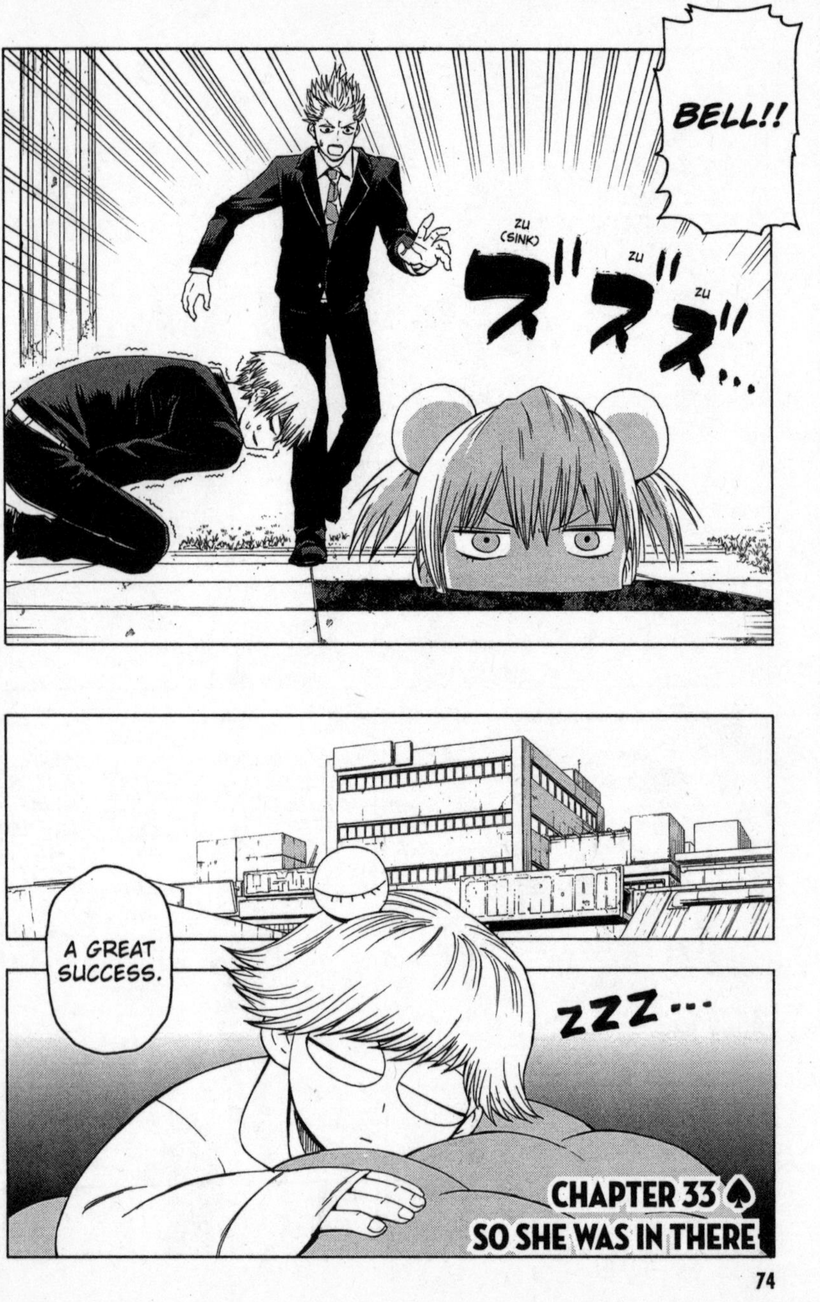
BELL!!
ZU (SINK) ZU ZU
ズズズ...
A GREAT SUCCESS.
ZZZ...
CHAPTER 33
SO SHE WAS IN THERE

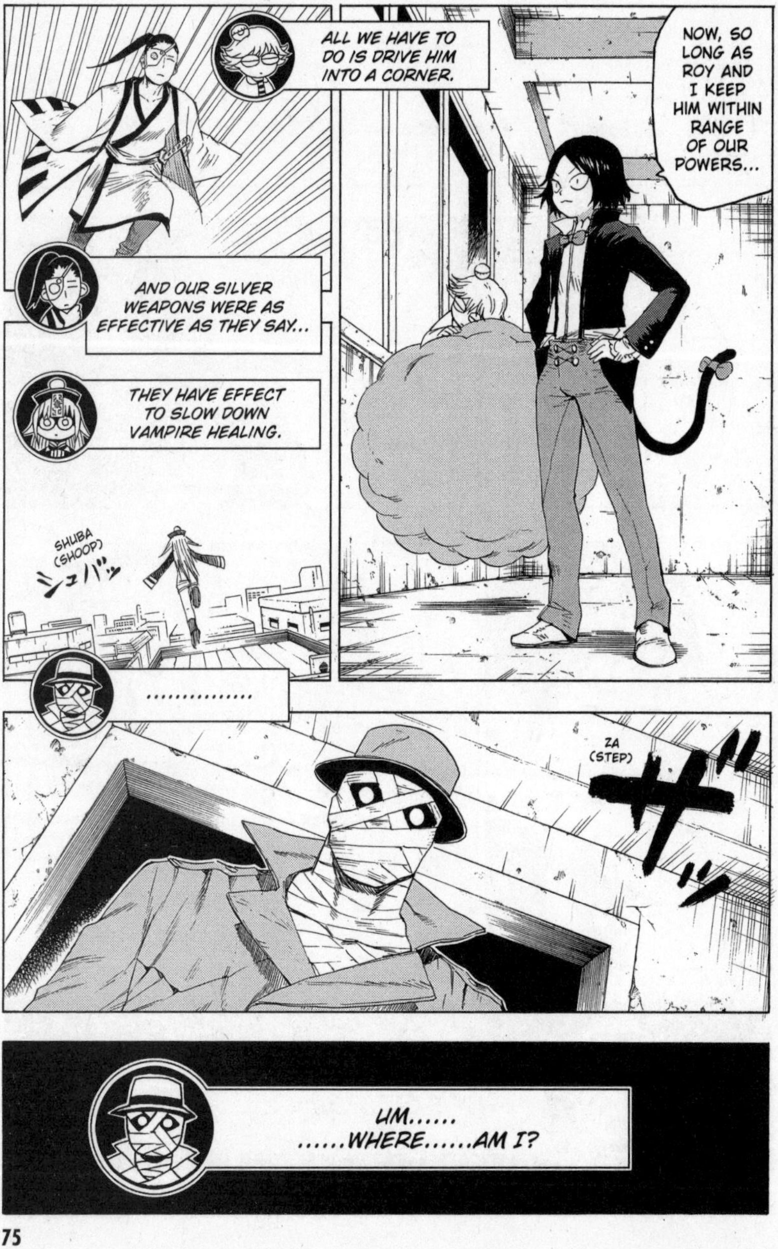
NOW, SO LONG AS ROY AND I KEEP HIM WITHIN RANGE OF OUR POWERS...
ALL WE HAVE TO DO IS DRIVE HIM INTO A CORNER.
AND OUR SILVER WEAPONS WERE AS EFFECTIVE AS THEY SAY...
THEY HAVE EFFECT TO SLOW DOWN VAMPIRE HEALING.
SHUBA (SHOOP)
シュバッ
....
ZA (STEP)
ザッ
UM......
......WHERE......AM I?

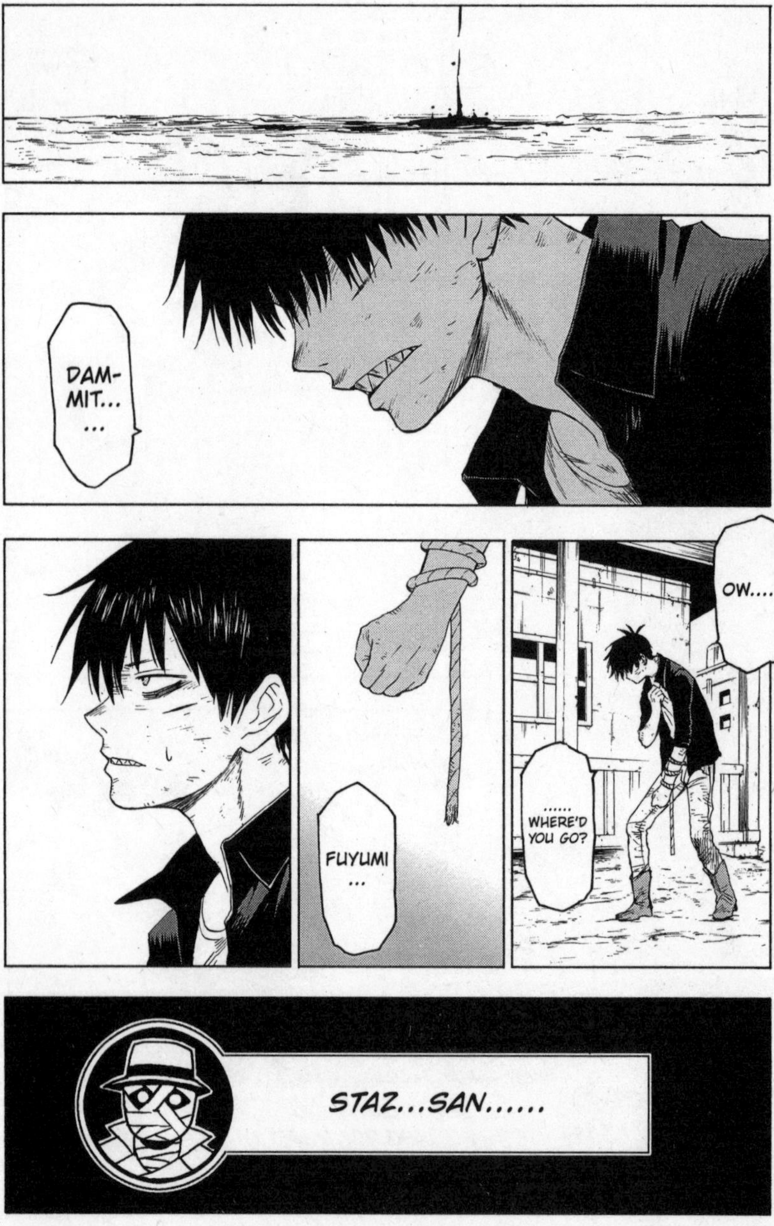
DAM-
MIT......
OW......
......WHERE'D YOU GO?
FUYUMI...
STAZ...SAN......

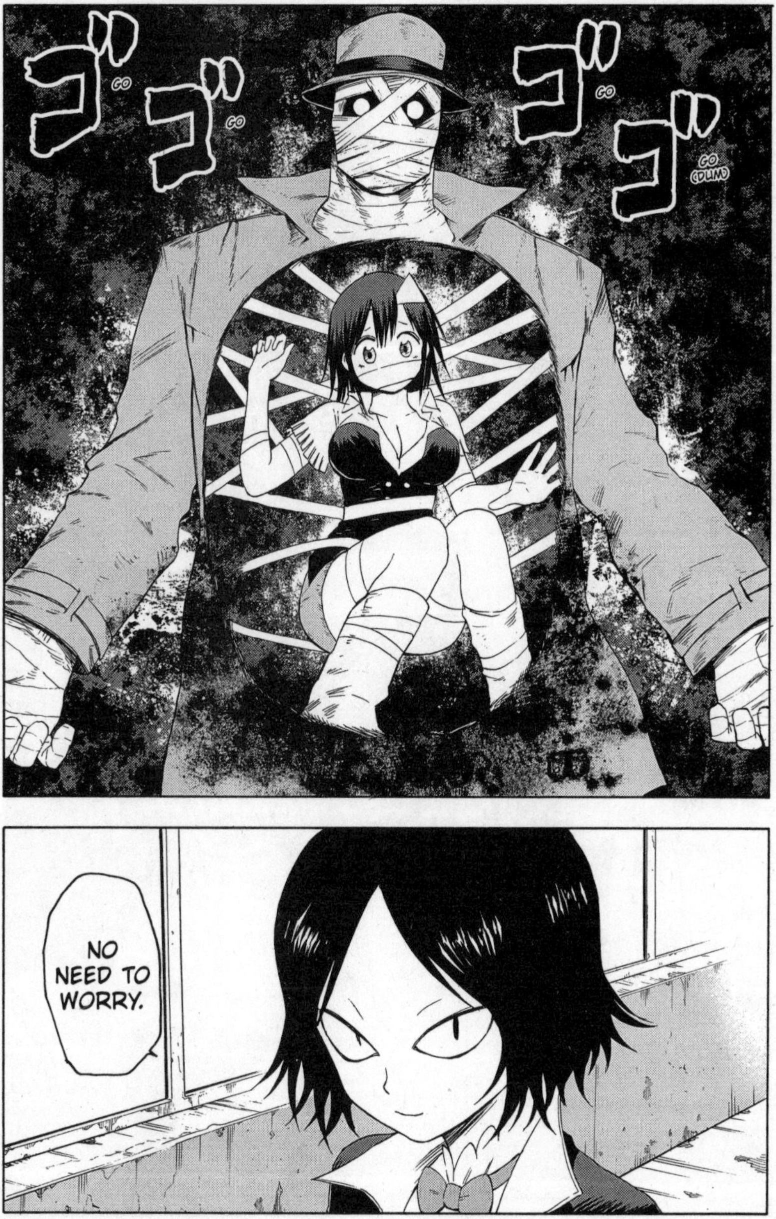
ゴゴゴゴ
GO GO GO GO (DUM)
NO NEED TO WORRY.

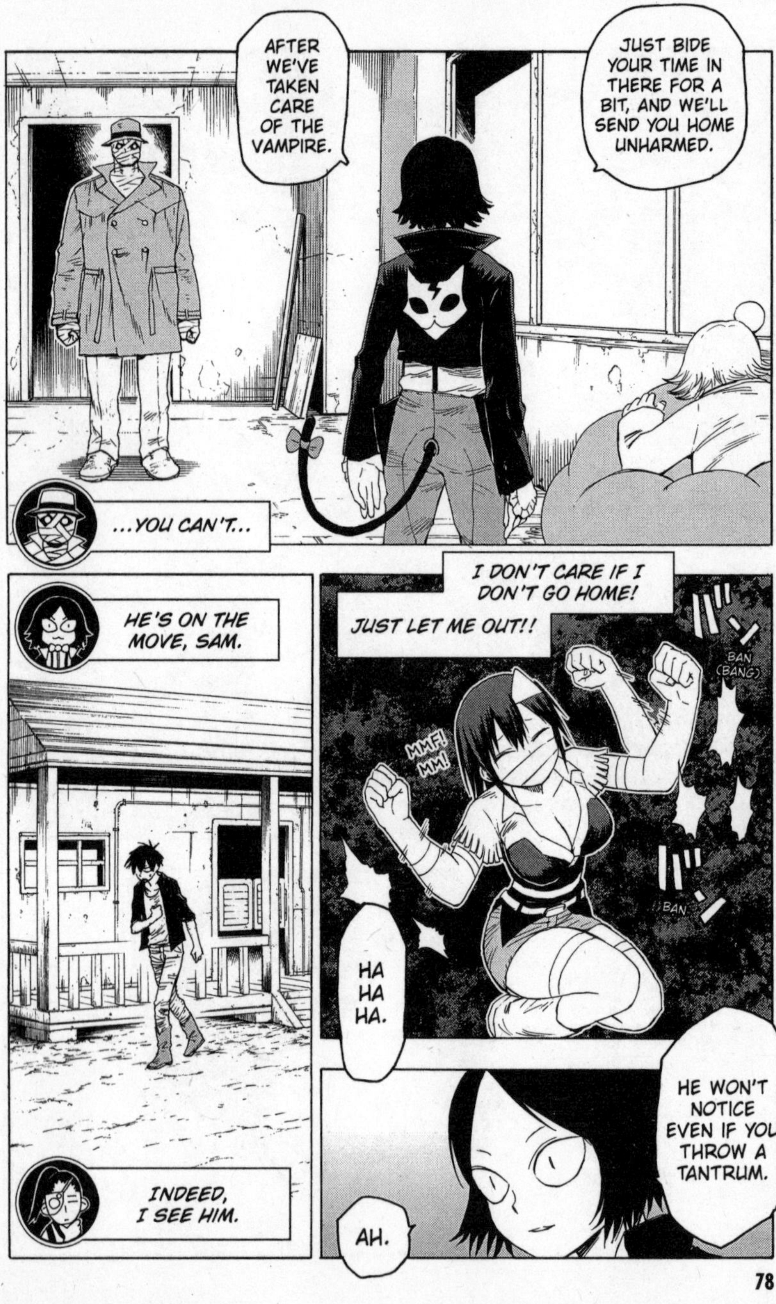
JUST BIDE YOUR TIME IN THERE FOR A BIT, AND WE'LL SEND YOU HOME UNHARMED.
AFTER WE'VE TAKEN CARE OF THE VAMPIRE.
...YOU CAN'T...
I DON'T CARE IF I DON'T GO HOME!
JUST LET ME OUT!!
BAN (BANG)
MMF! MM!
BAN
HA HA HA.
HE WON'T NOTICE EVEN IF YOU THROW A TANTRUM.
AH.
HE'S ON THE MOVE, SAM.
INDEED, I SEE HIM.

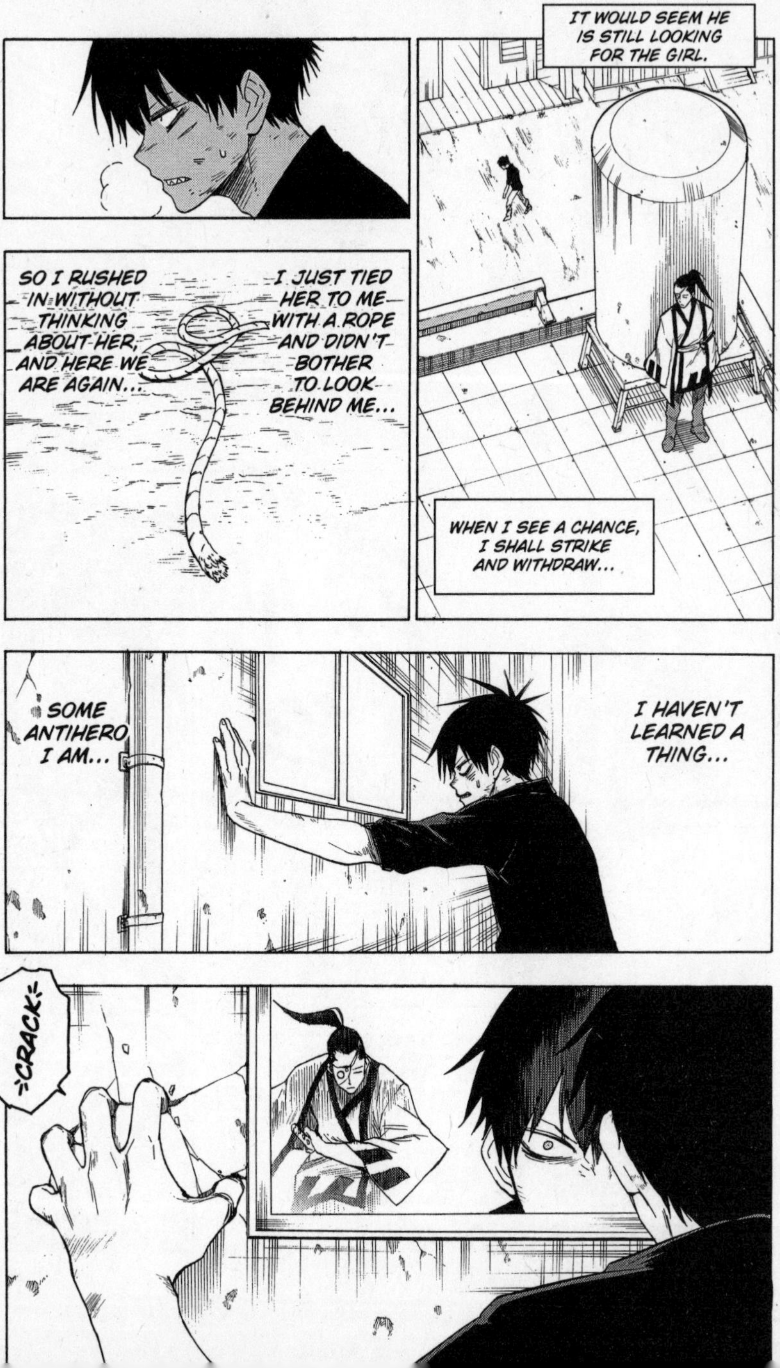
IT WOULD SEEM HE IS STILL LOOKING FOR THE GIRL.
WHEN I SEE A CHANCE, I SHALL STRIKE AND WITHDRAW...
I JUST TIED HER TO ME WITH A ROPE AND DIDN'T BOTHER TO LOOK BEHIND ME...
SO I RUSHED IN WITHOUT THINKING ABOUT HER, AND HERE WE ARE AGAIN...
I HAVEN'T LEARNED A THING...
SOME ANTIHERO I AM...
CRACK

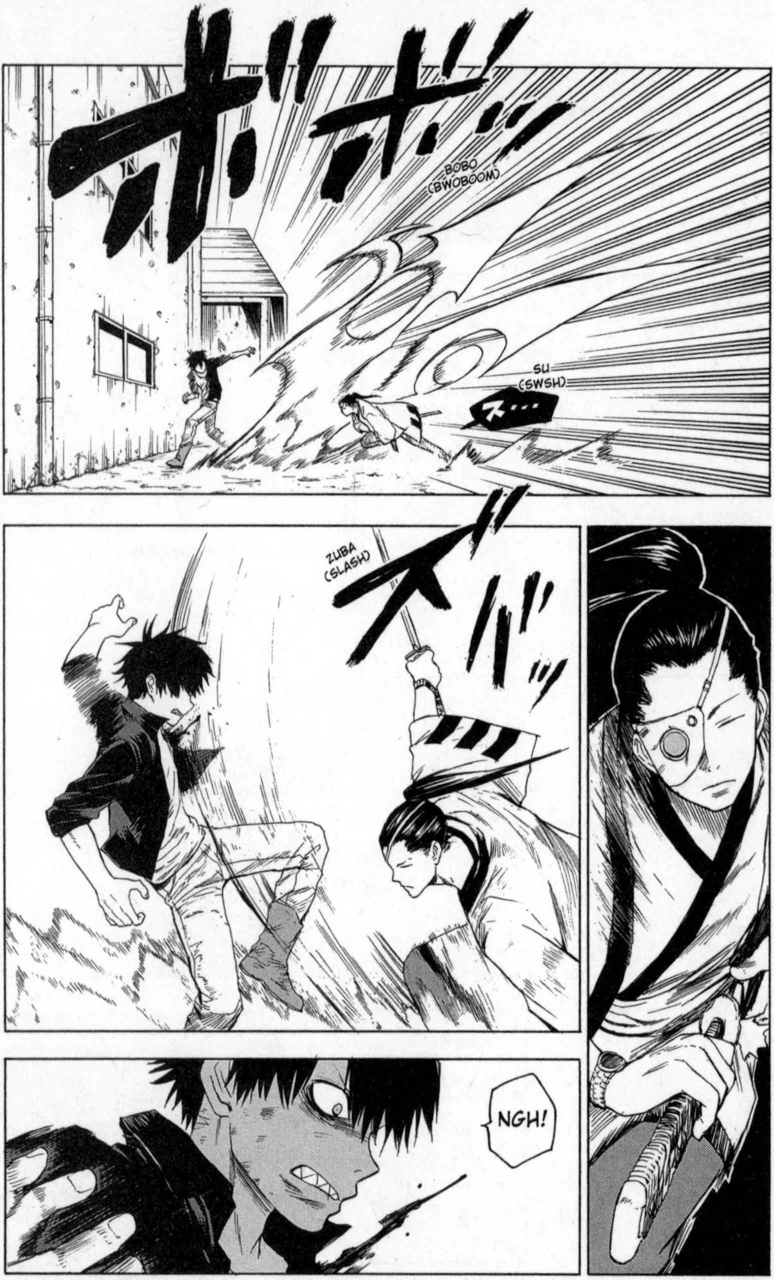
BOBO
(BWOBOOM)
SU
(SWSH)
ZUBA
(SLASH)
NGH!

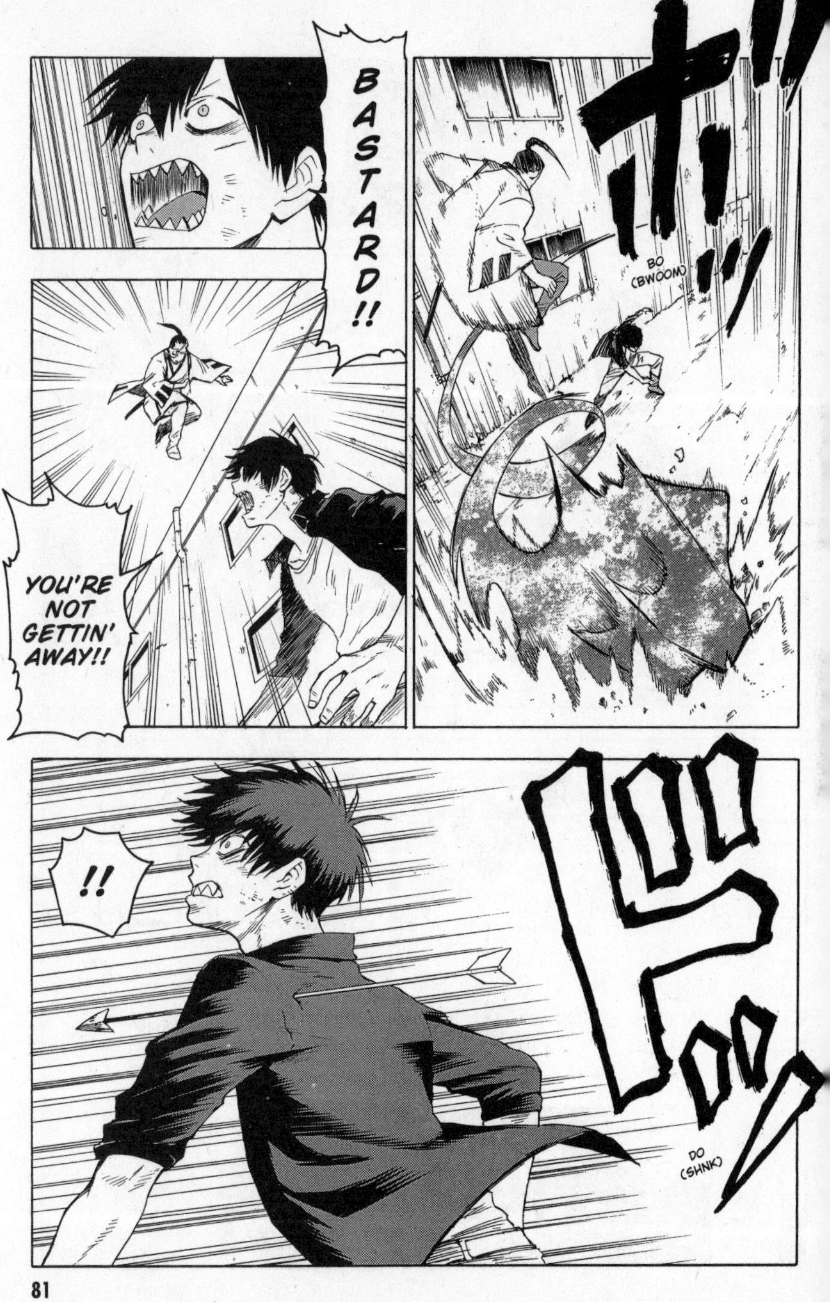
BO (BWOOM)
BASTARD!!
YOU'RE NOT GETTIN' AWAY!!
DO (SHNK)
!!

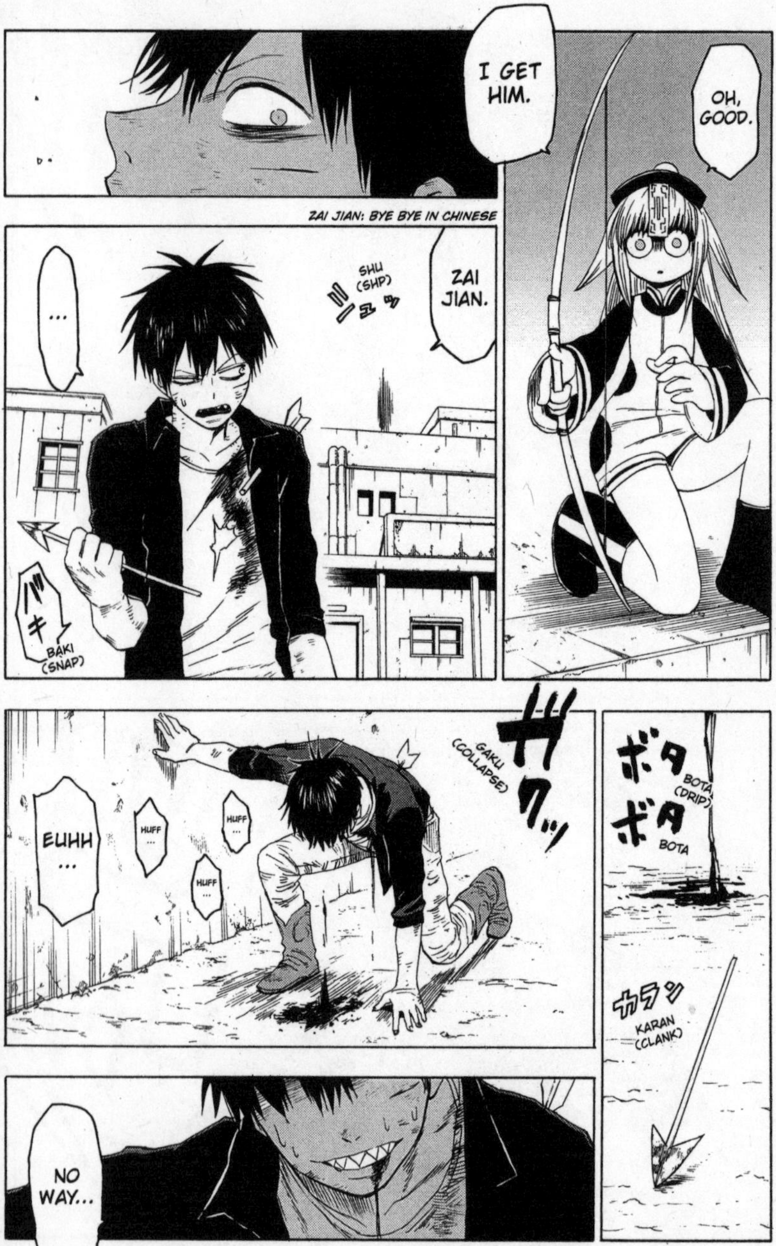
OH, GOOD.
I GET HIM.
ZAI JIAN: BYE BYE IN CHINESE
ZAI JIAN.
SHU (SHP)
...
BAKI (SNAP)
BOTA (DRIP)
BOTA
KARAN (CLANK)
GAKU (COLLAPSE)
HUFF ...
HUFF ...
HUFF ...
EUHH ...
NO WAY...

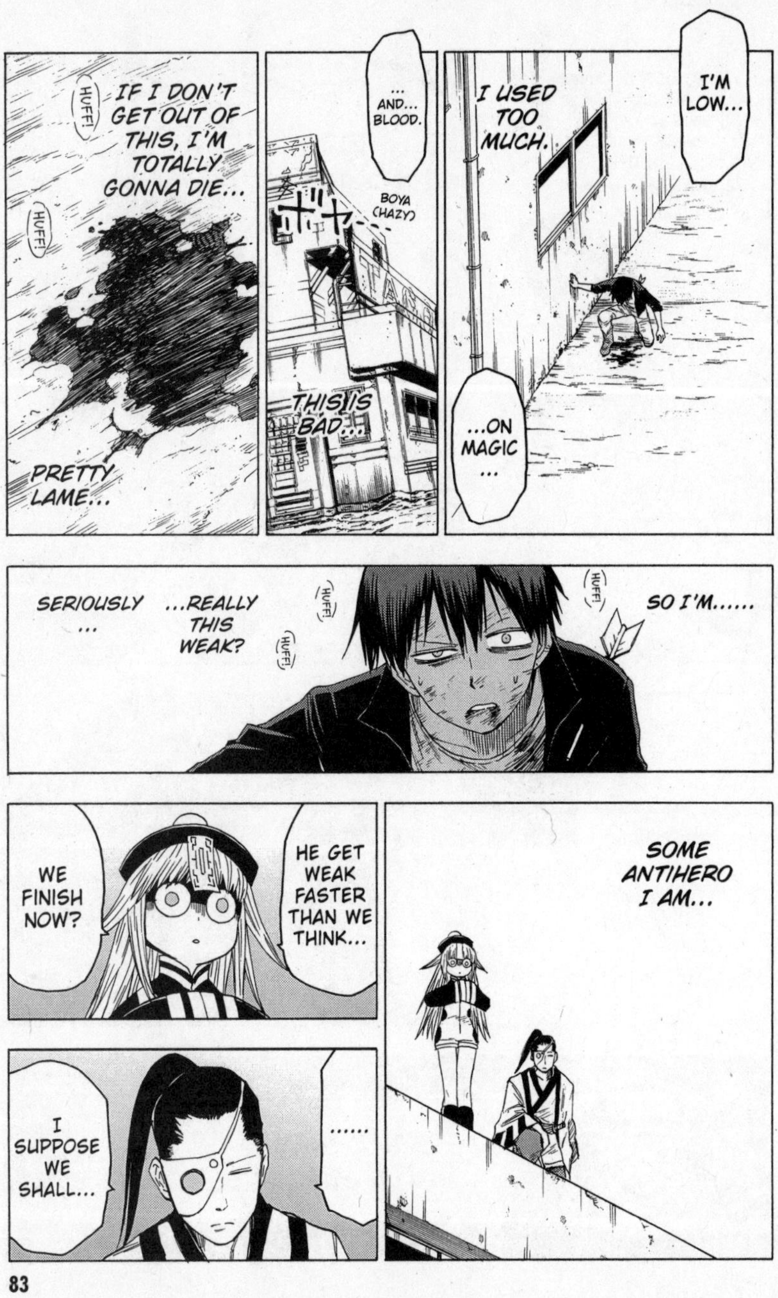
I'M LOW...
I USED TOO MUCH.
...ON MAGIC ...
... AND... BLOOD.
ボヤー
BOYA (HAZY)
THIS IS BAD...
HUFF!
IF I DON'T GET OUT OF THIS, I'M TOTALLY GONNA DIE...
HUFF!
PRETTY LAME...
SO I'M......
HUFF!
...REALLY THIS WEAK?
HUFF!
HUFF!
SERIOUSLY ...
SOME ANTIHERO I AM...
HE GET WEAK FASTER THAN WE THINK...
WE FINISH NOW?
......
I SUPPOSE WE SHALL...

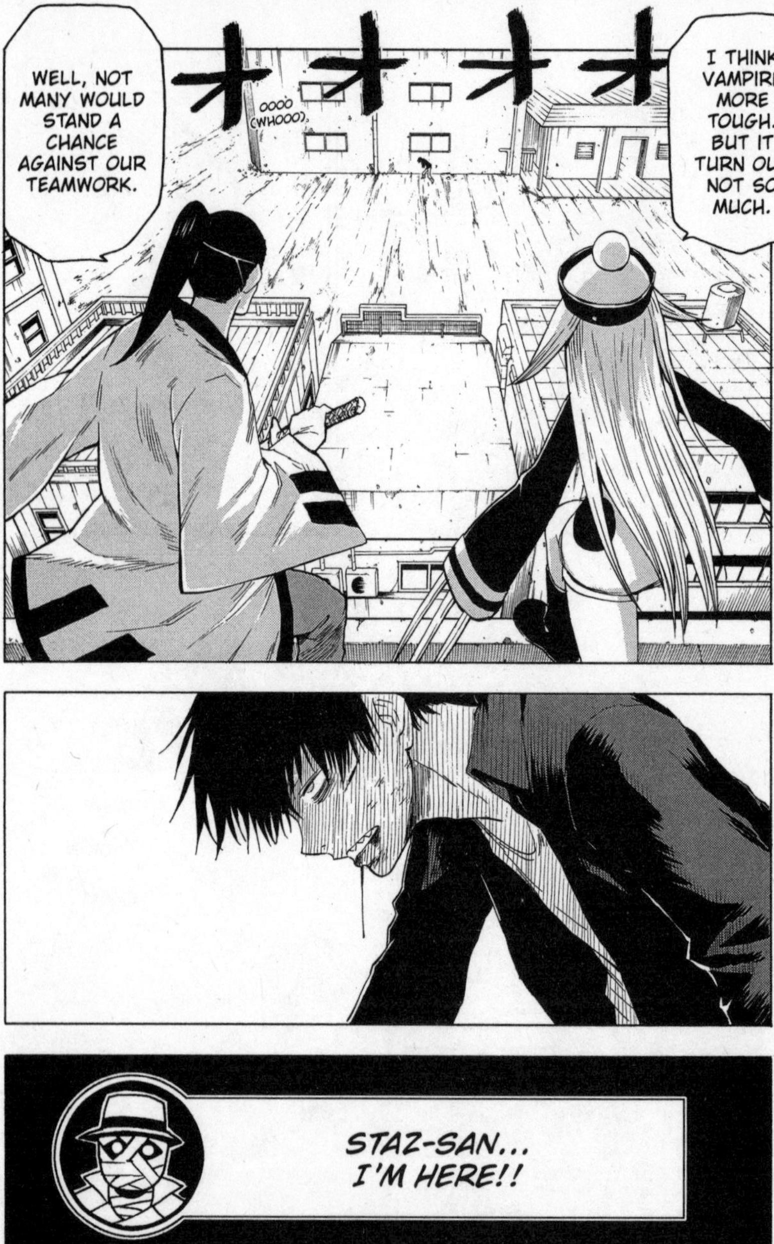
I THINK VAMPIRE MORE TOUGH. BUT IT TURN OUT NOT SO MUCH.
オオオオ
OOOO (WHOOO)
WELL, NOT MANY WOULD STAND A CHANCE AGAINST OUR TEAMWORK.
STAZ-SAN... I'M HERE!!

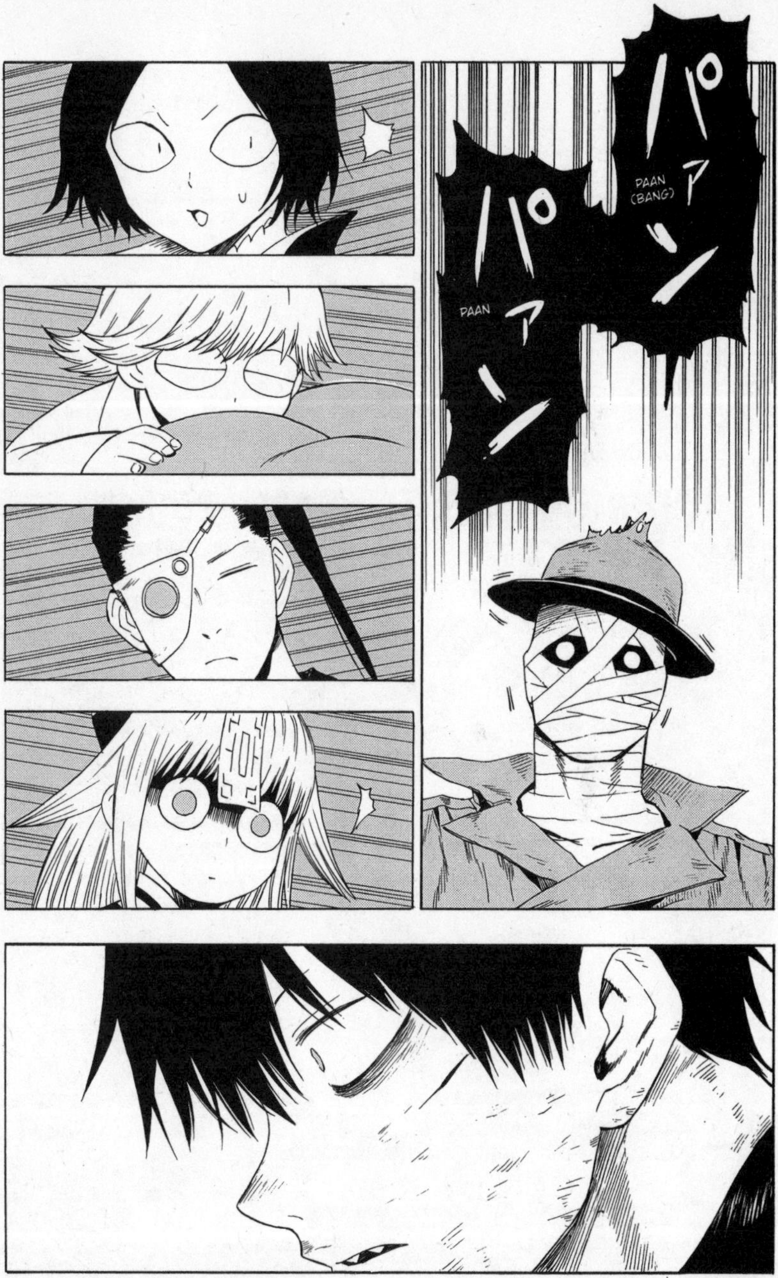
PAAN (BANG)
PAAN

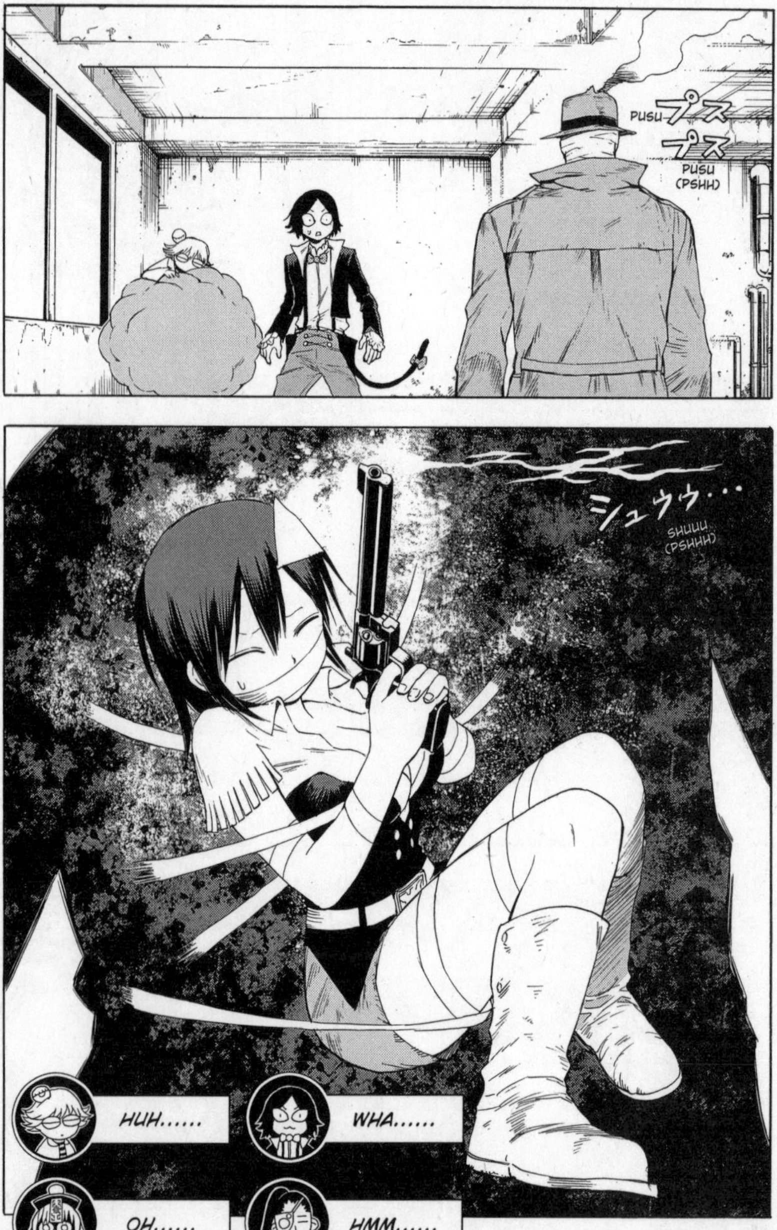
プス
PUSU
プス
PUSU
(PSHH)
シュウウ…
SHUUU
(PSHHH)
WHA......
HUH......
HMM......
OH......

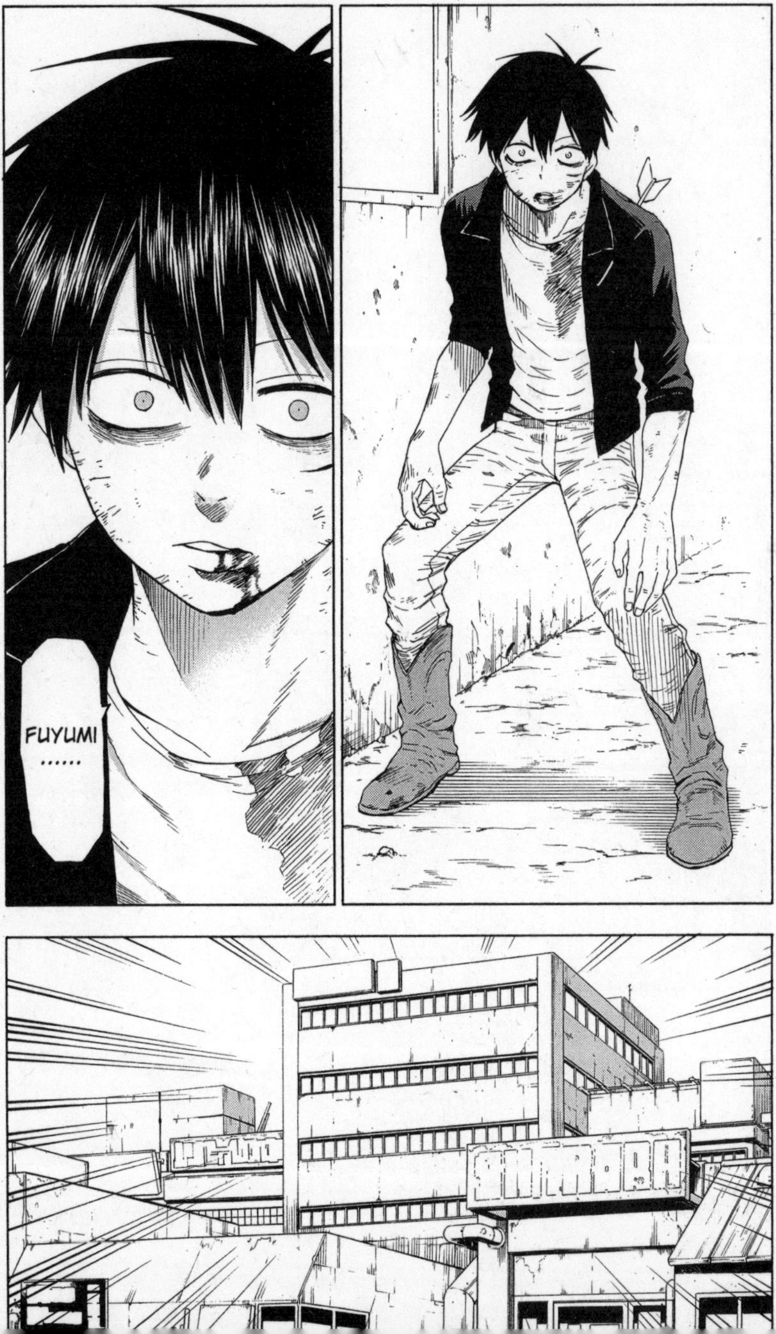
FUYUMI ......

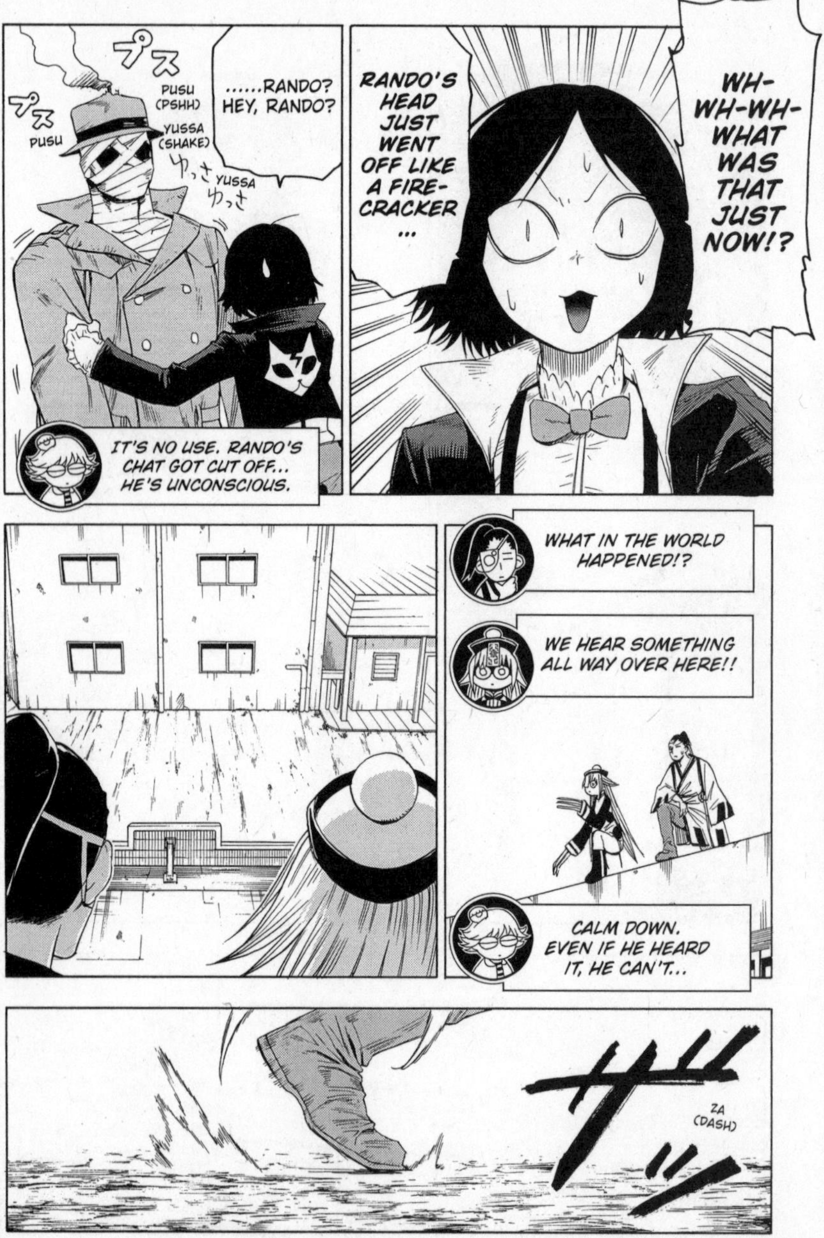
WH-WH-WH-WHAT WAS THAT JUST NOW!?
RANDO'S HEAD JUST WENT OFF LIKE A FIRE-CRACKER...
プス
PUSU (PSHH)
プス
PUSU
......RANDO? HEY, RANDO?
ゆっさ
YUSSA (SHAKE)
ゆっさ
YUSSA
IT'S NO USE. RANDO'S CHAT GOT CUT OFF... HE'S UNCONSCIOUS.
WHAT IN THE WORLD HAPPENED!?
WE HEAR SOMETHING ALL WAY OVER HERE!!
CALM DOWN. EVEN IF HE HEARD IT, HE CAN'T...
ザッ
ZA (DASH)

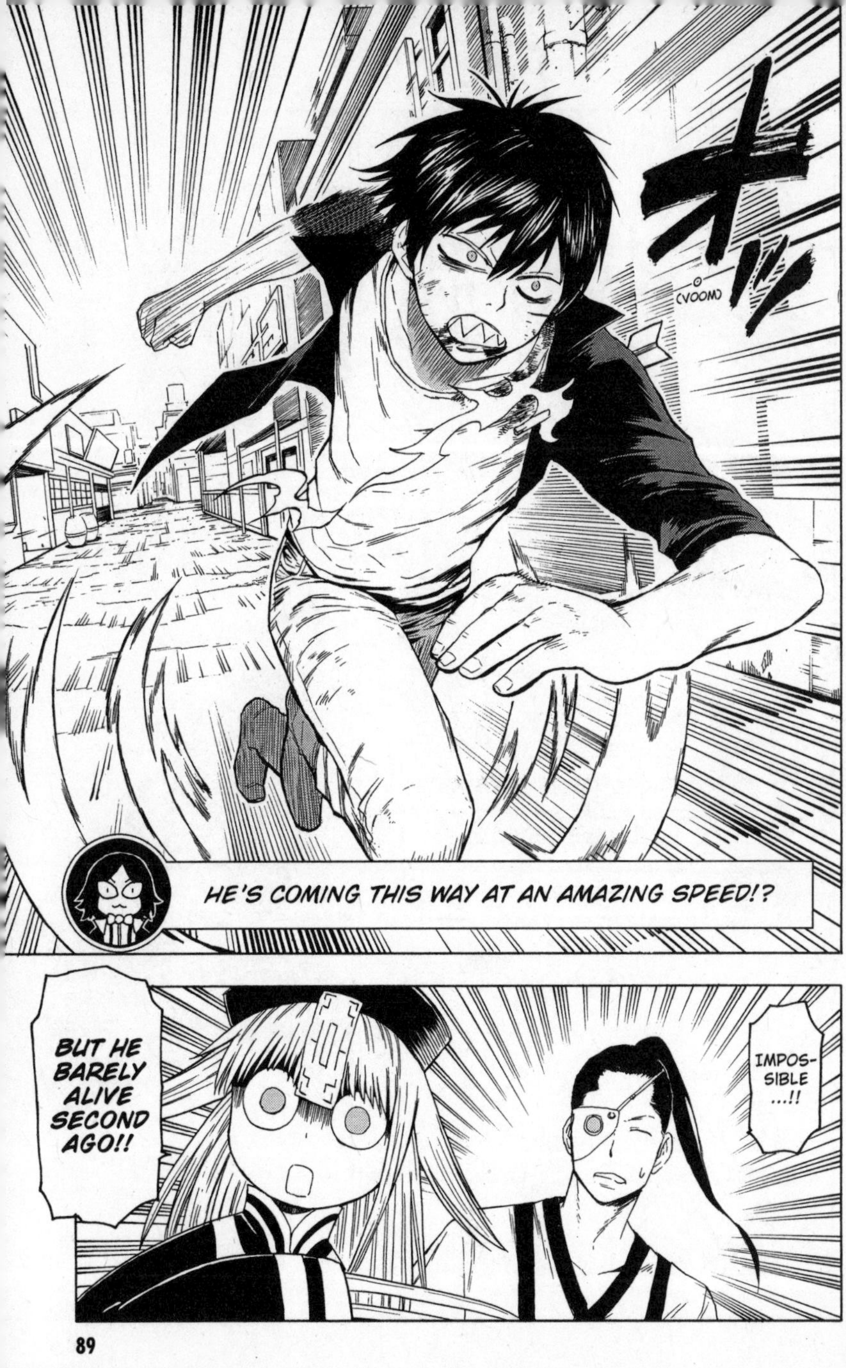
(VOOM)
HE'S COMING THIS WAY AT AN AMAZING SPEED!?
IMPOS-SIBLE ...!!
BUT HE BARELY ALIVE SECOND AGO!!

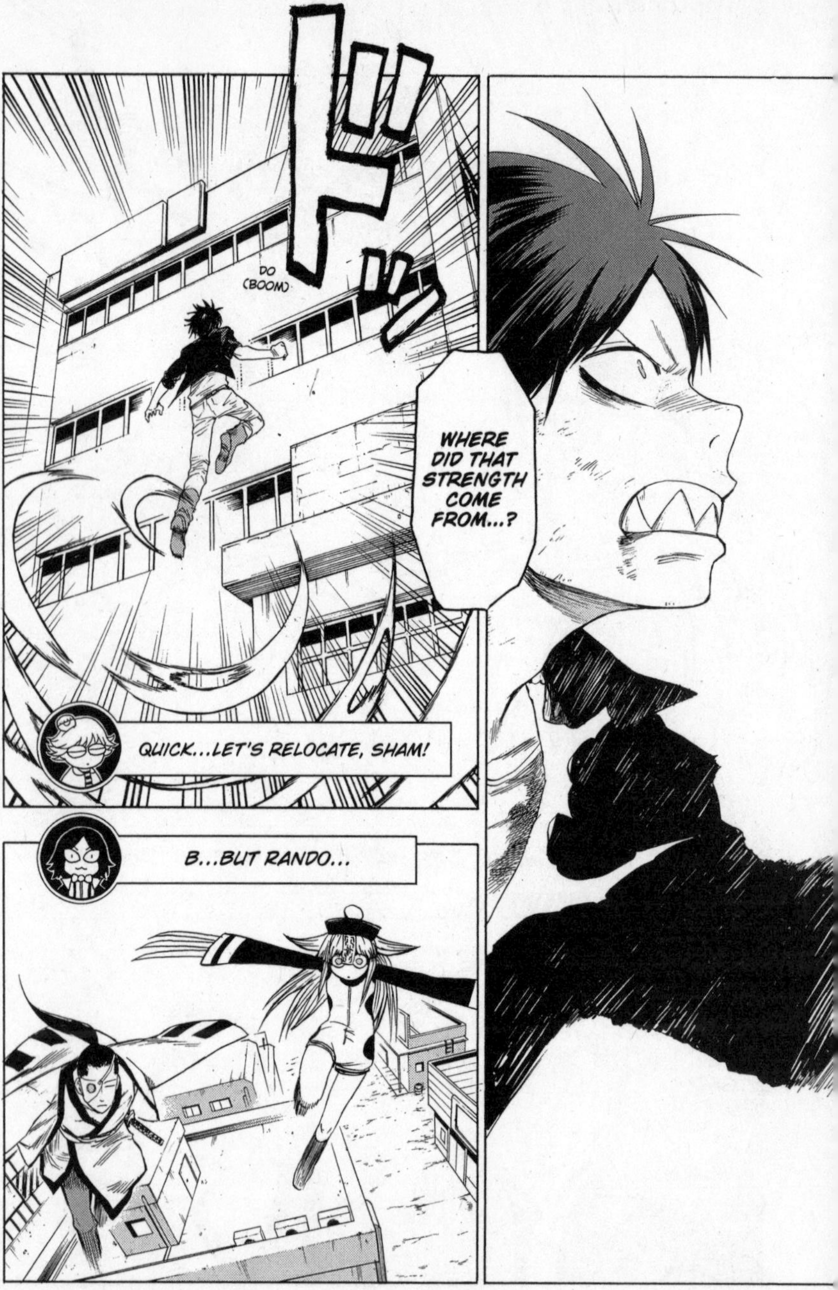
WHERE DID THAT STRENGTH COME FROM...?
DO (BOOM)
QUICK...LET'S RELOCATE, SHAM!
B...BUT RANDO...

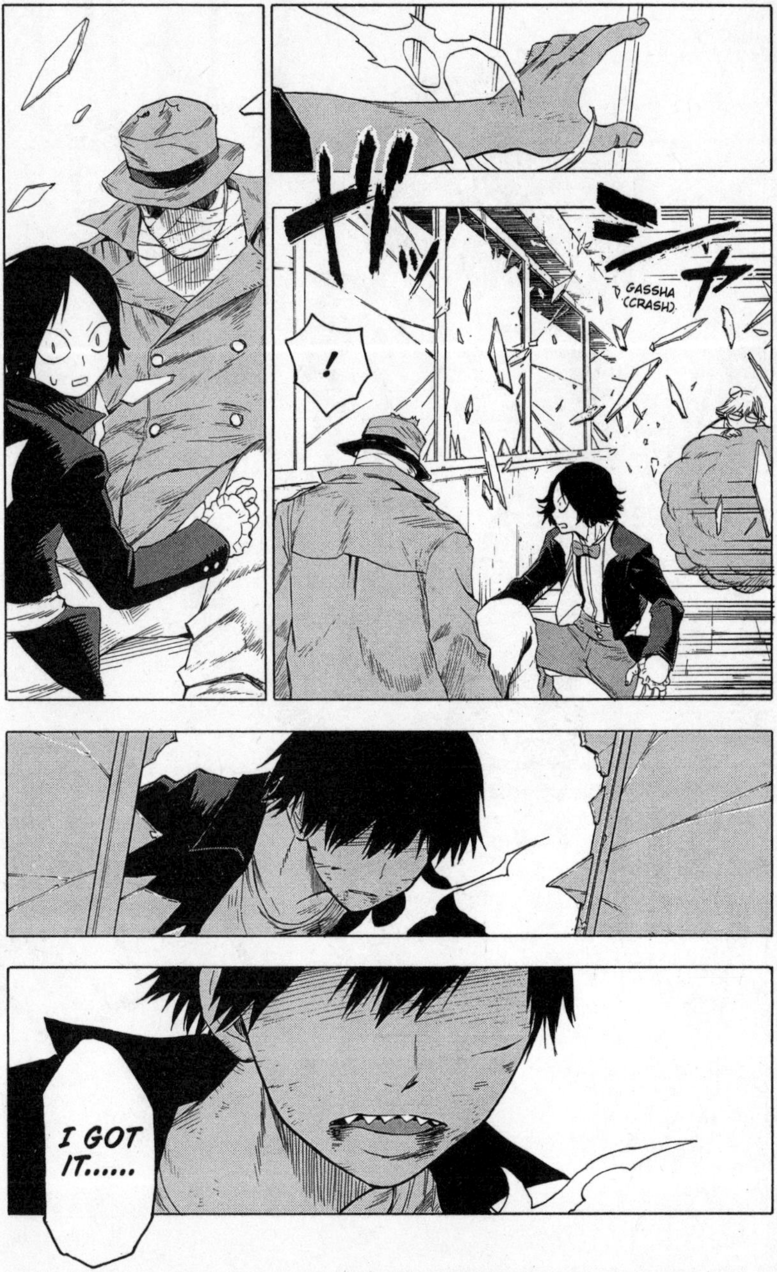
GASSHA (CRASH)
!
I GOT IT......

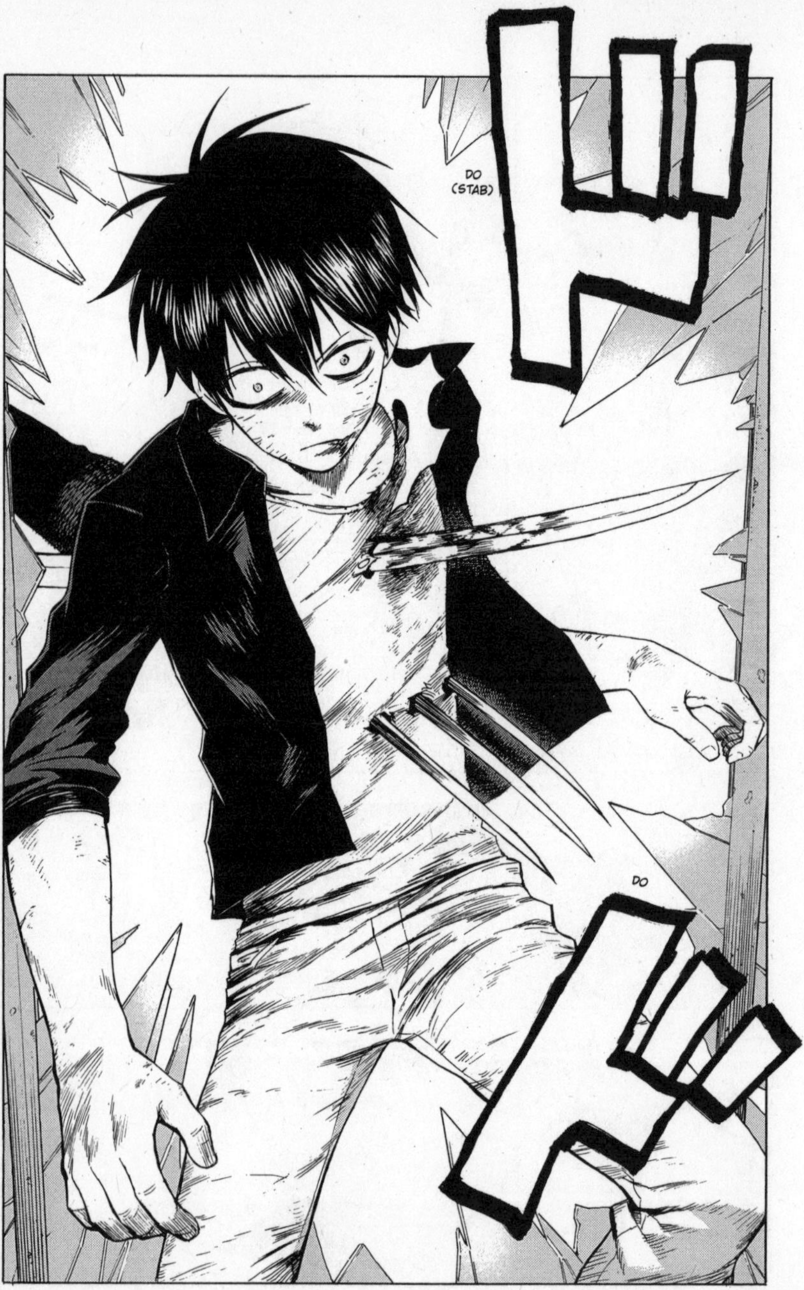
DO (STAB)
DO

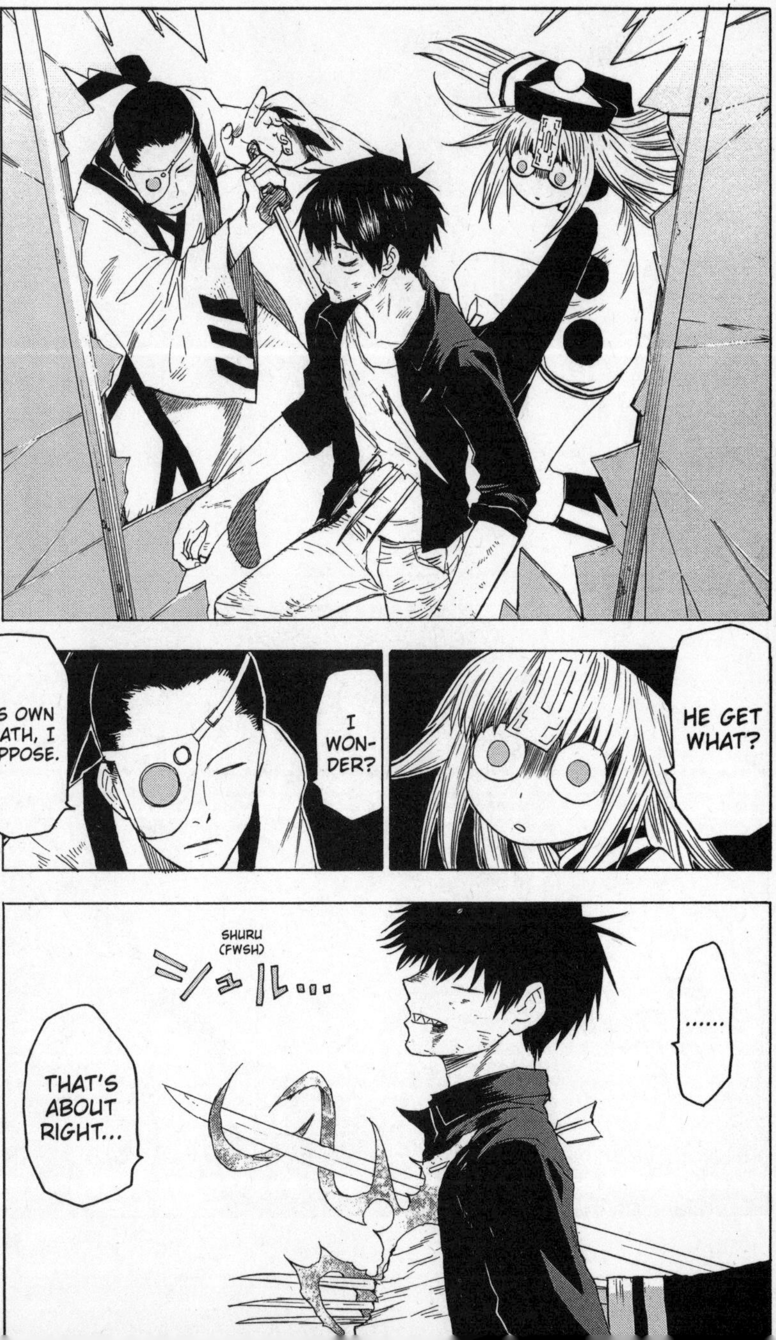
HE GET WHAT?
I WON-DER?
HIS OWN DEATH, I SUPPOSE.
......
SHURU (FWSH)
シュル...
THAT'S ABOUT RIGHT...

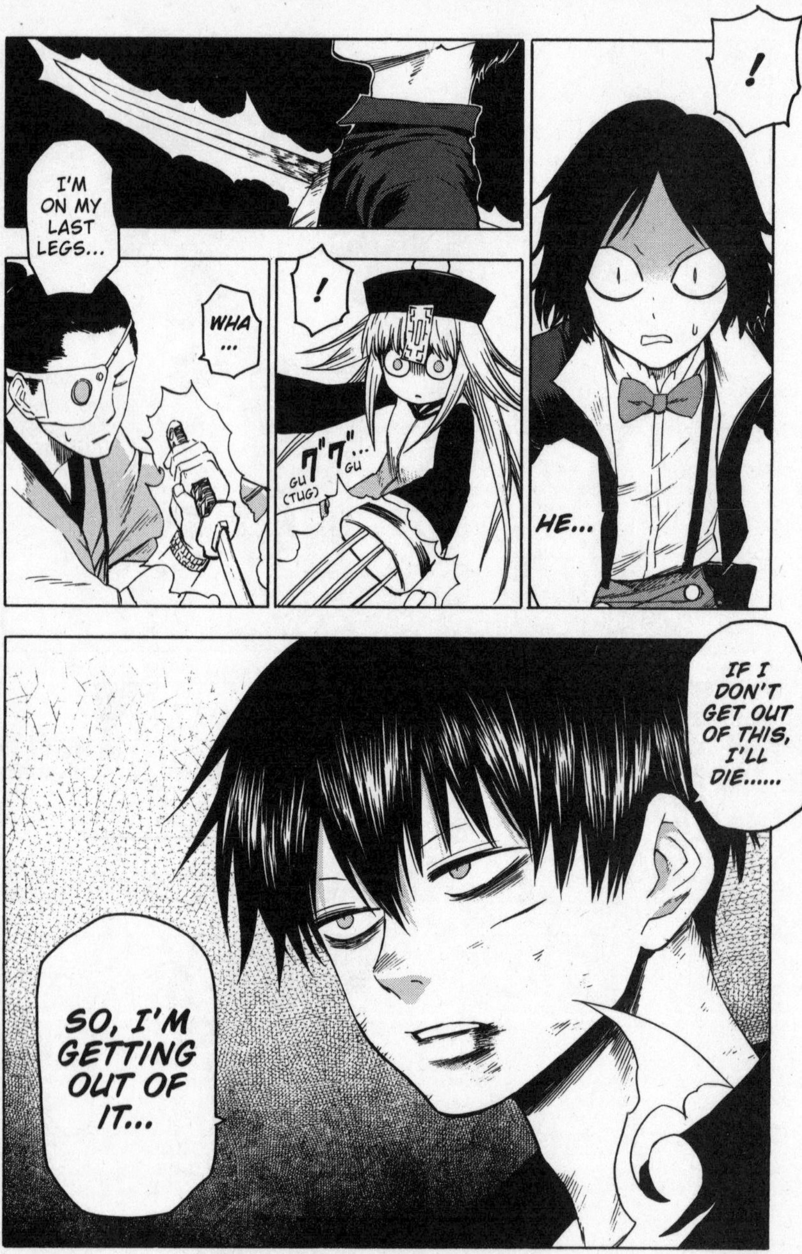
!
HE...
I'M ON MY LAST LEGS...
!
グッグッ…
GU GU (TUG)
WHA...
IF I DON'T GET OUT OF THIS, I'LL DIE......
SO, I'M GETTING OUT OF IT...

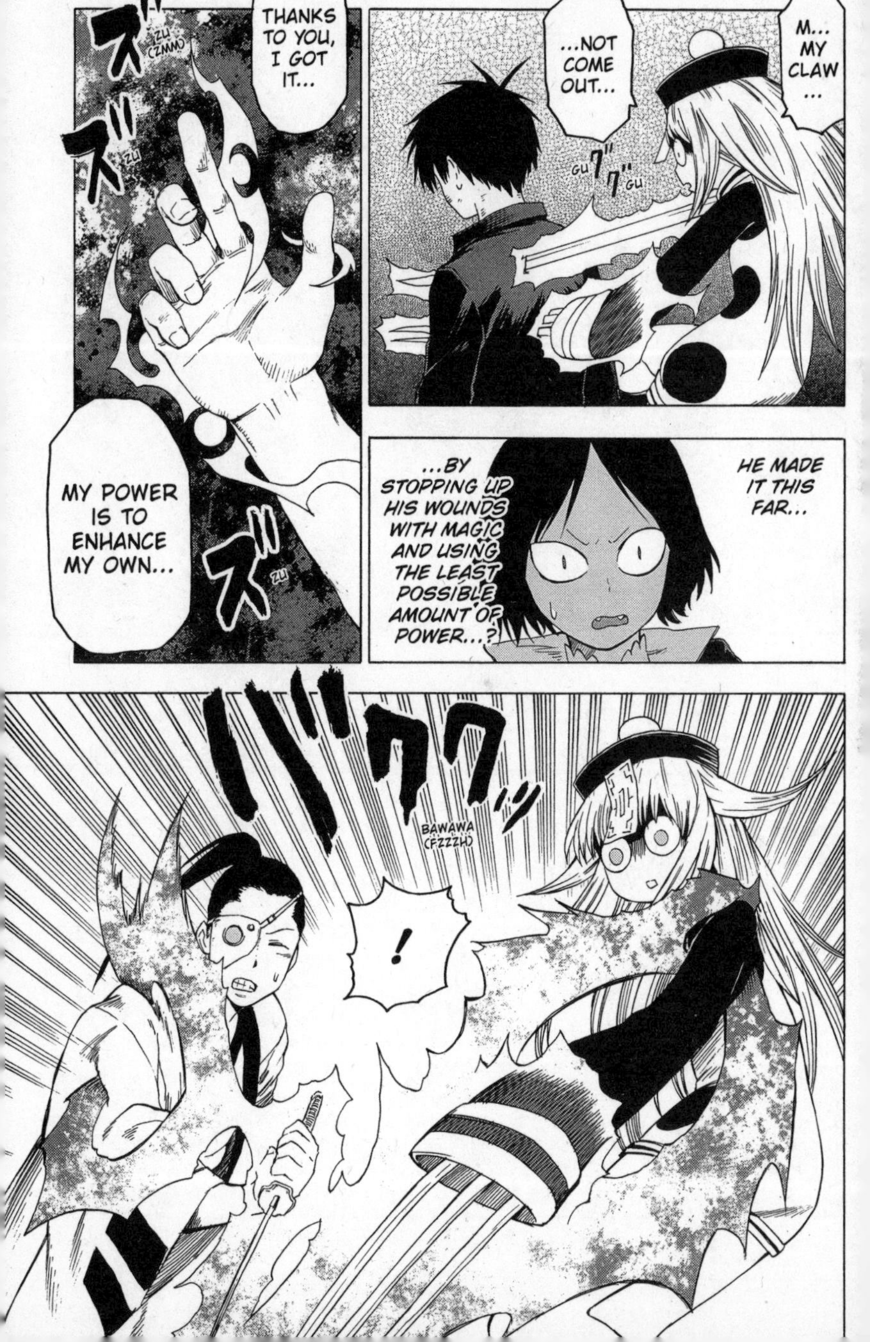
M... MY CLAW ...
...NOT COME OUT...
GU GU
THANKS TO YOU, I GOT IT...
ZU (ZMM)
ZU
MY POWER IS TO ENHANCE MY OWN...
ZU
HE MADE IT THIS FAR...
...BY STOPPING UP HIS WOUNDS WITH MAGIC AND USING THE LEAST POSSIBLE AMOUNT OF POWER...?
BAWAWA (FZZZH)
!

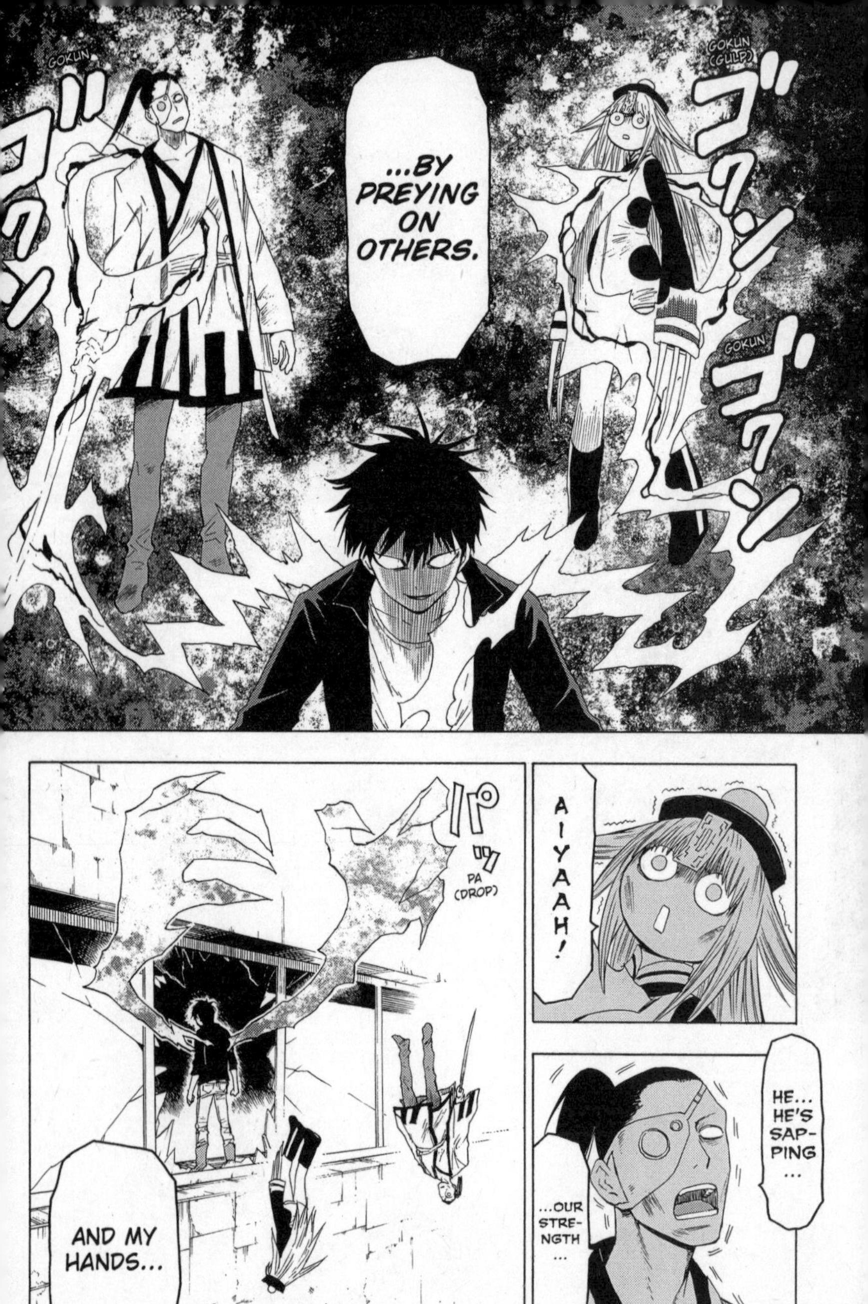
GOKUN (GULP)
GOKUN
...BY PREYING ON OTHERS.
GOKUN
AIYAAH!
HE... HE'S SAPPING...
...OUR STRENGTH...
PA (DROP)
AND MY HANDS...

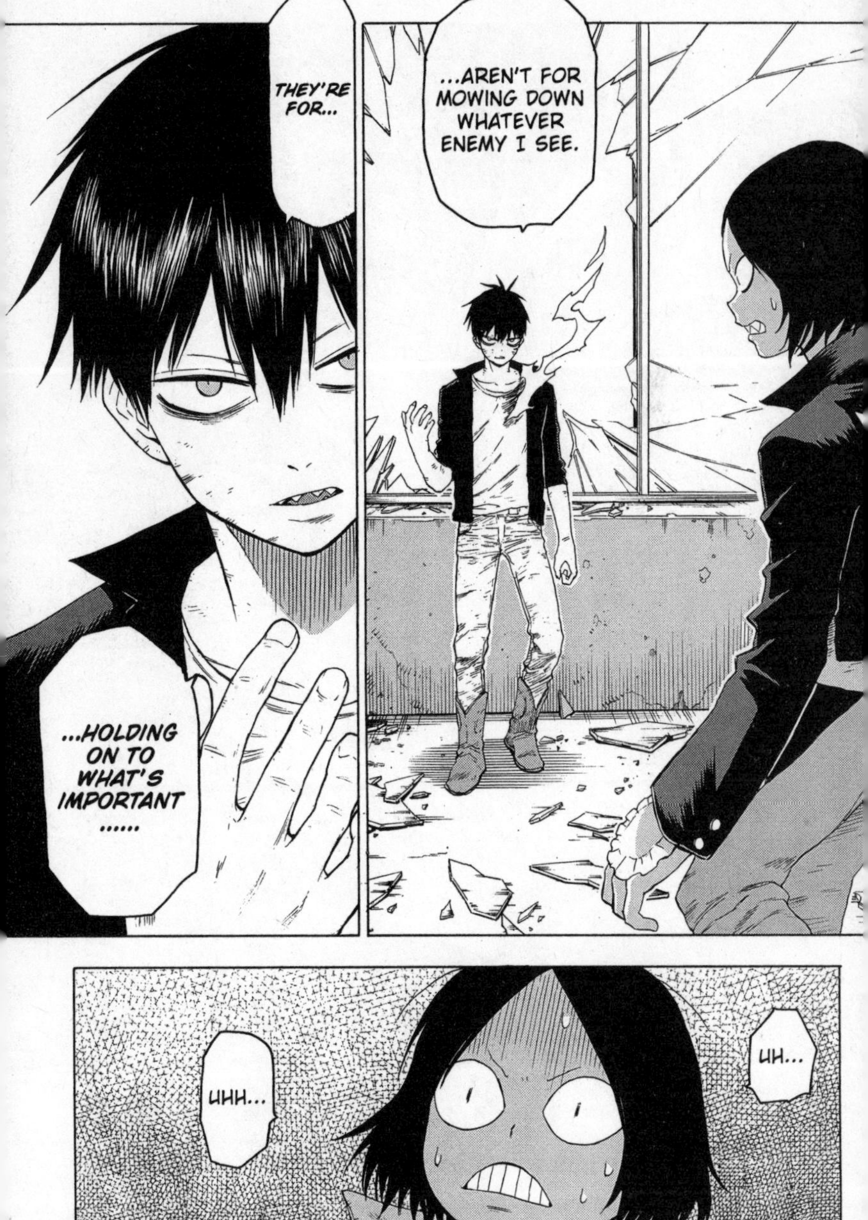
...AREN'T FOR MOWING DOWN WHATEVER ENEMY I SEE.
THEY'RE FOR...
...HOLDING ON TO WHAT'S IMPORTANT ......
UH...
UHH...

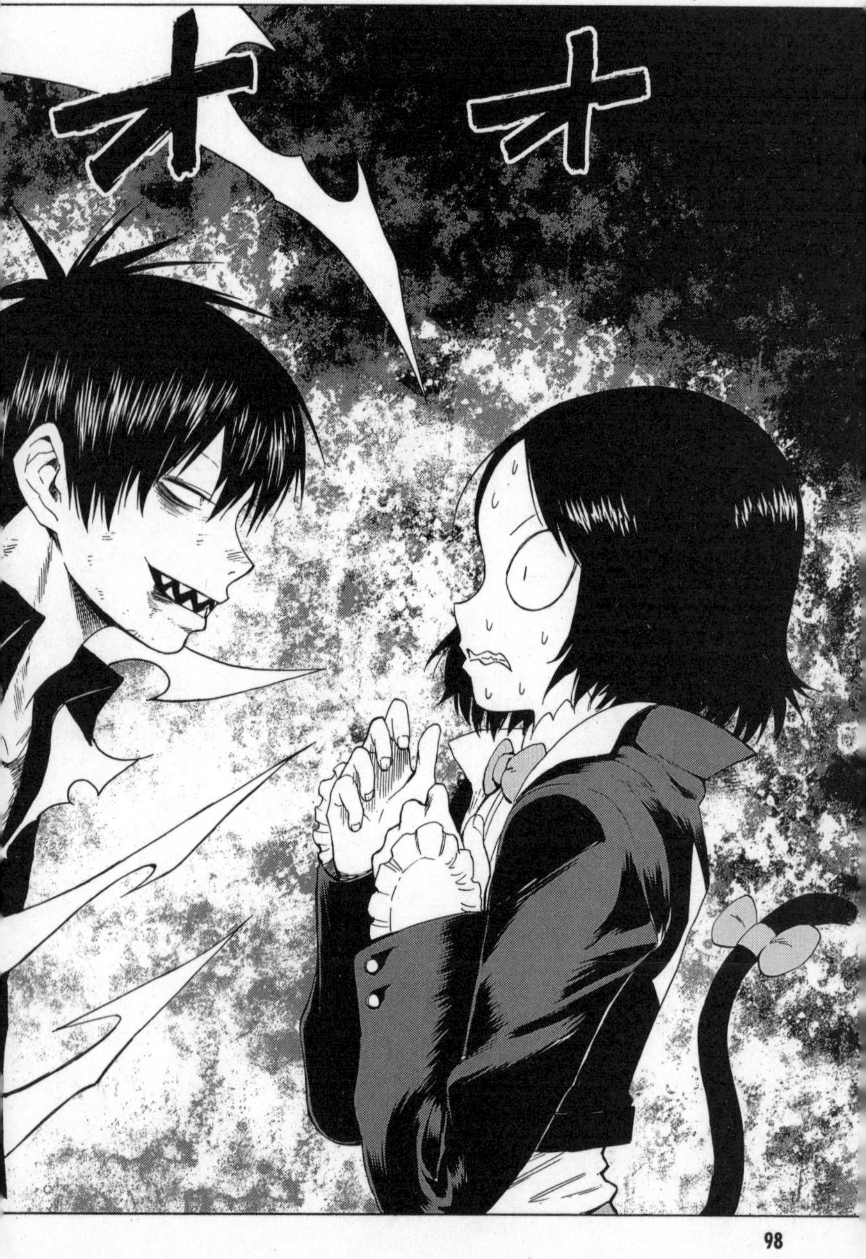
オオ

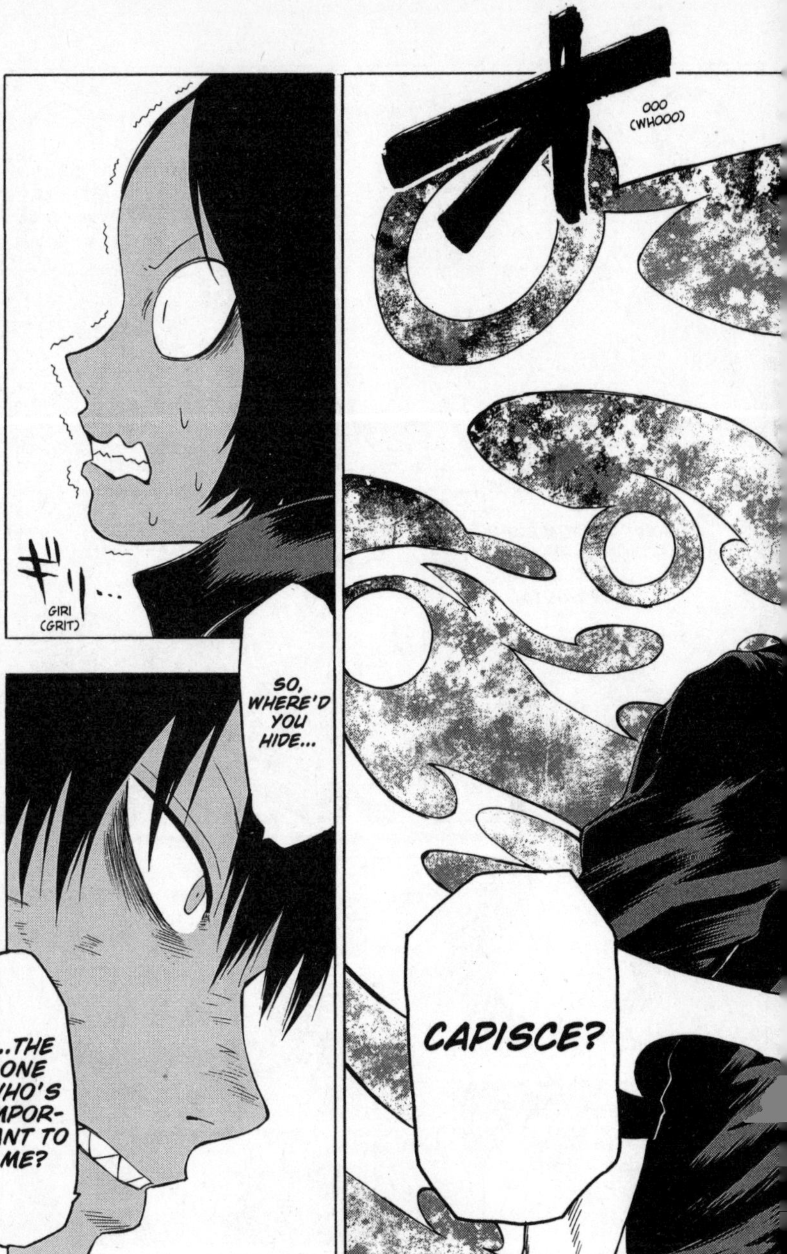

OOO
(WHOOO)
CAPISCE?
GIRI
(GRIT)
SO, WHERE'D YOU HIDE...
...THE ONE WHO'S IMPOR-TANT TO ME?

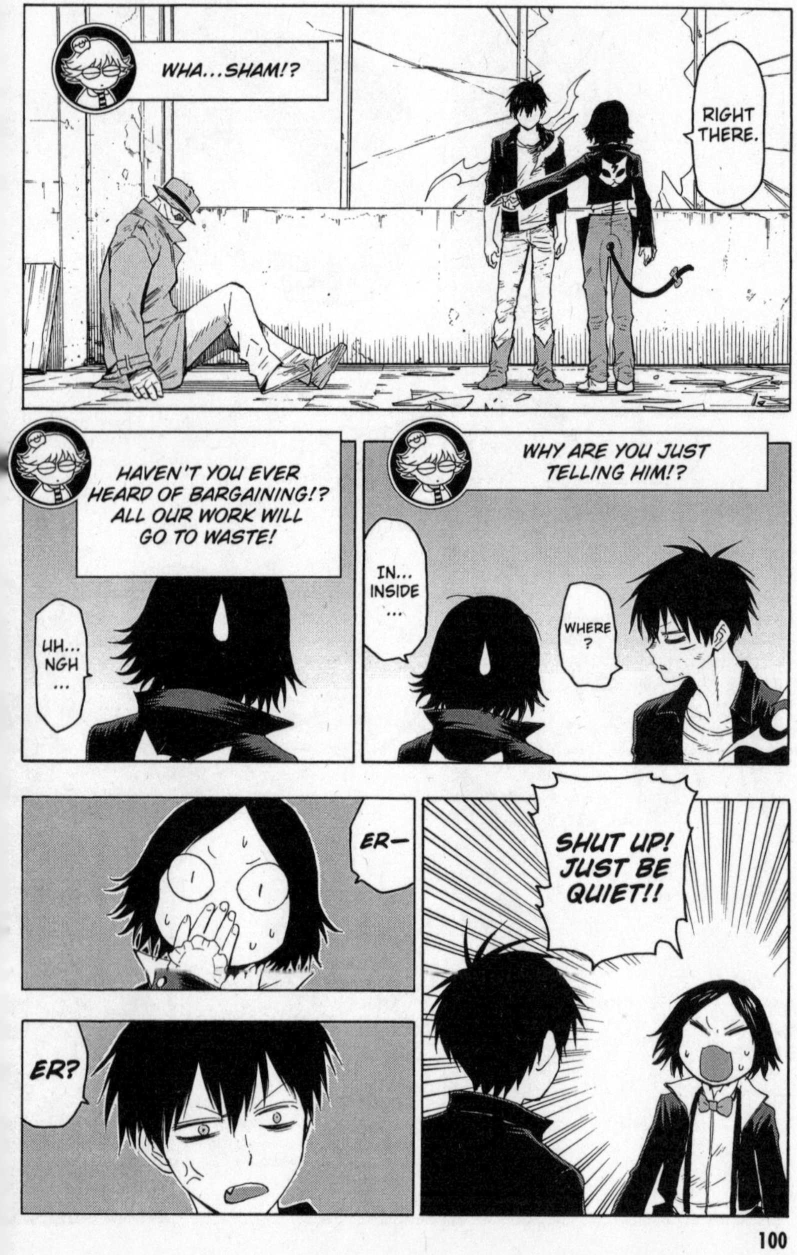
RIGHT THERE.
WHA...SHAM!?
WHERE?
IN... INSIDE...
WHY ARE YOU JUST TELLING HIM!?
HAVEN'T YOU EVER HEARD OF BARGAINING!? ALL OUR WORK WILL GO TO WASTE!
UH... NGH...
SHUT UP! JUST BE QUIET!!
ER—
ER?

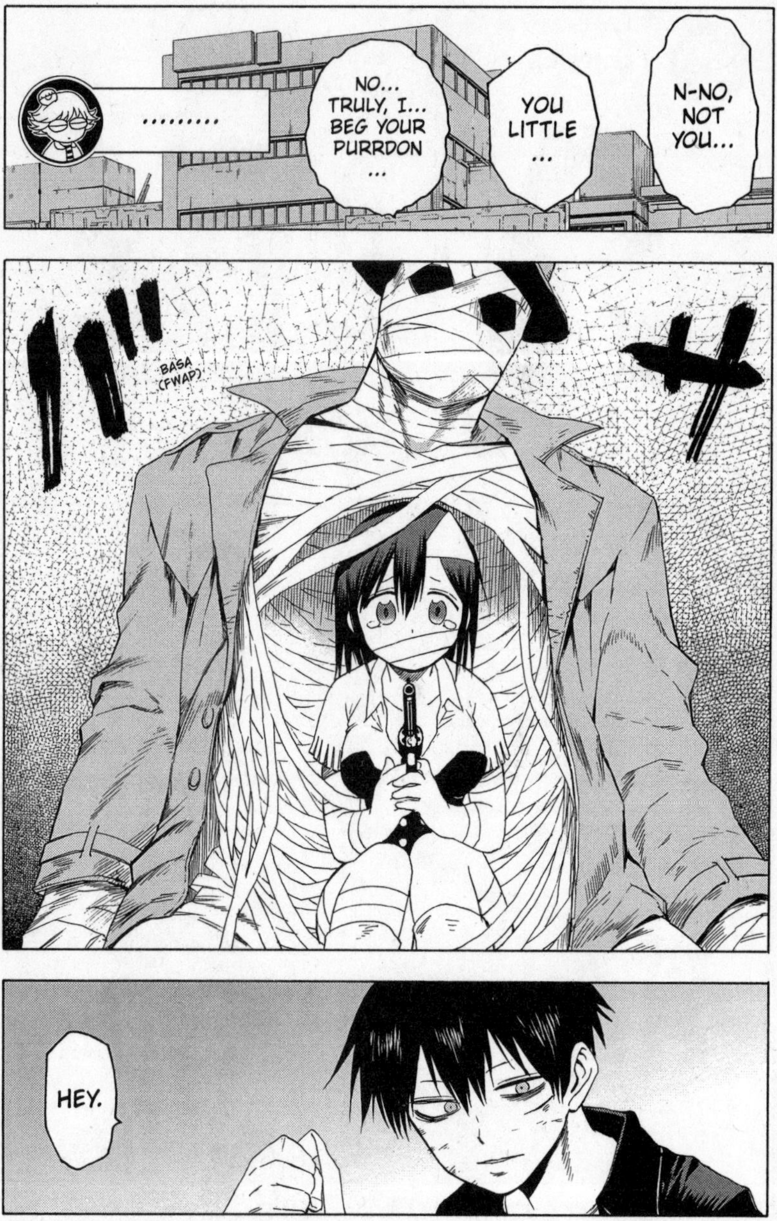
N-NO, NOT YOU...
YOU LITTLE ...
NO... TRULY, I... BEG YOUR PURRDON ...
....
BASA (FWAP)
HEY.

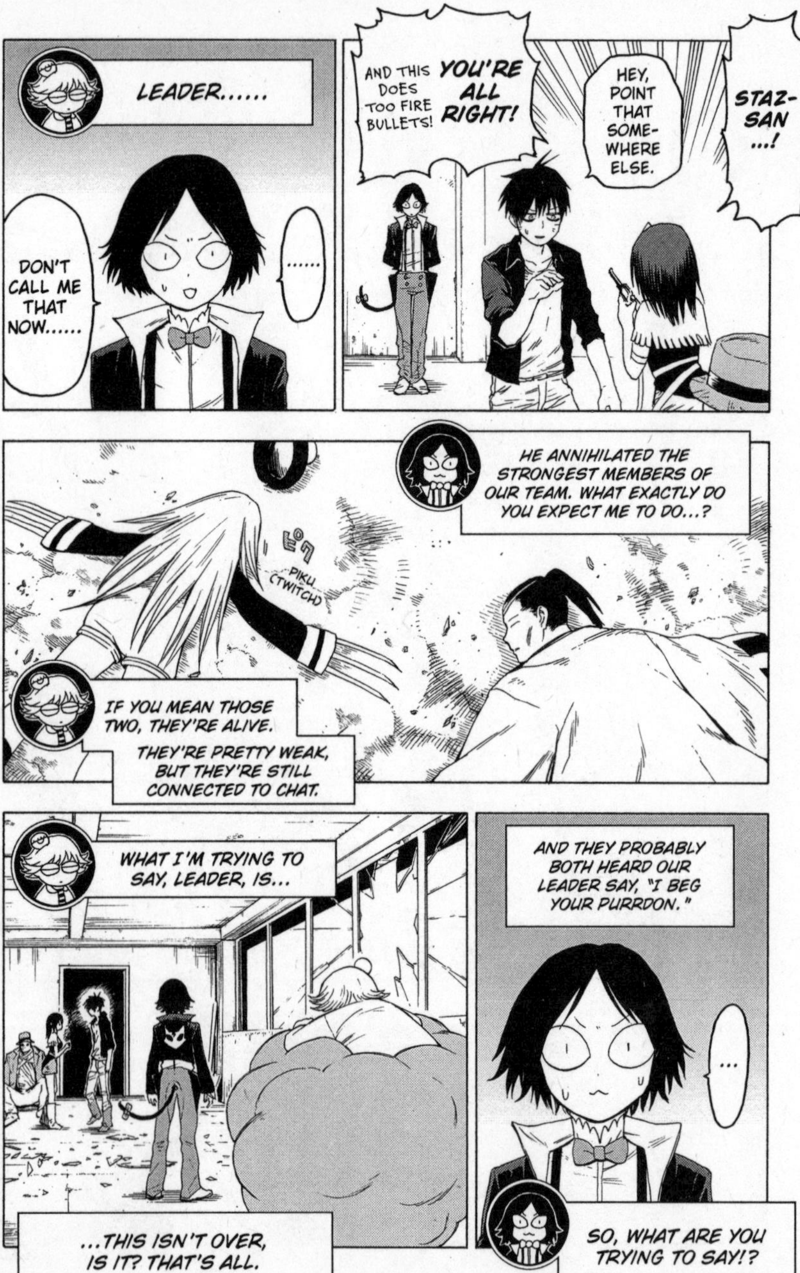
STAZ-SAN ...!
HEY, POINT THAT SOME-WHERE ELSE.
YOU'RE ALL RIGHT!
AND THIS DOES TOO FIRE BULLETS!
LEADER......
......
DON'T CALL ME THAT NOW......
HE ANNIHILATED THE STRONGEST MEMBERS OF OUR TEAM. WHAT EXACTLY DO YOU EXPECT ME TO DO...?
ピク
PIKU (TWITCH)
IF YOU MEAN THOSE TWO, THEY'RE ALIVE.
THEY'RE PRETTY WEAK, BUT THEY'RE STILL CONNECTED TO CHAT.
AND THEY PROBABLY BOTH HEARD OUR LEADER SAY, "I BEG YOUR PURRDON."
...
SO, WHAT ARE YOU TRYING TO SAY!?
WHAT I'M TRYING TO SAY, LEADER, IS...
...THIS ISN'T OVER, IS IT? THAT'S ALL.

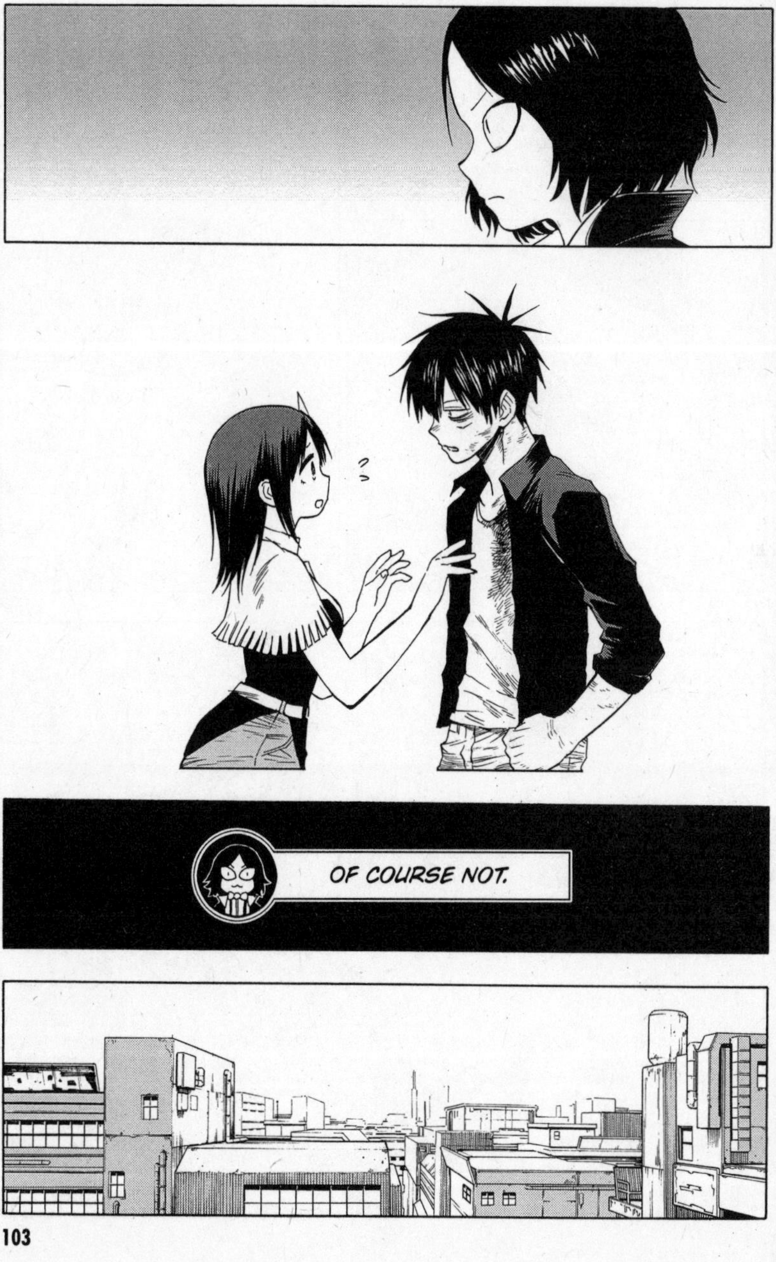
OF COURSE NOT.

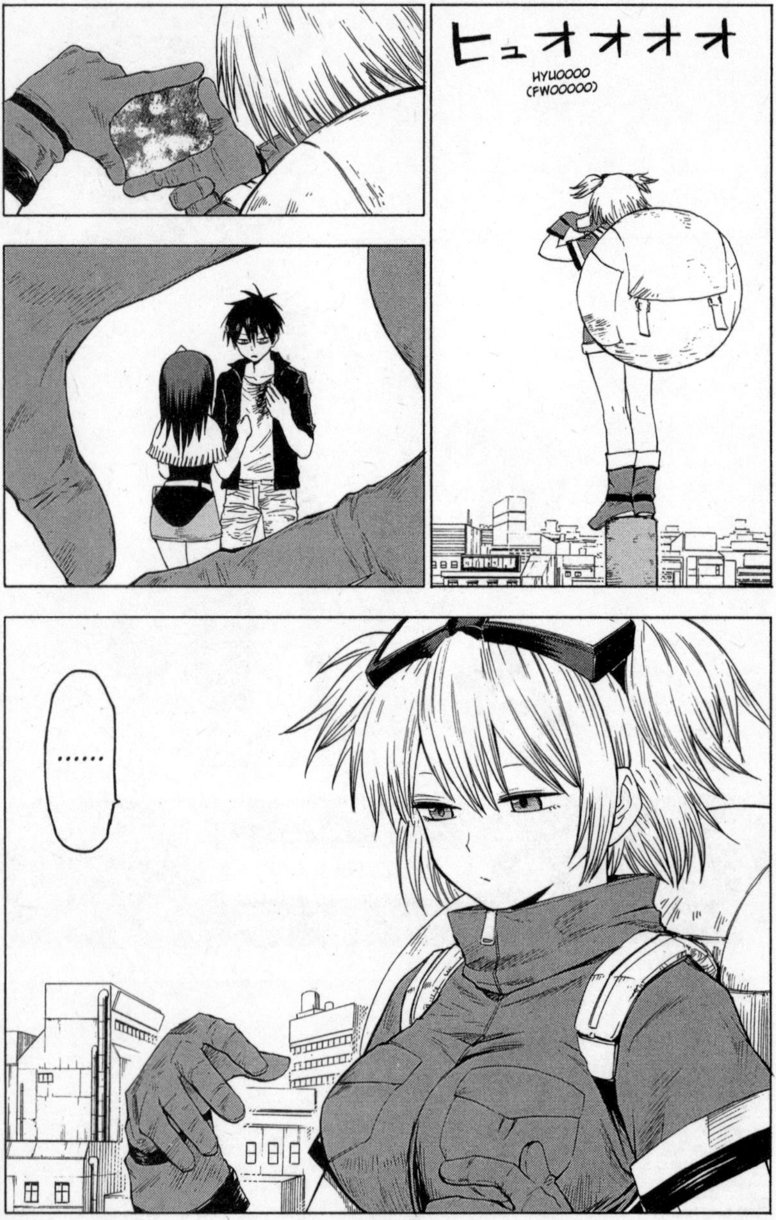
ヒュオオオオ
HYUOOOO
(FWOOOOO)
......

♠ To Be Continued ♠

BLOOD LAD

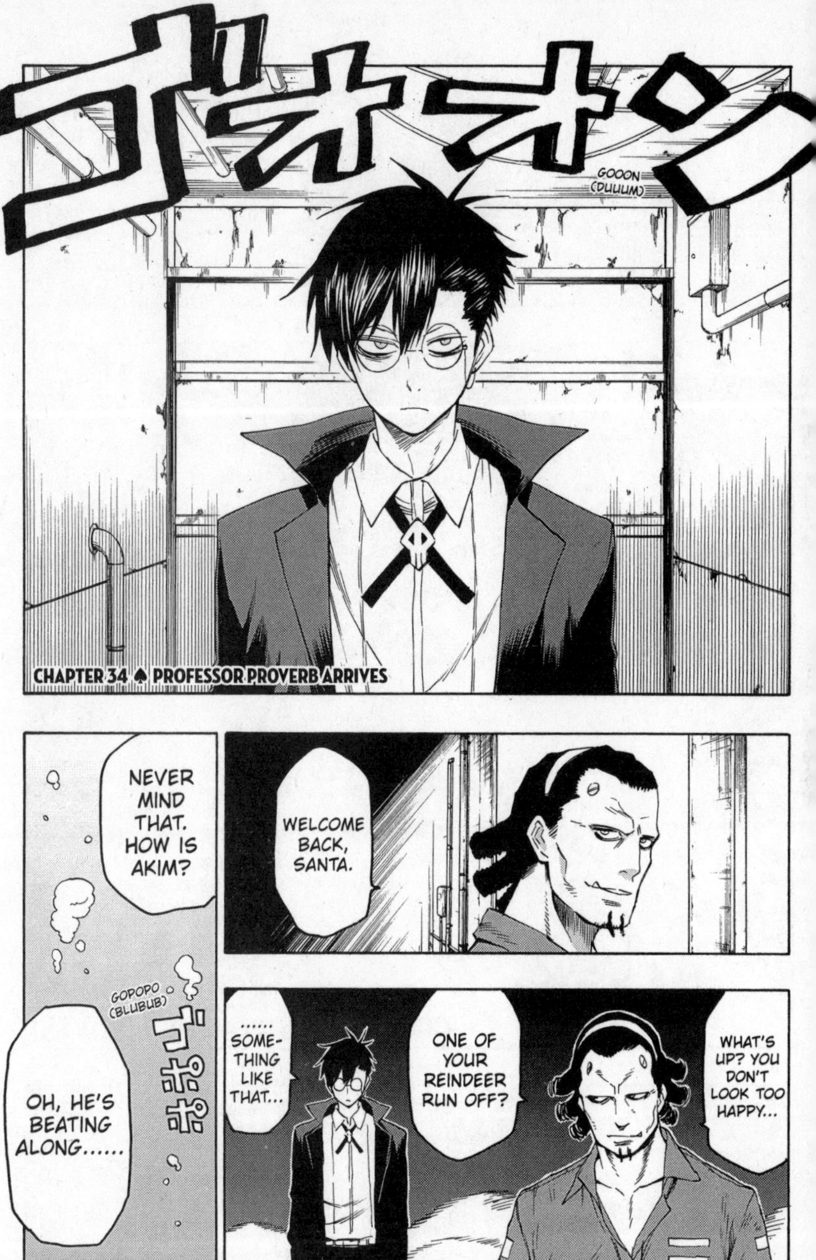
GOOON (DUUUM)
CHAPTER 34 ♠ PROFESSOR PROVERB ARRIVES
WELCOME BACK, SANTA.
WHAT'S UP? YOU DON'T LOOK TOO HAPPY...
ONE OF YOUR REINDEER RUN OFF?
......SOMETHING LIKE THAT...
NEVER MIND THAT. HOW IS AKIM?
GOPOPO (BLUBUB)
OH, HE'S BEATING ALONG......

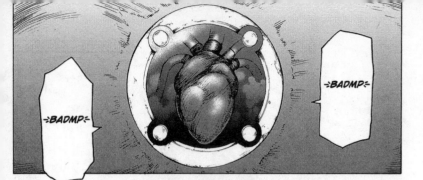

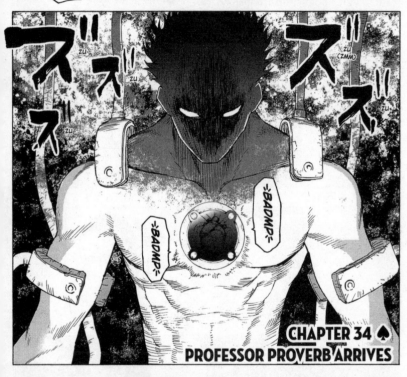

-BADMP-
-BADMP-
ZU (ZMM)
ZU
ZU
ZU
ZU
-BADMP-
-BADMP-
CHAPTER 34
PROFESSOR PROVERB ARRIVES
SO IT'S A SUCCESS ......

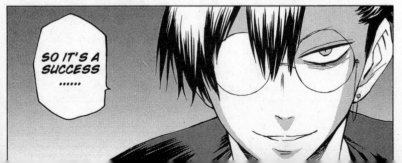

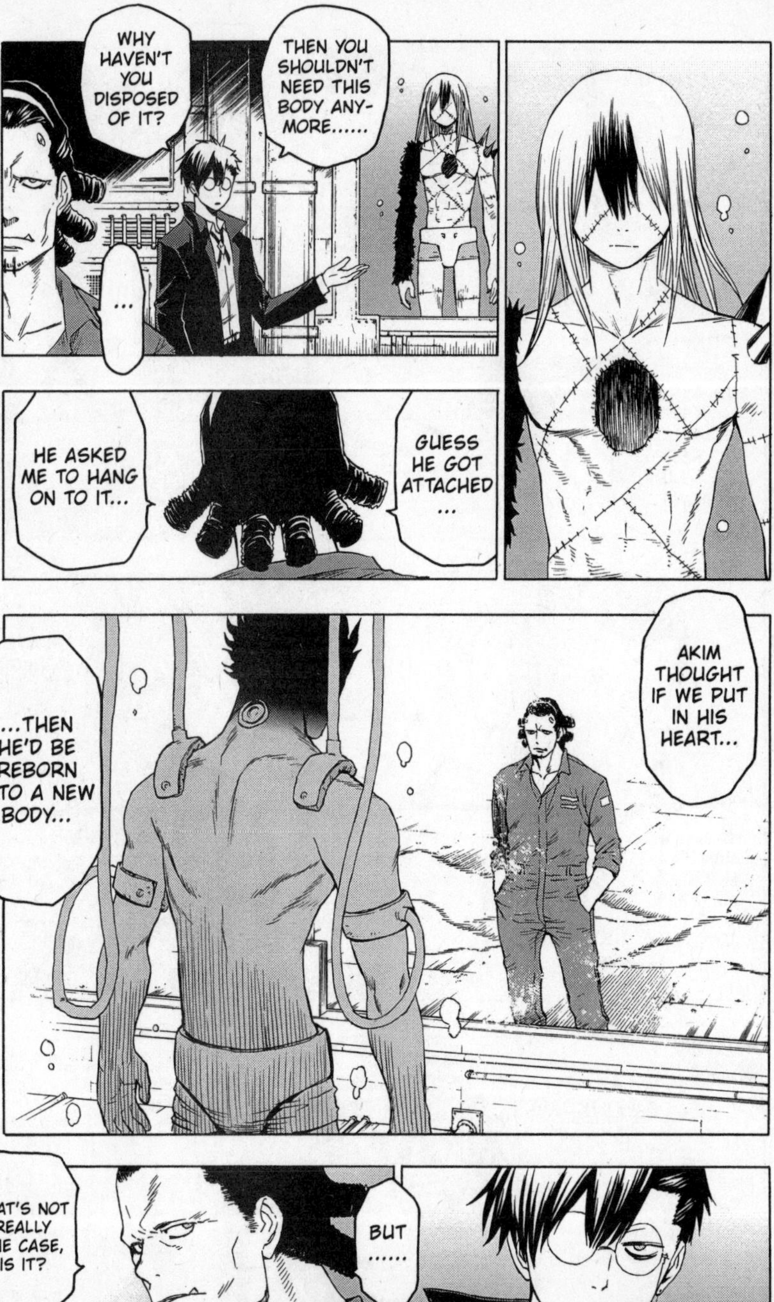
THEN YOU SHOULDN'T NEED THIS BODY ANY-MORE......
WHY HAVEN'T YOU DISPOSED OF IT?
...
GUESS HE GOT ATTACHED ...
HE ASKED ME TO HANG ON TO IT...
AKIM THOUGHT IF WE PUT IN HIS HEART...
...THEN HE'D BE REBORN INTO A NEW BODY...
BUT ......
THAT'S NOT REALLY THE CASE, IS IT?

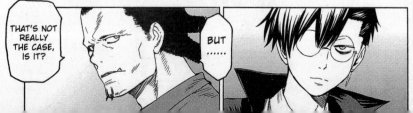

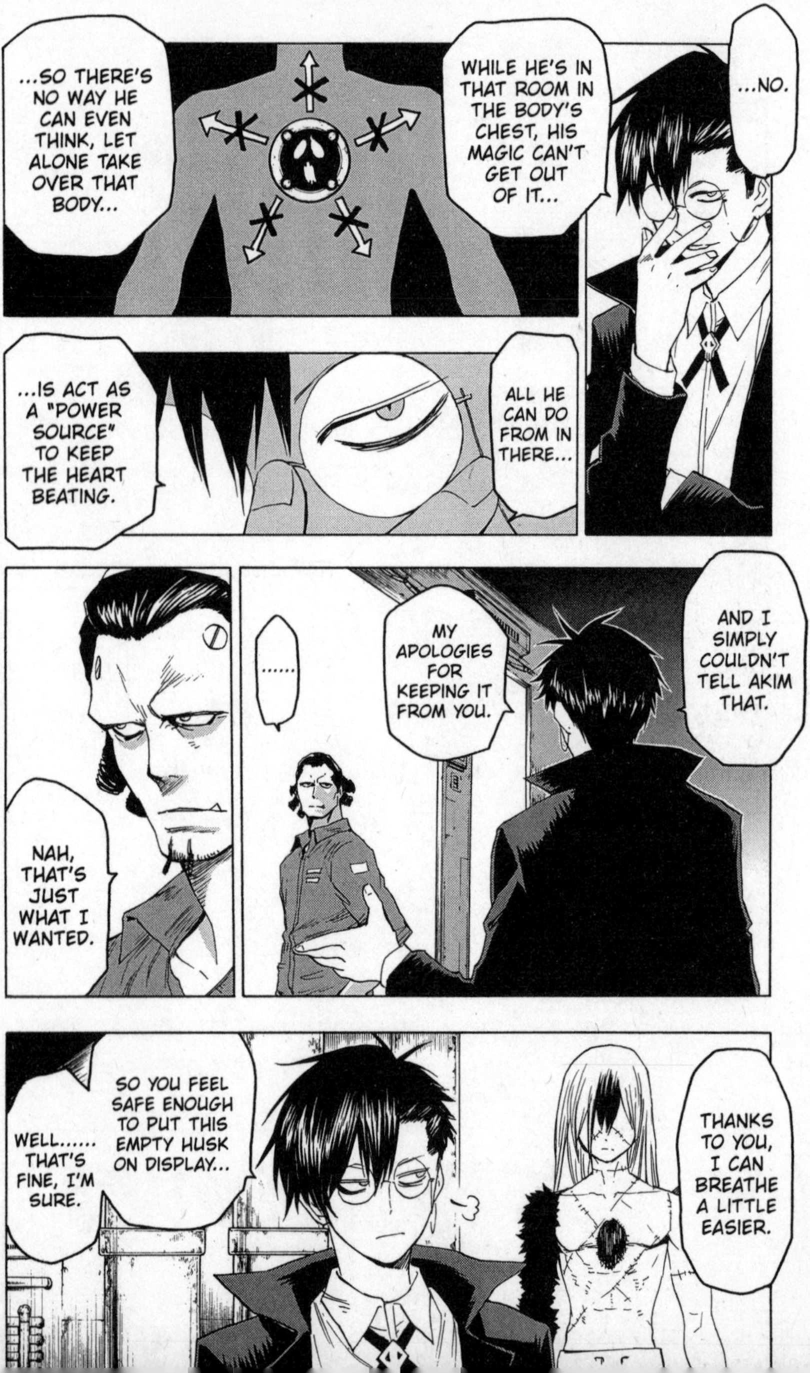
...NO.
WHILE HE'S IN THAT ROOM IN THE BODY'S CHEST, HIS MAGIC CAN'T GET OUT OF IT...
...SO THERE'S NO WAY HE CAN EVEN THINK, LET ALONE TAKE OVER THAT BODY...
ALL HE CAN DO FROM IN THERE...
...IS ACT AS A "POWER SOURCE" TO KEEP THE HEART BEATING.
AND I SIMPLY COULDN'T TELL AKIM THAT.
MY APOLOGIES FOR KEEPING IT FROM YOU.
......
NAH, THAT'S JUST WHAT I WANTED.
THANKS TO YOU, I CAN BREATHE A LITTLE EASIER.
SO YOU FEEL SAFE ENOUGH TO PUT THIS EMPTY HUSK ON DISPLAY...
WELL...... THAT'S FINE, I'M SURE.

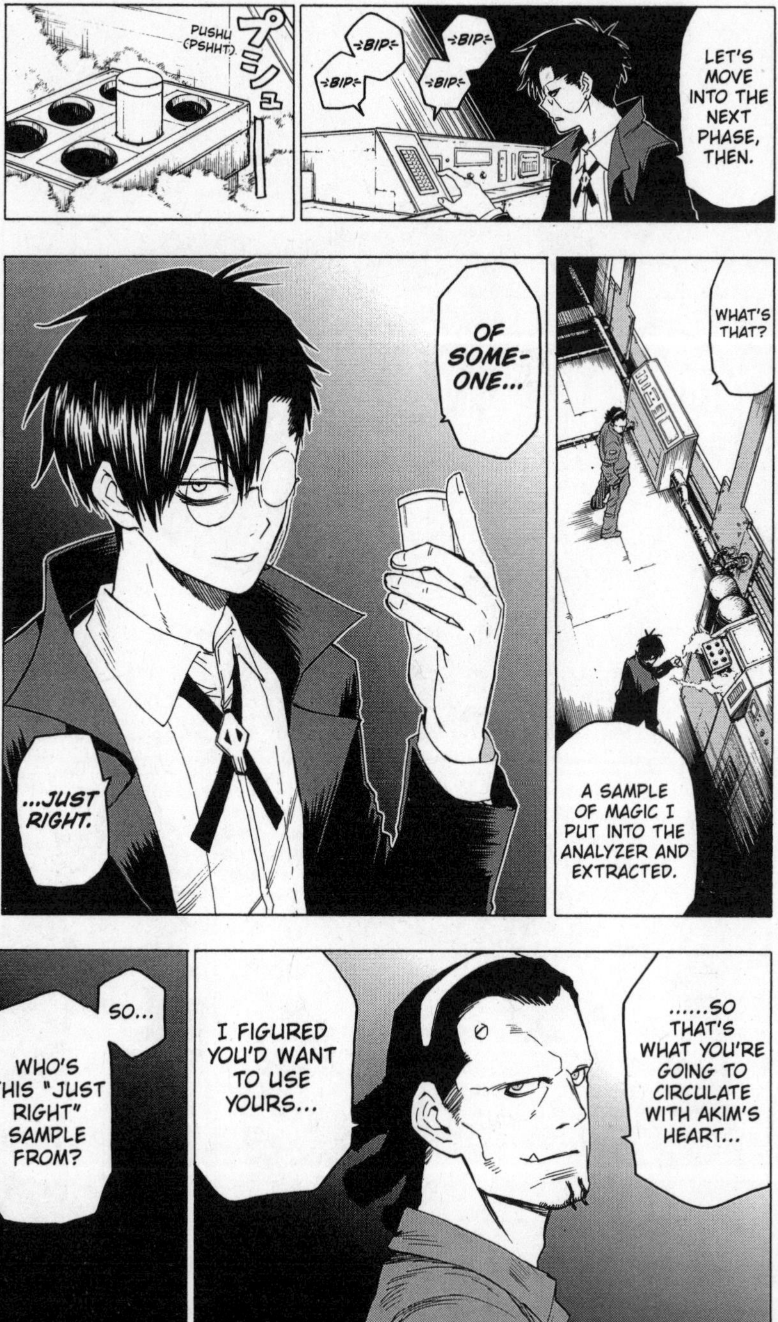
LET'S MOVE INTO THE NEXT PHASE, THEN.
BIP
BIP
BIP
BIP
プシュ
PUSHU (PSHHT)
WHAT'S THAT?
A SAMPLE OF MAGIC I PUT INTO THE ANALYZER AND EXTRACTED.
OF SOME-ONE...
...JUST RIGHT.
......SO THAT'S WHAT YOU'RE GOING TO CIRCULATE WITH AKIM'S HEART...
I FIGURED YOU'D WANT TO USE YOURS...
SO...
WHO'S THIS "JUST RIGHT" SAMPLE FROM?

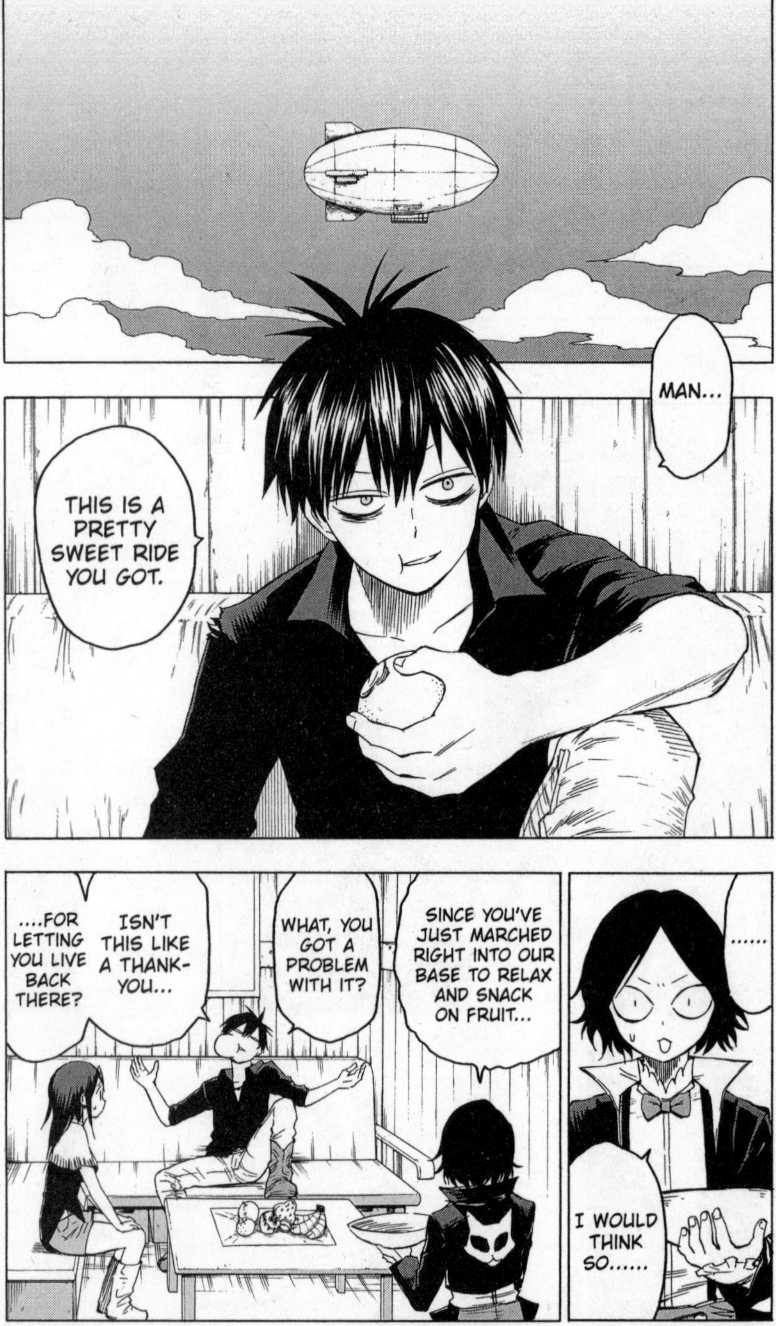
MAN...
THIS IS A PRETTY SWEET RIDE YOU GOT.
......
I WOULD THINK SO......
SINCE YOU'VE JUST MARCHED RIGHT INTO OUR BASE TO RELAX AND SNACK ON FRUIT...
WHAT, YOU GOT A PROBLEM WITH IT?
ISN'T THIS LIKE A THANK-YOU...
....FOR LETTING YOU LIVE BACK THERE?

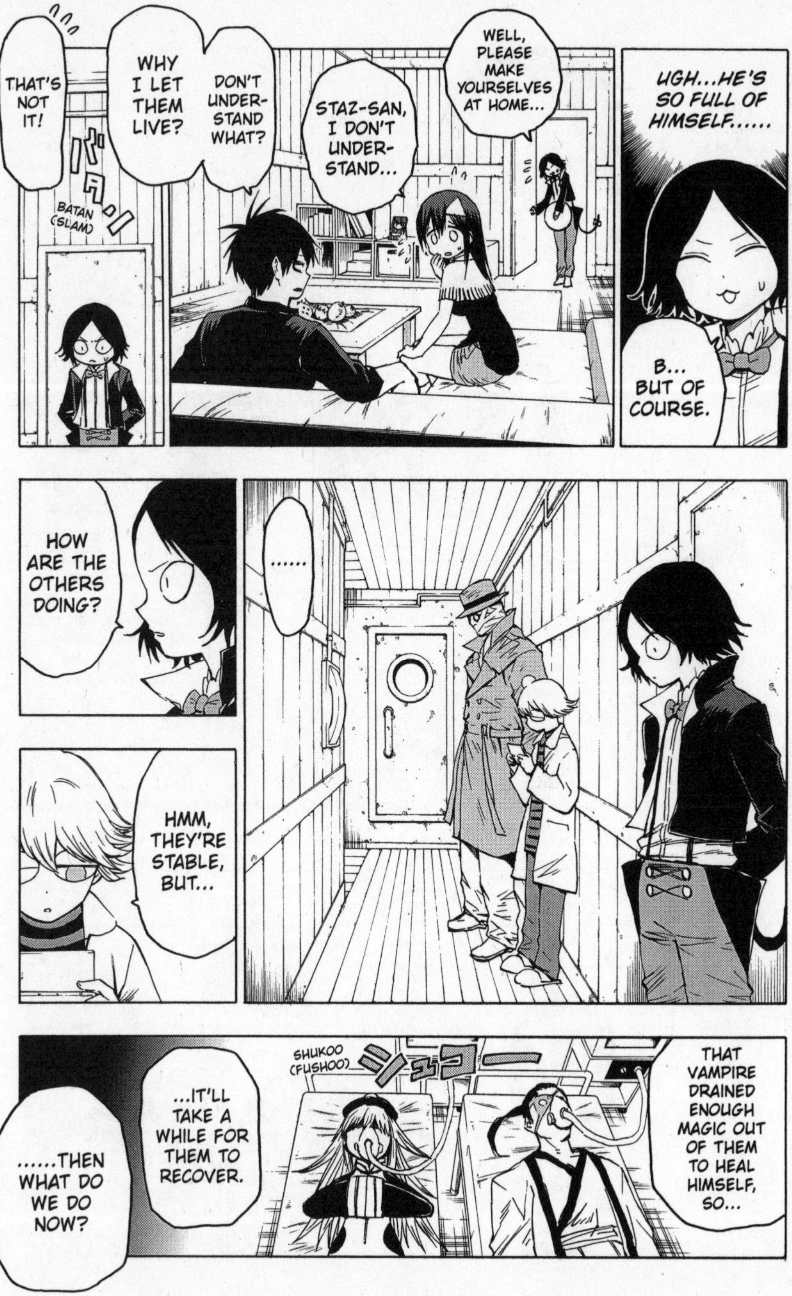
UGH...HE'S SO FULL OF HIMSELF......
B... BUT OF COURSE.
WELL, PLEASE MAKE YOURSELVES AT HOME...
STAZ-SAN, I DON'T UNDER-STAND...
DON'T UNDER-STAND WHAT?
WHY I LET THEM LIVE?
THAT'S NOT IT!
BATAN (SLAM)
......
HOW ARE THE OTHERS DOING?
HMM, THEY'RE STABLE, BUT...
THAT VAMPIRE DRAINED ENOUGH MAGIC OUT OF THEM TO HEAL HIMSELF, SO...
SHUKOO (FUSHOO)
...IT'LL TAKE A WHILE FOR THEM TO RECOVER.
......THEN WHAT DO WE DO NOW?

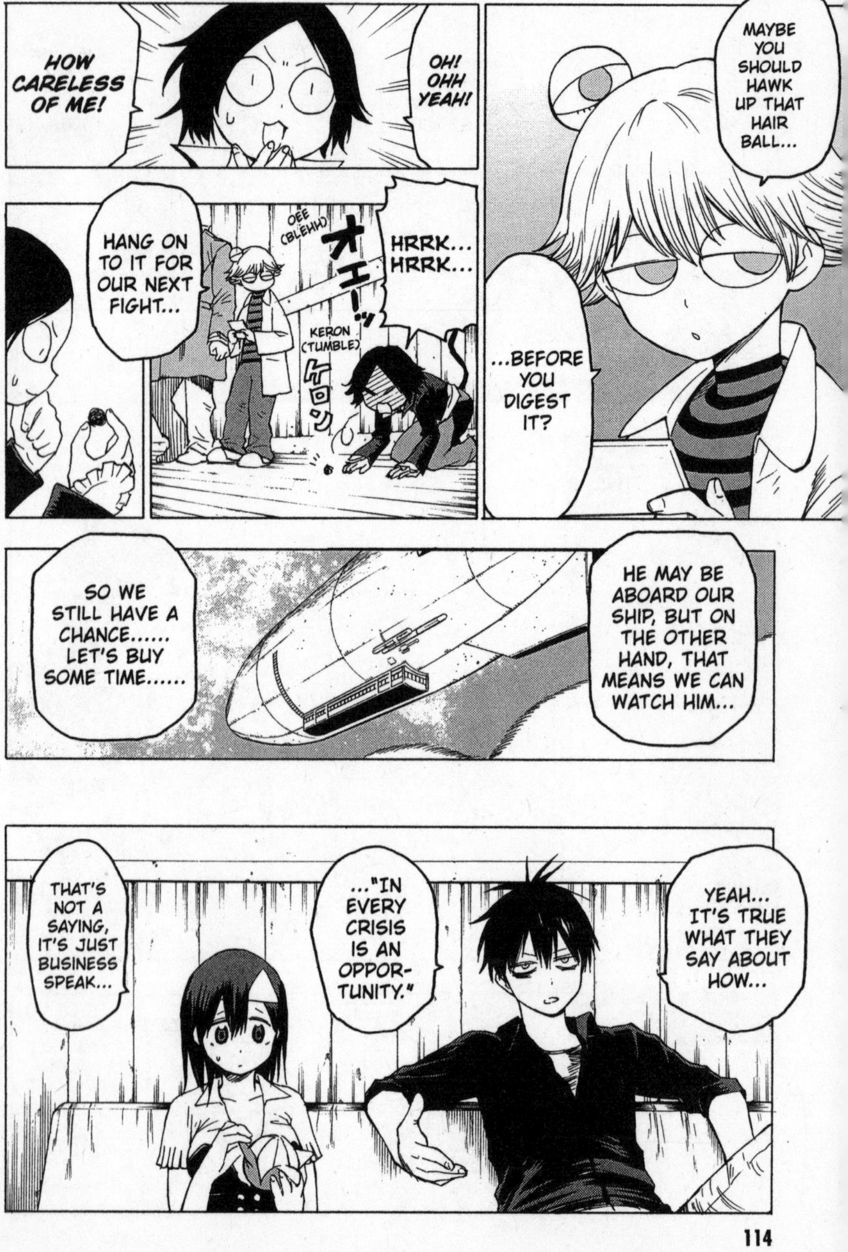
MAYBE YOU SHOULD HAWK UP THAT HAIR BALL...
...BEFORE YOU DIGEST IT?
OH! OHH YEAH!
HOW CARELESS OF ME!
HRRK... HRRK...
OEE (BLEHH)
KERON (TUMBLE)
HANG ON TO IT FOR OUR NEXT FIGHT...
HE MAY BE ABOARD OUR SHIP, BUT ON THE OTHER HAND, THAT MEANS WE CAN WATCH HIM...
SO WE STILL HAVE A CHANCE...... LET'S BUY SOME TIME......
YEAH... IT'S TRUE WHAT THEY SAY ABOUT HOW...
..."IN EVERY CRISIS IS AN OPPOR-TUNITY."
THAT'S NOT A SAYING, IT'S JUST BUSINESS SPEAK...

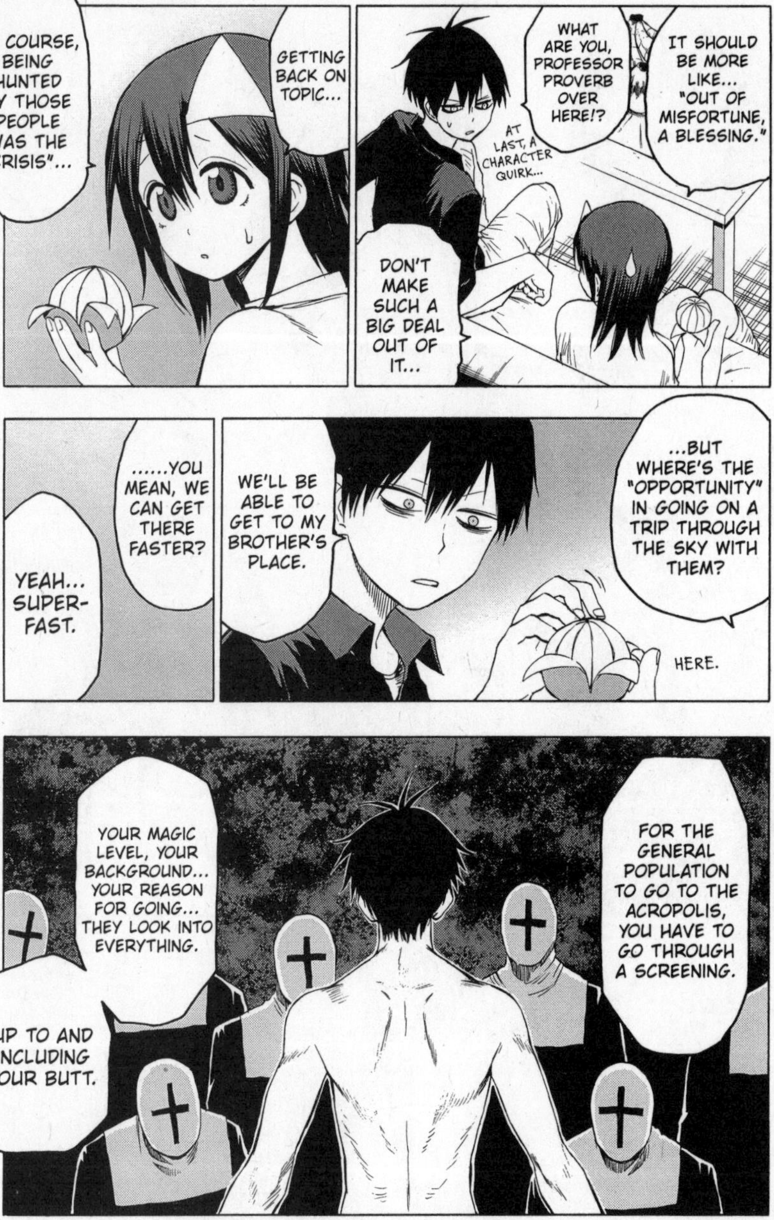
IT SHOULD BE MORE LIKE... "OUT OF MISFORTUNE, A BLESSING."
WHAT ARE YOU, PROFESSOR PROVERB OVER HERE!?
AT LAST, A CHARACTER QUIRK...
DON'T MAKE SUCH A BIG DEAL OUT OF IT...
GETTING BACK ON TOPIC...
OF COURSE, BEING HUNTED BY THOSE PEOPLE WAS THE "CRISIS"...
...BUT WHERE'S THE "OPPORTUNITY" IN GOING ON A TRIP THROUGH THE SKY WITH THEM?
HERE.
WE'LL BE ABLE TO GET TO MY BROTHER'S PLACE.
......YOU MEAN, WE CAN GET THERE FASTER?
YEAH... SUPER-FAST.
FOR THE GENERAL POPULATION TO GO TO THE ACROPOLIS, YOU HAVE TO GO THROUGH A SCREENING.
YOUR MAGIC LEVEL, YOUR BACKGROUND... YOUR REASON FOR GOING... THEY LOOK INTO EVERYTHING.
UP TO AND INCLUDING YOUR BUTT.

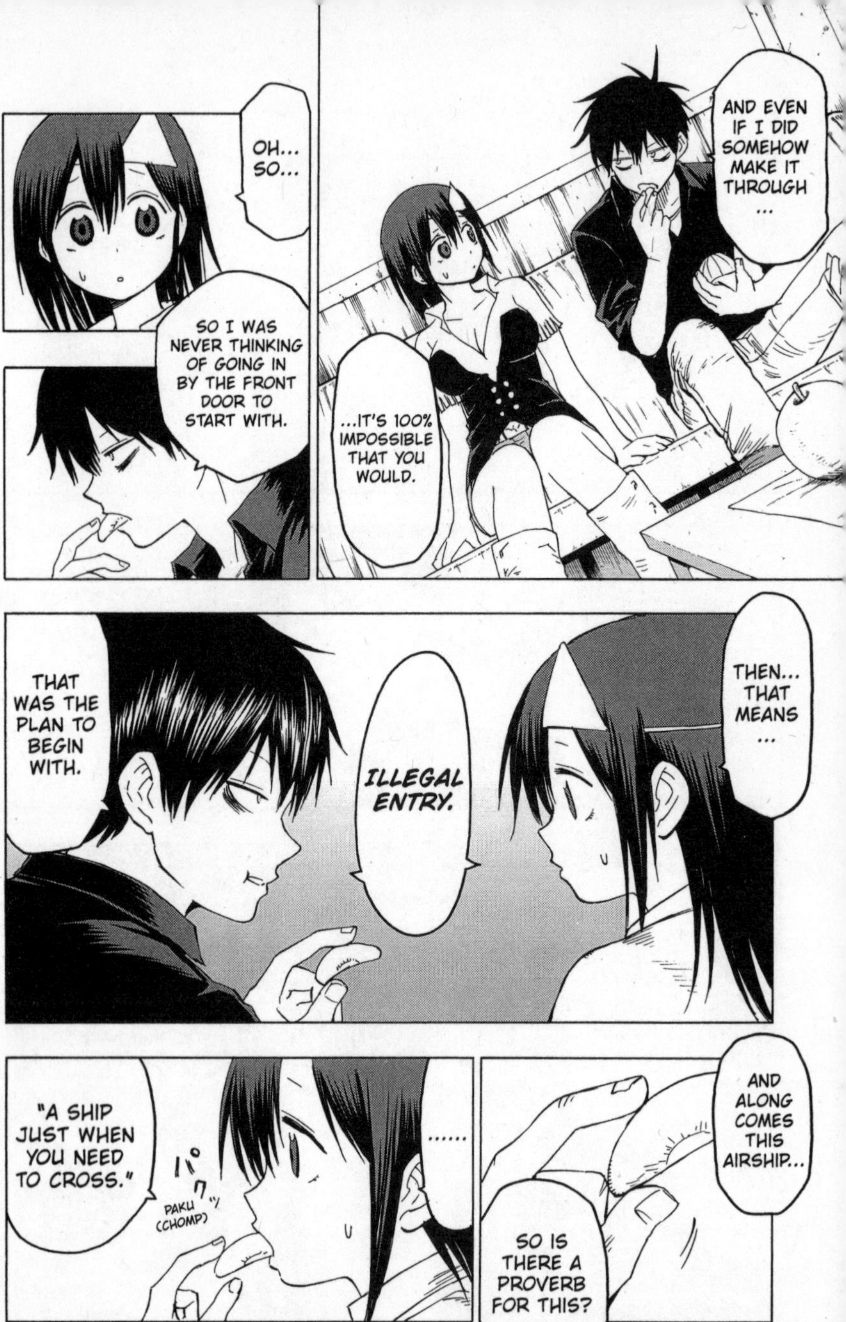
AND EVEN IF I DID SOMEHOW MAKE IT THROUGH ...
...IT'S 100% IMPOSSIBLE THAT YOU WOULD.
OH... SO...
SO I WAS NEVER THINKING OF GOING IN BY THE FRONT DOOR TO START WITH.
THEN... THAT MEANS ...
ILLEGAL ENTRY.
THAT WAS THE PLAN TO BEGIN WITH.
AND ALONG COMES THIS AIRSHIP...
SO IS THERE A PROVERB FOR THIS?
......
パクッ
PAKU (CHOMP)
"A SHIP JUST WHEN YOU NEED TO CROSS."

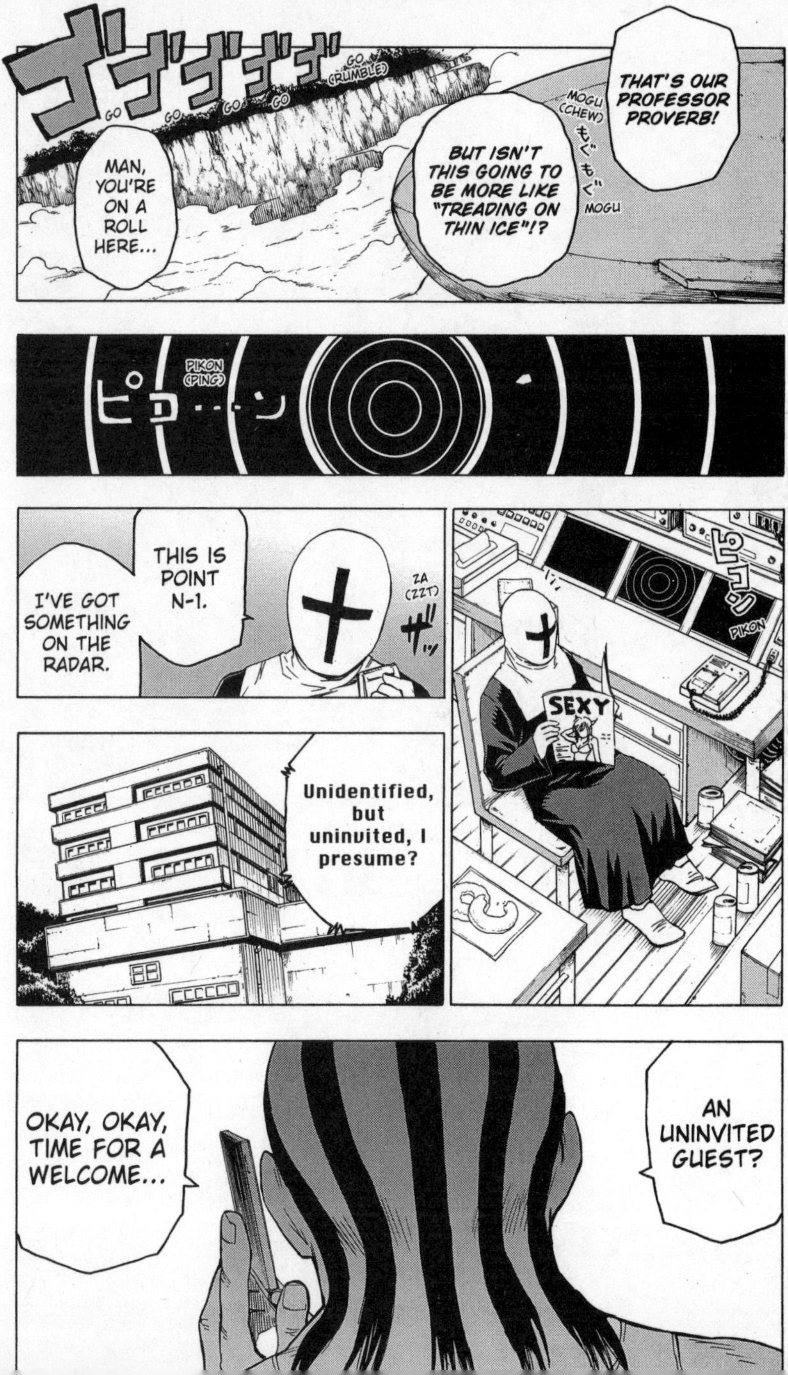
THAT'S OUR PROFESSOR PROVERB!
MOGU (CHEW) MOGU
もぐもぐ
BUT ISN'T THIS GOING TO BE MORE LIKE "TREADING ON THIN ICE"!?
ゴゴゴゴゴ
GO GO GO GO GO (RUMBLE)
MAN, YOU'RE ON A ROLL HERE...
PIKON (PING)
ピコ…ン
ピコン
PIKON
ZA (ZZT)
ザッ
THIS IS POINT N-1.
I'VE GOT SOMETHING ON THE RADAR.
SEXY
Unidentified, but uninvited, I presume?
AN UNINVITED GUEST?
OKAY, OKAY, TIME FOR A WELCOME...

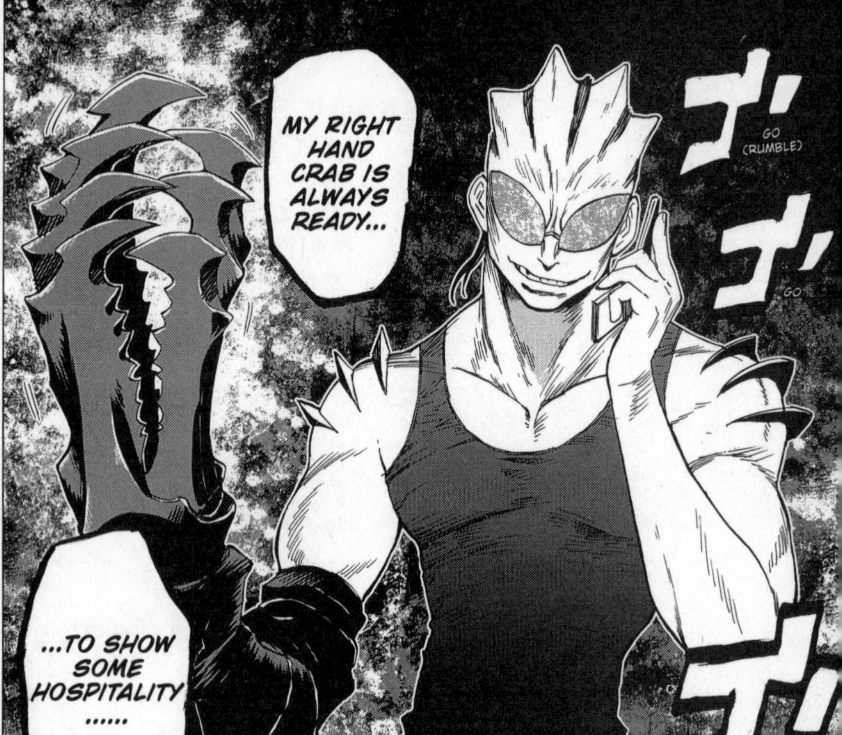
GO (RUMBLE)
GO
GO
MY RIGHT HAND CRAB IS ALWAYS READY...
...TO SHOW SOME HOSPITALITY ......

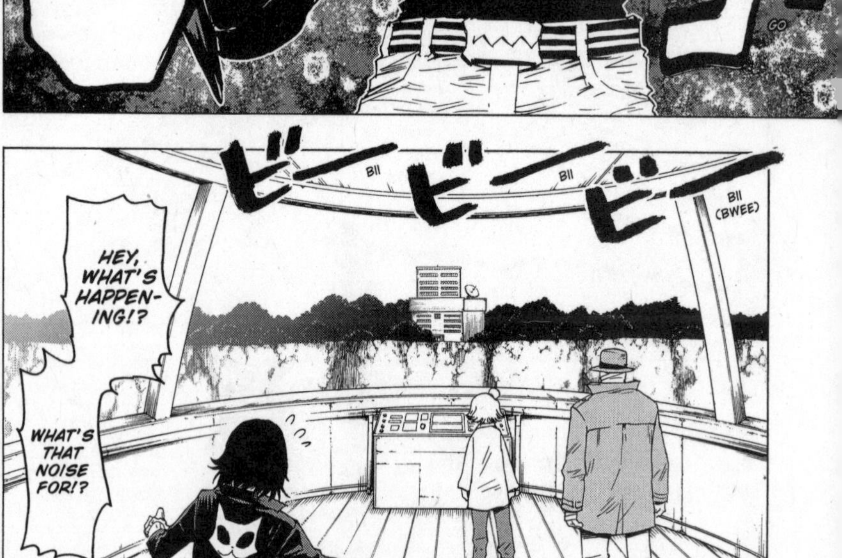
BII
BII
BII (BWEE)
HEY, WHAT'S HAPPEN-ING!?
WHAT'S THAT NOISE FOR!?

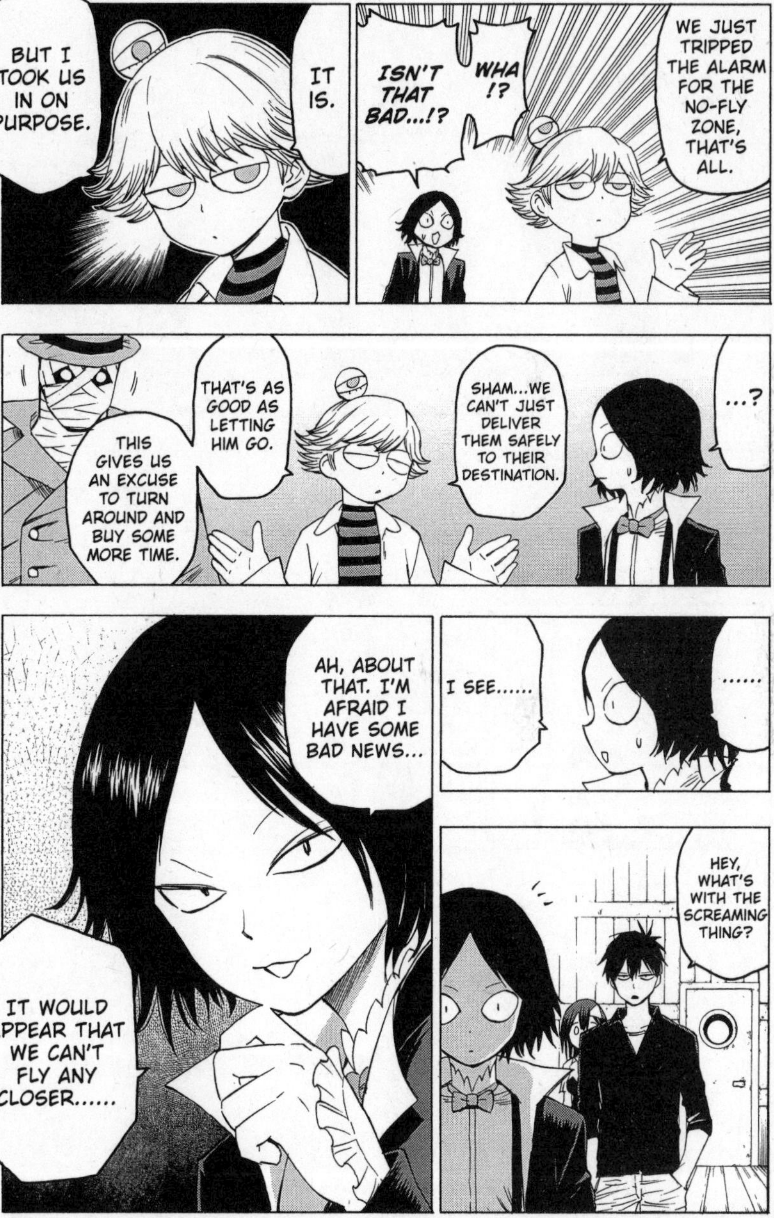

WE JUST TRIPPED THE ALARM FOR THE NO-FLY ZONE, THAT'S ALL.
WHA!?
ISN'T THAT BAD...!?
IT IS.
BUT I TOOK US IN ON PURPOSE.
...?
SHAM...WE CAN'T JUST DELIVER THEM SAFELY TO THEIR DESTINATION.
THAT'S AS GOOD AS LETTING HIM GO.
THIS GIVES US AN EXCUSE TO TURN AROUND AND BUY SOME MORE TIME.
......
I SEE......
HEY, WHAT'S WITH THE SCREAMING THING?
AH, ABOUT THAT. I'M AFRAID I HAVE SOME BAD NEWS...
IT WOULD APPEAR THAT WE CAN'T FLY ANY CLOSER......

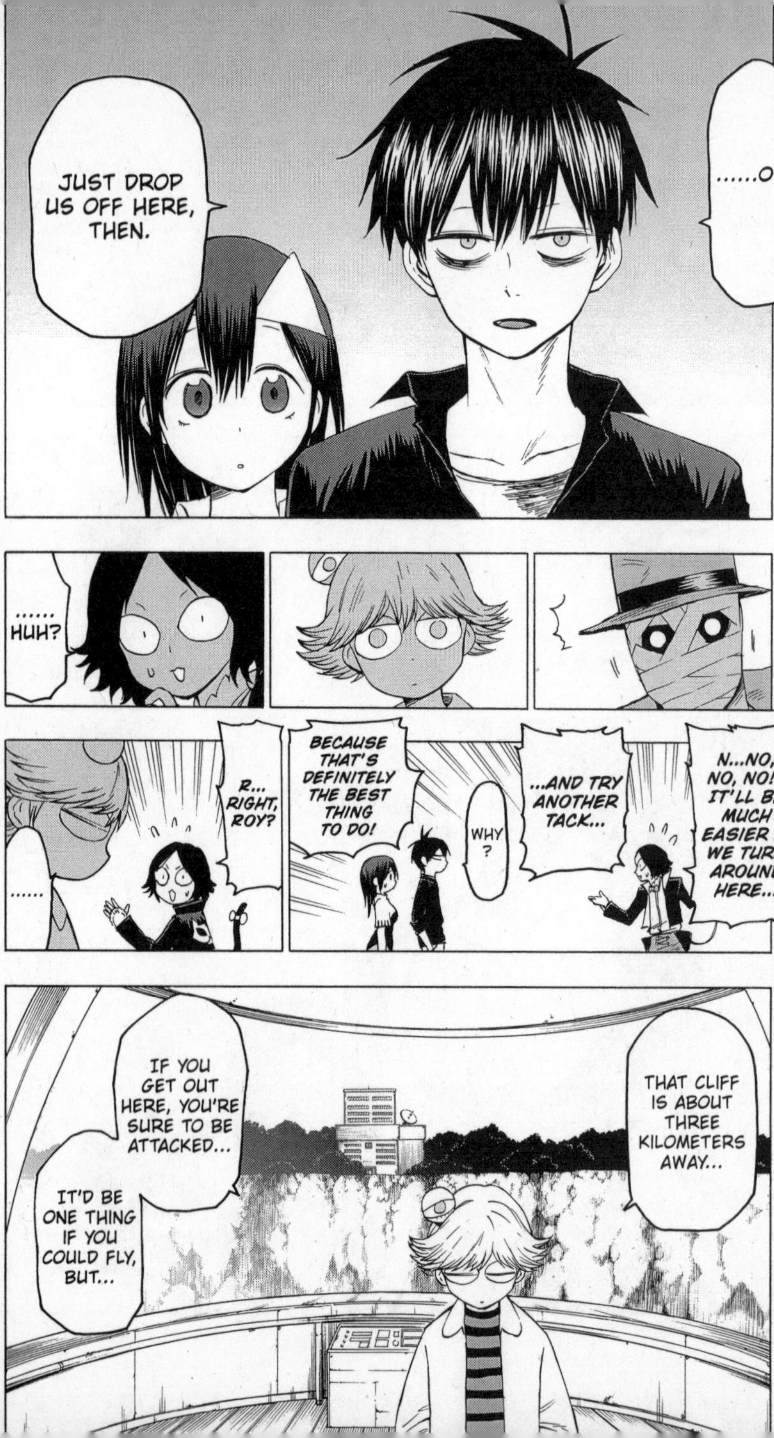

......OH.
JUST DROP US OFF HERE, THEN.
...... HUH?
N...NO, NO, NO!! IT'LL BE MUCH EASIER IF WE TURN AROUND HERE...
...AND TRY ANOTHER TACK...
WHY?
BECAUSE THAT'S DEFINITELY THE BEST THING TO DO!
R... RIGHT, ROY?
......
THAT CLIFF IS ABOUT THREE KILOMETERS AWAY...
IF YOU GET OUT HERE, YOU'RE SURE TO BE ATTACKED...
IT'D BE ONE THING IF YOU COULD FLY, BUT...

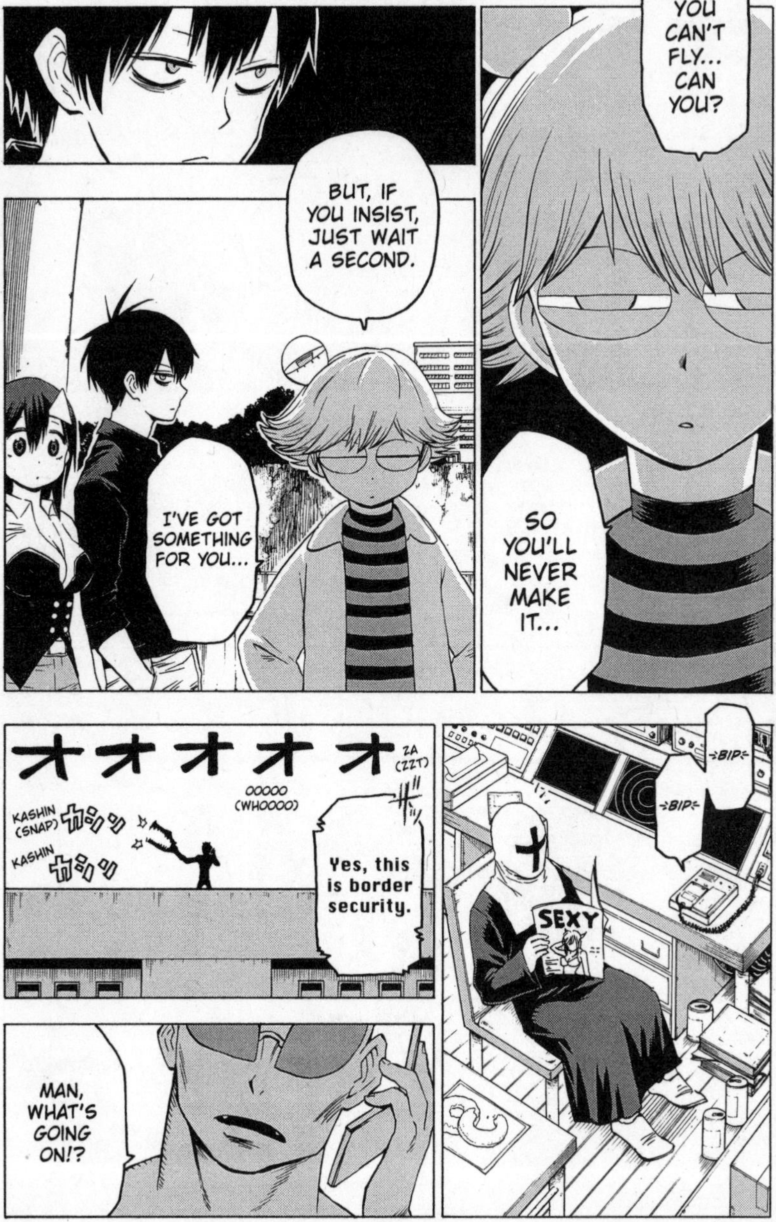

YOU CAN'T FLY... CAN YOU?
SO YOU'LL NEVER MAKE IT...
BUT, IF YOU INSIST, JUST WAIT A SECOND.
I'VE GOT SOMETHING FOR YOU...
BIP
BIP
ZA (ZZT)
Yes, this is border security.
オオオオオ
OOOOO (WHOOOO)
KASHIN (SNAP) カシッ
KASHIN カシッ
SEXY
MAN, WHAT'S GOING ON!?

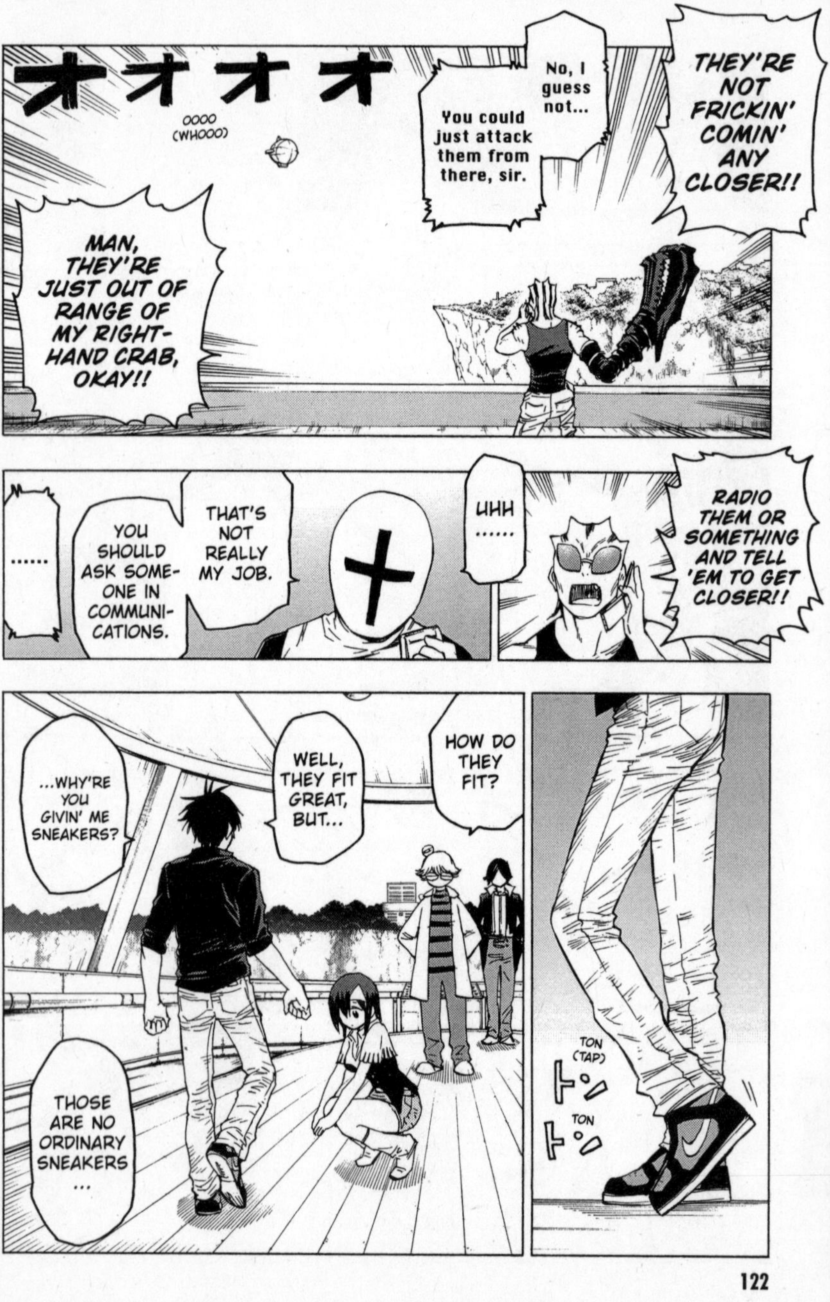
THEY'RE NOT FRICKIN' COMIN' ANY CLOSER!!
No, I guess not...
You could just attack them from there, sir.
オオオオ
OOOO (WHOOO)
MAN, THEY'RE JUST OUT OF RANGE OF MY RIGHT-HAND CRAB, OKAY!!
RADIO THEM OR SOMETHING AND TELL 'EM TO GET CLOSER!!
UHH ......
THAT'S NOT REALLY MY JOB.
YOU SHOULD ASK SOME-ONE IN COMMUNI-CATIONS.
......
TON (TAP)
トン
TON
トン
HOW DO THEY FIT?
WELL, THEY FIT GREAT, BUT...
...WHY'RE YOU GIVIN' ME SNEAKERS?
THOSE ARE NO ORDINARY SNEAKERS ...

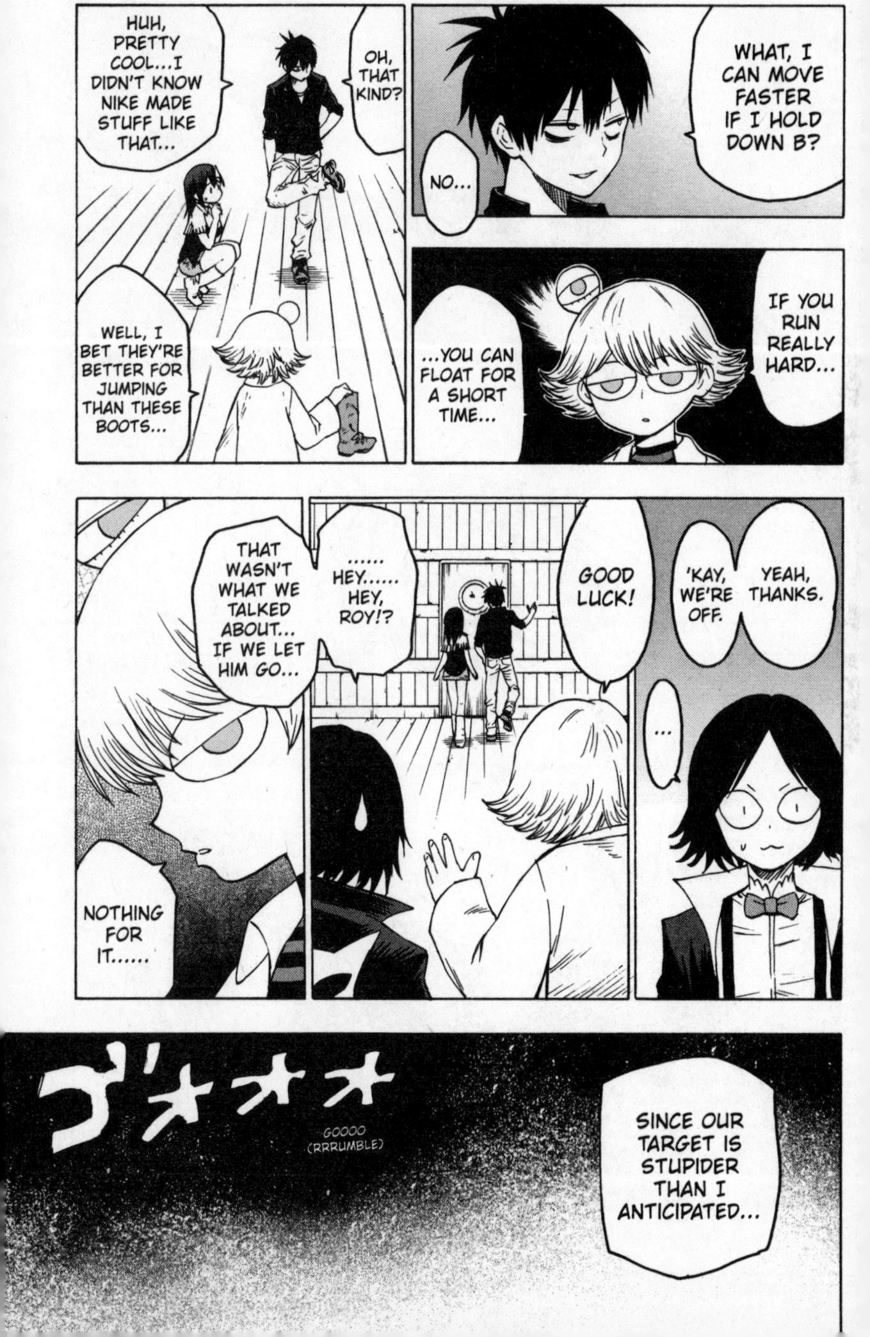
WHAT, I CAN MOVE FASTER IF I HOLD DOWN B?
NO...
IF YOU RUN REALLY HARD...
...YOU CAN FLOAT FOR A SHORT TIME...
OH, THAT KIND?
HUH, PRETTY COOL...I DIDN'T KNOW NIKE MADE STUFF LIKE THAT...
WELL, I BET THEY'RE BETTER FOR JUMPING THAN THESE BOOTS...
YEAH, THANKS.
'KAY, WE'RE OFF.
...
GOOD LUCK!
...... HEY...... HEY, ROY!?
THAT WASN'T WHAT WE TALKED ABOUT... IF WE LET HIM GO...
NOTHING FOR IT......
ゴオオオ
GOOOO (RRRUMBLE)
SINCE OUR TARGET IS STUPIDER THAN I ANTICIPATED...

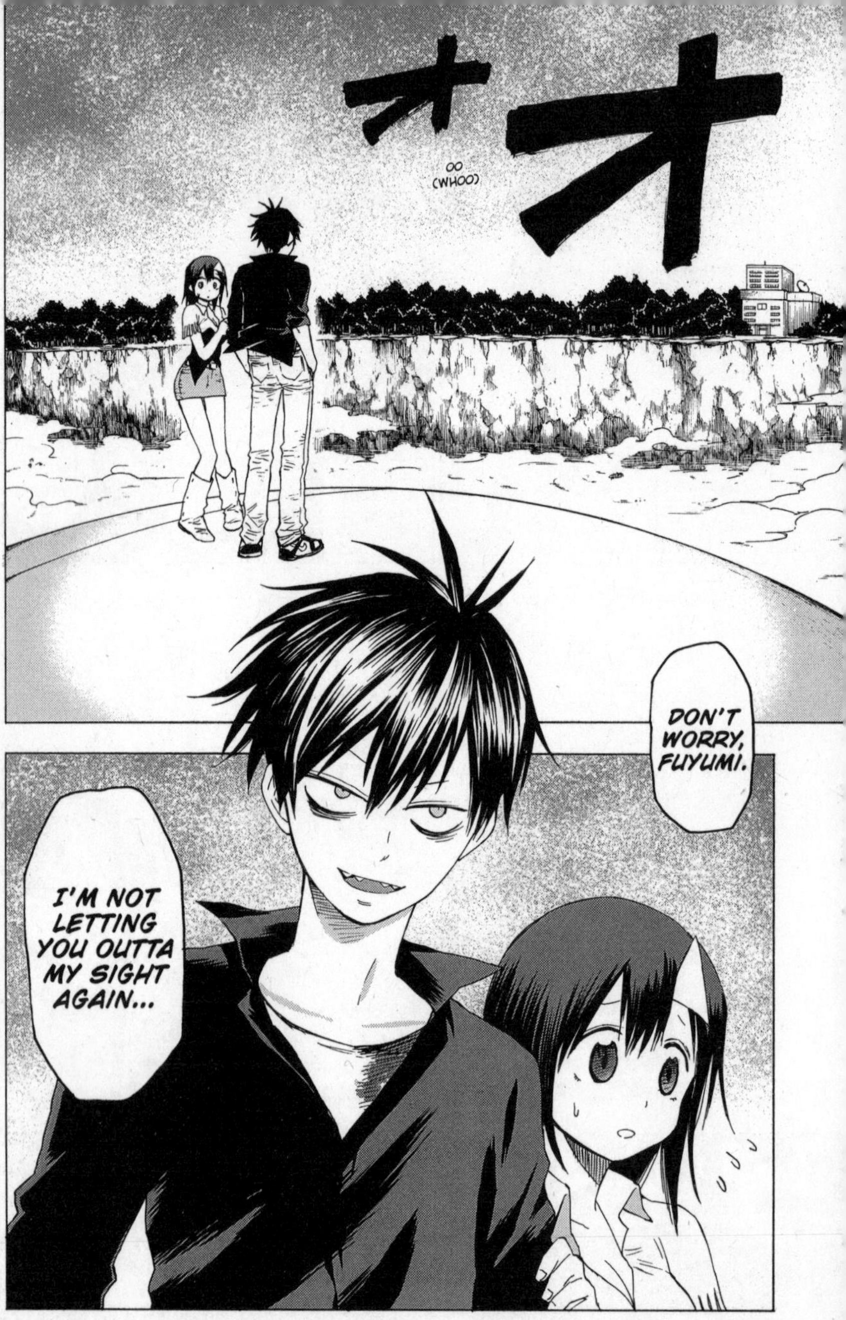
オオ
OO (WHOO)
DON'T WORRY, FUYUMI.
I'M NOT LETTING YOU OUTTA MY SIGHT AGAIN...

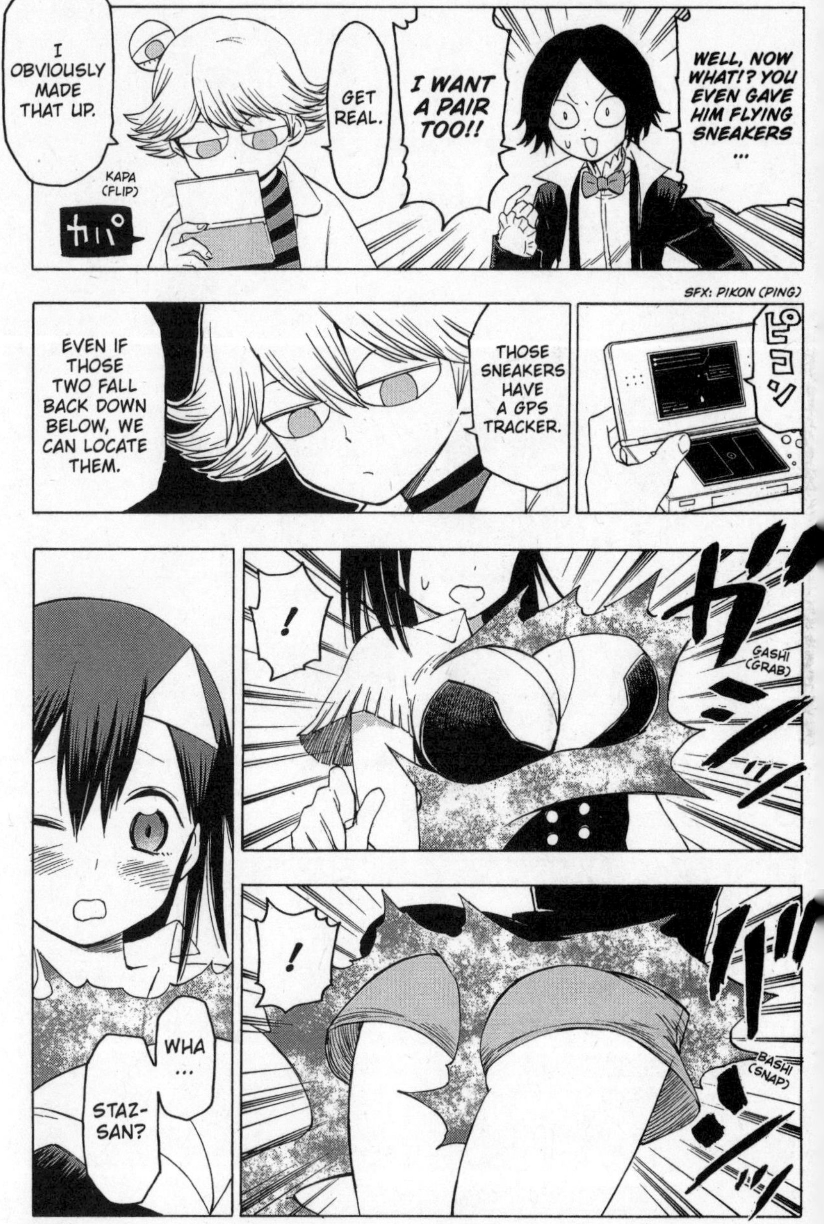
WELL, NOW WHAT!? YOU EVEN GAVE HIM FLYING SNEAKERS ...
I WANT A PAIR TOO!!
GET REAL.
I OBVIOUSLY MADE THAT UP.
KAPA (FLIP)
カパ
SFX: PIKON (PING)
ピコッ
THOSE SNEAKERS HAVE A GPS TRACKER.
EVEN IF THOSE TWO FALL BACK DOWN BELOW, WE CAN LOCATE THEM.
!
GASHI (GRAB)
!
BASHI (SNAP)
WHA ...
STAZ-SAN?

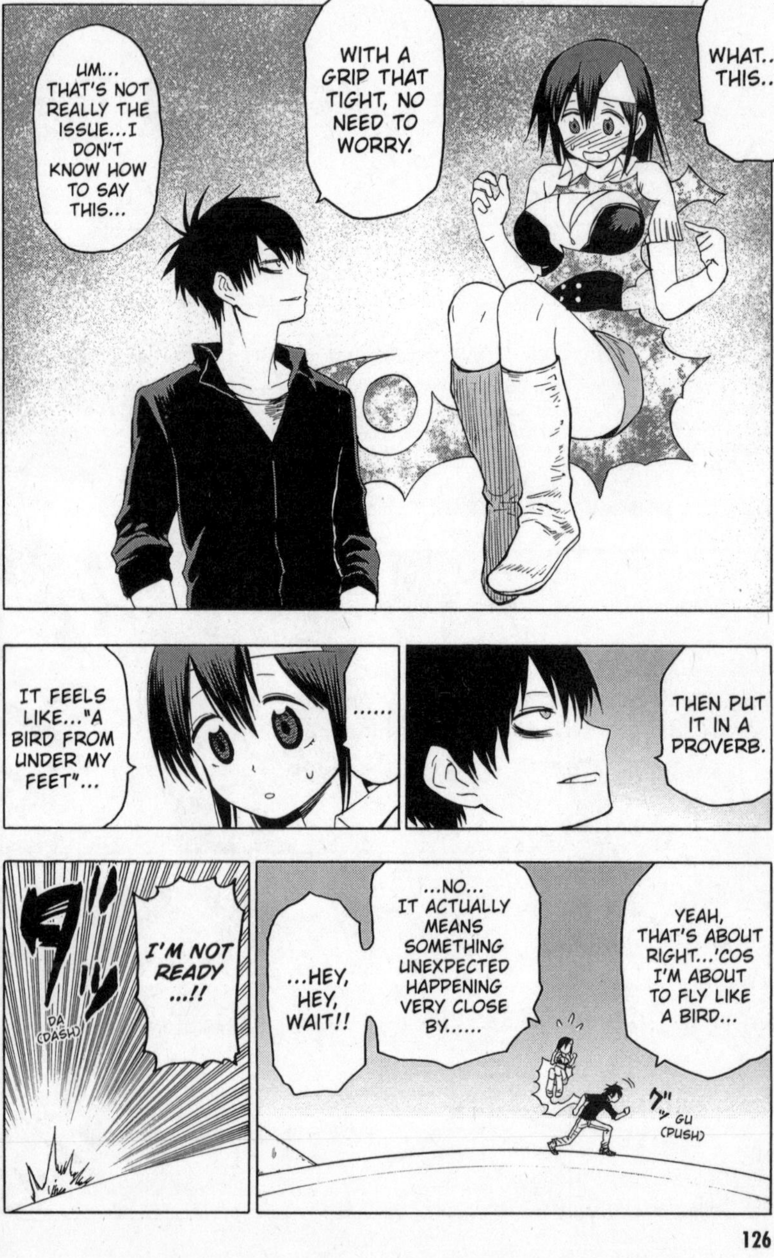
WHAT...IS THIS...?
WITH A GRIP THAT TIGHT, NO NEED TO WORRY.
UM... THAT'S NOT REALLY THE ISSUE...I DON'T KNOW HOW TO SAY THIS...
THEN PUT IT IN A PROVERB.
......
IT FEELS LIKE..."A BIRD FROM UNDER MY FEET"...
YEAH, THAT'S ABOUT RIGHT...'COS I'M ABOUT TO FLY LIKE A BIRD...
GU (PUSH)
...NO... IT ACTUALLY MEANS SOMETHING UNEXPECTED HAPPENING VERY CLOSE BY......
...HEY, HEY, WAIT!!
I'M NOT READY ...!!
DA (DASH)

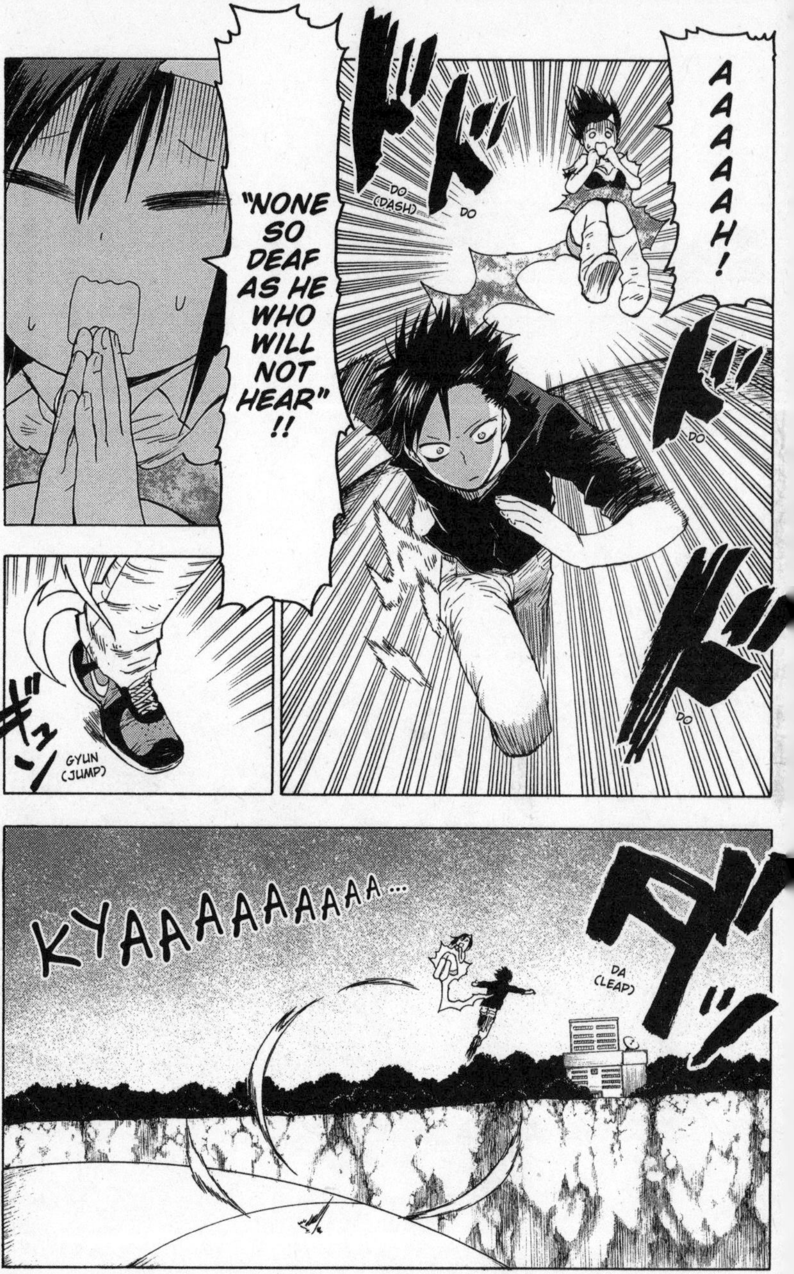
AAAAAAH!
DO (DASH)
DO
DO
DO
"NONE SO DEAF AS HE WHO WILL NOT HEAR" !!
GYUN (JUMP)
DA (LEAP)
KYAAAAAAAAAA...

THEY'RE HERE...

THEY'RE HERE, THEY'RE HERE, THEY'RE HEEERE!!

GUO
(ROOAR)

BIKI
(CRICK)

ベキ
BIKI

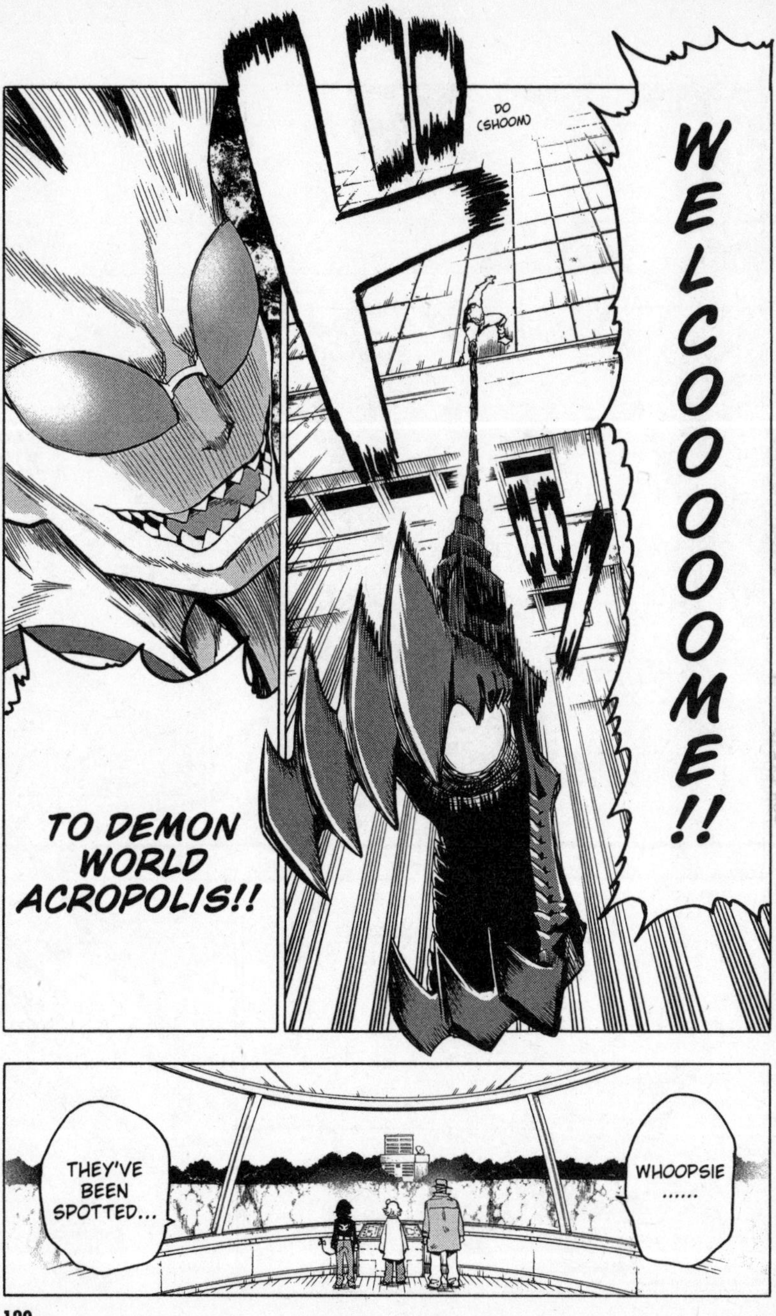
DO (SHOOM)
WELCOOOOOOME!!
TO DEMON WORLD ACROPOLIS!!
WHOOPSIE ......
THEY'VE BEEN SPOTTED...

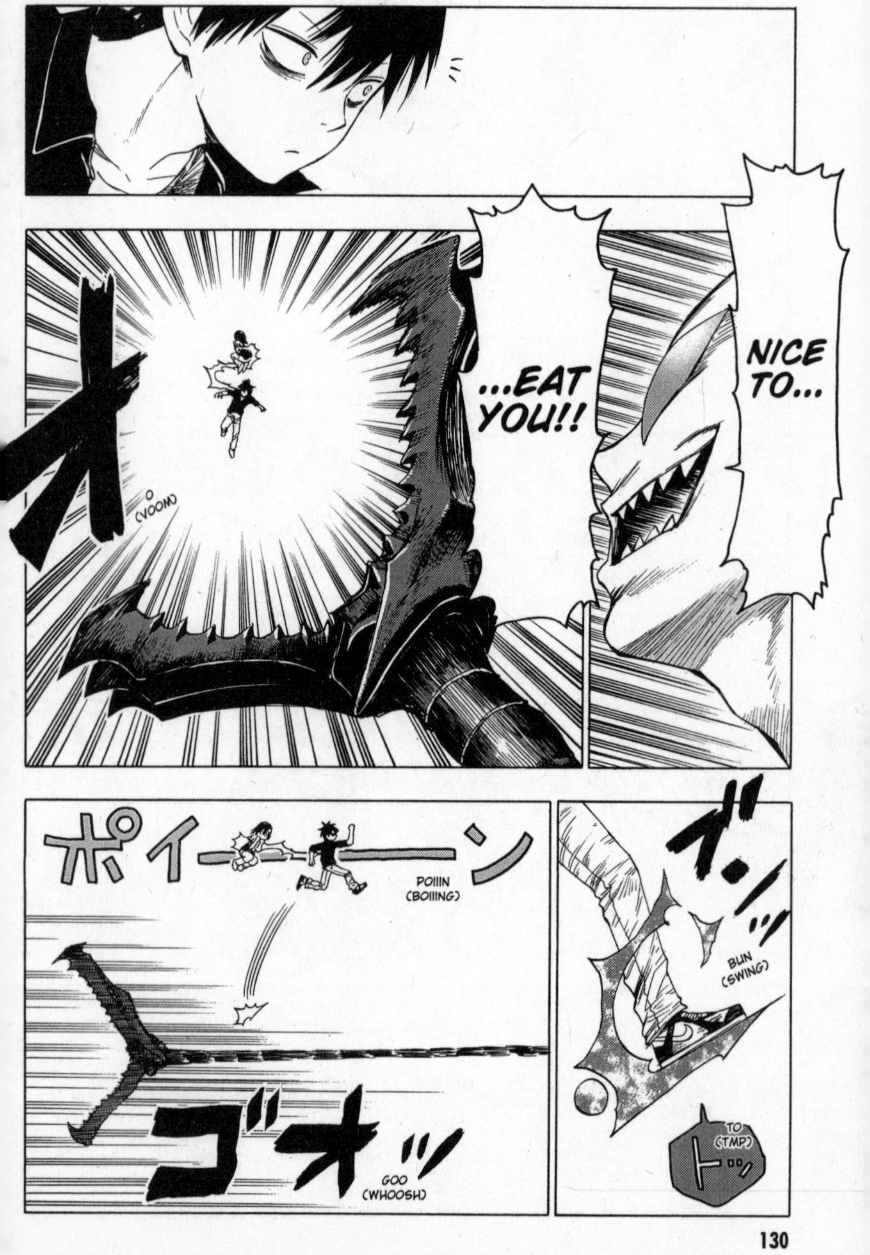
NICE TO...
...EAT YOU!!
オ
O (VOOM)
ブンッ
BUN (SWING)
トッ
TO (TMP)
ポイーーーン
POIIIN (BOIIING)
ゴオッ
GOO (WHOOSH)

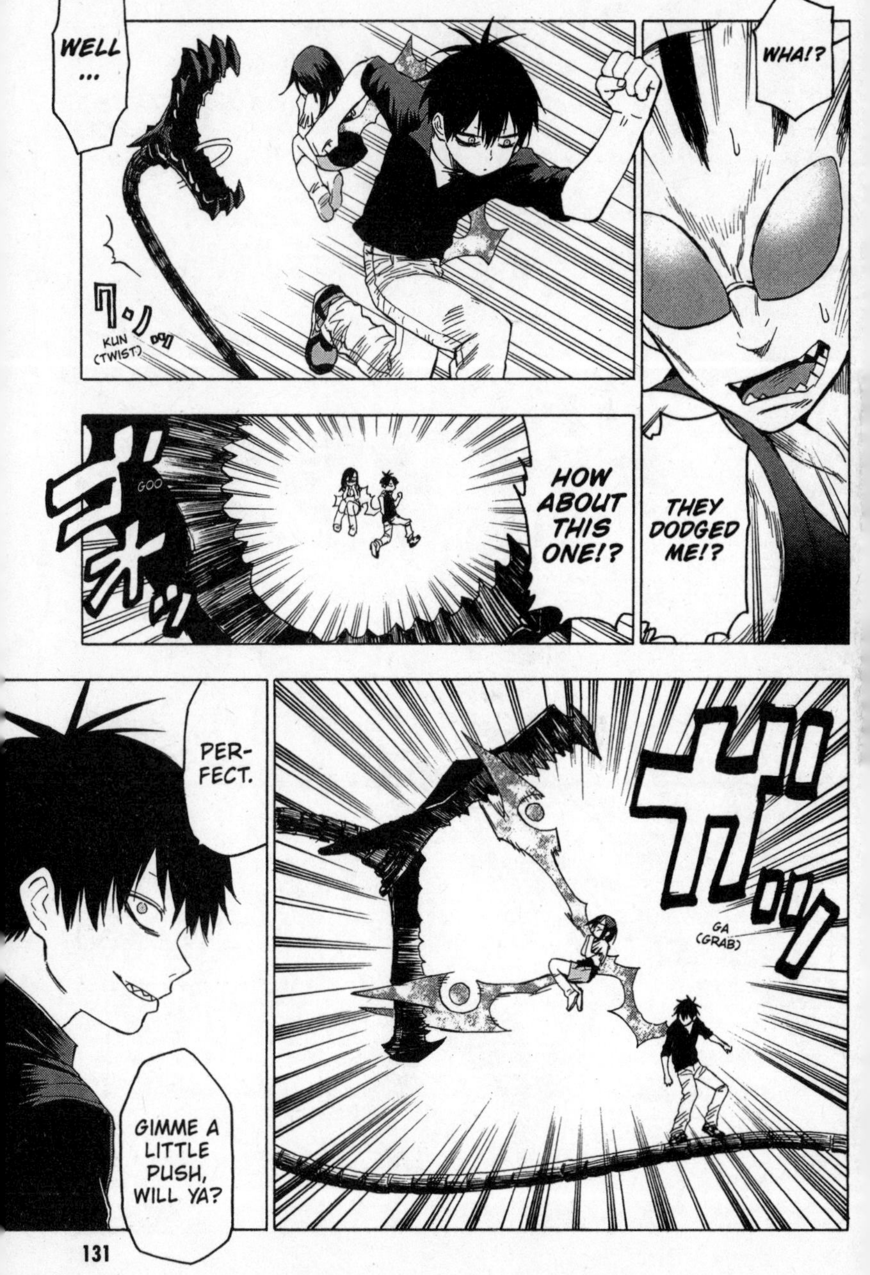
WHA!?
THEY DODGED ME!?
WELL ...
KUN (TWIST)
HOW ABOUT THIS ONE!?
GOO
GA (GRAB)
PER-FECT.
GIMME A LITTLE PUSH, WILL YA?

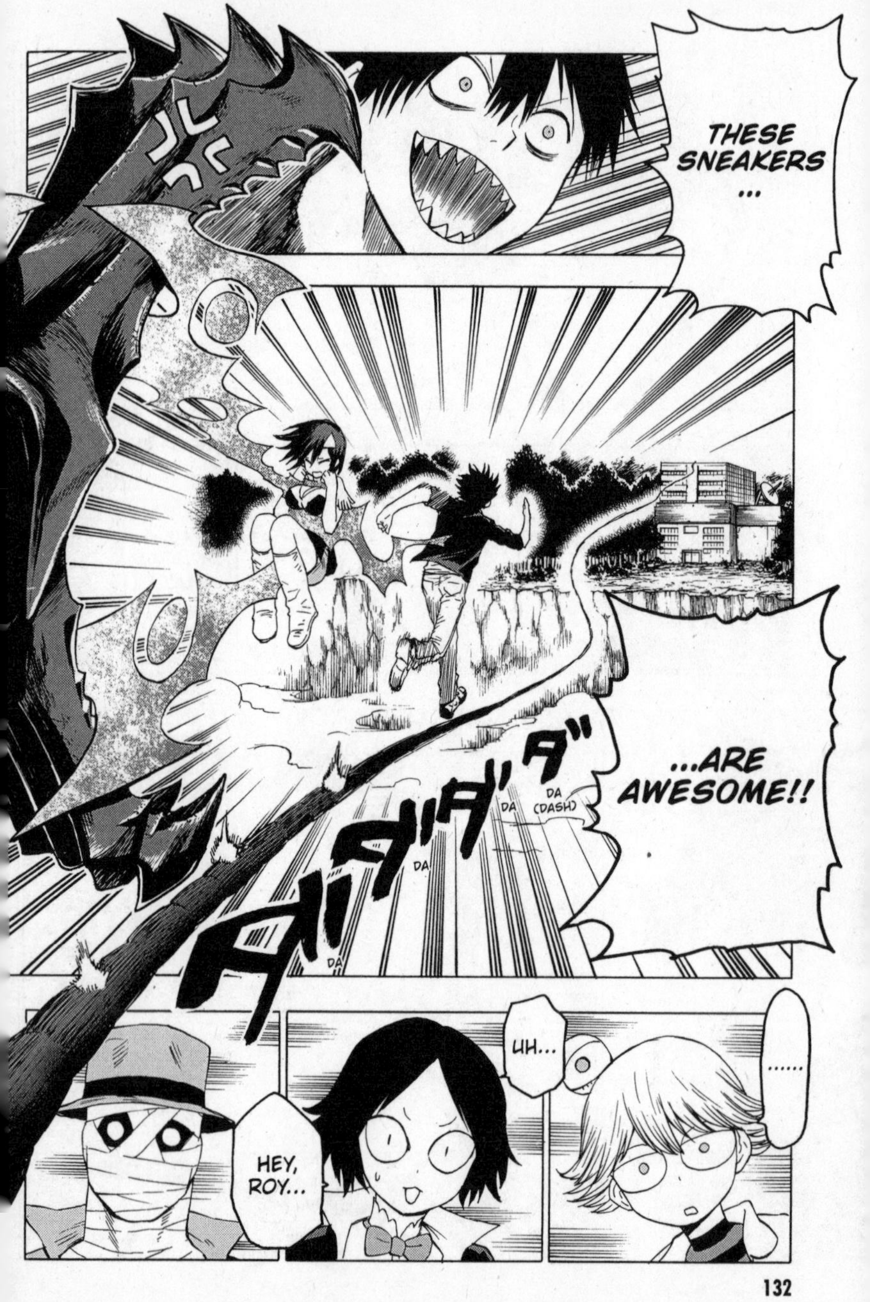
THESE SNEAKERS...
DA
DA (DASH)
DA
DA
...ARE AWESOME!!
......
UH...
HEY, ROY...

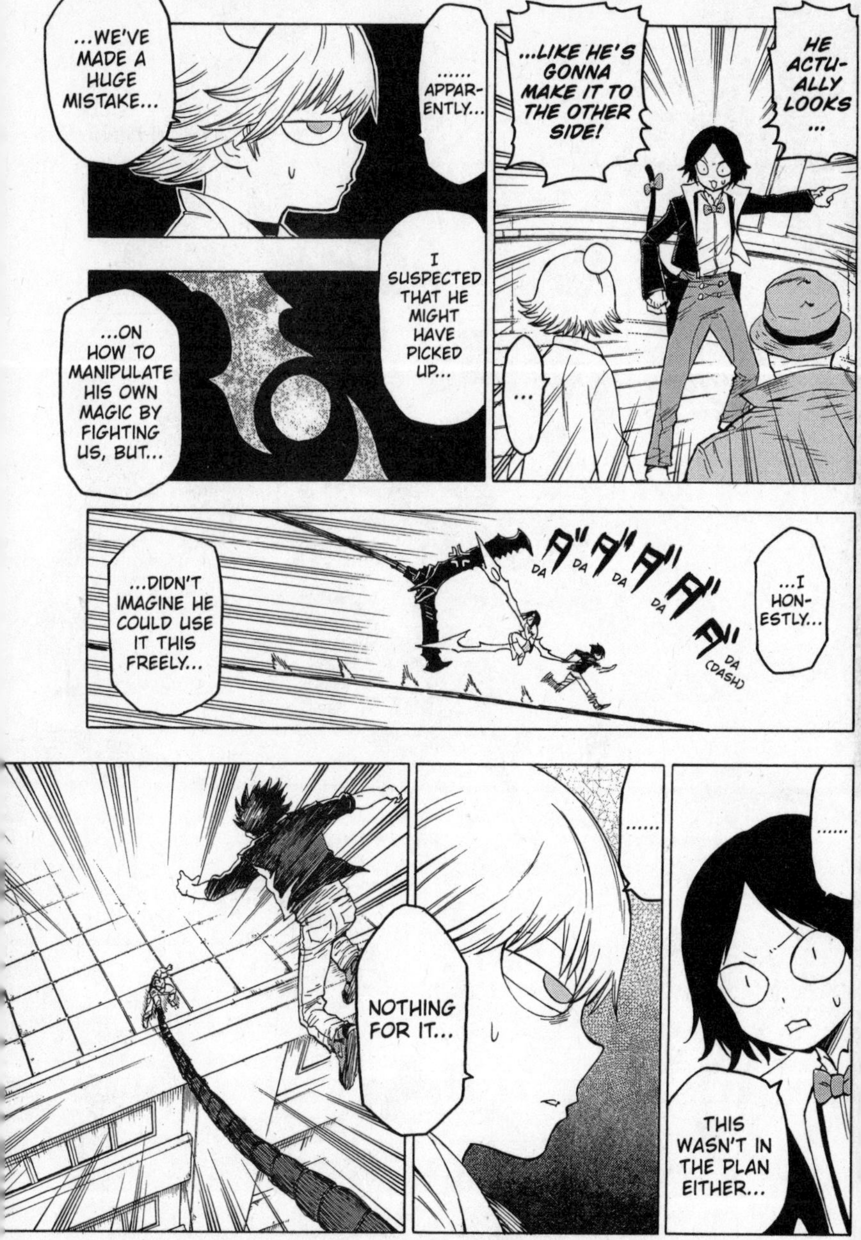
HE ACTU-ALLY LOOKS...
...LIKE HE'S GONNA MAKE IT TO THE OTHER SIDE!
...
......APPAR-ENTLY...
...WE'VE MADE A HUGE MISTAKE...
I SUSPECTED THAT HE MIGHT HAVE PICKED UP...
...ON HOW TO MANIPULATE HIS OWN MAGIC BY FIGHTING US, BUT...
...I HON-ESTLY...
DA DA DA DA DA DA (DASH)
...DIDN'T IMAGINE HE COULD USE IT THIS FREELY...
......
THIS WASN'T IN THE PLAN EITHER...
......
NOTHING FOR IT...

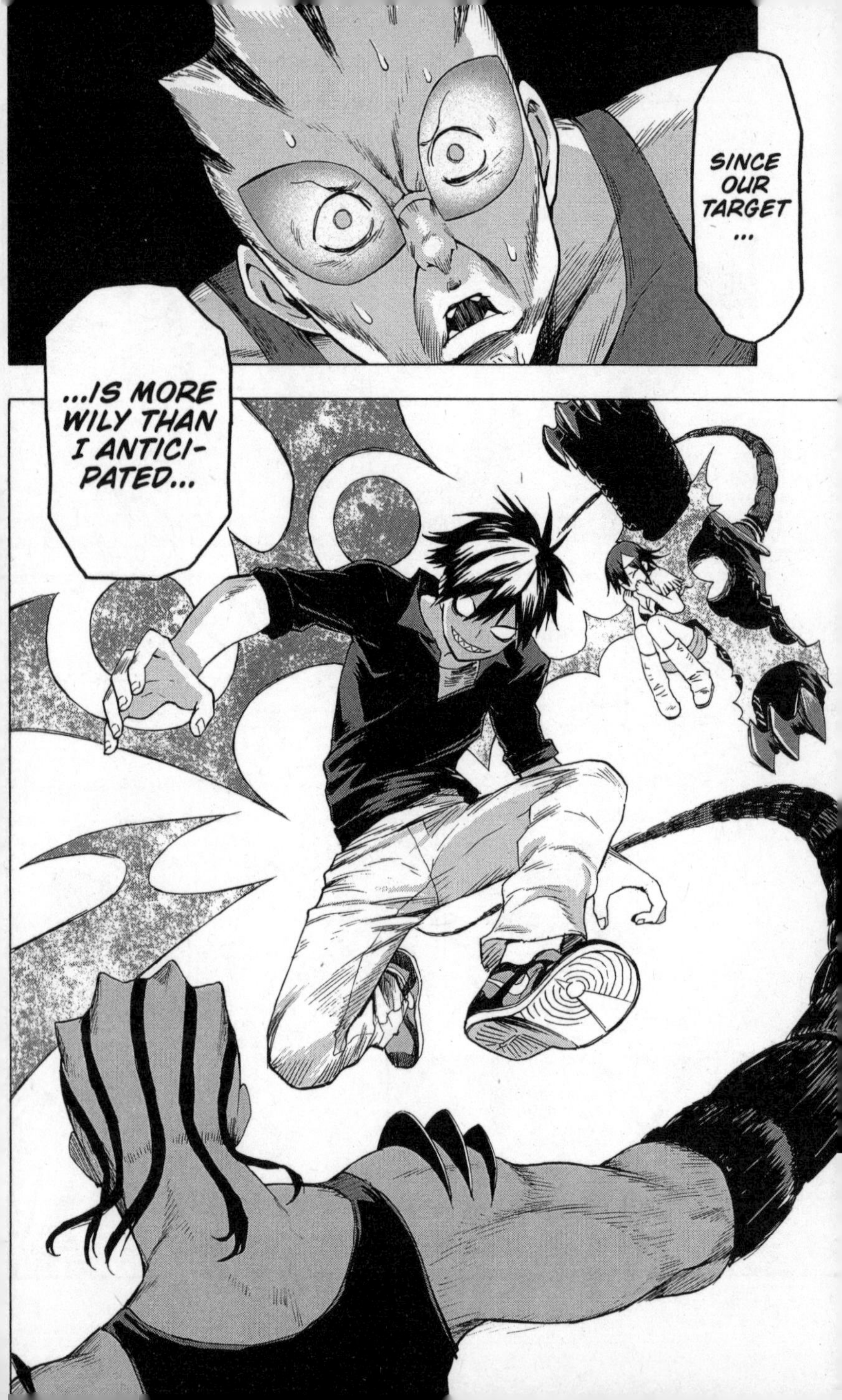
SINCE OUR TARGET ...
...IS MORE WILY THAN I ANTICI-PATED...

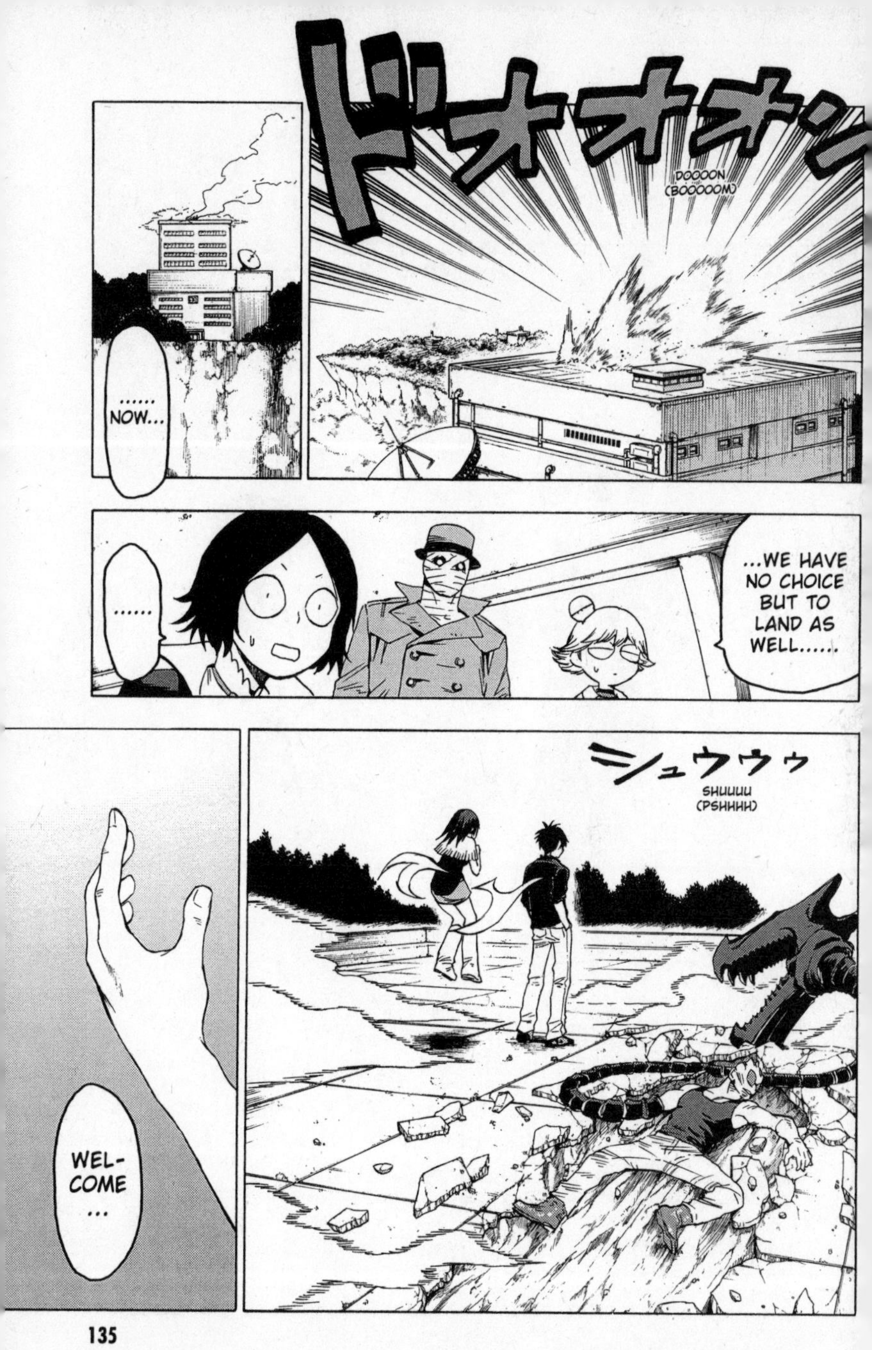
ドオオオン
DOOOON (BOOOOOM)
...... NOW...
...WE HAVE NO CHOICE BUT TO LAND AS WELL......
......
シュウウゥ
SHUUUU (PSHHHH)
WEL-COME ...

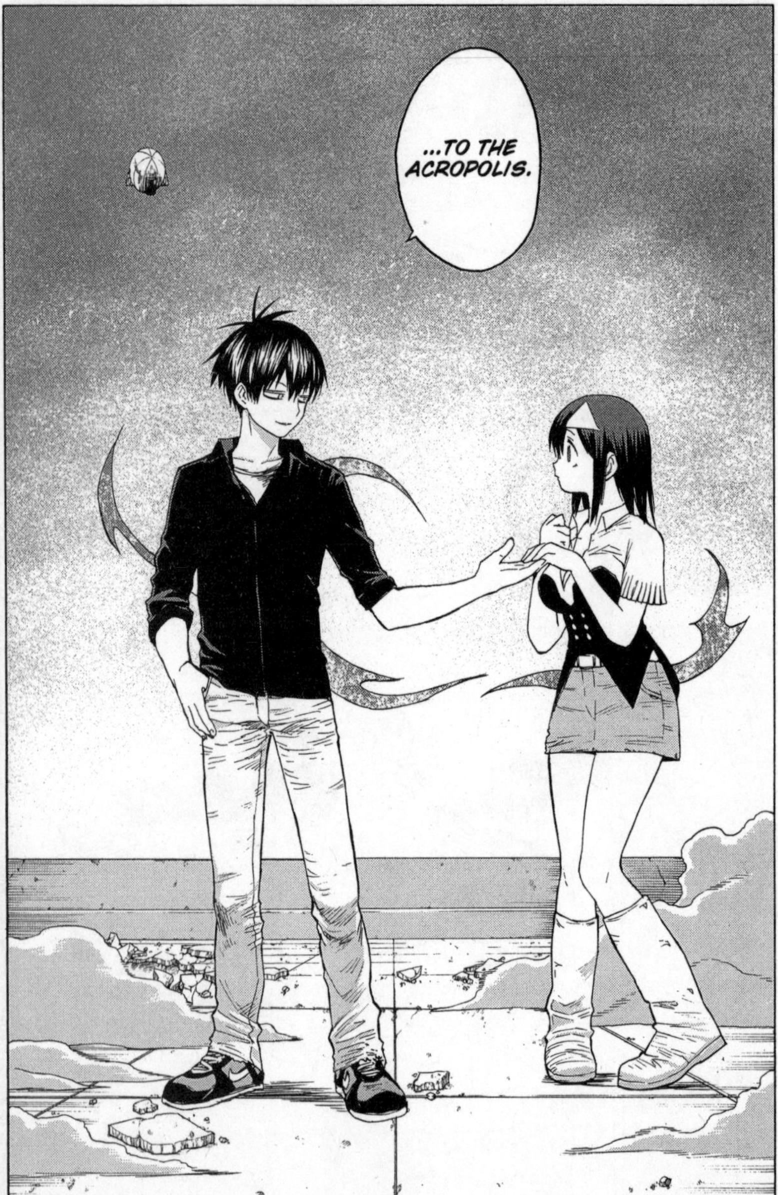
...TO THE ACROPOLIS.

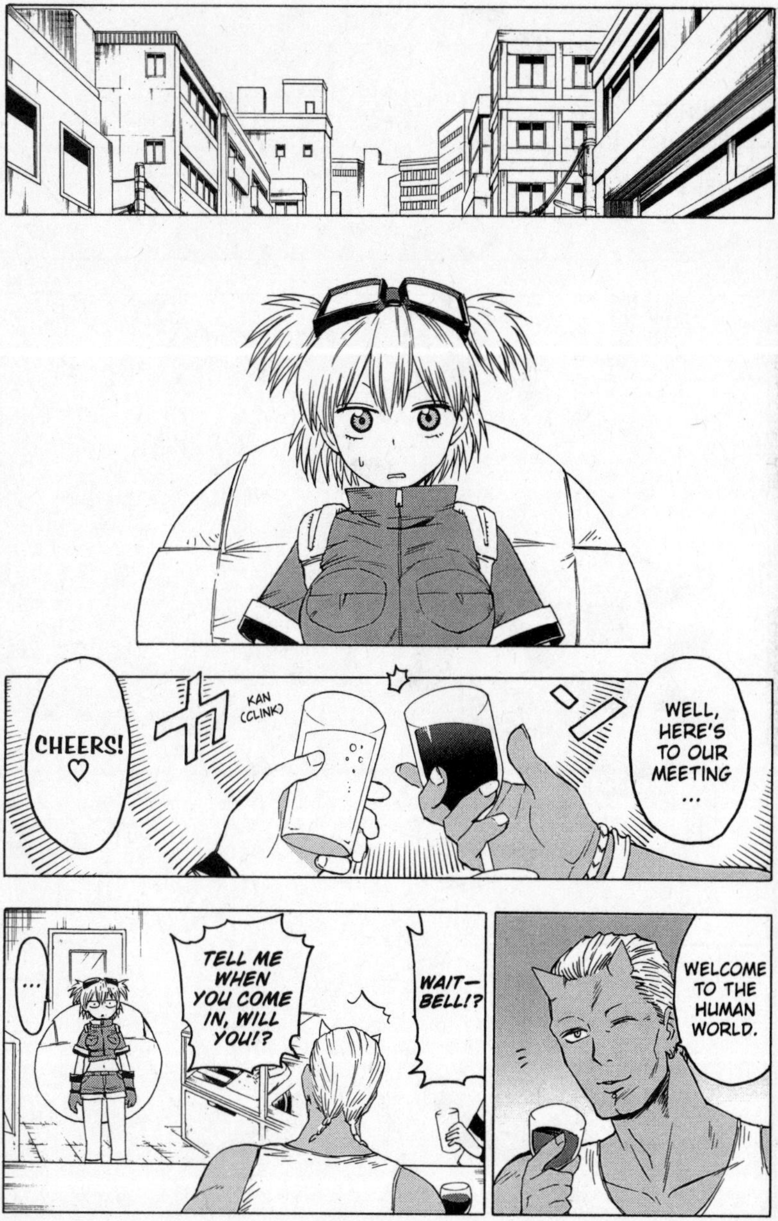
WELL, HERE'S TO OUR MEETING ...
KAN (CLINK)
CHEERS! ♡
WELCOME TO THE HUMAN WORLD.
WAIT— BELL!?
TELL ME WHEN YOU COME IN, WILL YOU!?
...

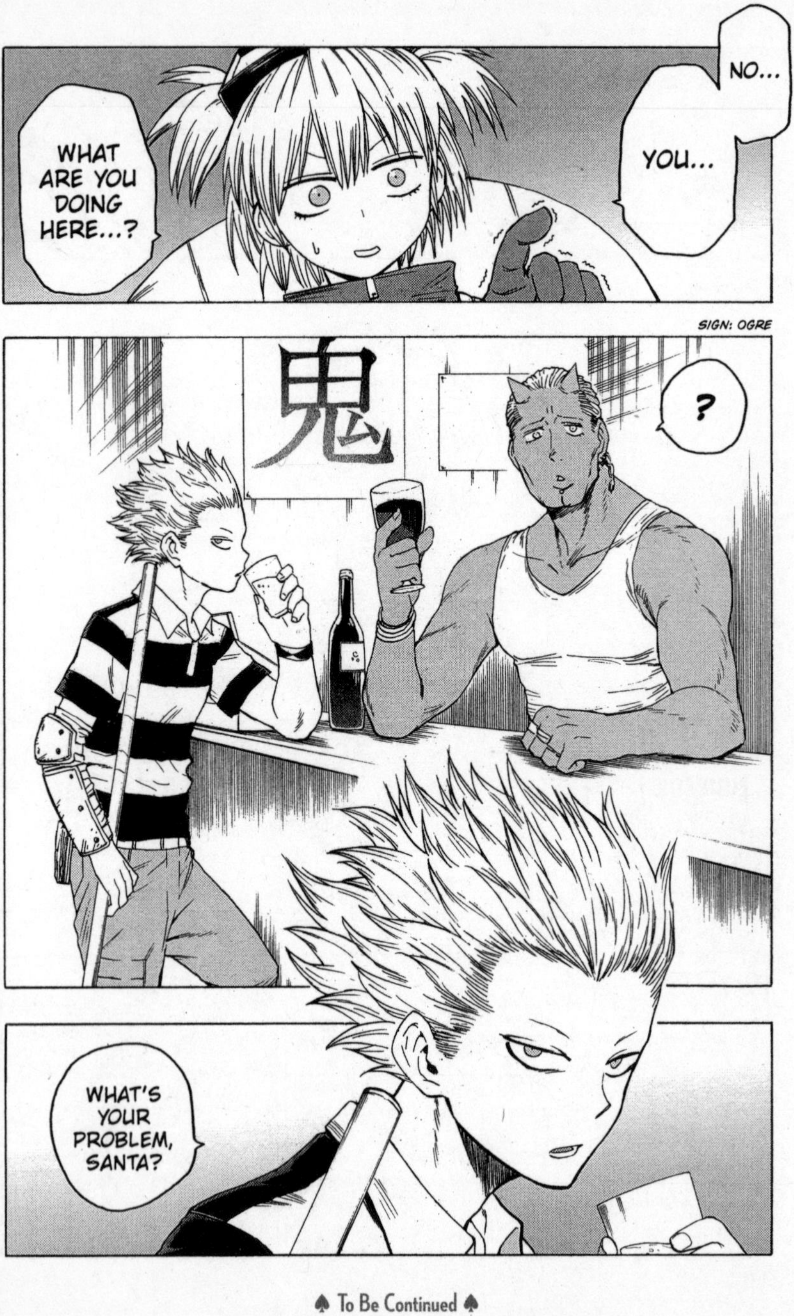
NO...
YOU...
WHAT ARE YOU DOING HERE...?
SIGN: OGRE
鬼
?
WHAT'S YOUR PROBLEM, SANTA?

♠ To Be Continued ♠

BLOOD LAD

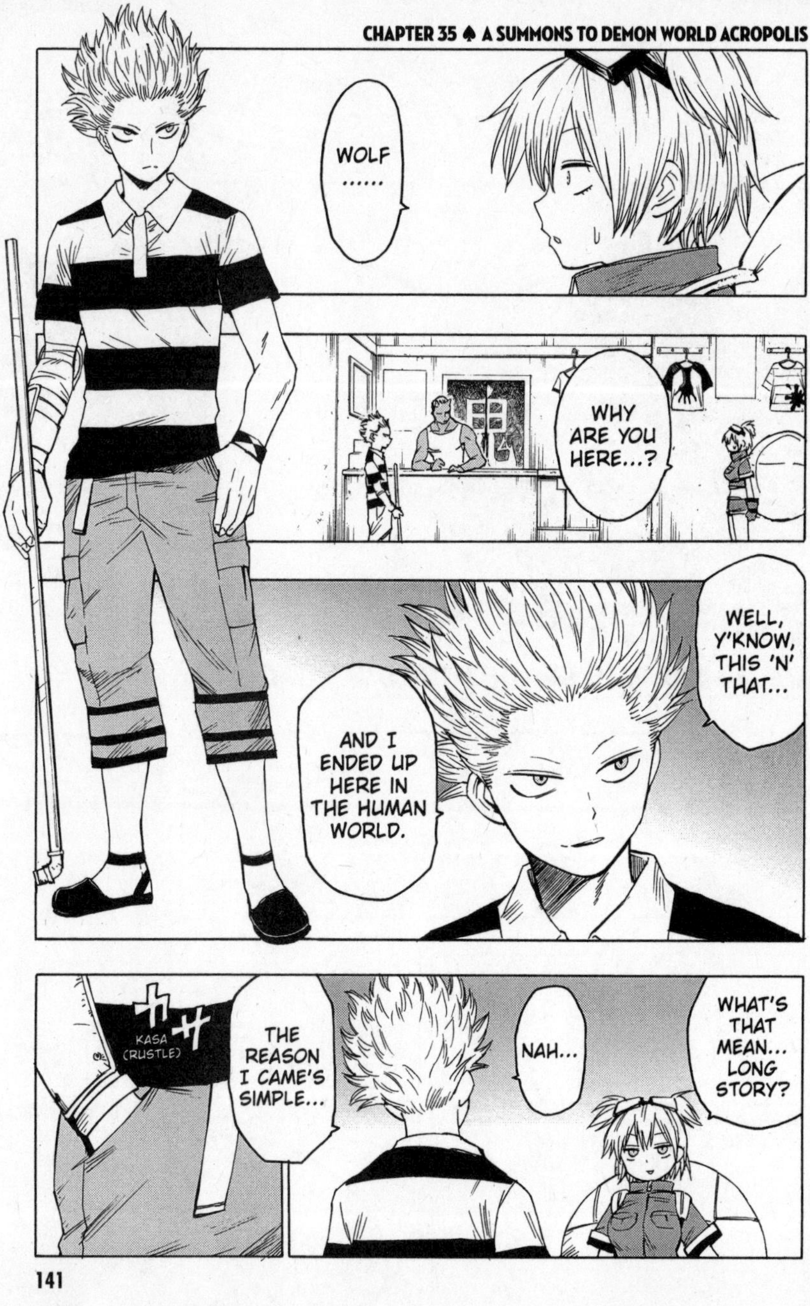
WOLF ......
WHY ARE YOU HERE...?
WELL, Y'KNOW, THIS 'N' THAT...
AND I ENDED UP HERE IN THE HUMAN WORLD.
WHAT'S THAT MEAN... LONG STORY?
NAH...
THE REASON I CAME'S SIMPLE...
KASA (RUSTLE)

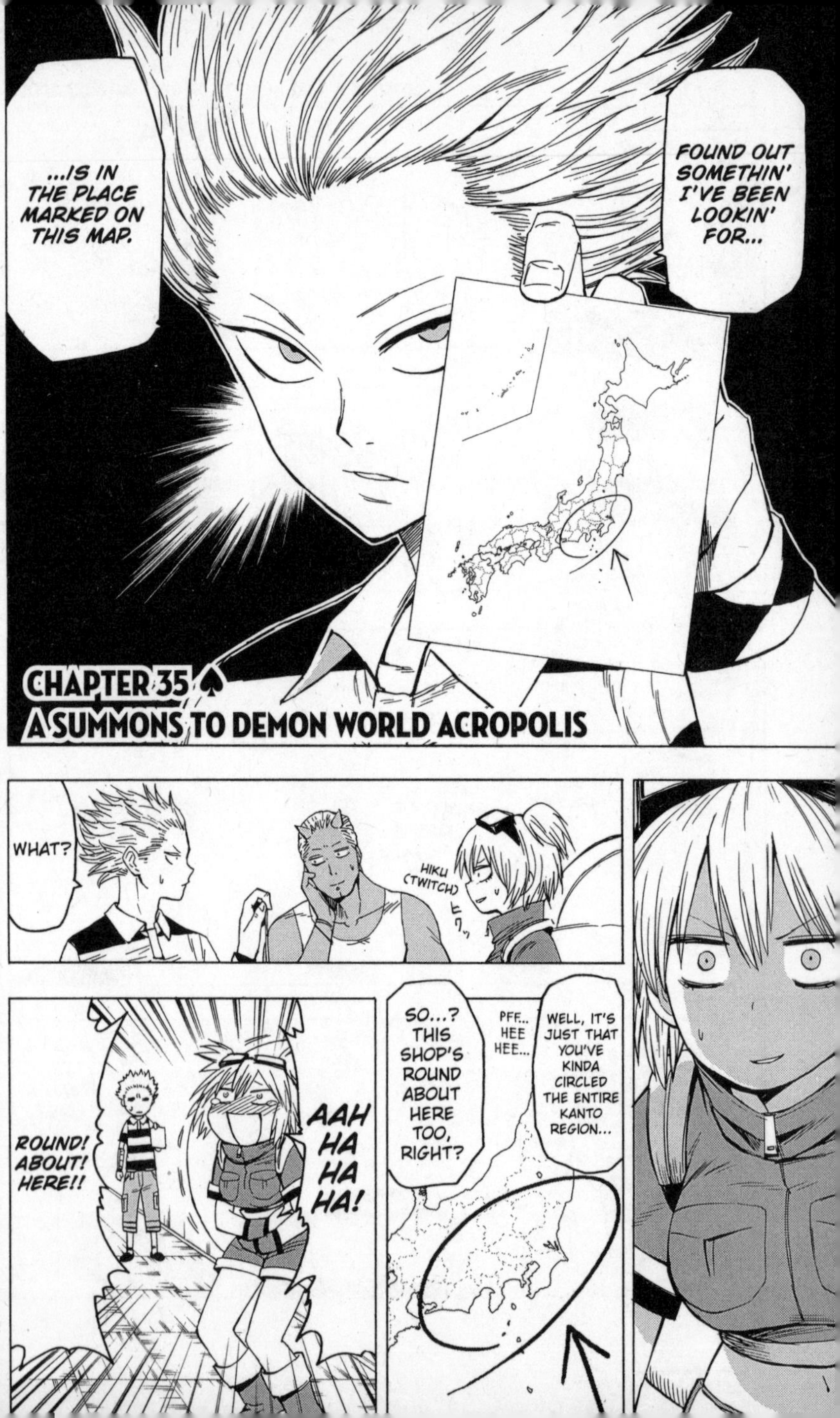
FOUND OUT SOMETHIN' I'VE BEEN LOOKIN' FOR...
...IS IN THE PLACE MARKED ON THIS MAP.
CHAPTER 35
A SUMMONS TO DEMON WORLD ACROPOLIS
HIKU (TWITCH)
ヒクッ
WHAT?
WELL, IT'S JUST THAT YOU'VE KINDA CIRCLED THE ENTIRE KANTO REGION...
PFF... HEE HEE...
SO...? THIS SHOP'S ROUND ABOUT HERE TOO, RIGHT?
AAH HA HA HA!
ROUND! ABOUT! HERE!!

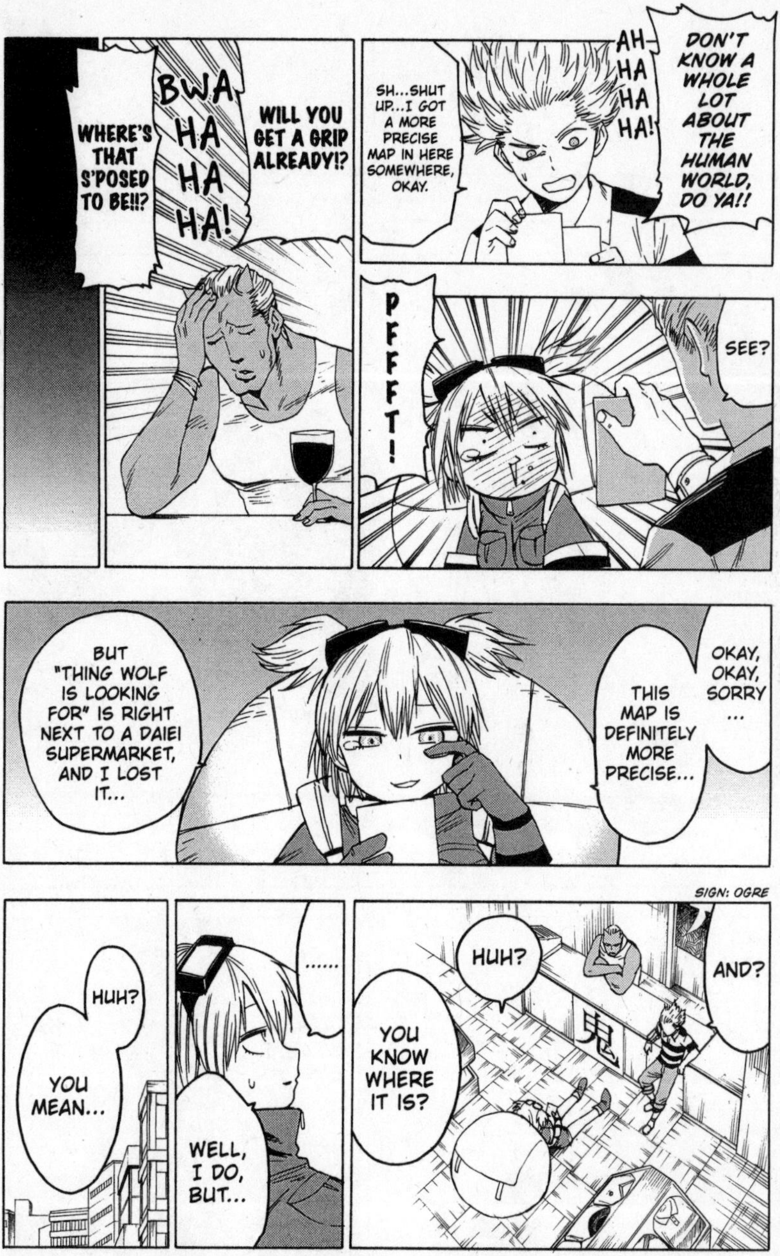
DON'T KNOW A WHOLE LOT ABOUT THE HUMAN WORLD, DO YA!!
AH-HA HA HA!
SH...SHUT UP...I GOT A MORE PRECISE MAP IN HERE SOMEWHERE, OKAY.
SEE?
PFFFT!
WILL YOU GET A GRIP ALREADY!?
BWA HA HA HA!
WHERE'S THAT S'POSED TO BE!!?
OKAY, OKAY, SORRY ...
THIS MAP IS DEFINITELY MORE PRECISE...
BUT "THING WOLF IS LOOKING FOR" IS RIGHT NEXT TO A DAIEI SUPERMARKET, AND I LOST IT...
SIGN: OGRE
AND?
HUH?
YOU KNOW WHERE IT IS?
......
WELL, I DO, BUT...
HUH?
YOU MEAN...

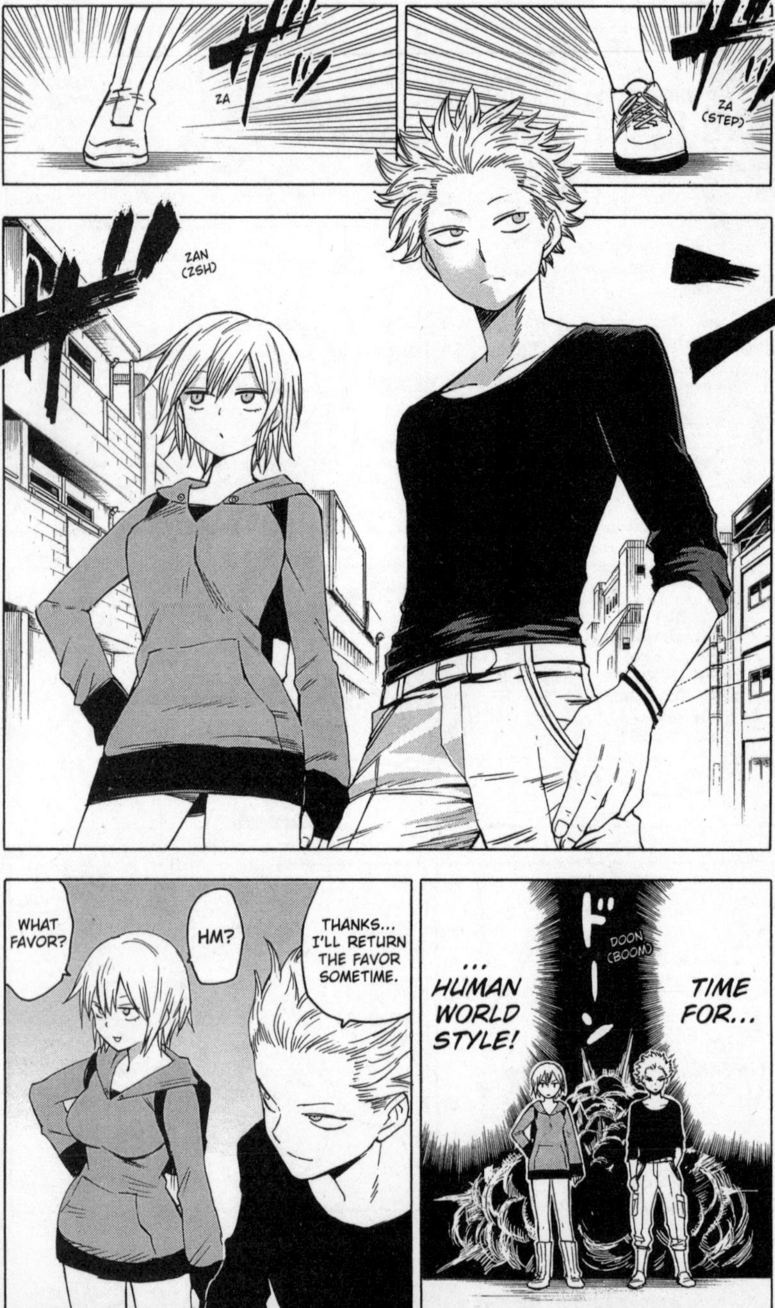
ザッ
ZA
(STEP)
ザッ
ZA
ザン
ZAN
(ZSH)
TIME FOR...
...HUMAN WORLD STYLE!
ドーン
DOON
(BOOM)
THANKS... I'LL RETURN THE FAVOR SOMETIME.
HM?
WHAT FAVOR?

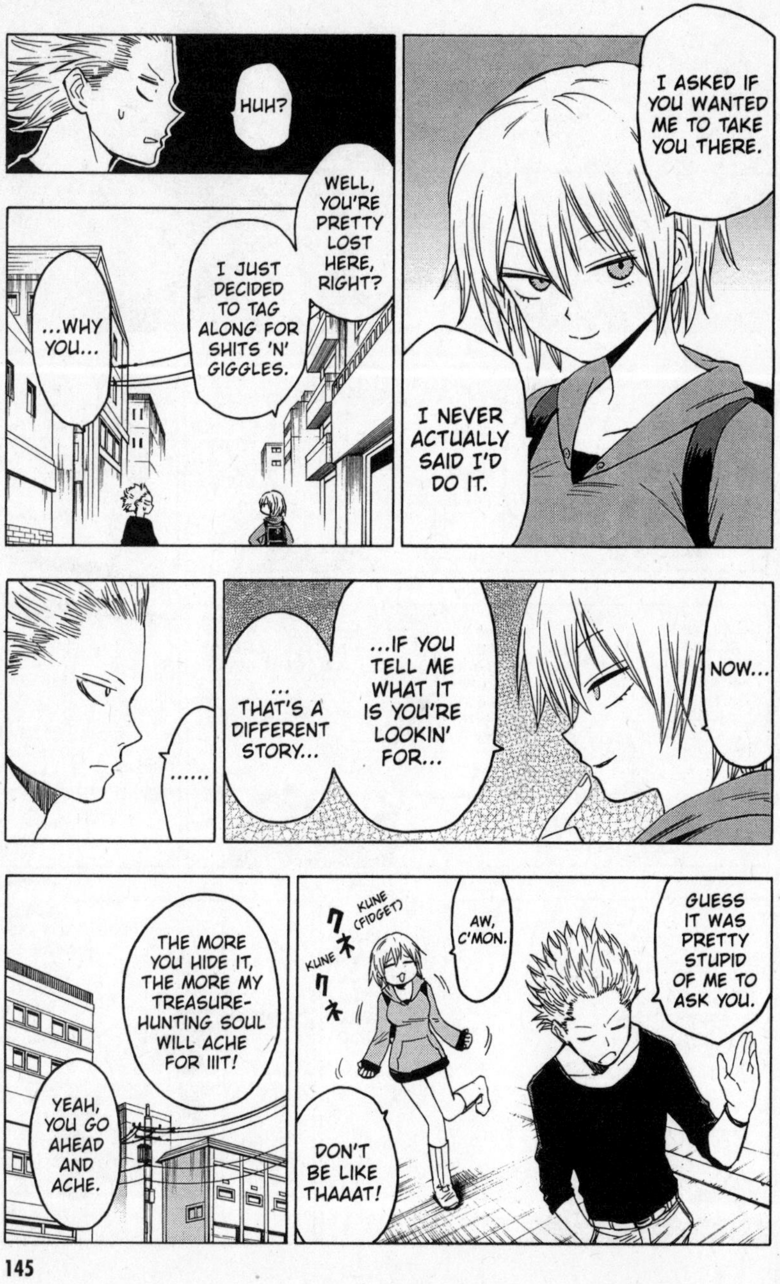
I ASKED IF YOU WANTED ME TO TAKE YOU THERE.
I NEVER ACTUALLY SAID I'D DO IT.
HUH?
WELL, YOU'RE PRETTY LOST HERE, RIGHT?
I JUST DECIDED TO TAG ALONG FOR SHITS 'N' GIGGLES.
...WHY YOU...
NOW...
...IF YOU TELL ME WHAT IT IS YOU'RE LOOKIN' FOR...
... THAT'S A DIFFERENT STORY...
......
GUESS IT WAS PRETTY STUPID OF ME TO ASK YOU.
AW, C'MON.
クネ KUNE (FIDGET)
クネ KUNE
DON'T BE LIKE THAAAT!
THE MORE YOU HIDE IT, THE MORE MY TREASURE-HUNTING SOUL WILL ACHE FOR IIIT!
YEAH, YOU GO AHEAD AND ACHE.

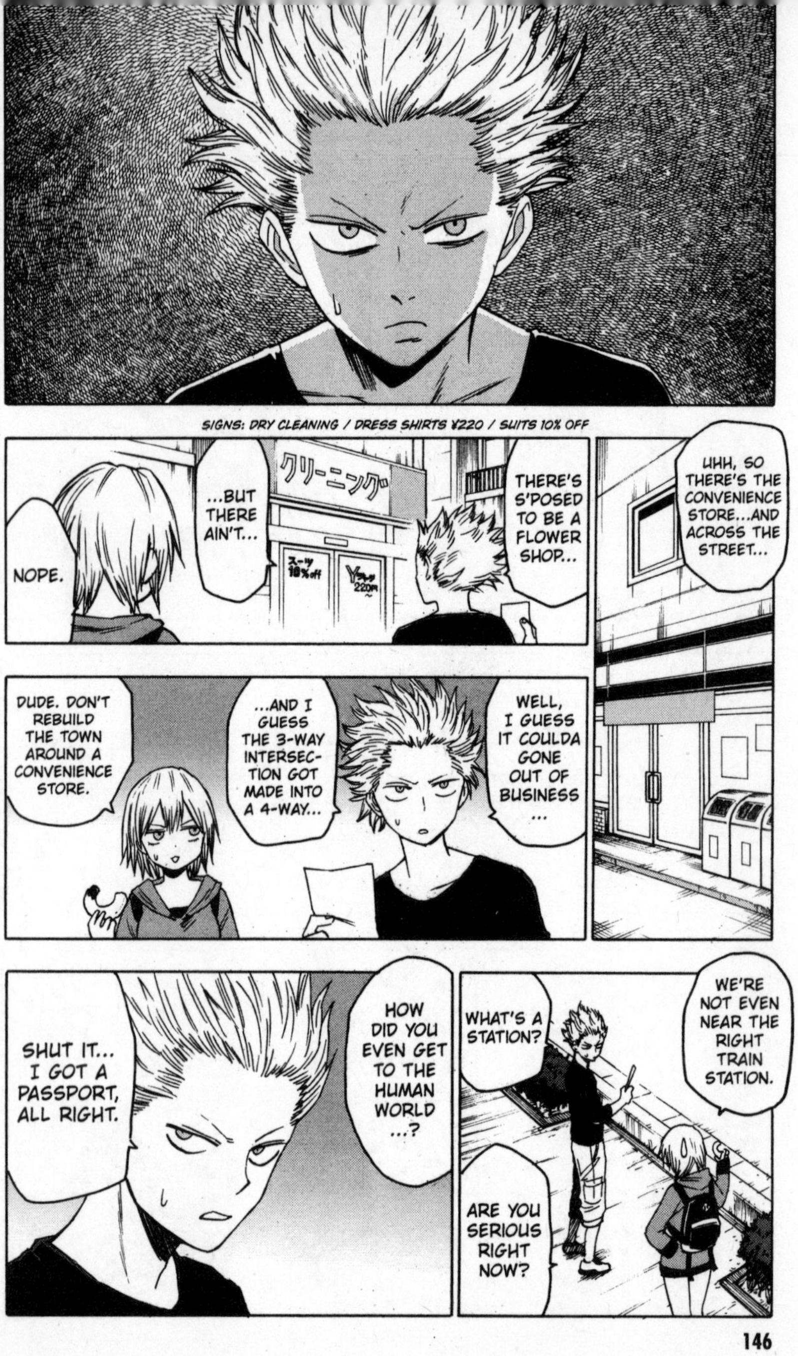
SIGNS: DRY CLEANING / DRESS SHIRTS ¥220 / SUITS 10% OFF
UHH, SO THERE'S THE CONVENIENCE STORE...AND ACROSS THE STREET...
THERE'S S'POSED TO BE A FLOWER SHOP...
クリーニング
...BUT THERE AIN'T...
NOPE.
WELL, I GUESS IT COULDA GONE OUT OF BUSINESS...
...AND I GUESS THE 3-WAY INTERSECTION GOT MADE INTO A 4-WAY...
DUDE. DON'T REBUILD THE TOWN AROUND A CONVENIENCE STORE.
WE'RE NOT EVEN NEAR THE RIGHT TRAIN STATION.
WHAT'S A STATION?
ARE YOU SERIOUS RIGHT NOW?
HOW DID YOU EVEN GET TO THE HUMAN WORLD...?
SHUT IT... I GOT A PASSPORT, ALL RIGHT.

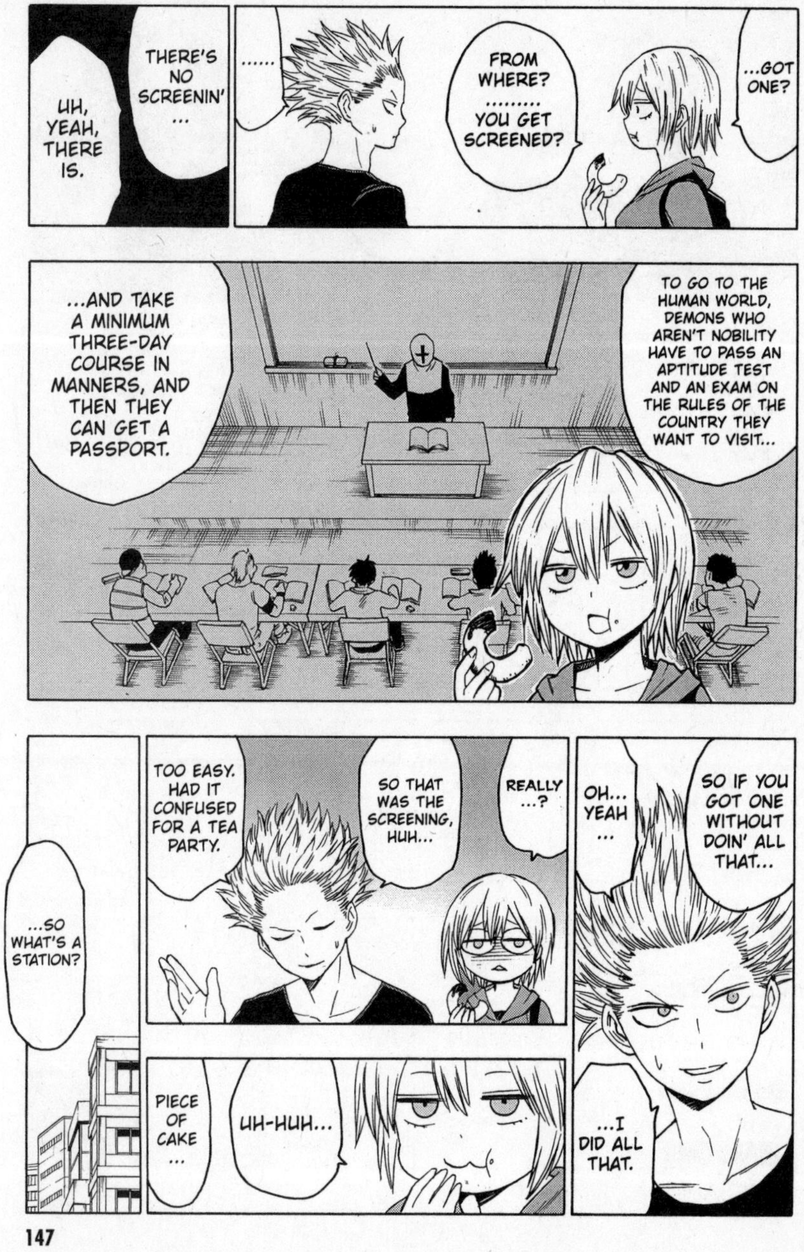
...GOT ONE?
FROM WHERE? .... YOU GET SCREENED?
......
THERE'S NO SCREENIN' ...
UH, YEAH, THERE IS.
TO GO TO THE HUMAN WORLD, DEMONS WHO AREN'T NOBILITY HAVE TO PASS AN APTITUDE TEST AND AN EXAM ON THE RULES OF THE COUNTRY THEY WANT TO VISIT...
...AND TAKE A MINIMUM THREE-DAY COURSE IN MANNERS, AND THEN THEY CAN GET A PASSPORT.
SO IF YOU GOT ONE WITHOUT DOIN' ALL THAT...
OH... YEAH ...
...I DID ALL THAT.
REALLY ...?
SO THAT WAS THE SCREENING, HUH...
TOO EASY. HAD IT CONFUSED FOR A TEA PARTY.
UH-HUH...
PIECE OF CAKE ...
...SO WHAT'S A STATION?

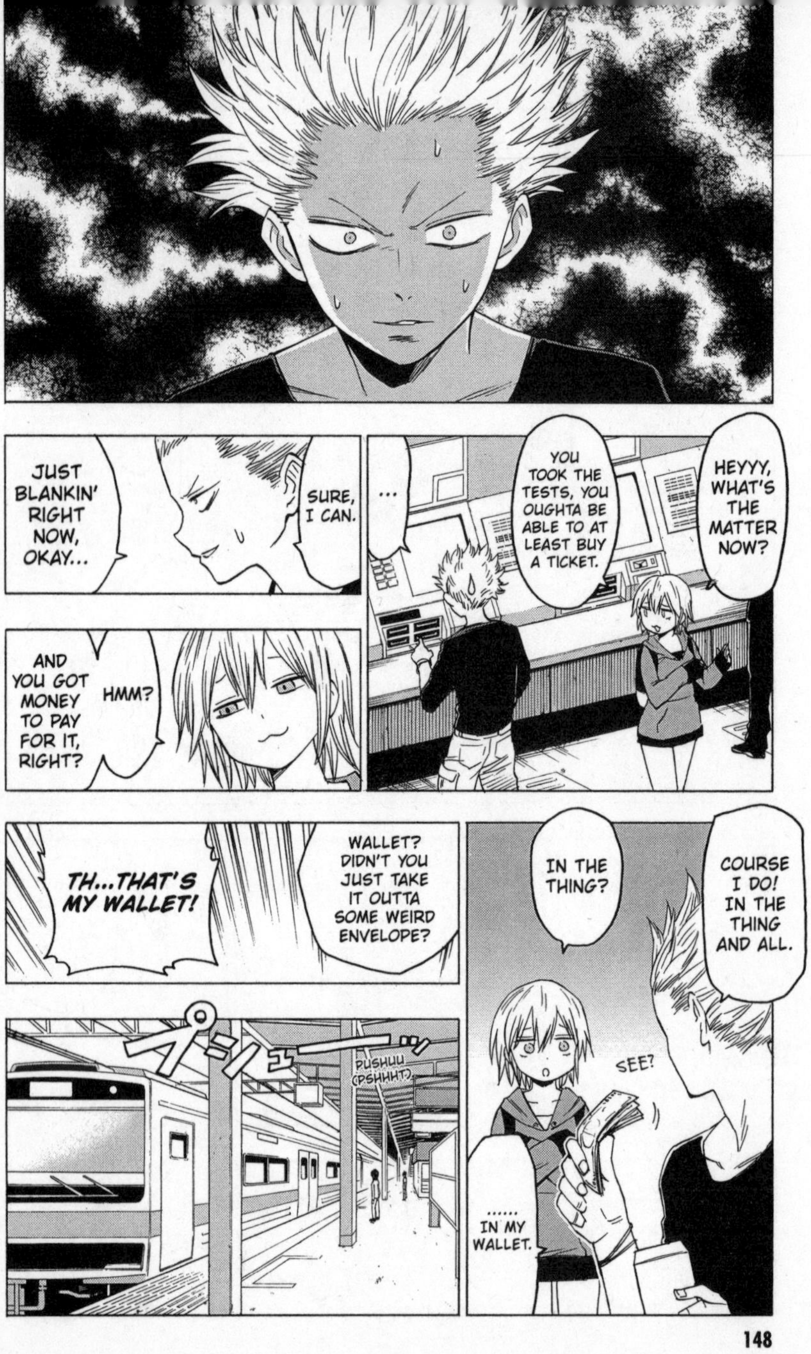
HEYYY, WHAT'S THE MATTER NOW?
YOU TOOK THE TESTS, YOU OUGHTA BE ABLE TO AT LEAST BUY A TICKET.
...
SURE, I CAN.
JUST BLANKIN' RIGHT NOW, OKAY...
HMM?
AND YOU GOT MONEY TO PAY FOR IT, RIGHT?
COURSE I DO! IN THE THING AND ALL.
IN THE THING?
SEE?
...... IN MY WALLET.
WALLET? DIDN'T YOU JUST TAKE IT OUTTA SOME WEIRD ENVELOPE?
TH...THAT'S MY WALLET!
PUSHUU (PSHHHT)

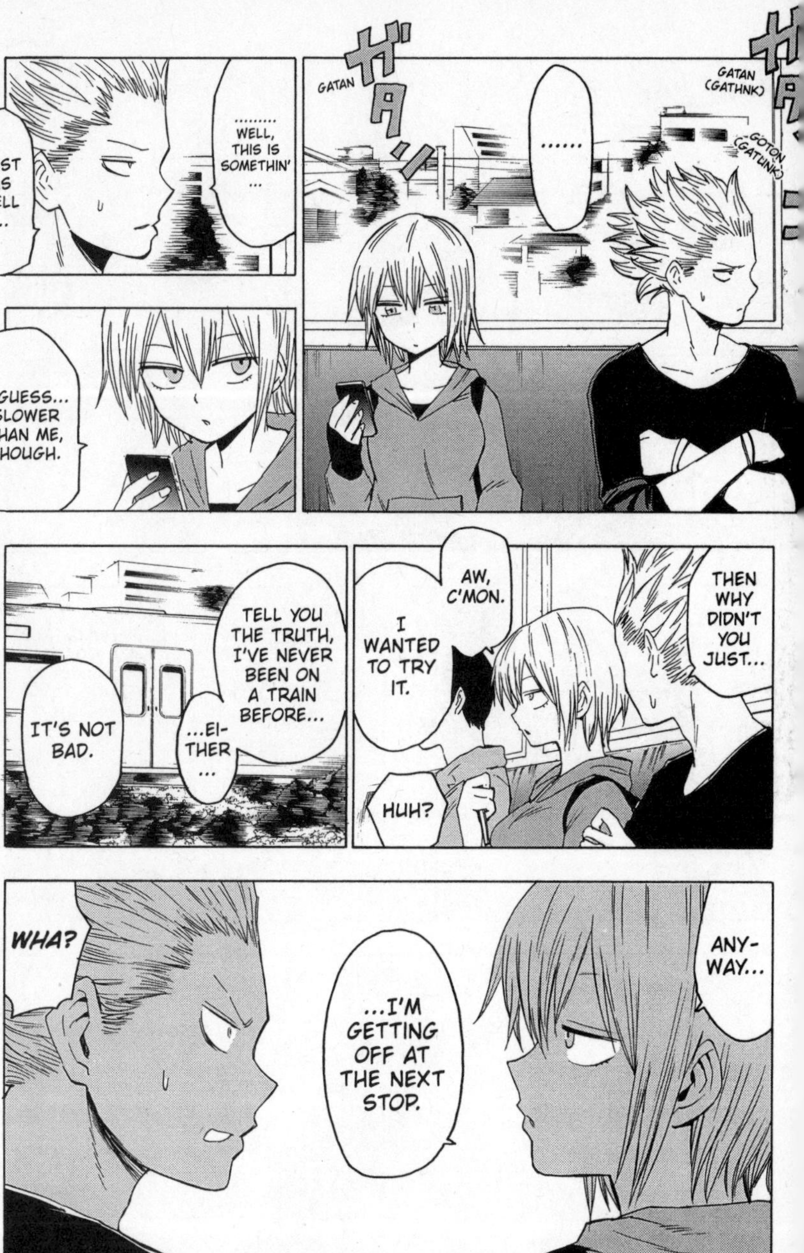
GATAN (GATHNK)
GOTON (GATUNK)
......
GATAN
.... WELL, THIS IS SOMETHIN' ...
FAST AS HELL ...
I GUESS... SLOWER THAN ME, THOUGH.
THEN WHY DIDN'T YOU JUST...
AW, C'MON.
I WANTED TO TRY IT.
HUH?
TELL YOU THE TRUTH, I'VE NEVER BEEN ON A TRAIN BEFORE...
...EI-THER ...
IT'S NOT BAD.
ANY-WAY...
...I'M GETTING OFF AT THE NEXT STOP.
WHA?

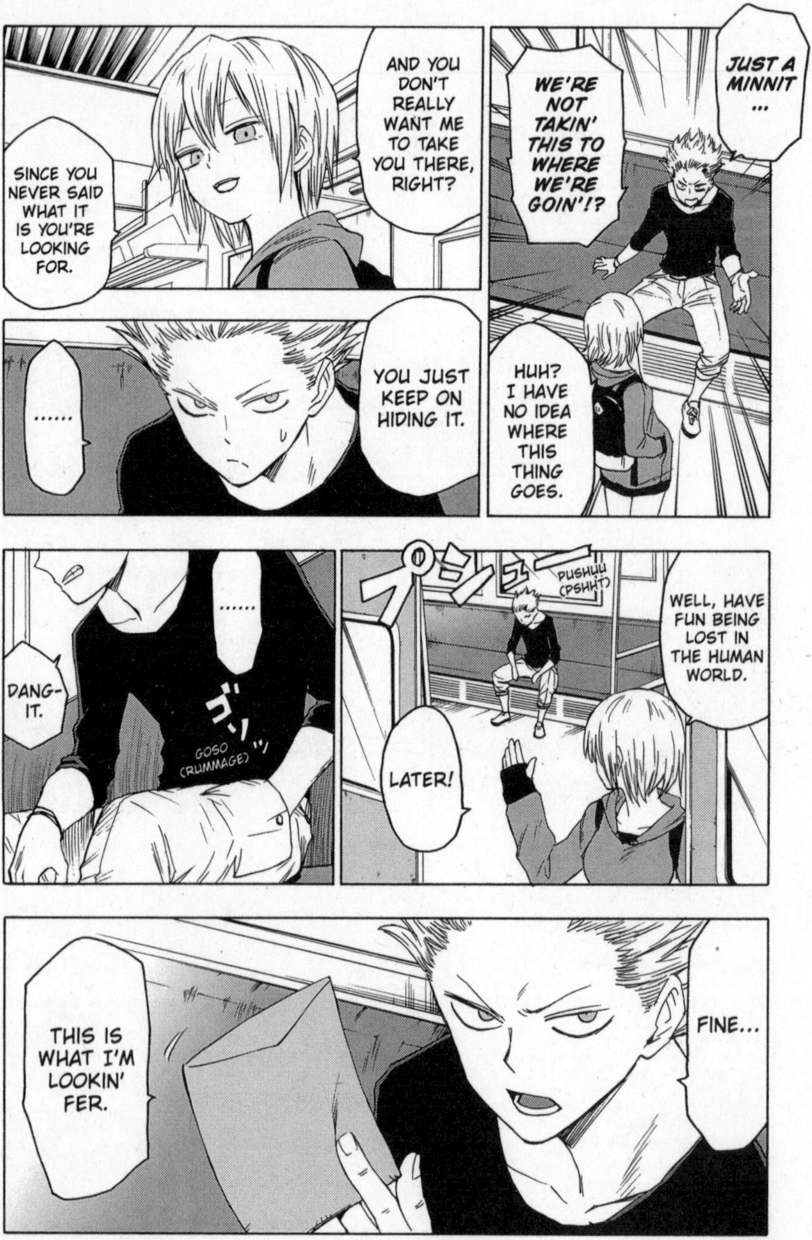
JUST A MINNIT ...
WE'RE NOT TAKIN' THIS TO WHERE WE'RE GOIN'!?
HUH? I HAVE NO IDEA WHERE THIS THING GOES.
AND YOU DON'T REALLY WANT ME TO TAKE YOU THERE, RIGHT?
SINCE YOU NEVER SAID WHAT IT IS YOU'RE LOOKING FOR.
YOU JUST KEEP ON HIDING IT.
......
プシュー
PUSHUU (PSHHT)
WELL, HAVE FUN BEING LOST IN THE HUMAN WORLD.
LATER!
......
ゴソッ
GOSO (RUMMAGE)
DANG-IT.
FINE...
THIS IS WHAT I'M LOOKIN' FER.

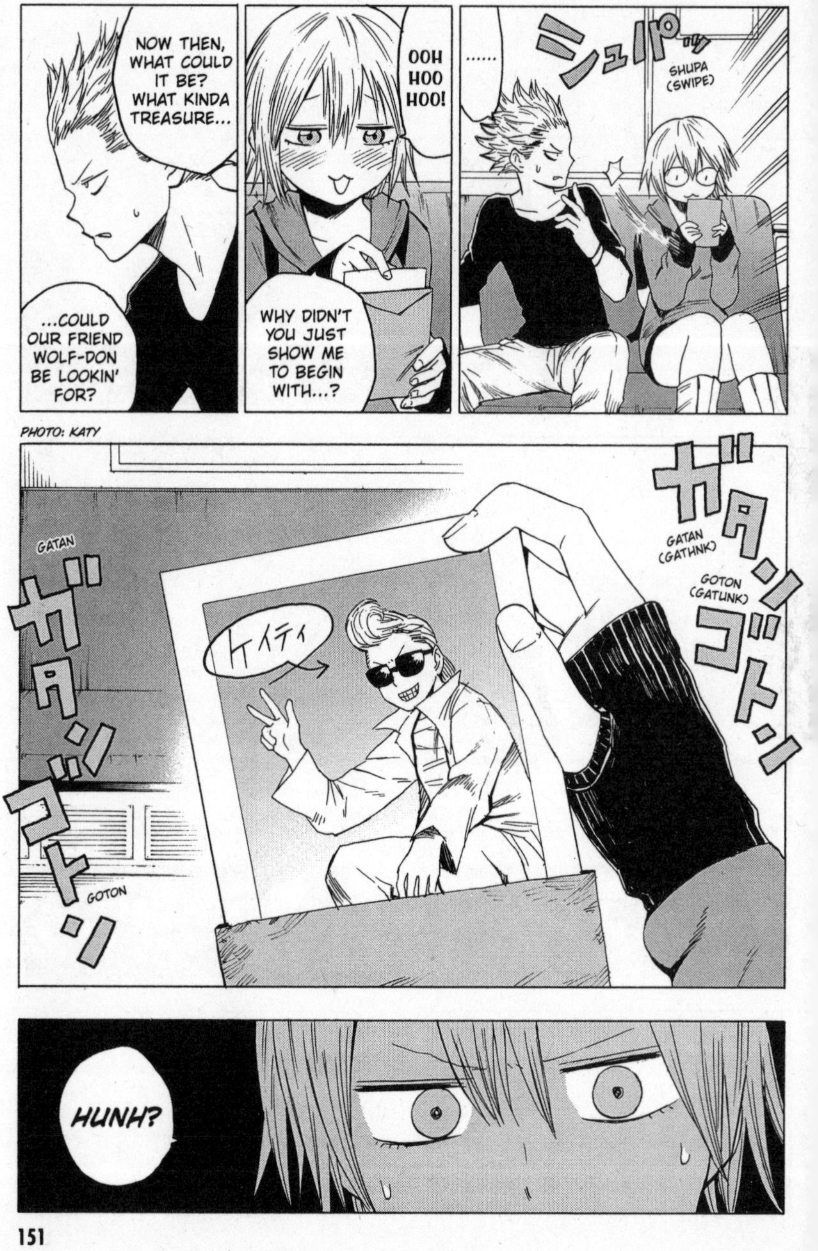
NOW THEN, WHAT COULD IT BE? WHAT KINDA TREASURE...
...COULD OUR FRIEND WOLF-DON BE LOOKIN' FOR?
OOH HOO HOO!
WHY DIDN'T YOU JUST SHOW ME TO BEGIN WITH...?
......
シュパッ
SHUPA (SWIPE)
PHOTO: KATY
ガタン
GATAN (GATHNK)
ゴトン
GOTON (GATUNK)
ケイティ
GATAN
ガタン
ゴトン
GOTON
HUNH?

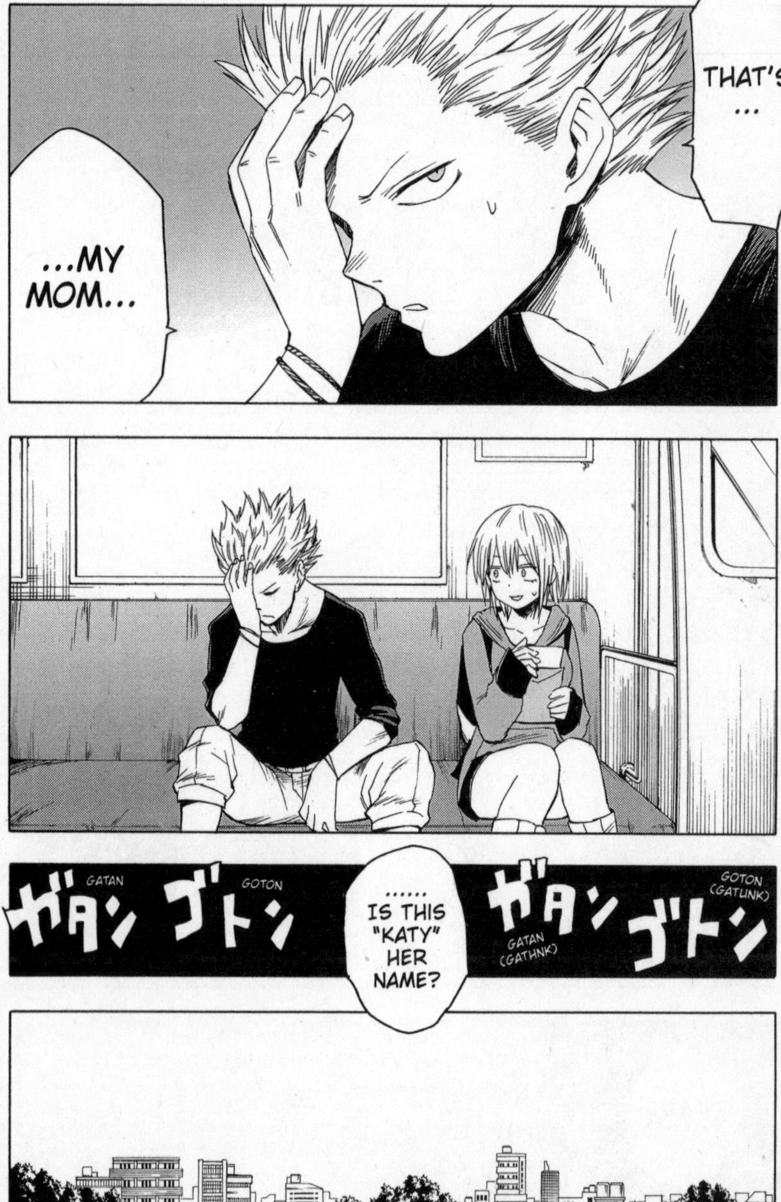
THAT'S ...
...MY MOM...
ゴトン GOTON (GATUNK)
ガタン GATAN (GATHNK)
...... IS THIS "KATY" HER NAME?
ゴトン GOTON
ガタン GATAN

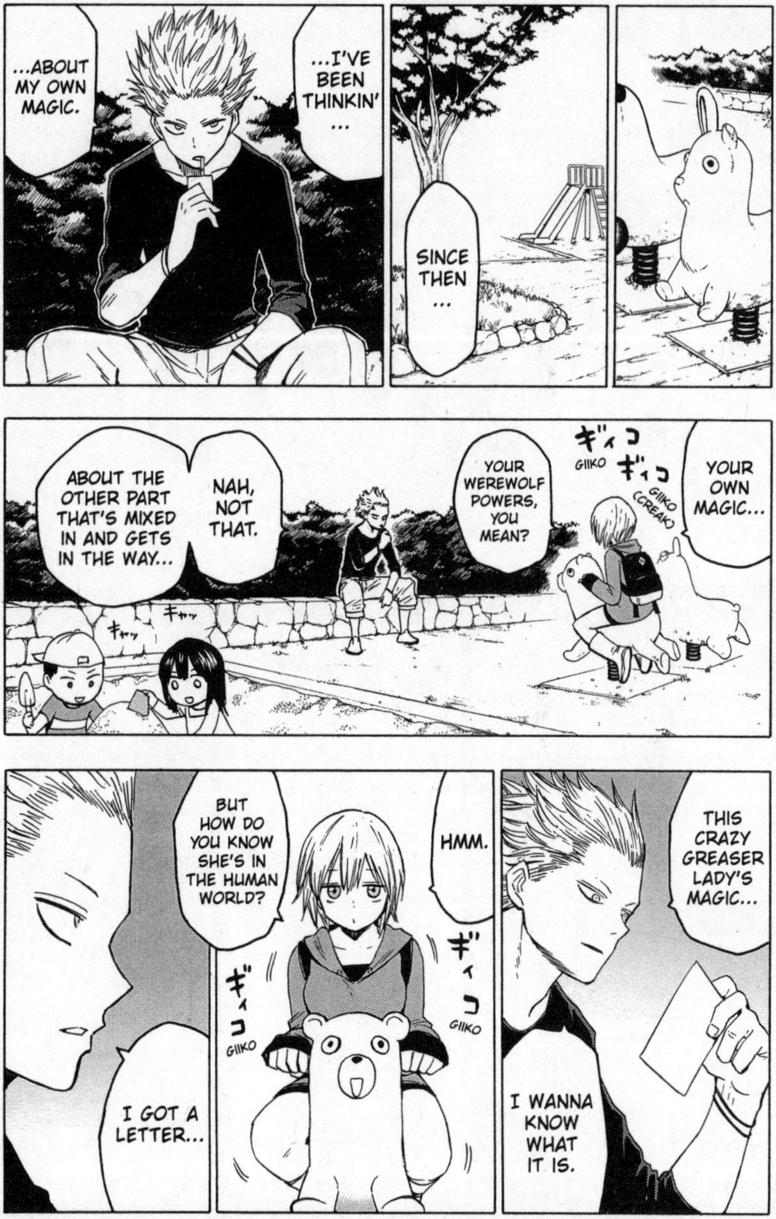
SINCE THEN...
...I'VE BEEN THINKIN'...
...ABOUT MY OWN MAGIC.
YOUR OWN MAGIC...
ギィコ
GIIKO
ギィコ
GIIKO (CREAK)
YOUR WEREWOLF POWERS, YOU MEAN?
NAH, NOT THAT.
ABOUT THE OTHER PART THAT'S MIXED IN AND GETS IN THE WAY...
キャッ
キャッ
THIS CRAZY GREASER LADY'S MAGIC...
I WANNA KNOW WHAT IT IS.
HMM.
ギィコ
GIIKO
BUT HOW DO YOU KNOW SHE'S IN THE HUMAN WORLD?
ギィコ
GIIKO
I GOT A LETTER...

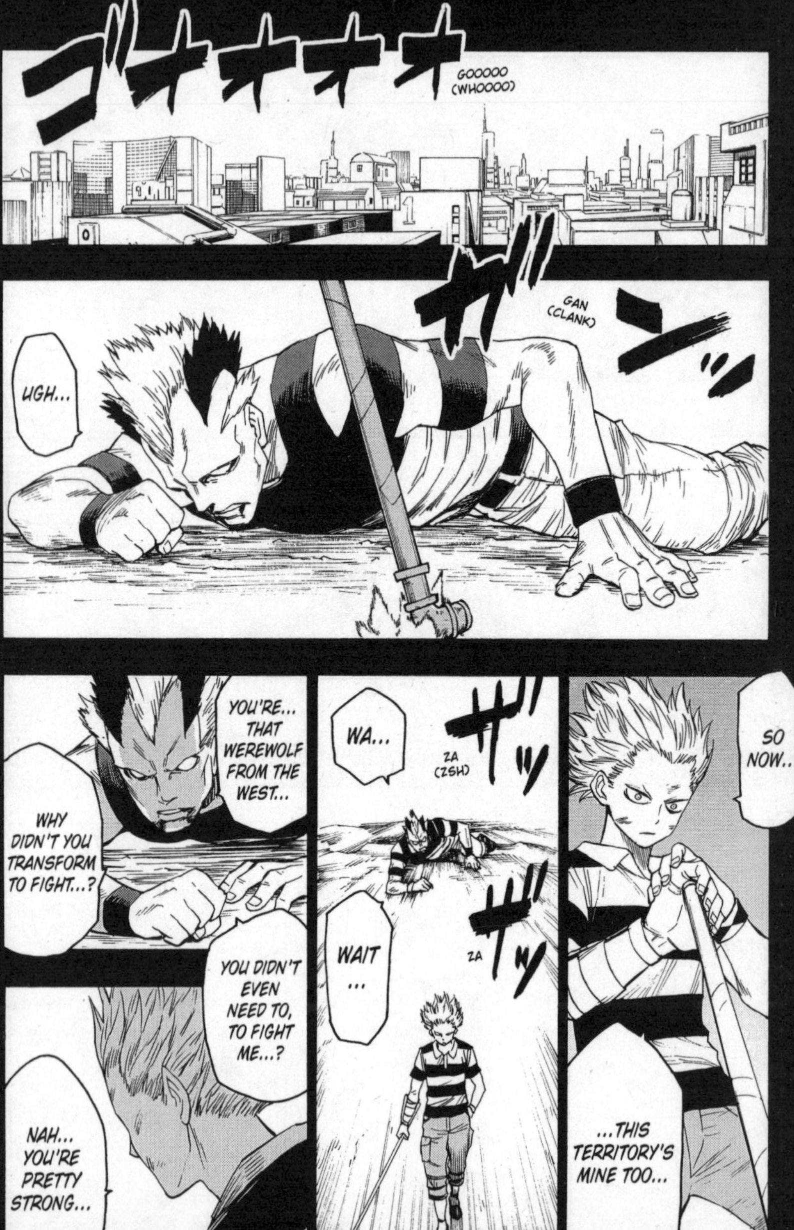
GOOOOO (WHOOOO)
GAN (CLANK)
UGH...
SO NOW...
...THIS TERRITORY'S MINE TOO...
ZA (ZSH)
WA...
ZA
WAIT ...
YOU'RE... THAT WEREWOLF FROM THE WEST...
WHY DIDN'T YOU TRANSFORM TO FIGHT...?
YOU DIDN'T EVEN NEED TO, TO FIGHT ME...?
NAH... YOU'RE PRETTY STRONG...

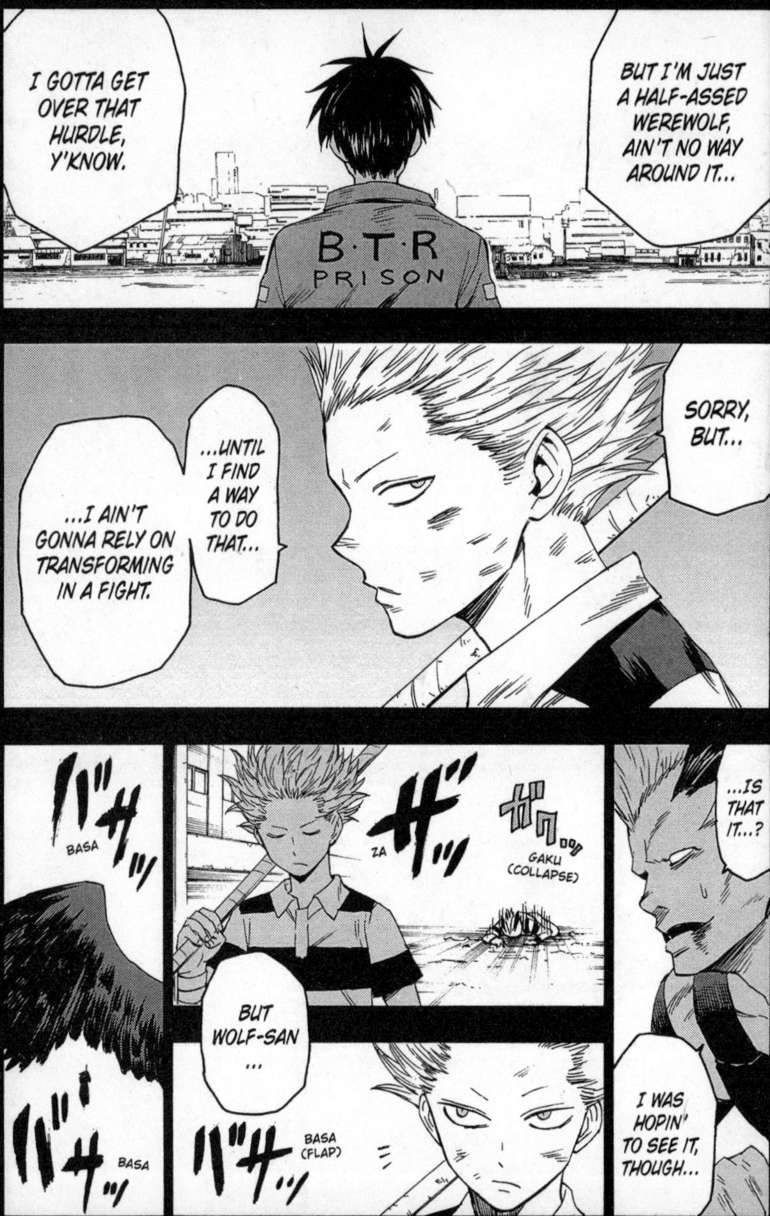
BUT I'M JUST A HALF-ASSED WEREWOLF, AIN'T NO WAY AROUND IT...
I GOTTA GET OVER THAT HURDLE, Y'KNOW.
B·T·R PRISON
SORRY, BUT...
...UNTIL I FIND A WAY TO DO THAT...
...I AIN'T GONNA RELY ON TRANSFORMING IN A FIGHT.
...IS THAT IT...?
I WAS HOPIN' TO SEE IT, THOUGH...
GAKU (COLLAPSE)
ZA
BUT WOLF-SAN ...
BASA (FLAP)
BASA
BASA

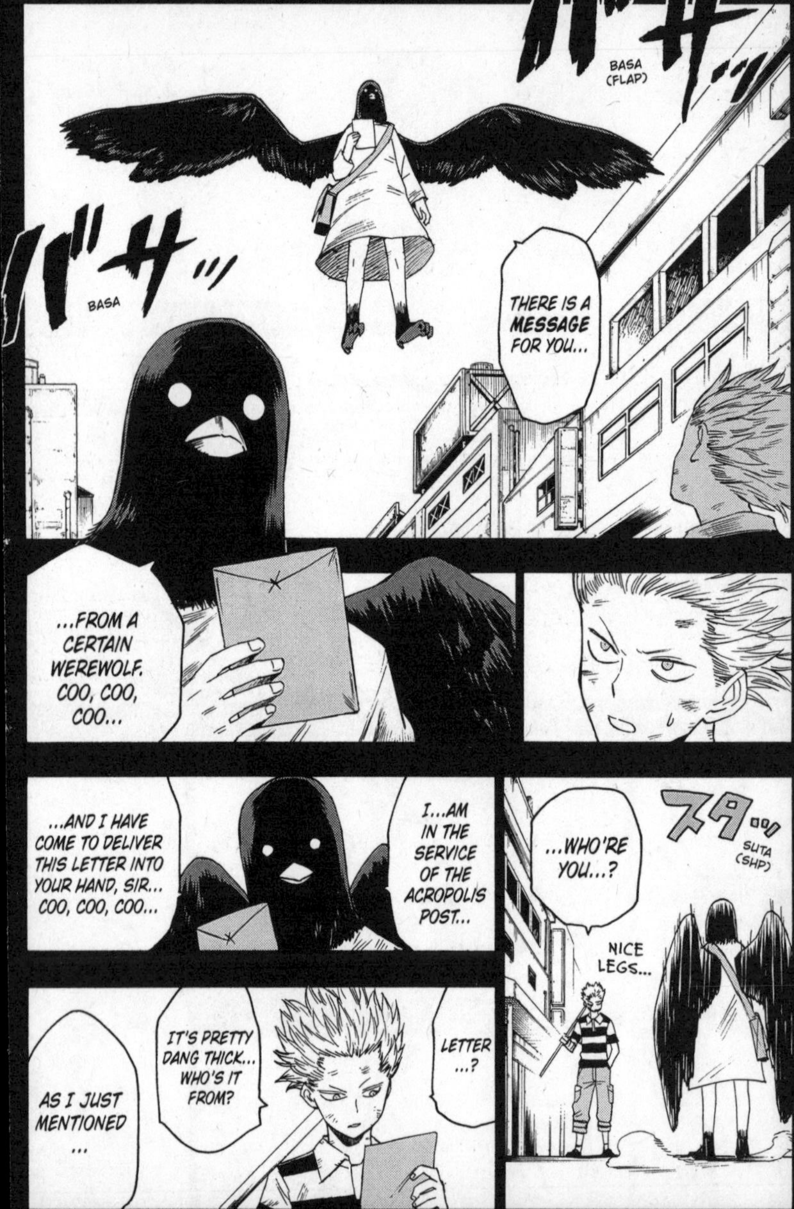
BASA (FLAP)
BASA
THERE IS A MESSAGE FOR YOU...
...FROM A CERTAIN WEREWOLF. COO, COO, COO...
...WHO'RE YOU...?
SUTA (SHP)
NICE LEGS...
I...AM IN THE SERVICE OF THE ACROPOLIS POST...
...AND I HAVE COME TO DELIVER THIS LETTER INTO YOUR HAND, SIR... COO, COO, COO...
LETTER ...?
IT'S PRETTY DANG THICK... WHO'S IT FROM?
AS I JUST MENTIONED ...

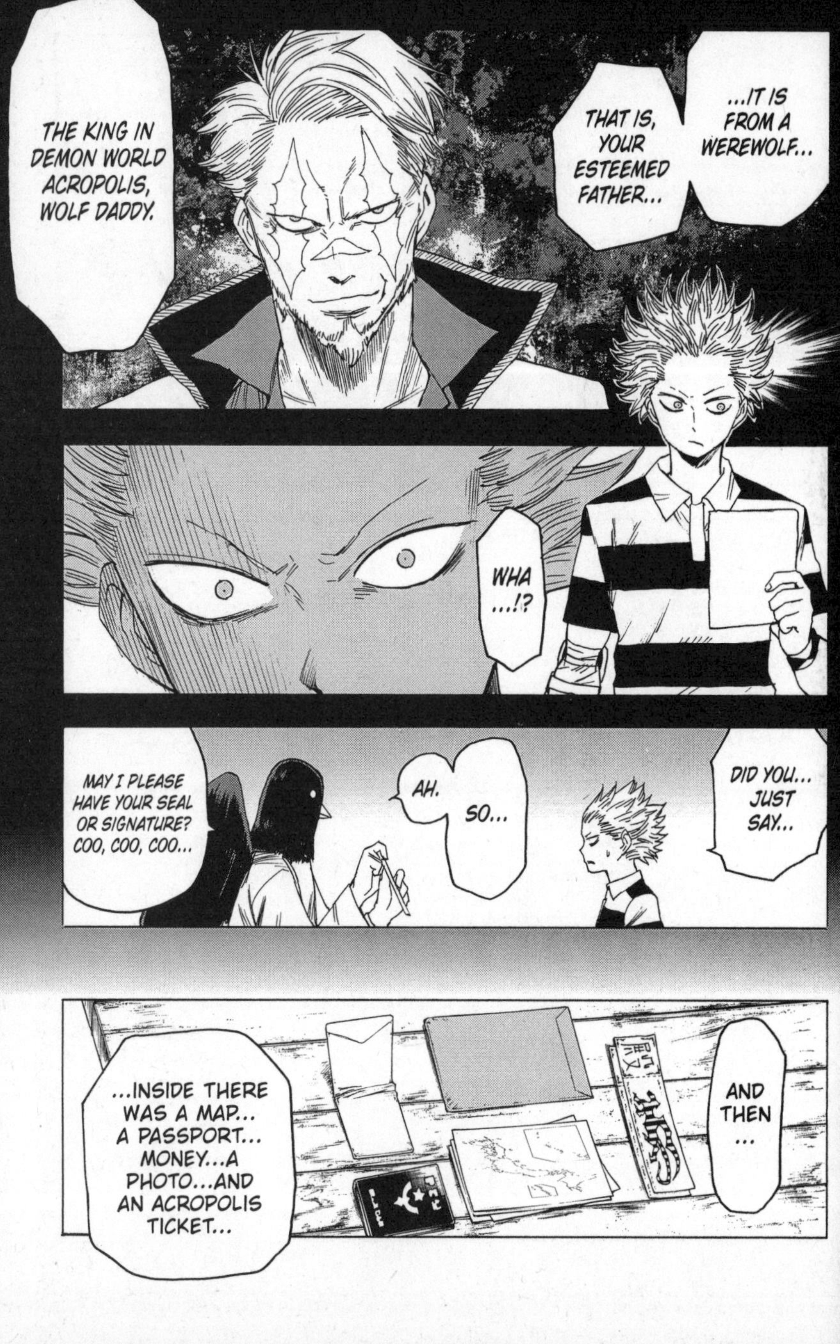
...IT IS FROM A WEREWOLF...
THAT IS, YOUR ESTEEMED FATHER...
THE KING IN DEMON WORLD ACROPOLIS, WOLF DADDY.
WHA ...!?
DID YOU... JUST SAY...
AH.
SO...
MAY I PLEASE HAVE YOUR SEAL OR SIGNATURE? COO, COO, COO...
AND THEN ...
...INSIDE THERE WAS A MAP... A PASSPORT... MONEY...A PHOTO...AND AN ACROPOLIS TICKET...

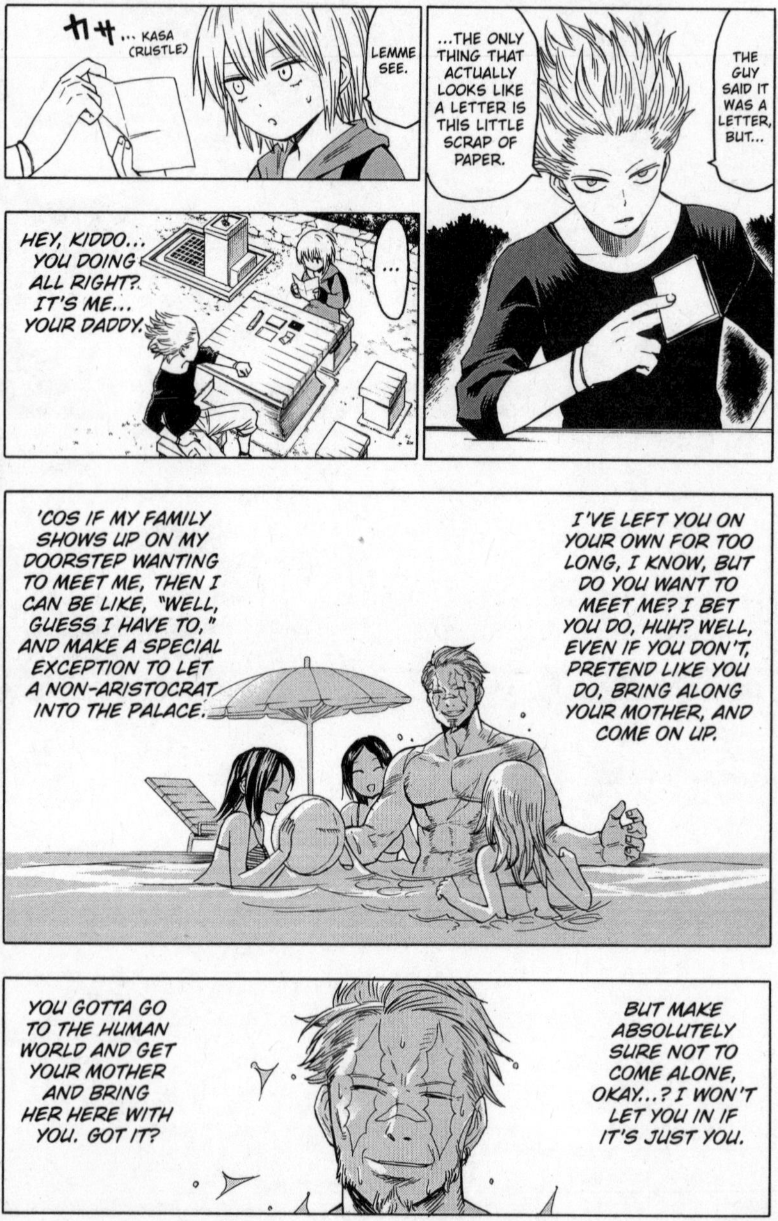
THE GUY SAID IT WAS A LETTER, BUT...
...THE ONLY THING THAT ACTUALLY LOOKS LIKE A LETTER IS THIS LITTLE SCRAP OF PAPER.
LEMME SEE.
カサ... KASA (RUSTLE)
...
HEY, KIDDO... YOU DOING ALL RIGHT? IT'S ME... YOUR DADDY.
I'VE LEFT YOU ON YOUR OWN FOR TOO LONG, I KNOW, BUT DO YOU WANT TO MEET ME? I BET YOU DO, HUH? WELL, EVEN IF YOU DON'T, PRETEND LIKE YOU DO, BRING ALONG YOUR MOTHER, AND COME ON UP.
'COS IF MY FAMILY SHOWS UP ON MY DOORSTEP WANTING TO MEET ME, THEN I CAN BE LIKE, "WELL, GUESS I HAVE TO," AND MAKE A SPECIAL EXCEPTION TO LET A NON-ARISTOCRAT INTO THE PALACE.
BUT MAKE ABSOLUTELY SURE NOT TO COME ALONE, OKAY...? I WON'T LET YOU IN IF IT'S JUST YOU.
YOU GOTTA GO TO THE HUMAN WORLD AND GET YOUR MOTHER AND BRING HER HERE WITH YOU. GOT IT?

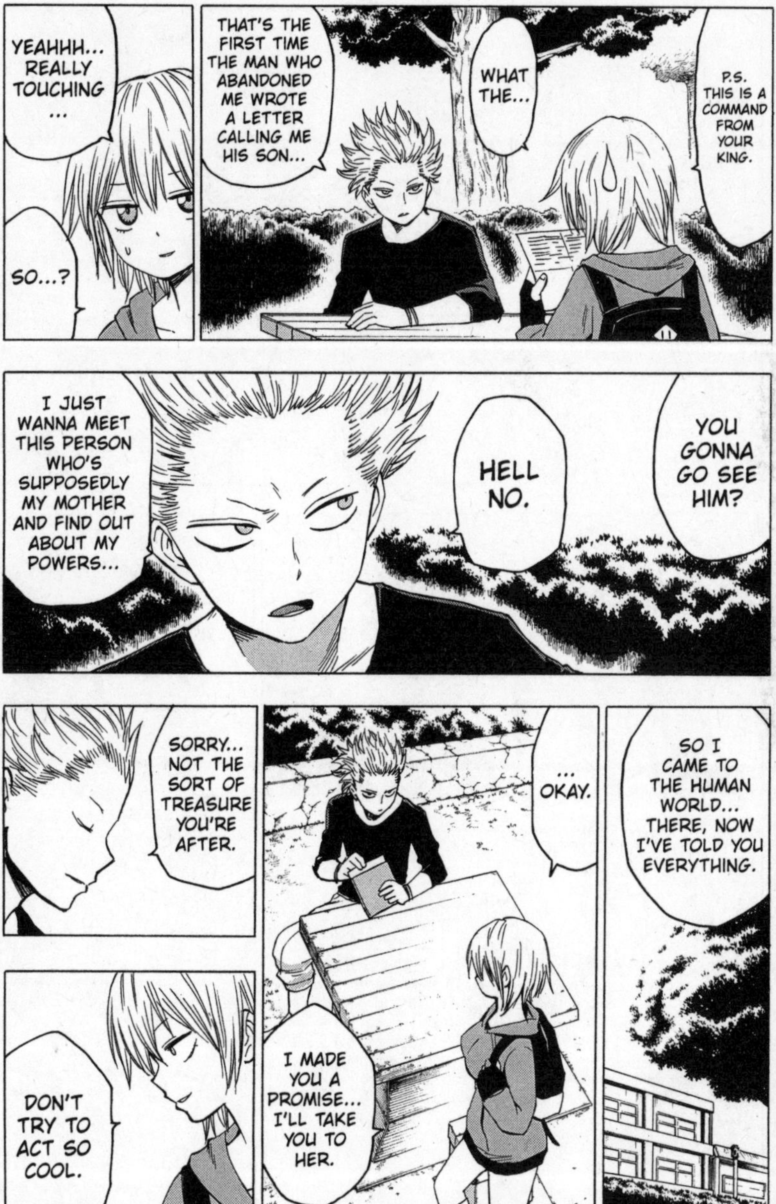
P.S. THIS IS A COMMAND FROM YOUR KING.
WHAT THE...
THAT'S THE FIRST TIME THE MAN WHO ABANDONED ME WROTE A LETTER CALLING ME HIS SON...
YEAHHH... REALLY TOUCHING ...
SO...?
YOU GONNA GO SEE HIM?
HELL NO.
I JUST WANNA MEET THIS PERSON WHO'S SUPPOSEDLY MY MOTHER AND FIND OUT ABOUT MY POWERS...
SO I CAME TO THE HUMAN WORLD... THERE, NOW I'VE TOLD YOU EVERYTHING.
... OKAY.
I MADE YOU A PROMISE... I'LL TAKE YOU TO HER.
SORRY... NOT THE SORT OF TREASURE YOU'RE AFTER.
DON'T TRY TO ACT SO COOL.

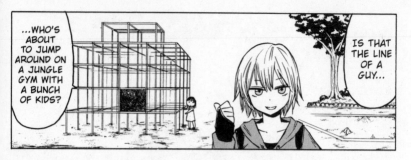

IS THAT THE LINE OF A GUY...
...WHO'S ABOUT TO JUMP AROUND ON A JUNGLE GYM WITH A BUNCH OF KIDS?
SHUN (SHP)
シュッ
THERE WE GO...
FLOWER SHOP IN FRONT OF A CON-VENIENCE STORE... 3-WAY INTER-SECTION ...
IT'S DEFI-NITELY AROUND HERE.
?
UH-OH. HEY, DON'T PUT YOUR HEAD IN THERE, IT'S NOT SAFE, OKAY?
BYE, TEACH-ER.
UH-HUH. GET HOME SAFE.
BYE.

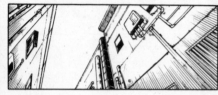

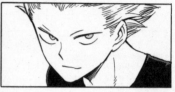

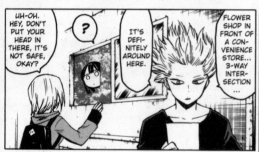

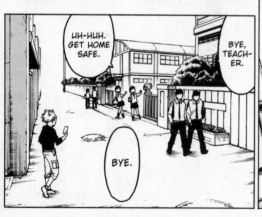

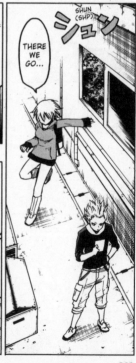

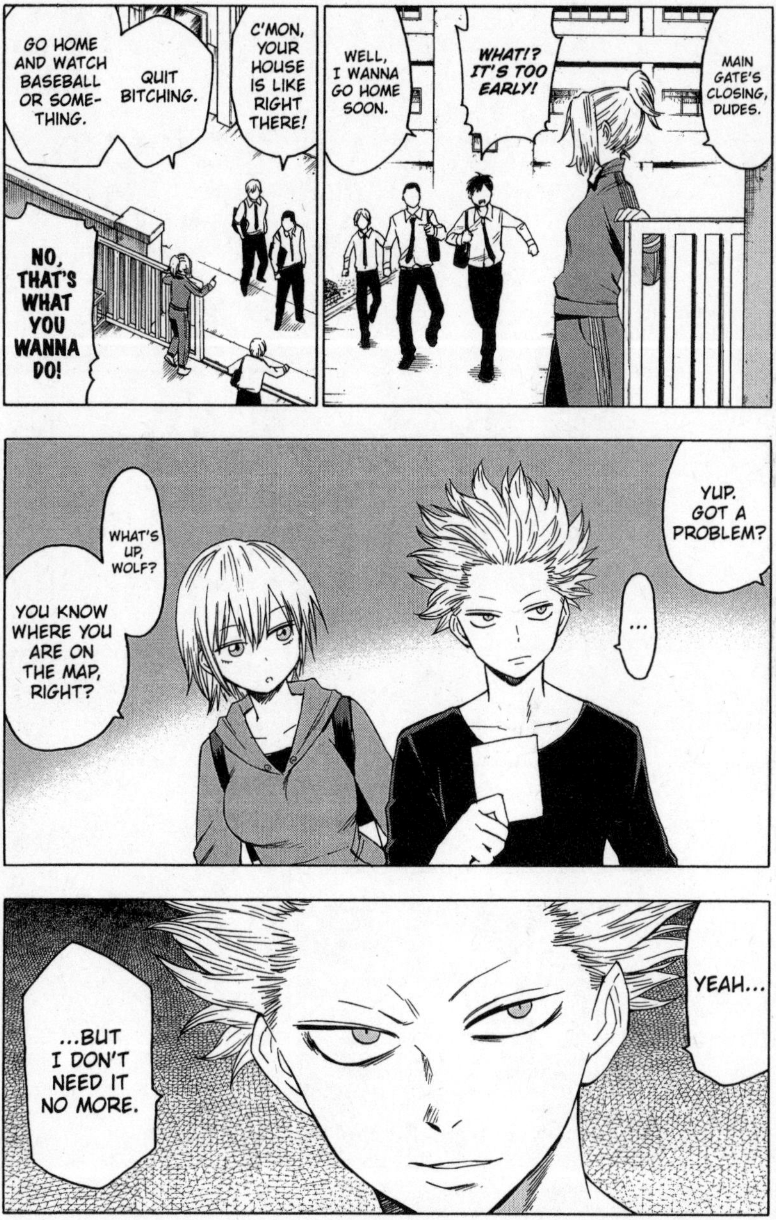
MAIN GATE'S CLOSING, DUDES.
WHAT!? IT'S TOO EARLY!
WELL, I WANNA GO HOME SOON.
C'MON, YOUR HOUSE IS LIKE RIGHT THERE!
QUIT BITCHING.
GO HOME AND WATCH BASEBALL OR SOME-THING.
NO, THAT'S WHAT YOU WANNA DO!
YUP. GOT A PROBLEM?
...
WHAT'S UP, WOLF?
YOU KNOW WHERE YOU ARE ON THE MAP, RIGHT?
YEAH...
...BUT I DON'T NEED IT NO MORE.

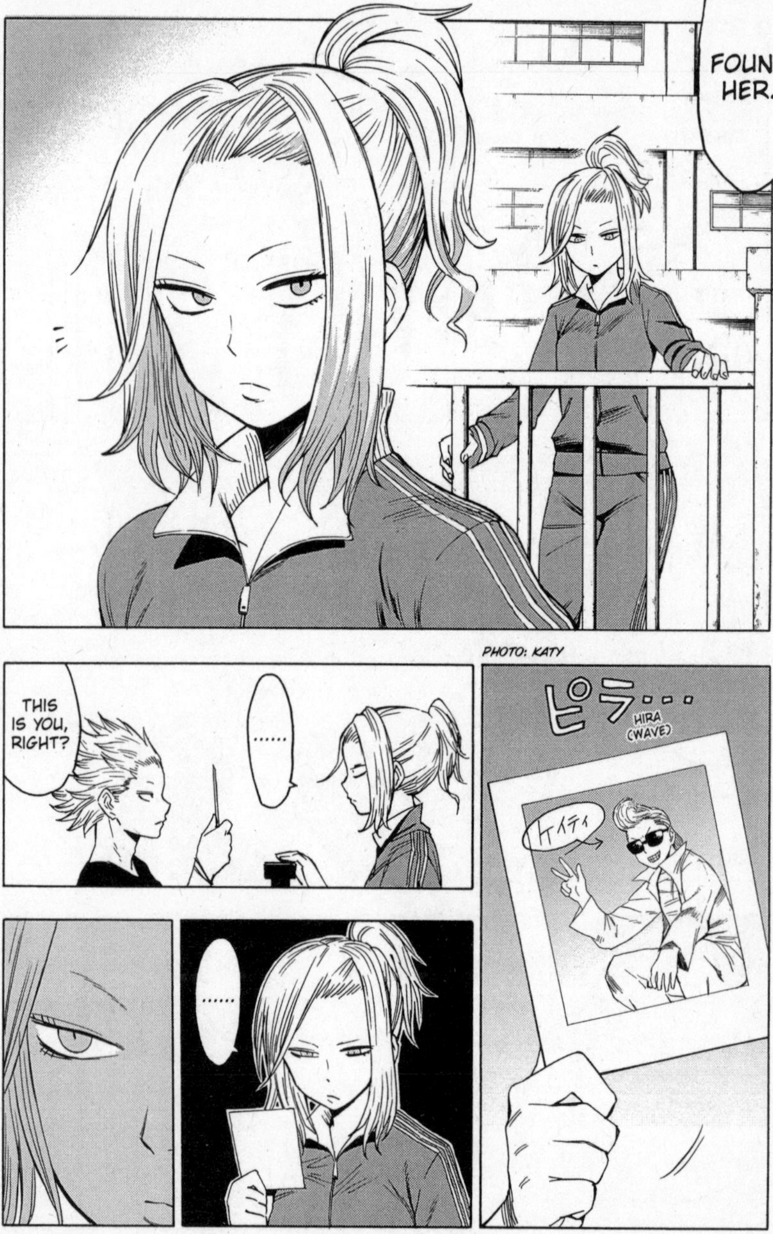
FOUND HER.
PHOTO: KATY
ピラ…
HIRA (WAVE)
ケイティ
THIS IS YOU, RIGHT?
......
......

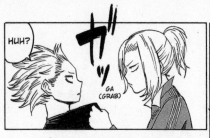

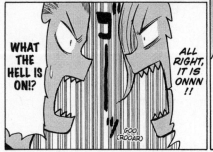

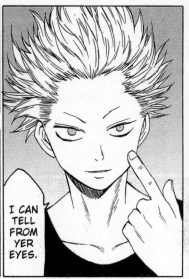

I CAN TELL FROM YER EYES.
HUH?
GA (GRAB)
ALL RIGHT, IT IS ONNN!!
GOO (ROOAR)
WHAT THE HELL IS ON!?
'BOUT TIME YOU SHOWED UP! SO COME TO DO YOUR BOSS'S BIDDING, LAPDOG!?
THE HELL ARE YOU EVEN TALKIN' ABOUT!? I AIN'T NO DOG!!
OH YEAH, THEN WHAT ARE YA!?
A WOLF!
A WOLF, HUH!? THAT'D BE YOUR OWNER!!
NO, I'M A WOLF TOO!!
HUH!?
NO MISTAKE HERE...
WELL, NOW THAT YOU SAY SO, YOU DO KINDA LOOK LIKE HIM!
YEAH, I'VE BEEN SAYIN'!!
THEY'RE FAMILY, ALL RIGHT...

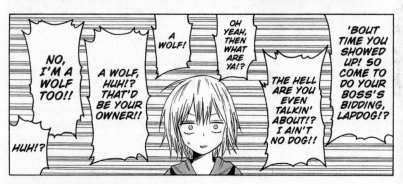

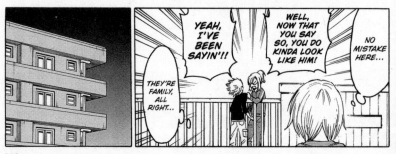

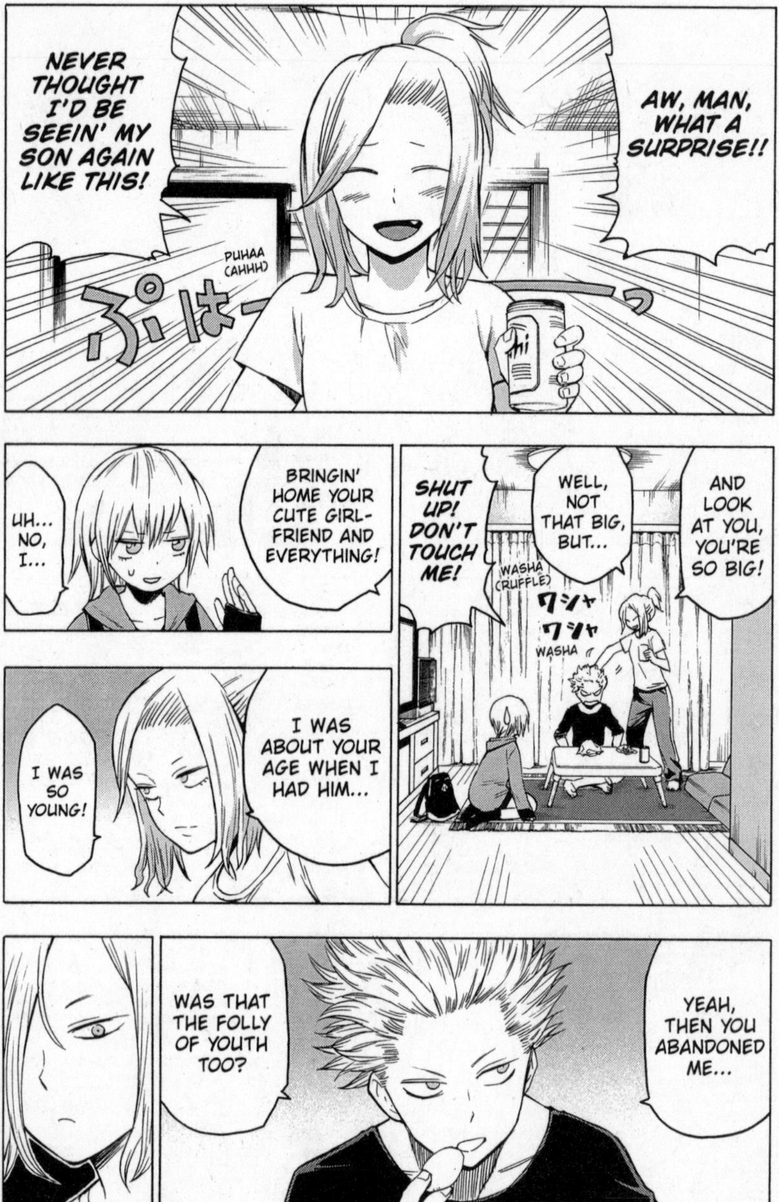
AW, MAN, WHAT A SURPRISE!!
NEVER THOUGHT I'D BE SEEIN' MY SON AGAIN LIKE THIS!
PUHAA (AHHH)
ぷはーっ
AND LOOK AT YOU, YOU'RE SO BIG!
WELL, NOT THAT BIG, BUT...
SHUT UP! DON'T TOUCH ME!
WASHA (RUFFLE)
ワシャ
ワシャ
WASHA
BRINGIN' HOME YOUR CUTE GIRL-FRIEND AND EVERYTHING!
UH... NO, I...
I WAS ABOUT YOUR AGE WHEN I HAD HIM...
I WAS SO YOUNG!
YEAH, THEN YOU ABANDONED ME...
WAS THAT THE FOLLY OF YOUTH TOO?

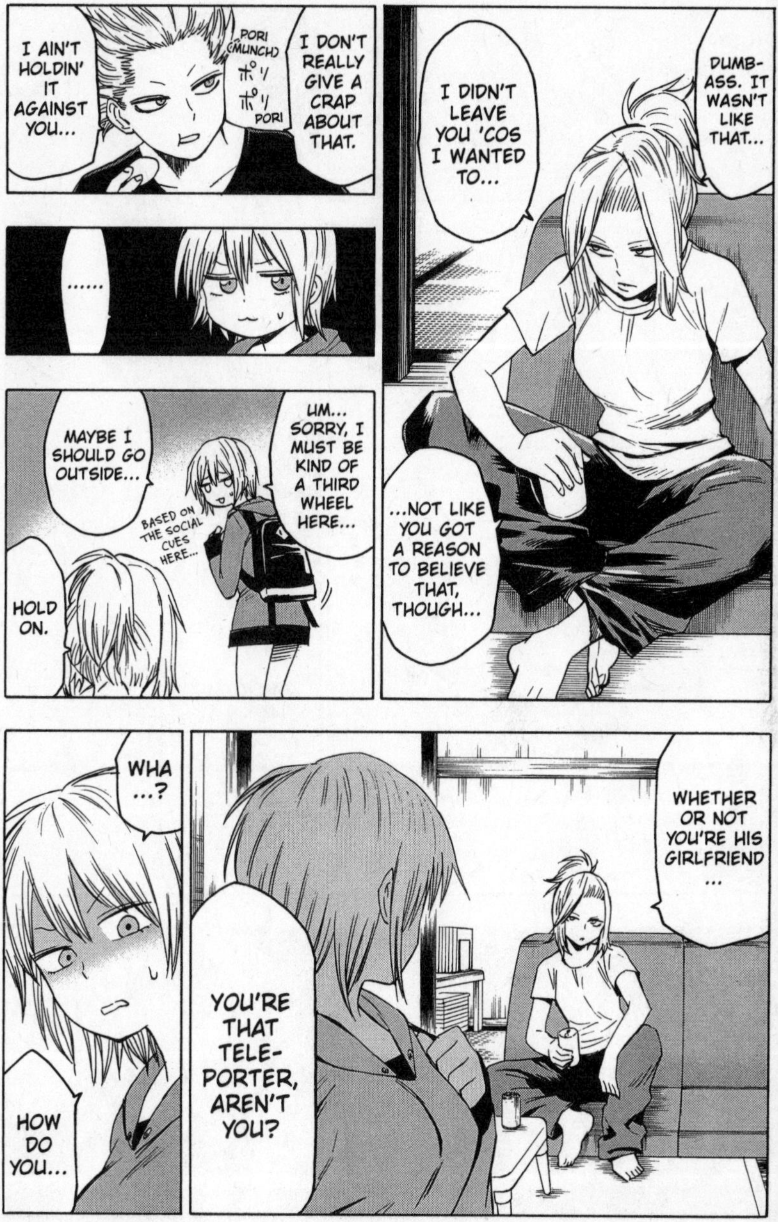
DUMB-ASS. IT WASN'T LIKE THAT...
I DIDN'T LEAVE YOU 'COS I WANTED TO...
...NOT LIKE YOU GOT A REASON TO BELIEVE THAT, THOUGH...
I DON'T REALLY GIVE A CRAP ABOUT THAT.
PORI (MUNCH) ポリ ポリ PORI
I AIN'T HOLDIN' IT AGAINST YOU...
......
UM... SORRY, I MUST BE KIND OF A THIRD WHEEL HERE...
BASED ON THE SOCIAL CUES HERE...
MAYBE I SHOULD GO OUTSIDE...
HOLD ON.
WHETHER OR NOT YOU'RE HIS GIRLFRIEND ...
YOU'RE THAT TELE-PORTER, AREN'T YOU?
WHA ...?
HOW DO YOU...

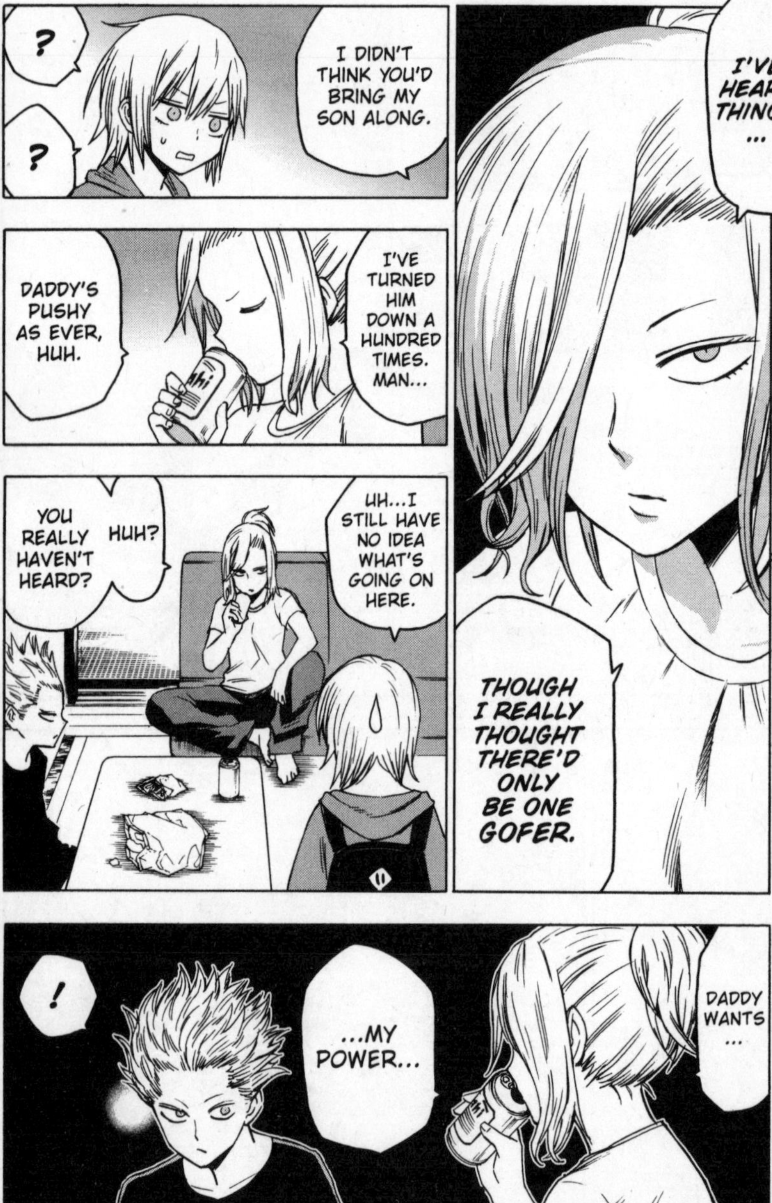
I'VE HEARD THINGS...
THOUGH I REALLY THOUGHT THERE'D ONLY BE ONE GOFER.
I DIDN'T THINK YOU'D BRING MY SON ALONG.
?
?
I'VE TURNED HIM DOWN A HUNDRED TIMES. MAN...
DADDY'S PUSHY AS EVER, HUH.
UH...I STILL HAVE NO IDEA WHAT'S GOING ON HERE.
HUH?
YOU REALLY HAVEN'T HEARD?
DADDY WANTS...
...MY POWER...
!

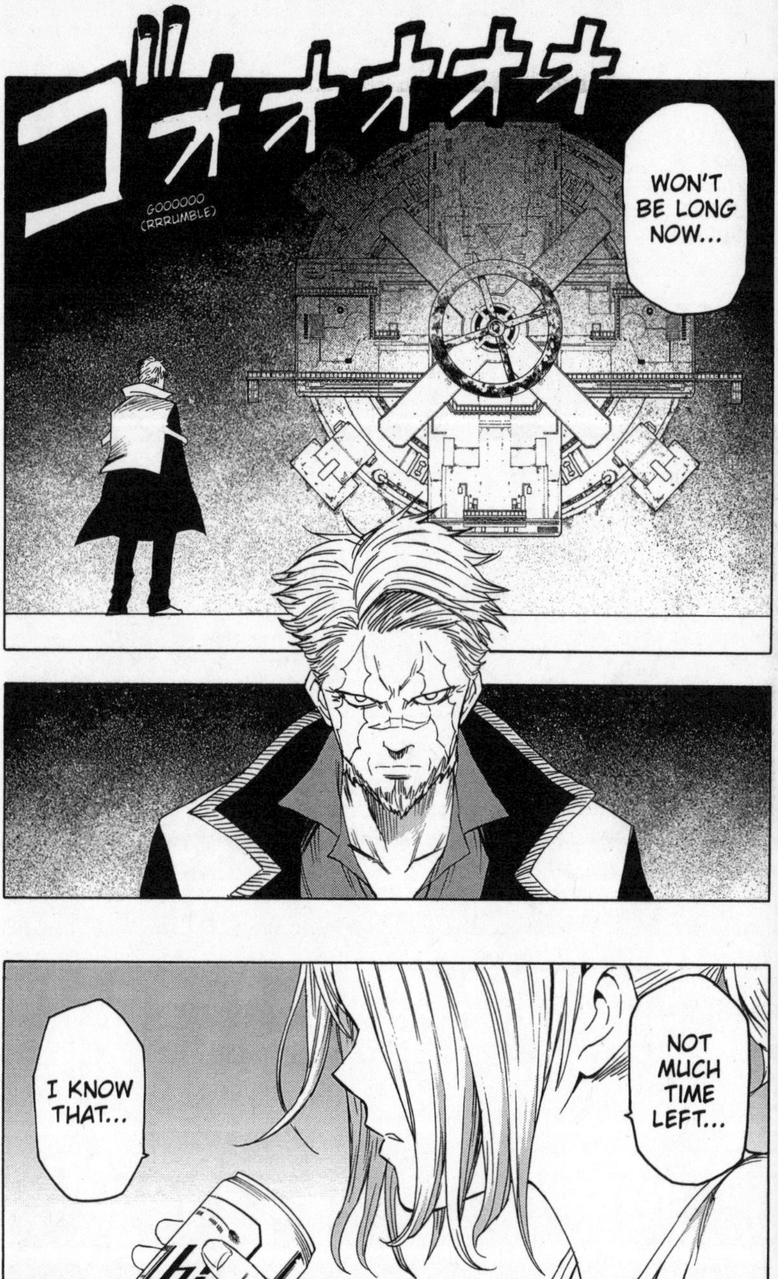
WON'T BE LONG NOW...
ゴオオオオオ
GOOOOOO (RRRUMBLE)
NOT MUCH TIME LEFT...
I KNOW THAT...

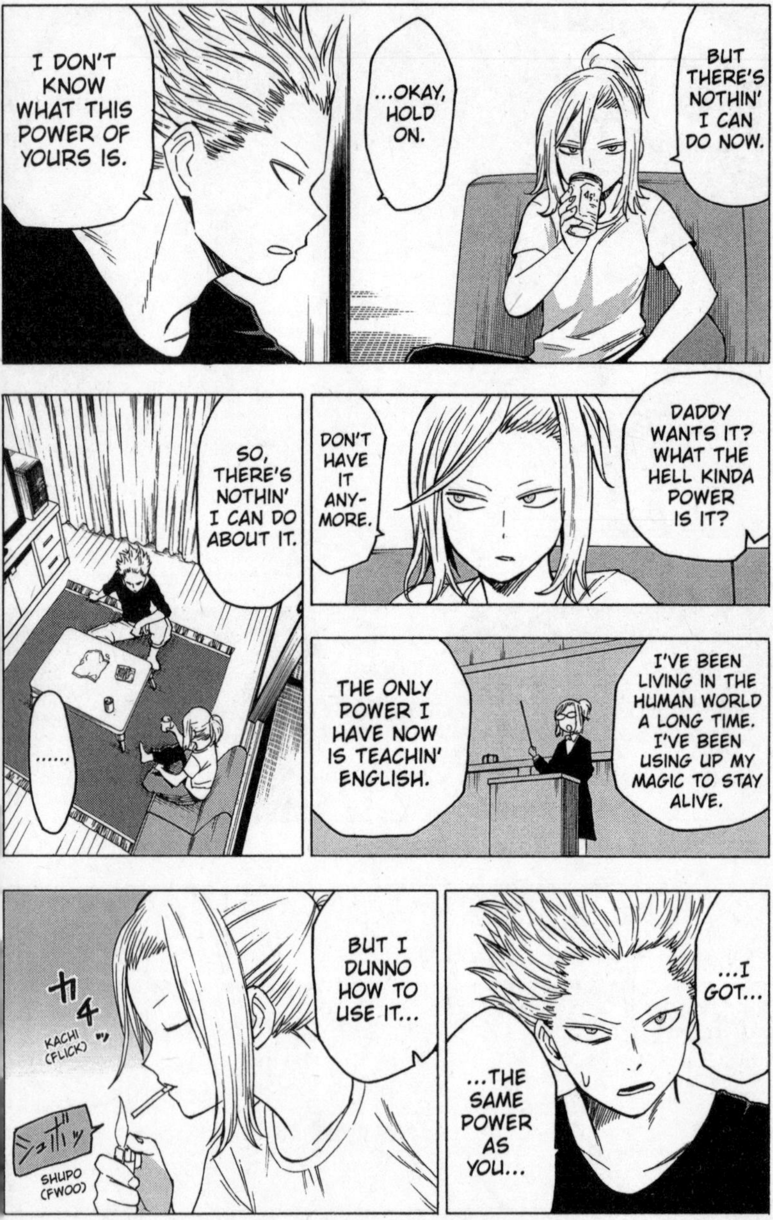
BUT THERE'S NOTHIN' I CAN DO NOW.
...OKAY, HOLD ON.
I DON'T KNOW WHAT THIS POWER OF YOURS IS.
DADDY WANTS IT? WHAT THE HELL KINDA POWER IS IT?
DON'T HAVE IT ANYMORE.
I'VE BEEN LIVING IN THE HUMAN WORLD A LONG TIME. I'VE BEEN USING UP MY MAGIC TO STAY ALIVE.
THE ONLY POWER I HAVE NOW IS TEACHIN' ENGLISH.
SO, THERE'S NOTHIN' I CAN DO ABOUT IT.
......
...I GOT...
...THE SAME POWER AS YOU...
BUT I DUNNO HOW TO USE IT...
カチッ
KACHI (FLICK)
シュボッ
SHUPO (FWOO)

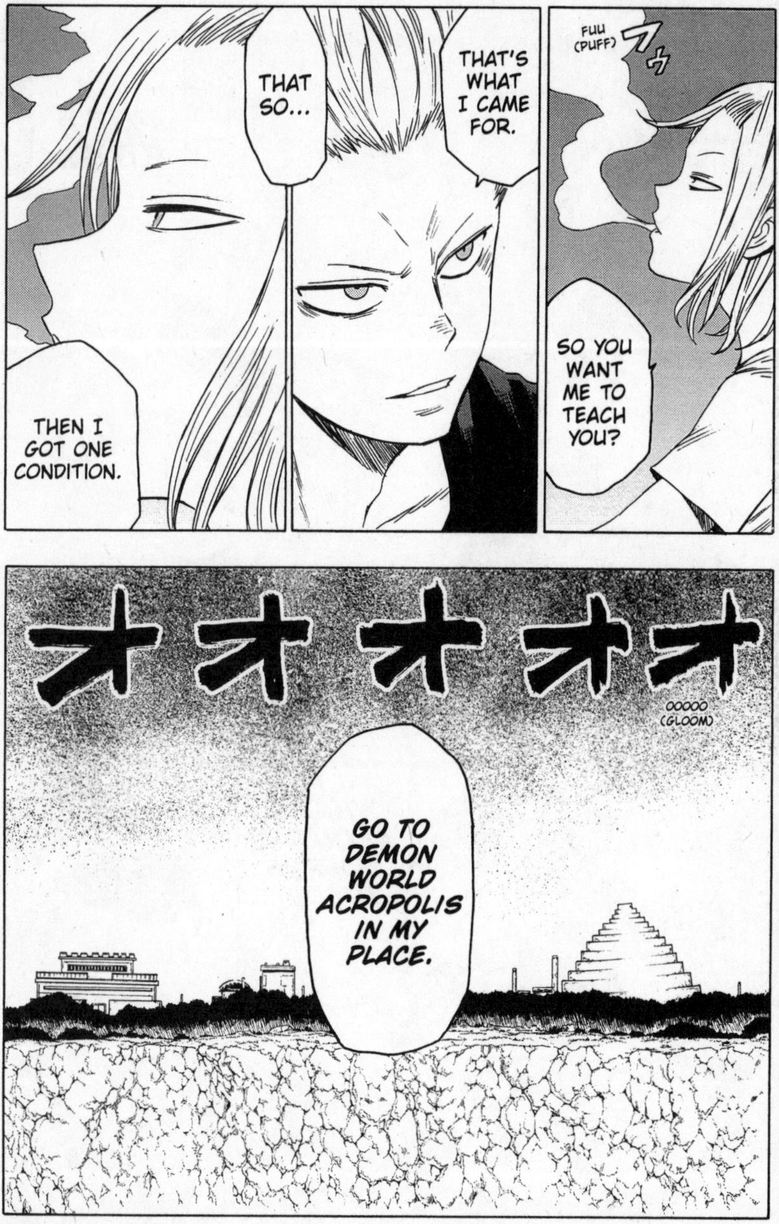
FUU (PUFF)
SO YOU WANT ME TO TEACH YOU?
THAT'S WHAT I CAME FOR.
THAT SO...
THEN I GOT ONE CONDITION.
オオオオオ
OOOOO (GLOOM)
GO TO DEMON WORLD ACROPOLIS IN MY PLACE.

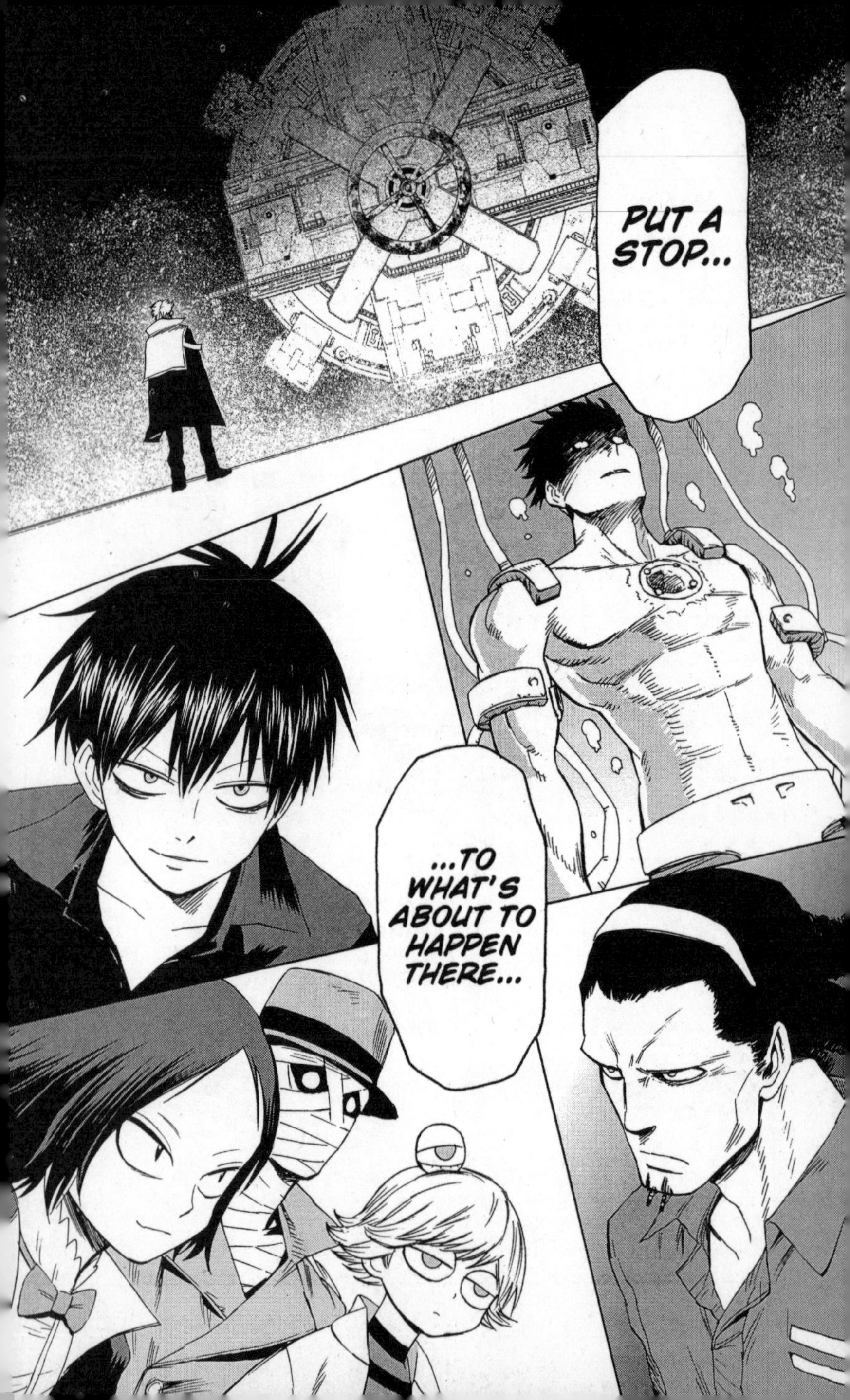
PUT A STOP...
...TO WHAT'S ABOUT TO HAPPEN THERE...

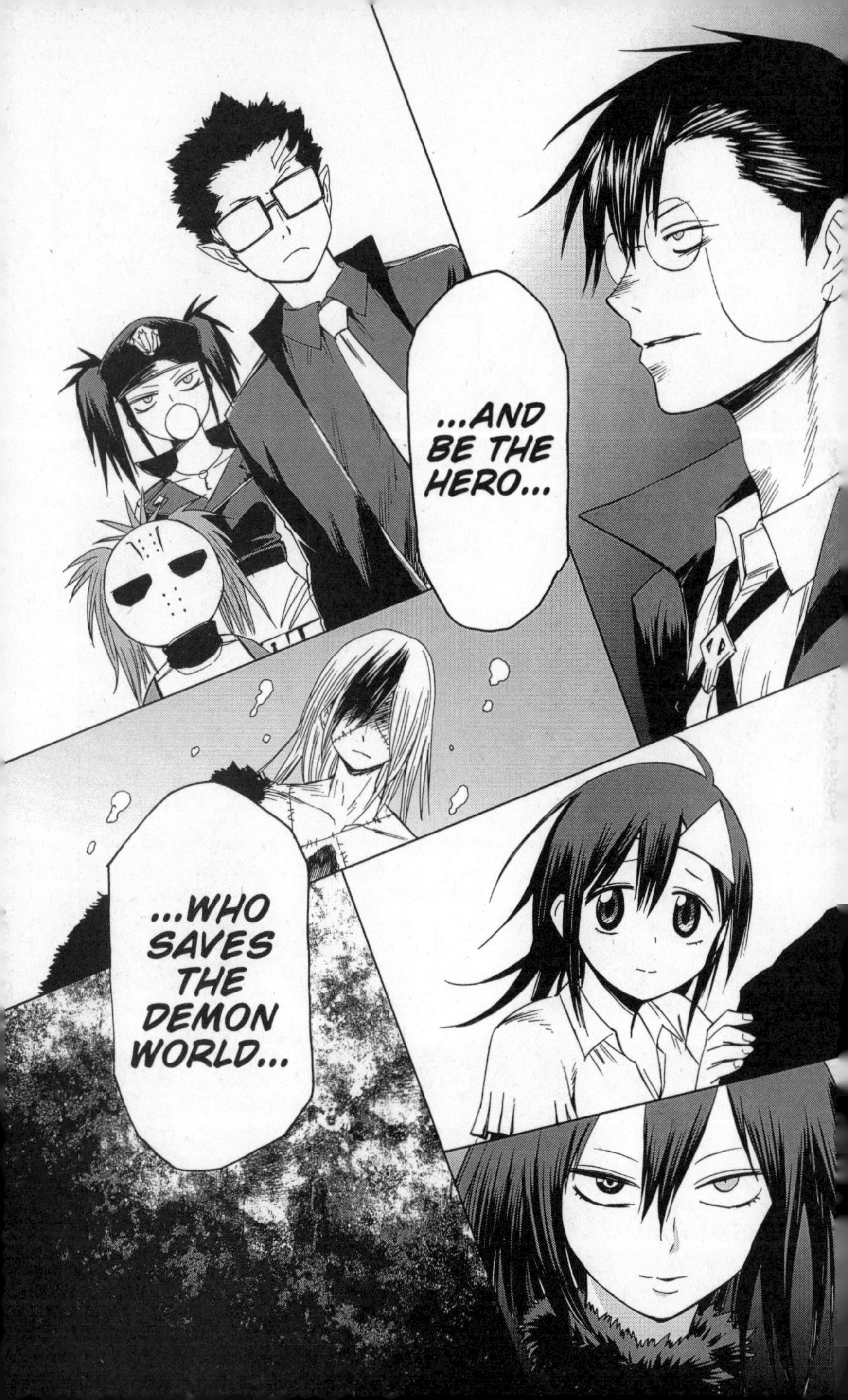
...AND BE THE HERO...
...WHO SAVES THE DEMON WORLD...

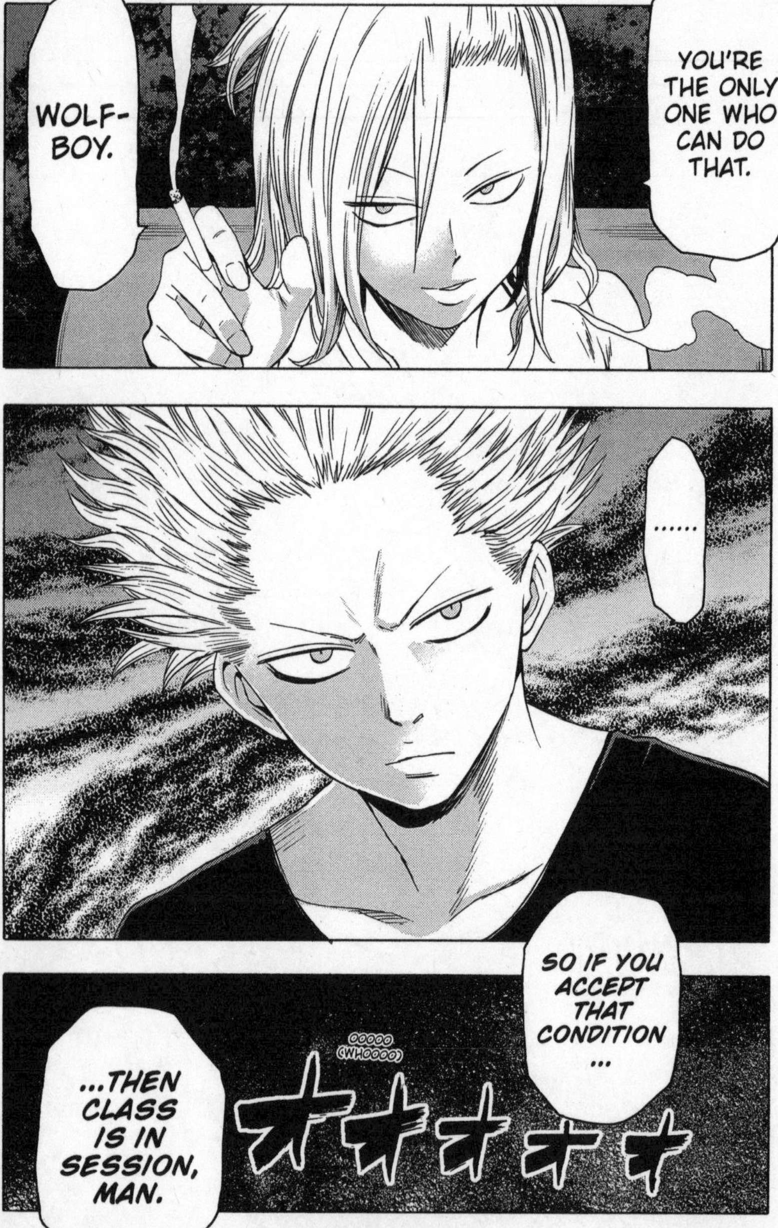
YOU'RE THE ONLY ONE WHO CAN DO THAT.
WOLF-BOY.
......
SO IF YOU ACCEPT THAT CONDITION ...
オオオオオ
OOOOO (WHOOOO)
...THEN CLASS IS IN SESSION, MAN.

♠ To Be Continued ♠

To Be Continued.

BLODD LAD

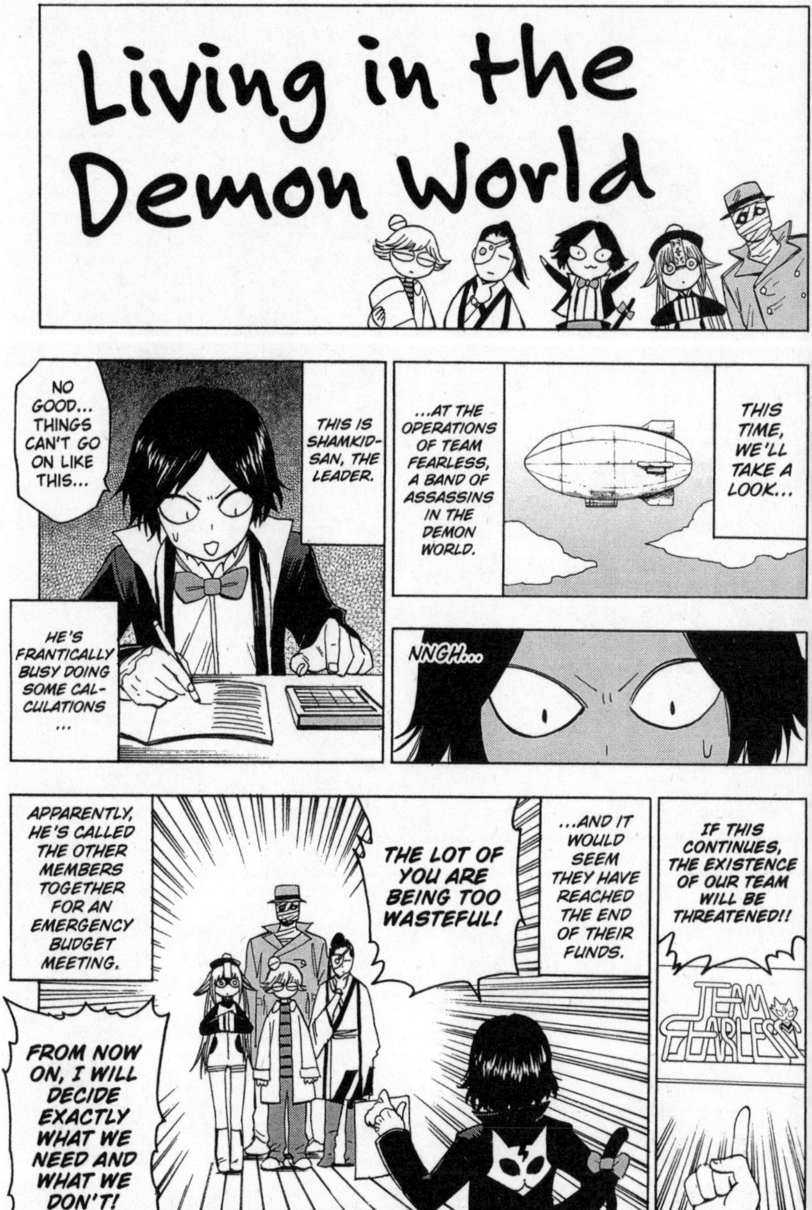
Living in the Demon World
THIS TIME, WE'LL TAKE A LOOK...
...AT THE OPERATIONS OF TEAM FEARLESS, A BAND OF ASSASSINS IN THE DEMON WORLD.
NNGH...
THIS IS SHAMKID-SAN, THE LEADER.
NO GOOD... THINGS CAN'T GO ON LIKE THIS...
HE'S FRANTICALLY BUSY DOING SOME CAL-CULATIONS ...
IF THIS CONTINUES, THE EXISTENCE OF OUR TEAM WILL BE THREATENED!!
TEAM FEARLESS
...AND IT WOULD SEEM THEY HAVE REACHED THE END OF THEIR FUNDS.
THE LOT OF YOU ARE BEING TOO WASTEFUL!
APPARENTLY, HE'S CALLED THE OTHER MEMBERS TOGETHER FOR AN EMERGENCY BUDGET MEETING.
FROM NOW ON, I WILL DECIDE EXACTLY WHAT WE NEED AND WHAT WE DON'T!

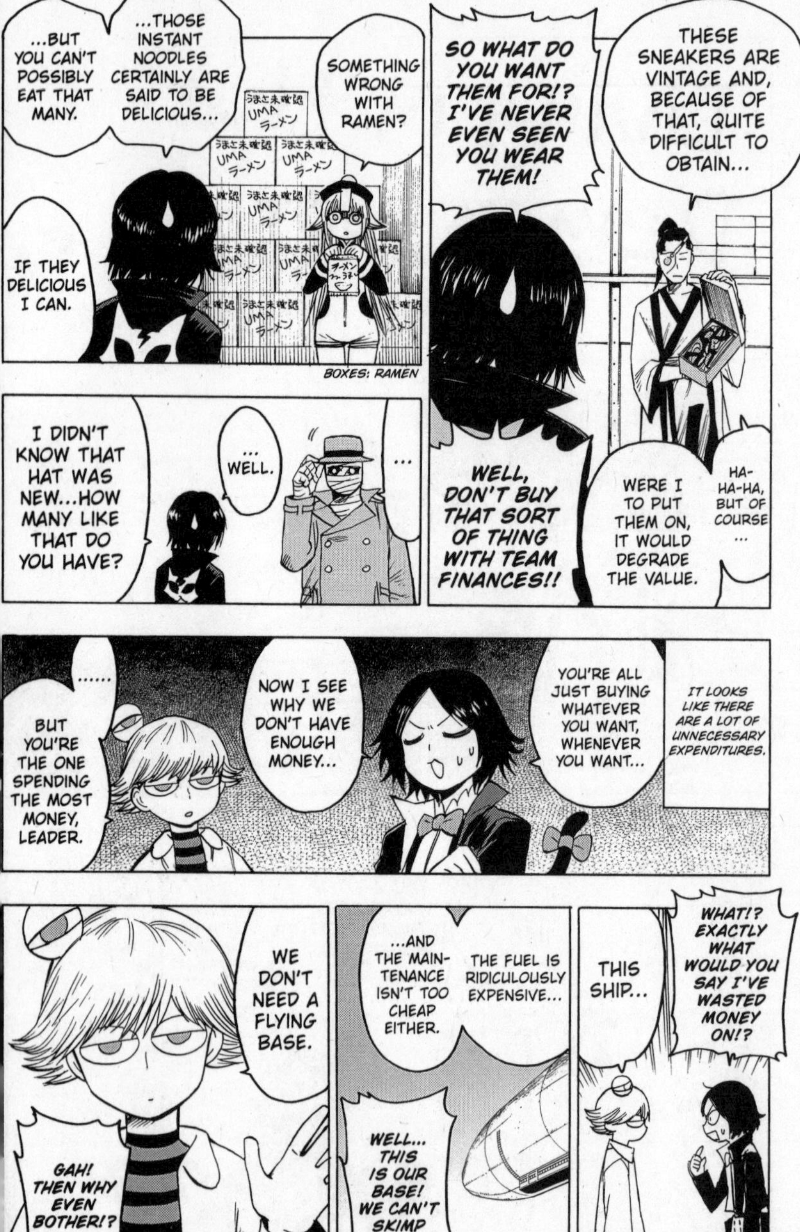
THESE SNEAKERS ARE VINTAGE AND, BECAUSE OF THAT, QUITE DIFFICULT TO OBTAIN...
SO WHAT DO YOU WANT THEM FOR!? I'VE NEVER EVEN SEEN YOU WEAR THEM!
HA-HA-HA, BUT OF COURSE...
WERE I TO PUT THEM ON, IT WOULD DEGRADE THE VALUE.
WELL, DON'T BUY THAT SORT OF THING WITH TEAM FINANCES!!
SOMETHING WRONG WITH RAMEN?
...THOSE INSTANT NOODLES CERTAINLY ARE SAID TO BE DELICIOUS...
...BUT YOU CAN'T POSSIBLY EAT THAT MANY.
IF THEY DELICIOUS I CAN.
BOXES: RAMEN
...
... WELL.
I DIDN'T KNOW THAT HAT WAS NEW...HOW MANY LIKE THAT DO YOU HAVE?
IT LOOKS LIKE THERE ARE A LOT OF UNNECESSARY EXPENDITURES.
YOU'RE ALL JUST BUYING WHATEVER YOU WANT, WHENEVER YOU WANT...
NOW I SEE WHY WE DON'T HAVE ENOUGH MONEY...
......
BUT YOU'RE THE ONE SPENDING THE MOST MONEY, LEADER.
WHAT!? EXACTLY WHAT WOULD YOU SAY I'VE WASTED MONEY ON!?
THIS SHIP...
THE FUEL IS RIDICULOUSLY EXPENSIVE...
...AND THE MAIN-TENANCE ISN'T TOO CHEAP EITHER.
WELL... THIS IS OUR BASE! WE CAN'T SKIMP ON IT!
WE DON'T NEED A FLYING BASE.
GAH! THEN WHY EVEN BOTHER!?

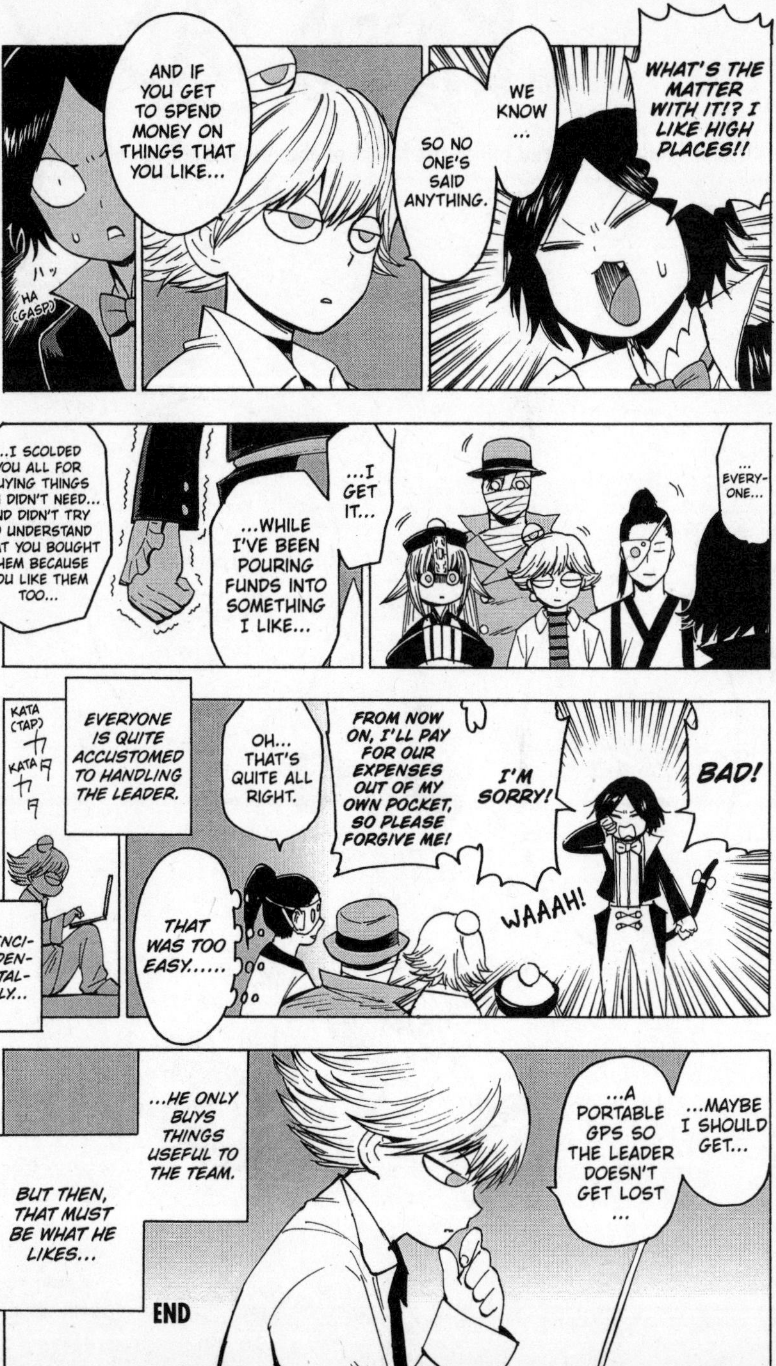
WHAT'S THE MATTER WITH IT!? I LIKE HIGH PLACES!!
WE KNOW...
SO NO ONE'S SAID ANYTHING.
AND IF YOU GET TO SPEND MONEY ON THINGS THAT YOU LIKE...
ハッ
HA (GASP)
...EVERYONE...
...I GET IT...
...WHILE I'VE BEEN POURING FUNDS INTO SOMETHING I LIKE...
...I SCOLDED YOU ALL FOR BUYING THINGS YOU DIDN'T NEED... AND DIDN'T TRY TO UNDERSTAND THAT YOU BOUGHT THEM BECAUSE YOU LIKE THEM TOO...
BAD!
I'M SORRY!
FROM NOW ON, I'LL PAY FOR OUR EXPENSES OUT OF MY OWN POCKET, SO PLEASE FORGIVE ME!
WAAAH!
OH... THAT'S QUITE ALL RIGHT.
THAT WAS TOO EASY......
EVERYONE IS QUITE ACCUSTOMED TO HANDLING THE LEADER.
KATA (TAP)
カタ
KATA
カタ
INCIDENTALLY...
...MAYBE I SHOULD GET...
...A PORTABLE GPS SO THE LEADER DOESN'T GET LOST...
...HE ONLY BUYS THINGS USEFUL TO THE TEAM.
BUT THEN, THAT MUST BE WHAT HE LIKES...
END

BLOOD LAD 7

These images appeared under the jacket of the original edition of *Blood Lad*!

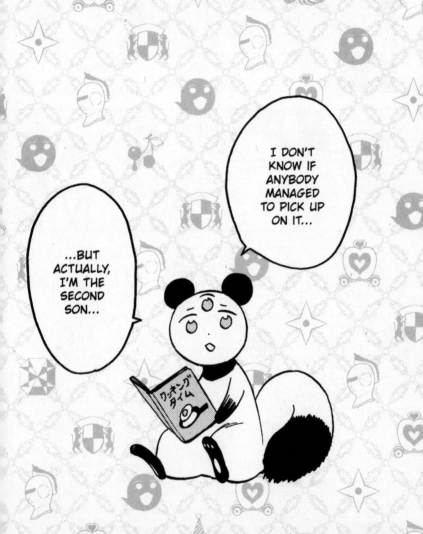

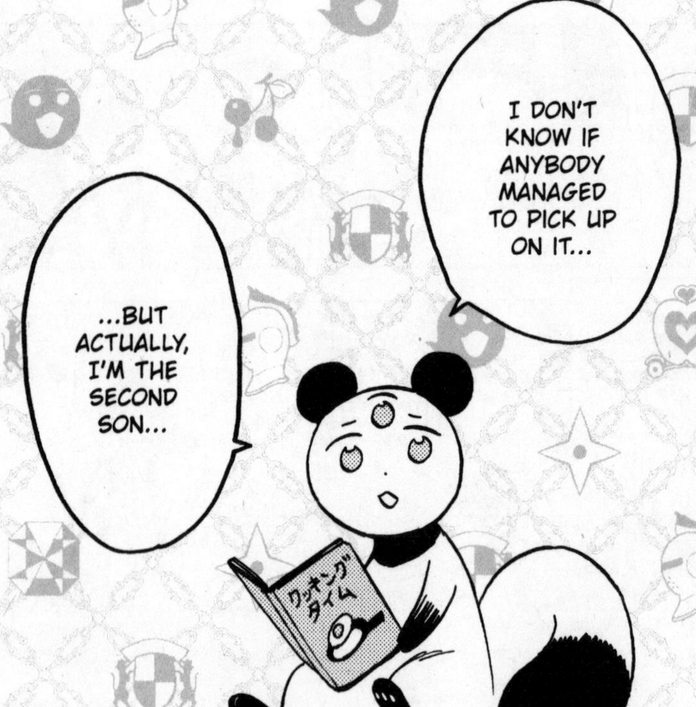
I DON'T KNOW IF ANYBODY MANAGED TO PICK UP ON IT...
...BUT ACTUALLY, I'M THE SECOND SON...

BOOK: COOKING TIME
NOTE: THE "JIROU" IN MAMEJIROU IS A NAME ENDING FOR THE SECOND SON IN A FAMILY. IT WOULD BE OBVIOUS FROM READING HIS NAME.

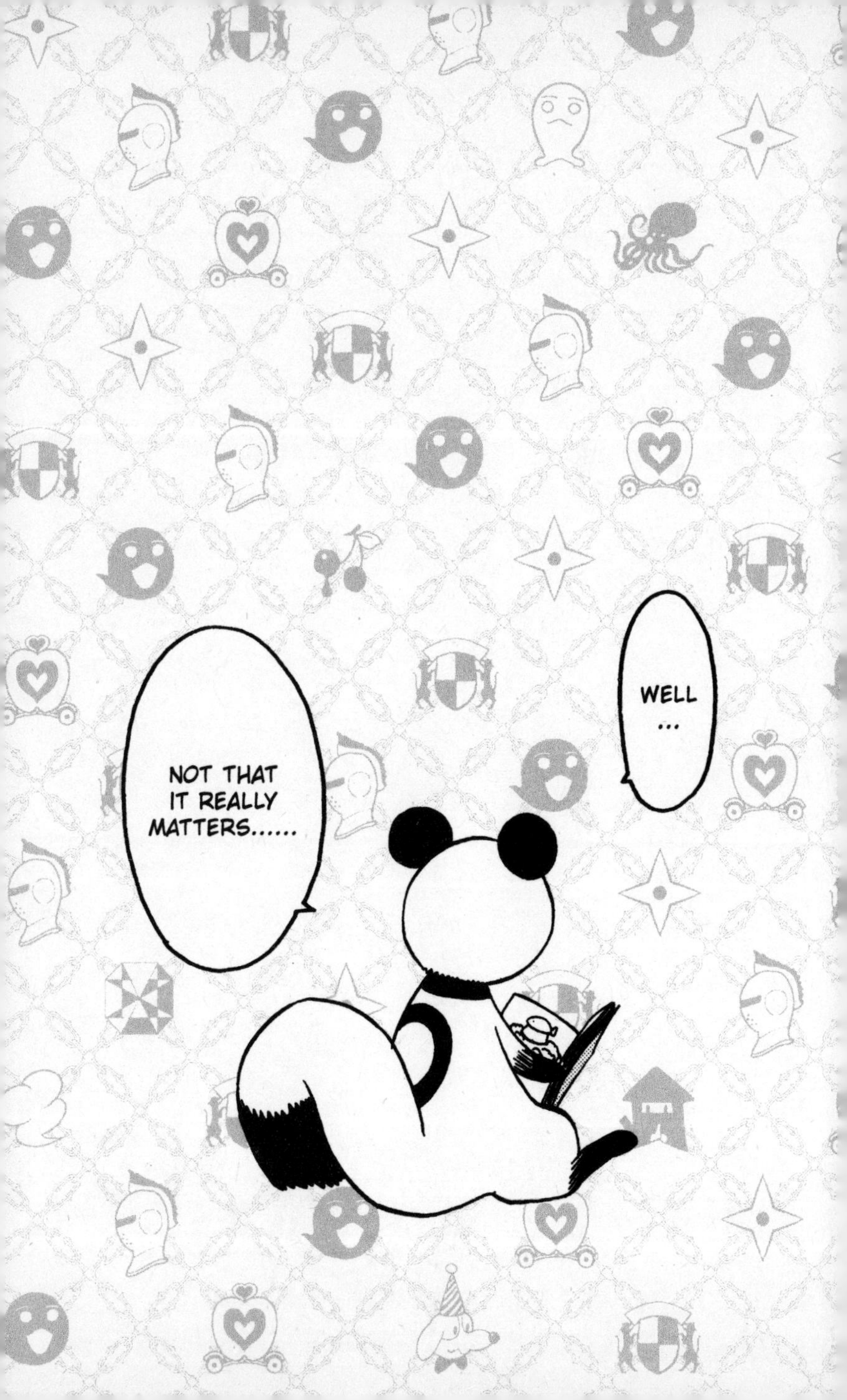
WELL ...
NOT THAT IT REALLY MATTERS......

BLOOD LAD

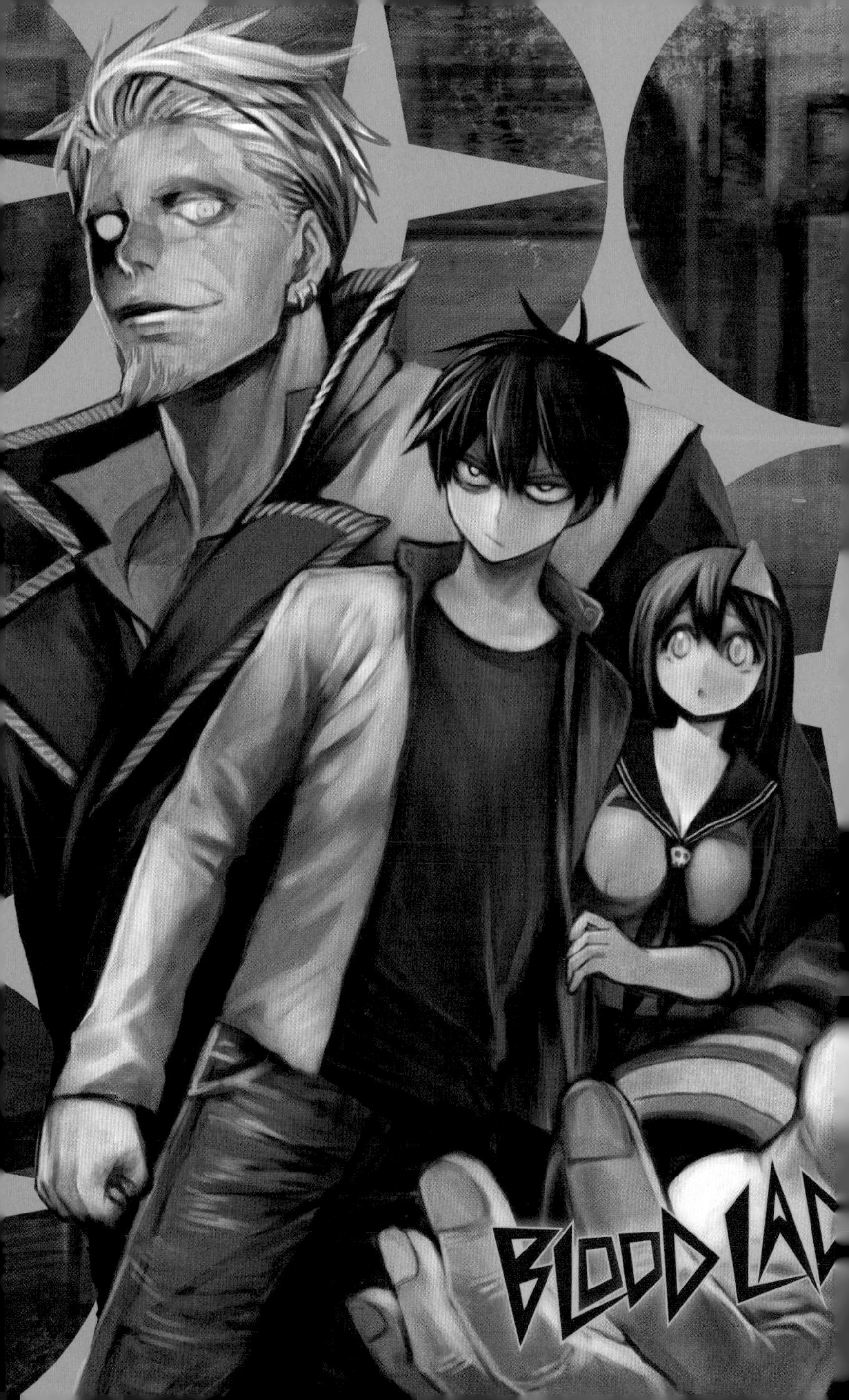
BLOOD LAD

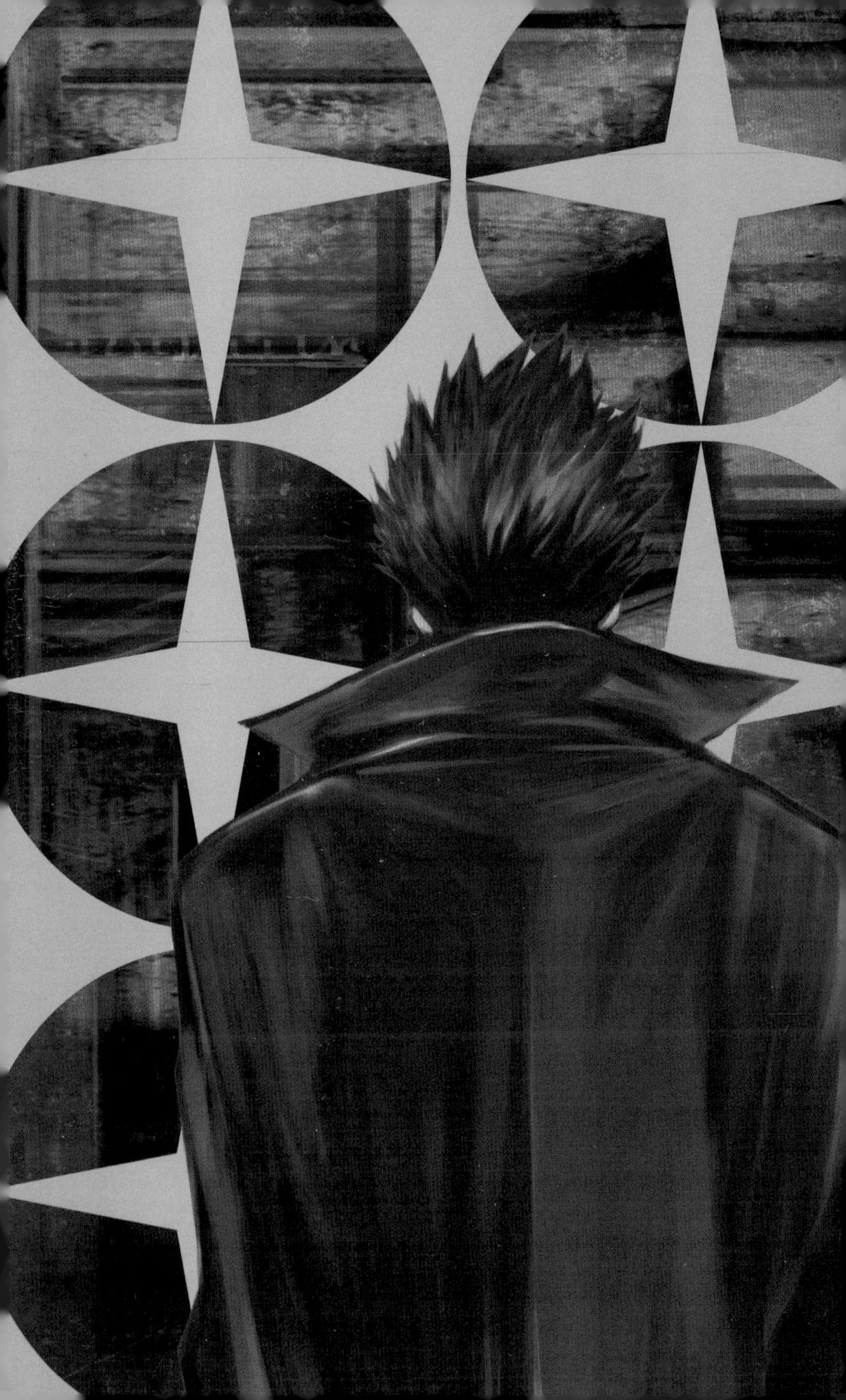

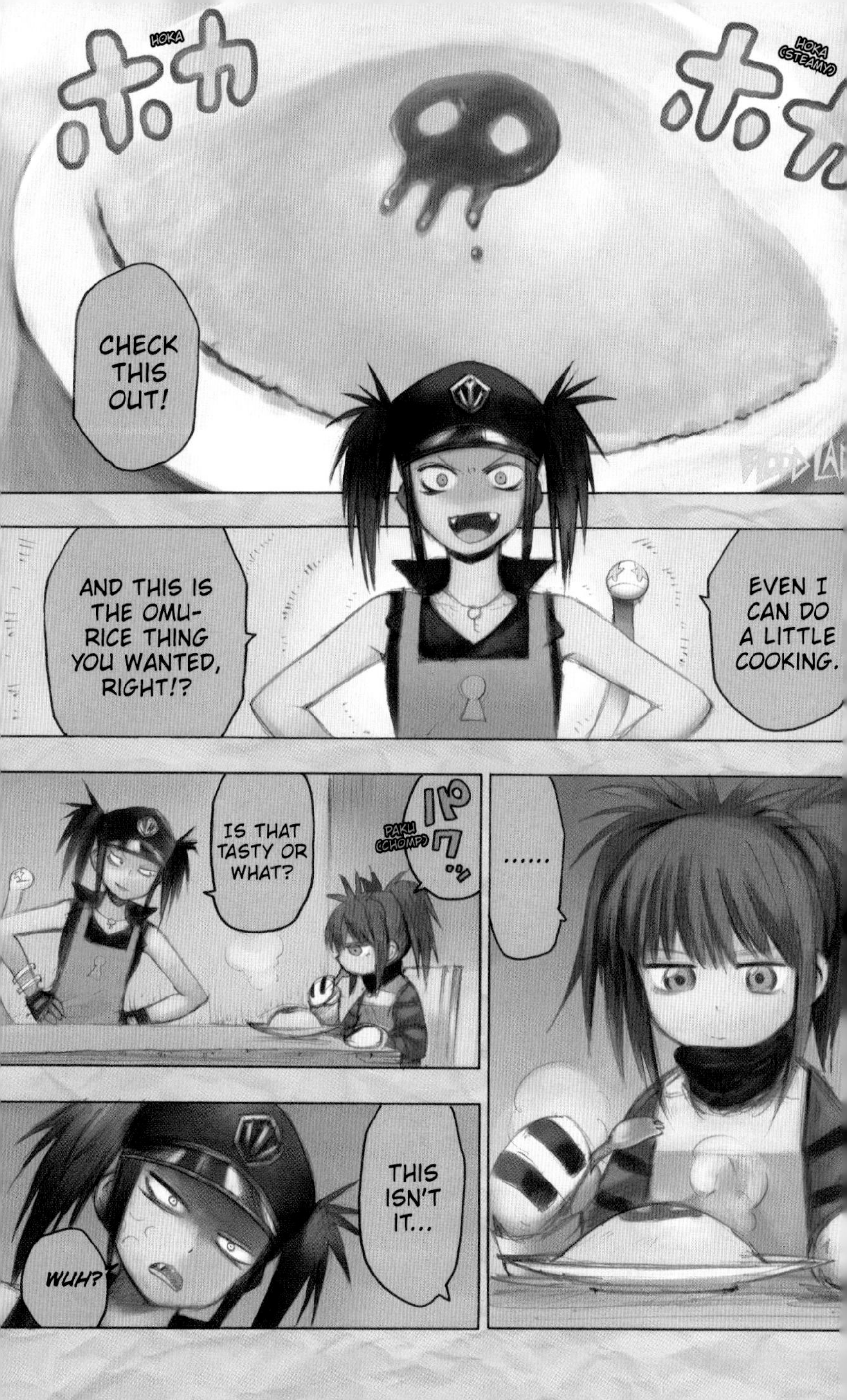
HOKA (STEAMY)
HOKA
CHECK THIS OUT!
EVEN I CAN DO A LITTLE COOKING.
AND THIS IS THE OMU-RICE THING YOU WANTED, RIGHT!?
......
PAKU (CHOMP)
IS THAT TASTY OR WHAT?
THIS ISN'T IT...
WUH?

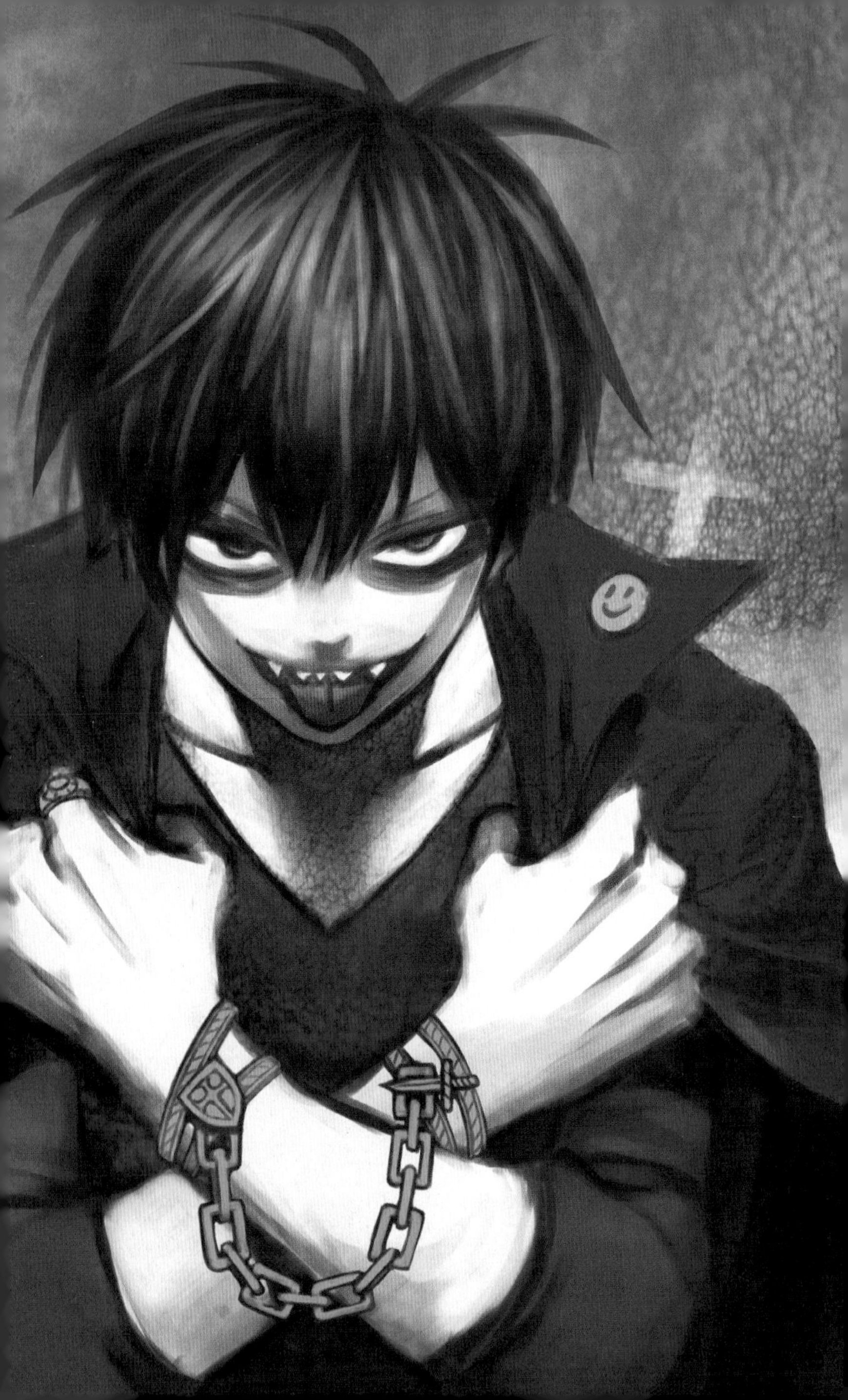

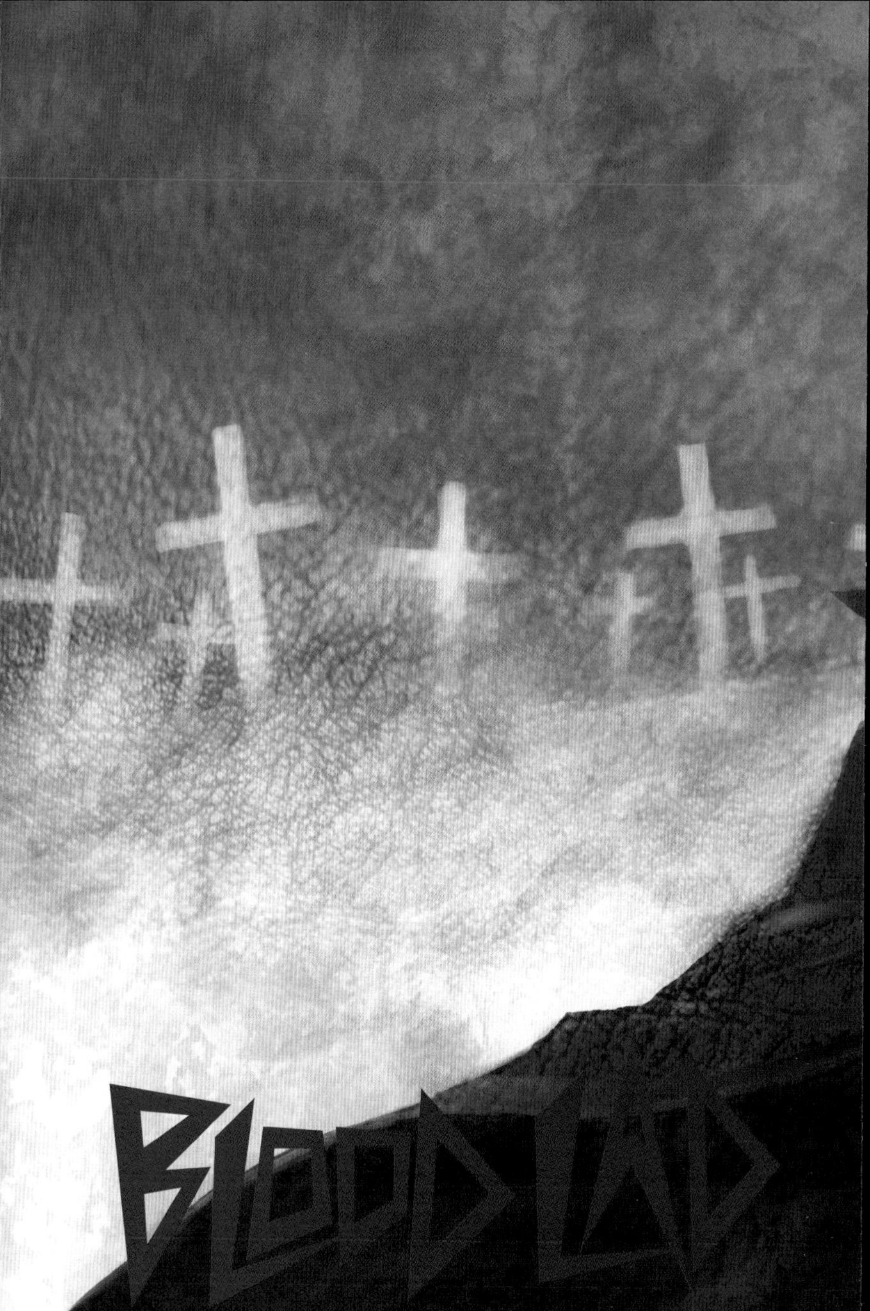
BLOOD LAD

CHAPTER 36 ♠ BREAK INTO THE ACROPOLIS CAVES!

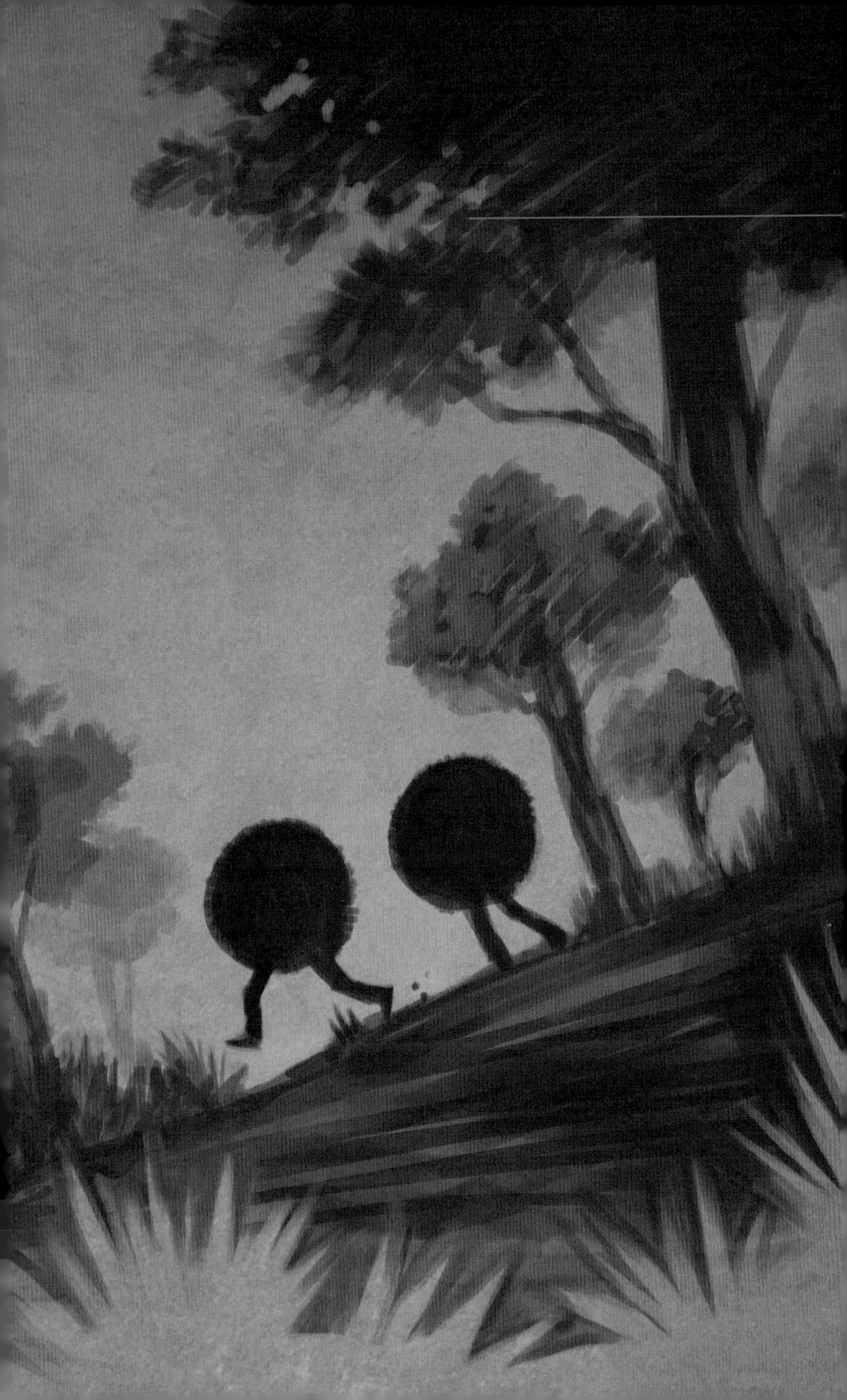

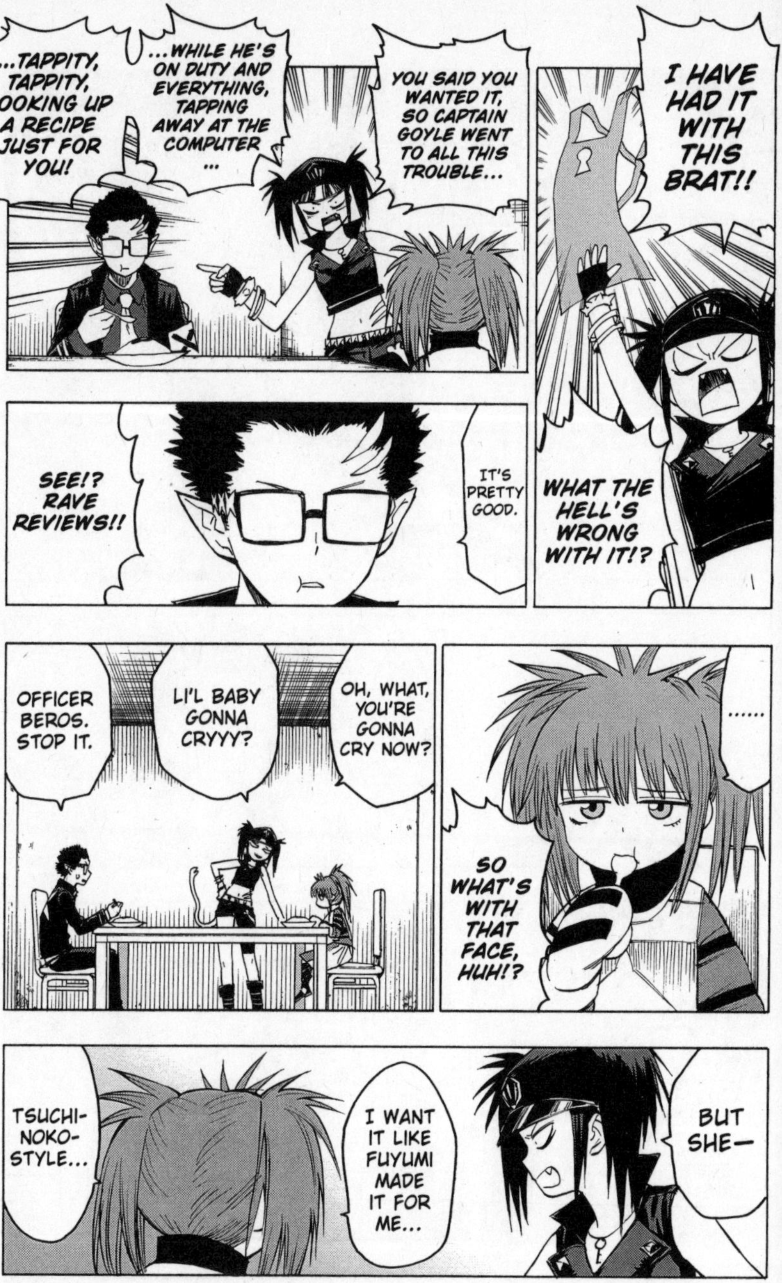
I HAVE HAD IT WITH THIS BRAT!!
WHAT THE HELL'S WRONG WITH IT!?
YOU SAID YOU WANTED IT, SO CAPTAIN GOYLE WENT TO ALL THIS TROUBLE...
...WHILE HE'S ON DUTY AND EVERYTHING, TAPPING AWAY AT THE COMPUTER ...
...TAPPITY, TAPPITY, LOOKING UP A RECIPE JUST FOR YOU!
IT'S PRETTY GOOD.
SEE!? RAVE REVIEWS!!
......
SO WHAT'S WITH THAT FACE, HUH!?
OH, WHAT, YOU'RE GONNA CRY NOW?
LI'L BABY GONNA CRYYY?
OFFICER BEROS. STOP IT.
BUT SHE—
I WANT IT LIKE FUYUMI MADE IT FOR ME...
TSUCHI-NOKO-STYLE...

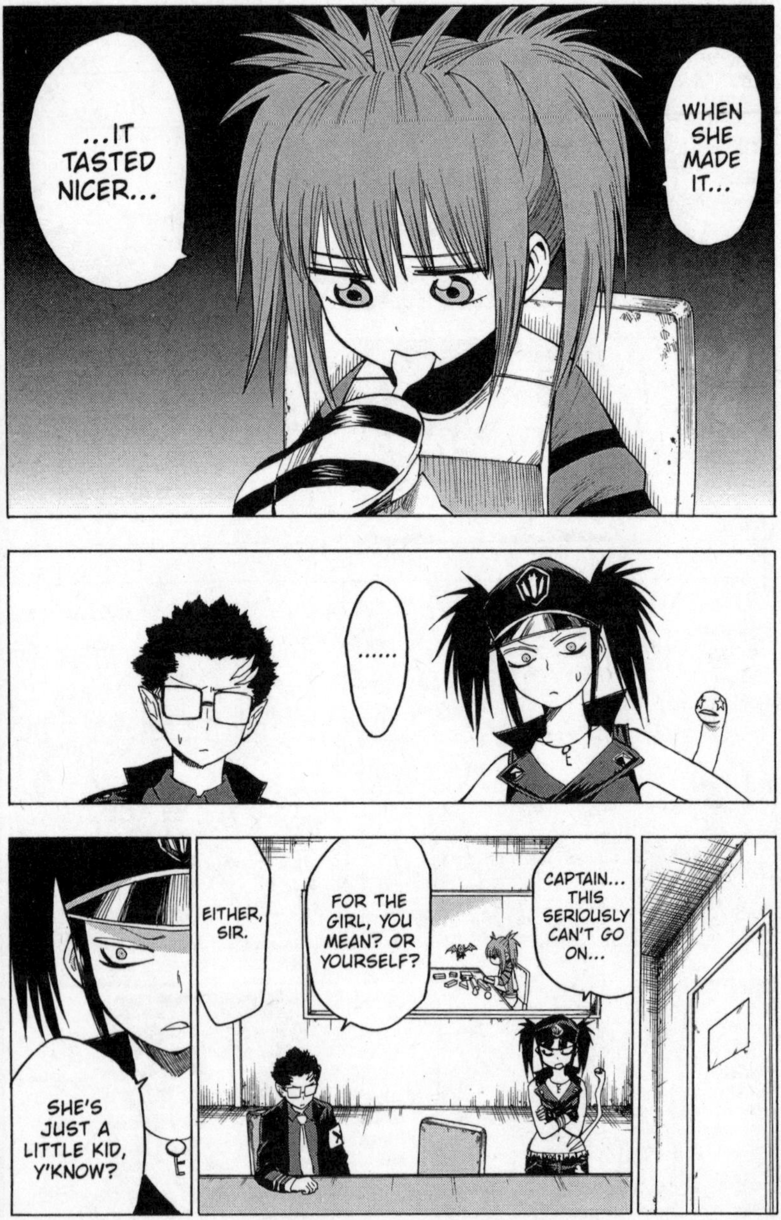
WHEN SHE MADE IT...
...IT TASTED NICER...
......
CAPTAIN... THIS SERIOUSLY CAN'T GO ON...
FOR THE GIRL, YOU MEAN? OR YOURSELF?
EITHER, SIR.
SHE'S JUST A LITTLE KID, Y'KNOW?

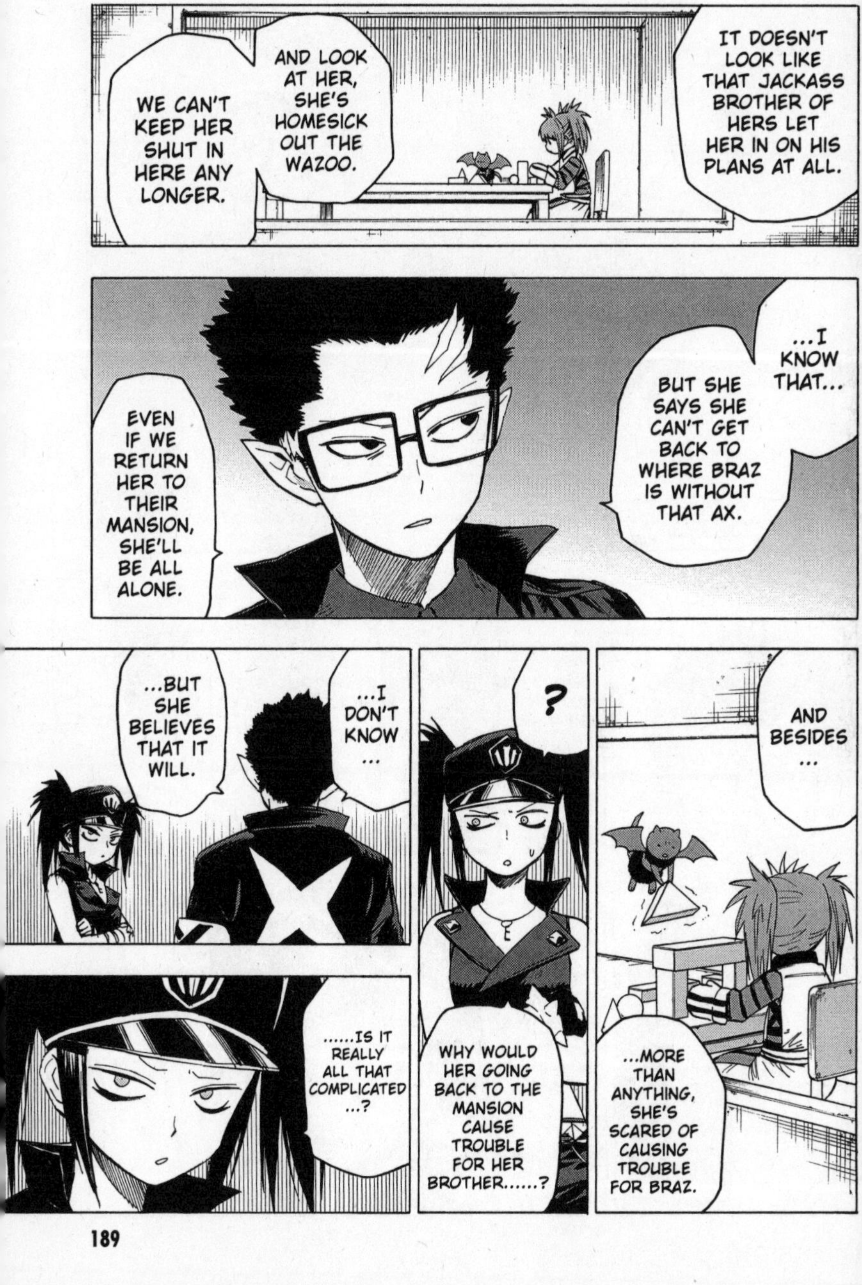
IT DOESN'T LOOK LIKE THAT JACKASS BROTHER OF HERS LET HER IN ON HIS PLANS AT ALL.
AND LOOK AT HER, SHE'S HOMESICK OUT THE WAZOO.
WE CAN'T KEEP HER SHUT IN HERE ANY LONGER.
...I KNOW THAT...
BUT SHE SAYS SHE CAN'T GET BACK TO WHERE BRAZ IS WITHOUT THAT AX.
EVEN IF WE RETURN HER TO THEIR MANSION, SHE'LL BE ALL ALONE.
AND BESIDES ...
...MORE THAN ANYTHING, SHE'S SCARED OF CAUSING TROUBLE FOR BRAZ.
?
WHY WOULD HER GOING BACK TO THE MANSION CAUSE TROUBLE FOR HER BROTHER......?
...I DON'T KNOW ...
...BUT SHE BELIEVES THAT IT WILL.
......IS IT REALLY ALL THAT COMPLICATED ...?

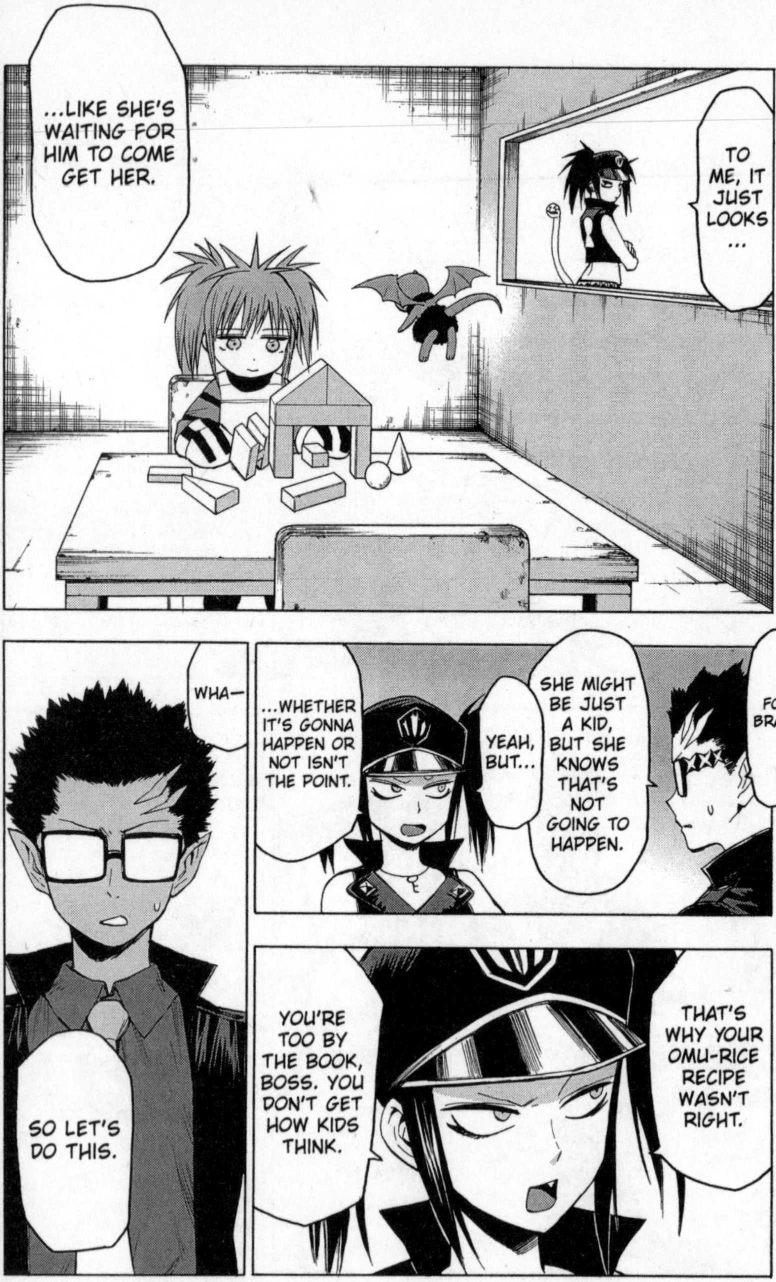
TO ME, IT JUST LOOKS...
...LIKE SHE'S WAITING FOR HIM TO COME GET HER.
FOR BRAZ?
SHE MIGHT BE JUST A KID, BUT SHE KNOWS THAT'S NOT GOING TO HAPPEN.
YEAH, BUT...
...WHETHER IT'S GONNA HAPPEN OR NOT ISN'T THE POINT.
THAT'S WHY YOUR OMU-RICE RECIPE WASN'T RIGHT.
YOU'RE TOO BY THE BOOK, BOSS. YOU DON'T GET HOW KIDS THINK.
WHA—
SO LET'S DO THIS.

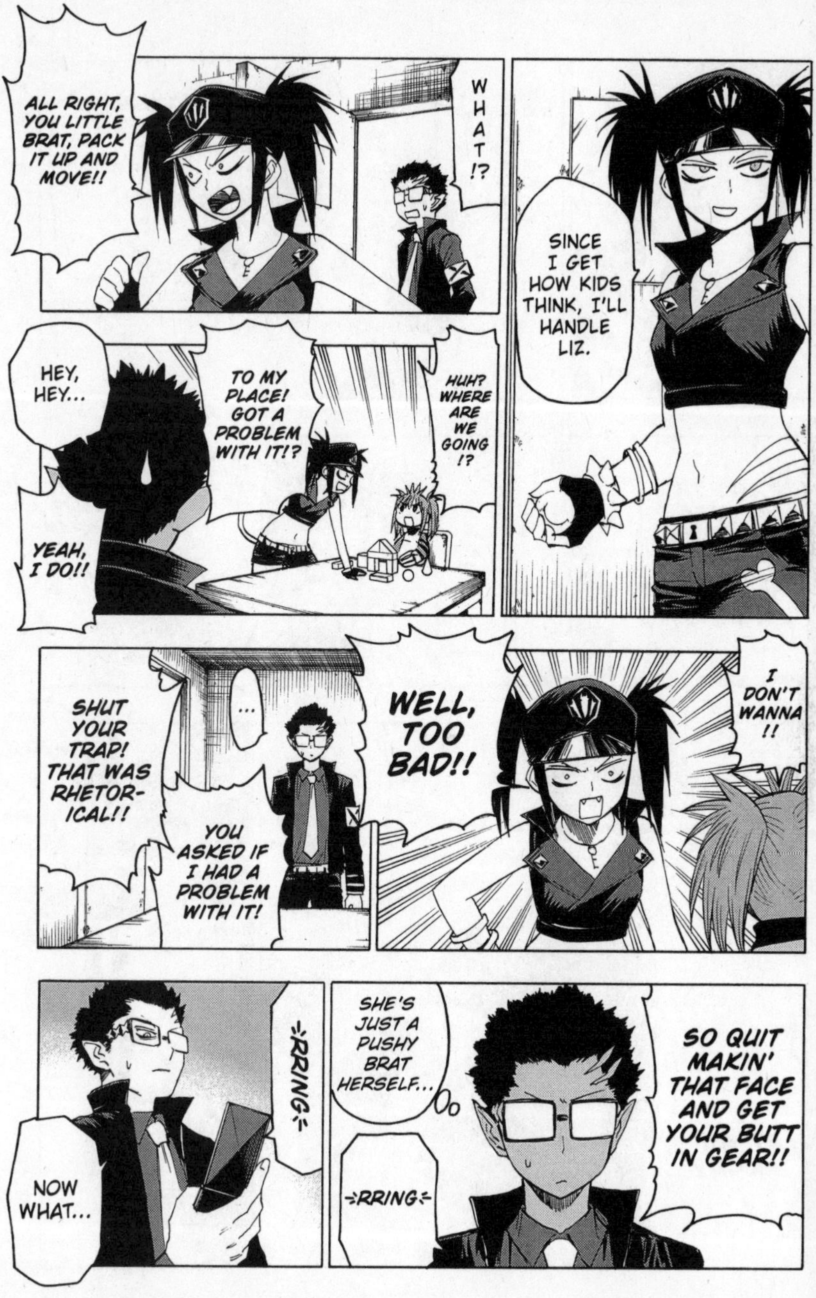
SINCE I GET HOW KIDS THINK, I'LL HANDLE LIZ.
WHAT!?
ALL RIGHT, YOU LITTLE BRAT, PACK IT UP AND MOVE!!
HUH? WHERE ARE WE GOING!?
TO MY PLACE! GOT A PROBLEM WITH IT!?
HEY, HEY...
YEAH, I DO!!
I DON'T WANNA!!
WELL, TOO BAD!!
...
YOU ASKED IF I HAD A PROBLEM WITH IT!
SHUT YOUR TRAP! THAT WAS RHETORICAL!!
SO QUIT MAKIN' THAT FACE AND GET YOUR BUTT IN GEAR!!
SHE'S JUST A PUSHY BRAT HERSELF...
RRING
RRING
NOW WHAT...

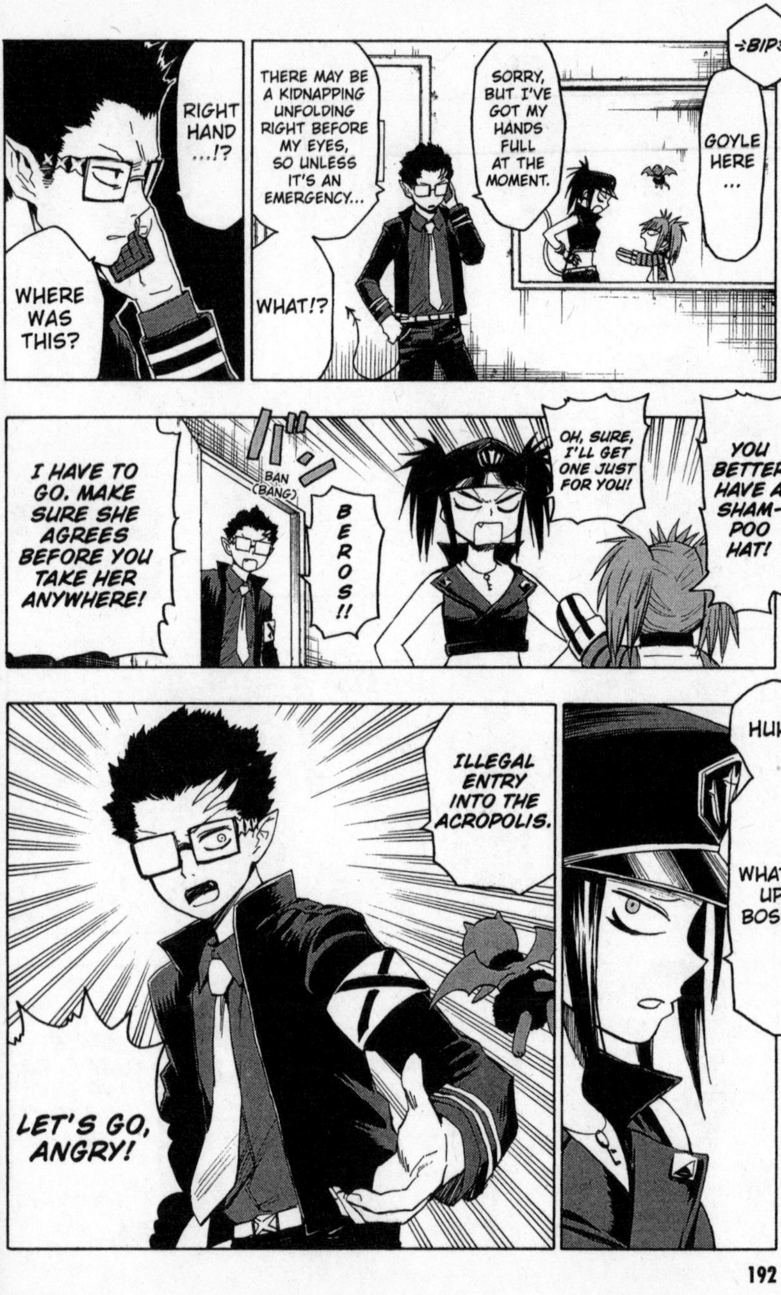
BIP
GOYLE HERE...
SORRY, BUT I'VE GOT MY HANDS FULL AT THE MOMENT.
THERE MAY BE A KIDNAPPING UNFOLDING RIGHT BEFORE MY EYES, SO UNLESS IT'S AN EMERGENCY...
WHAT!?
RIGHT HAND...!?
WHERE WAS THIS?
YOU BETTER HAVE A SHAMPOO HAT!
OH, SURE, I'LL GET ONE JUST FOR YOU!
BEROS!!
BAN (BANG)
I HAVE TO GO. MAKE SURE SHE AGREES BEFORE YOU TAKE HER ANYWHERE!
HUH?
WHAT'S UP, BOSS?
ILLEGAL ENTRY INTO THE ACROPOLIS.
LET'S GO, ANGRY!

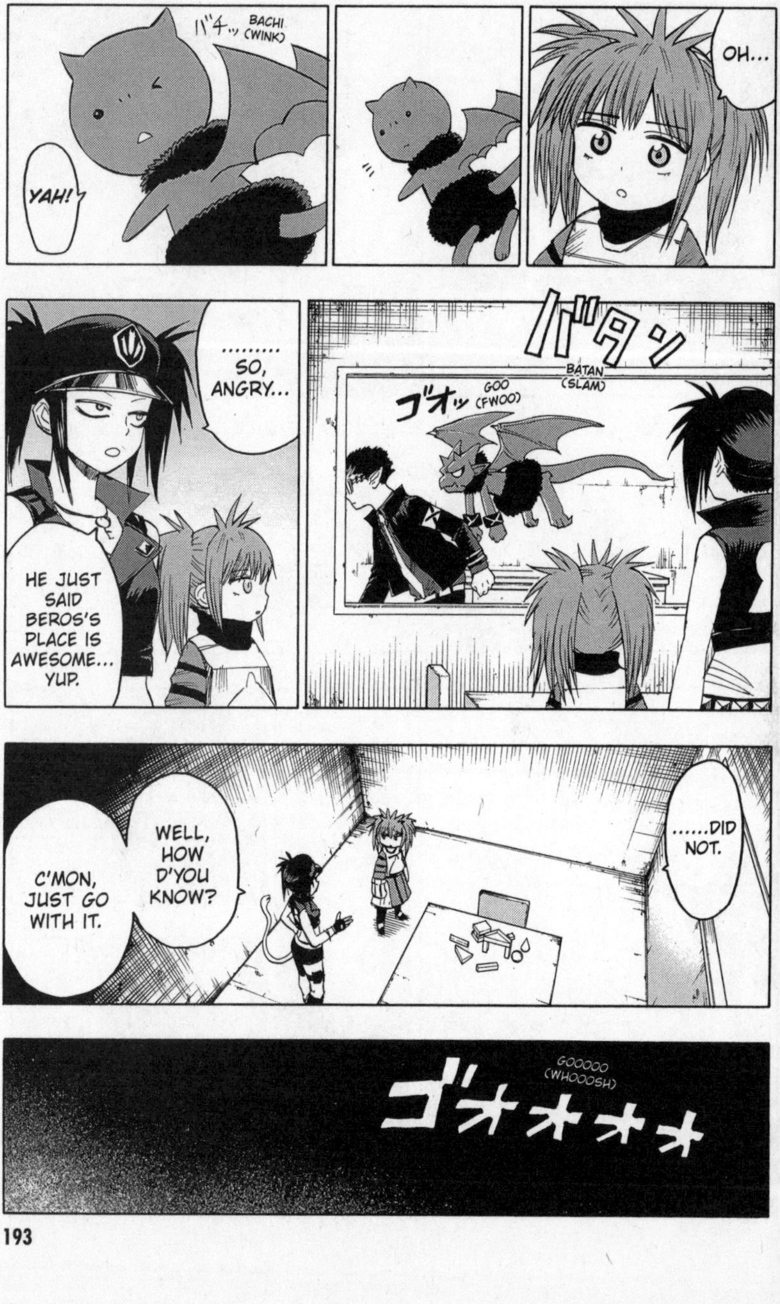
OH...
バチッ
BACHI (WINK)
YAH!
バタン
BATAN (SLAM)
ゴオッ
GOO (FWOO)
....
SO, ANGRY...
HE JUST SAID BEROS'S PLACE IS AWESOME... YUP.
......DID NOT.
WELL, HOW D'YOU KNOW?
C'MON, JUST GO WITH IT.
GOOOOO (WHOOOSH)
ゴオオオオ

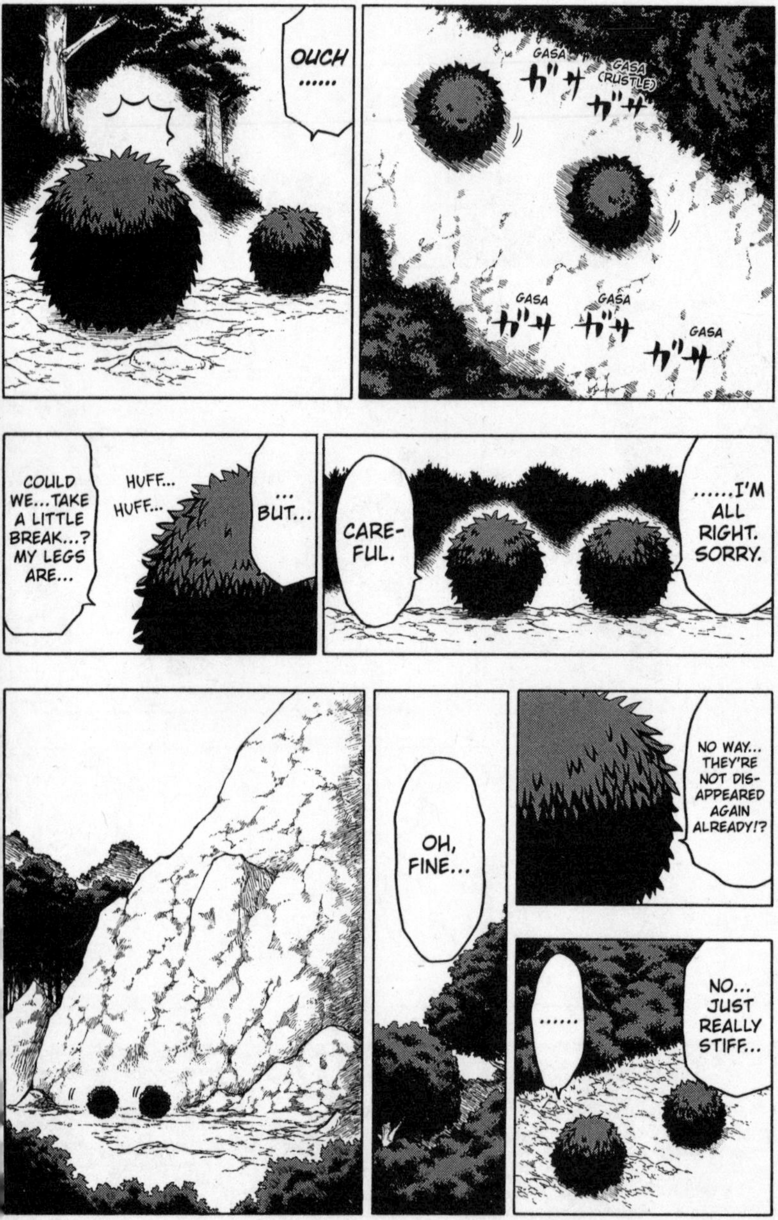
GASA ガサ
GASA (RUSTLE) ガサ
GASA ガサ
GASA ガサ
GASA ガサ
OUCH ......
......I'M ALL RIGHT. SORRY.
CARE-FUL.
... BUT...
HUFF... HUFF...
COULD WE...TAKE A LITTLE BREAK...? MY LEGS ARE...
NO WAY... THEY'RE NOT DIS-APPEARED AGAIN ALREADY!?
NO... JUST REALLY STIFF...
......
OH, FINE...

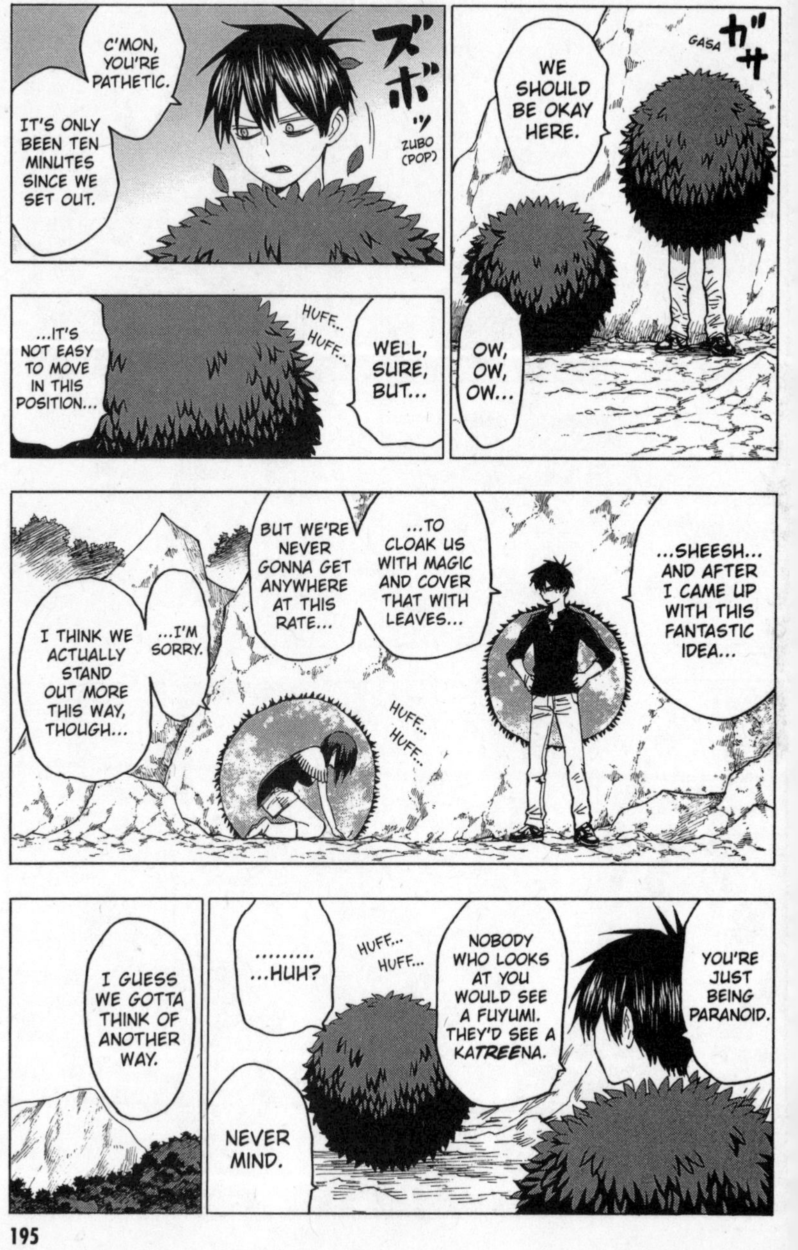
ガサ
GASA
WE SHOULD BE OKAY HERE.
OW, OW, OW...
ズボッ
ZUBO (POP)
C'MON, YOU'RE PATHETIC.
IT'S ONLY BEEN TEN MINUTES SINCE WE SET OUT.
WELL, SURE, BUT...
HUFF... HUFF...
...IT'S NOT EASY TO MOVE IN THIS POSITION...
...SHEESH... AND AFTER I CAME UP WITH THIS FANTASTIC IDEA...
...TO CLOAK US WITH MAGIC AND COVER THAT WITH LEAVES...
HUFF... HUFF...
BUT WE'RE NEVER GONNA GET ANYWHERE AT THIS RATE...
...I'M SORRY.
I THINK WE ACTUALLY STAND OUT MORE THIS WAY, THOUGH...
YOU'RE JUST BEING PARANOID.
NOBODY WHO LOOKS AT YOU WOULD SEE A FUYUMI. THEY'D SEE A KATREENA.
HUFF... HUFF...
....HUH?
NEVER MIND.
I GUESS WE GOTTA THINK OF ANOTHER WAY.

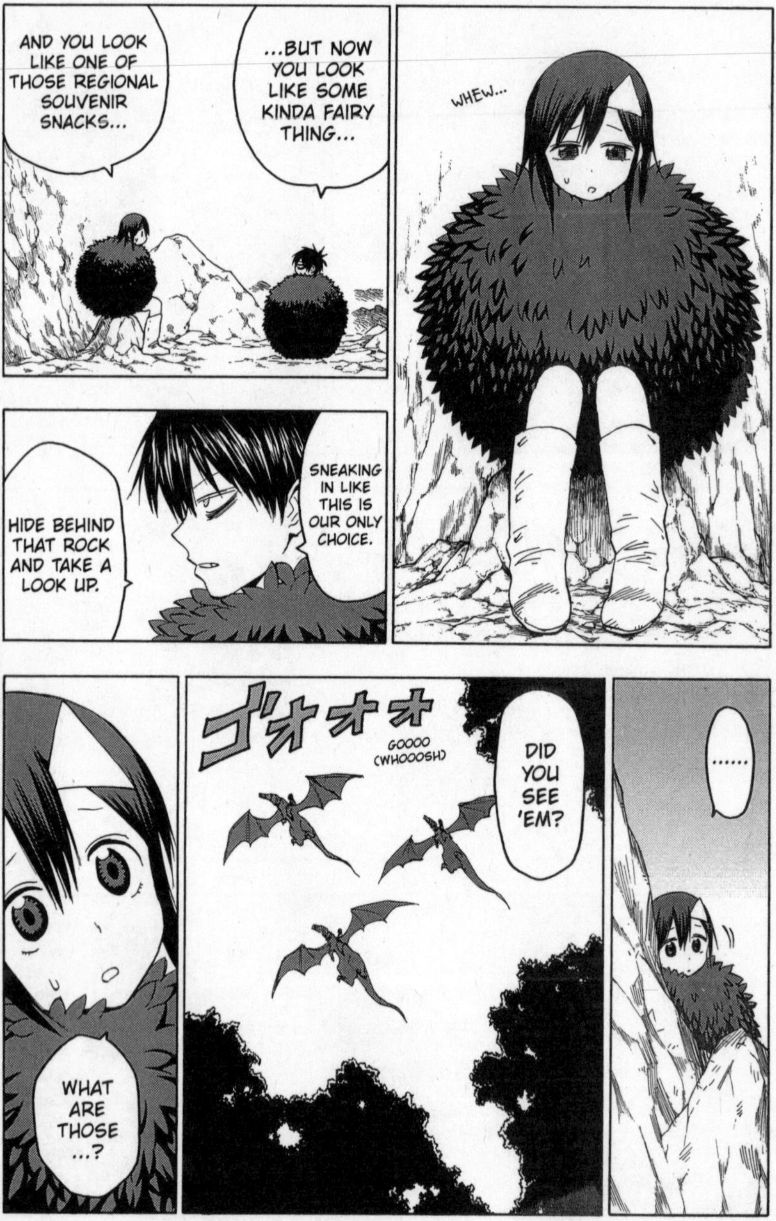
WHEW...
...BUT NOW YOU LOOK LIKE SOME KINDA FAIRY THING...
AND YOU LOOK LIKE ONE OF THOSE REGIONAL SOUVENIR SNACKS...
SNEAKING IN LIKE THIS IS OUR ONLY CHOICE.
HIDE BEHIND THAT ROCK AND TAKE A LOOK UP.
......
DID YOU SEE 'EM?
ゴオオオ
GOOOO (WHOOOSH)
WHAT ARE THOSE ...?

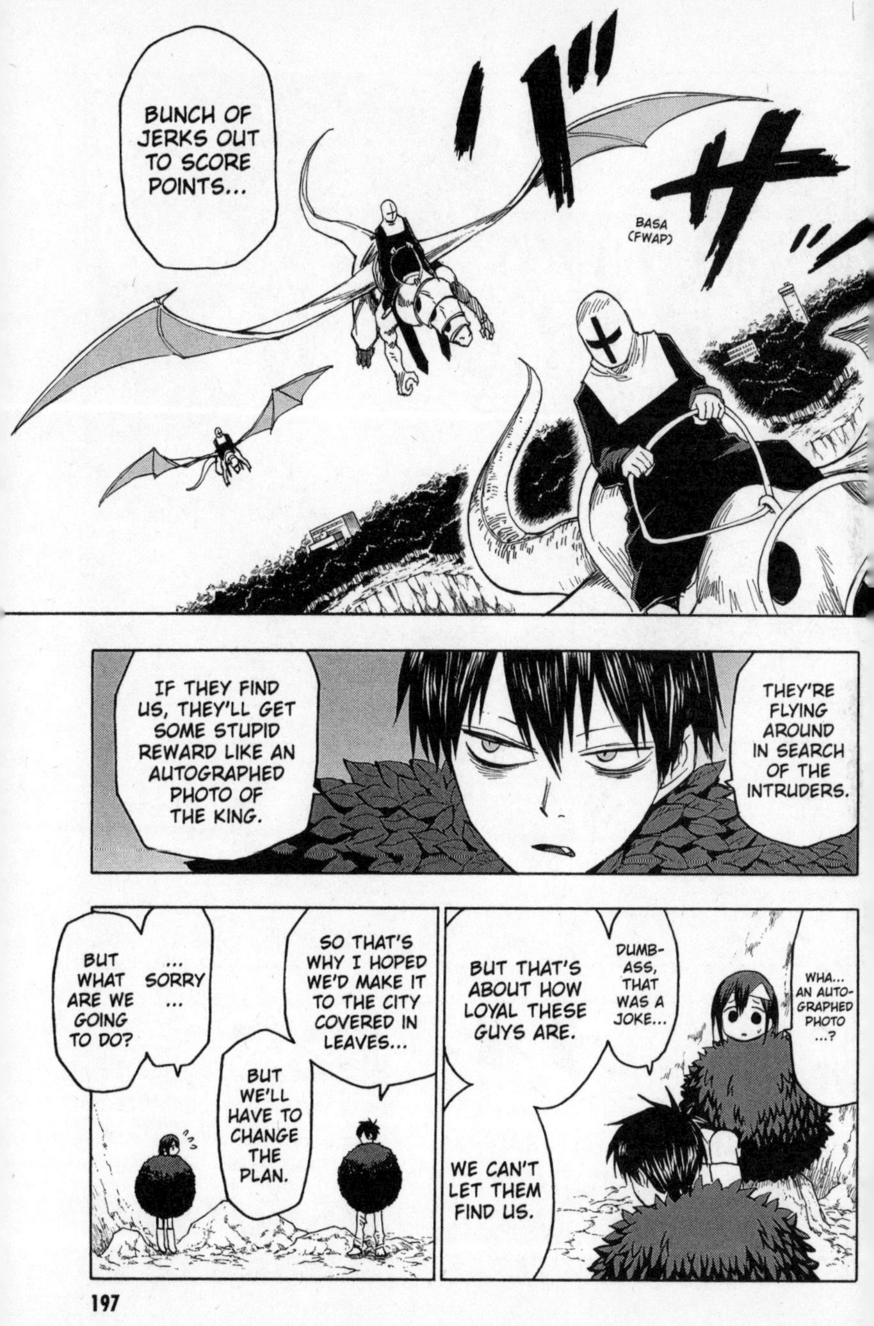
BASA (FWAP)
BUNCH OF JERKS OUT TO SCORE POINTS...
THEY'RE FLYING AROUND IN SEARCH OF THE INTRUDERS.
IF THEY FIND US, THEY'LL GET SOME STUPID REWARD LIKE AN AUTOGRAPHED PHOTO OF THE KING.
WHA... AN AUTO-GRAPHED PHOTO ...?
DUMB-ASS, THAT WAS A JOKE...
BUT THAT'S ABOUT HOW LOYAL THESE GUYS ARE.
WE CAN'T LET THEM FIND US.
SO THAT'S WHY I HOPED WE'D MAKE IT TO THE CITY COVERED IN LEAVES...
BUT WE'LL HAVE TO CHANGE THE PLAN.
... SORRY ...
BUT WHAT ARE WE GOING TO DO?

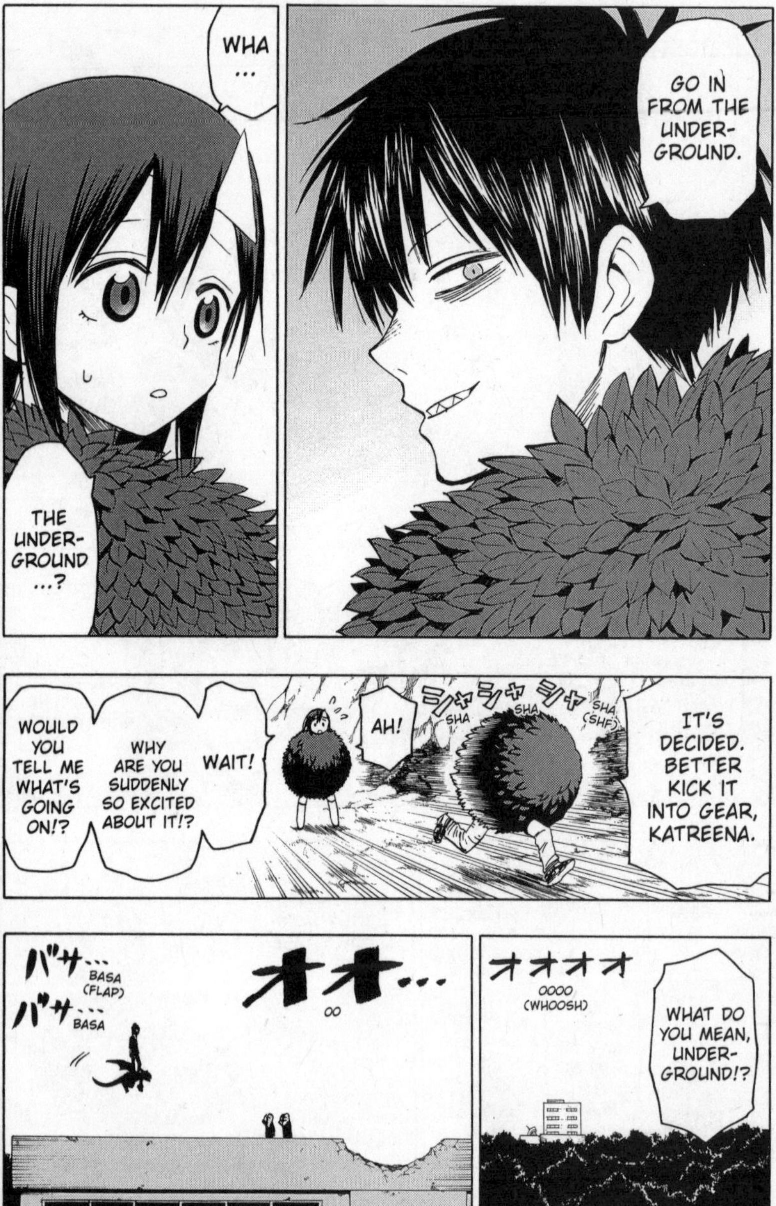
GO IN FROM THE UNDER-GROUND.
WHA ...
THE UNDER-GROUND ...?
IT'S DECIDED. BETTER KICK IT INTO GEAR, KATREENA.
シャシャシャ
SHA SHA SHA (SHF)
AH!
WAIT!
WHY ARE YOU SUDDENLY SO EXCITED ABOUT IT!?
WOULD YOU TELL ME WHAT'S GOING ON!?
オオオオ
OOOO (WHOOSH)
WHAT DO YOU MEAN, UNDER-GROUND!?
オオ…
OO
バサ…
BASA (FLAP)
バサ…
BASA

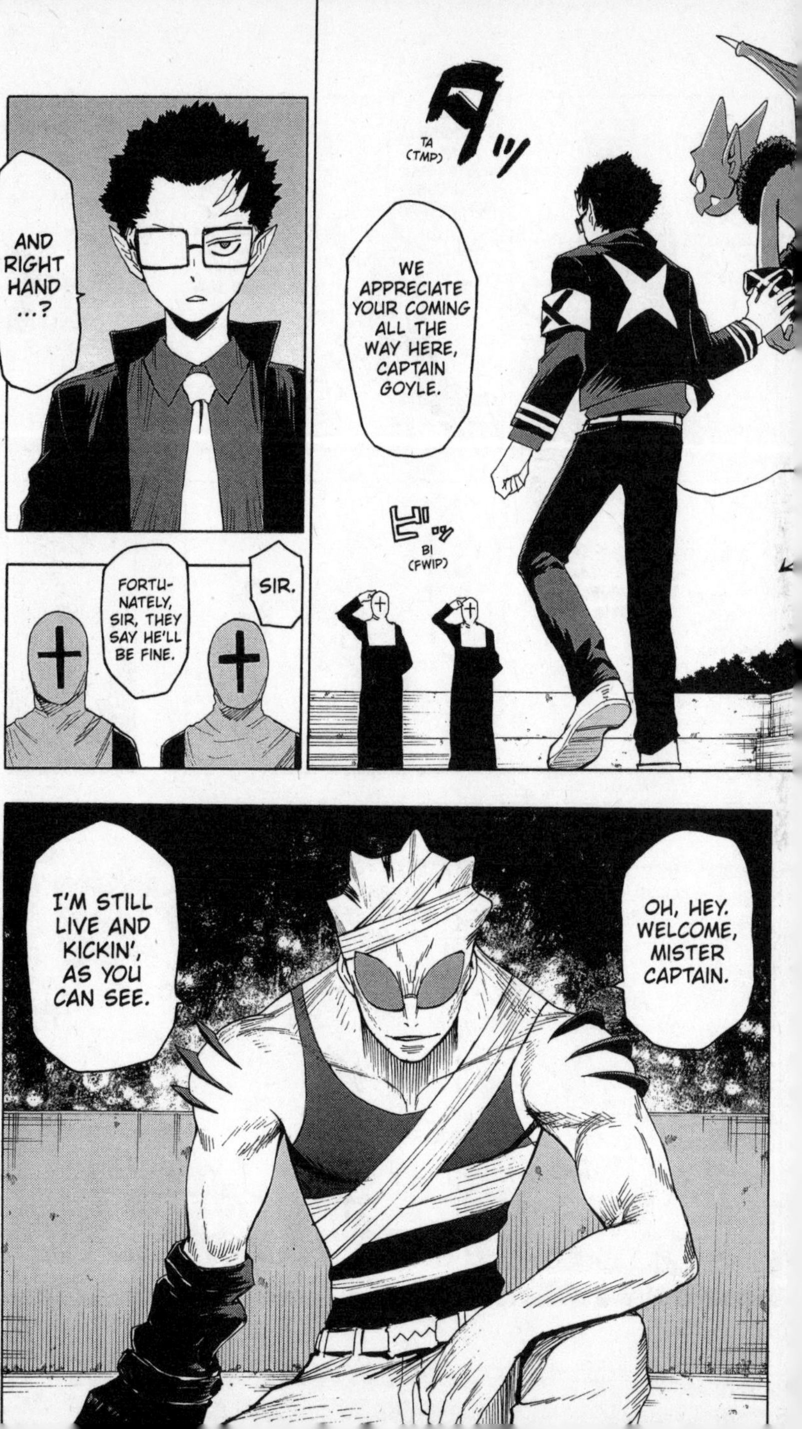

タッ
TA (TMP)
WE APPRECIATE YOUR COMING ALL THE WAY HERE, CAPTAIN GOYLE.
ビッ
BI (FWIP)
AND RIGHT HAND ...?
SIR.
FORTUNATELY, SIR, THEY SAY HE'LL BE FINE.
OH, HEY. WELCOME, MISTER CAPTAIN.
I'M STILL LIVE AND KICKIN', AS YOU CAN SEE.

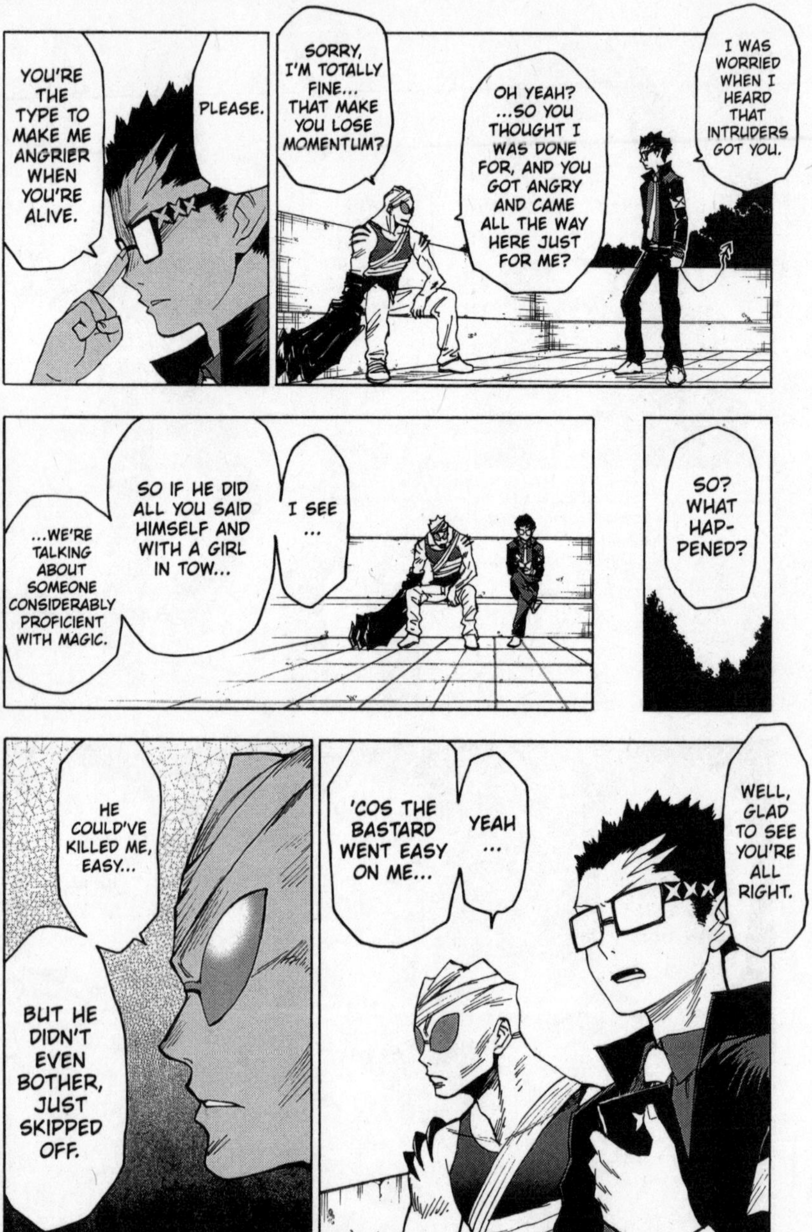
I WAS WORRIED WHEN I HEARD THAT INTRUDERS GOT YOU.
OH YEAH? ...SO YOU THOUGHT I WAS DONE FOR, AND YOU GOT ANGRY AND CAME ALL THE WAY HERE JUST FOR ME?
SORRY, I'M TOTALLY FINE... THAT MAKE YOU LOSE MOMENTUM?
PLEASE.
YOU'RE THE TYPE TO MAKE ME ANGRIER WHEN YOU'RE ALIVE.
SO? WHAT HAP-PENED?
I SEE ...
SO IF HE DID ALL YOU SAID HIMSELF AND WITH A GIRL IN TOW...
...WE'RE TALKING ABOUT SOMEONE CONSIDERABLY PROFICIENT WITH MAGIC.
WELL, GLAD TO SEE YOU'RE ALL RIGHT.
YEAH ...
'COS THE BASTARD WENT EASY ON ME...
HE COULD'VE KILLED ME, EASY...
BUT HE DIDN'T EVEN BOTHER, JUST SKIPPED OFF.

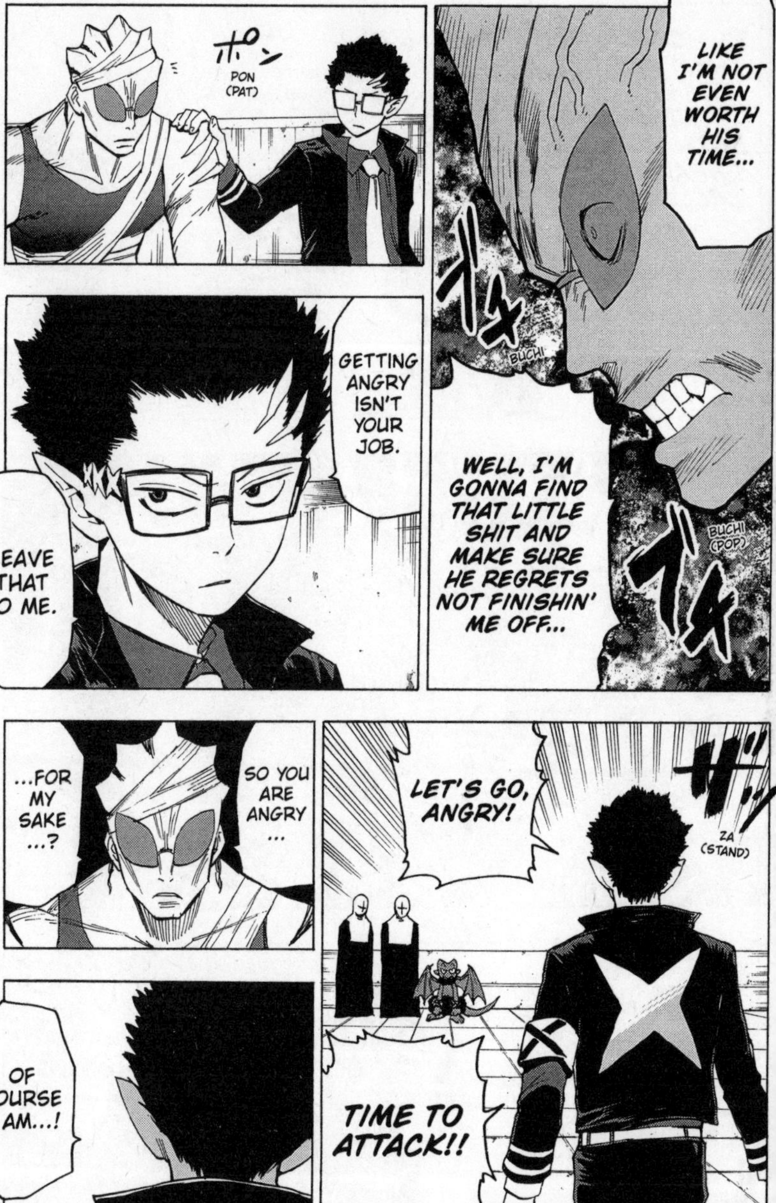

LIKE I'M NOT EVEN WORTH HIS TIME...
BUCHI
WELL, I'M GONNA FIND THAT LITTLE SHIT AND MAKE SURE HE REGRETS NOT FINISHIN' ME OFF...
BUCHI (POP)
ポン
PON (PAT)
GETTING ANGRY ISN'T YOUR JOB.
LEAVE THAT TO ME.
ZA (STAND)
LET'S GO, ANGRY!
TIME TO ATTACK!!
SO YOU ARE ANGRY...
...FOR MY SAKE...?
OF COURSE I AM...!

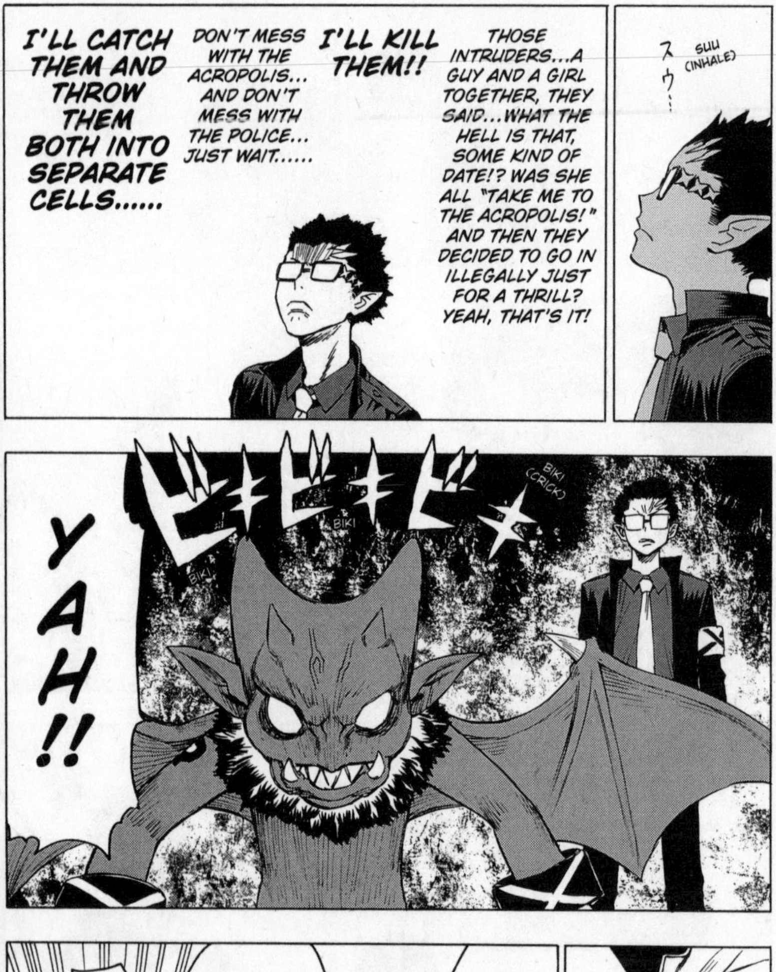
スゥ…
SUU (INHALE)
THOSE INTRUDERS...A GUY AND A GIRL TOGETHER, THEY SAID...WHAT THE HELL IS THAT, SOME KIND OF DATE!? WAS SHE ALL "TAKE ME TO THE ACROPOLIS!" AND THEN THEY DECIDED TO GO IN ILLEGALLY JUST FOR A THRILL? YEAH, THAT'S IT!
I'LL KILL THEM!!
DON'T MESS WITH THE ACROPOLIS... AND DON'T MESS WITH THE POLICE... JUST WAIT......
I'LL CATCH THEM AND THROW THEM BOTH INTO SEPARATE CELLS......
BIKI (CRICK)
BIKI
BIKI
YAH!!
WHOA...
I'LL BE PURSUING THE INTRUDERS FROM NOW ON.
RADIO THE OTHERS AND TELL THEM TO FOLLOW ME.
YES, SIR!

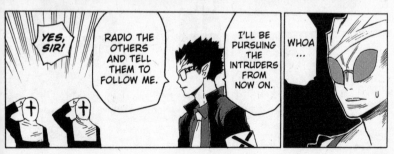

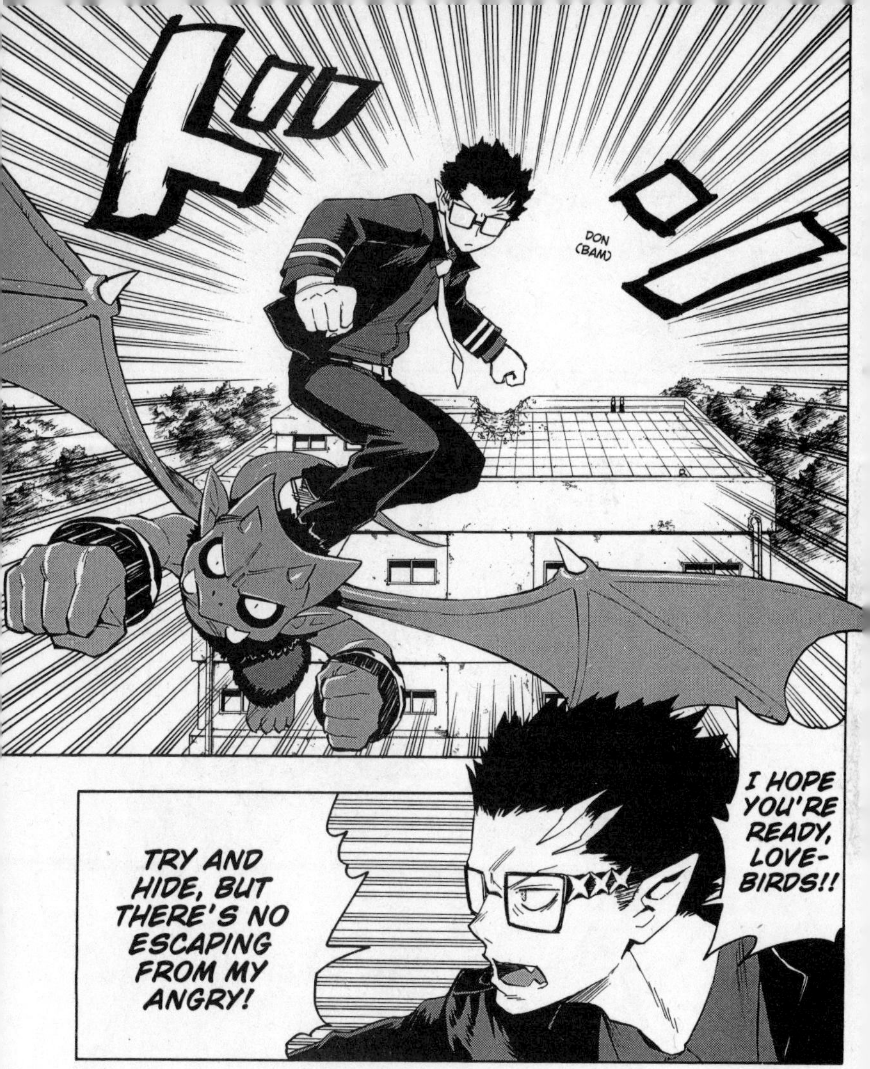
DON
(BAM)
I HOPE YOU'RE READY, LOVE-BIRDS!!
TRY AND HIDE, BUT THERE'S NO ESCAPING FROM MY ANGRY!
DOHYUN
(ZOOOM)

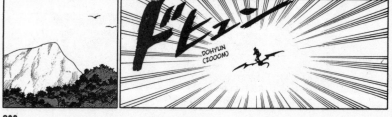

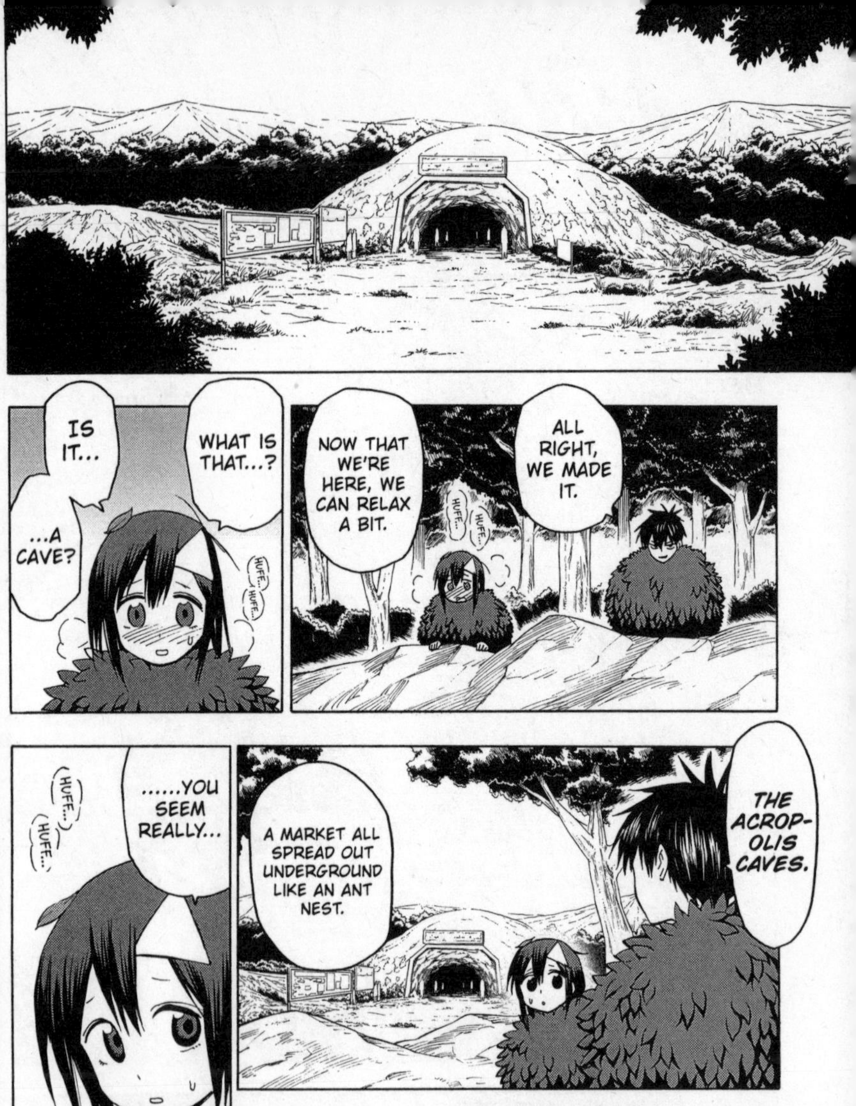
ALL RIGHT, WE MADE IT.
NOW THAT WE'RE HERE, WE CAN RELAX A BIT.
HUFF... HUFF...
WHAT IS THAT...?
IS IT...
...A CAVE?
HUFF... HUFF...
THE ACROP-OLIS CAVES.
A MARKET ALL SPREAD OUT UNDERGROUND LIKE AN ANT NEST.
WELL, IT'S GONNA BE PRETTY ROUND-ABOUT...
...BUT IT'S KIND OF A MAZE AND UNDERGROUND TO BOOT. CAN'T BEAT THAT FOR STAYING HIDDEN.
(HUFF...) (HUFF...)
......YOU SEEM REALLY...
...HAPPY ABOUT IT...

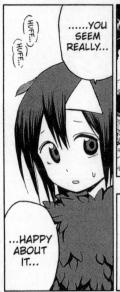

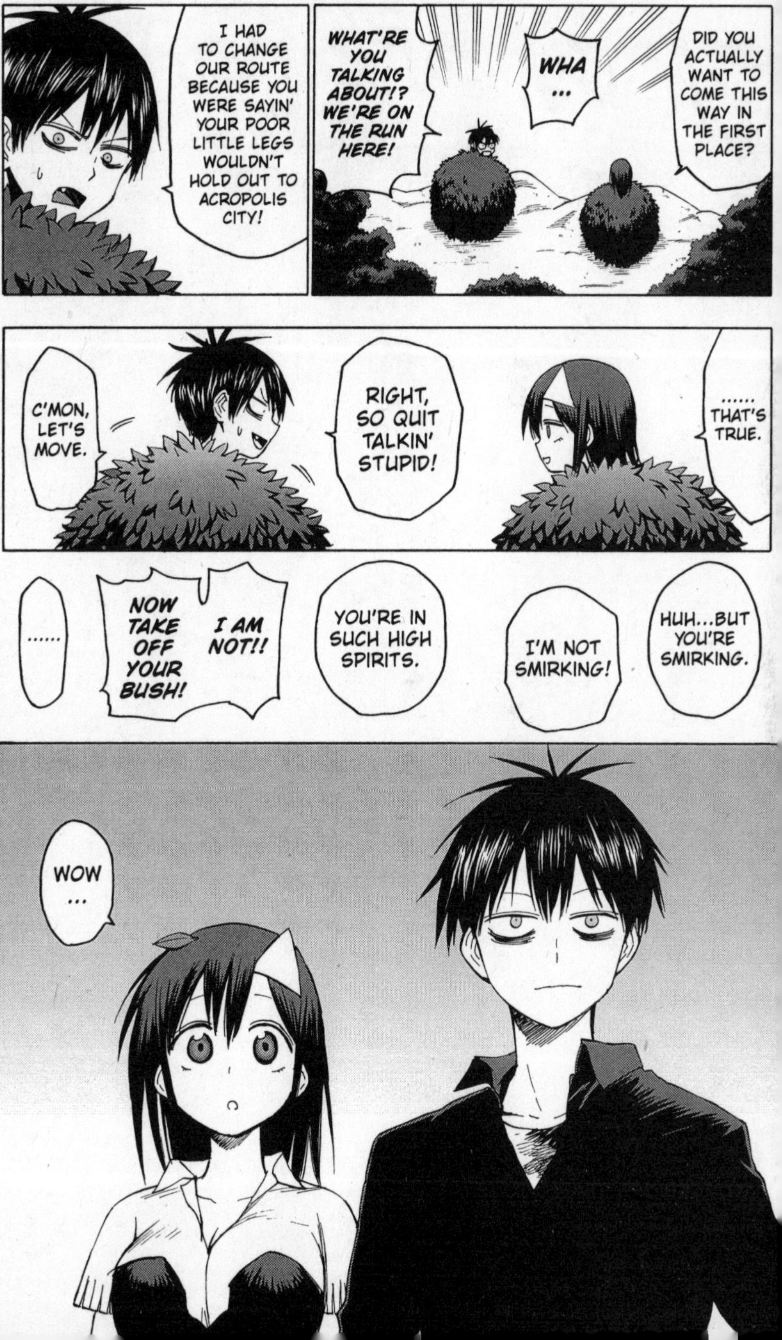
DID YOU ACTUALLY WANT TO COME THIS WAY IN THE FIRST PLACE?
WHA ...
WHAT'RE YOU TALKING ABOUT!? WE'RE ON THE RUN HERE!
I HAD TO CHANGE OUR ROUTE BECAUSE YOU WERE SAYIN' YOUR POOR LITTLE LEGS WOULDN'T HOLD OUT TO ACROPOLIS CITY!
...... THAT'S TRUE.
RIGHT, SO QUIT TALKIN' STUPID!
C'MON, LET'S MOVE.
HUH...BUT YOU'RE SMIRKING.
I'M NOT SMIRKING!
YOU'RE IN SUCH HIGH SPIRITS.
I AM NOT!!
NOW TAKE OFF YOUR BUSH!
......
WOW ...

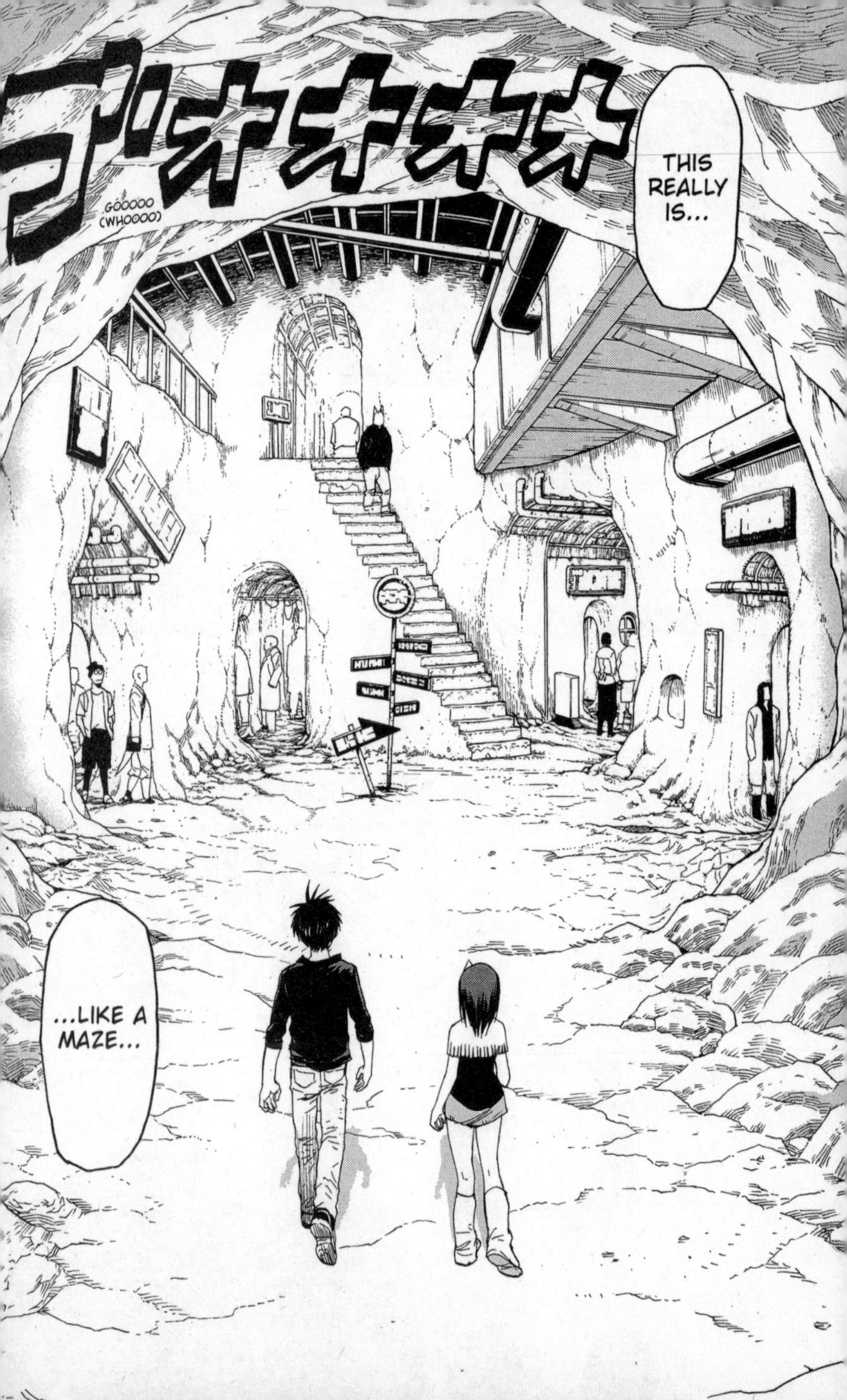
THIS REALLY IS...
GOOOOO (WHOOOO)
....
...LIKE A MAZE...

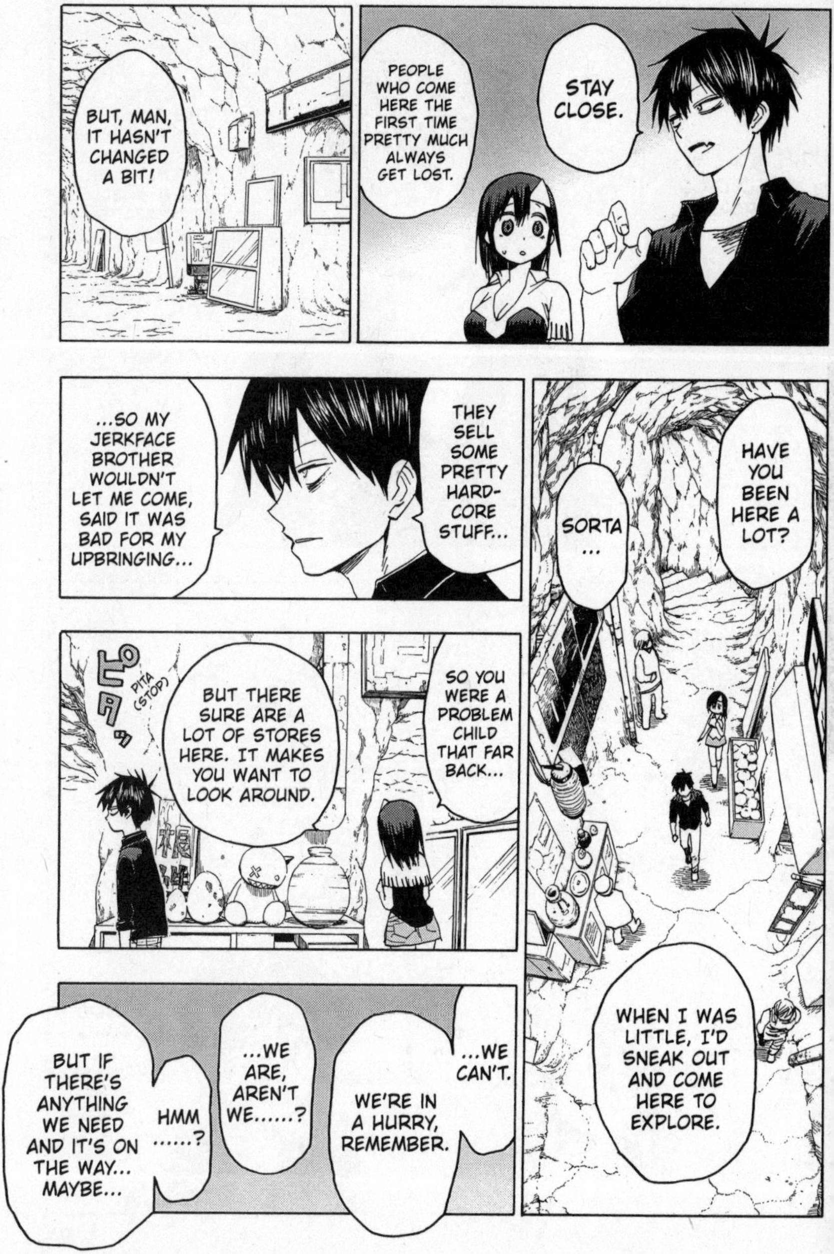
STAY CLOSE.
PEOPLE WHO COME HERE THE FIRST TIME PRETTY MUCH ALWAYS GET LOST.
BUT, MAN, IT HASN'T CHANGED A BIT!
HAVE YOU BEEN HERE A LOT?
SORTA...
WHEN I WAS LITTLE, I'D SNEAK OUT AND COME HERE TO EXPLORE.
THEY SELL SOME PRETTY HARD-CORE STUFF...
...SO MY JERKFACE BROTHER WOULDN'T LET ME COME, SAID IT WAS BAD FOR MY UPBRINGING...
SO YOU WERE A PROBLEM CHILD THAT FAR BACK...
BUT THERE SURE ARE A LOT OF STORES HERE. IT MAKES YOU WANT TO LOOK AROUND.
PITA (STOP)
...WE CAN'T.
WE'RE IN A HURRY, REMEMBER.
...WE ARE, AREN'T WE......?
HMM ......?
BUT IF THERE'S ANYTHING WE NEED AND IT'S ON THE WAY... MAYBE...

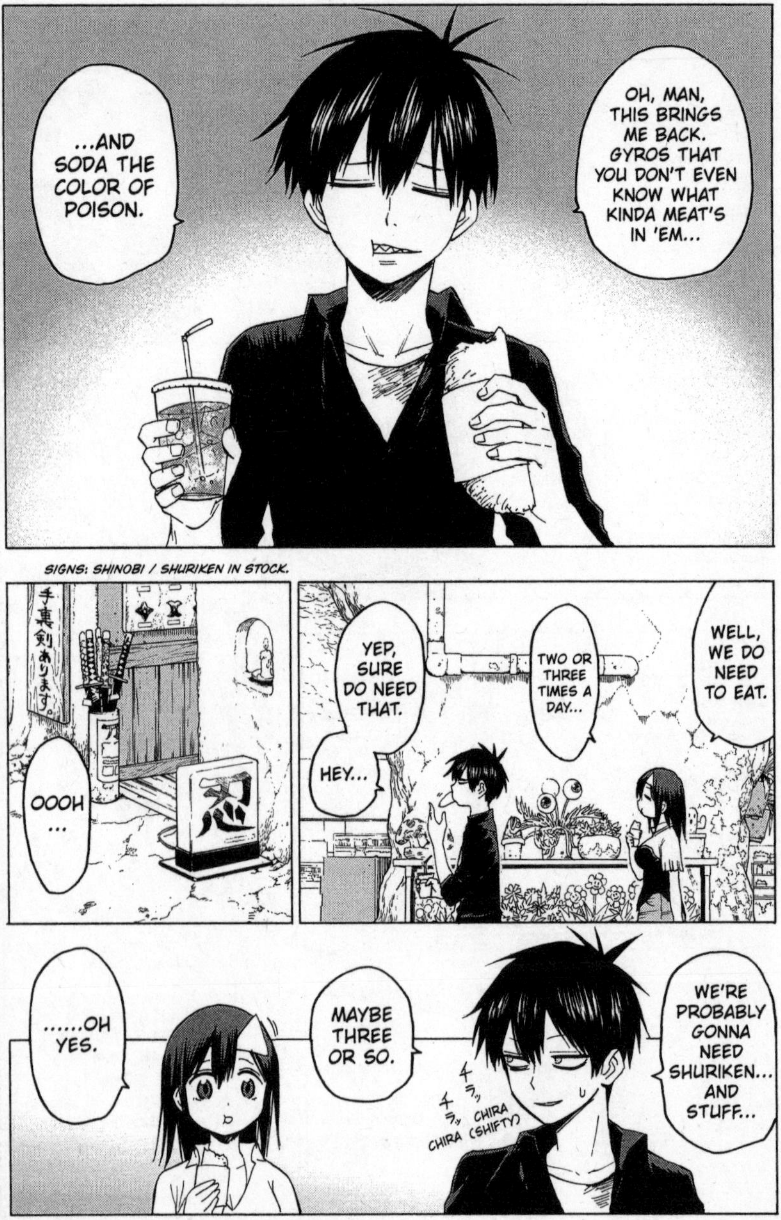
OH, MAN, THIS BRINGS ME BACK. GYROS THAT YOU DON'T EVEN KNOW WHAT KINDA MEAT'S IN 'EM...
...AND SODA THE COLOR OF POISON.
SIGNS: SHINOBI / SHURIKEN IN STOCK.
WELL, WE DO NEED TO EAT.
TWO OR THREE TIMES A DAY...
YEP, SURE DO NEED THAT.
HEY...
手裏剣あります。
忍
OOOH ...
WE'RE PROBABLY GONNA NEED SHURIKEN... AND STUFF...
チラッ チラッ
CHIRA CHIRA (SHIFTY)
MAYBE THREE OR SO.
......OH YES.

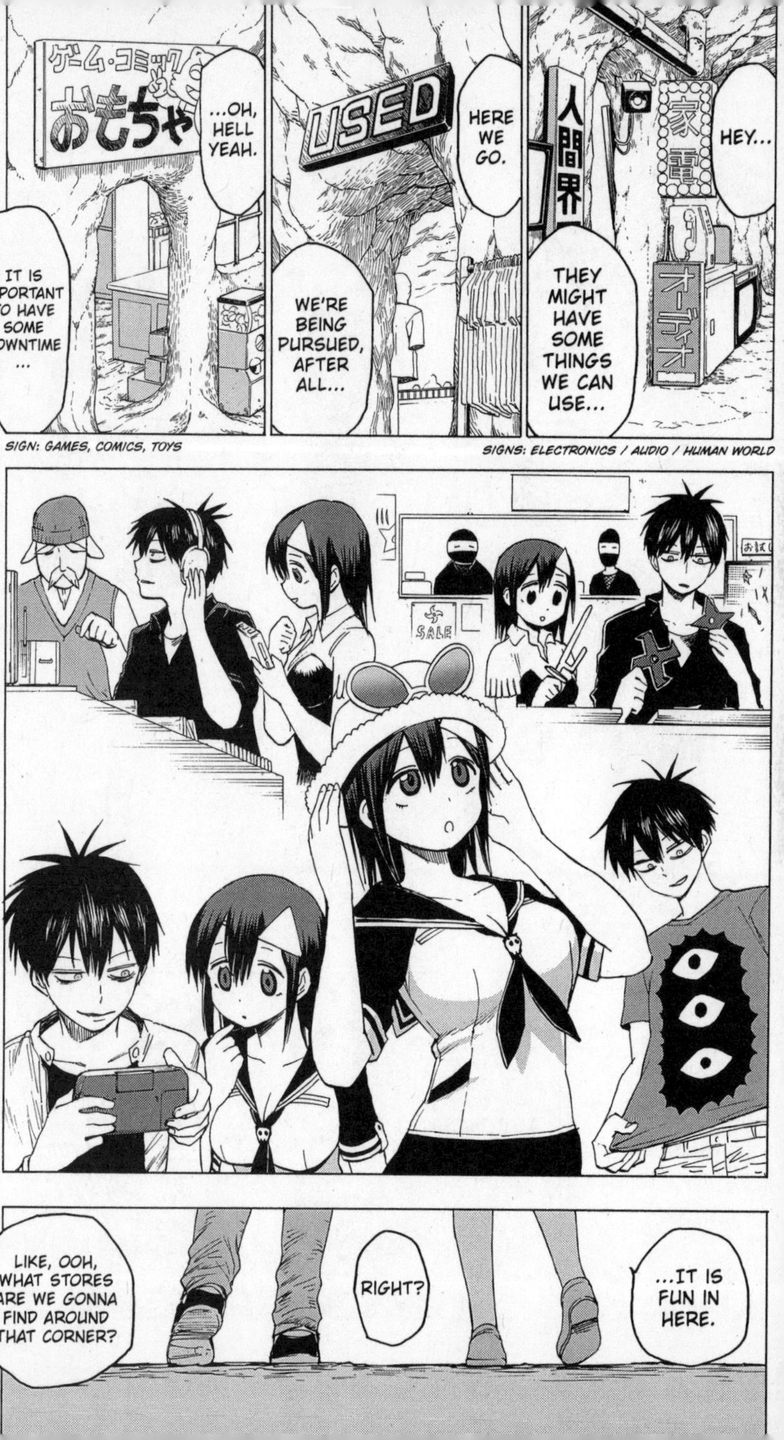
家電
HEY...
人間界
THEY MIGHT HAVE SOME THINGS WE CAN USE...
オーディオ
USED
HERE WE GO.
WE'RE BEING PURSUED, AFTER ALL...
ゲーム・コミック
おもちゃ
...OH, HELL YEAH.
IT IS IMPORTANT TO HAVE SOME DOWNTIME...
SIGNS: ELECTRONICS / AUDIO / HUMAN WORLD
SIGN: GAMES, COMICS, TOYS
SALE
...IT IS FUN IN HERE.
RIGHT?
LIKE, OOH, WHAT STORES ARE WE GONNA FIND AROUND THAT CORNER?

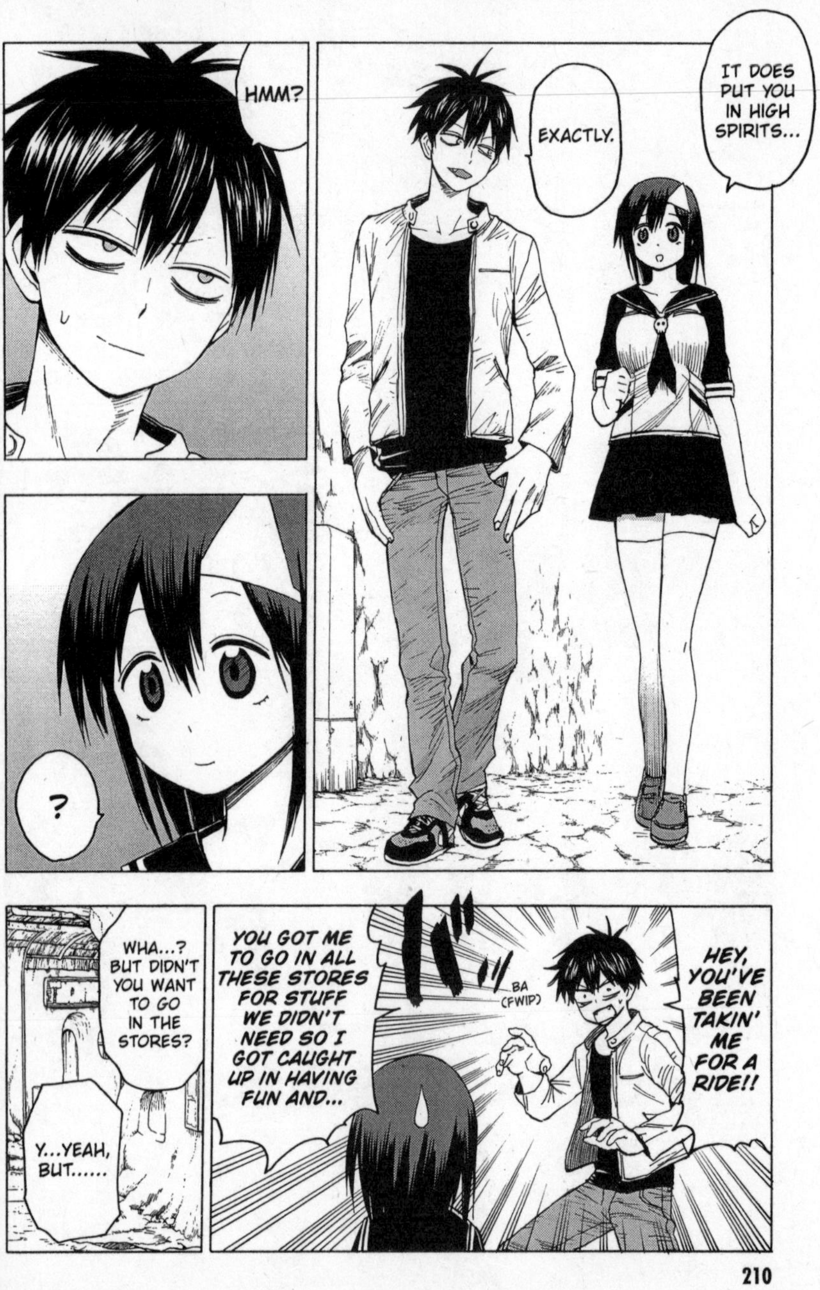
IT DOES PUT YOU IN HIGH SPIRITS...
EXACTLY.
HMM?
?
HEY, YOU'VE BEEN TAKIN' ME FOR A RIDE!!
BA (FWIP)
YOU GOT ME TO GO IN ALL THESE STORES FOR STUFF WE DIDN'T NEED SO I GOT CAUGHT UP IN HAVING FUN AND...
WHA...? BUT DIDN'T YOU WANT TO GO IN THE STORES?
Y...YEAH, BUT......

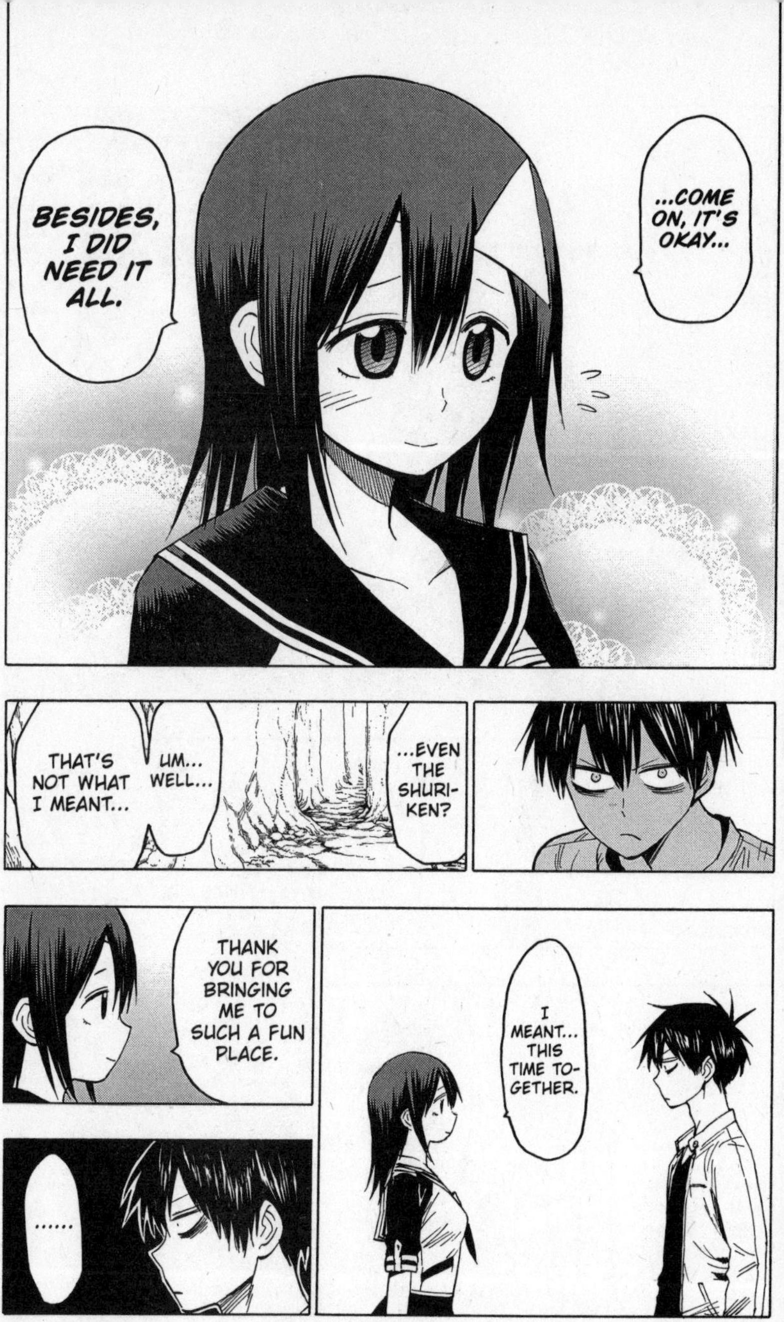
...COME ON, IT'S OKAY...
BESIDES, I DID NEED IT ALL.
...EVEN THE SHURIKEN?
UM... WELL...
THAT'S NOT WHAT I MEANT...
I MEANT... THIS TIME TOGETHER.
THANK YOU FOR BRINGING ME TO SUCH A FUN PLACE.
......

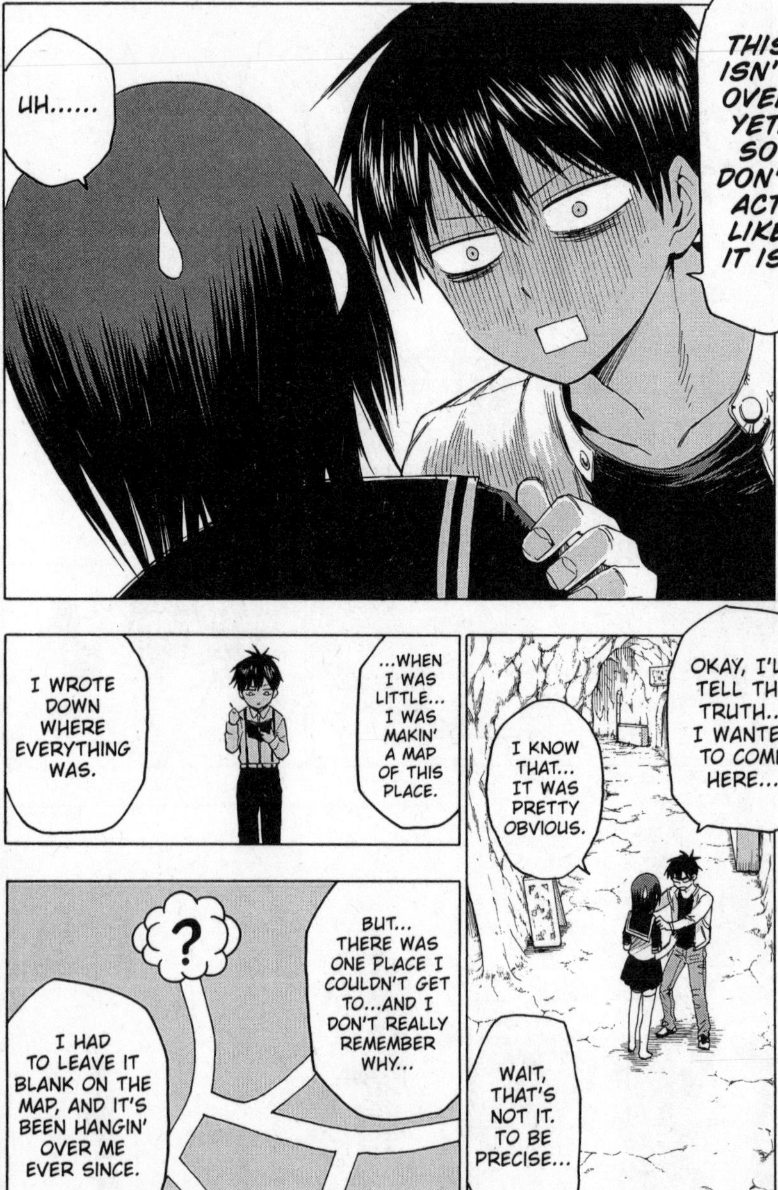
THIS ISN'T OVER YET. SO DON'T ACT LIKE IT IS.
UH......
OKAY, I'LL TELL THE TRUTH... I WANTED TO COME HERE...
I KNOW THAT... IT WAS PRETTY OBVIOUS.
WAIT, THAT'S NOT IT. TO BE PRECISE...
...WHEN I WAS LITTLE... I WAS MAKIN' A MAP OF THIS PLACE.
I WROTE DOWN WHERE EVERYTHING WAS.
BUT... THERE WAS ONE PLACE I COULDN'T GET TO...AND I DON'T REALLY REMEMBER WHY...
?
I HAD TO LEAVE IT BLANK ON THE MAP, AND IT'S BEEN HANGIN' OVER ME EVER SINCE.

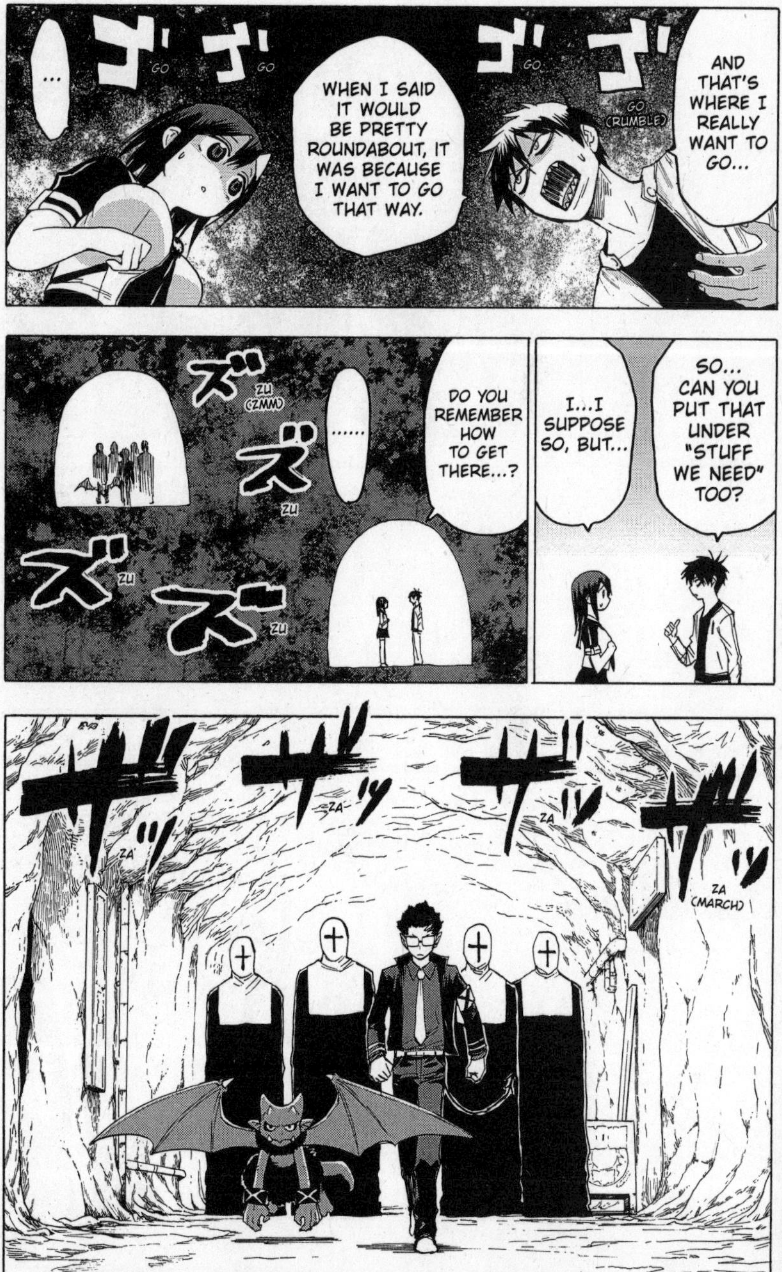
AND THAT'S WHERE I REALLY WANT TO GO...
GO (RUMBLE)
GO
WHEN I SAID IT WOULD BE PRETTY ROUNDABOUT, IT WAS BECAUSE I WANT TO GO THAT WAY.
GO
GO
...
SO... CAN YOU PUT THAT UNDER "STUFF WE NEED" TOO?
I...I SUPPOSE SO, BUT...
DO YOU REMEMBER HOW TO GET THERE...?
......
ZU (ZMM)
ZU
ZU
ZU
ZA (MARCH)
ZA
ZA
ZA

SIGN: FRUIT

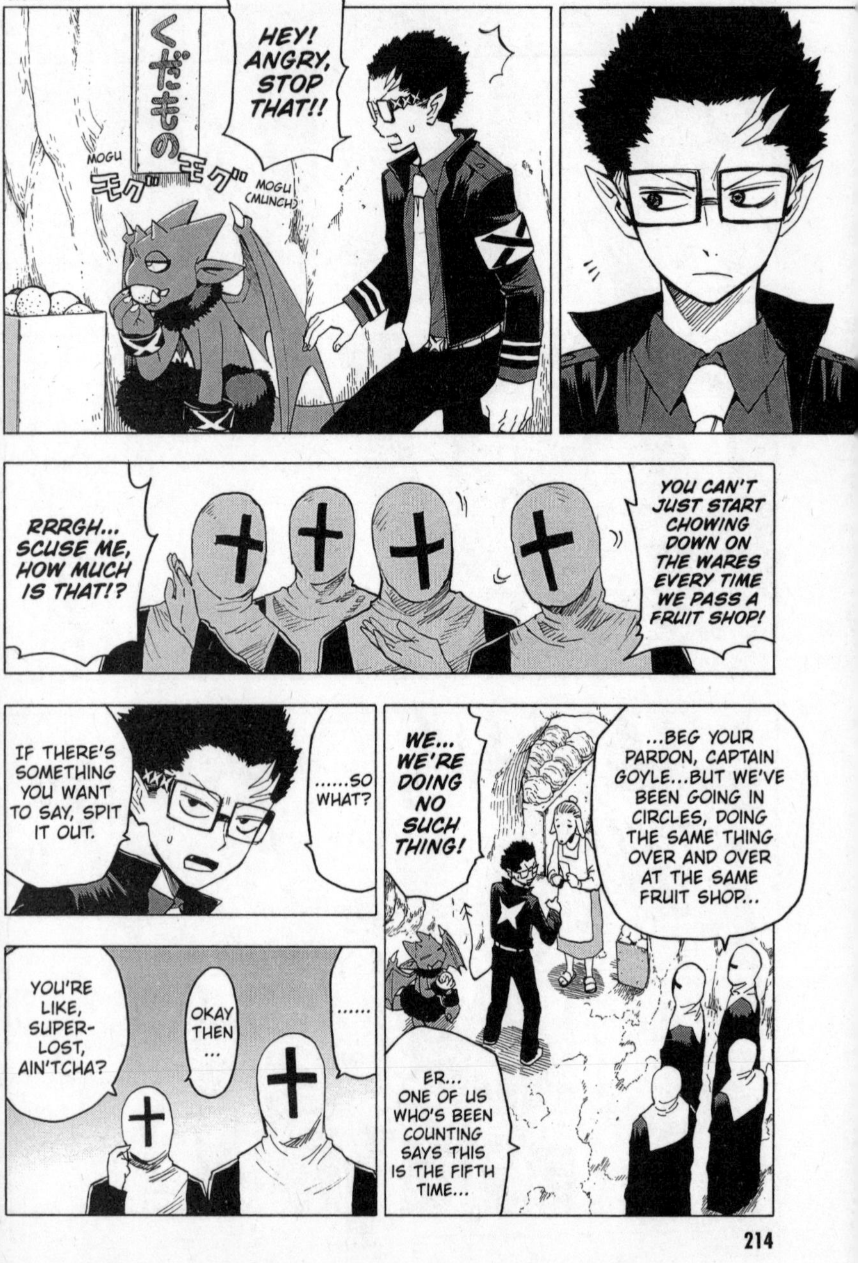

HEY! ANGRY, STOP THAT!!
くだもの
MOGU モグ
MOGU モグ (MUNCH)
YOU CAN'T JUST START CHOWING DOWN ON THE WARES EVERY TIME WE PASS A FRUIT SHOP!
RRRGH... SCUSE ME, HOW MUCH IS THAT!?
...BEG YOUR PARDON, CAPTAIN GOYLE...BUT WE'VE BEEN GOING IN CIRCLES, DOING THE SAME THING OVER AND OVER AT THE SAME FRUIT SHOP...
WE... WE'RE DOING NO SUCH THING!
ER... ONE OF US WHO'S BEEN COUNTING SAYS THIS IS THE FIFTH TIME...
......SO WHAT?
IF THERE'S SOMETHING YOU WANT TO SAY, SPIT IT OUT.
......
OKAY THEN ...
YOU'RE LIKE, SUPER-LOST, AIN'TCHA?

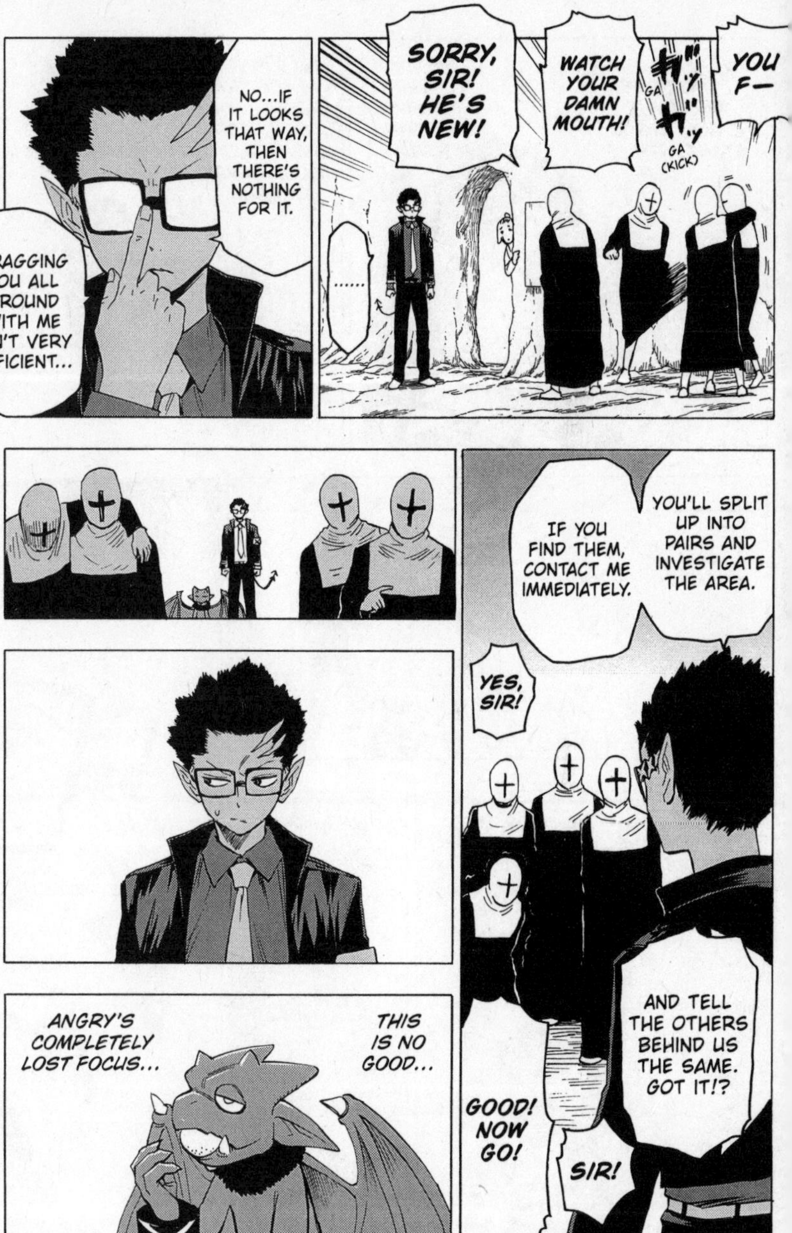
YOU F—
GA GA (KICK)
WATCH YOUR DAMN MOUTH!
SORRY, SIR! HE'S NEW!
......
NO...IF IT LOOKS THAT WAY, THEN THERE'S NOTHING FOR IT.
DRAGGING YOU ALL AROUND WITH ME ISN'T VERY EFFICIENT...
YOU'LL SPLIT UP INTO PAIRS AND INVESTIGATE THE AREA.
IF YOU FIND THEM, CONTACT ME IMMEDIATELY.
YES, SIR!
AND TELL THE OTHERS BEHIND US THE SAME. GOT IT!?
GOOD! NOW GO!
SIR!
THIS IS NO GOOD...
ANGRY'S COMPLETELY LOST FOCUS...

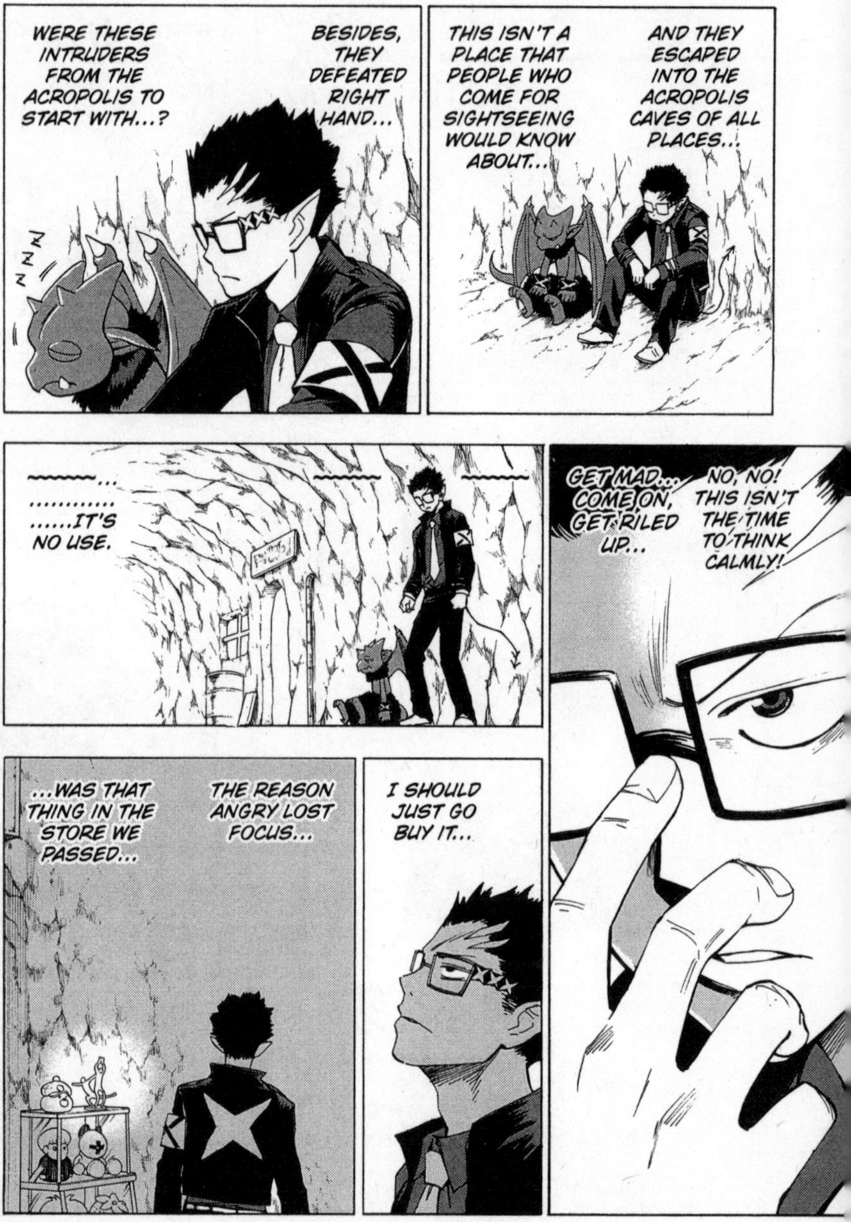
AND THEY ESCAPED INTO THE ACROPOLIS CAVES OF ALL PLACES...
THIS ISN'T A PLACE THAT PEOPLE WHO COME FOR SIGHTSEEING WOULD KNOW ABOUT...
BESIDES, THEY DEFEATED RIGHT HAND...
WERE THESE INTRUDERS FROM THE ACROPOLIS TO START WITH...?
NO, NO! THIS ISN'T THE TIME TO THINK CALMLY!
GET MAD... COME ON, GET RILED UP...
~~~~~~
~~~~~~
~~~~~~...
....
......IT'S NO USE.
I SHOULD JUST GO BUY IT...
THE REASON ANGRY LOST FOCUS...
...WAS THAT THING IN THE STORE WE PASSED...
~~~~~~

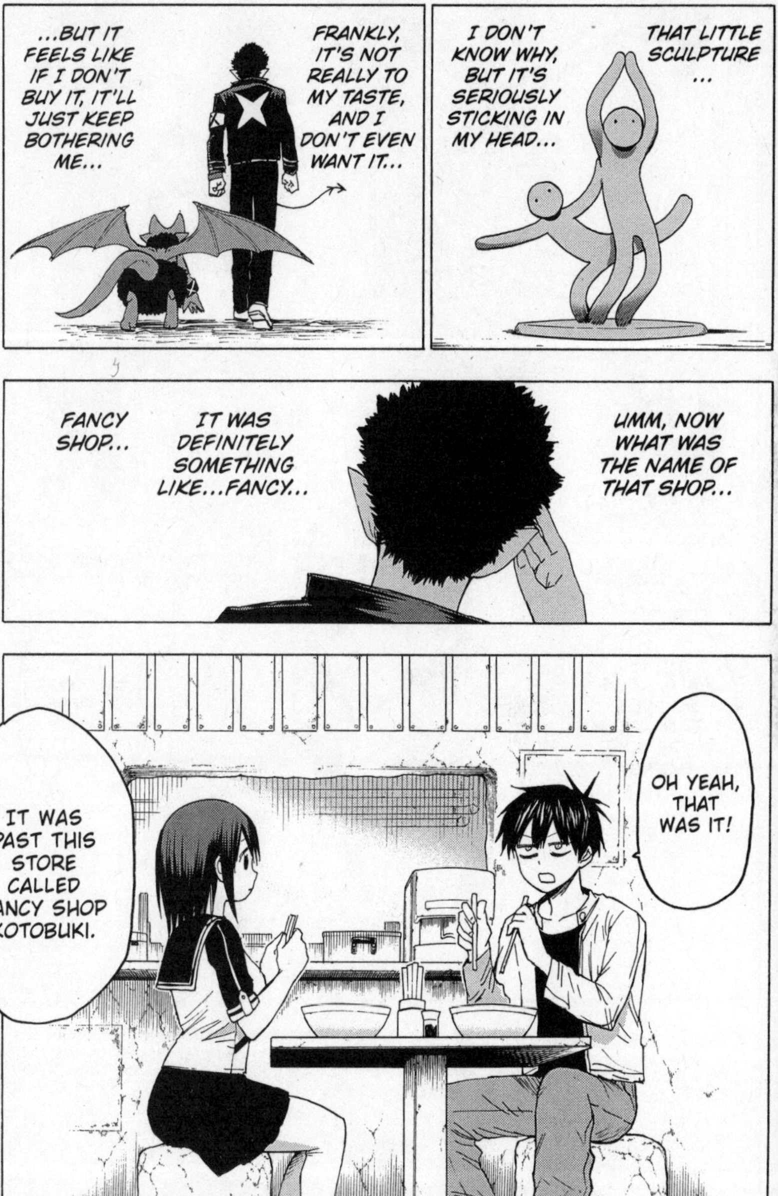
THAT LITTLE SCULPTURE...
I DON'T KNOW WHY, BUT IT'S SERIOUSLY STICKING IN MY HEAD...
FRANKLY, IT'S NOT REALLY TO MY TASTE, AND I DON'T EVEN WANT IT...
...BUT IT FEELS LIKE IF I DON'T BUY IT, IT'LL JUST KEEP BOTHERING ME...
UMM, NOW WHAT WAS THE NAME OF THAT SHOP...
IT WAS DEFINITELY SOMETHING LIKE...FANCY...
FANCY SHOP...
OH YEAH, THAT WAS IT!
IT WAS PAST THIS STORE CALLED FANCY SHOP KOTOBUKI.

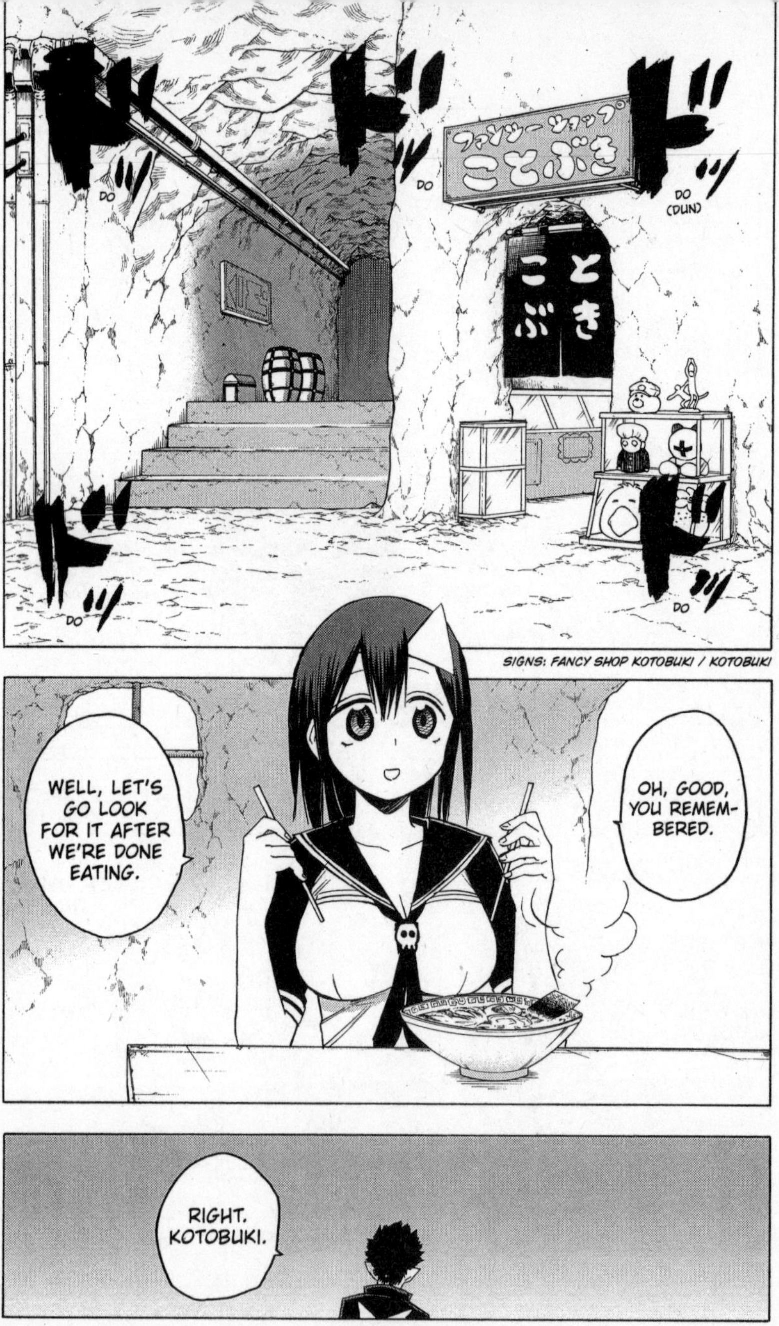
DO (DUN)
DO
DO
DO
DO
SIGNS: FANCY SHOP KOTOBUKI / KOTOBUKI
OH, GOOD, YOU REMEMBERED.
WELL, LET'S GO LOOK FOR IT AFTER WE'RE DONE EATING.
RIGHT. KOTOBUKI.

♠ To Be Continued ♠

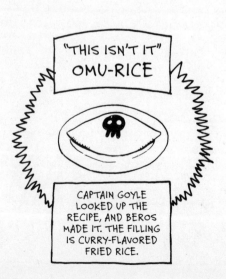

"THIS ISN'T IT"
OMU-RICE

CAPTAIN GOYLE
LOOKED UP THE
RECIPE, AND BEROS
MADE IT. THE FILLING
IS CURRY-FLAVORED
FRIED RICE.

BLOOD LAD

CHAPTER 37 ♠ EXPERIENCE ADULT RELAXATION!

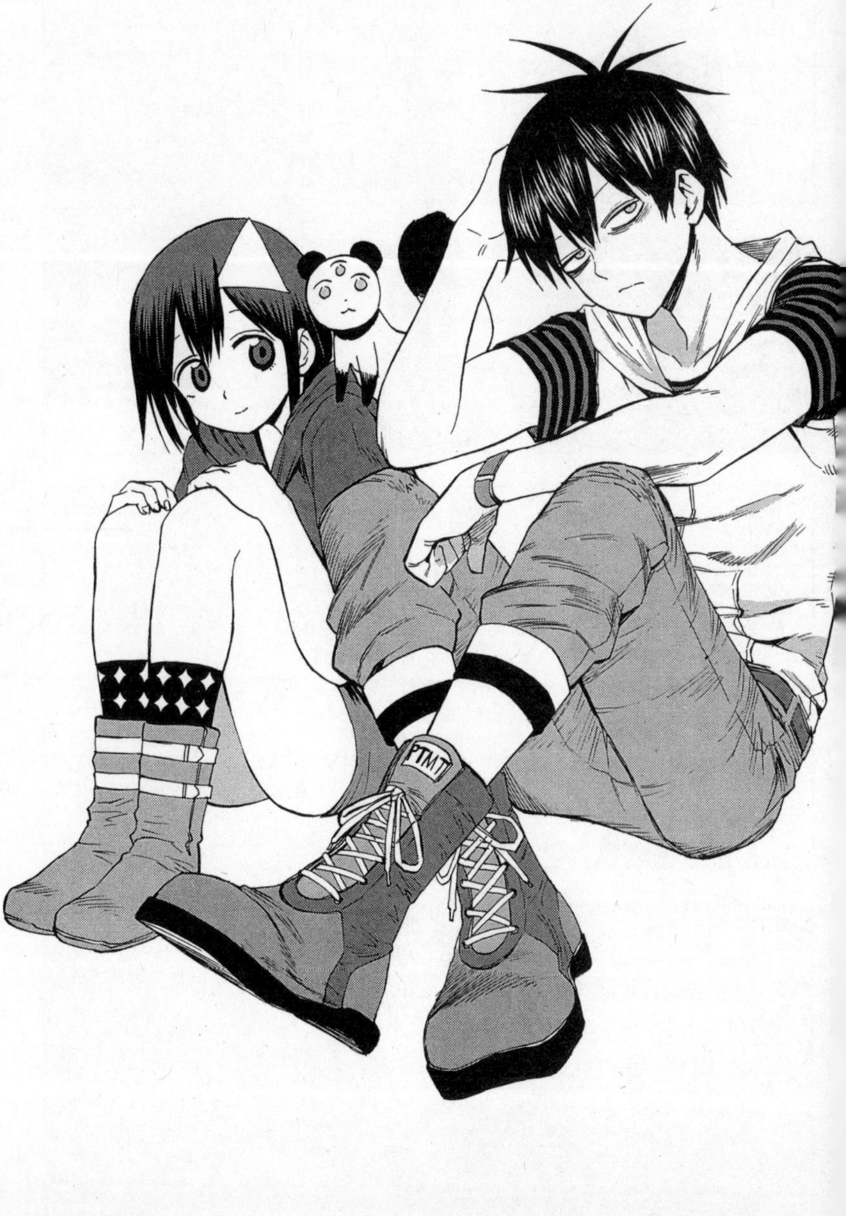
PTMT

SIGN: FANCY SHOP KOTOBUKI / CURTAINS: KOTOBUKI

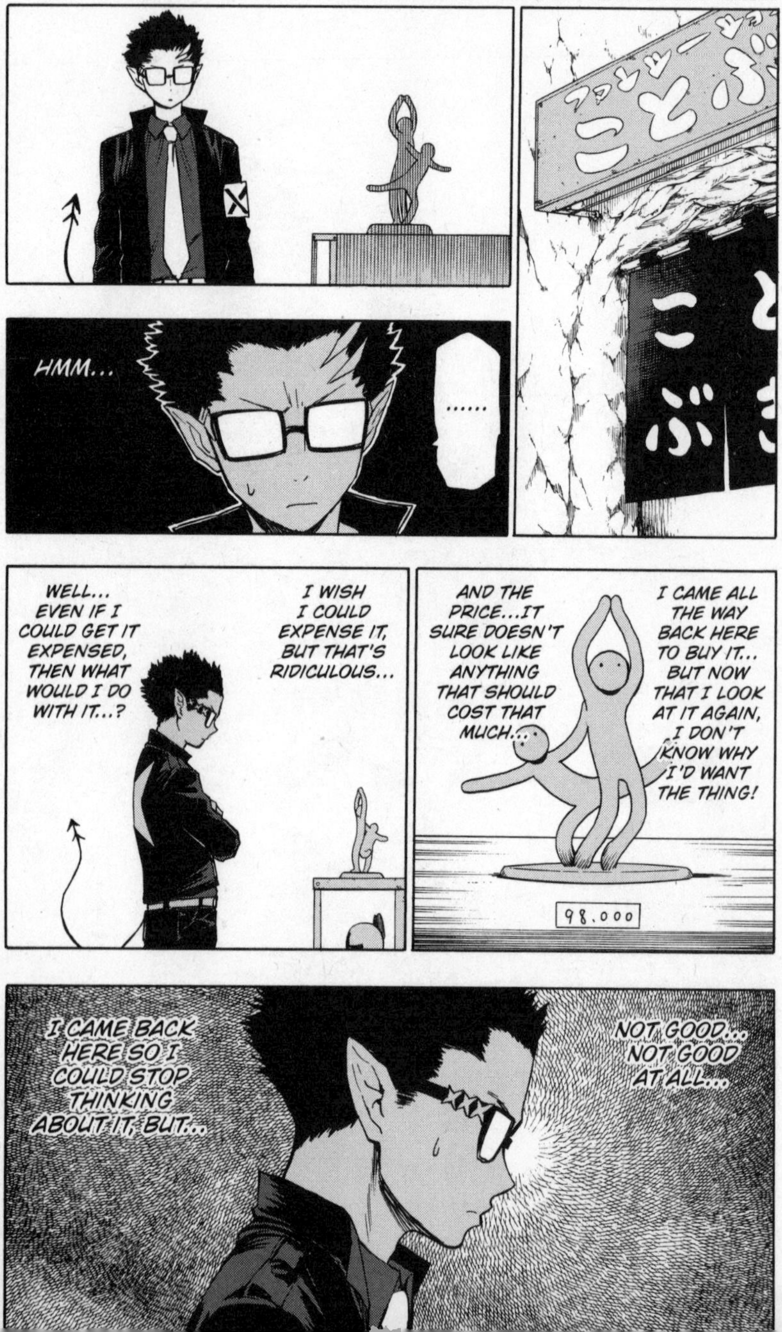
......
HMM...
I CAME ALL THE WAY BACK HERE TO BUY IT... BUT NOW THAT I LOOK AT IT AGAIN, I DON'T KNOW WHY I'D WANT THE THING!
AND THE PRICE...IT SURE DOESN'T LOOK LIKE ANYTHING THAT SHOULD COST THAT MUCH...
98.000
I WISH I COULD EXPENSE IT, BUT THAT'S RIDICULOUS...
WELL... EVEN IF I COULD GET IT EXPENSED, THEN WHAT WOULD I DO WITH IT...?
NOT GOOD... NOT GOOD AT ALL...
I CAME BACK HERE SO I COULD STOP THINKING ABOUT IT, BUT...

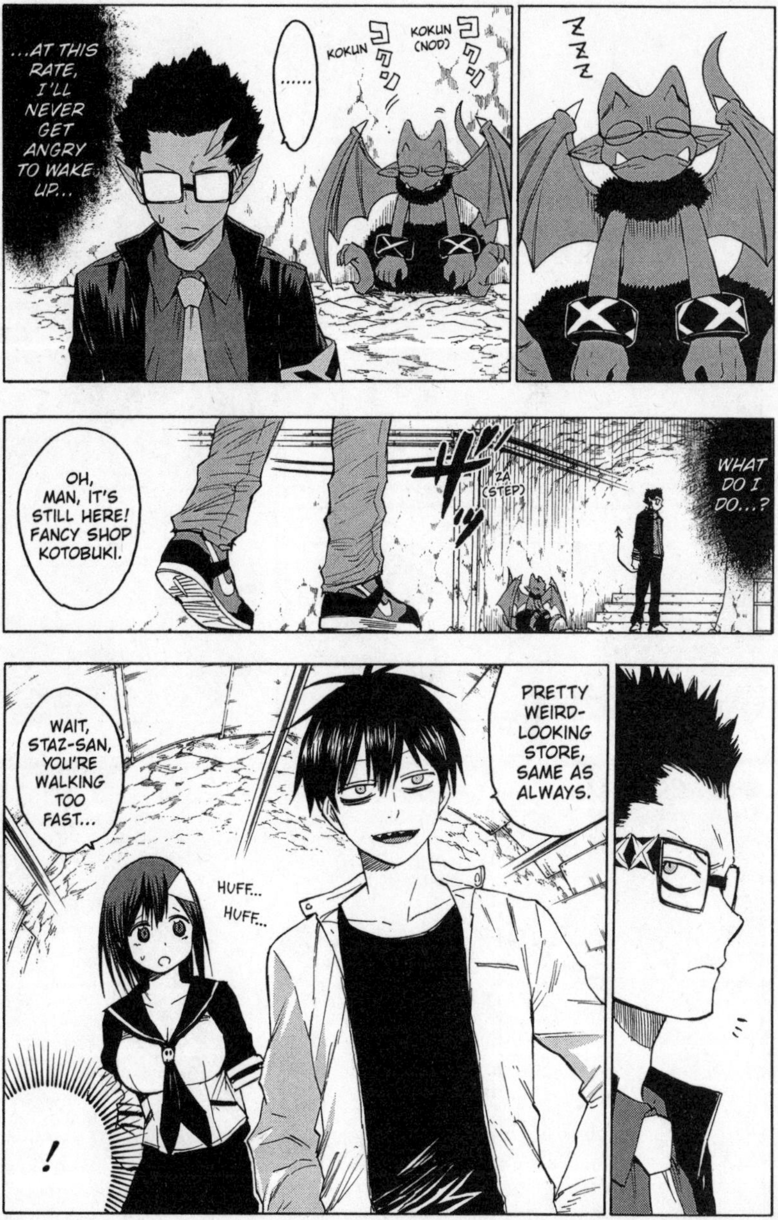
Z Z Z
KOKUN (NOD)
KOKUN
......
...AT THIS RATE, I'LL NEVER GET ANGRY TO WAKE UP...
WHAT DO I DO...?
ZA (STEP)
OH, MAN, IT'S STILL HERE! FANCY SHOP KOTOBUKI.
PRETTY WEIRD-LOOKING STORE, SAME AS ALWAYS.
WAIT, STAZ-SAN, YOU'RE WALKING TOO FAST...
HUFF... HUFF...
!

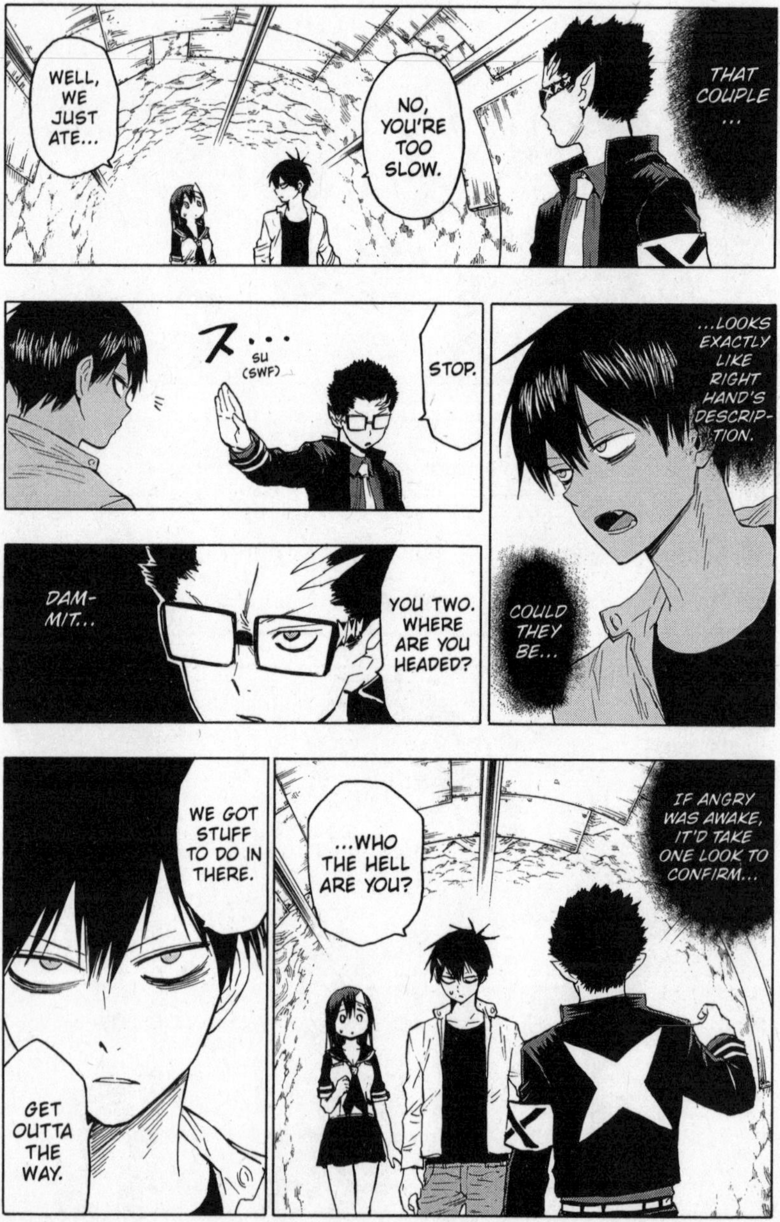
THAT COUPLE...
NO, YOU'RE TOO SLOW.
WELL, WE JUST ATE...
...LOOKS EXACTLY LIKE RIGHT HAND'S DESCRIPTION.
COULD THEY BE...
STOP.
ス...
SU (SWF)
YOU TWO. WHERE ARE YOU HEADED?
DAM-MIT...
IF ANGRY WAS AWAKE, IT'D TAKE ONE LOOK TO CONFIRM...
...WHO THE HELL ARE YOU?
WE GOT STUFF TO DO IN THERE.
GET OUTTA THE WAY.

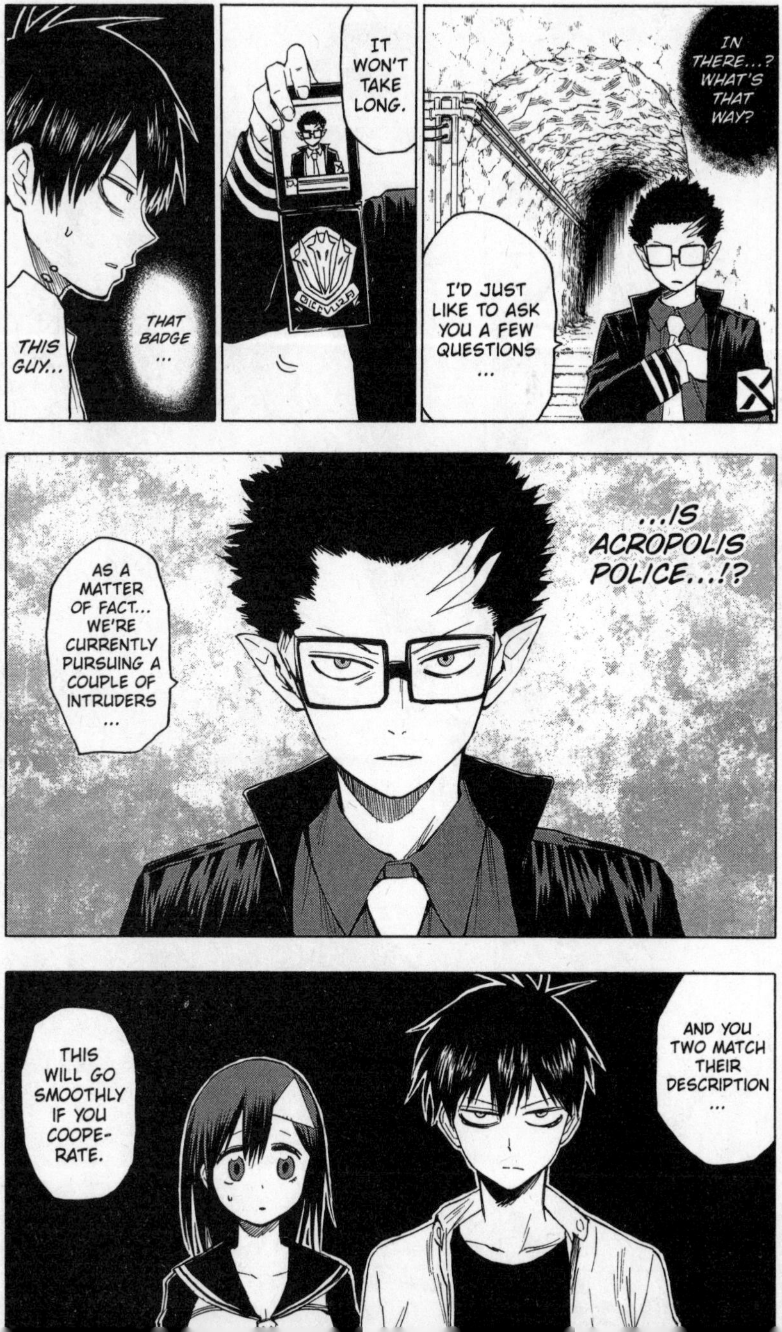
IN THERE...? WHAT'S THAT WAY?
I'D JUST LIKE TO ASK YOU A FEW QUESTIONS ...
IT WON'T TAKE LONG.
THAT BADGE ...
THIS GUY...
...IS ACROPOLIS POLICE...!?
AS A MATTER OF FACT... WE'RE CURRENTLY PURSUING A COUPLE OF INTRUDERS ...
AND YOU TWO MATCH THEIR DESCRIPTION ...
THIS WILL GO SMOOTHLY IF YOU COOPE-RATE.

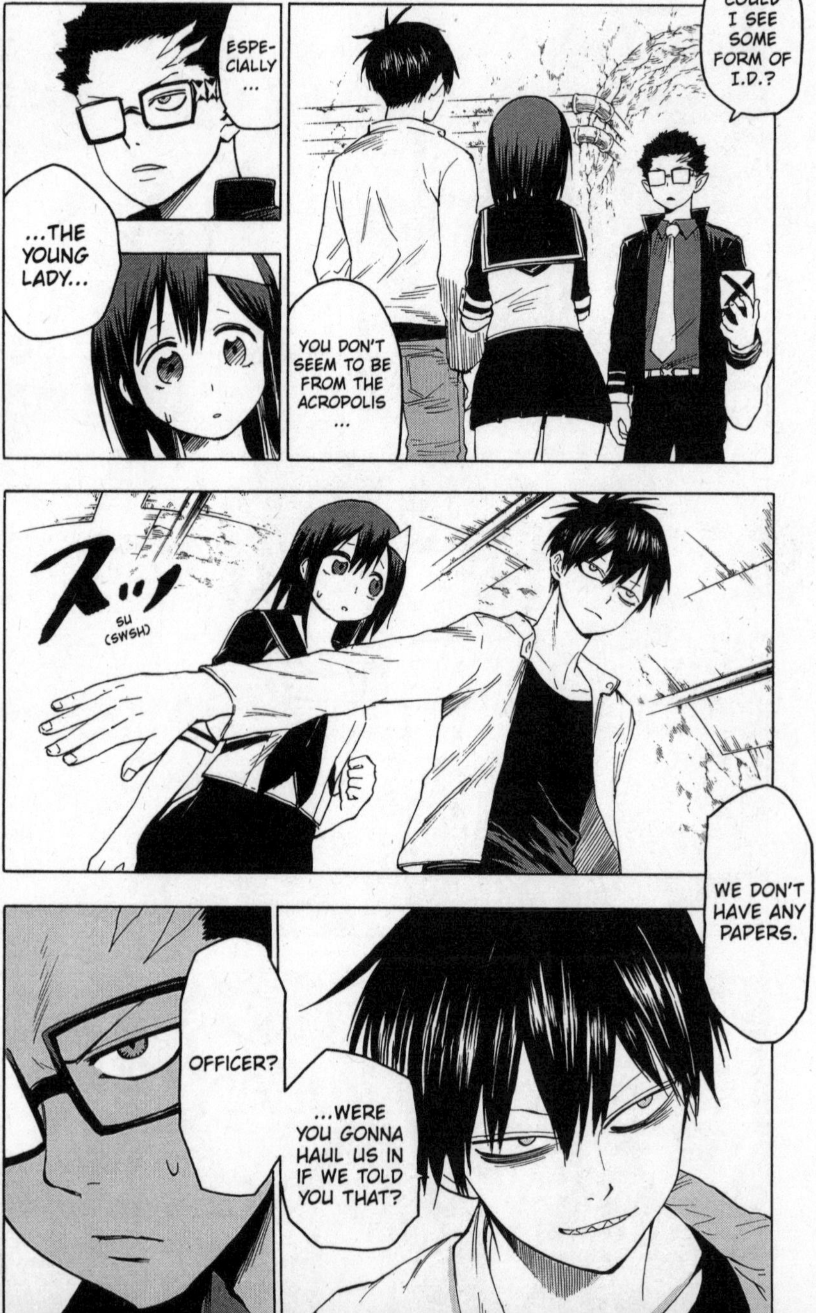
COULD I SEE SOME FORM OF I.D.?
YOU DON'T SEEM TO BE FROM THE ACROPOLIS...
ESPE-CIALLY...
...THE YOUNG LADY...
スッ
SU (SWSH)
WE DON'T HAVE ANY PAPERS.
OFFICER?
...WERE YOU GONNA HAUL US IN IF WE TOLD YOU THAT?

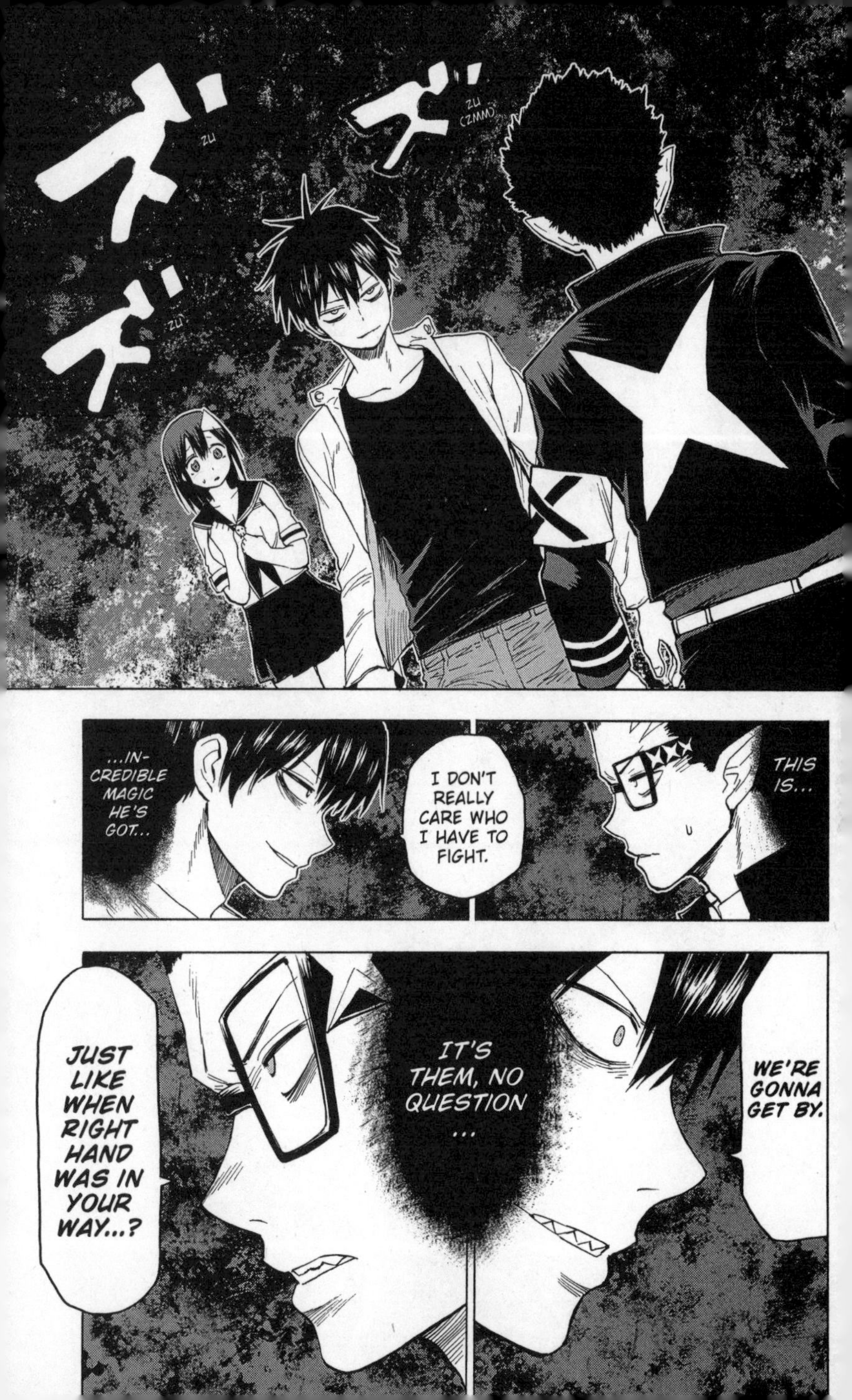
ZU (ZMMM)
ZU
ZU
THIS IS...
I DON'T REALLY CARE WHO I HAVE TO FIGHT.
...IN-CREDIBLE MAGIC HE'S GOT...
WE'RE GONNA GET BY.
IT'S THEM, NO QUESTION...
JUST LIKE WHEN RIGHT HAND WAS IN YOUR WAY...?

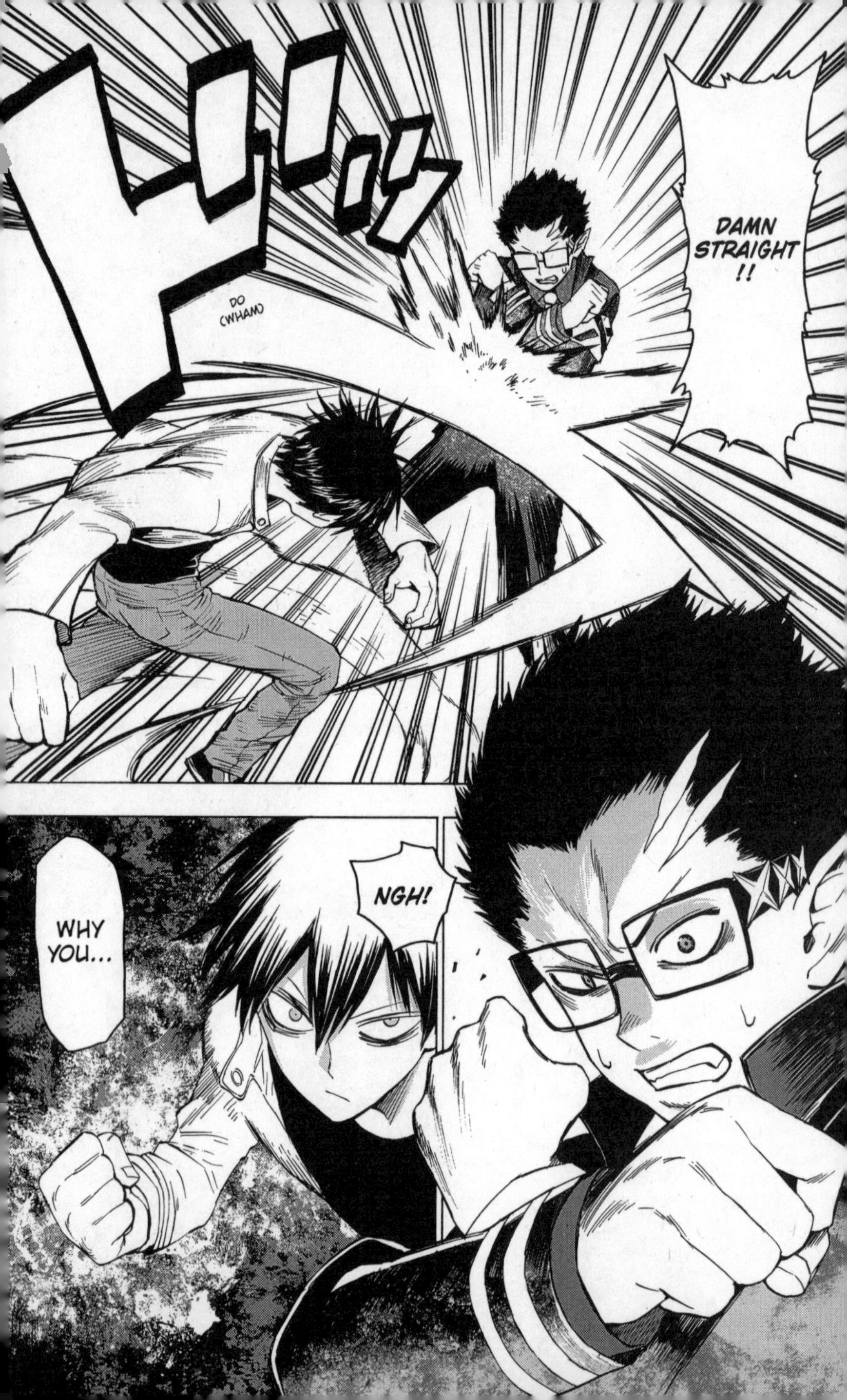
DAMN STRAIGHT!!
DO (WHAM)
NGH!
WHY YOU...

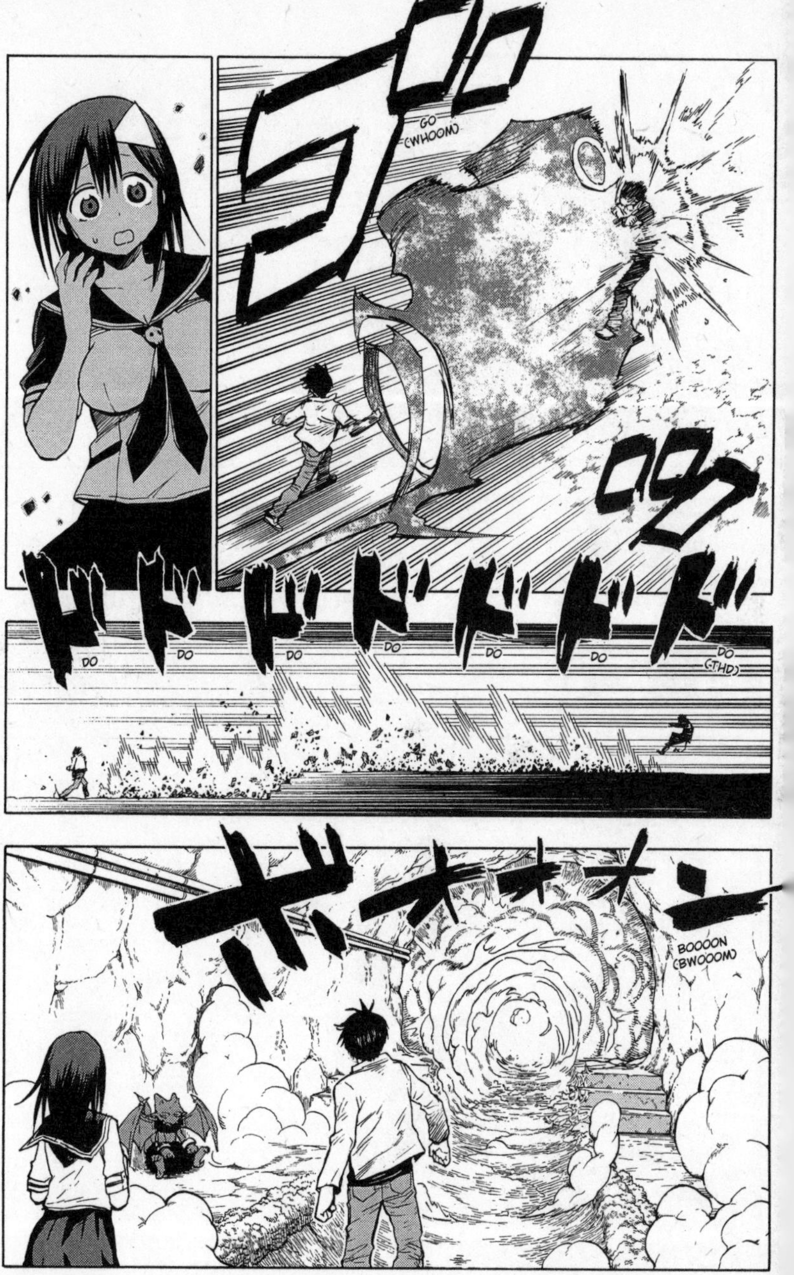
ゴ
GO (WHOOM)
ドドドドドドド
DO
DO
DO
DO
DO
DO
DO (THD)
ボオオオン
BOOOON (BWOOOM)

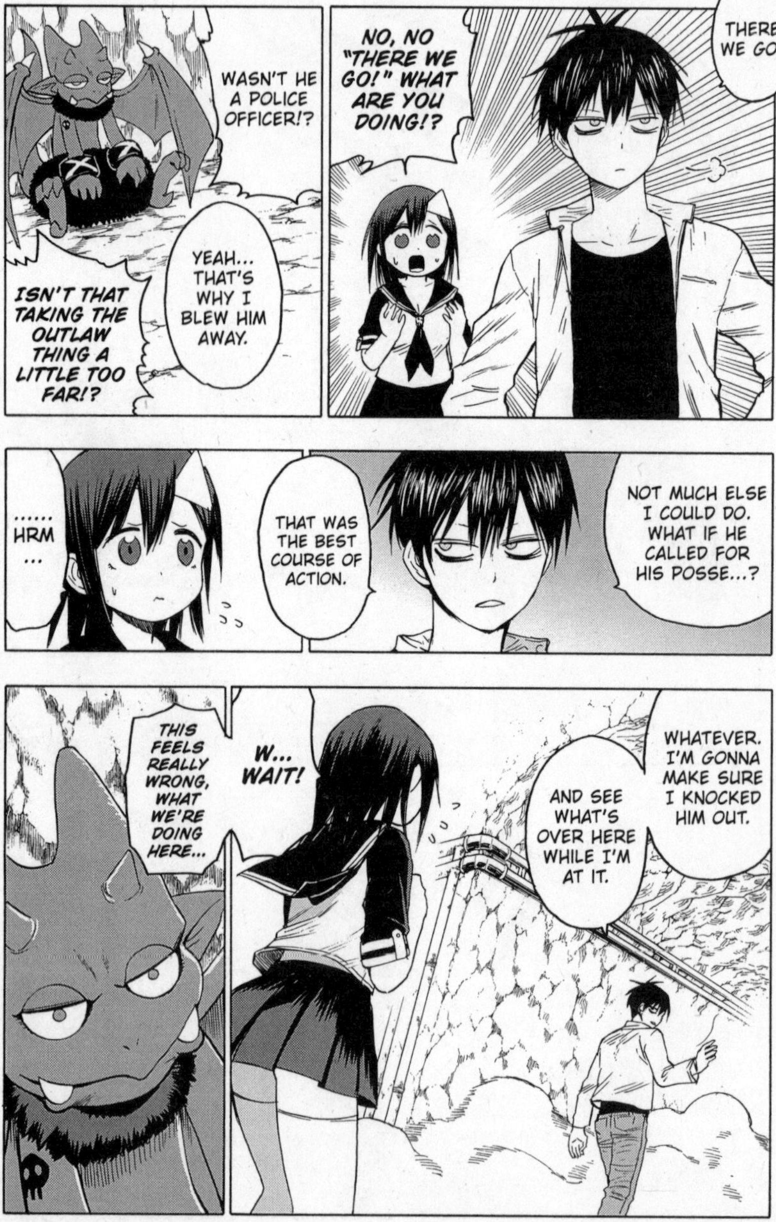
THERE WE GO!
NO, NO "THERE WE GO!" WHAT ARE YOU DOING!?
WASN'T HE A POLICE OFFICER!?
YEAH... THAT'S WHY I BLEW HIM AWAY.
ISN'T THAT TAKING THE OUTLAW THING A LITTLE TOO FAR!?
NOT MUCH ELSE I COULD DO. WHAT IF HE CALLED FOR HIS POSSE...?
THAT WAS THE BEST COURSE OF ACTION.
...... HRM ...
WHATEVER. I'M GONNA MAKE SURE I KNOCKED HIM OUT.
AND SEE WHAT'S OVER HERE WHILE I'M AT IT.
W... WAIT!
THIS FEELS REALLY WRONG, WHAT WE'RE DOING HERE...

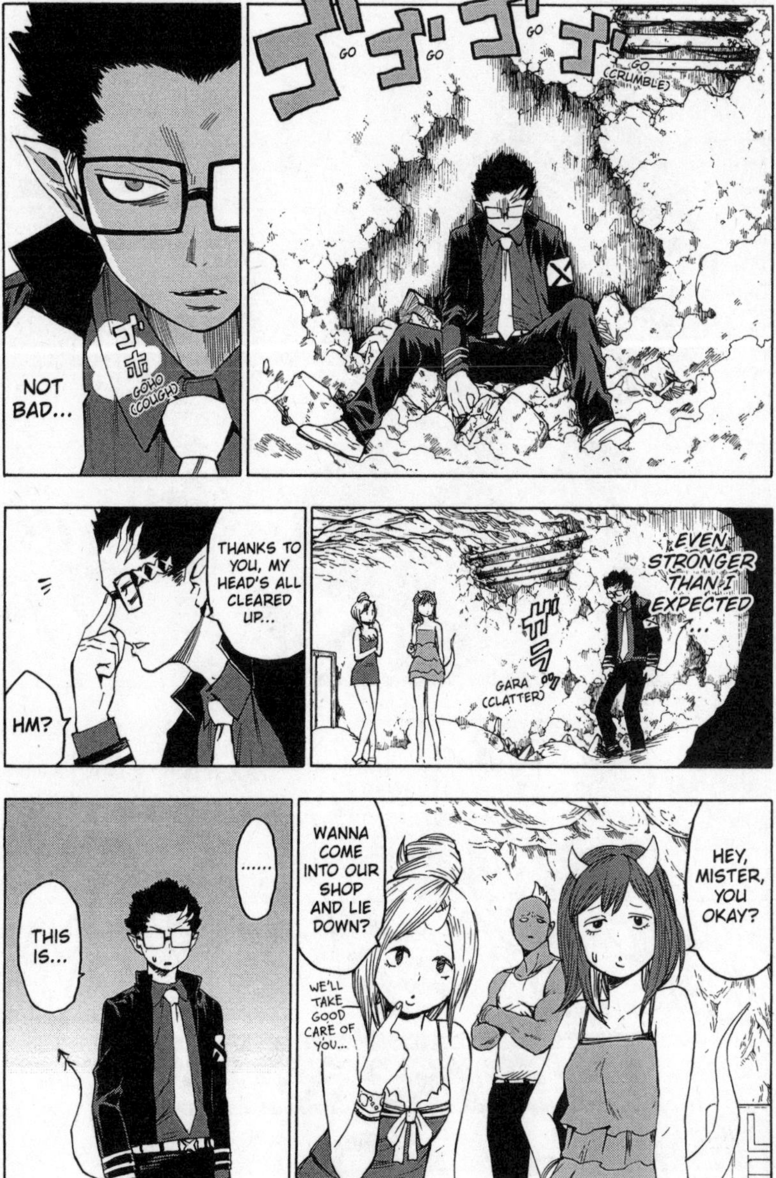
ゴゴゴゴ
GO GO GO GO
(CRUMBLE)
ゴホ
GOHO (COUGH)
NOT BAD...
EVEN STRONGER THAN I EXPECTED...
ガラ
GARA (CLATTER)
THANKS TO YOU, MY HEAD'S ALL CLEARED UP...
HM?
HEY, MISTER, YOU OKAY?
WANNA COME INTO OUR SHOP AND LIE DOWN?
WE'LL TAKE GOOD CARE OF YOU...
......
THIS IS...

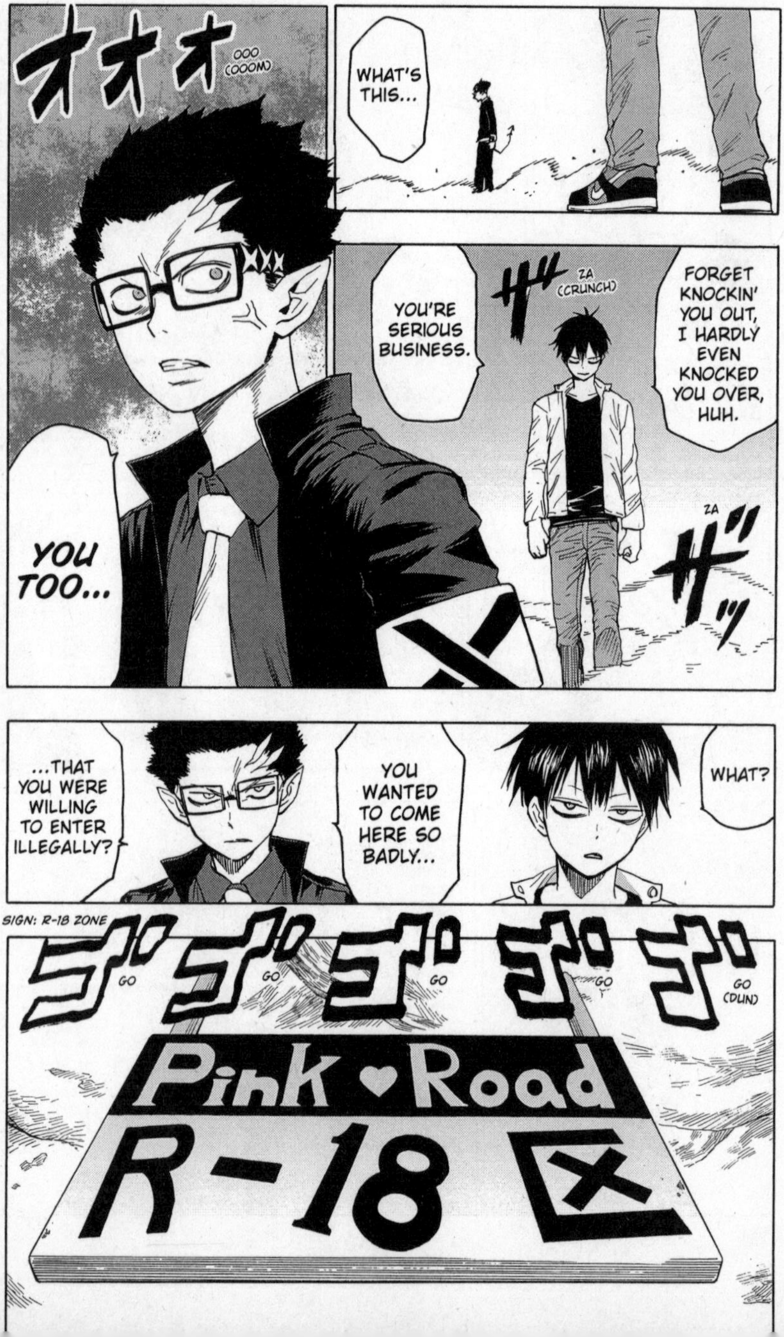
WHAT'S THIS...
FORGET KNOCKIN' YOU OUT, I HARDLY EVEN KNOCKED YOU OVER, HUH.
ZA (CRUNCH)
YOU'RE SERIOUS BUSINESS.
ZA
OOO (OOOM)
YOU TOO...
WHAT?
YOU WANTED TO COME HERE SO BADLY...
...THAT YOU WERE WILLING TO ENTER ILLEGALLY?
SIGN: R-18 ZONE
GO
GO
GO
GO
GO (DUN)
Pink♥Road
R-18 区

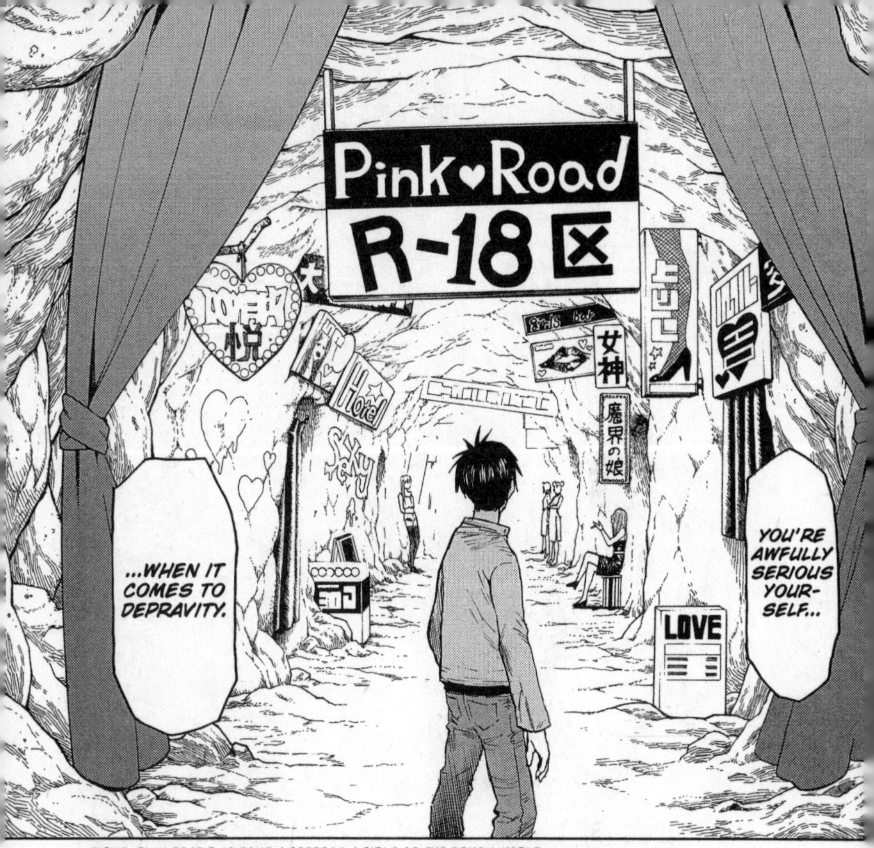
Pink♥Road
R-18 区
女神
魔界の娘
Hotel
LOVE
YOU'RE AWFULLY SERIOUS YOURSELF...
...WHEN IT COMES TO DEPRAVITY.

SIGNS: PINK ROAD R-18 ZONE / GODDESS / GIRLS OF THE DEMON WORLD

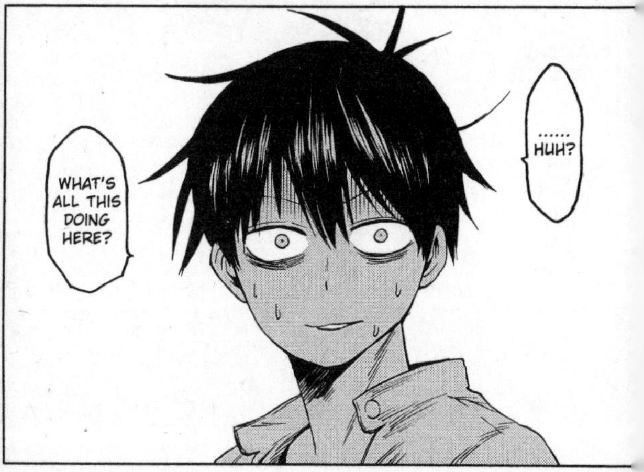
......HUH?
WHAT'S ALL THIS DOING HERE?

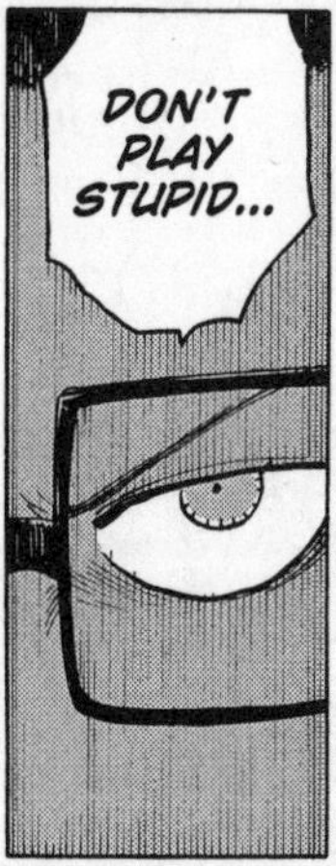
DON'T PLAY STUPID...

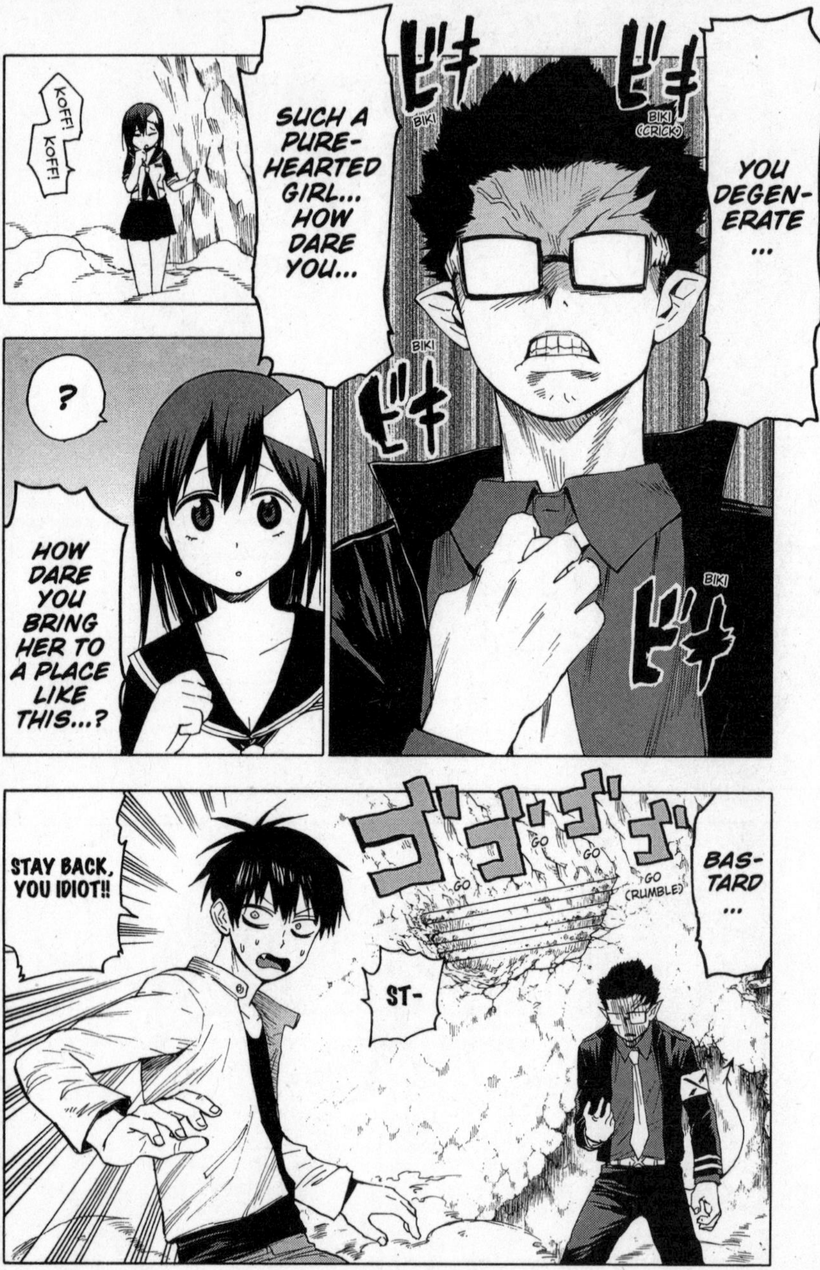
YOU DEGENERATE...
BIKI (CRICK)
BIKI
SUCH A PURE-HEARTED GIRL... HOW DARE YOU...
BIKI
BIKI
KOFF! KOFF!
?
HOW DARE YOU BRING HER TO A PLACE LIKE THIS...?
BASTARD...
GO GO GO GO (RUMBLE)
ST-
STAY BACK, YOU IDIOT!!

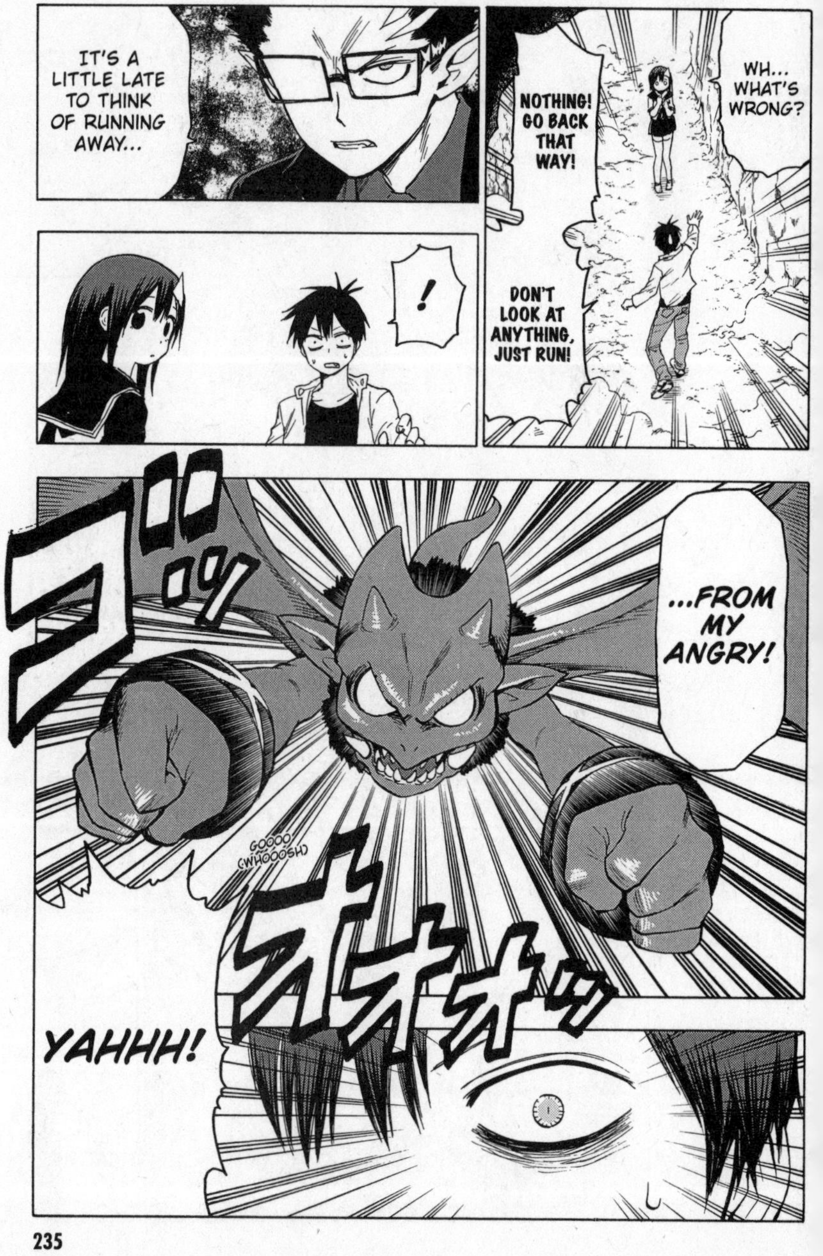
WH... WHAT'S WRONG?
NOTHING! GO BACK THAT WAY!
DON'T LOOK AT ANYTHING, JUST RUN!
IT'S A LITTLE LATE TO THINK OF RUNNING AWAY...
!
...FROM MY ANGRY!
GOOOO (WHOOOSH)
YAHHH!

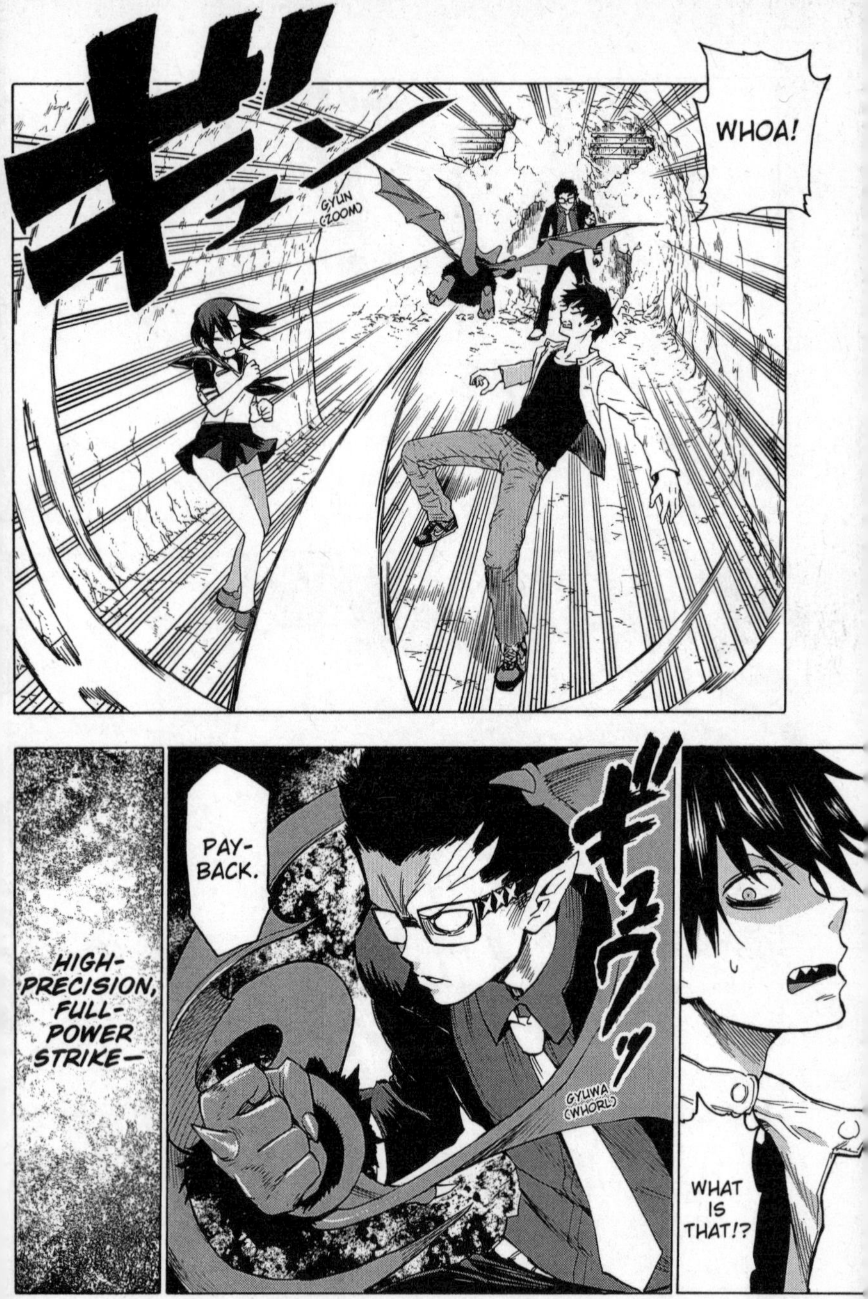
WHOA!
GYUN (ZOOM)
WHAT IS THAT!?
PAY-BACK.
GYUWA (WHORL)
HIGH-PRECISION, FULL-POWER STRIKE—

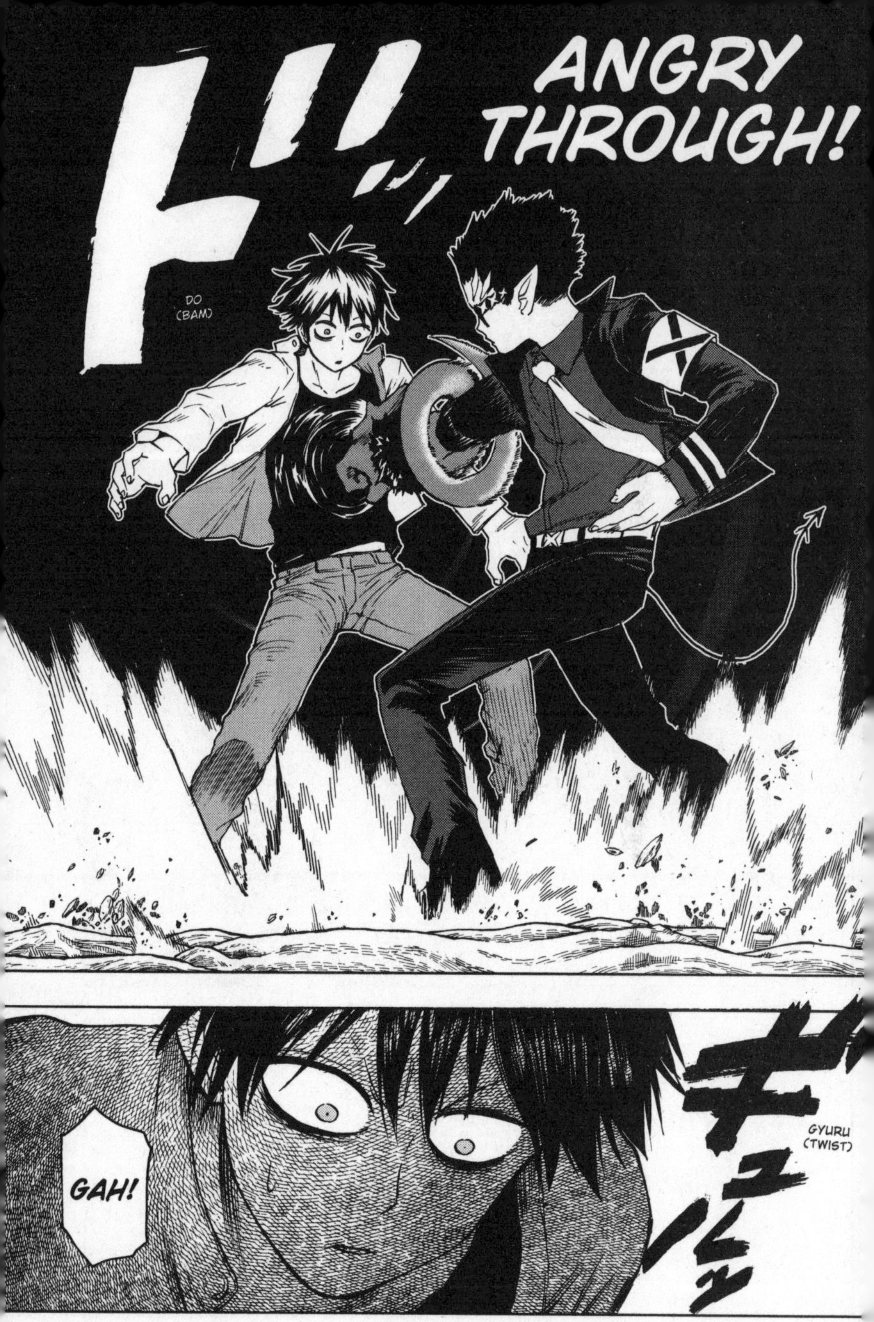
ANGRY THROUGH!
DO (BAM)
GYURU (TWIST)
GAH!

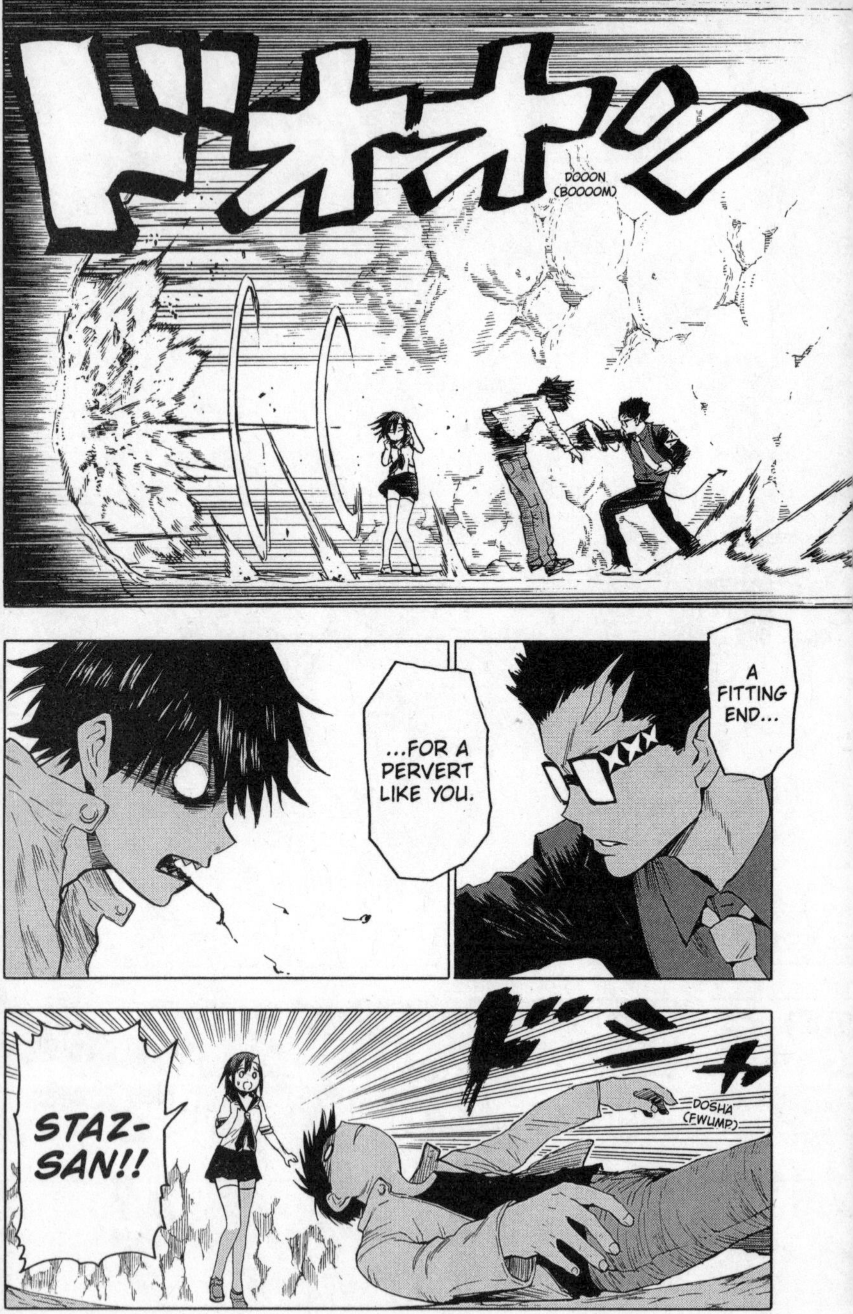
DOOON
(BOOOOM)
A FITTING END...
...FOR A PERVERT LIKE YOU.
DOSHA
(FWUMP)
STAZ-SAN!!

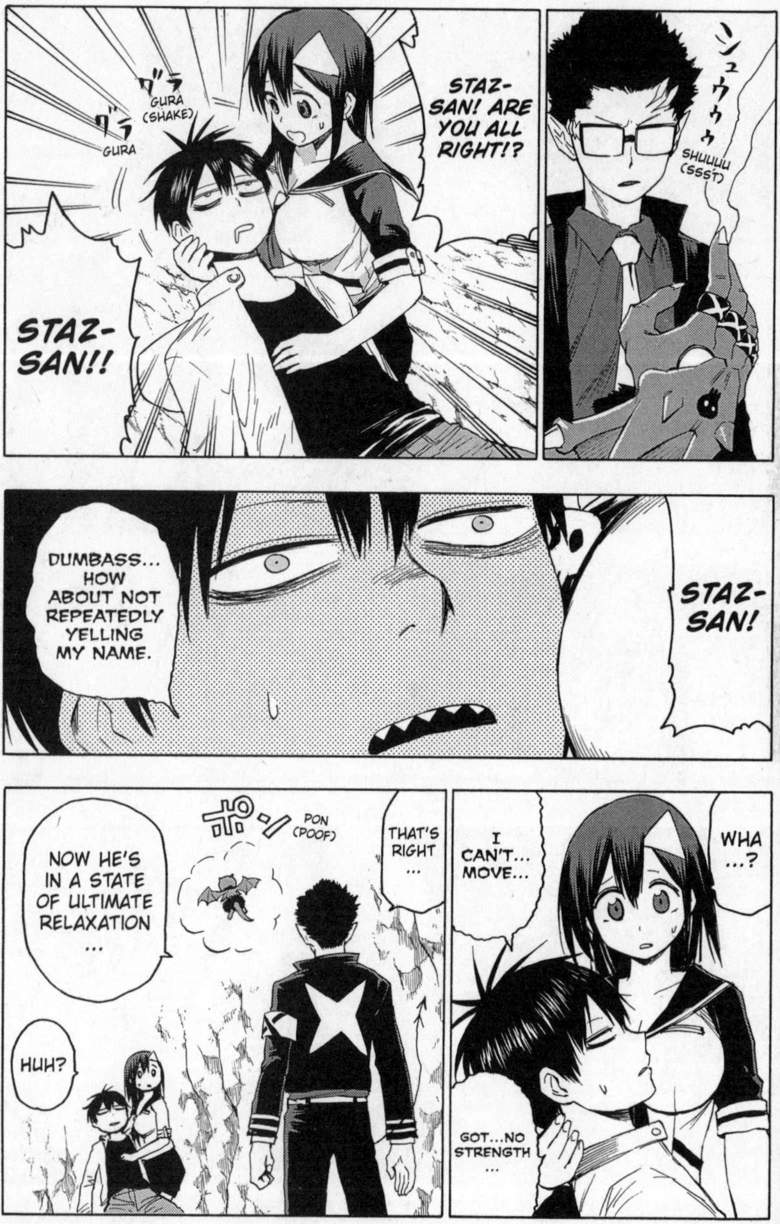

シュウウゥ
SHUUUUU (SSST)
STAZ-SAN! ARE YOU ALL RIGHT!?
グラ
GURA (SHAKE)
グラ
GURA
STAZ-SAN!!
STAZ-SAN!
DUMBASS... HOW ABOUT NOT REPEATEDLY YELLING MY NAME.
WHA ...?
I CAN'T... MOVE...
GOT...NO STRENGTH ...
THAT'S RIGHT ...
ポン
PON (POOF)
NOW HE'S IN A STATE OF ULTIMATE RELAXATION ...
HUH?

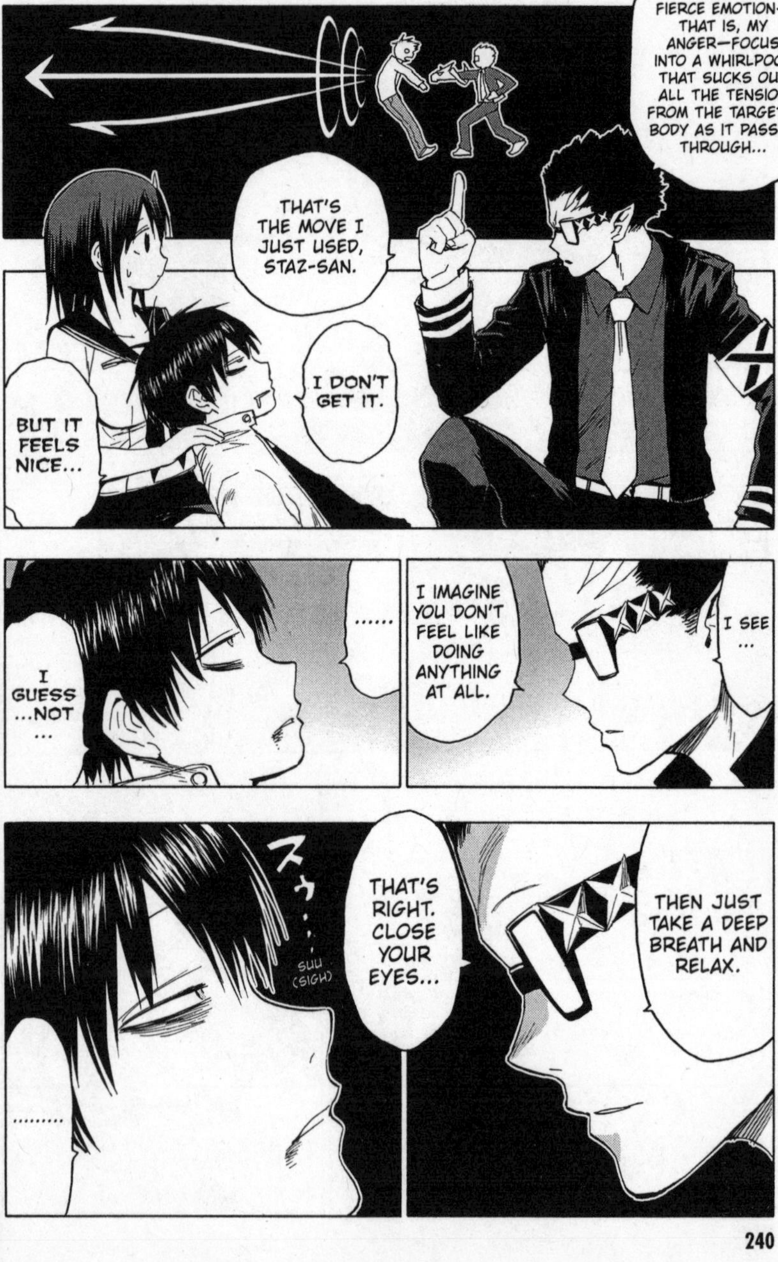
WAVES OF FIERCE EMOTION—THAT IS, MY ANGER—FOCUS INTO A WHIRLPOOL THAT SUCKS OUT ALL THE TENSION FROM THE TARGET'S BODY AS IT PASSES THROUGH...
THAT'S THE MOVE I JUST USED, STAZ-SAN.
I DON'T GET IT.
BUT IT FEELS NICE...
I SEE ...
I IMAGINE YOU DON'T FEEL LIKE DOING ANYTHING AT ALL.
......
I GUESS ...NOT ...
THEN JUST TAKE A DEEP BREATH AND RELAX.
THAT'S RIGHT. CLOSE YOUR EYES...
スゥ...
SUU (SIGH)
....

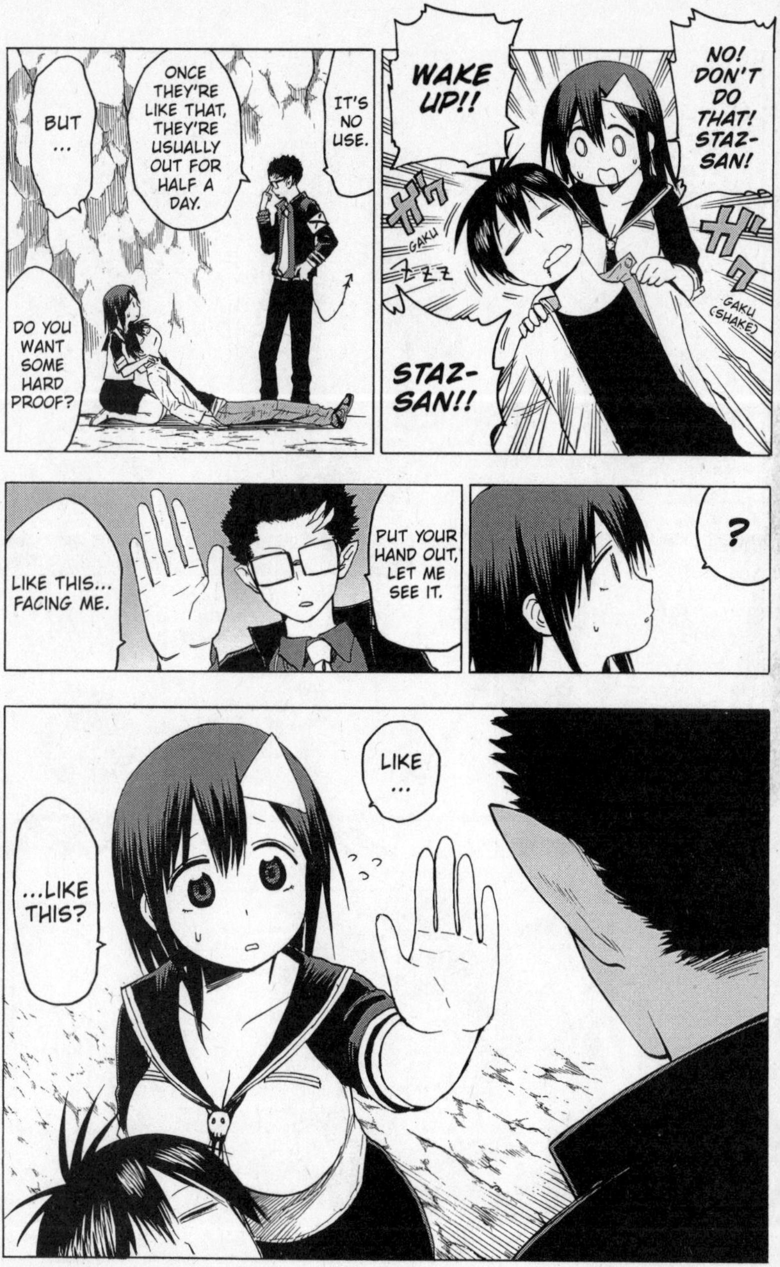
NO! DON'T DO THAT! STAZ-SAN!
WAKE UP!!
GAKU (SHAKE)
GAKU
ZZZ
STAZ-SAN!!
IT'S NO USE.
ONCE THEY'RE LIKE THAT, THEY'RE USUALLY OUT FOR HALF A DAY.
BUT ...
DO YOU WANT SOME HARD PROOF?
?
PUT YOUR HAND OUT, LET ME SEE IT.
LIKE THIS... FACING ME.
LIKE ...
...LIKE THIS?

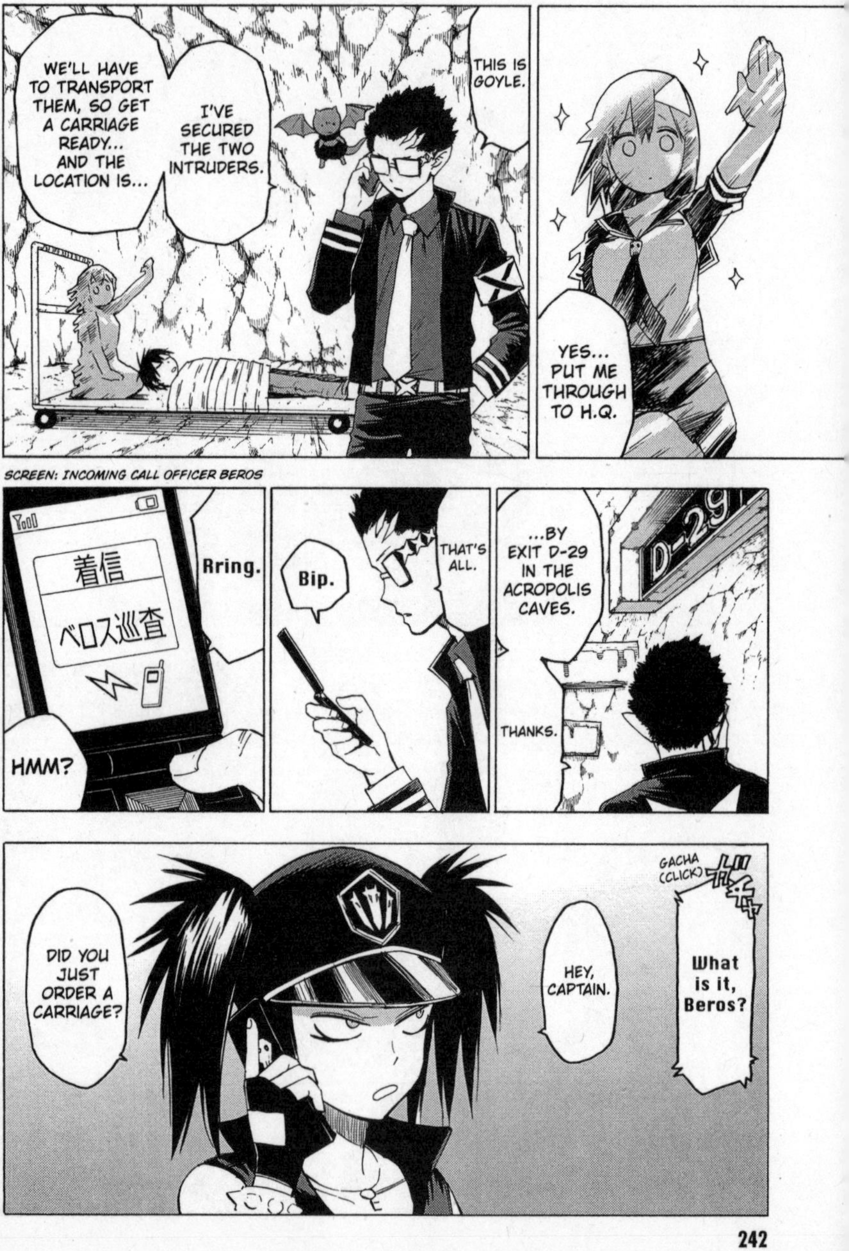
YES... PUT ME THROUGH TO H.Q.
THIS IS GOYLE.
I'VE SECURED THE TWO INTRUDERS.
WE'LL HAVE TO TRANSPORT THEM, SO GET A CARRIAGE READY... AND THE LOCATION IS...
...BY EXIT D-29 IN THE ACROPOLIS CAVES.
D-29
THANKS.
THAT'S ALL.
Bip.
Rring.
着信
ベロス巡査
HMM?
SCREEN: INCOMING CALL OFFICER BEROS
GACHA (CLICK)
What is it, Beros?
HEY, CAPTAIN.
DID YOU JUST ORDER A CARRIAGE?

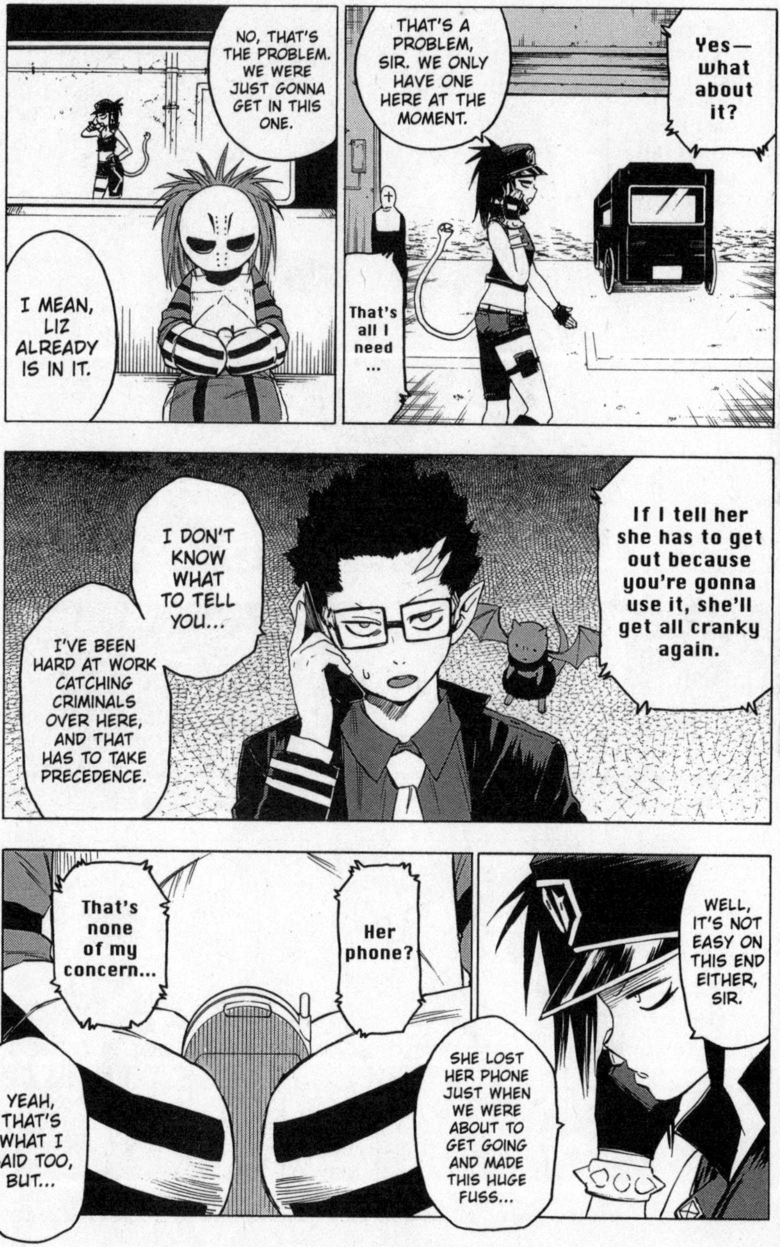
Yes—what about it?
THAT'S A PROBLEM, SIR. WE ONLY HAVE ONE HERE AT THE MOMENT.
That's all I need...
NO, THAT'S THE PROBLEM. WE WERE JUST GONNA GET IN THIS ONE.
I MEAN, LIZ ALREADY IS IN IT.
If I tell her she has to get out because you're gonna use it, she'll get all cranky again.
I DON'T KNOW WHAT TO TELL YOU...
I'VE BEEN HARD AT WORK CATCHING CRIMINALS OVER HERE, AND THAT HAS TO TAKE PRECEDENCE.
WELL, IT'S NOT EASY ON THIS END EITHER, SIR.
SHE LOST HER PHONE JUST WHEN WE WERE ABOUT TO GET GOING AND MADE THIS HUGE FUSS...
Her phone?
That's none of my concern...
YEAH, THAT'S WHAT I SAID TOO, BUT...

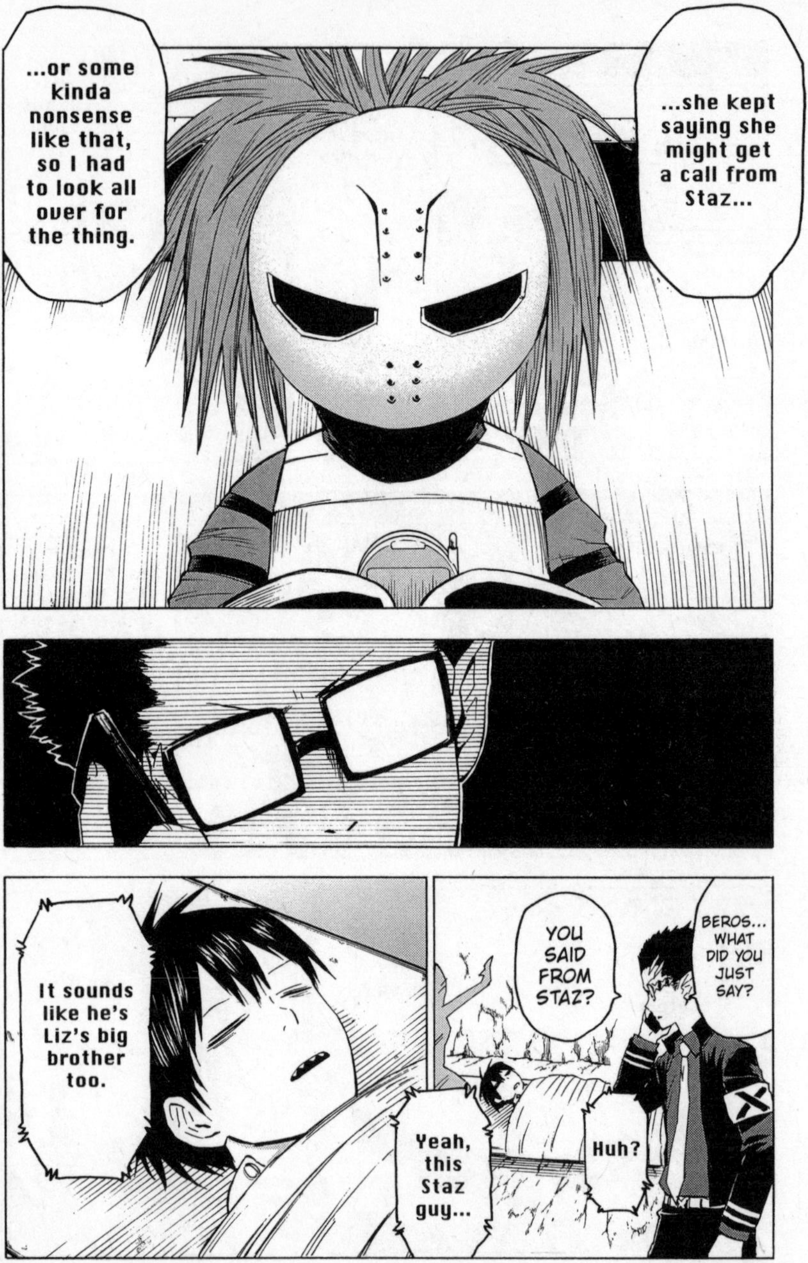
...she kept saying she might get a call from Staz...
...or some kinda nonsense like that, so I had to look all over for the thing.
BEROS... WHAT DID YOU JUST SAY?
YOU SAID FROM STAZ?
Huh?
Yeah, this Staz guy...
It sounds like he's Liz's big brother too.

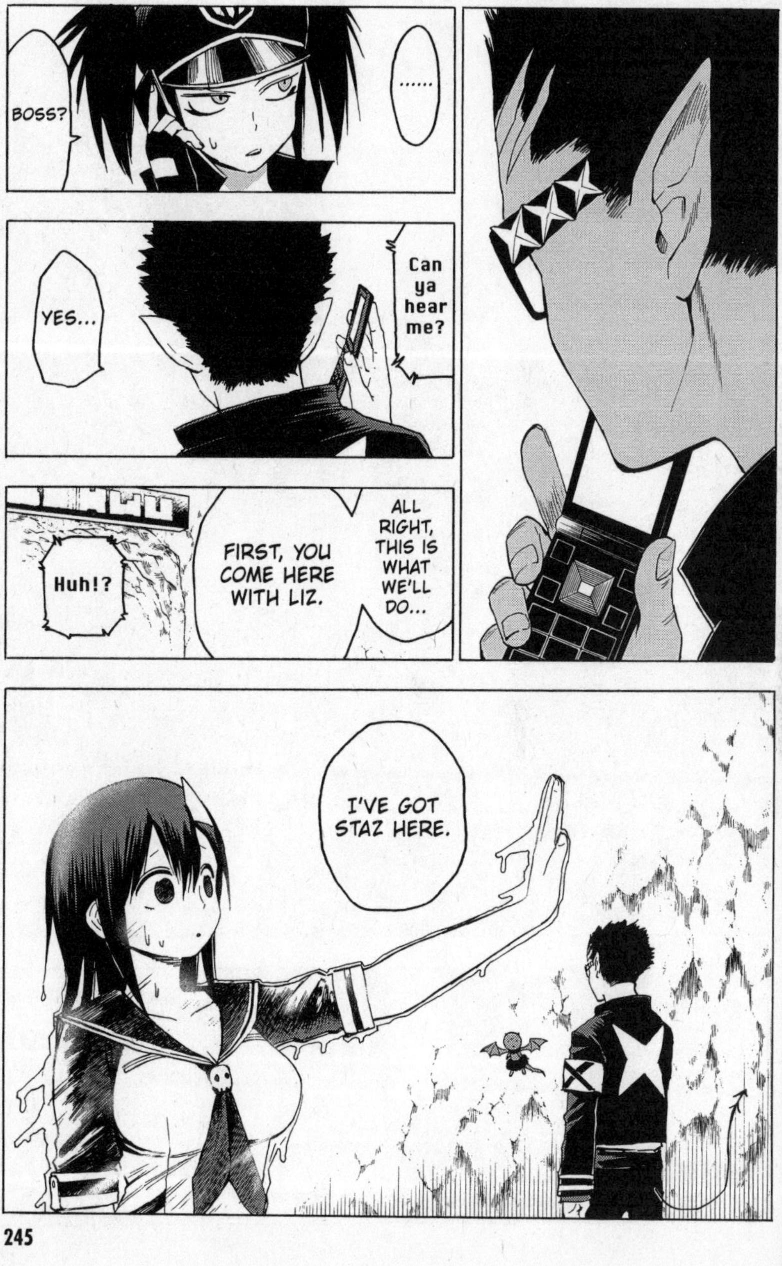
......
BOSS?
Can ya hear me?
YES...
ALL RIGHT, THIS IS WHAT WE'LL DO...
FIRST, YOU COME HERE WITH LIZ.
Huh!?
I'VE GOT STAZ HERE.

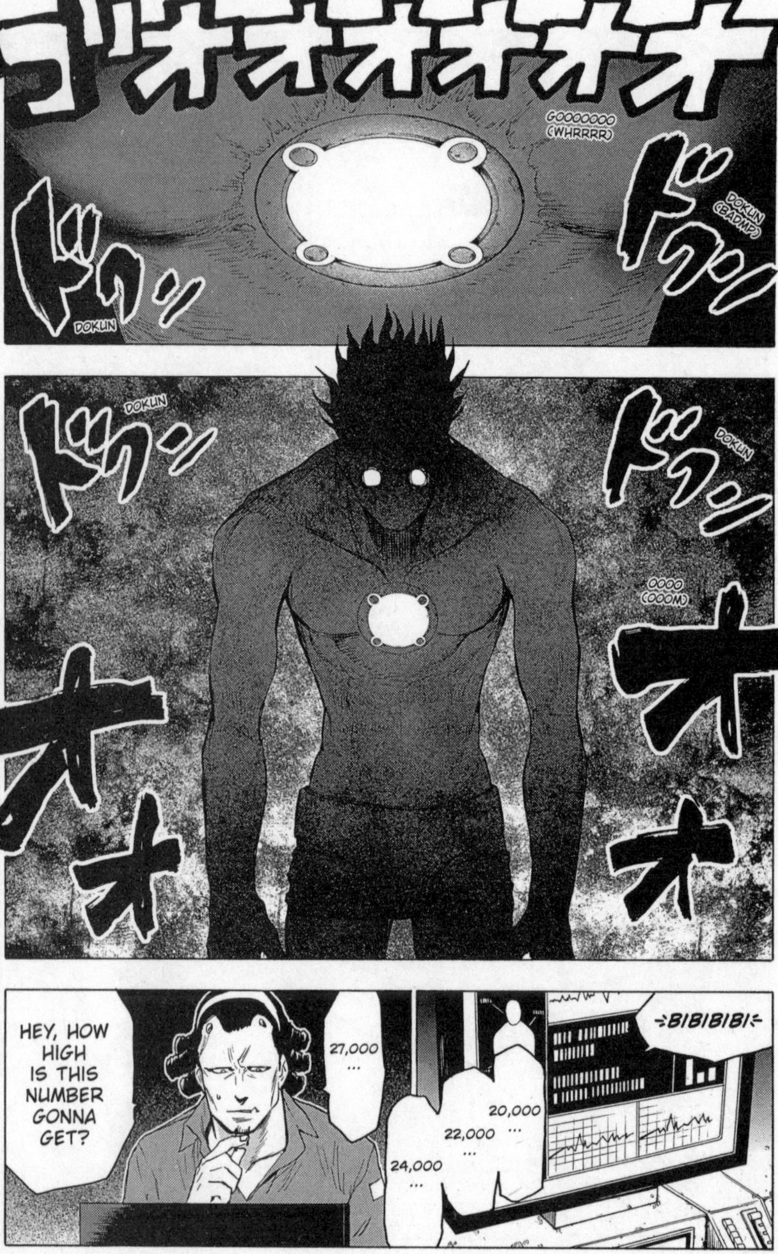
ゴオオオオオオオ
GOOOOOOO (WHRRRR)
ドクン
DOKUN (BADMP)
ドクン
DOKUN
ドクン
DOKUN
オオ
OOOO (OOOM)
ドクン
DOKUN
オオ
≈BIBIBIBI≈
20,000 ...
22,000 ...
24,000 ...
27,000 ...
HEY, HOW HIGH IS THIS NUMBER GONNA GET?

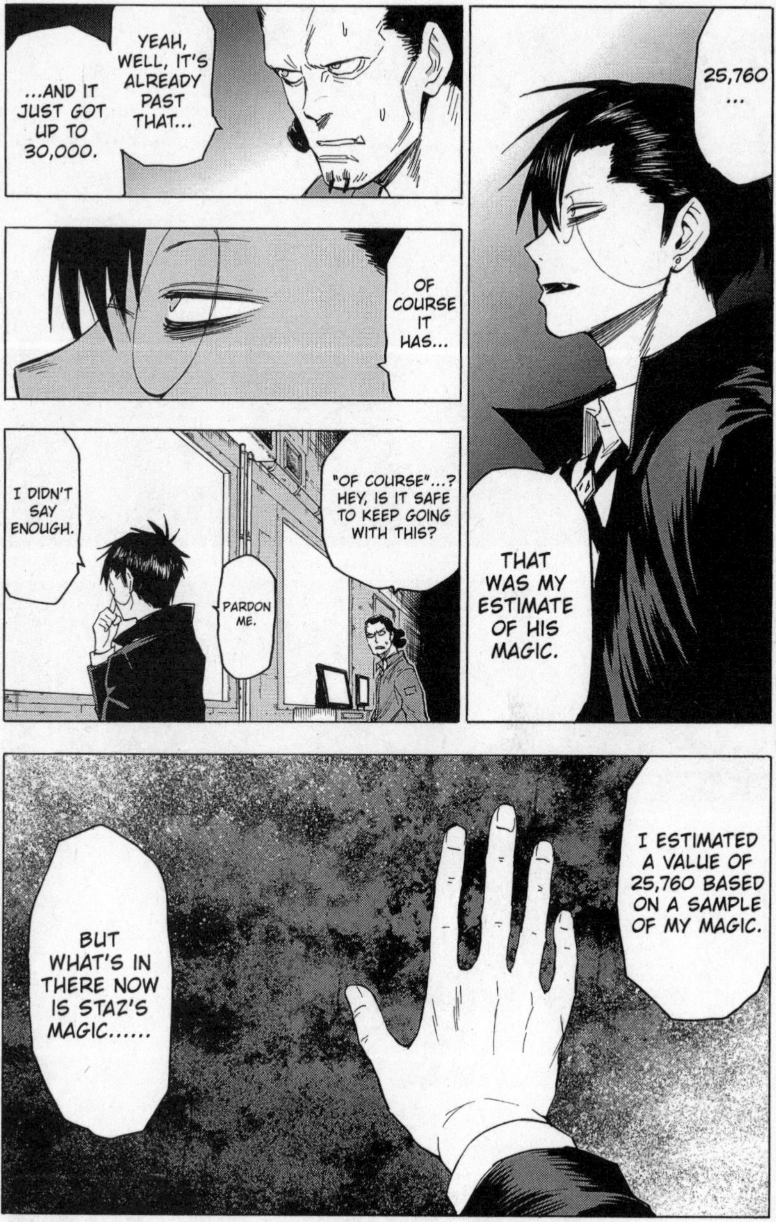
25,760 ...
THAT WAS MY ESTIMATE OF HIS MAGIC.
YEAH, WELL, IT'S ALREADY PAST THAT...
...AND IT JUST GOT UP TO 30,000.
OF COURSE IT HAS...
"OF COURSE"...? HEY, IS IT SAFE TO KEEP GOING WITH THIS?
PARDON ME.
I DIDN'T SAY ENOUGH.
I ESTIMATED A VALUE OF 25,760 BASED ON A SAMPLE OF MY MAGIC.
BUT WHAT'S IN THERE NOW IS STAZ'S MAGIC......

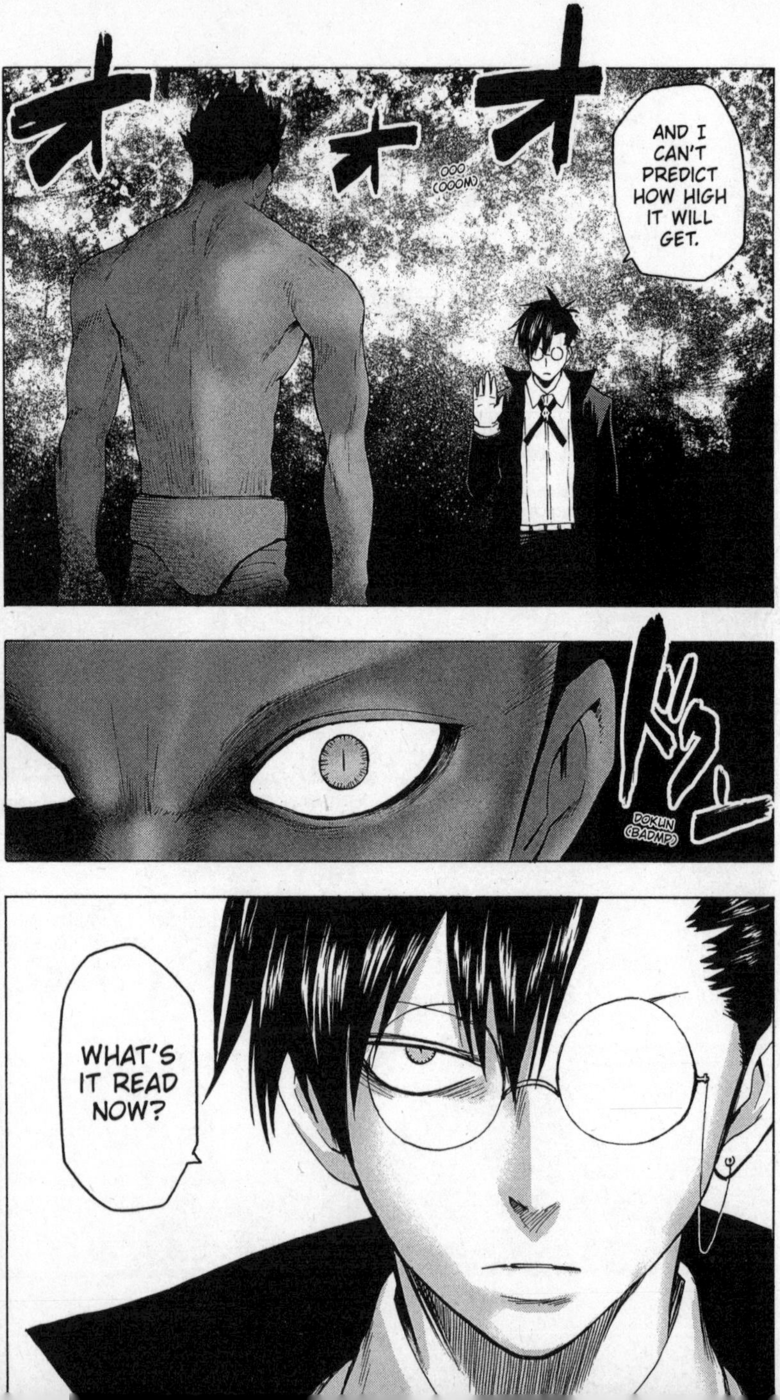
AND I CAN'T PREDICT HOW HIGH IT WILL GET.
OOO (OOOM)
DOKUN (BADMP)
WHAT'S IT READ NOW?

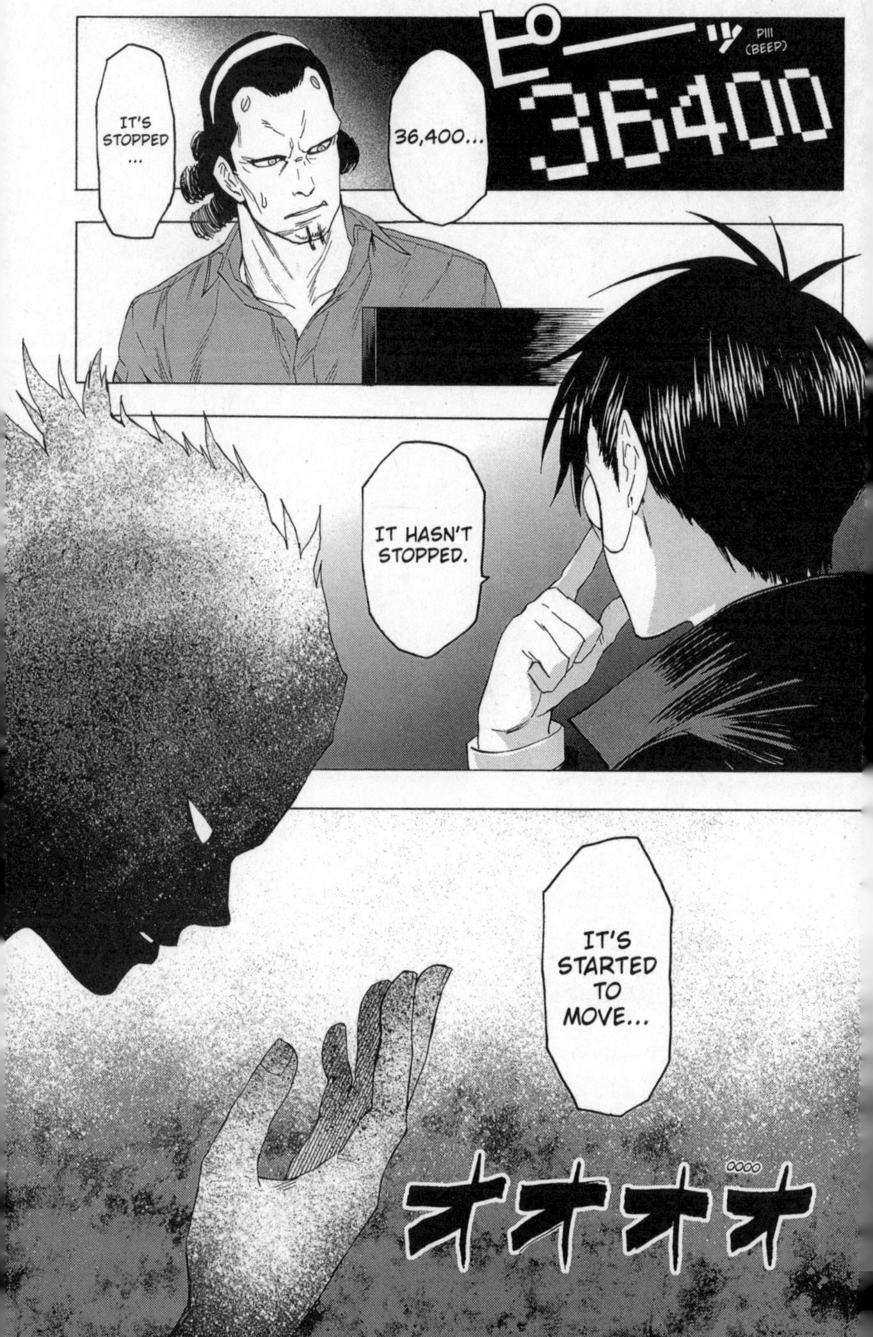
ピーーッ
PIII (BEEP)
36400
36,400...
IT'S STOPPED ...
IT HASN'T STOPPED.
IT'S STARTED TO MOVE...
オオオオ
OOOO

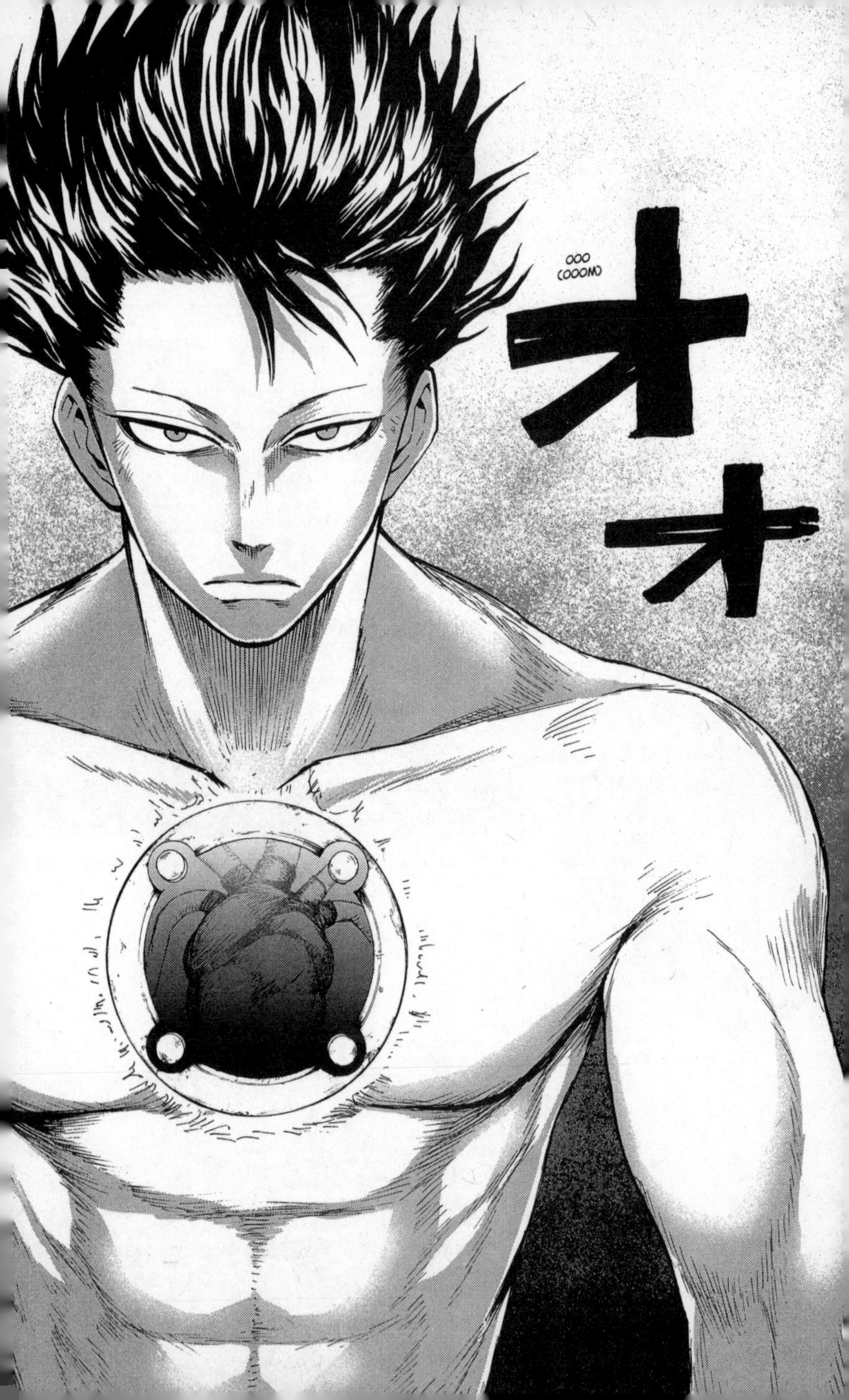
オオ
(WOOO)
OOO

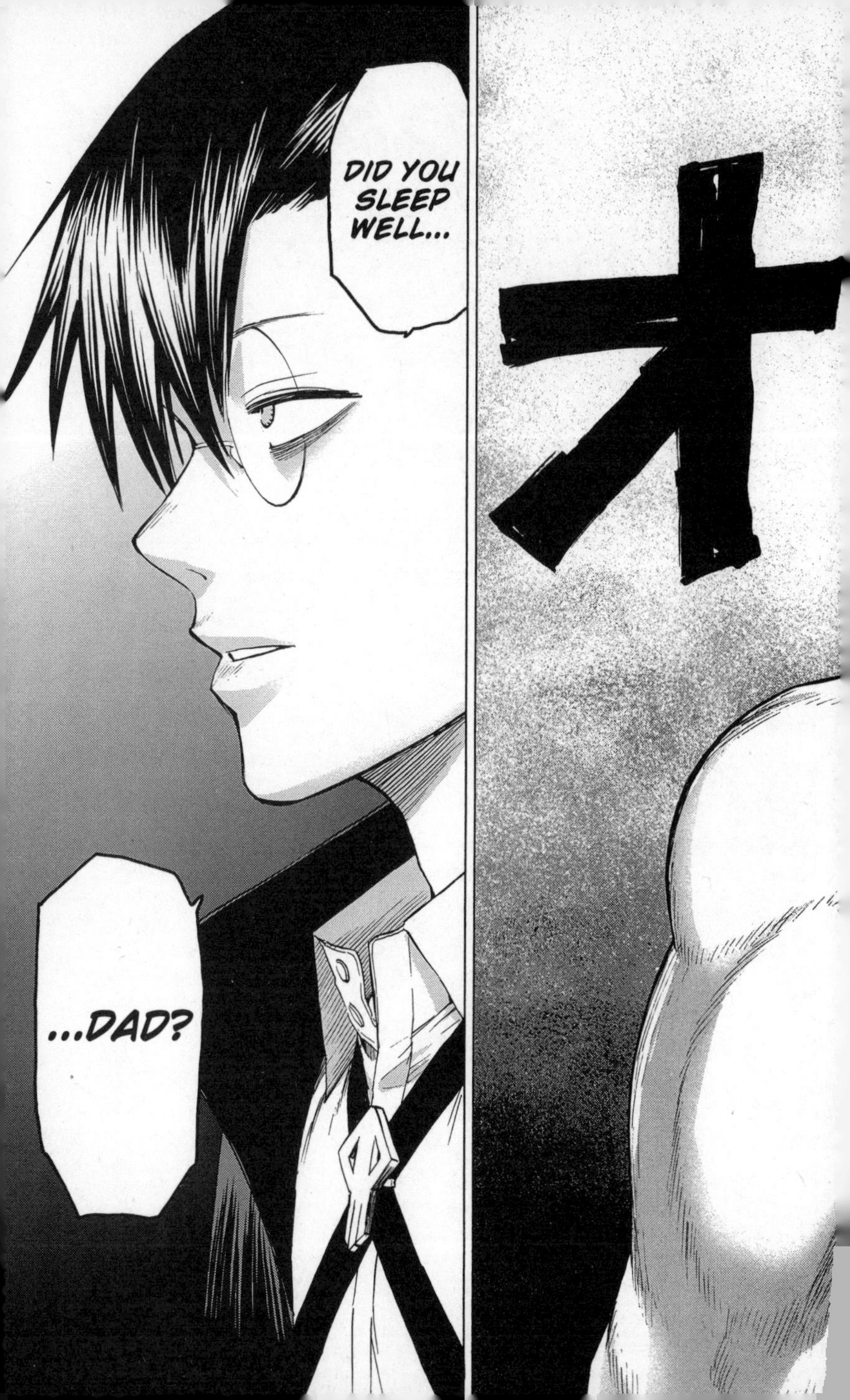
オ
DID YOU SLEEP WELL...
...DAD?

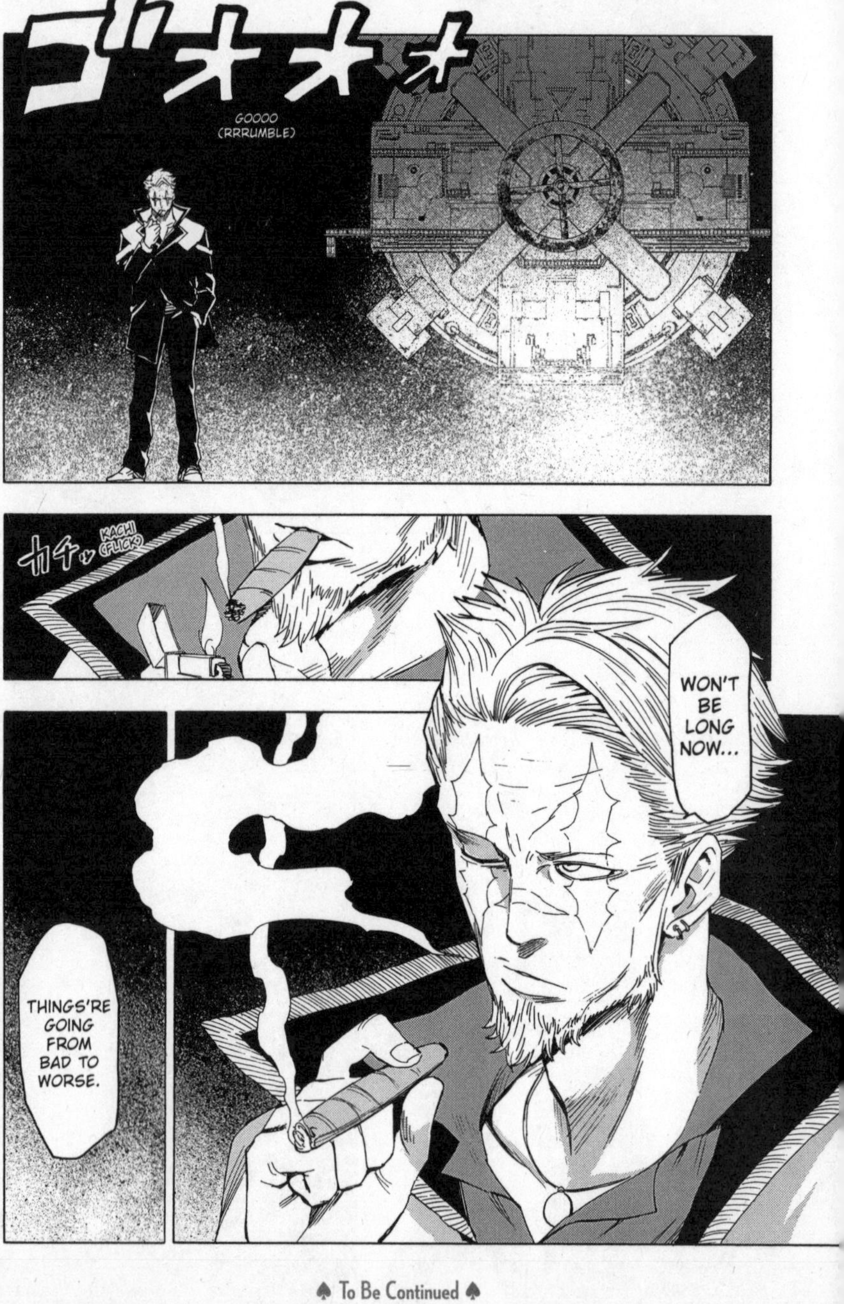
ゴオオオ
GOOOO (RRRUMBLE)
カチッ
KACHI (FLICK)
WON'T BE LONG NOW...
THINGS'RE GOING FROM BAD TO WORSE.

♠ To Be Continued ♠

FABLED CREATURE
KATREENA

A SPIRIT
STUCK IN A
BUSH, LOOKING
SOMEHOW
APOLOGETIC.
KNOWS A LOT
OF PROVERBS.

BLOOD LAD

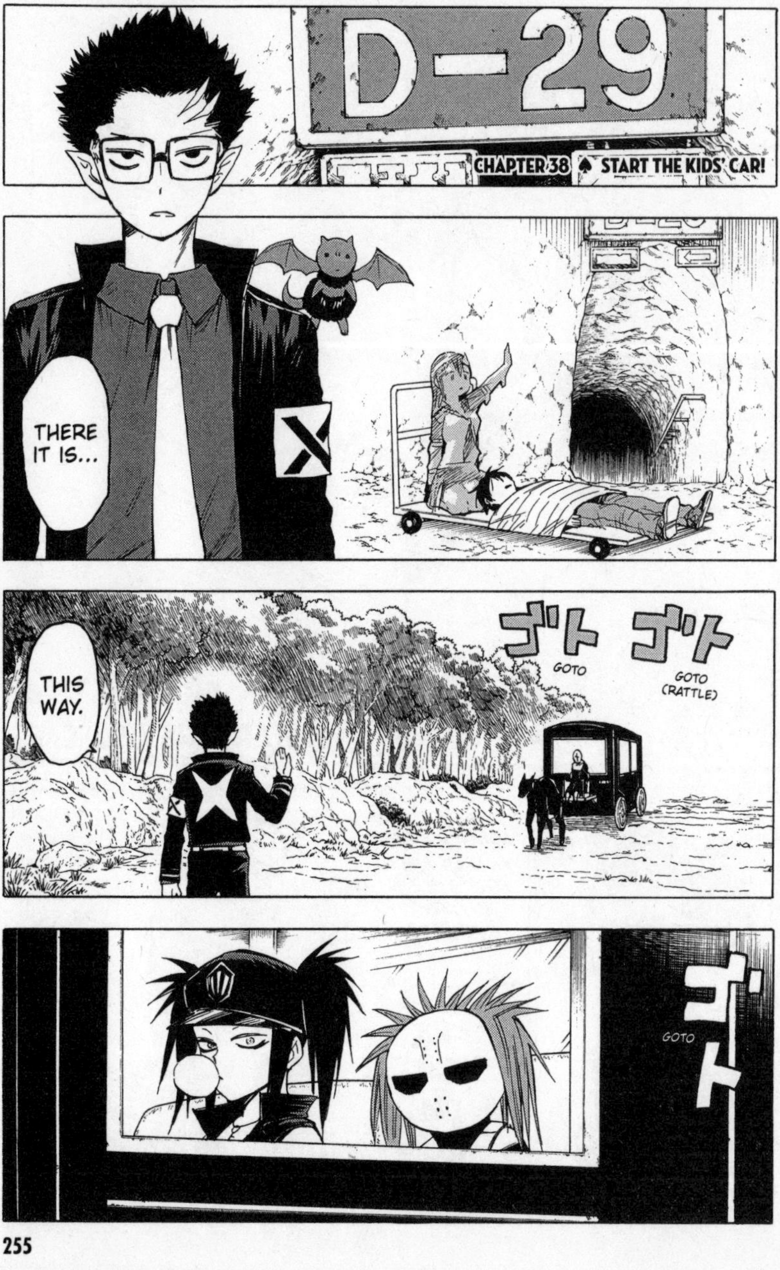
D-29
CHAPTER 38 ♠ START THE KIDS' CAR!
THERE IT IS...
ゴト
GOTO
ゴト
GOTO (RATTLE)
THIS WAY.
ゴト
GOTO

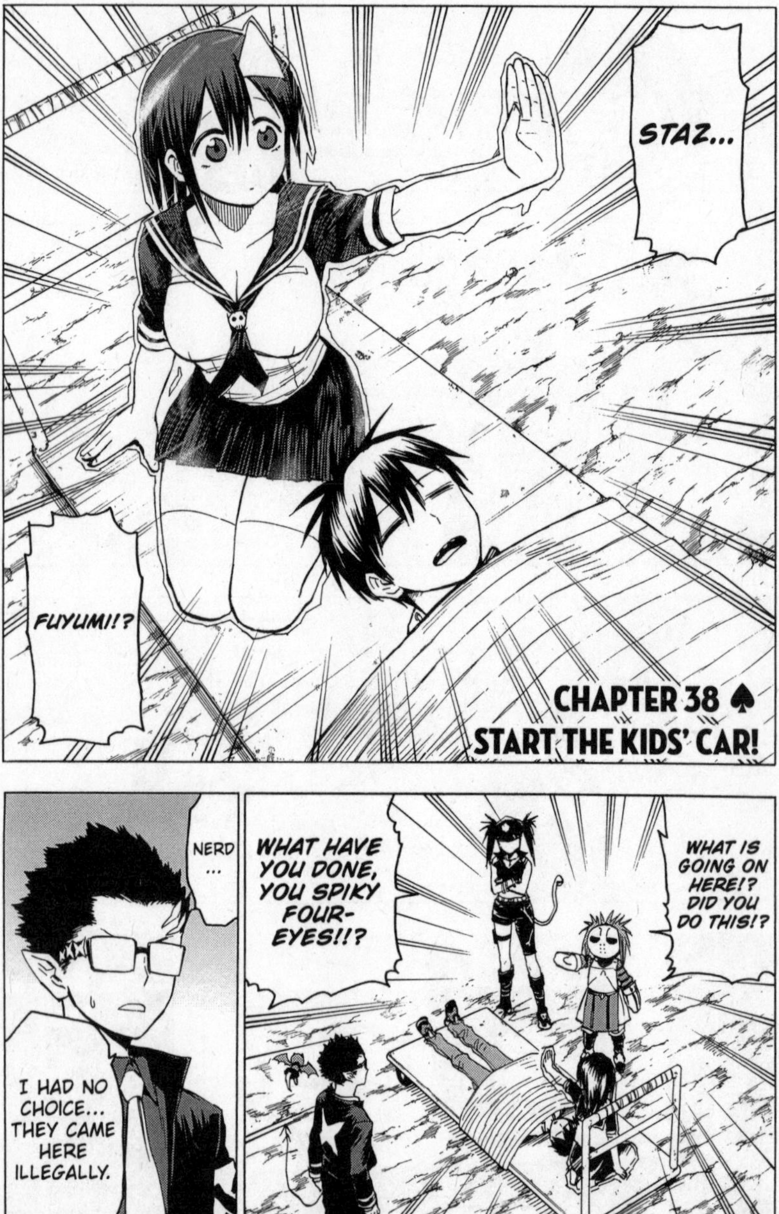
STAZ...
FUYUMI!?
CHAPTER 38 ♠
START THE KIDS' CAR!
WHAT IS GOING ON HERE!? DID YOU DO THIS!?
WHAT HAVE YOU DONE, YOU SPIKY FOUR-EYES!!?
NERD ...
I HAD NO CHOICE... THEY CAME HERE ILLEGALLY.

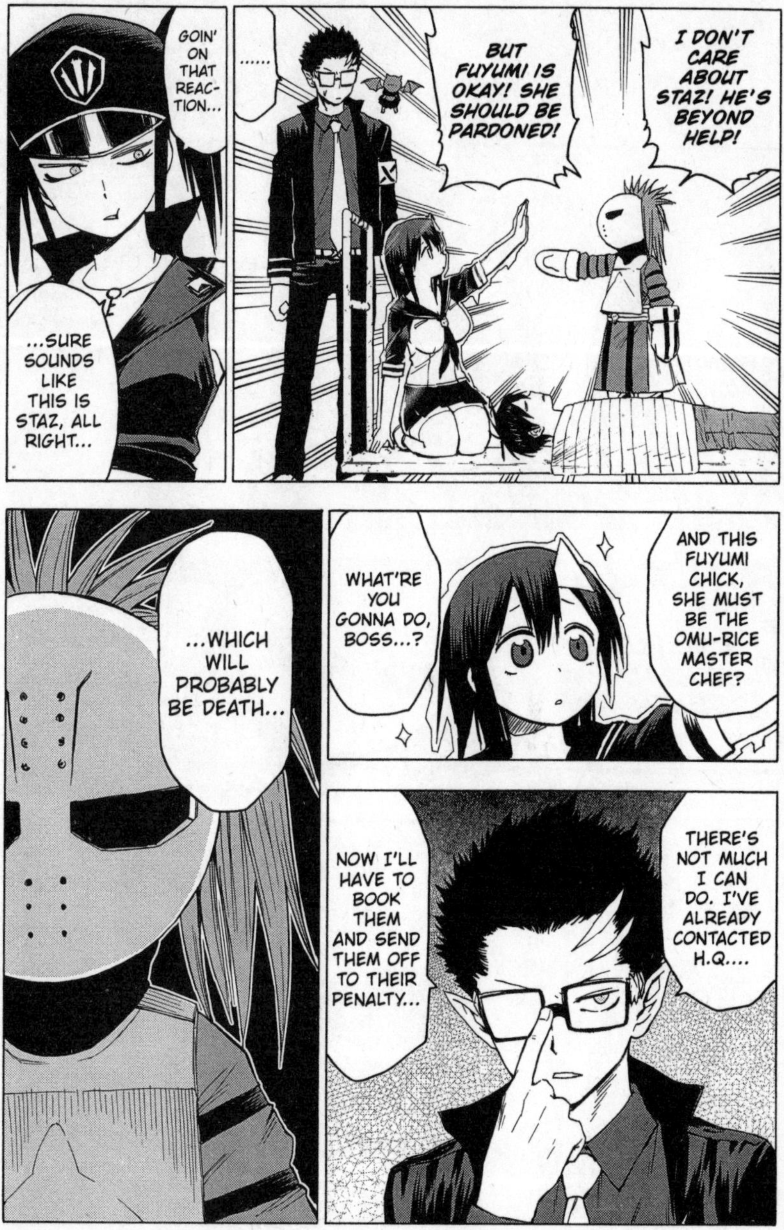
I DON'T CARE ABOUT STAZ! HE'S BEYOND HELP!
BUT FUYUMI IS OKAY! SHE SHOULD BE PARDONED!
......
GOIN' ON THAT REACTION...
...SURE SOUNDS LIKE THIS IS STAZ, ALL RIGHT...
AND THIS FUYUMI CHICK, SHE MUST BE THE OMU-RICE MASTER CHEF?
WHAT'RE YOU GONNA DO, BOSS...?
THERE'S NOT MUCH I CAN DO. I'VE ALREADY CONTACTED H.Q....
NOW I'LL HAVE TO BOOK THEM AND SEND THEM OFF TO THEIR PENALTY...
...WHICH WILL PROBABLY BE DEATH...

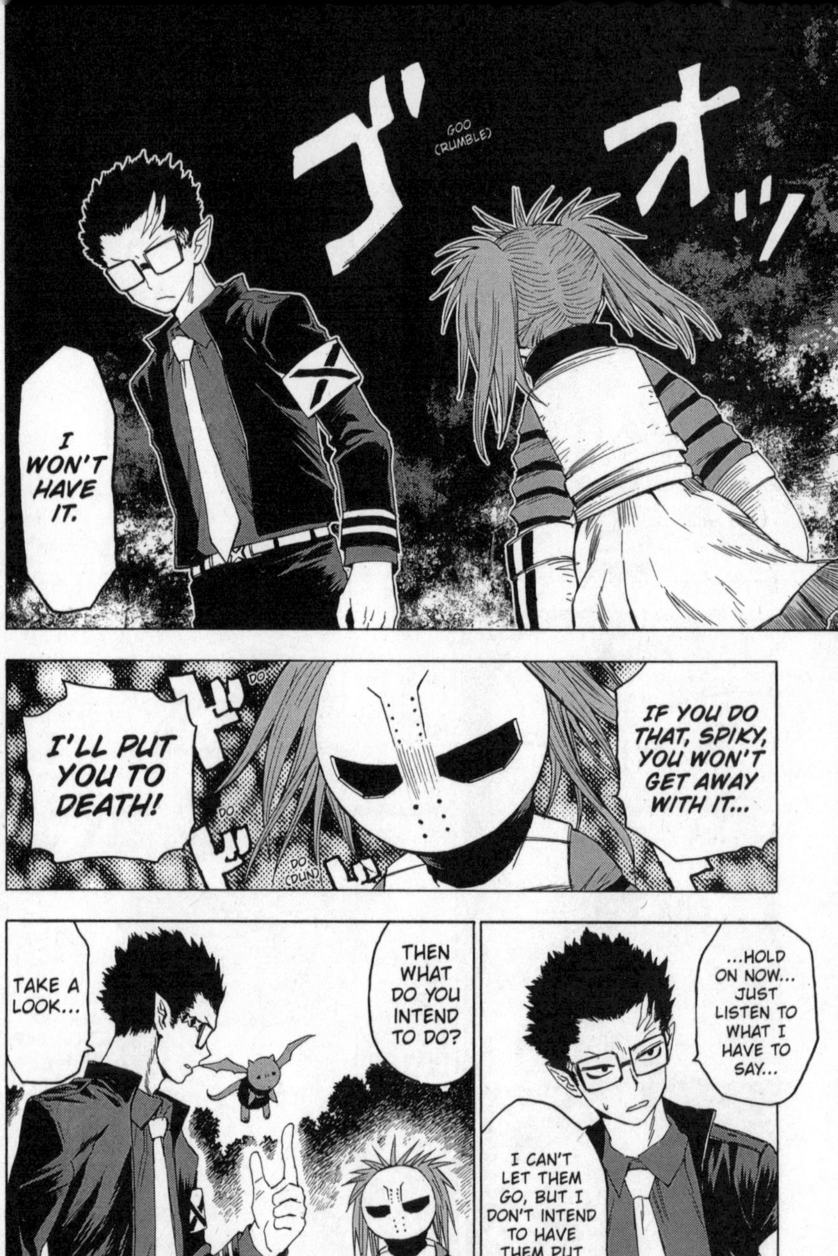
GOO (RUMBLE)
I WON'T HAVE IT.
IF YOU DO THAT, SPIKY, YOU WON'T GET AWAY WITH IT...
DO
I'LL PUT YOU TO DEATH!
DO
DO (DUN)
...HOLD ON NOW... JUST LISTEN TO WHAT I HAVE TO SAY...
I CAN'T LET THEM GO, BUT I DON'T INTEND TO HAVE THEM PUT TO DEATH EITHER.
THEN WHAT DO YOU INTEND TO DO?
TAKE A LOOK...

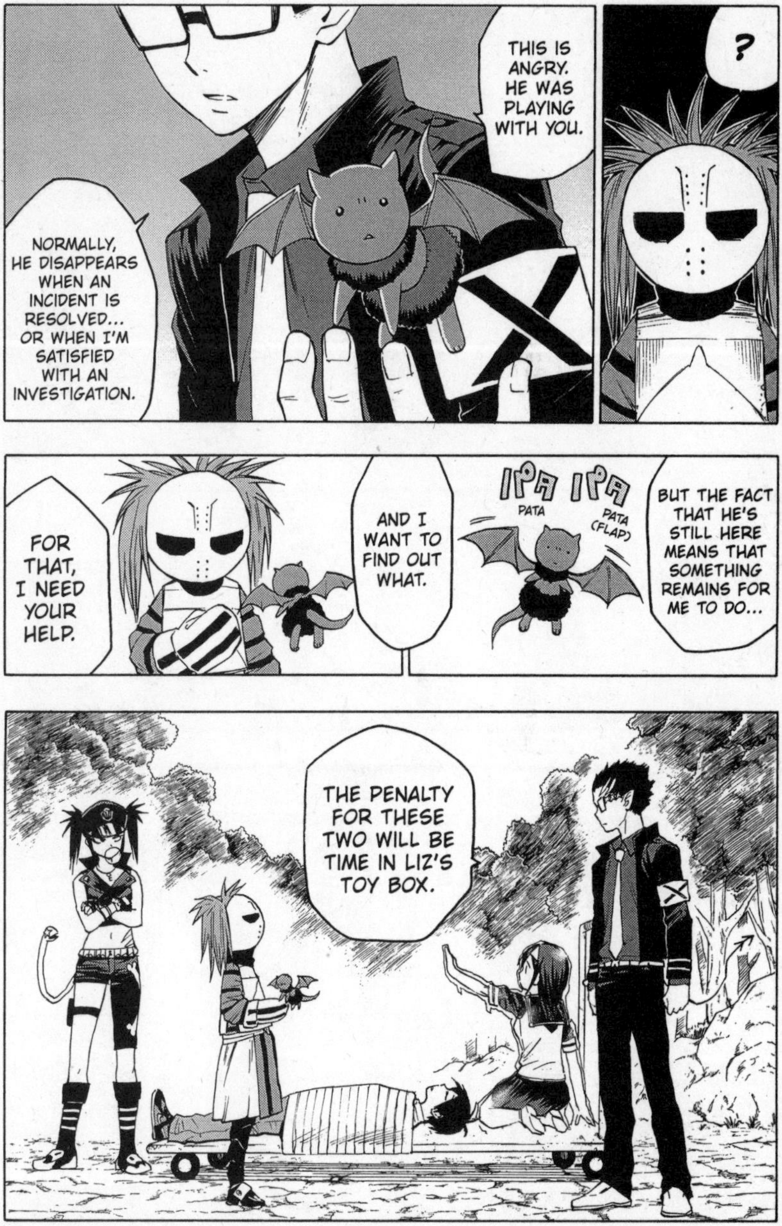
?
THIS IS ANGRY. HE WAS PLAYING WITH YOU.
NORMALLY, HE DISAPPEARS WHEN AN INCIDENT IS RESOLVED... OR WHEN I'M SATISFIED WITH AN INVESTIGATION.
BUT THE FACT THAT HE'S STILL HERE MEANS THAT SOMETHING REMAINS FOR ME TO DO...
PATA PATA (FLAP)
AND I WANT TO FIND OUT WHAT.
FOR THAT, I NEED YOUR HELP.
THE PENALTY FOR THESE TWO WILL BE TIME IN LIZ'S TOY BOX.

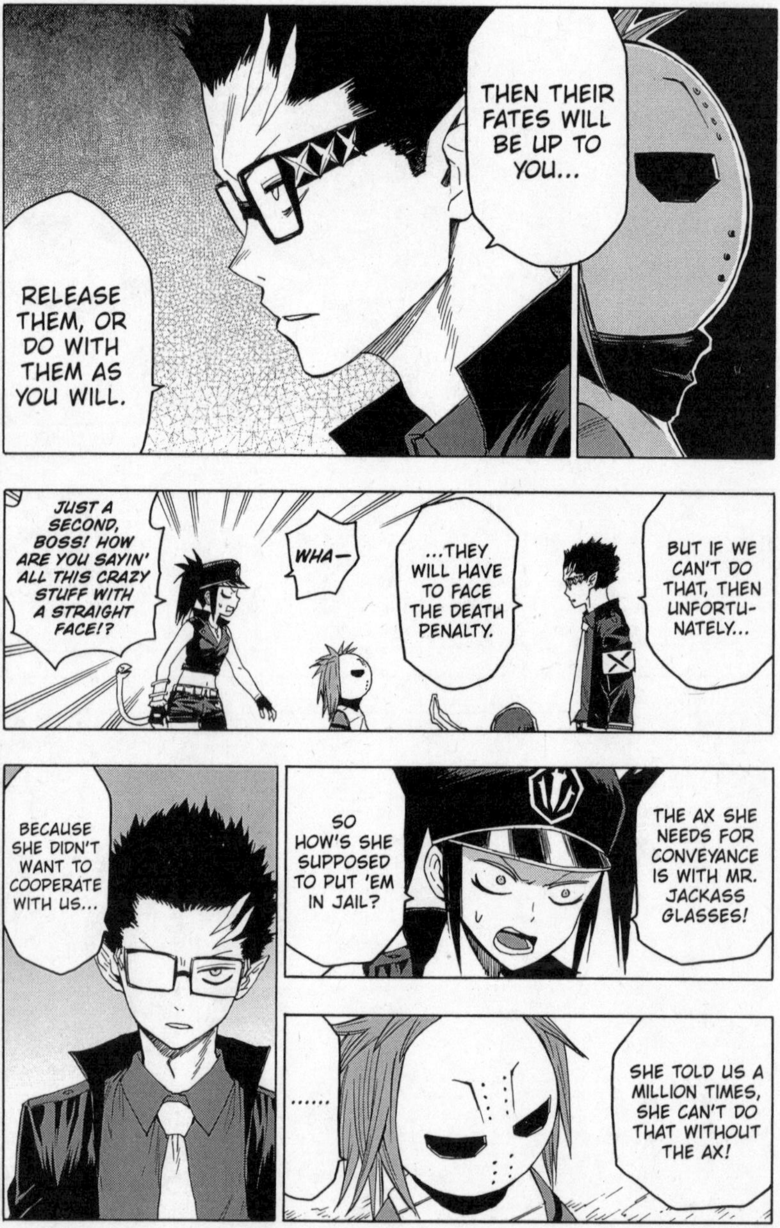
THEN THEIR FATES WILL BE UP TO YOU...
RELEASE THEM, OR DO WITH THEM AS YOU WILL.
BUT IF WE CAN'T DO THAT, THEN UNFORTUNATELY...
...THEY WILL HAVE TO FACE THE DEATH PENALTY.
WHA—
JUST A SECOND, BOSS! HOW ARE YOU SAYIN' ALL THIS CRAZY STUFF WITH A STRAIGHT FACE!?
THE AX SHE NEEDS FOR CONVEYANCE IS WITH MR. JACKASS GLASSES!
SO HOW'S SHE SUPPOSED TO PUT 'EM IN JAIL?
SHE TOLD US A MILLION TIMES, SHE CAN'T DO THAT WITHOUT THE AX!
......
BECAUSE SHE DIDN'T WANT TO COOPERATE WITH US...

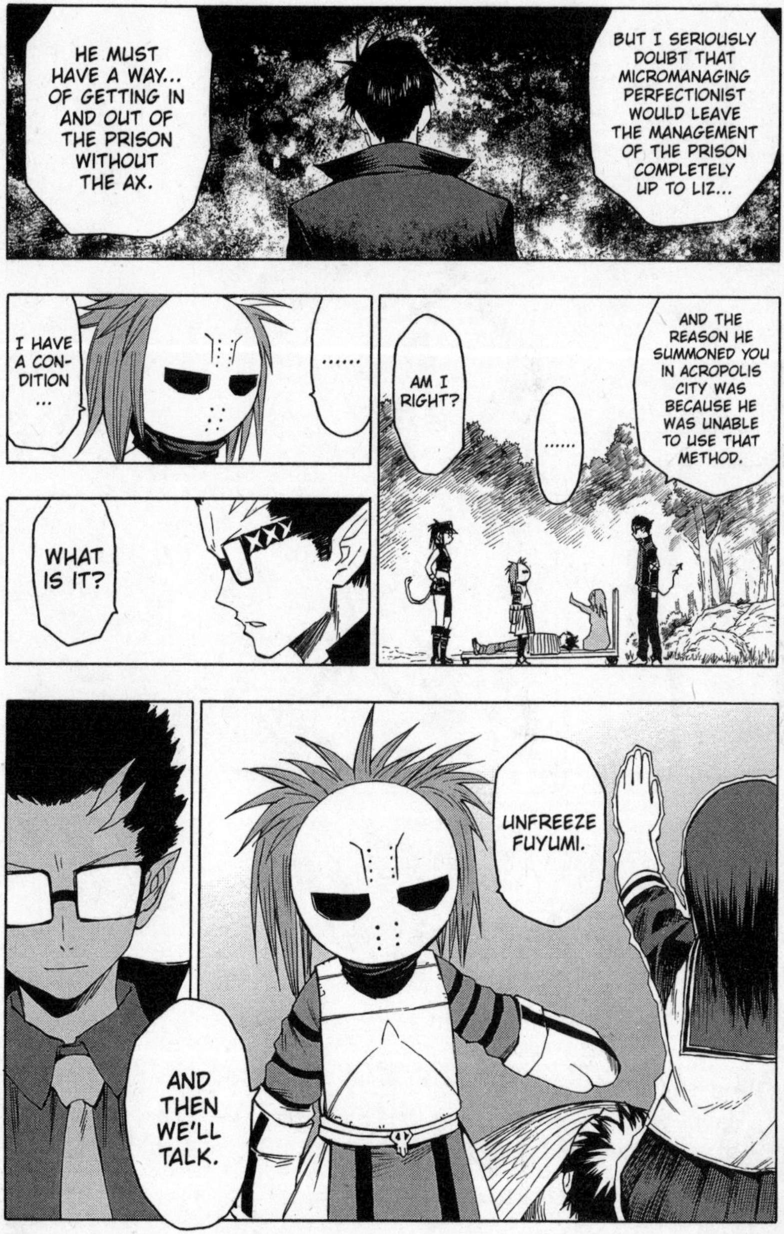
BUT I SERIOUSLY DOUBT THAT MICROMANAGING PERFECTIONIST WOULD LEAVE THE MANAGEMENT OF THE PRISON COMPLETELY UP TO LIZ...
HE MUST HAVE A WAY... OF GETTING IN AND OUT OF THE PRISON WITHOUT THE AX.
AND THE REASON HE SUMMONED YOU IN ACROPOLIS CITY WAS BECAUSE HE WAS UNABLE TO USE THAT METHOD.
......
AM I RIGHT?
......
I HAVE A CONDITION ...
WHAT IS IT?
UNFREEZE FUYUMI.
AND THEN WE'LL TALK.

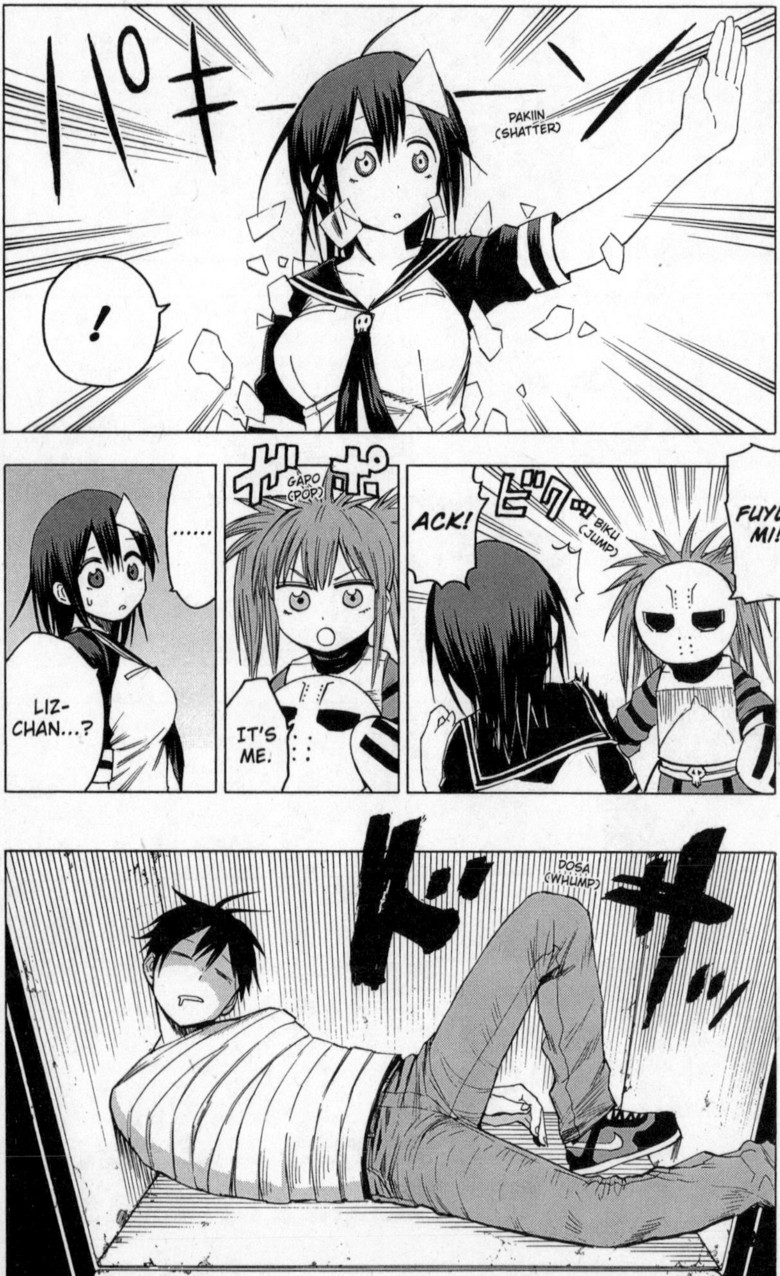
PAKIIN (SHATTER)
!
FUYU-MI!
BIKU (JUMP)
ACK!
GAPO (POP)
IT'S ME.
......
LIZ-CHAN...?
DOSA (WHUMP)

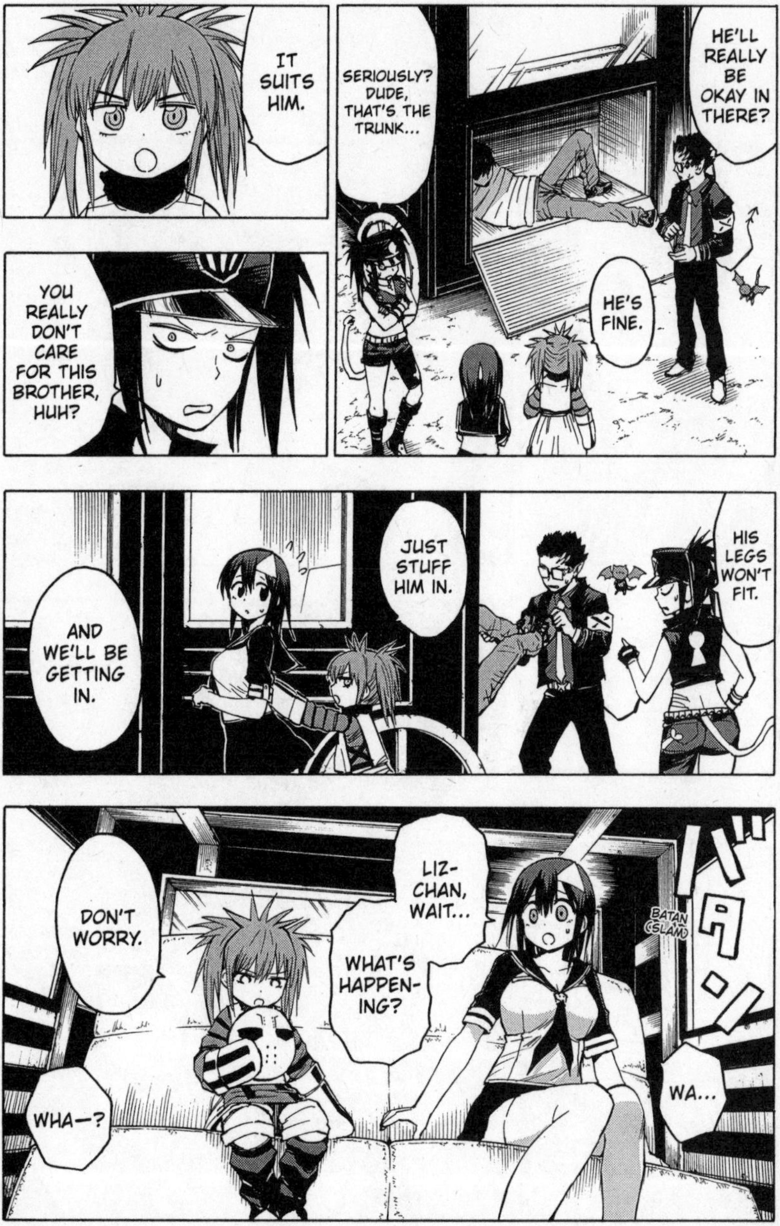
HE'LL REALLY BE OKAY IN THERE?
SERIOUSLY? DUDE, THAT'S THE TRUNK...
HE'S FINE.
IT SUITS HIM.
YOU REALLY DON'T CARE FOR THIS BROTHER, HUH?
HIS LEGS WON'T FIT.
JUST STUFF HIM IN.
AND WE'LL BE GETTING IN.
BATAN (SLAM)
WA...
LIZ-CHAN, WAIT...
WHAT'S HAPPENING?
DON'T WORRY.
WHA—?

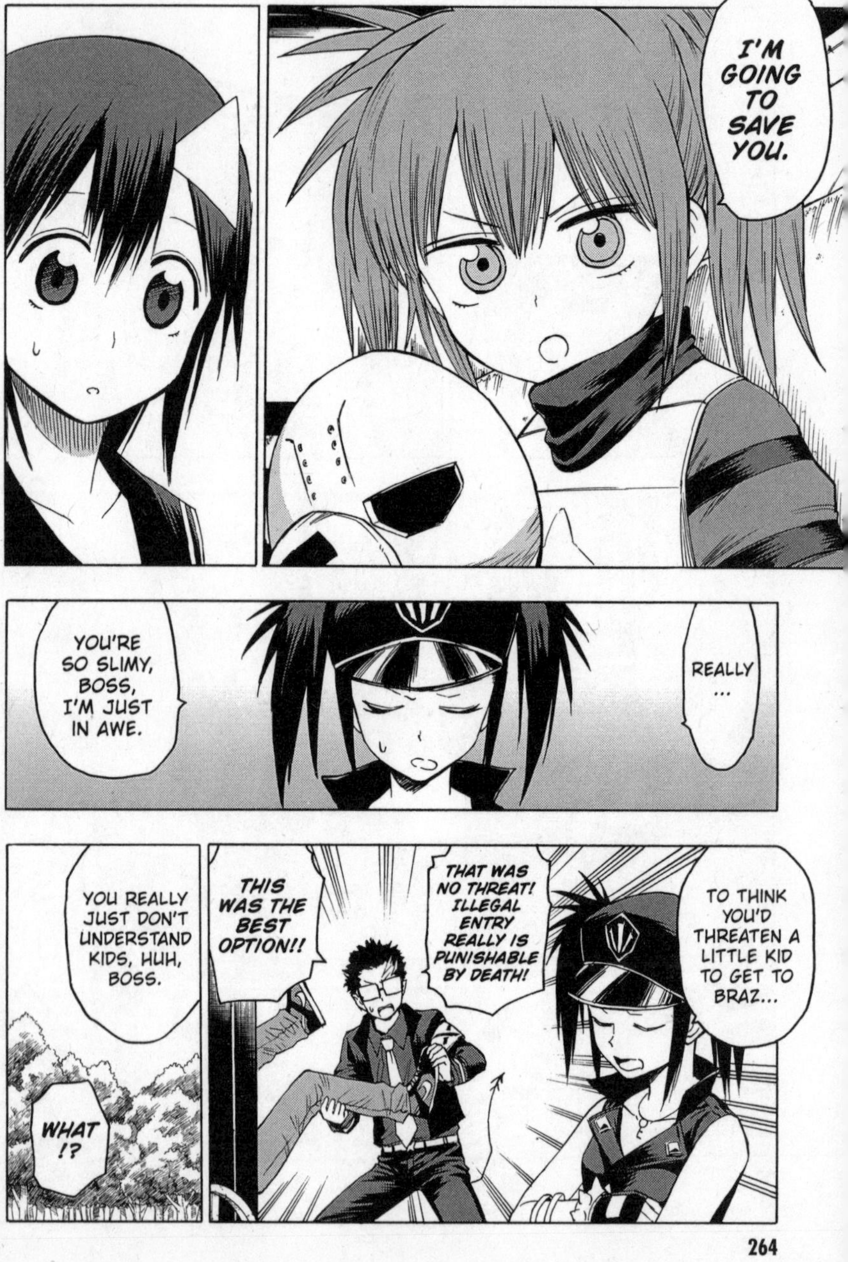
I'M GOING TO SAVE YOU.
REALLY...
YOU'RE SO SLIMY, BOSS, I'M JUST IN AWE.
TO THINK YOU'D THREATEN A LITTLE KID TO GET TO BRAZ...
THAT WAS NO THREAT! ILLEGAL ENTRY REALLY IS PUNISHABLE BY DEATH!
THIS WAS THE BEST OPTION!!
YOU REALLY JUST DON'T UNDERSTAND KIDS, HUH, BOSS.
WHAT!?

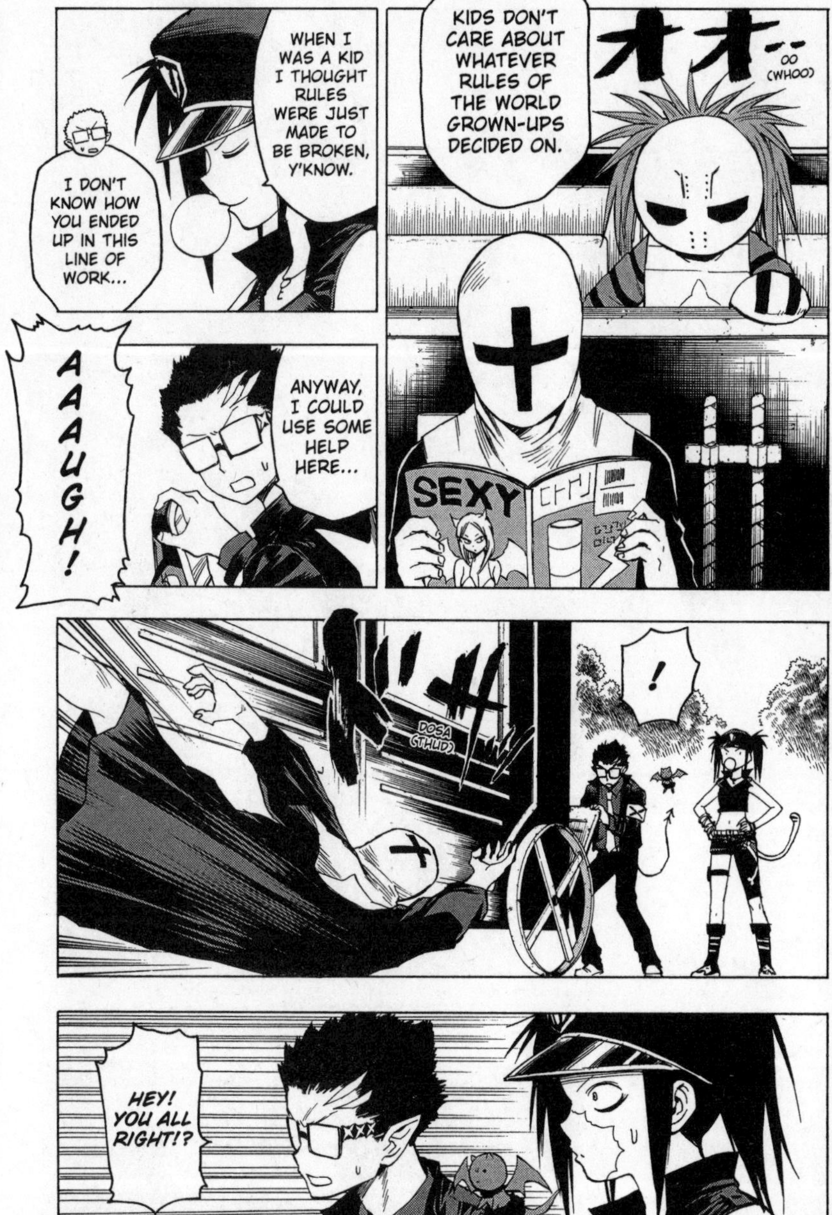
KIDS DON'T CARE ABOUT WHATEVER RULES OF THE WORLD GROWN-UPS DECIDED ON.
オオー
OO (WHOO)
WHEN I WAS A KID I THOUGHT RULES WERE JUST MADE TO BE BROKEN, Y'KNOW.
I DON'T KNOW HOW YOU ENDED UP IN THIS LINE OF WORK...
ANYWAY, I COULD USE SOME HELP HERE...
AAAAUGH!
SEXY
!
DOSA (THUD)
HEY! YOU ALL RIGHT!?

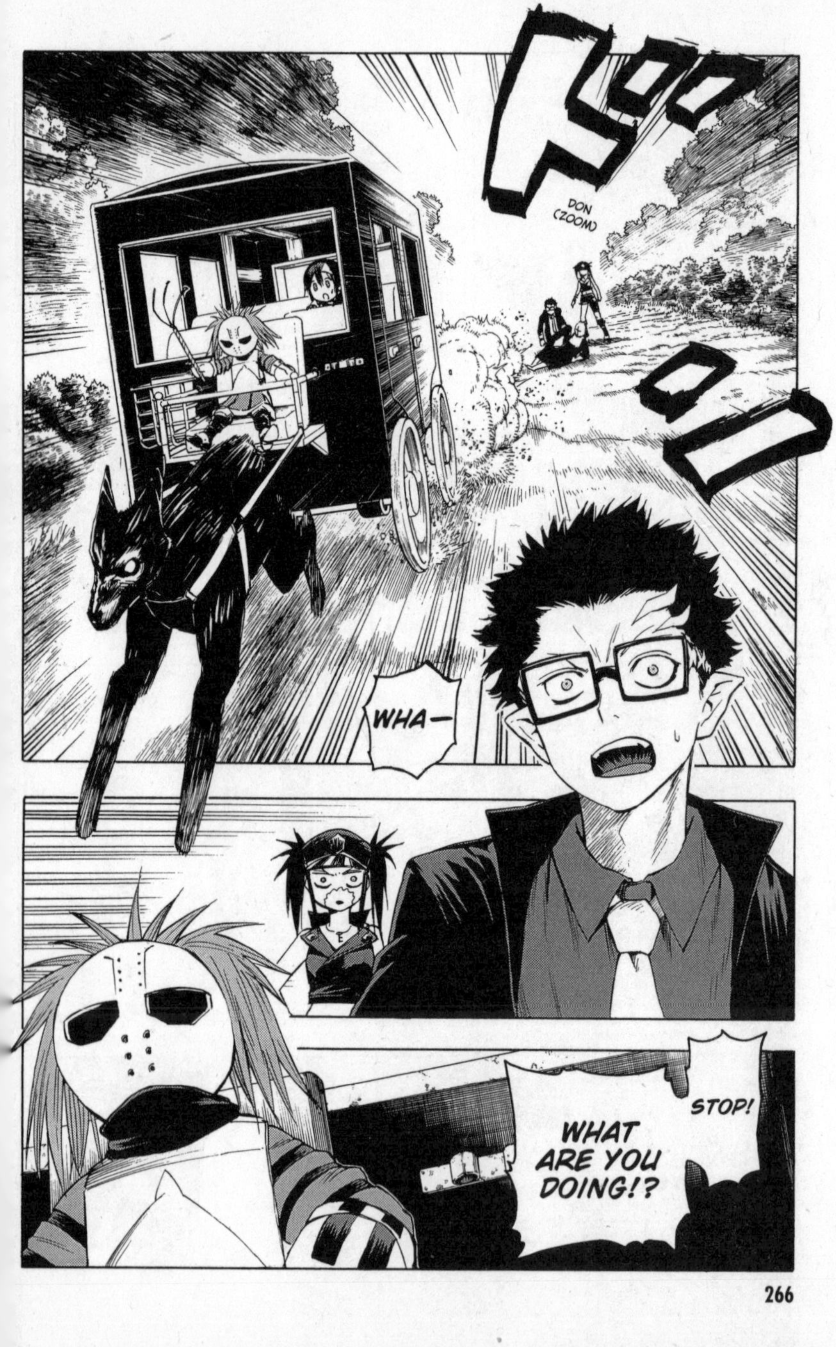
DON
(ZOOM)
WHA—
STOP!
WHAT ARE YOU DOING!?

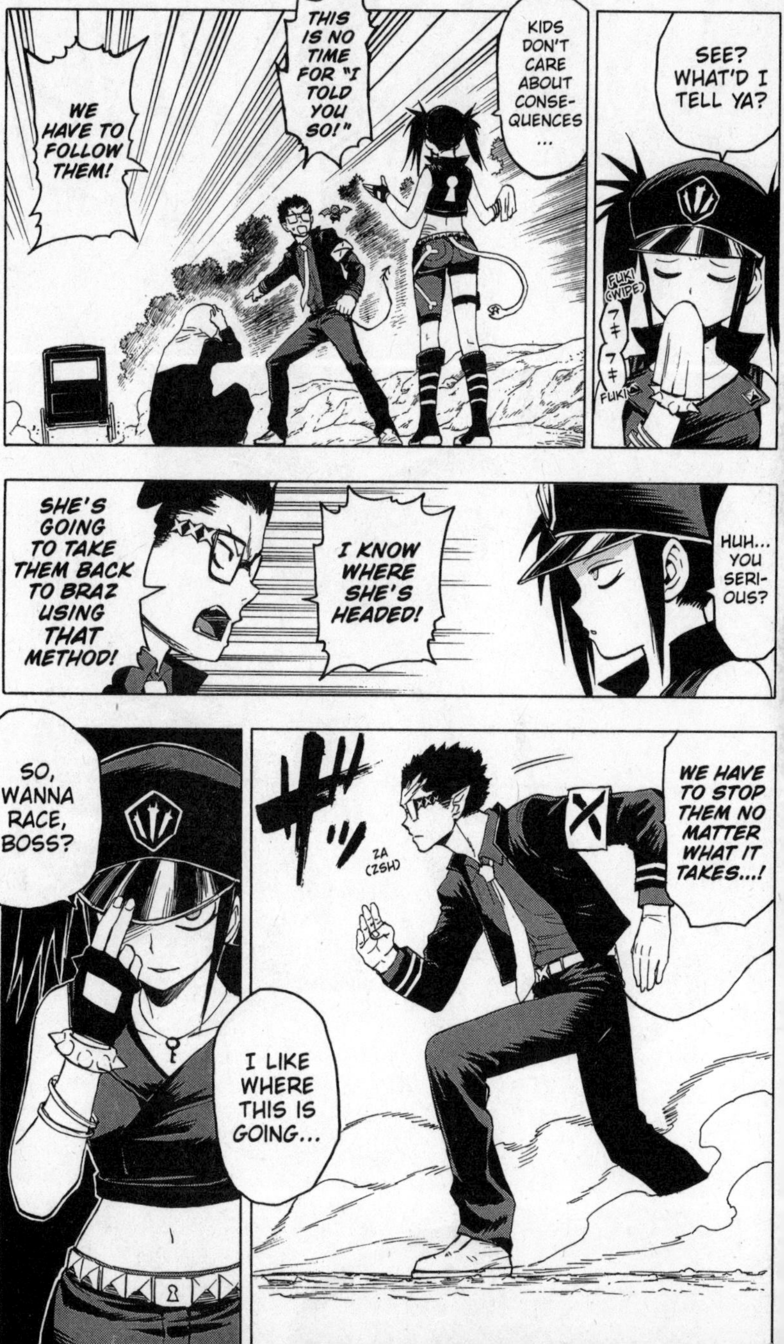
SEE? WHAT'D I TELL YA?
FUKI (WIPE)
フキ
フキ
FUKI
KIDS DON'T CARE ABOUT CONSE-QUENCES...
THIS IS NO TIME FOR "I TOLD YOU SO!"
WE HAVE TO FOLLOW THEM!
HUH... YOU SERI-OUS?
I KNOW WHERE SHE'S HEADED!
SHE'S GOING TO TAKE THEM BACK TO BRAZ USING THAT METHOD!
WE HAVE TO STOP THEM NO MATTER WHAT IT TAKES...!
ZA (ZSH)
SO, WANNA RACE, BOSS?
I LIKE WHERE THIS IS GOING...

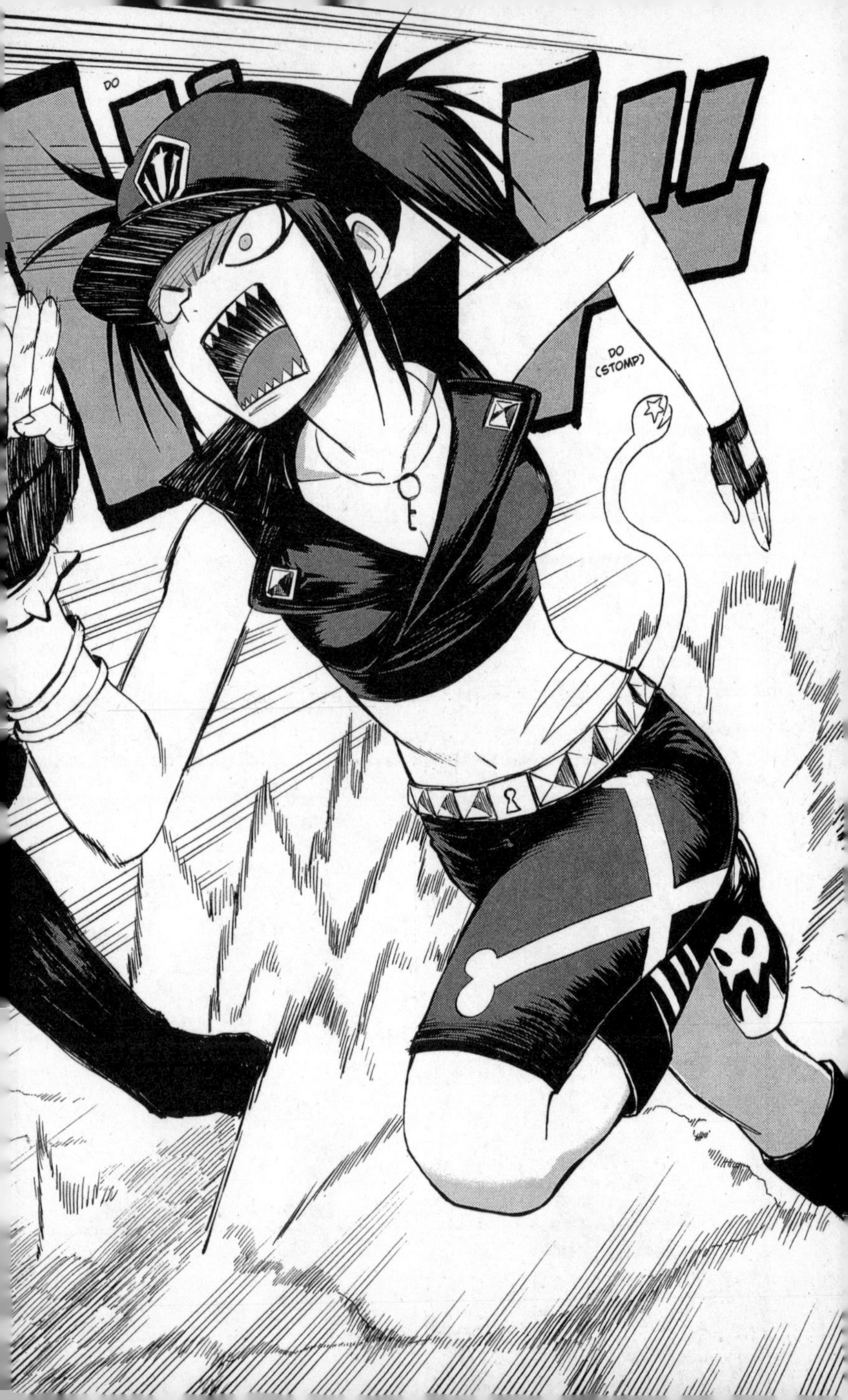
DO
DO
(STOMP)

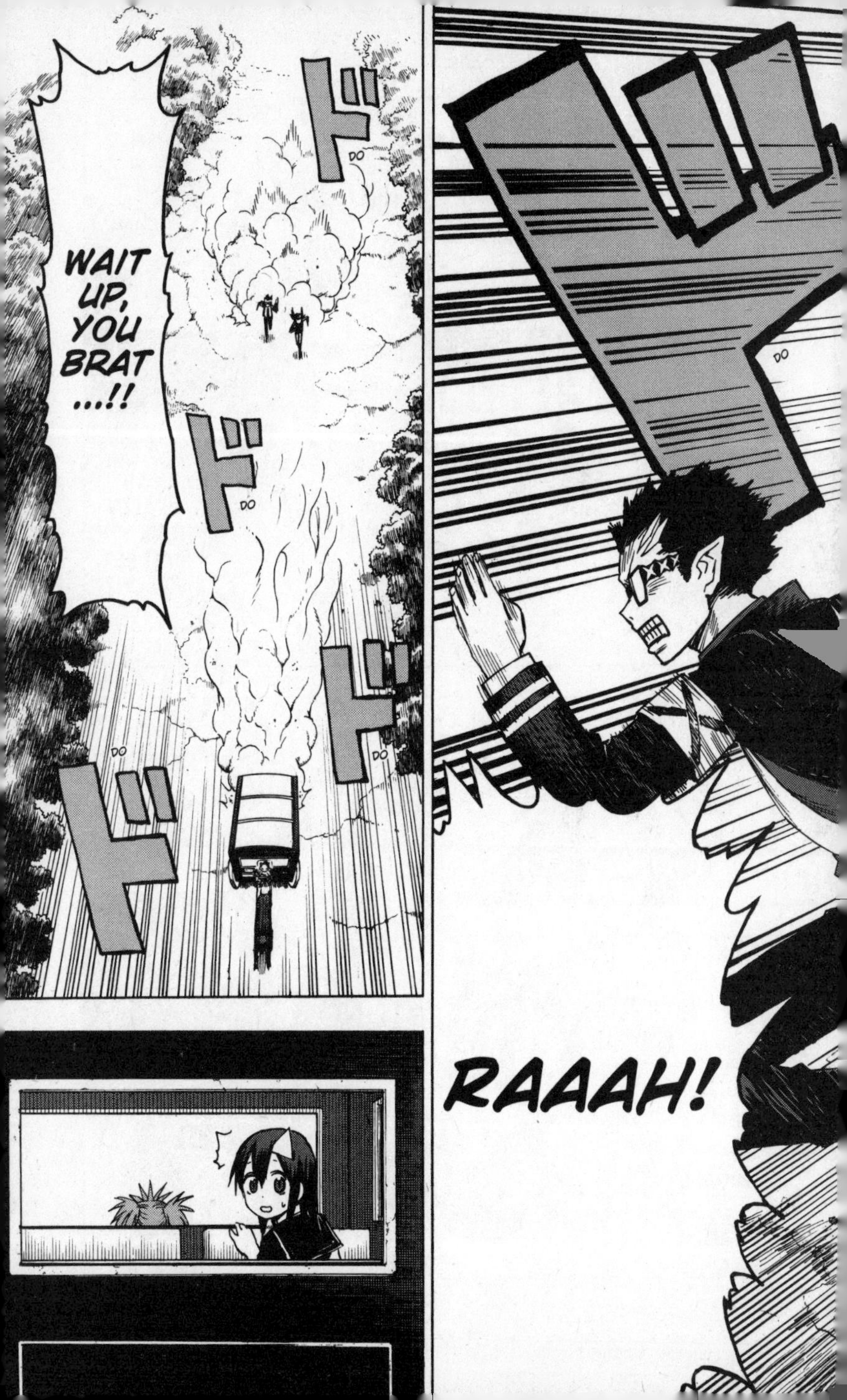
DO
RAAAH!
ド DO
WAIT UP, YOU BRAT ...!!
ド DO
ド DO
ド DO

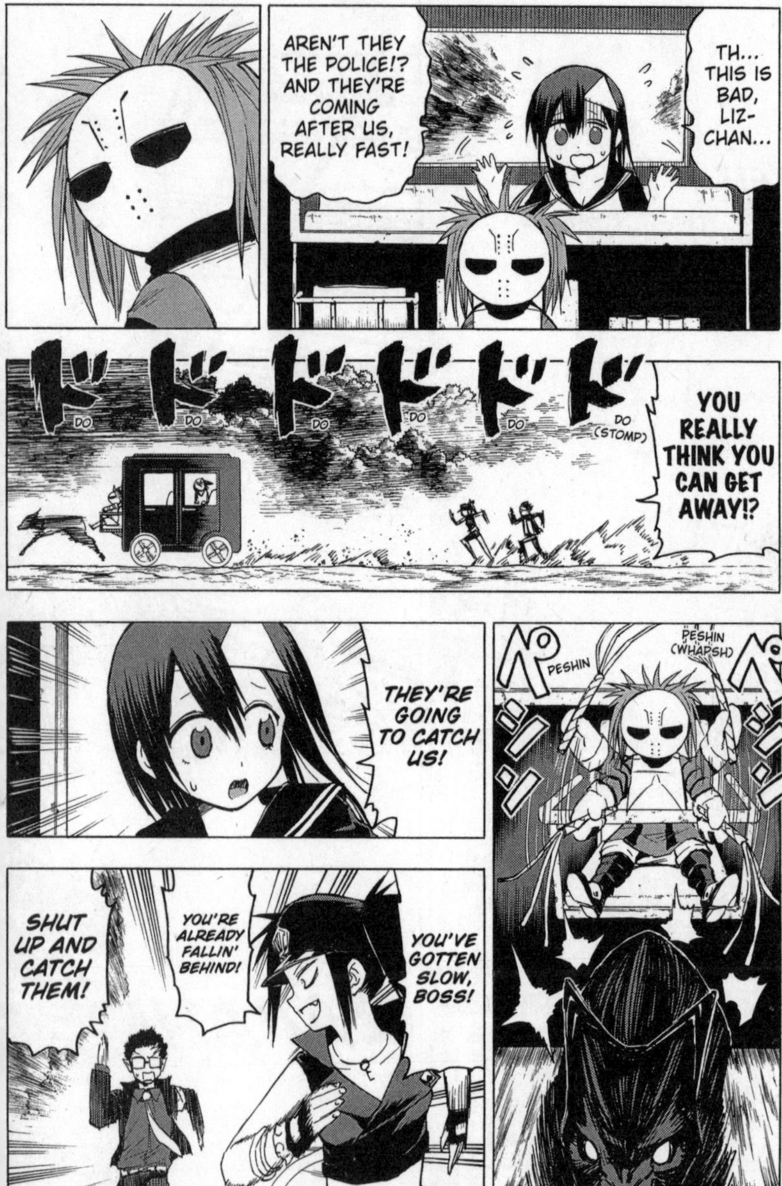
TH... THIS IS BAD, LIZ-CHAN...
AREN'T THEY THE POLICE!? AND THEY'RE COMING AFTER US, REALLY FAST!
YOU REALLY THINK YOU CAN GET AWAY!?
ド DO (STOMP)
ド DO
ド DO
ド DO
ド DO
ド DO
ペ PESHIN (WHAPSH)
ペ PESHIN
THEY'RE GOING TO CATCH US!
YOU'VE GOTTEN SLOW, BOSS!
YOU'RE ALREADY FALLIN' BEHIND!
SHUT UP AND CATCH THEM!

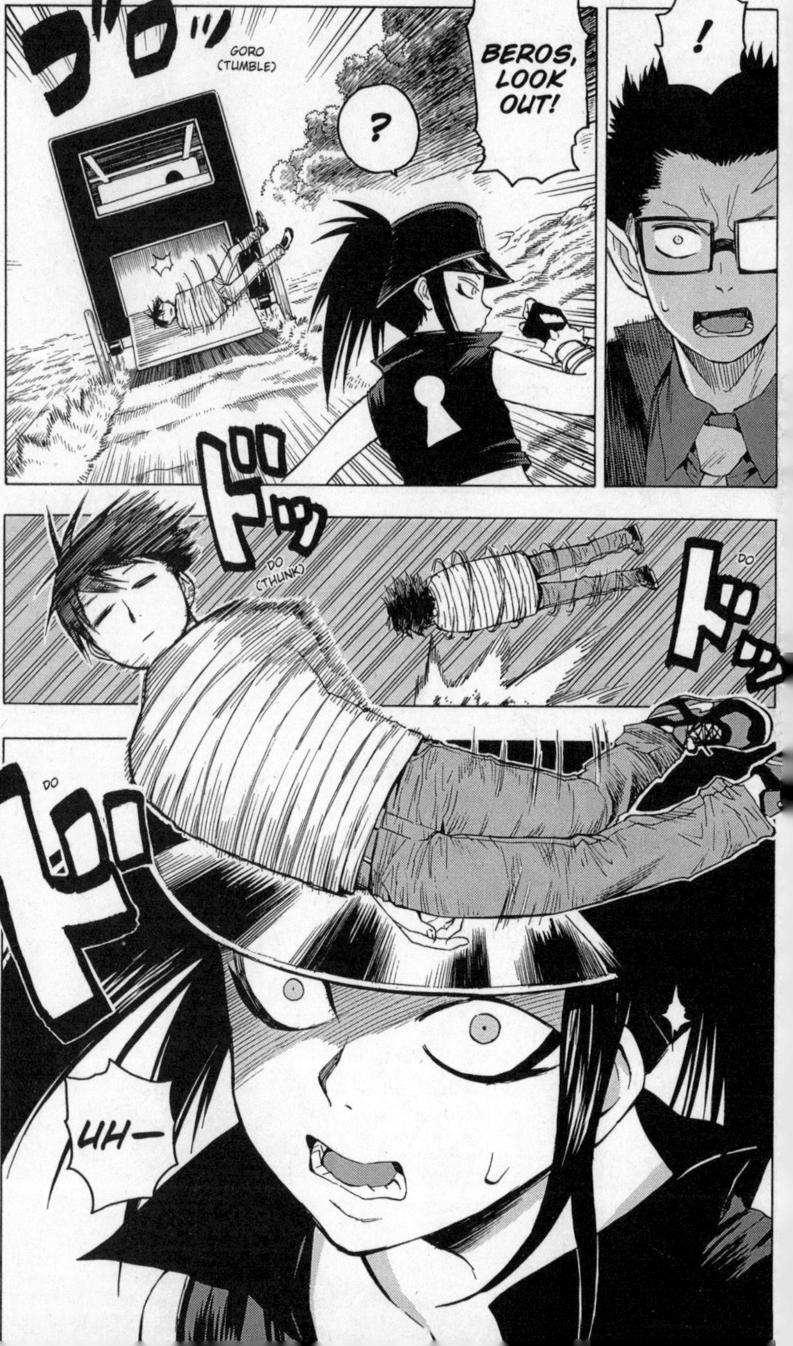
!
BEROS, LOOK OUT!
?
GORO (TUMBLE)
DO
DO (THUNK)
DO
UH—

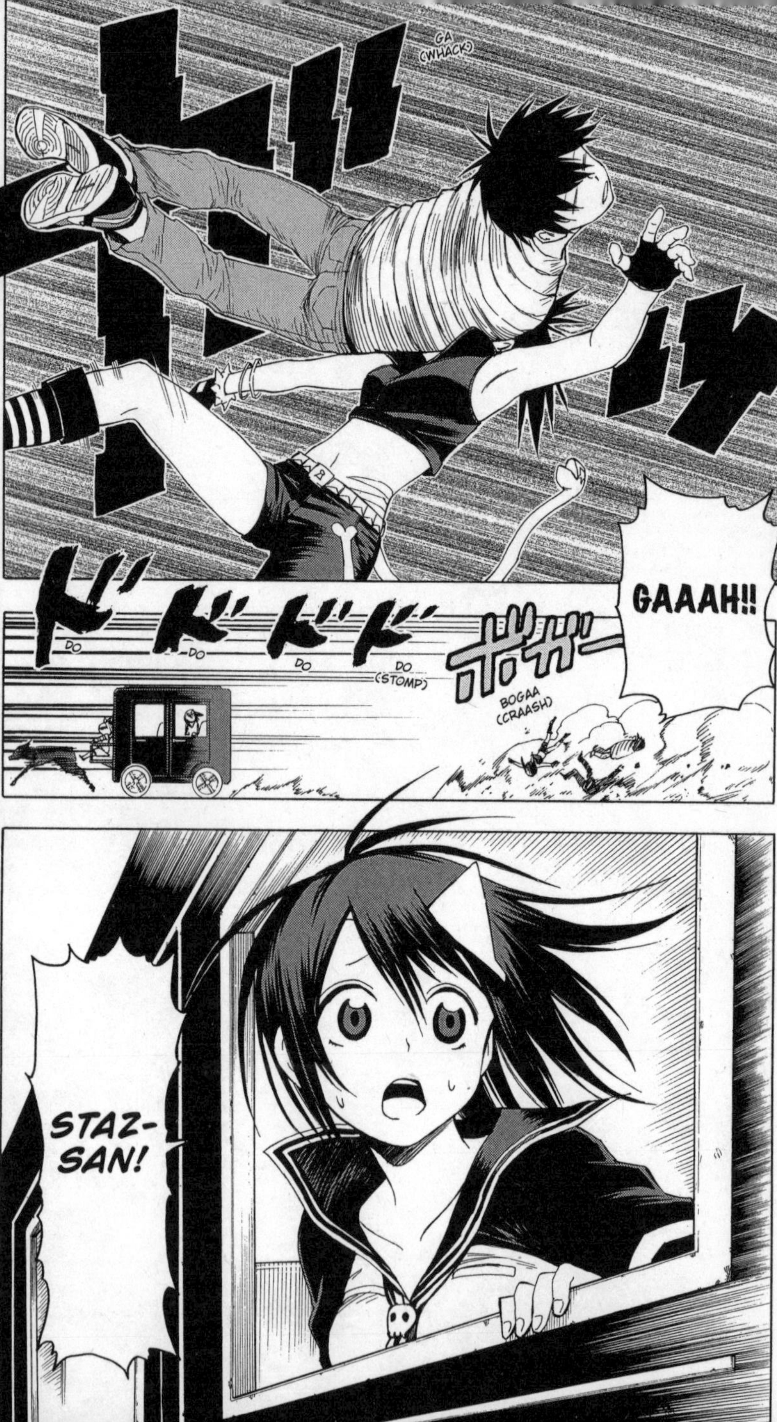
GA
(WHACK)
DO
DO
DO
DO
(STOMP)
BOGAA
(CRAASH)
GAAAH!!
STAZ-SAN!

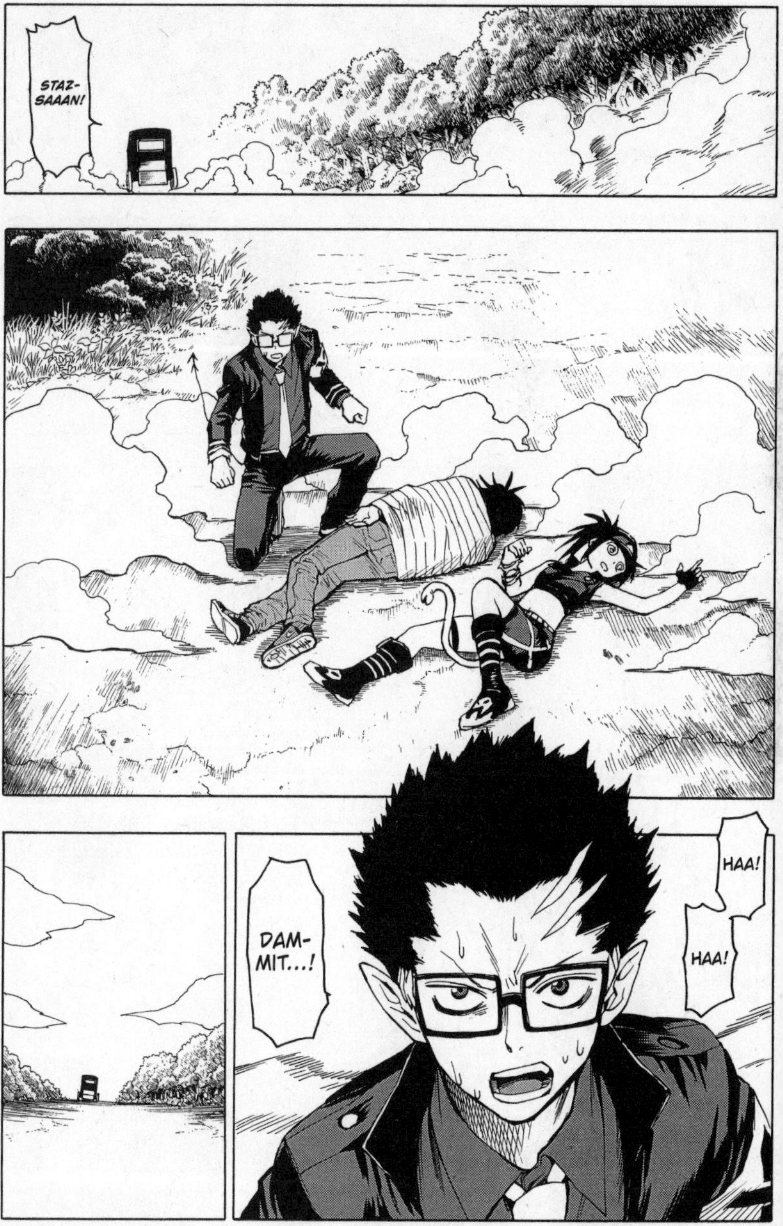
STAZ-SAAAN!
HAA!
HAA!
DAM-MIT...!

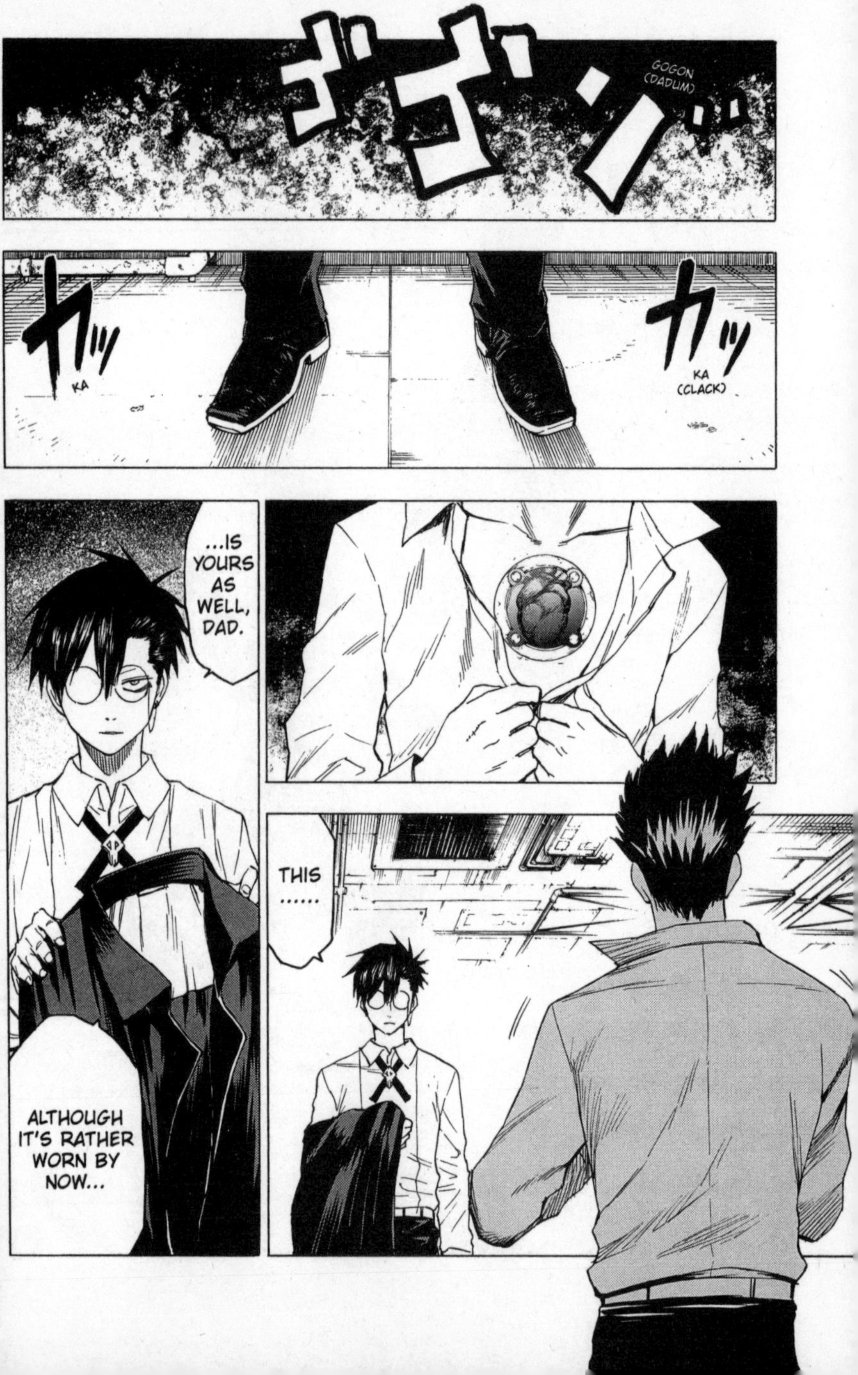
ゴゴン
GOGON (DADUM)
カッ
KA (CLACK)
カッ
KA
THIS ......
...IS YOURS AS WELL, DAD.
ALTHOUGH IT'S RATHER WORN BY NOW...

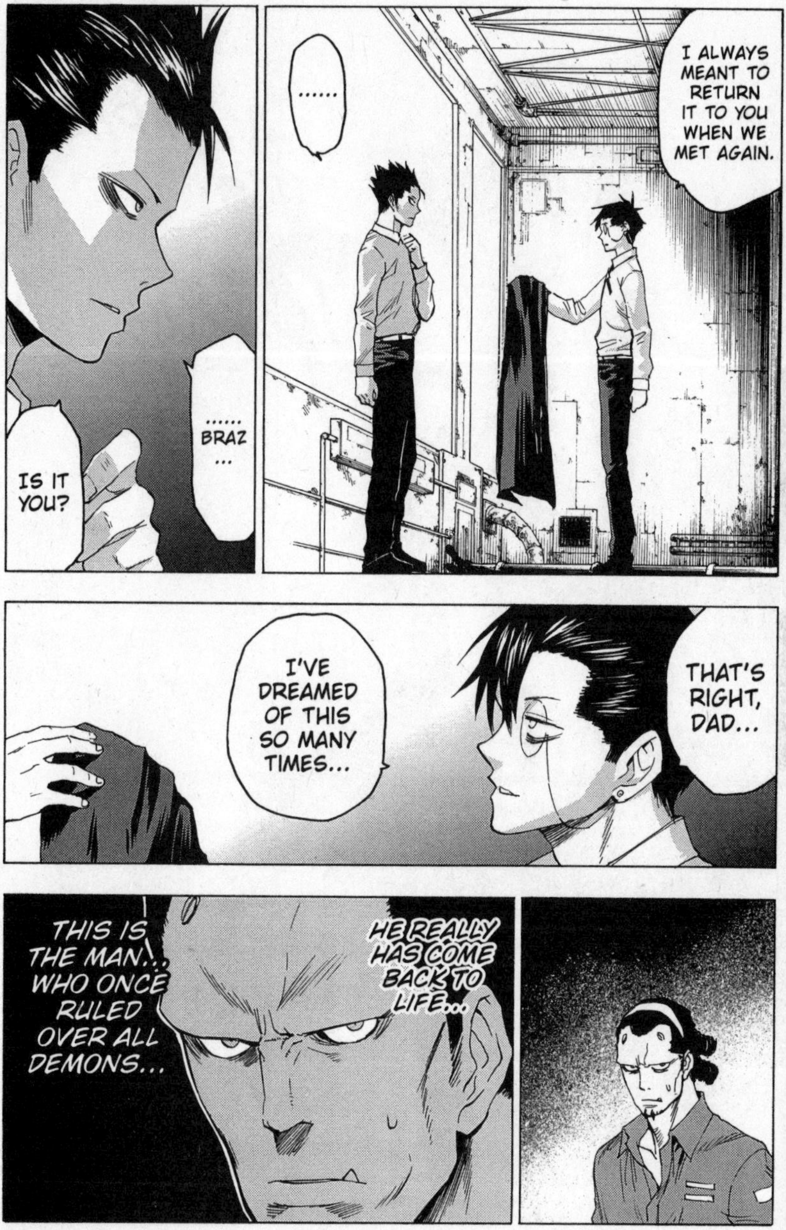
I ALWAYS MEANT TO RETURN IT TO YOU WHEN WE MET AGAIN.
......
...... BRAZ ...
IS IT YOU?
THAT'S RIGHT, DAD...
I'VE DREAMED OF THIS SO MANY TIMES...
HE REALLY HAS COME BACK TO LIFE...
THIS IS THE MAN... WHO ONCE RULED OVER ALL DEMONS...

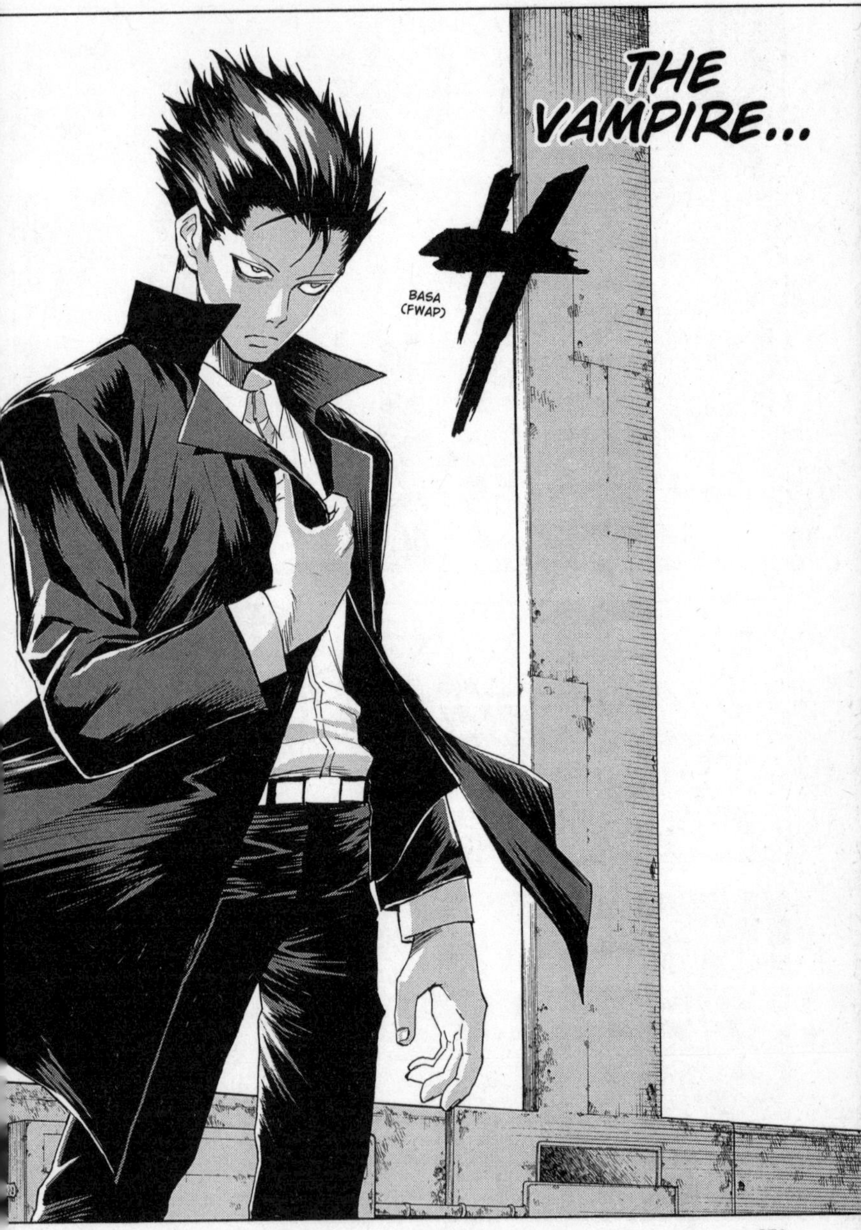
THE VAMPIRE...
BASA
(FWAP)

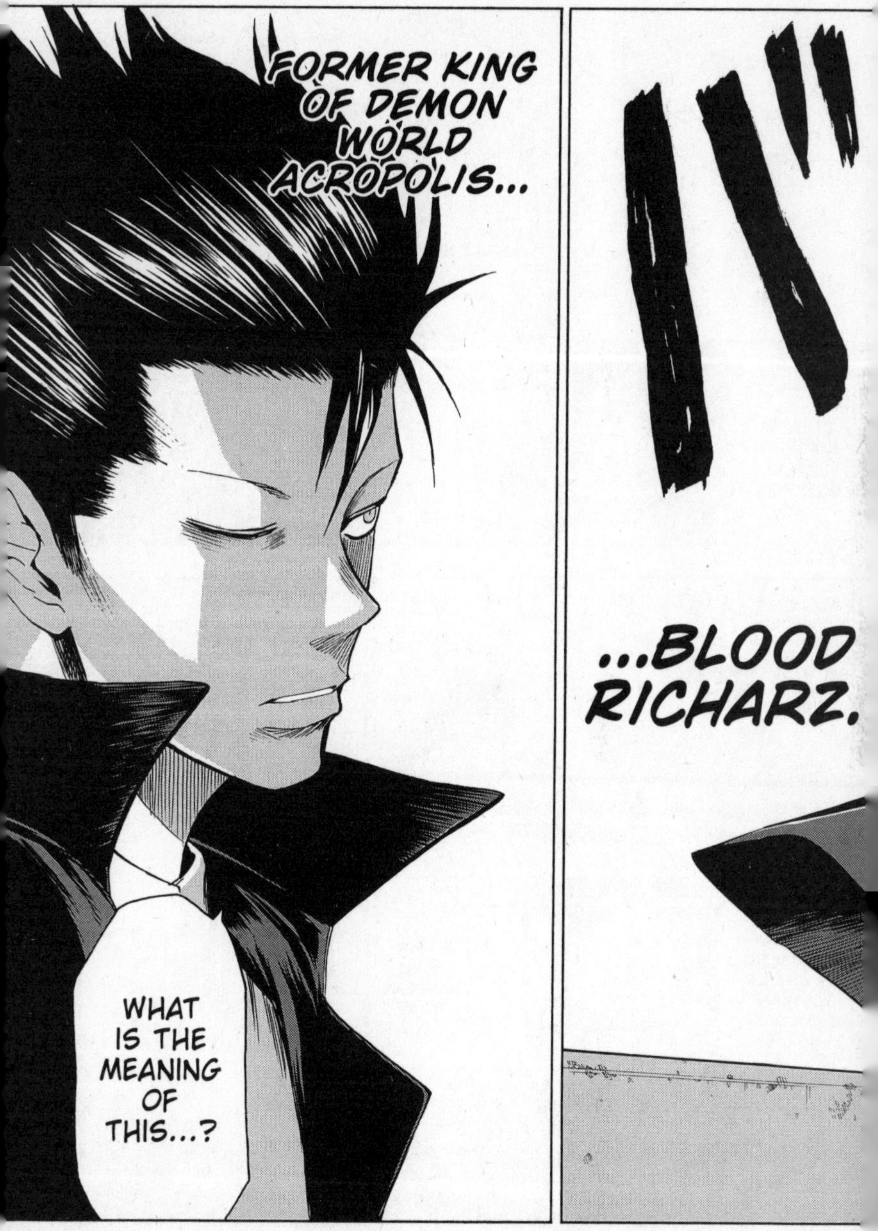
FORMER KING OF DEMON WORLD ACROPOLIS...
WHAT IS THE MEANING OF THIS...?
バ
...BLOOD RICHARZ.

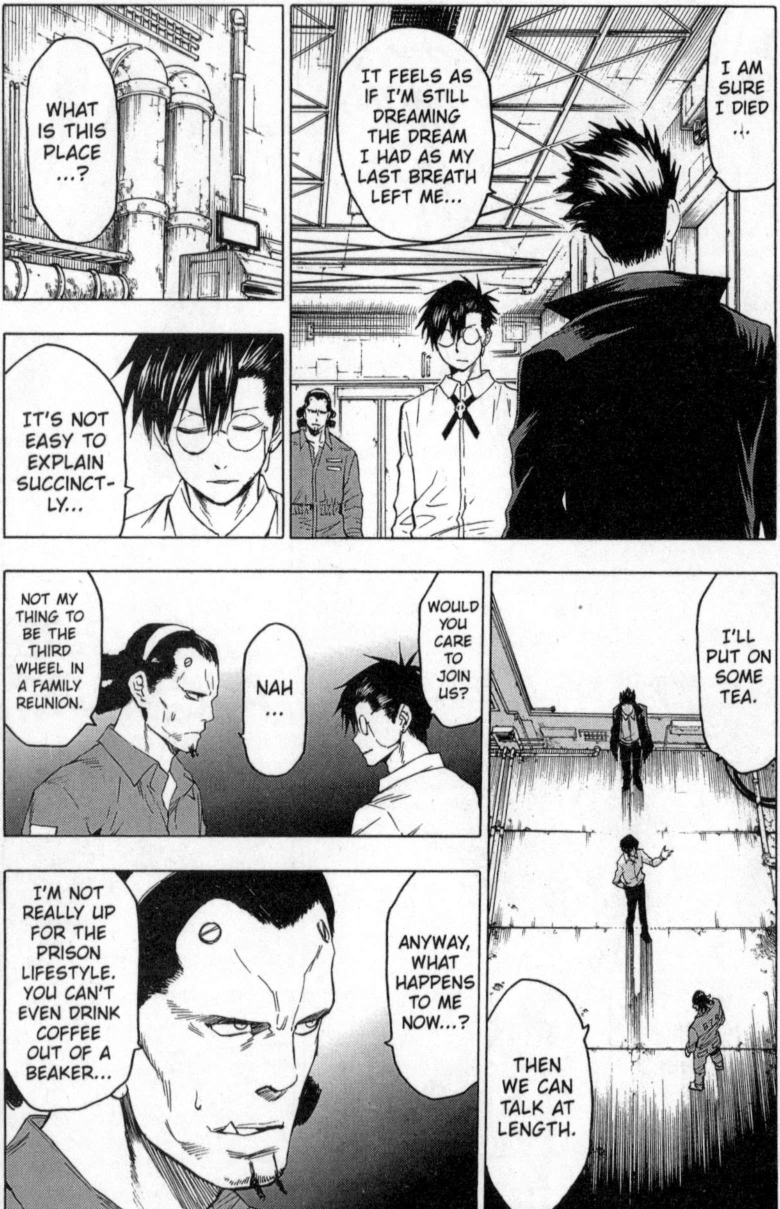
I AM SURE I DIED ...
IT FEELS AS IF I'M STILL DREAMING THE DREAM I HAD AS MY LAST BREATH LEFT ME...
WHAT IS THIS PLACE ...?
IT'S NOT EASY TO EXPLAIN SUCCINCT-LY...
I'LL PUT ON SOME TEA.
THEN WE CAN TALK AT LENGTH.
WOULD YOU CARE TO JOIN US?
NAH ...
NOT MY THING TO BE THE THIRD WHEEL IN A FAMILY REUNION.
ANYWAY, WHAT HAPPENS TO ME NOW...?
I'M NOT REALLY UP FOR THE PRISON LIFESTYLE. YOU CAN'T EVEN DRINK COFFEE OUT OF A BEAKER...

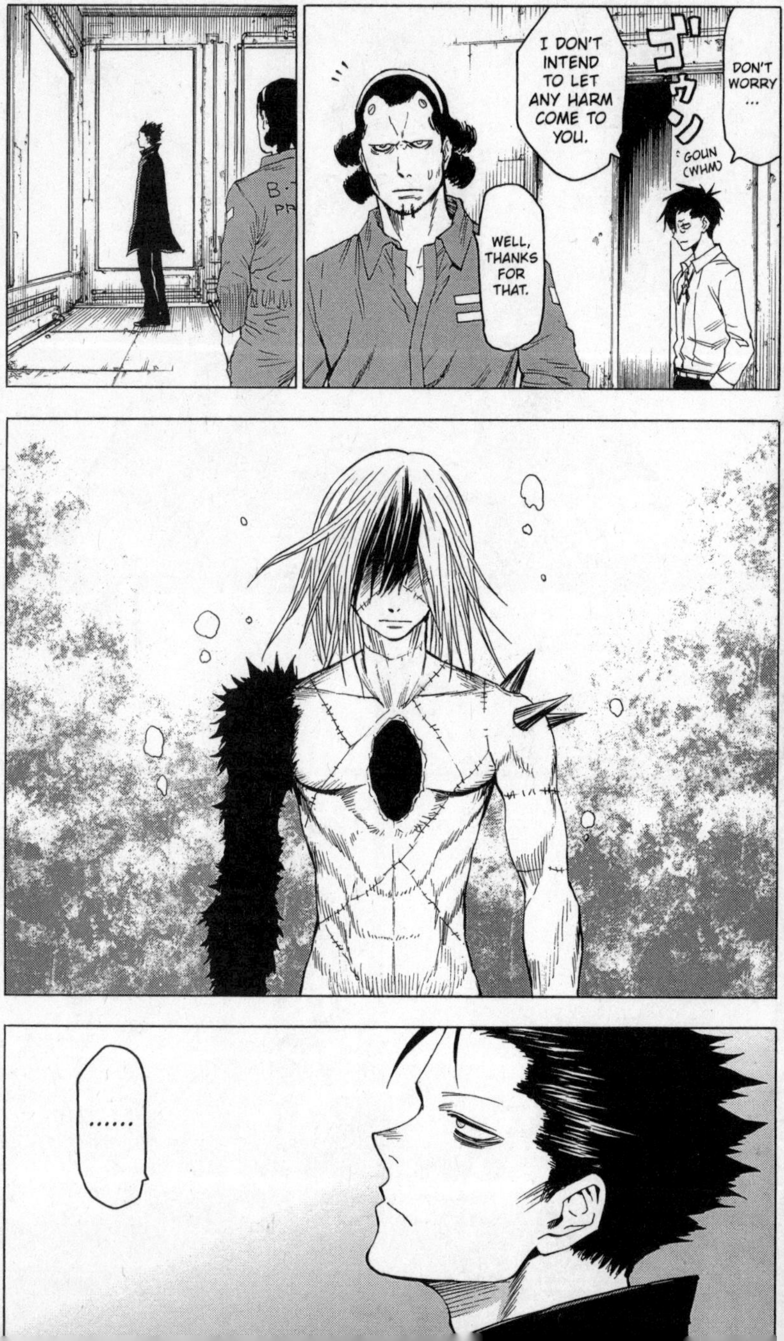
DON'T WORRY ...
ゴウン
GOUN (WHM)
I DON'T INTEND TO LET ANY HARM COME TO YOU.
WELL, THANKS FOR THAT.
....

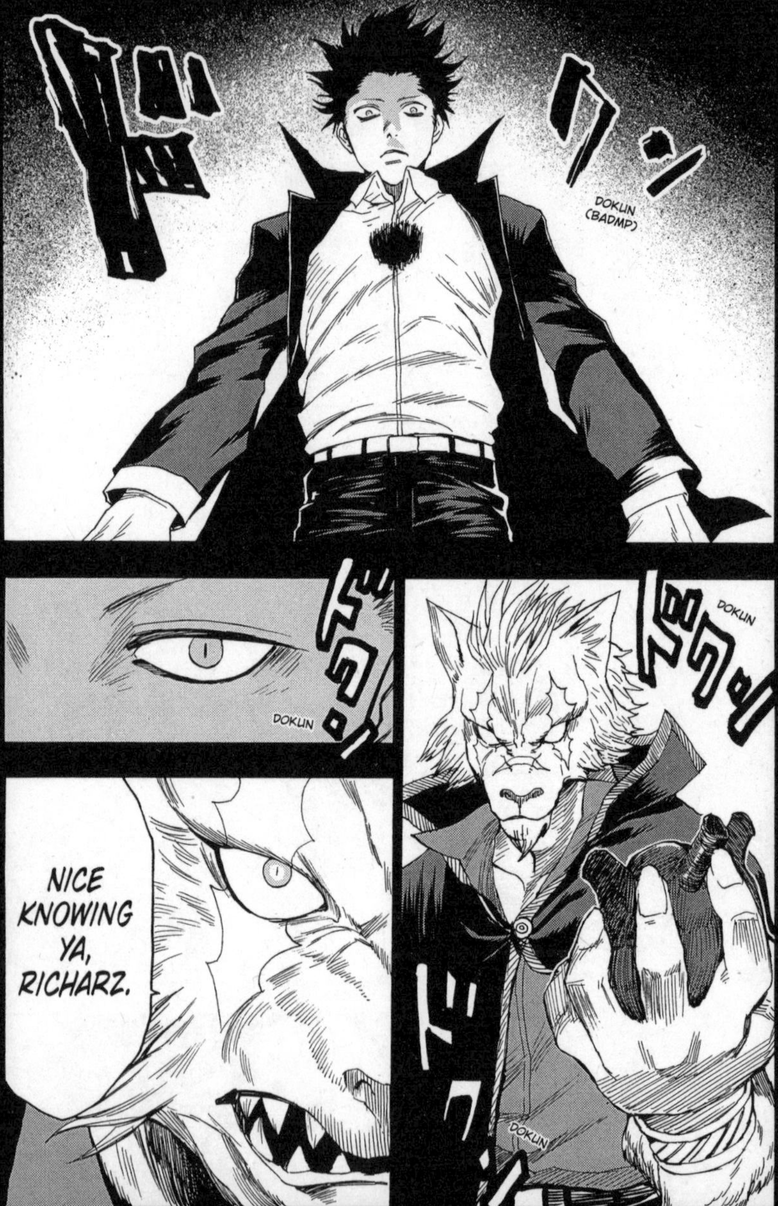
DOKUN (BADMP)
DOKUN
DOKUN
DOKUN
NICE KNOWING YA, RICHARZ.

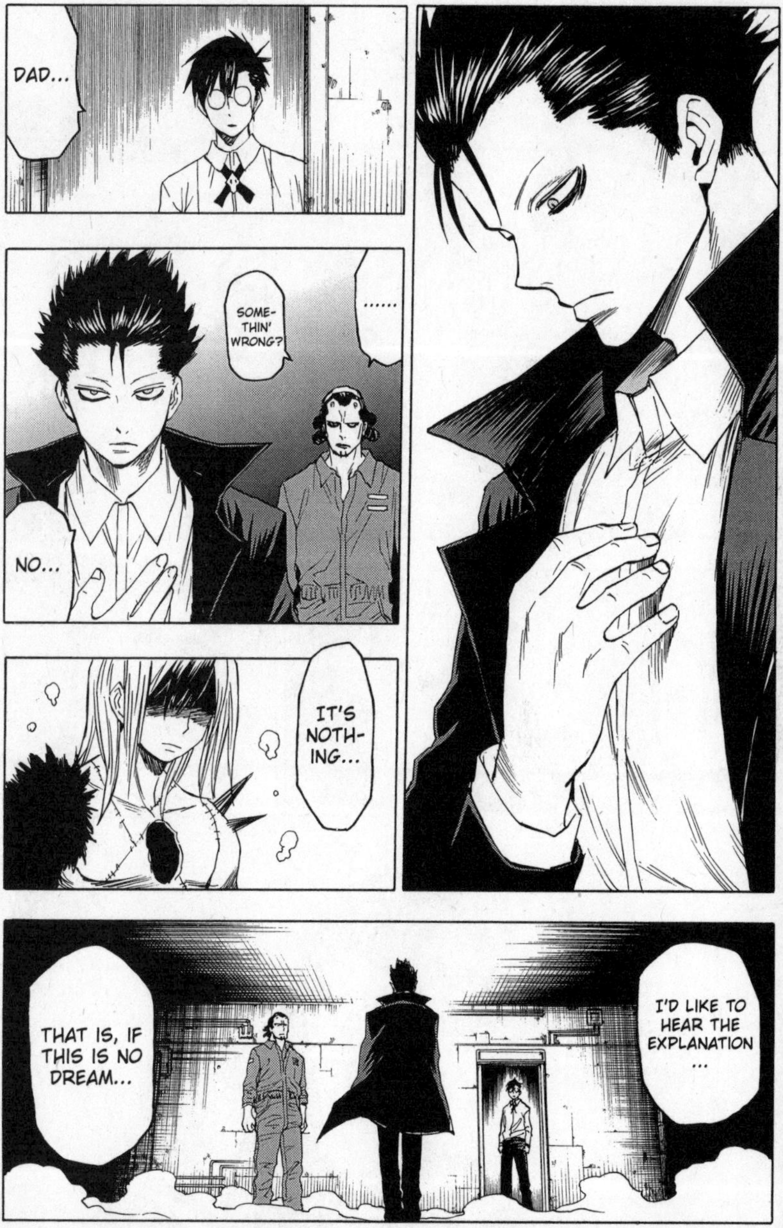
DAD...
......
SOME-THIN' WRONG?
NO...
IT'S NOTH-ING...
I'D LIKE TO HEAR THE EXPLANATION ...
THAT IS, IF THIS IS NO DREAM...

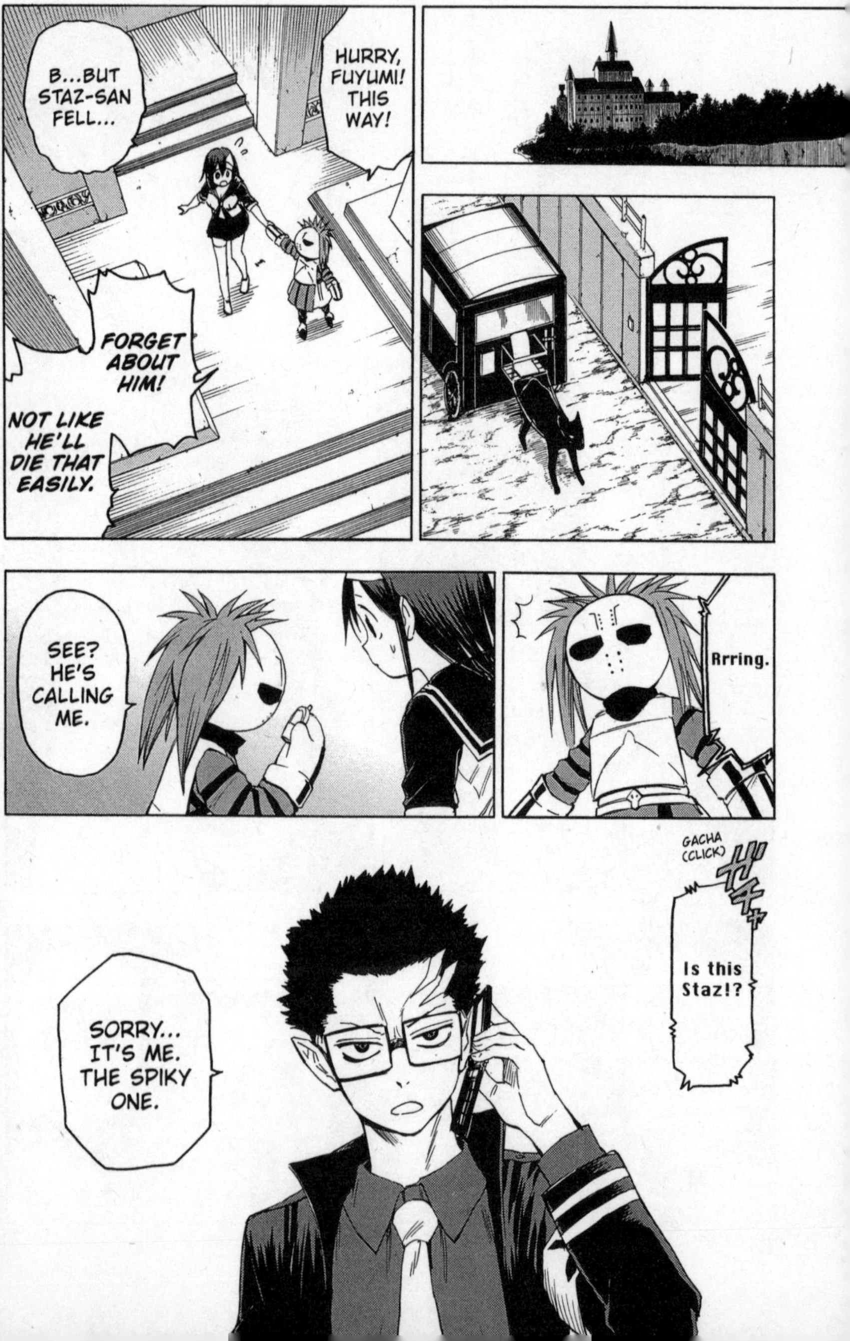
HURRY, FUYUMI! THIS WAY!
B...BUT STAZ-SAN FELL...
FORGET ABOUT HIM!
NOT LIKE HE'LL DIE THAT EASILY.
Rrring.
SEE? HE'S CALLING ME.
GACHA (CLICK)
Is this Staz!?
SORRY... IT'S ME. THE SPIKY ONE.

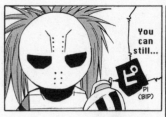

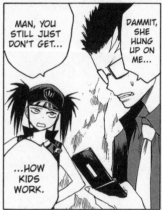

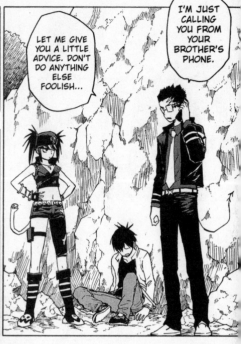

I'M JUST CALLING YOU FROM YOUR BROTHER'S PHONE.
LET ME GIVE YOU A LITTLE ADVICE. DON'T DO ANYTHING ELSE FOOLISH...
You can still...
PI (BIP)
DAMMIT, SHE HUNG UP ON ME...
MAN, YOU STILL JUST DON'T GET...
...HOW KIDS WORK.
ALL RIGHT...! YOU TALK TO HER, THEN.
SHE'S NOT GONNA PICK UP AGAIN.
HOW DO YOU KNOW!?
'COS YOU PUT HER IN A TIGHT SPOT...
THIS IS ALREADY BEYOND ANYTHING LIZ CAN DEAL WITH ON HER OWN.
AND THERE'S ONLY ONE THING KIDS DO IN A SITUATION LIKE THAT.

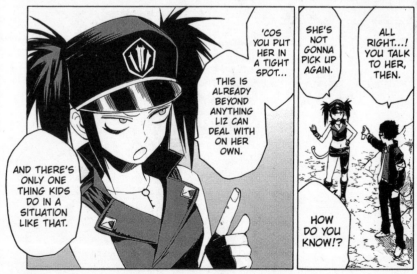

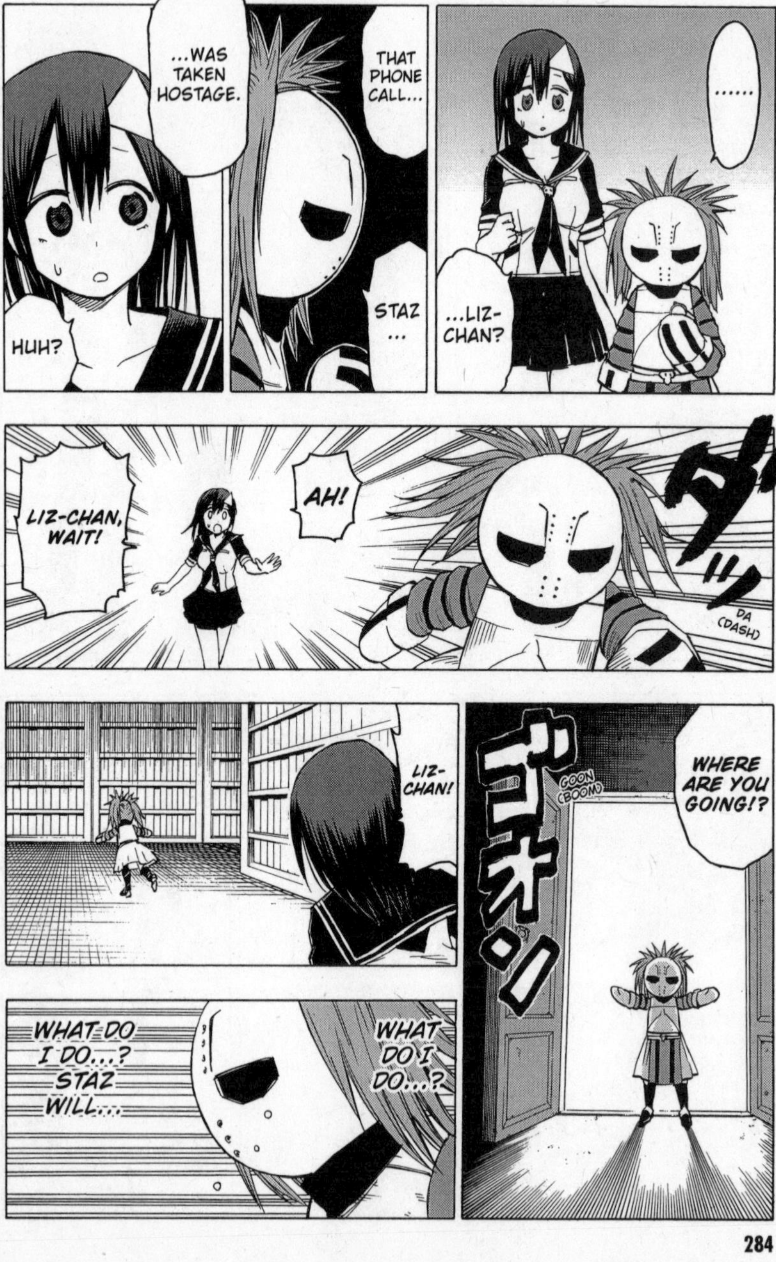
......
...LIZ-CHAN?
THAT PHONE CALL...
STAZ ...
...WAS TAKEN HOSTAGE.
HUH?
DA (DASH)
AH!
LIZ-CHAN, WAIT!
WHERE ARE YOU GOING!?
GOON (BOOM)
LIZ-CHAN!
WHAT DO I DO...?
WHAT DO I DO...? STAZ WILL...

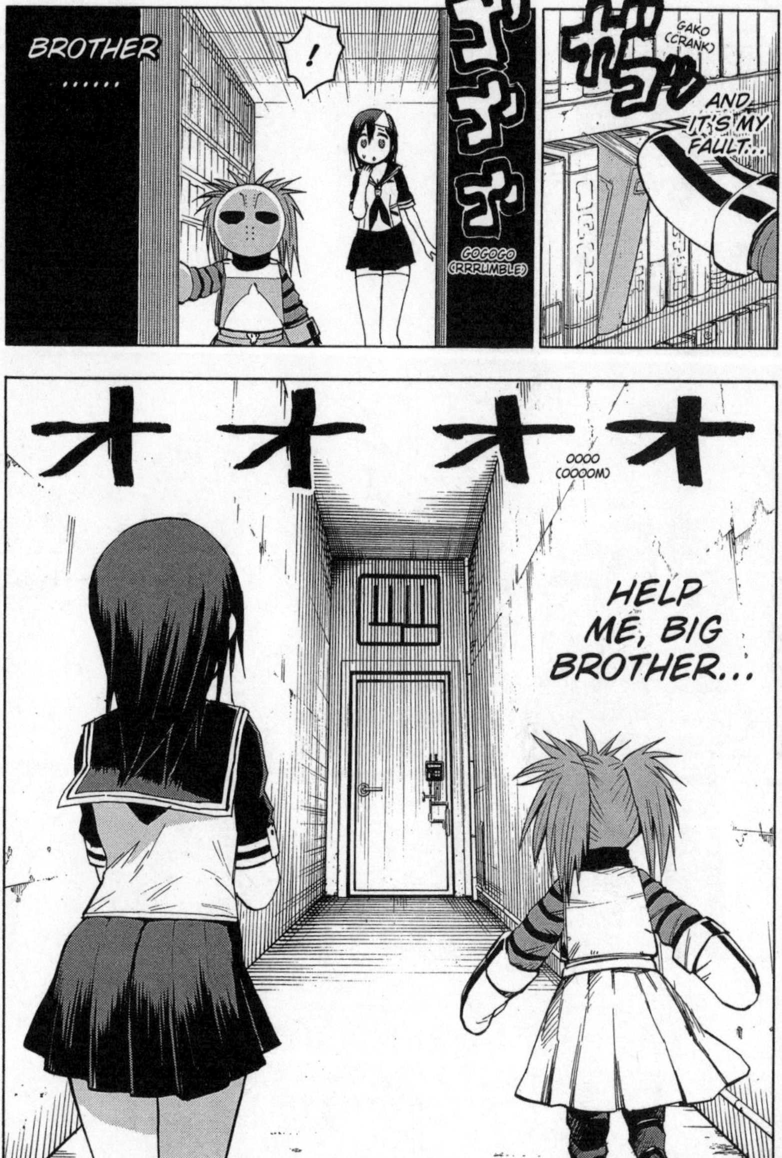
GAKO (CRANK)
AND IT'S MY FAULT...
GOGOGO (RRRUMBLE)
!
BROTHER ......
OOOO (OOOOM)
HELP ME, BIG BROTHER...

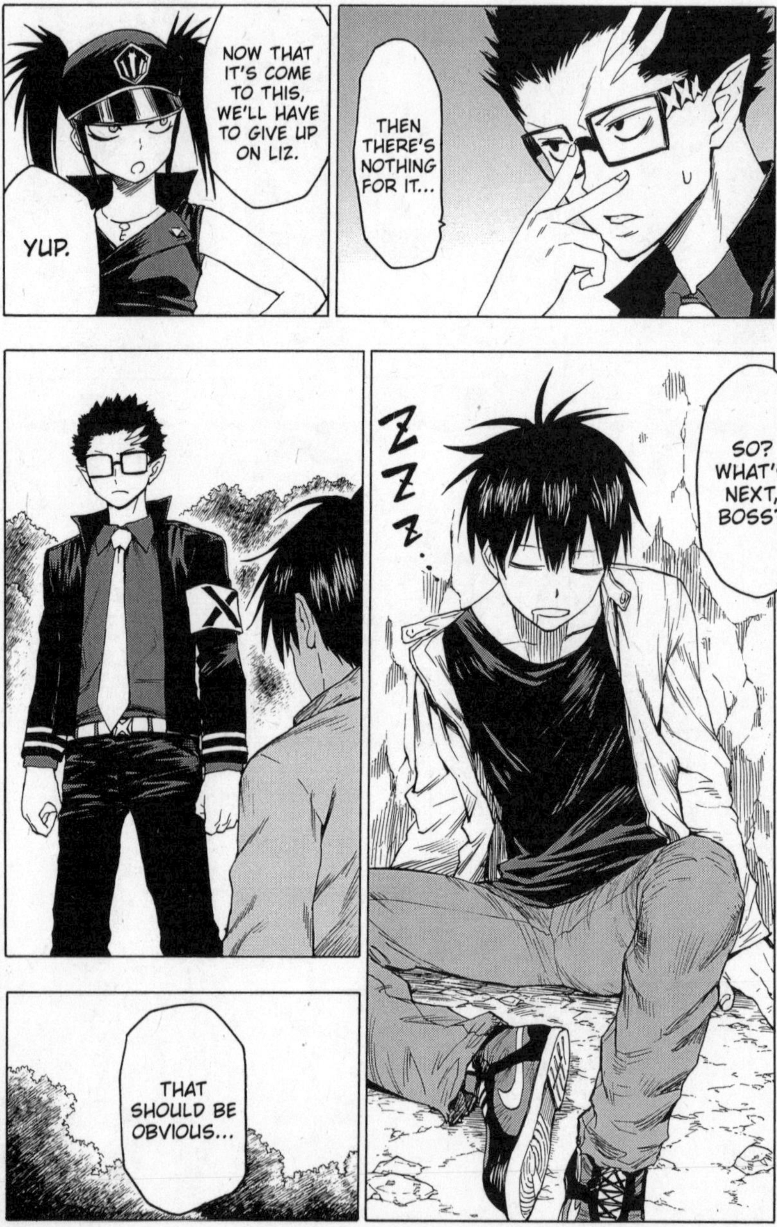
THEN THERE'S NOTHING FOR IT...
NOW THAT IT'S COME TO THIS, WE'LL HAVE TO GIVE UP ON LIZ.
YUP.
SO? WHAT'S NEXT, BOSS?
ZZZ...
THAT SHOULD BE OBVIOUS...

♠ To Be Continued ♠

TOTALLY INSIGNIFICANT
STATUE

A SLOPPILY MADE
STATUE THAT LOOKS
LIKE THE LITTLE
GUY IN THE BACK
WAS ADDED ON JUST
BECAUSE THERE
WAS EXTRA SPACE.

BLOOD LAD

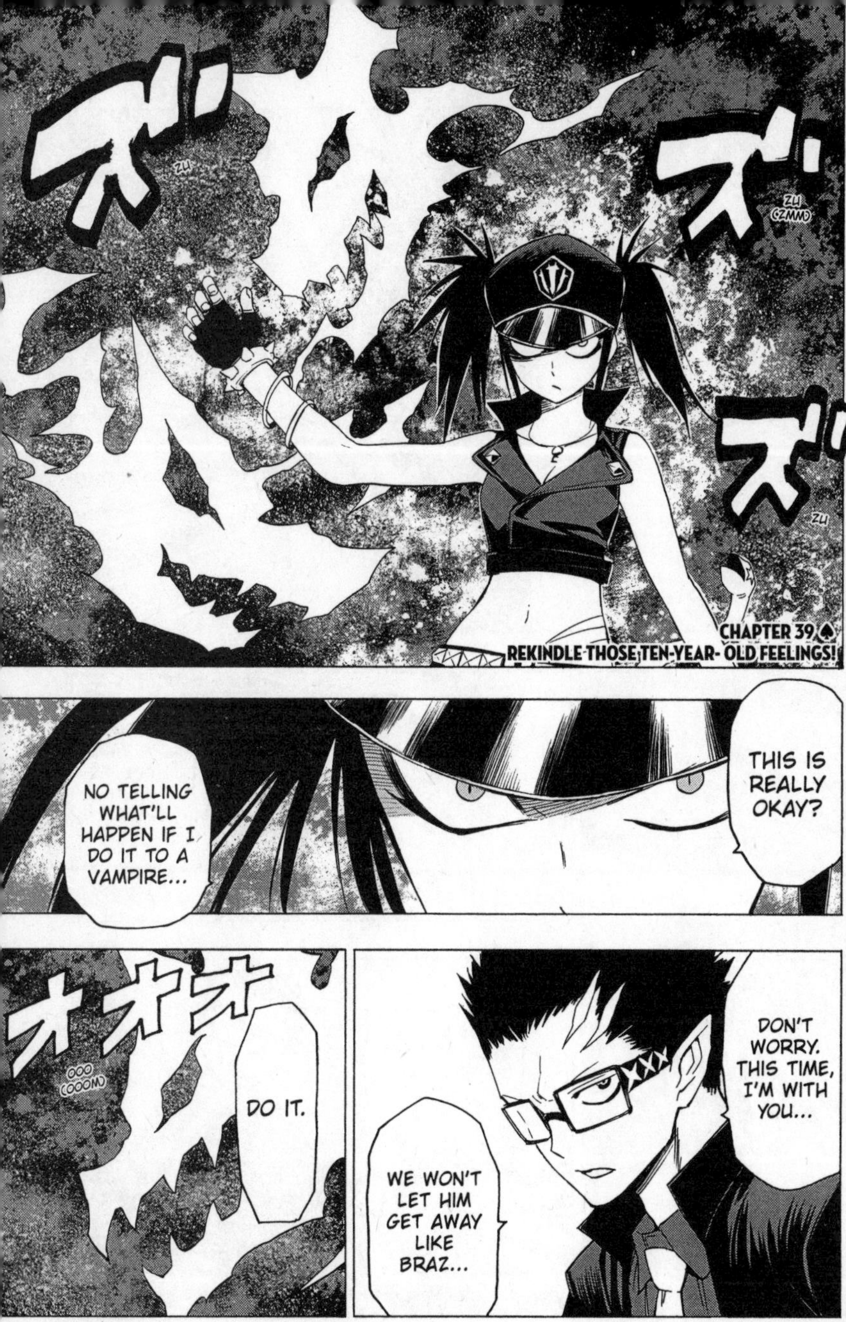
ZU (ZMM)
ZU
ZU
CHAPTER 39
REKINDLE THOSE TEN-YEAR- OLD FEELINGS!
THIS IS REALLY OKAY?
NO TELLING WHAT'LL HAPPEN IF I DO IT TO A VAMPIRE...
DON'T WORRY. THIS TIME, I'M WITH YOU...
WE WON'T LET HIM GET AWAY LIKE BRAZ...
DO IT.
OOO (OOOM)

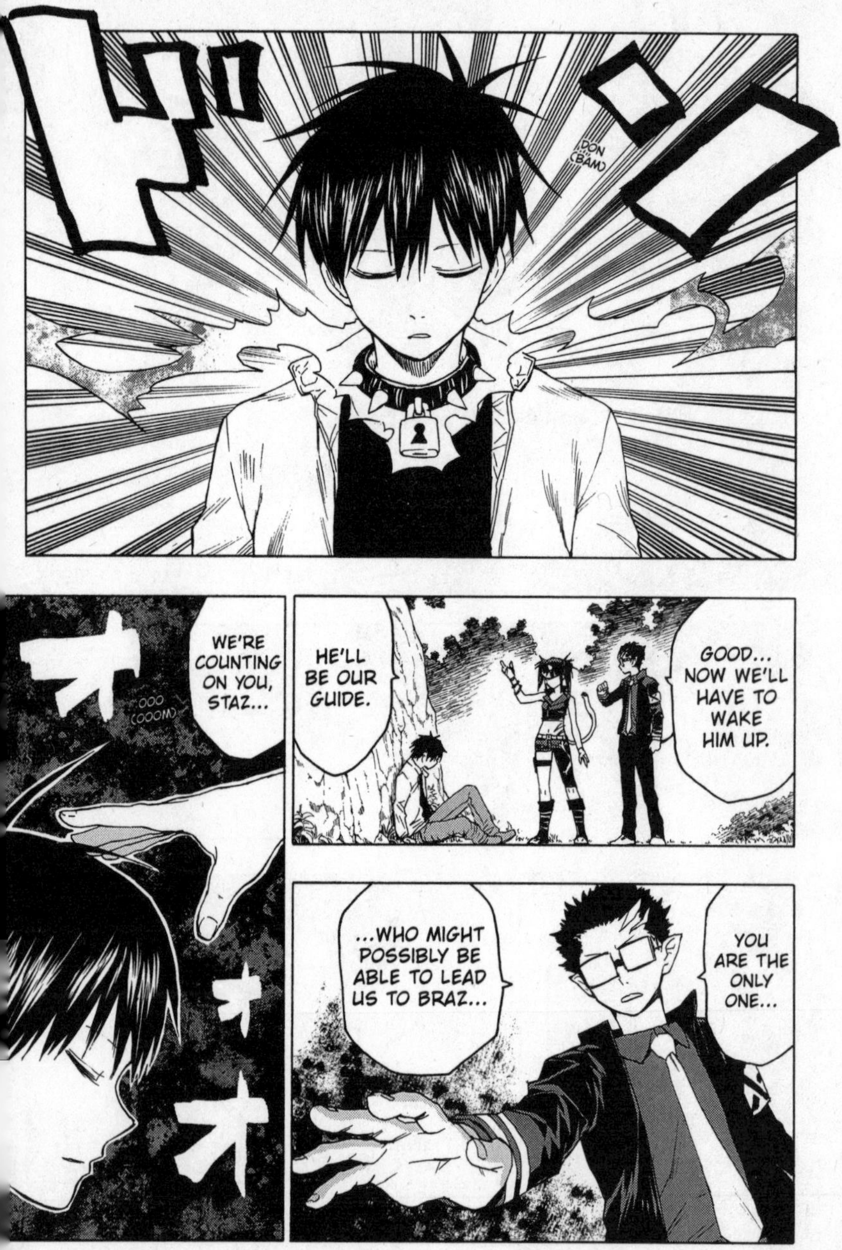
DON (BAM)
GOOD... NOW WE'LL HAVE TO WAKE HIM UP.
HE'LL BE OUR GUIDE.
YOU ARE THE ONLY ONE...
...WHO MIGHT POSSIBLY BE ABLE TO LEAD US TO BRAZ...
WE'RE COUNTING ON YOU, STAZ...
OOO (OOOM)

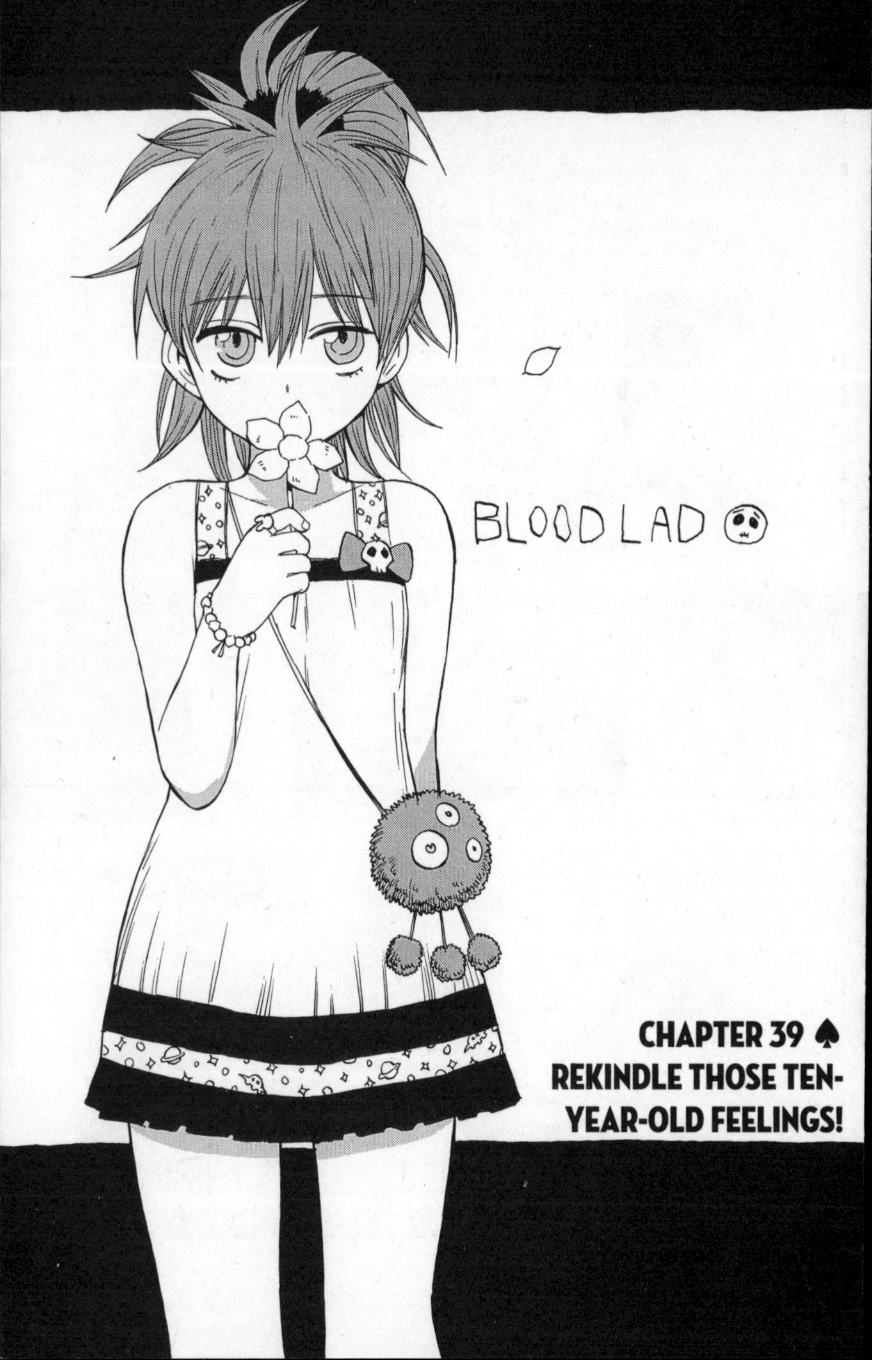
BLOOD LAD
CHAPTER 39 ♠
REKINDLE THOSE TEN-YEAR-OLD FEELINGS!

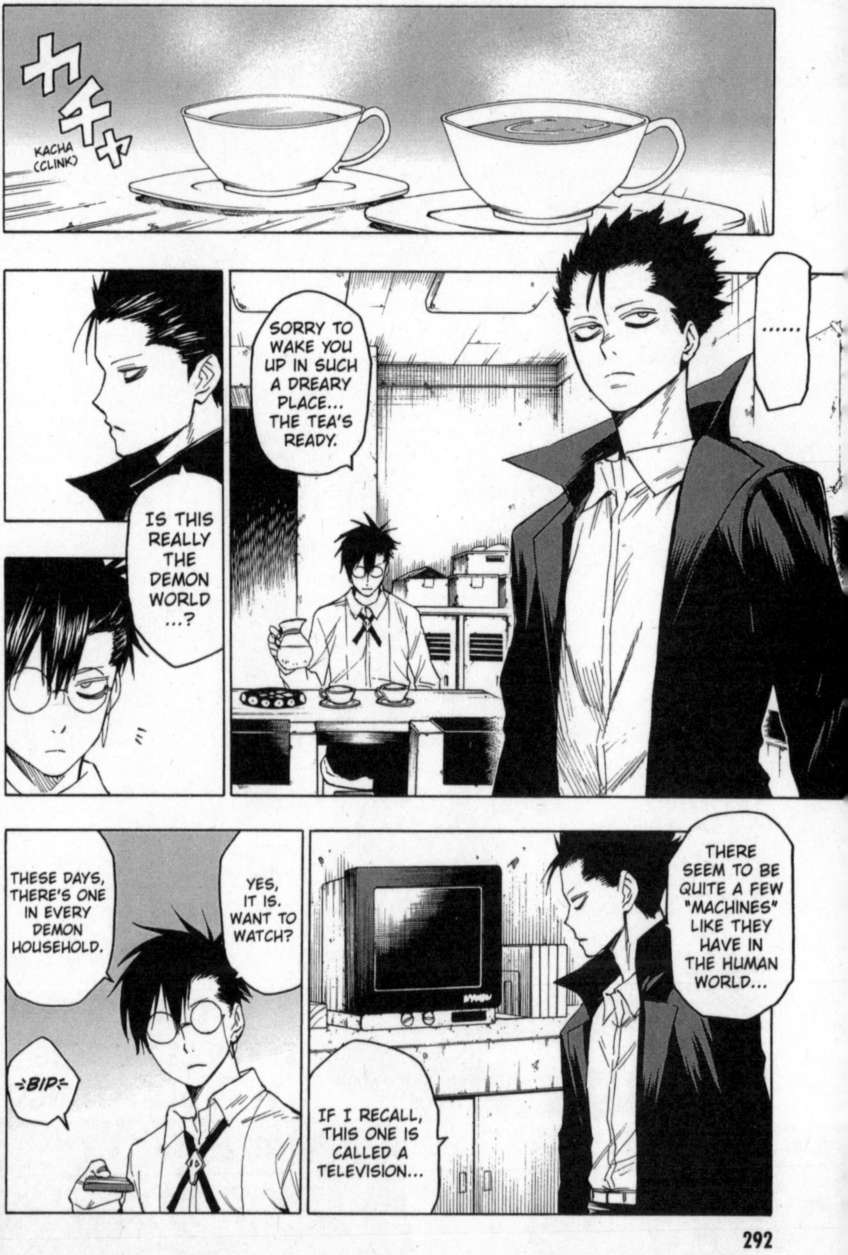
KACHA (CLINK)
......
SORRY TO WAKE YOU UP IN SUCH A DREARY PLACE... THE TEA'S READY.
IS THIS REALLY THE DEMON WORLD ...?
THERE SEEM TO BE QUITE A FEW "MACHINES" LIKE THEY HAVE IN THE HUMAN WORLD...
IF I RECALL, THIS ONE IS CALLED A TELEVISION...
YES, IT IS. WANT TO WATCH?
THESE DAYS, THERE'S ONE IN EVERY DEMON HOUSEHOLD.
BIP

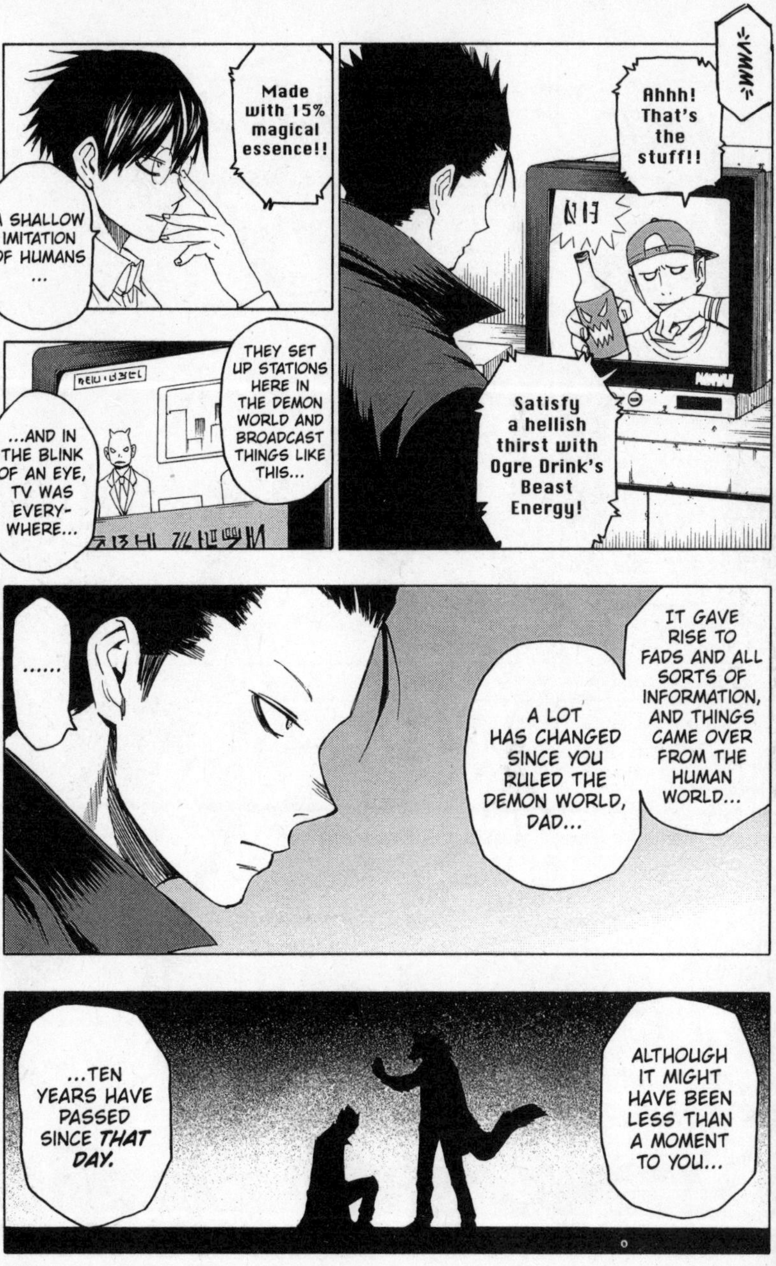
YMM
Ahhh! That's the stuff!!
Satisfy a hellish thirst with Ogre Drink's Beast Energy!
Made with 15% magical essence!!
A SHALLOW IMITATION OF HUMANS ...
THEY SET UP STATIONS HERE IN THE DEMON WORLD AND BROADCAST THINGS LIKE THIS...
...AND IN THE BLINK OF AN EYE, TV WAS EVERY-WHERE...
IT GAVE RISE TO FADS AND ALL SORTS OF INFORMATION, AND THINGS CAME OVER FROM THE HUMAN WORLD...
A LOT HAS CHANGED SINCE YOU RULED THE DEMON WORLD, DAD...
......
ALTHOUGH IT MIGHT HAVE BEEN LESS THAN A MOMENT TO YOU...
...TEN YEARS HAVE PASSED SINCE *THAT DAY.*

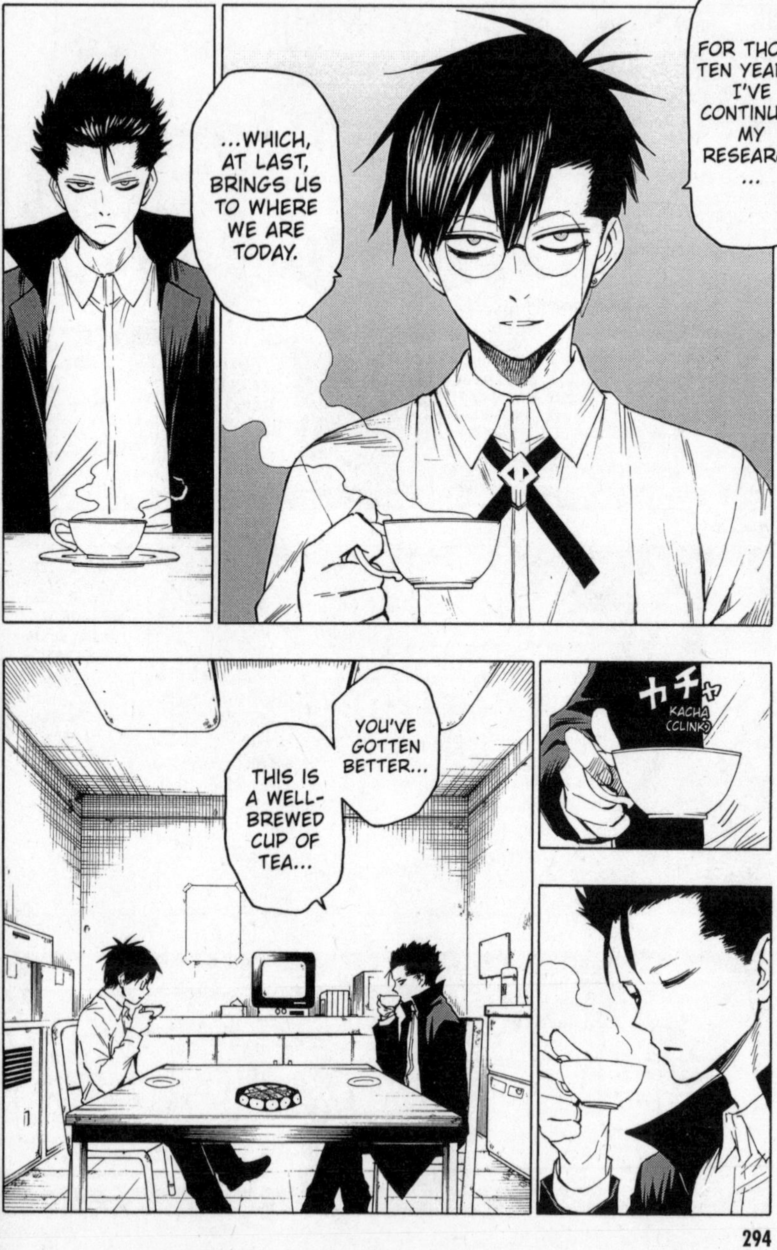
FOR THOSE TEN YEARS, I'VE CONTINUED MY RESEARCH ...
...WHICH, AT LAST, BRINGS US TO WHERE WE ARE TODAY.
カチャ
KACHA (CLINK)
YOU'VE GOTTEN BETTER...
THIS IS A WELL-BREWED CUP OF TEA...

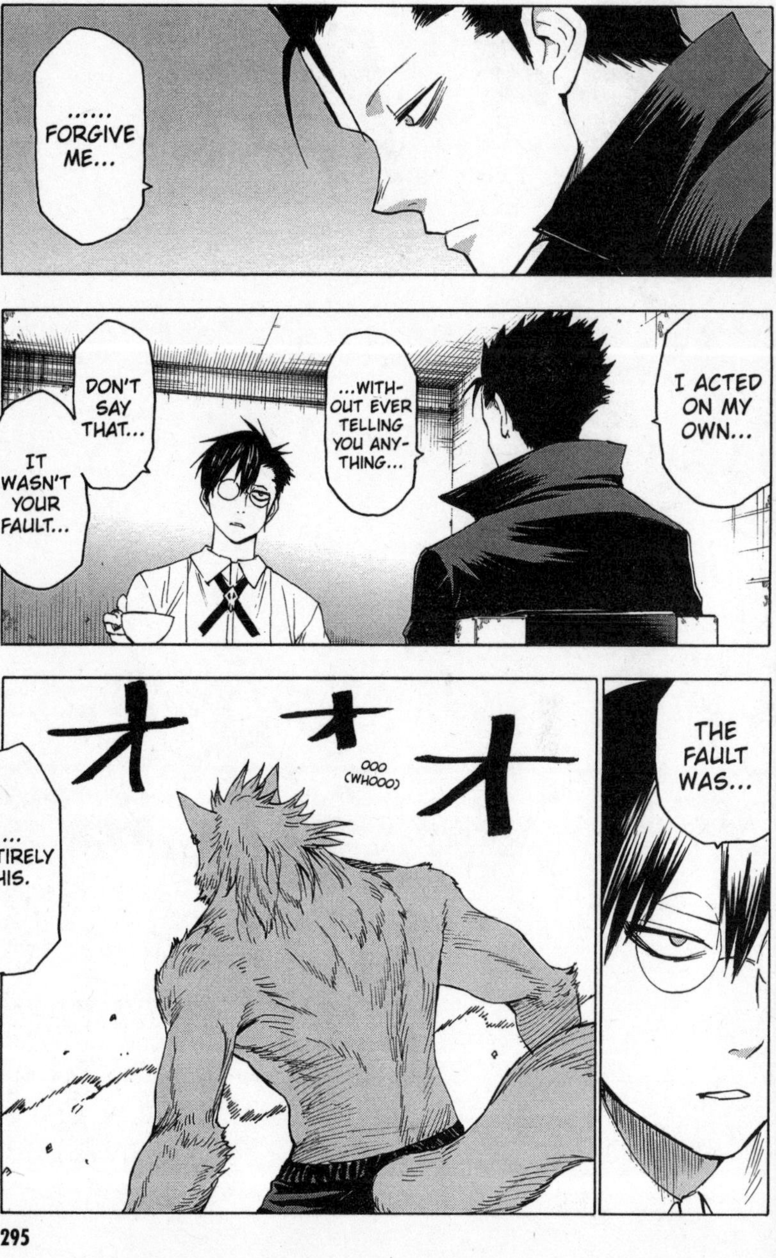

...... FORGIVE ME...
I ACTED ON MY OWN...
...WITH-OUT EVER TELLING YOU ANY-THING...
DON'T SAY THAT...
IT WASN'T YOUR FAULT...
THE FAULT WAS...
オオオ
OOO (WHOOO)
... ENTIRELY HIS.

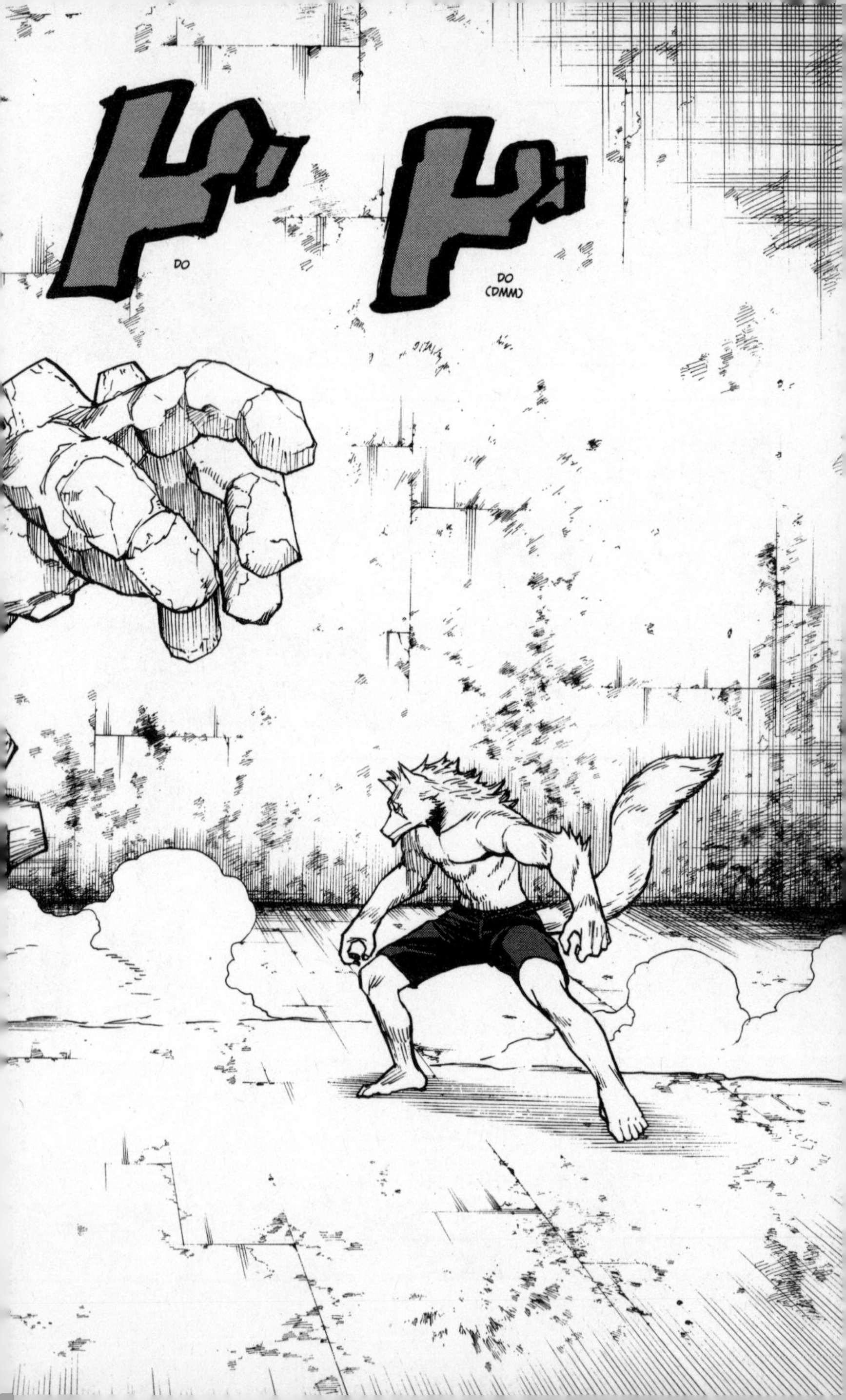
ドド
DO
DO
(DMM)

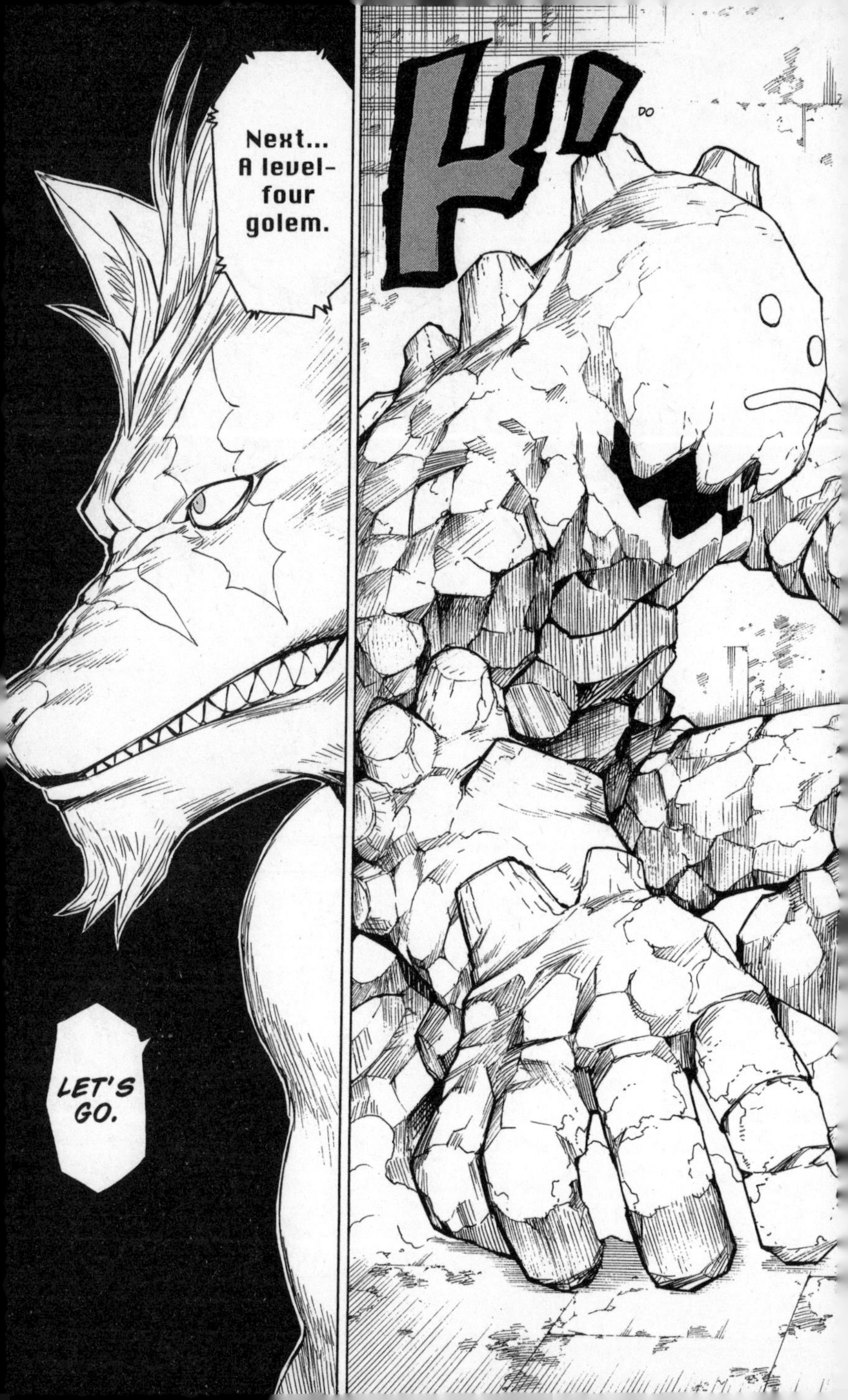
DO
Next... A level-four golem.
LET'S GO.

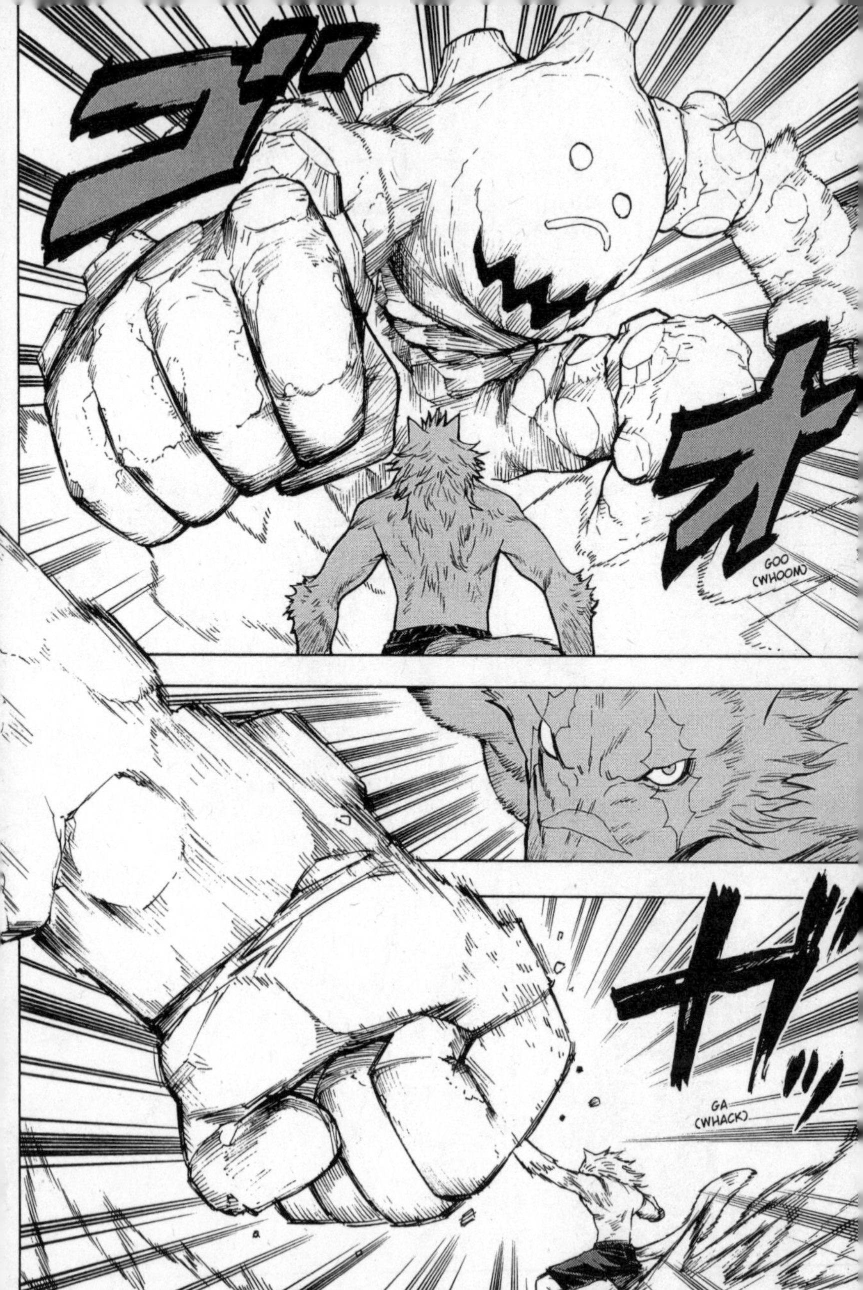
GOO
(WHOOM)
GA
(WHACK)

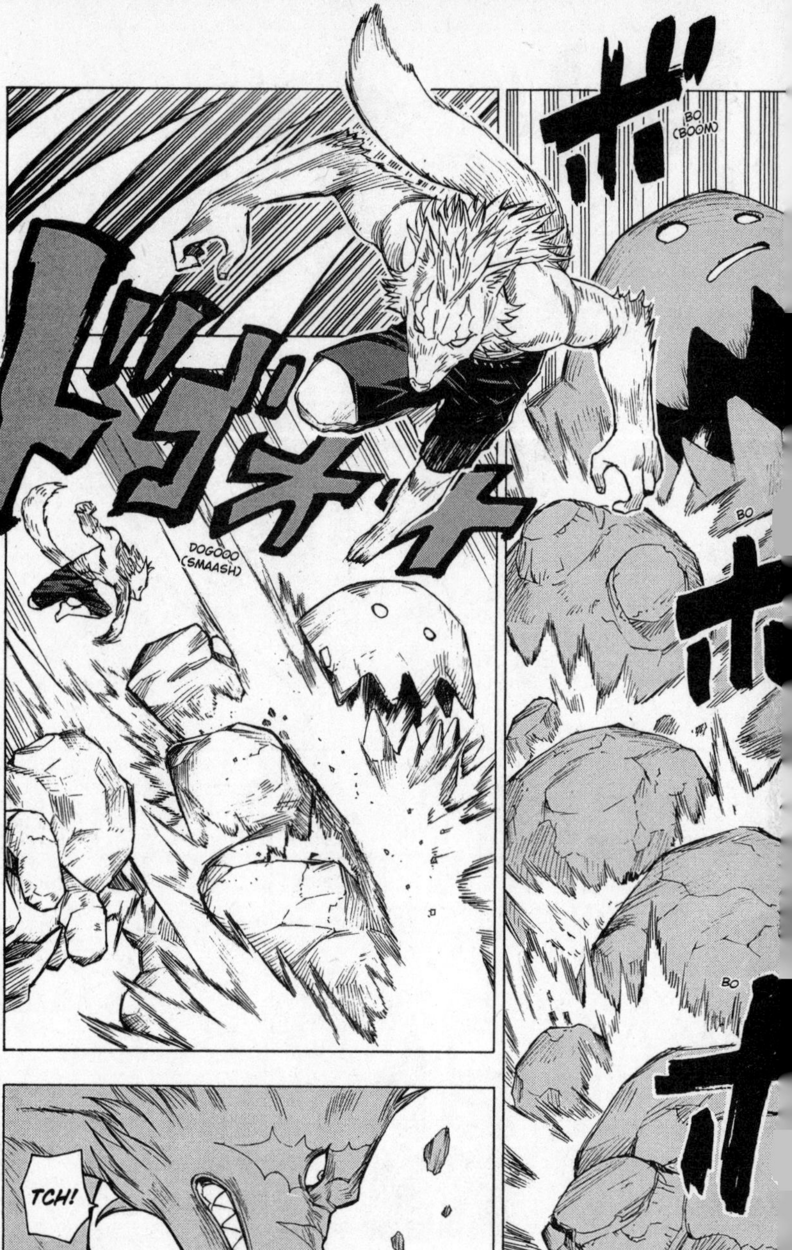
BO
(BOOM)
BO
BO
DOGOOO
(SMAASH)
TCH!

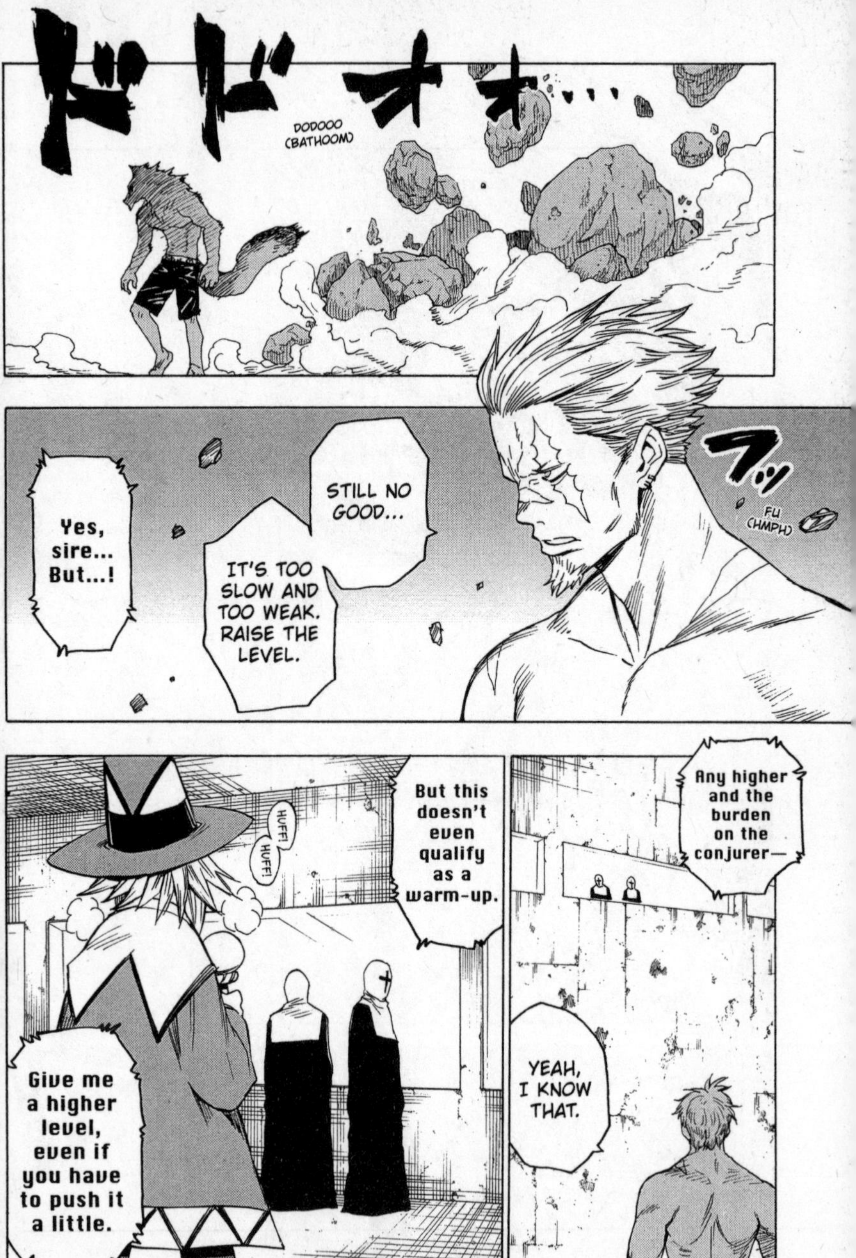
ドドオォ…
DODOOO (BATHOOM)
フッ
FU (HMPH)
STILL NO GOOD…
IT'S TOO SLOW AND TOO WEAK. RAISE THE LEVEL.
Yes, sire… But…!
Any higher and the burden on the conjurer—
YEAH, I KNOW THAT.
But this doesn't even qualify as a warm-up.
HUFF!
HUFF!
Give me a higher level, even if you have to push it a little.

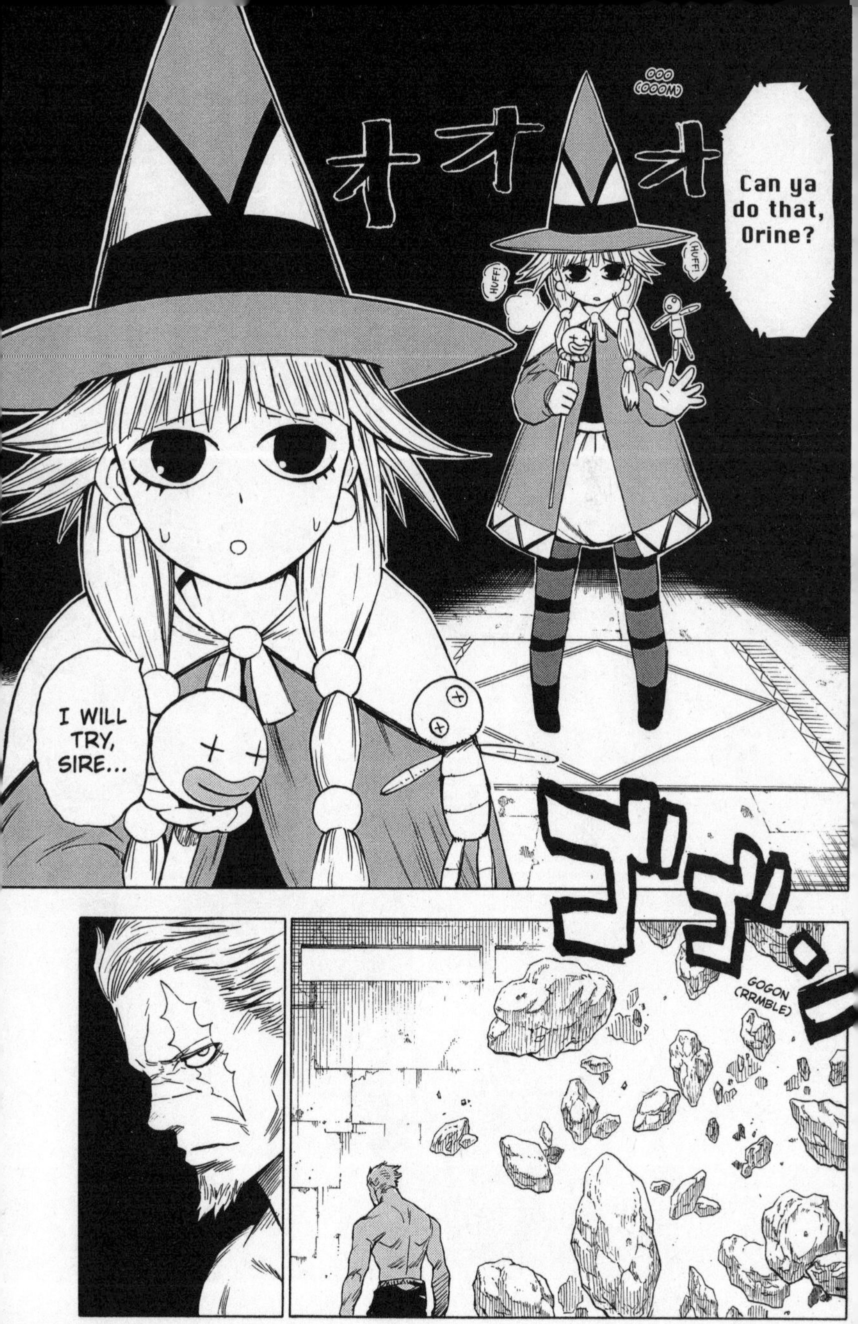
OOO
(COOOM)
Can ya do that, Orine?
HUFF!
HUFF!
I WILL TRY, SIRE...
GOGON
(RRMBLE)

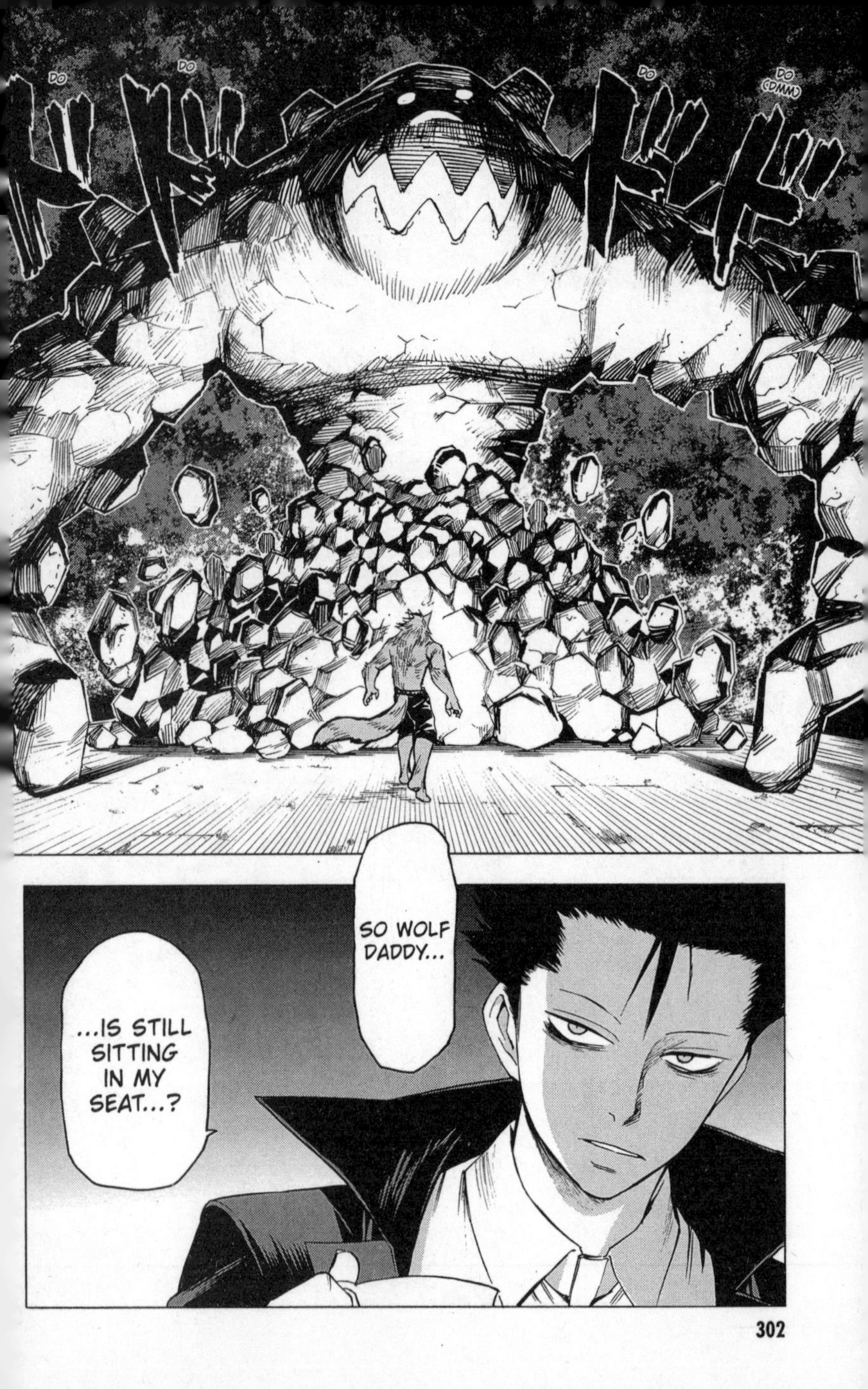
DO (DMM)
DO
DO
DO
SO WOLF DADDY...
...IS STILL SITTING IN MY SEAT...?

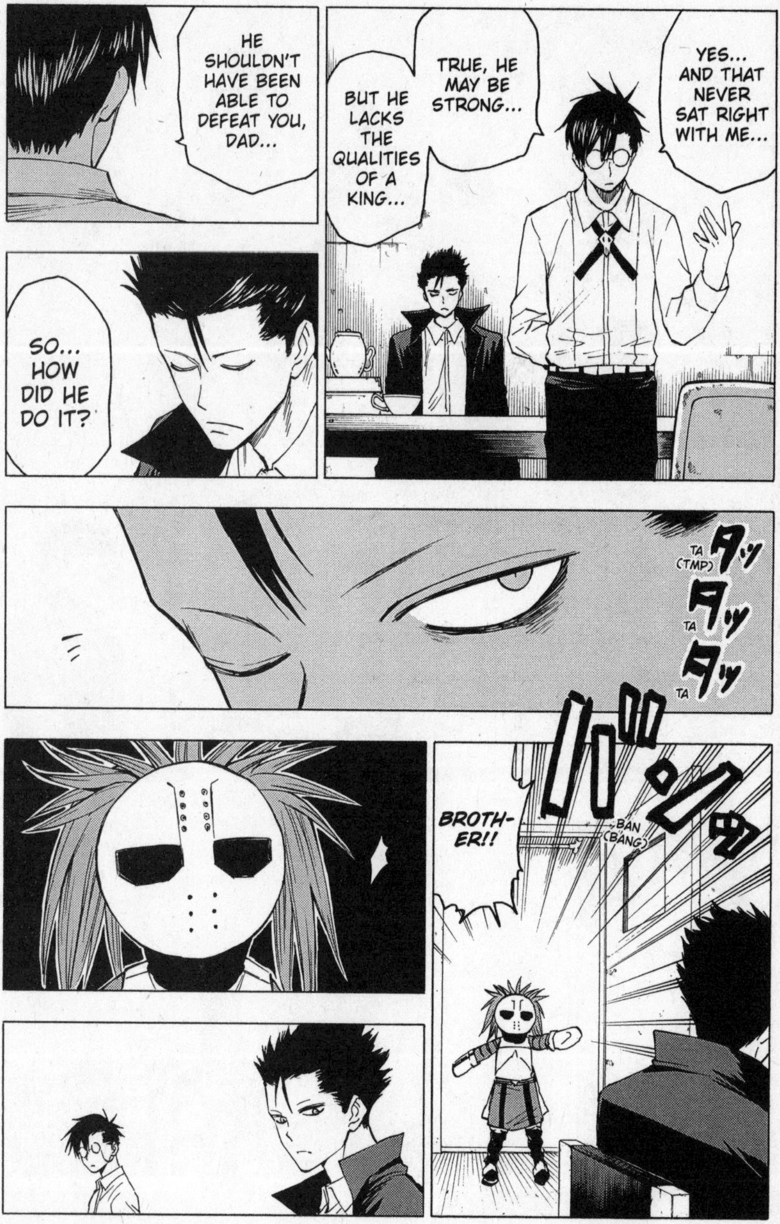
YES... AND THAT NEVER SAT RIGHT WITH ME...
TRUE, HE MAY BE STRONG...
BUT HE LACKS THE QUALITIES OF A KING...
HE SHOULDN'T HAVE BEEN ABLE TO DEFEAT YOU, DAD...
SO... HOW DID HE DO IT?
タッ TA (TMP)
タッ TA
タッ TA
バン BAN (BANG)
BROTHER!!

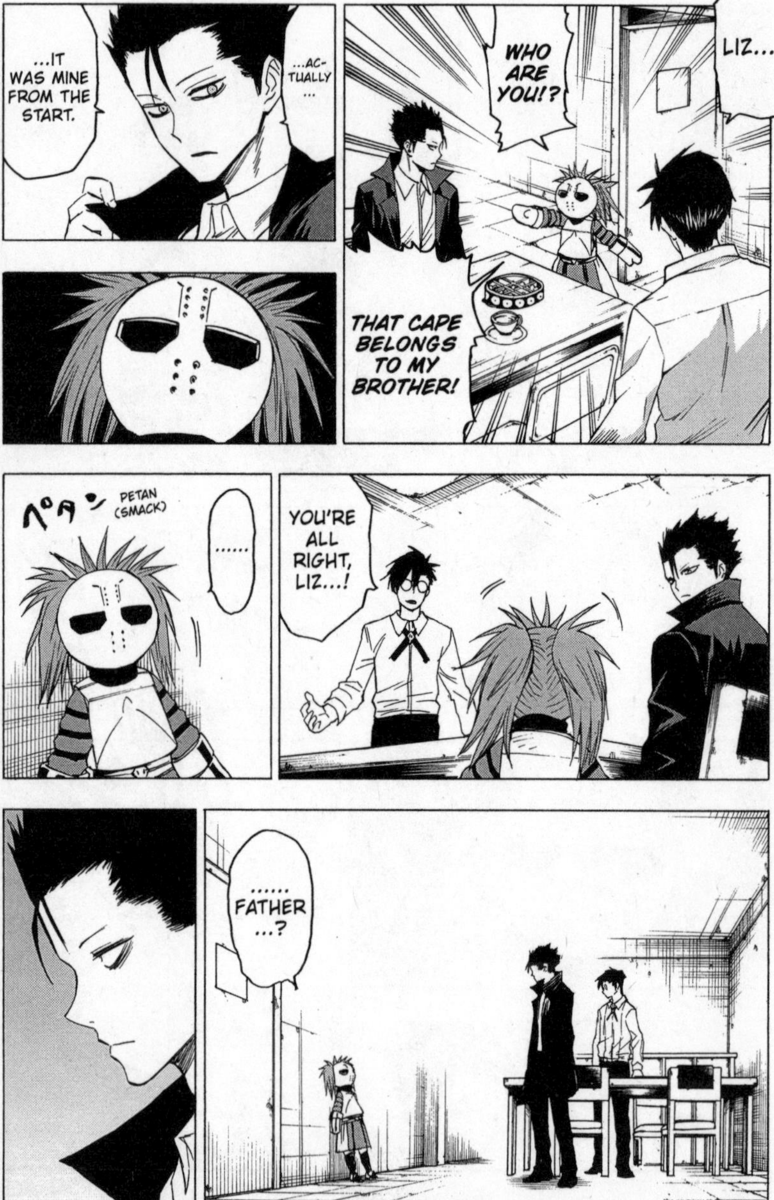
LIZ...!
WHO ARE YOU!?
THAT CAPE BELONGS TO MY BROTHER!
...ACTUALLY ...
...IT WAS MINE FROM THE START.
YOU'RE ALL RIGHT, LIZ...!
......
ペタン PETAN (SMACK)
...... FATHER ...?

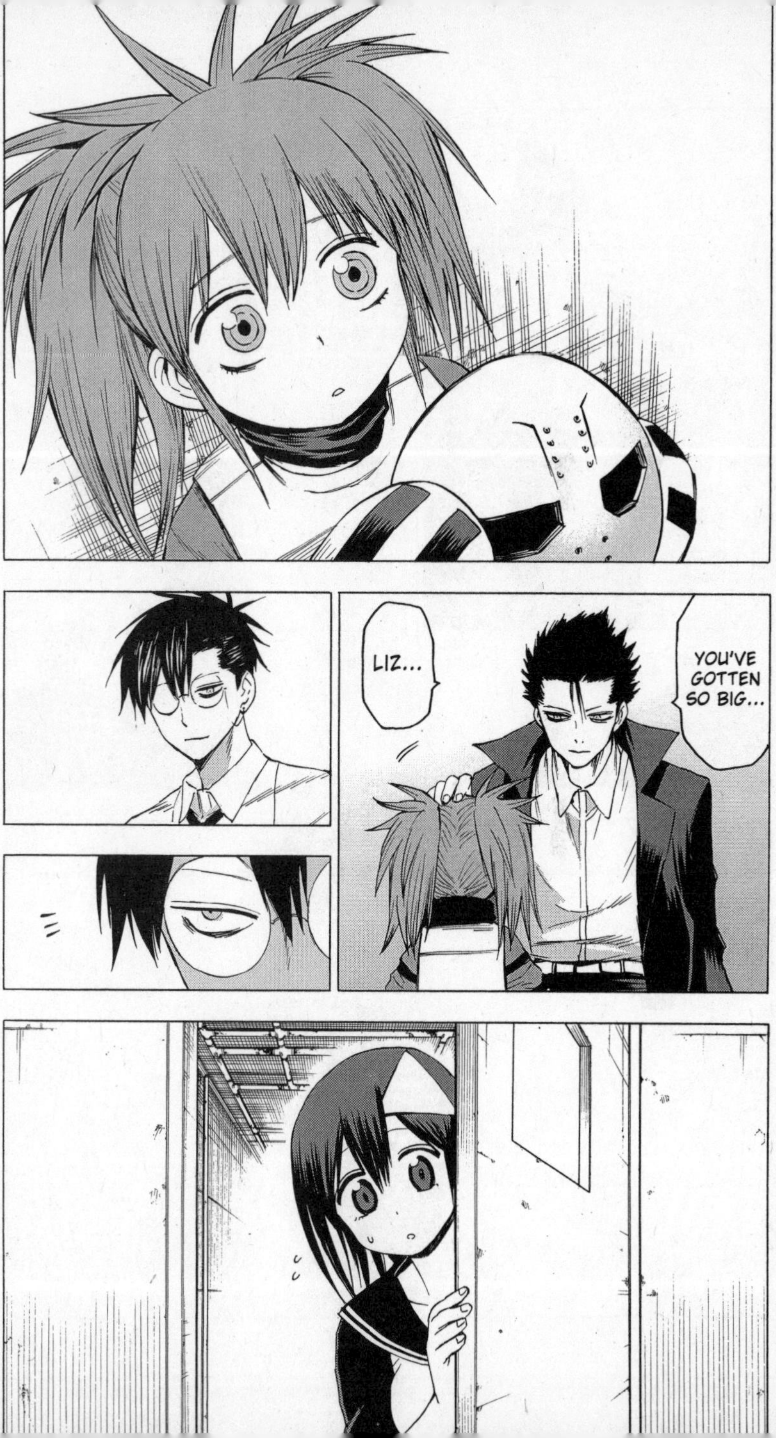
YOU'VE GOTTEN SO BIG...
LIZ...

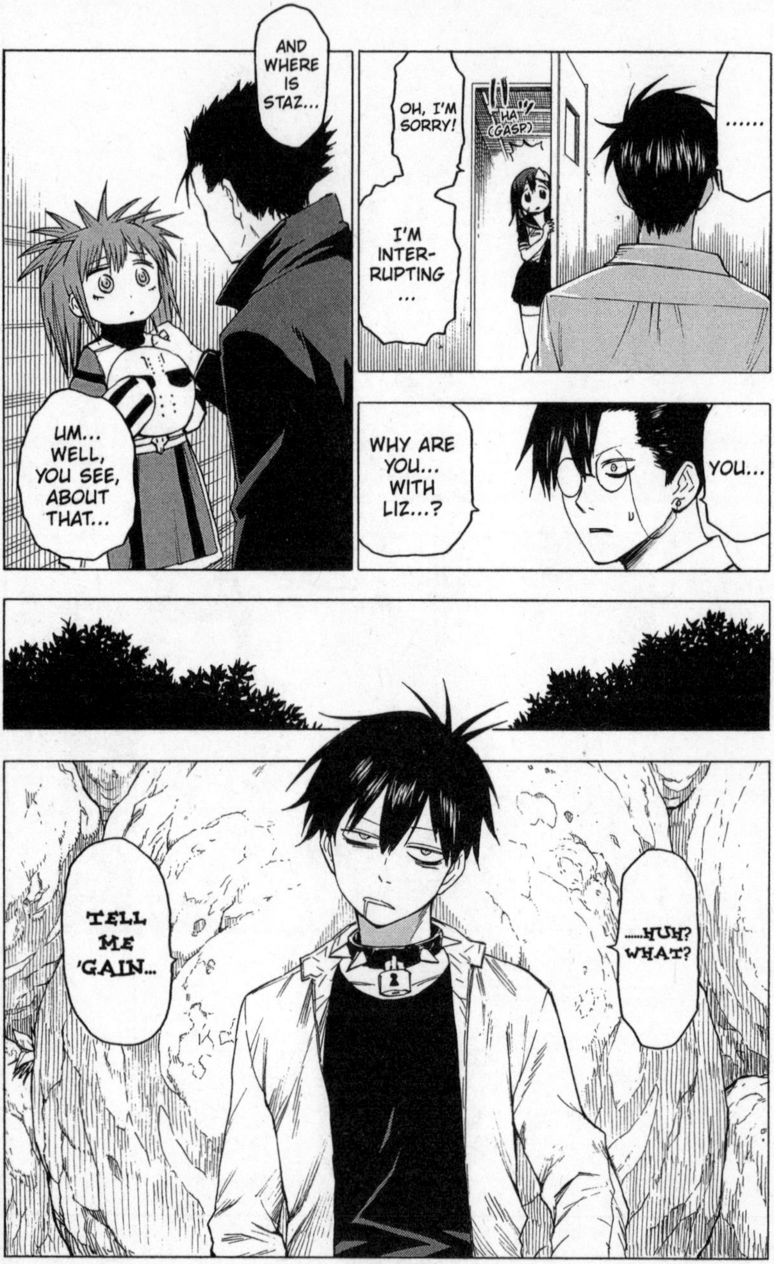
......
HA (GASP)
OH, I'M SORRY!
I'M INTERRUPTING...
YOU...
WHY ARE YOU... WITH LIZ...?
AND WHERE IS STAZ...
UM... WELL, YOU SEE, ABOUT THAT...
......HUH? WHAT?
TELL ME 'GAIN...

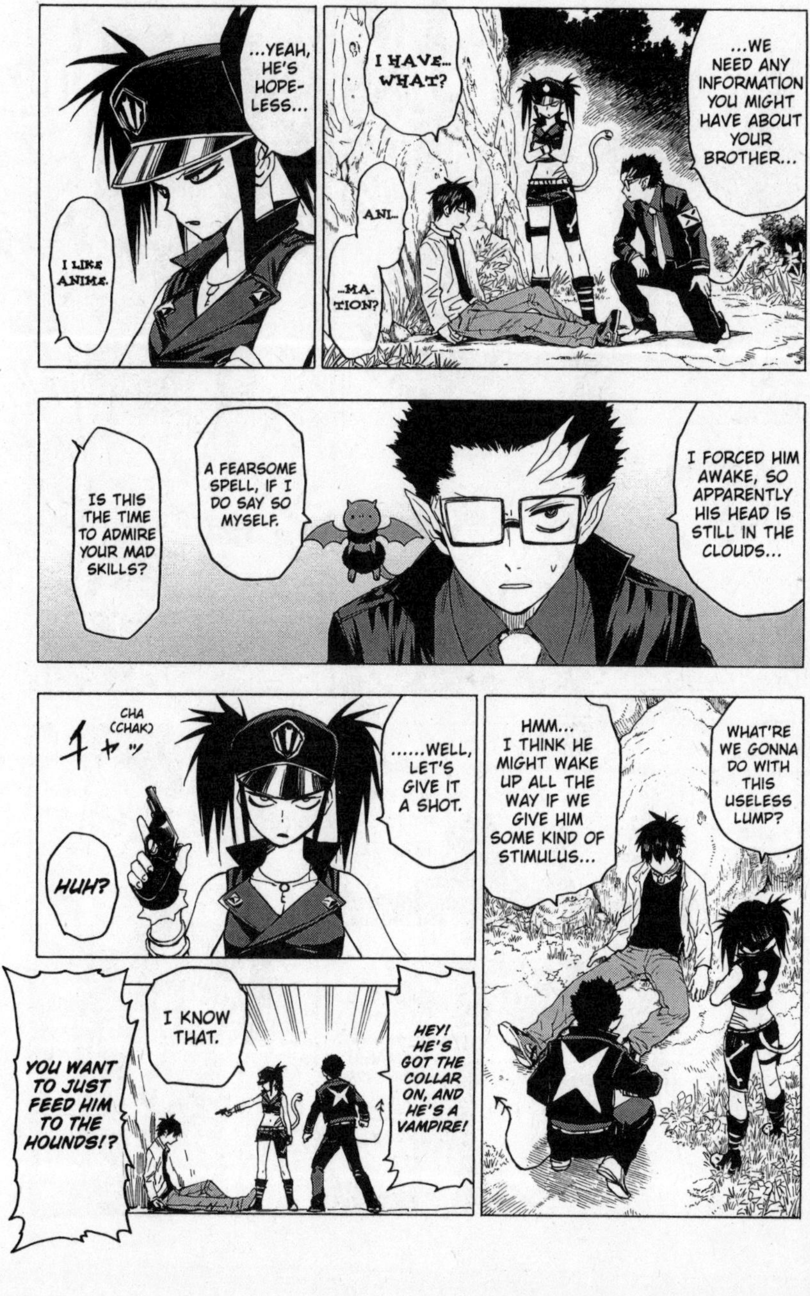
...WE NEED ANY INFORMATION YOU MIGHT HAVE ABOUT YOUR BROTHER...
I HAVE... WHAT?
ANI...
...MA-TION?
...YEAH, HE'S HOPE-LESS...
I LIKE ANIME.
I FORCED HIM AWAKE, SO APPARENTLY HIS HEAD IS STILL IN THE CLOUDS...
A FEARSOME SPELL, IF I DO SAY SO MYSELF.
IS THIS THE TIME TO ADMIRE YOUR MAD SKILLS?
WHAT'RE WE GONNA DO WITH THIS USELESS LUMP?
HMM... I THINK HE MIGHT WAKE UP ALL THE WAY IF WE GIVE HIM SOME KIND OF STIMULUS...
......WELL, LET'S GIVE IT A SHOT.
チャッ
CHA (CHAK)
HUH?
HEY! HE'S GOT THE COLLAR ON, AND HE'S A VAMPIRE!
I KNOW THAT.
YOU WANT TO JUST FEED HIM TO THE HOUNDS!?

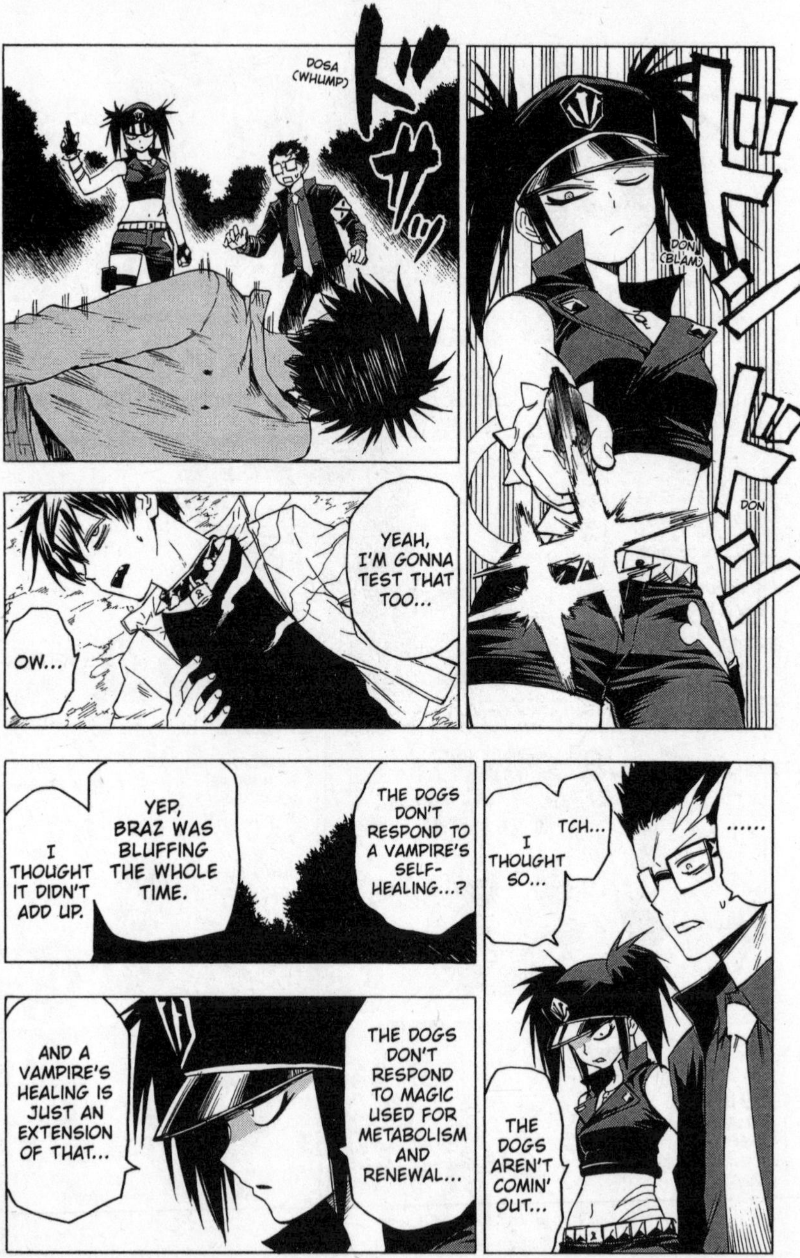
DON (BLAM)
DON
DOSA (WHUMP)
YEAH, I'M GONNA TEST THAT TOO...
OW...
......
TCH... I THOUGHT SO...
THE DOGS AREN'T COMIN' OUT...
THE DOGS DON'T RESPOND TO A VAMPIRE'S SELF-HEALING...?
YEP, BRAZ WAS BLUFFING THE WHOLE TIME.
I THOUGHT IT DIDN'T ADD UP.
THE DOGS DON'T RESPOND TO MAGIC USED FOR METABOLISM AND RENEWAL...
AND A VAMPIRE'S HEALING IS JUST AN EXTENSION OF THAT...

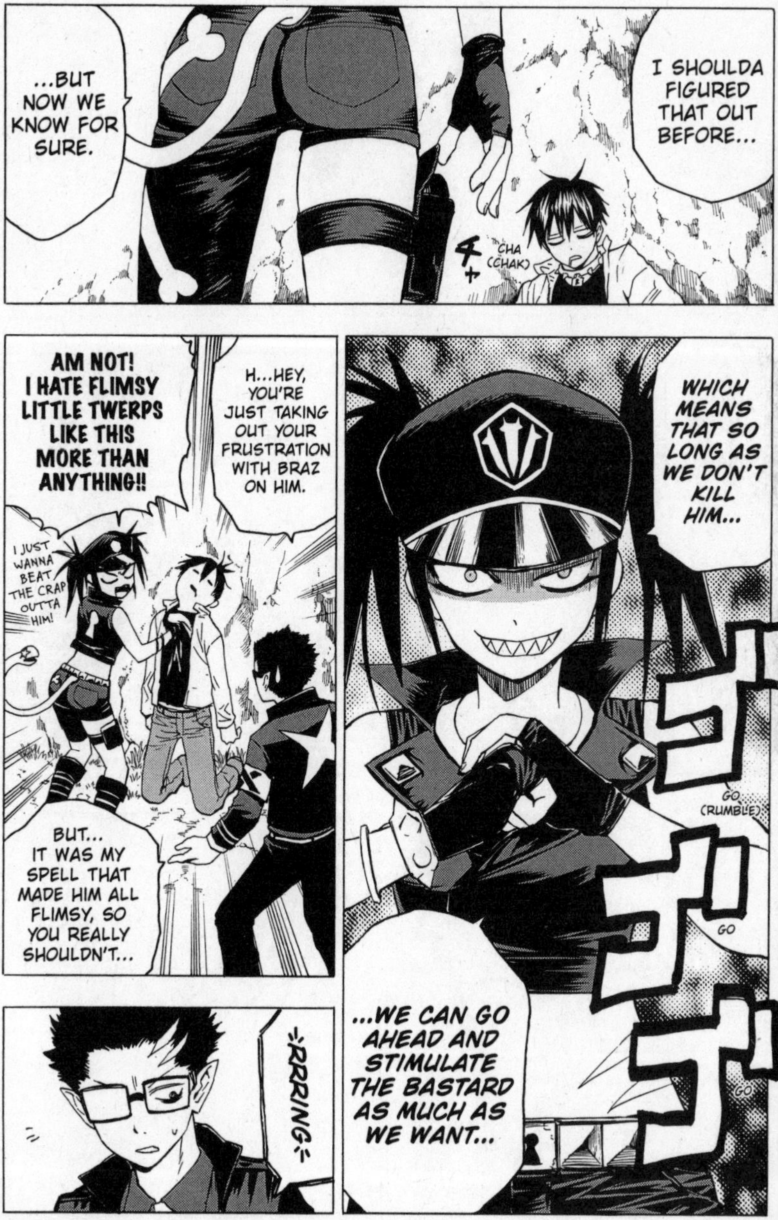

I SHOULDA FIGURED THAT OUT BEFORE...
CHA (CHAK)
...BUT NOW WE KNOW FOR SURE.
WHICH MEANS THAT SO LONG AS WE DON'T KILL HIM...
GO (RUMBLE)
GO
...WE CAN GO AHEAD AND STIMULATE THE BASTARD AS MUCH AS WE WANT...
GO
H...HEY, YOU'RE JUST TAKING OUT YOUR FRUSTRATION WITH BRAZ ON HIM.
AM NOT! I HATE FLIMSY LITTLE TWERPS LIKE THIS MORE THAN ANYTHING!!
I JUST WANNA BEAT THE CRAP OUTTA HIM!
BUT... IT WAS MY SPELL THAT MADE HIM ALL FLIMSY, SO YOU REALLY SHOULDN'T...
RRRING

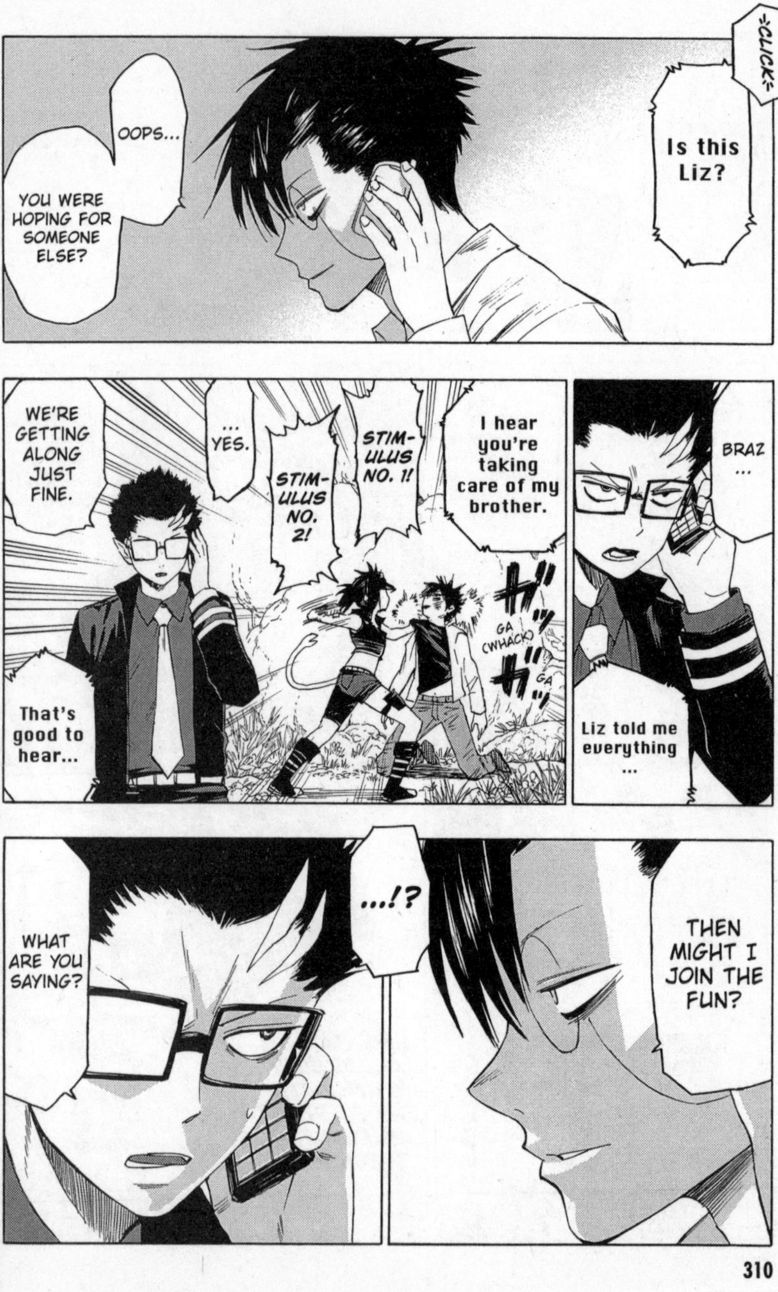
CLICK
Is this Liz?
OOPS...
YOU WERE HOPING FOR SOMEONE ELSE?
BRAZ ...
Liz told me everything ...
I hear you're taking care of my brother.
GA (WHACK)
GA
STIM-ULUS NO. 1!
STIM-ULUS NO. 2!
... YES.
WE'RE GETTING ALONG JUST FINE.
That's good to hear...
THEN MIGHT I JOIN THE FUN?
...!?
WHAT ARE YOU SAYING?

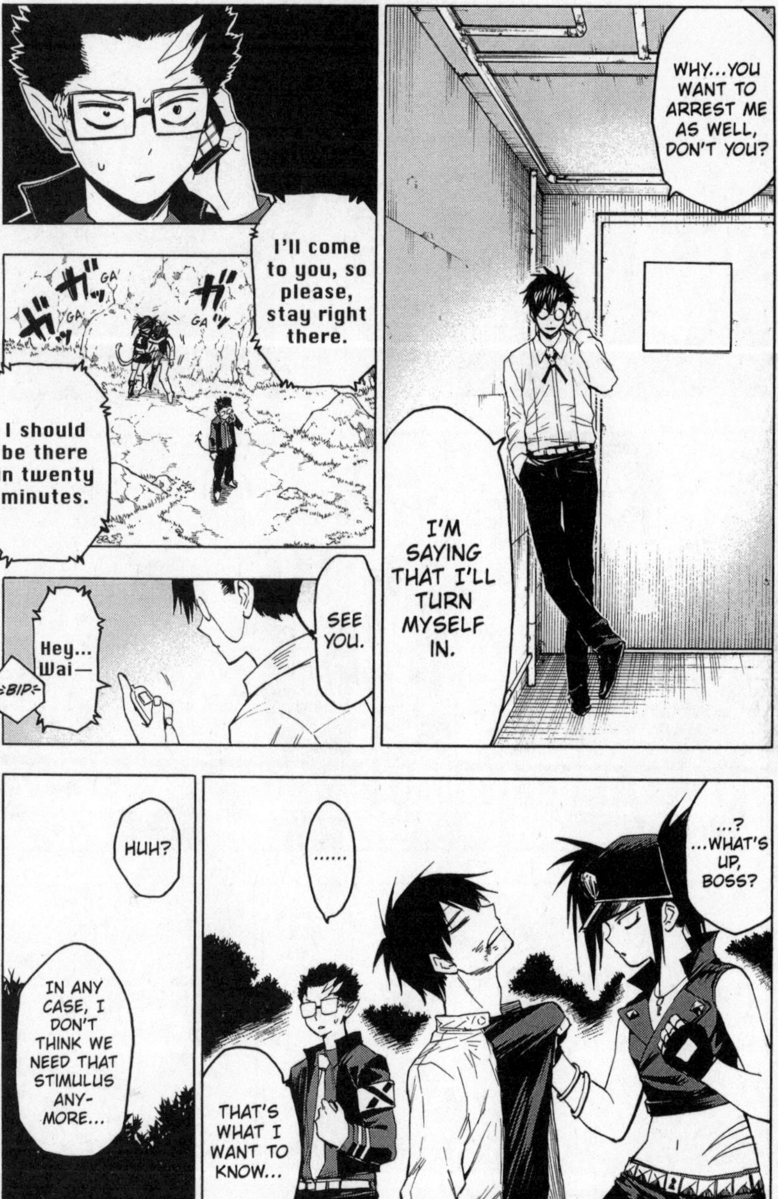
WHY...YOU WANT TO ARREST ME AS WELL, DON'T YOU?
I'M SAYING THAT I'LL TURN MYSELF IN.
I'll come to you, so please, stay right there.
GA
GA
GA
I should be there in twenty minutes.
SEE YOU.
Hey... Wai—
BIP
...? ...WHAT'S UP, BOSS?
......
THAT'S WHAT I WANT TO KNOW...
HUH?
IN ANY CASE, I DON'T THINK WE NEED THAT STIMULUS ANY-MORE...

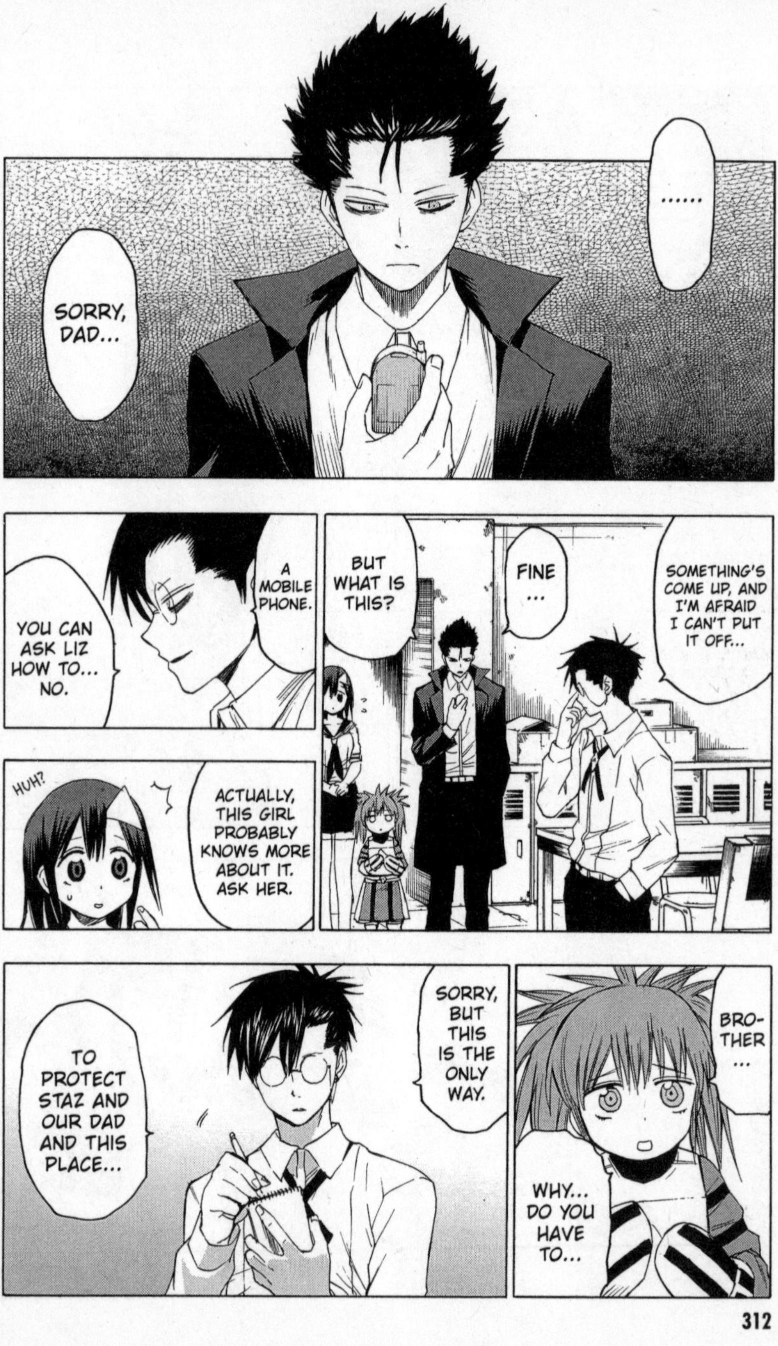
......
SORRY, DAD...
SOMETHING'S COME UP, AND I'M AFRAID I CAN'T PUT IT OFF...
FINE ...
BUT WHAT IS THIS?
A MOBILE PHONE.
YOU CAN ASK LIZ HOW TO... NO.
ACTUALLY, THIS GIRL PROBABLY KNOWS MORE ABOUT IT. ASK HER.
HUH?
BROTHER...
WHY... DO YOU HAVE TO...
SORRY, BUT THIS IS THE ONLY WAY.
TO PROTECT STAZ AND OUR DAD AND THIS PLACE...

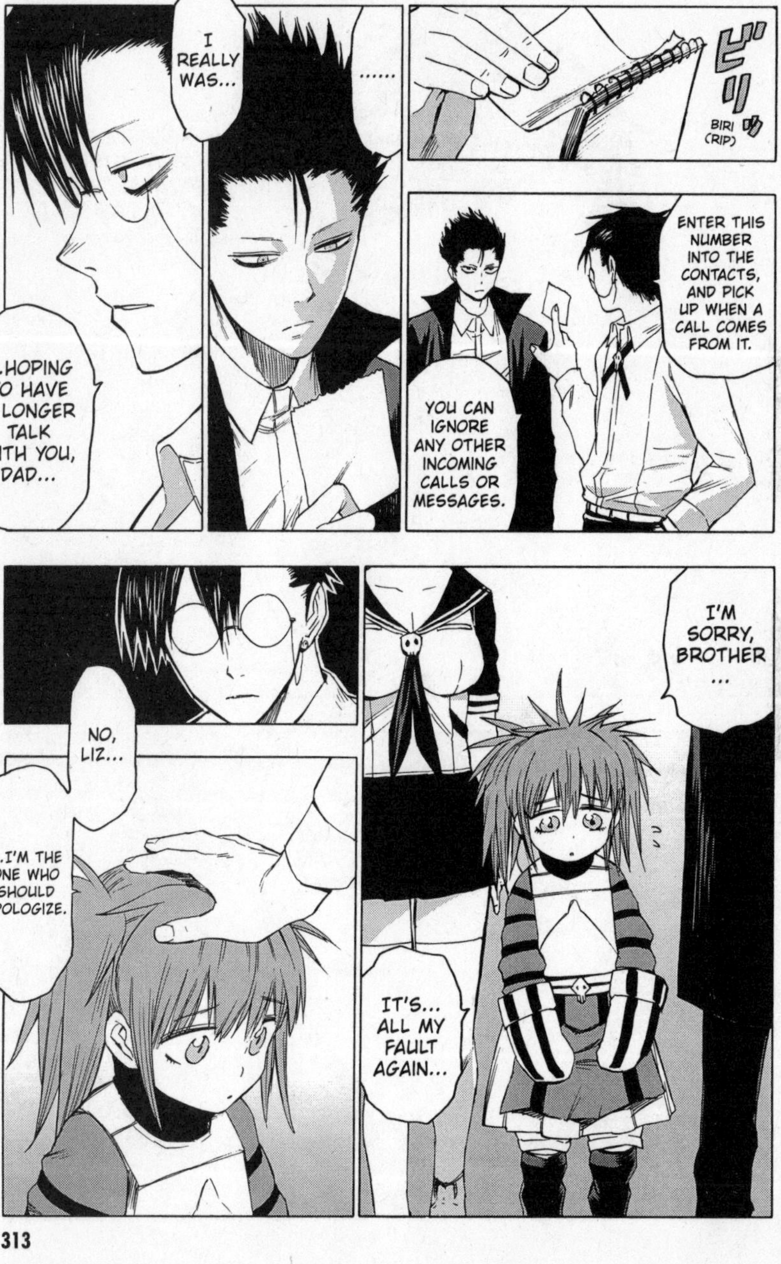
ビリッ
BIRI (RIP)
ENTER THIS NUMBER INTO THE CONTACTS, AND PICK UP WHEN A CALL COMES FROM IT.
YOU CAN IGNORE ANY OTHER INCOMING CALLS OR MESSAGES.
......
I REALLY WAS...
...HOPING TO HAVE A LONGER TALK WITH YOU, DAD...
I'M SORRY, BROTHER ...
IT'S... ALL MY FAULT AGAIN...
NO, LIZ...
...I'M THE ONE WHO SHOULD APOLOGIZE.

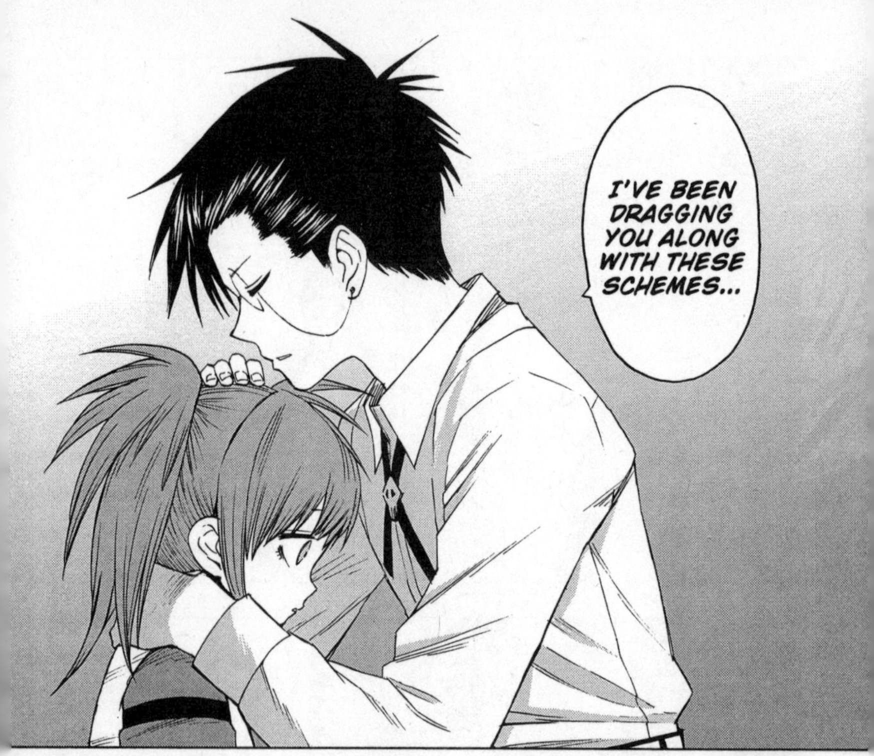
I'VE BEEN DRAGGING YOU ALONG WITH THESE SCHEMES...

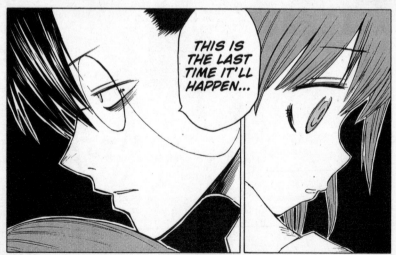

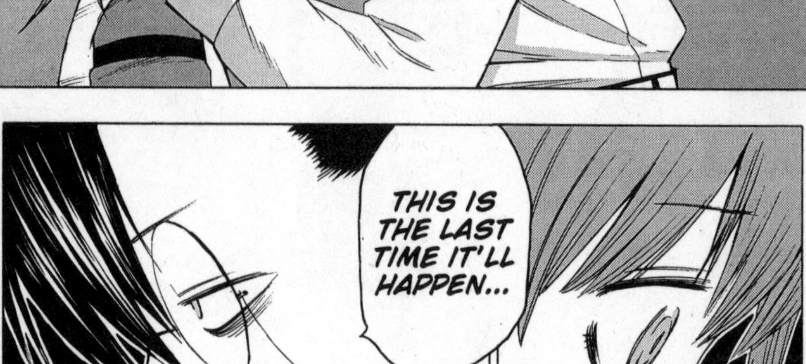
THIS IS THE LAST TIME IT'LL HAPPEN...

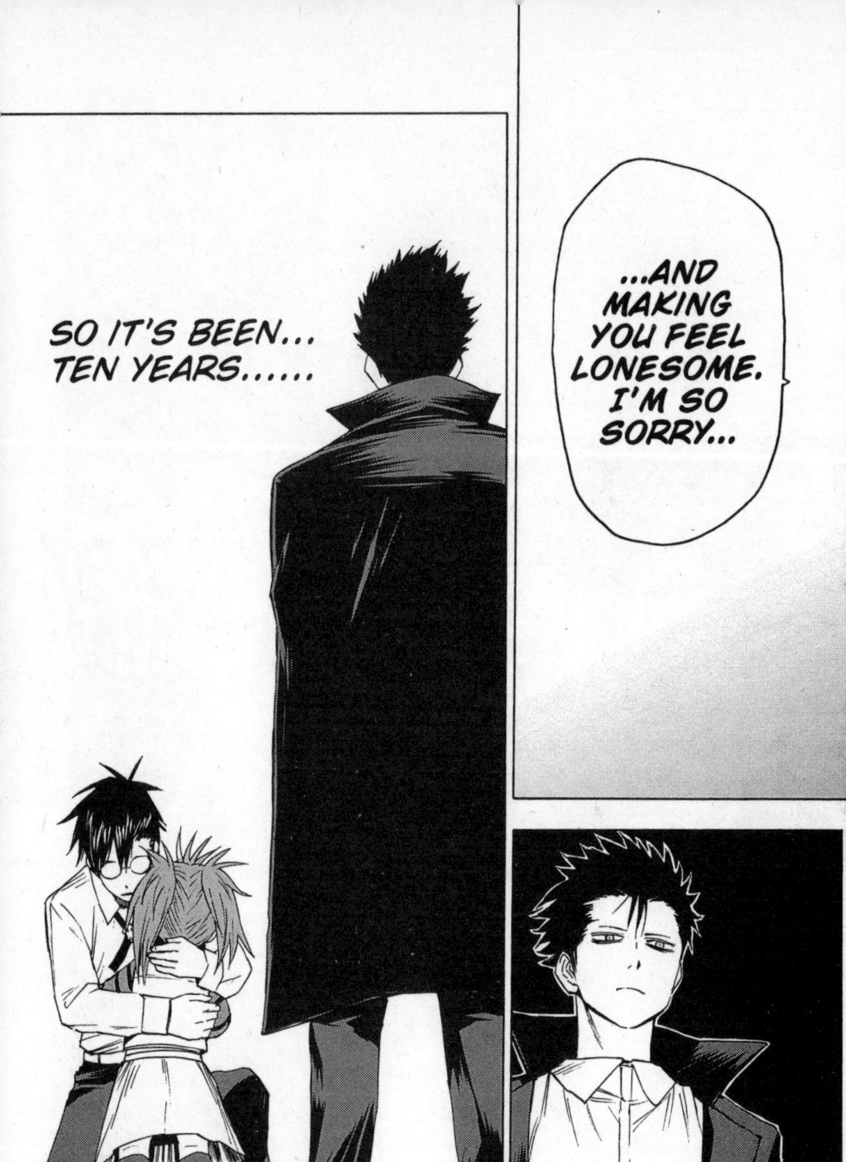
...AND MAKING YOU FEEL LONESOME. I'M SO SORRY...
SO IT'S BEEN... TEN YEARS......

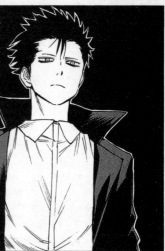

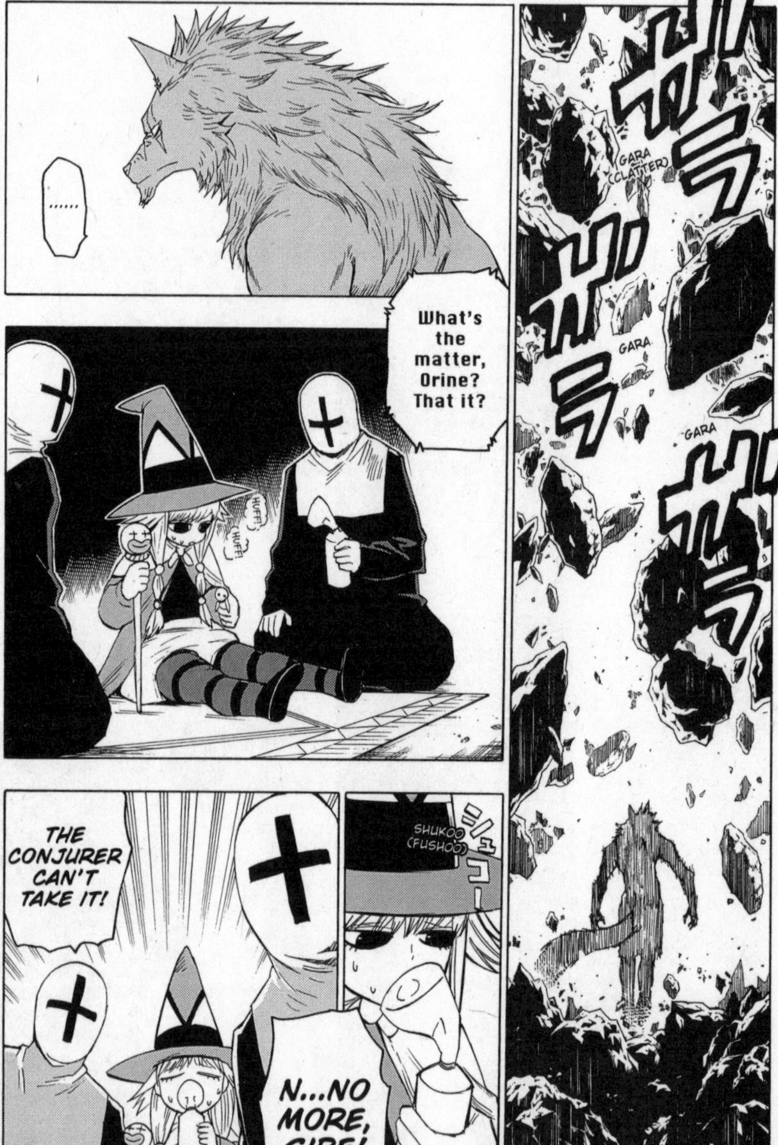
GARA (CLATTER)
GARA
GARA
......
What's the matter, Orine? That it?
HUFF!
HUFF!
SHUKOO (FUSHOO)
THE CONJURER CAN'T TAKE IT!
N...NO MORE, SIRE!

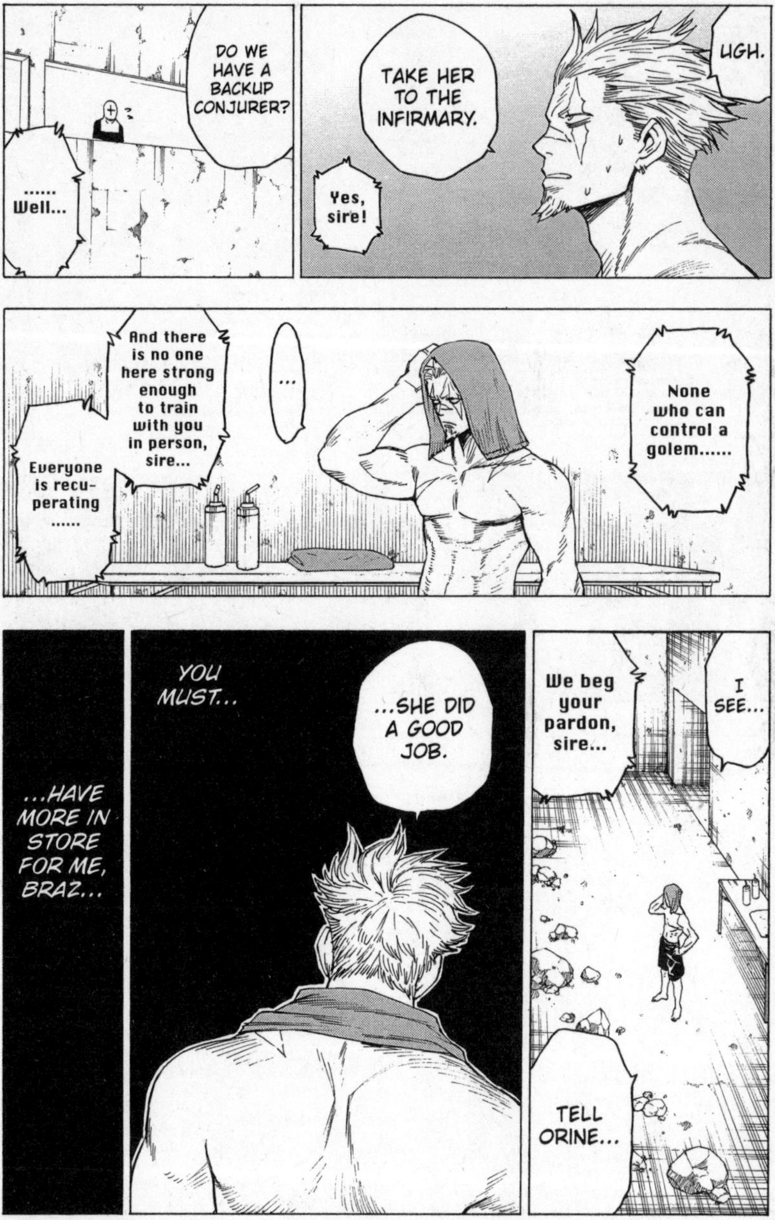
UGH.
TAKE HER TO THE INFIRMARY.
Yes, sire!
DO WE HAVE A BACKUP CONJURER?
...... Well...
None who can control a golem......
...
And there is no one here strong enough to train with you in person, sire...
Everyone is recuperating ......
I SEE...
We beg your pardon, sire...
TELL ORINE...
...SHE DID A GOOD JOB.
YOU MUST...
...HAVE MORE IN STORE FOR ME, BRAZ...

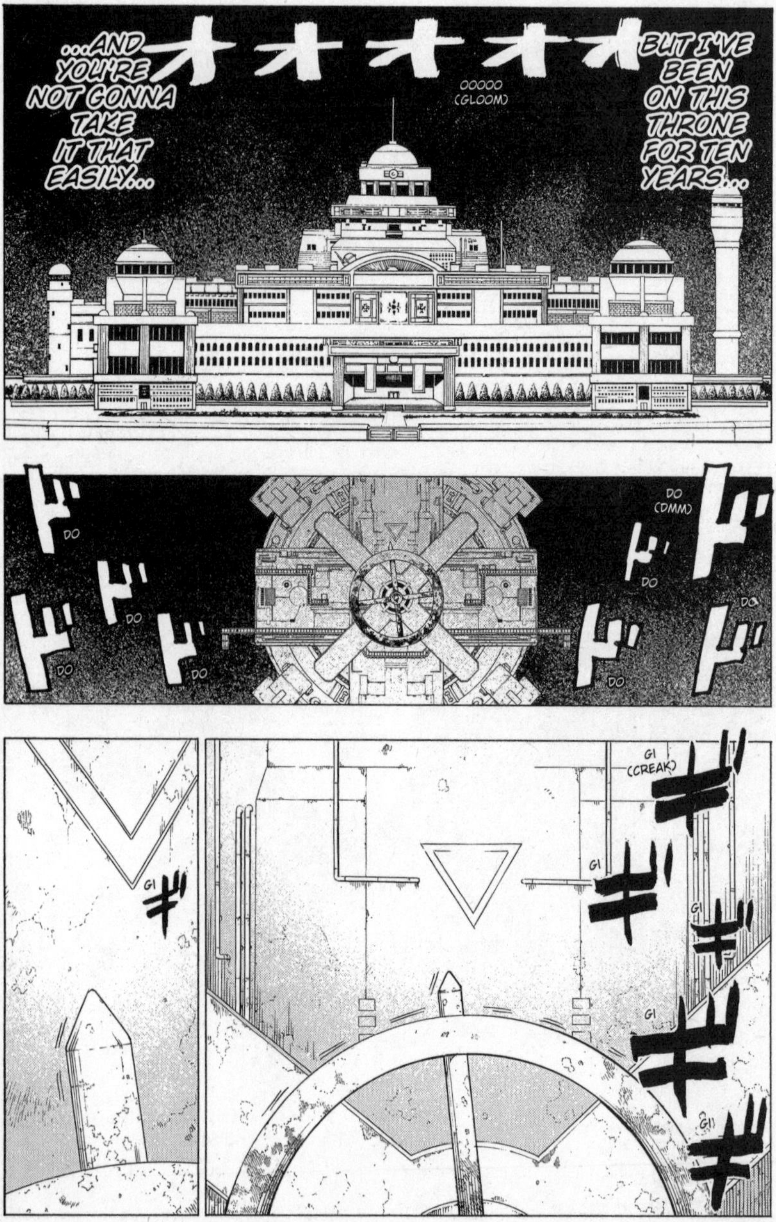
BUT I'VE BEEN ON THIS THRONE FOR TEN YEARS...
OOOOO (GLOOM)
...AND YOU'RE NOT GONNA TAKE IT THAT EASILY...
DO (DMM)
DO
DO
DO
DO
DO
DO
DO
GI (CREAK)
GI
GI
GI
GI
GI

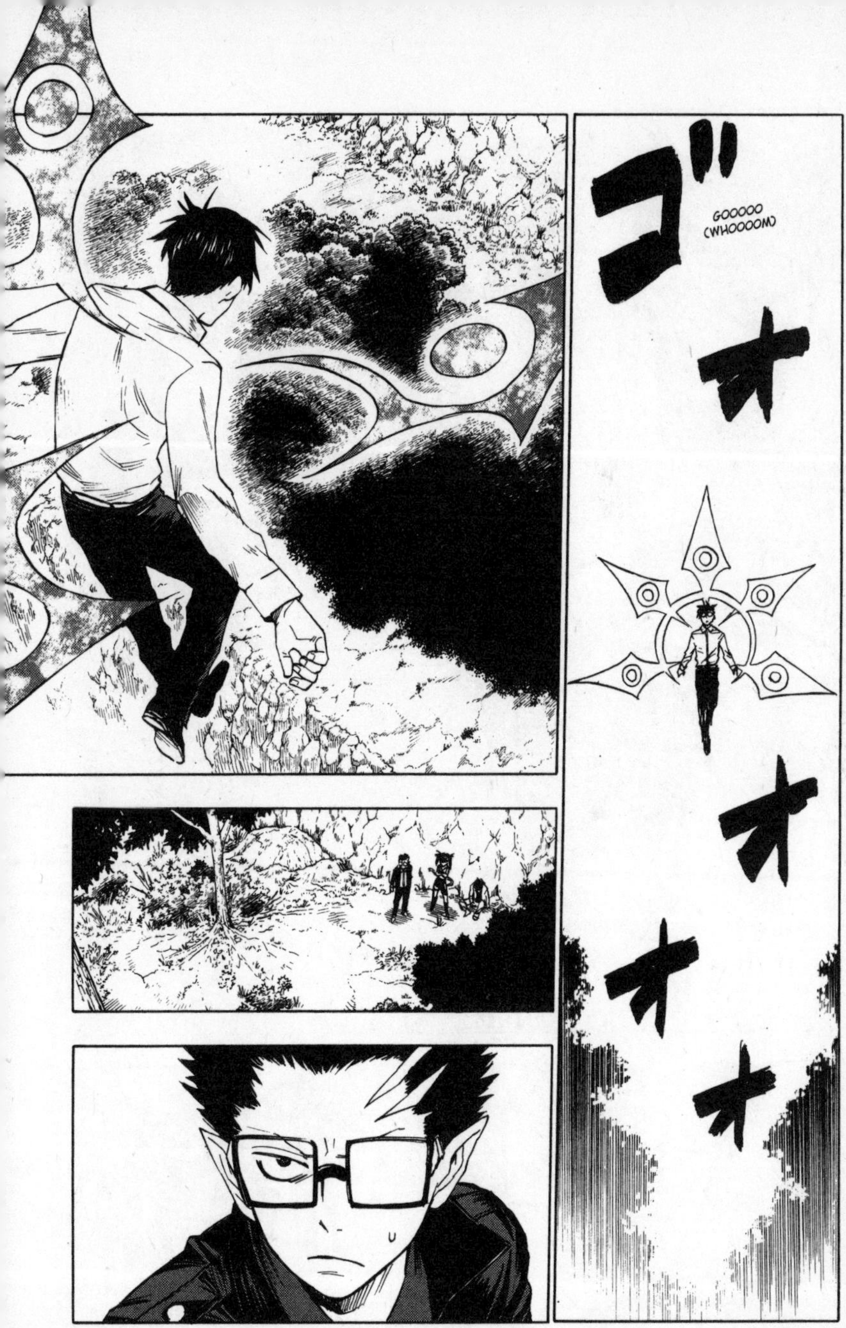
ゴォォォォ
GOOOOO
(WHOOOOM)

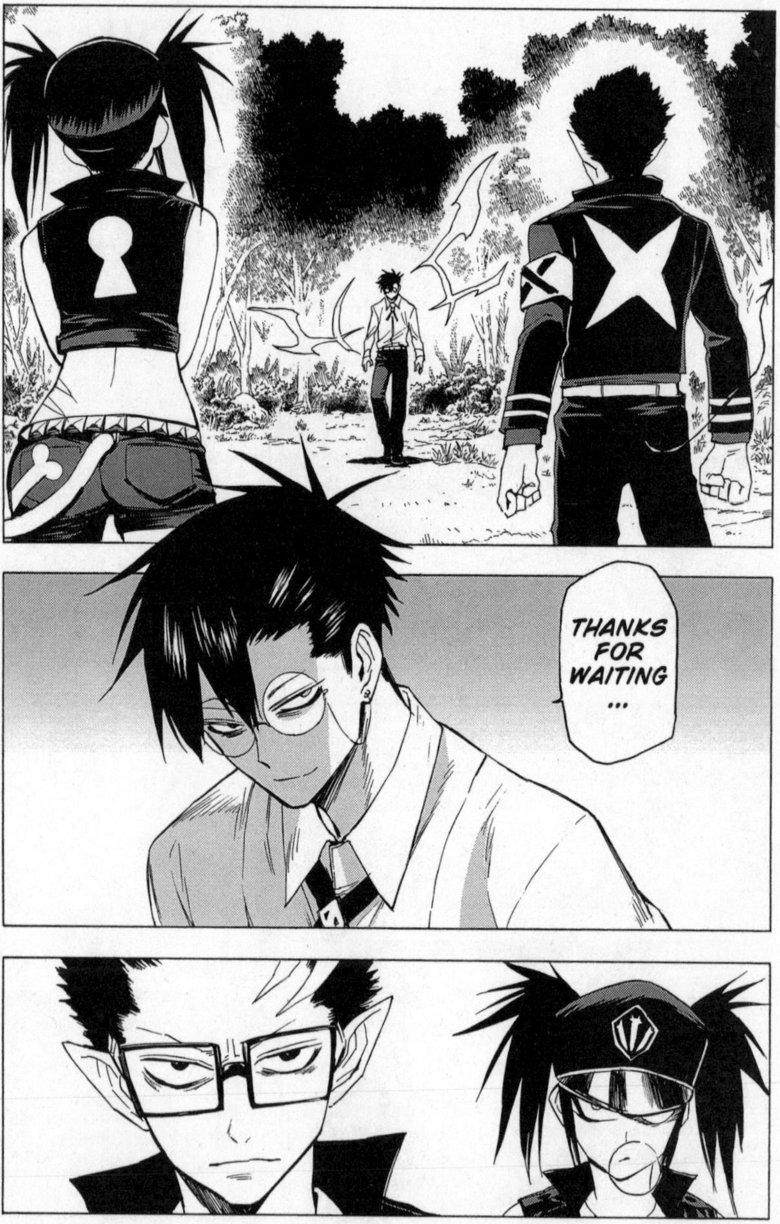
THANKS FOR WAITING ...

♠ To Be Continued ♠

OGRE DRINK'S
BEAST ENERGY

A BEVERAGE WHOSE
SELLING POINT IS THE
15% CONCENTRATED
MAGICAL ESSENCE
FROM DEMON WORLD
ACROPOLIS. BUT
THE CARBONATION
IS A LITTLE MUCH.

BLOOD LAD

CHAPTER 40 ♠ MEET ON THAT DAY, AT THAT HOUR, AT THAT PLACE!

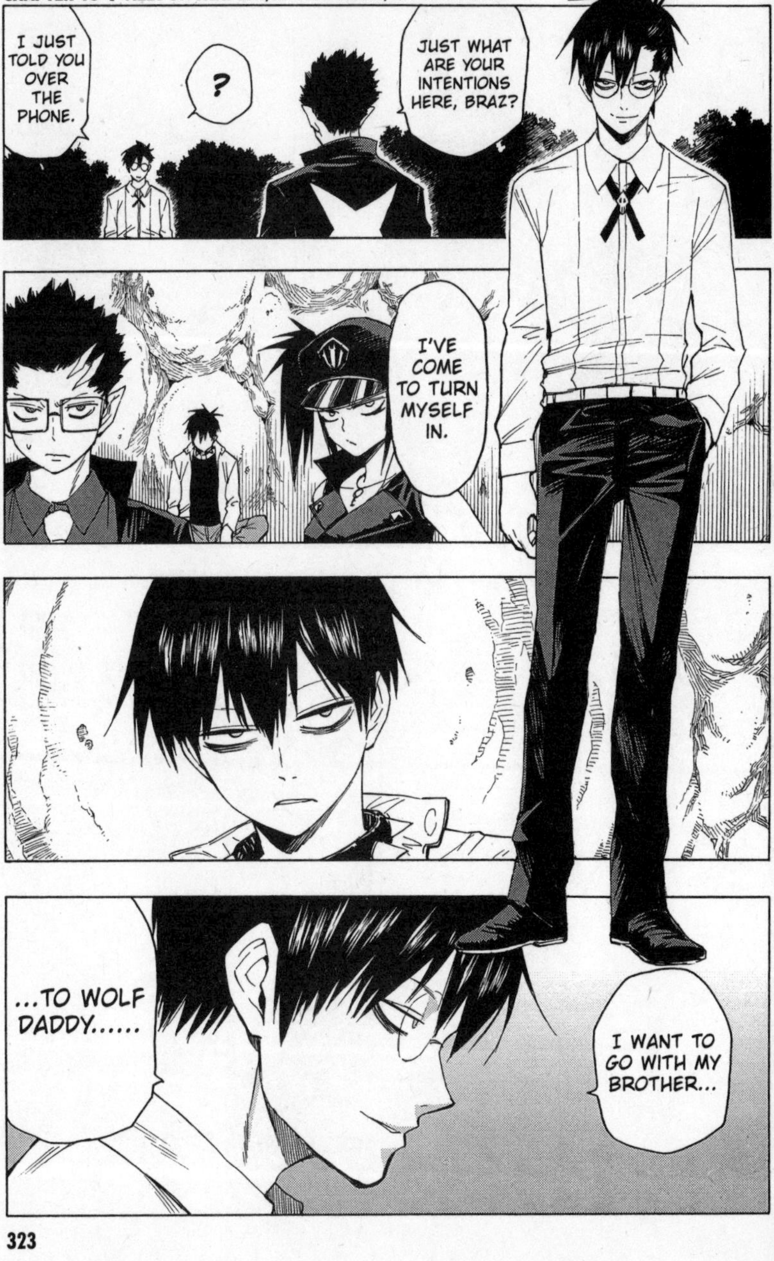
JUST WHAT ARE YOUR INTENTIONS HERE, BRAZ?
?
I JUST TOLD YOU OVER THE PHONE.
I'VE COME TO TURN MYSELF IN.
I WANT TO GO WITH MY BROTHER...
...TO WOLF DADDY......

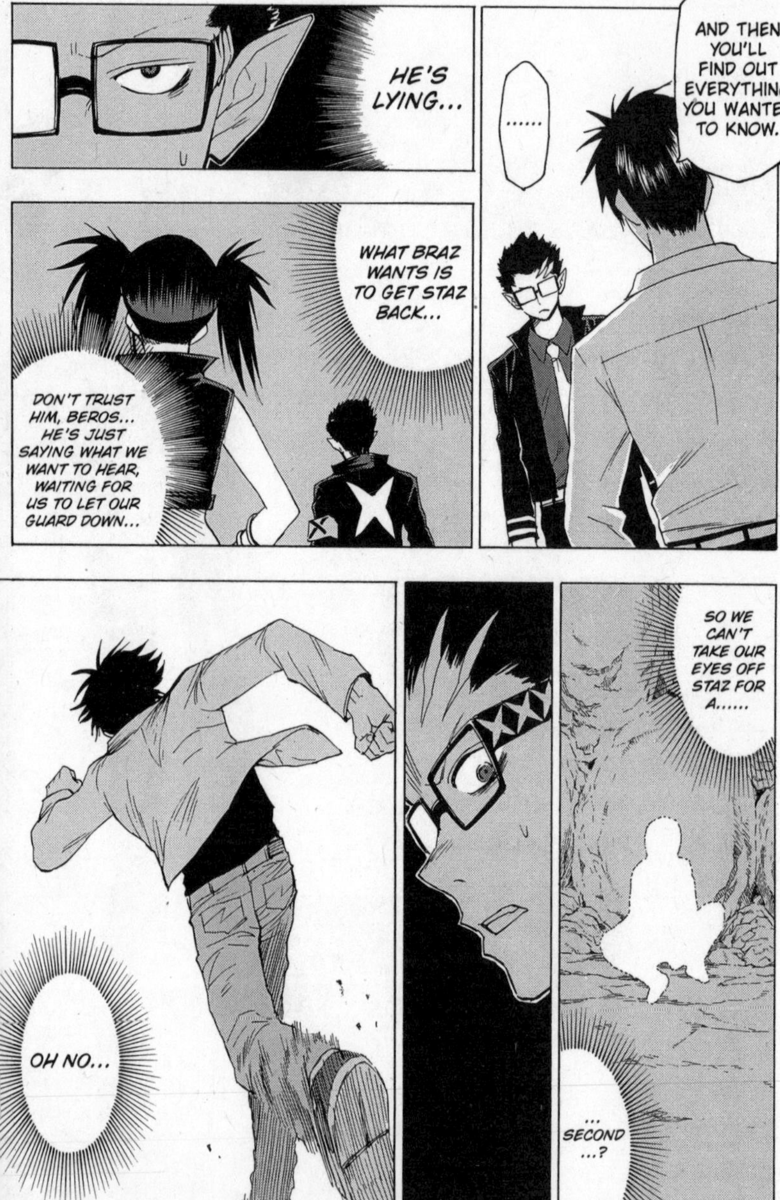
AND THEN YOU'LL FIND OUT EVERYTHING YOU WANTED TO KNOW.
......
HE'S LYING...
WHAT BRAZ WANTS IS TO GET STAZ BACK...
DON'T TRUST HIM, BEROS... HE'S JUST SAYING WHAT WE WANT TO HEAR, WAITING FOR US TO LET OUR GUARD DOWN...
SO WE CAN'T TAKE OUR EYES OFF STAZ FOR A......
...SECOND...?
OH NO...

CHAPTER 40 ♠ MEET ON THAT DAY, AT THAT HOUR, AT THAT PLACE!

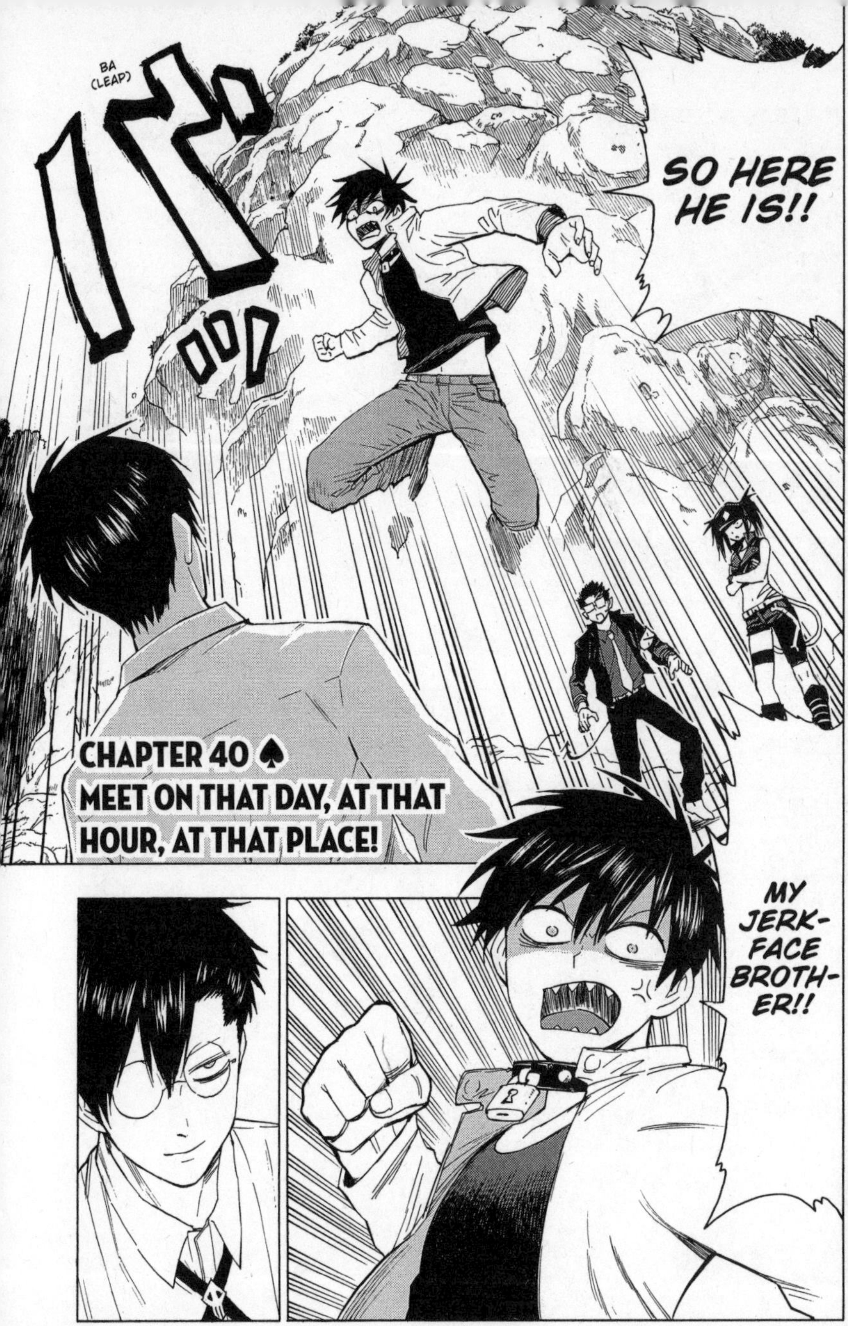
SO HERE HE IS!!
BA
(LEAP)
MY JERK-FACE BROTHER!!

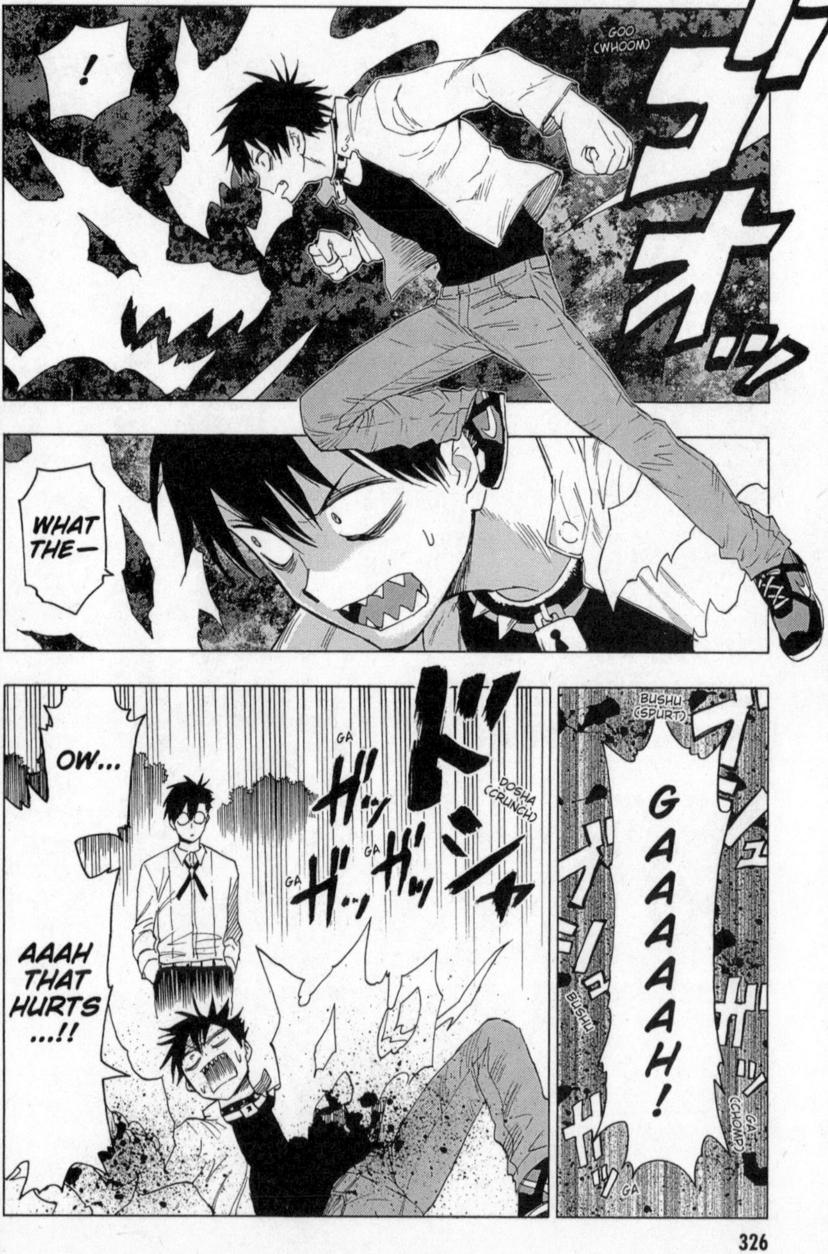
GOO (WHOOM)
!
WHAT THE—
BUSHU (SPURT)
GAAAAAAH!
BUSHU
GA (CHOMP)
GA
DOSHA (CRUNCH)
GA
GA
GA
OW...
AAAH THAT HURTS ...!!

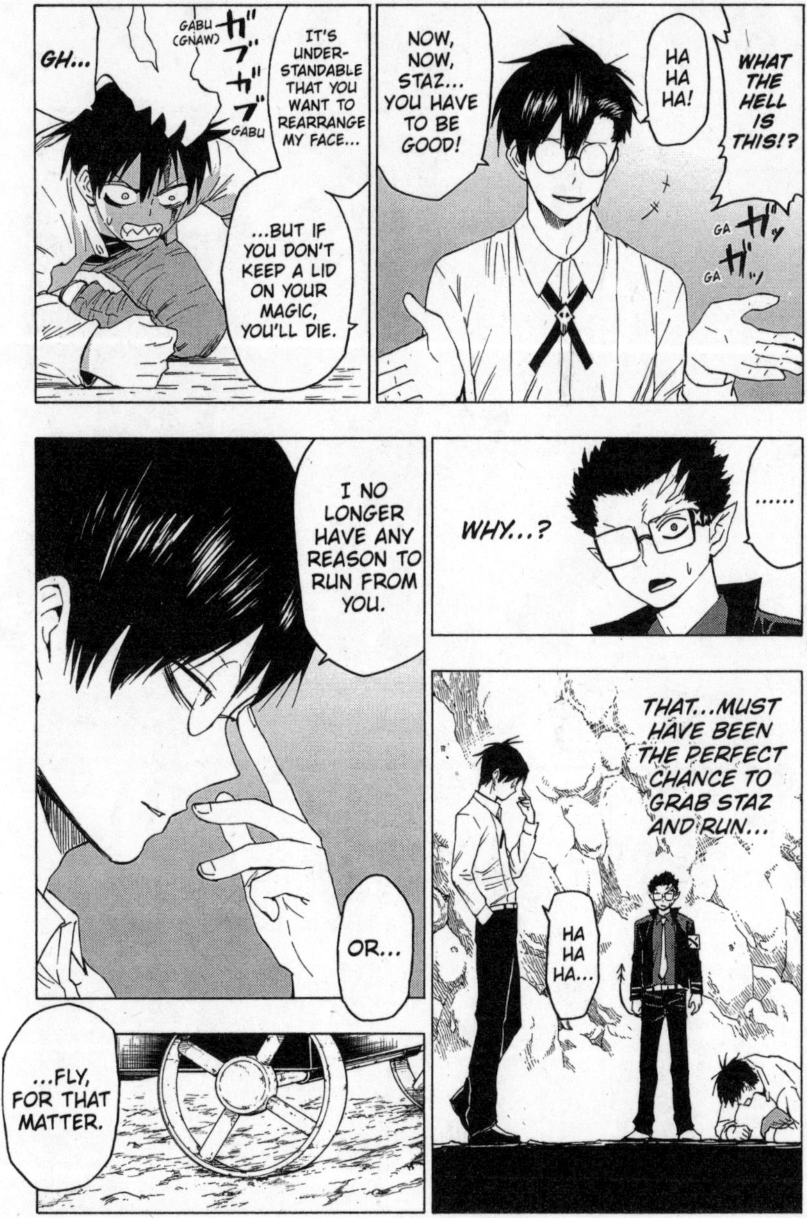
WHAT THE HELL IS THIS!?
HA HA HA!
GA
GA
NOW, NOW, STAZ... YOU HAVE TO BE GOOD!
IT'S UNDER-STANDABLE THAT YOU WANT TO REARRANGE MY FACE...
GABU (GNAW)
GABU
GH...
...BUT IF YOU DON'T KEEP A LID ON YOUR MAGIC, YOU'LL DIE.
......
WHY...?
THAT...MUST HAVE BEEN THE PERFECT CHANCE TO GRAB STAZ AND RUN...
HA HA HA...
I NO LONGER HAVE ANY REASON TO RUN FROM YOU.
OR...
...FLY, FOR THAT MATTER.

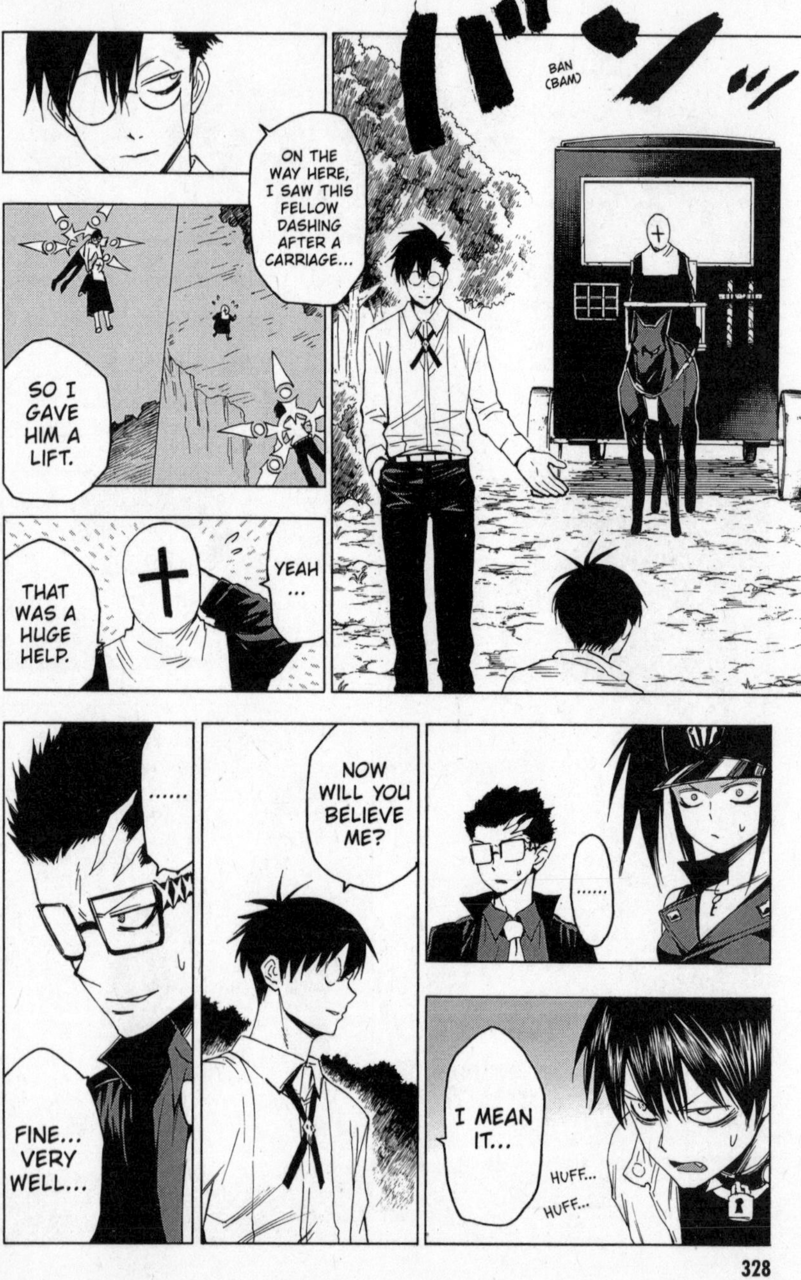
BAN (BAM)
ON THE WAY HERE, I SAW THIS FELLOW DASHING AFTER A CARRIAGE...
SO I GAVE HIM A LIFT.
YEAH ...
THAT WAS A HUGE HELP.
......
I MEAN IT...
HUFF... HUFF...
NOW WILL YOU BELIEVE ME?
......
FINE... VERY WELL...

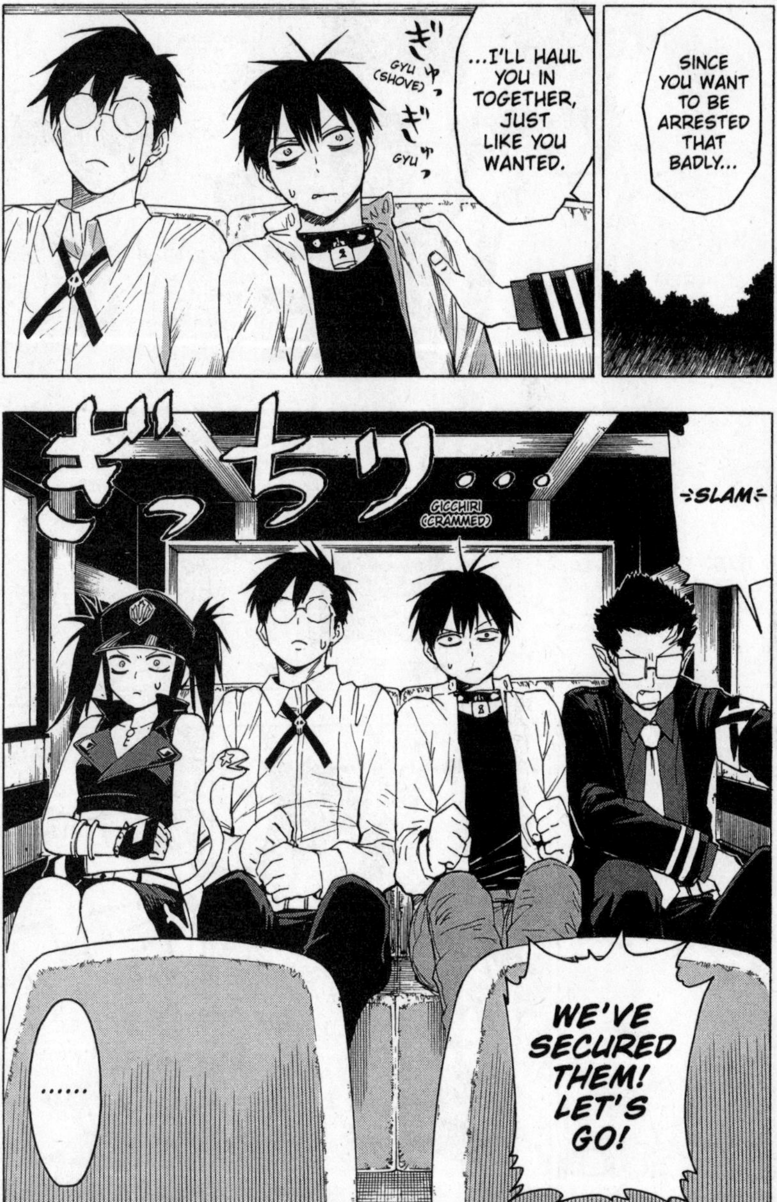
SINCE YOU WANT TO BE ARRESTED THAT BADLY...
...I'LL HAUL YOU IN TOGETHER, JUST LIKE YOU WANTED.
ぎゅっ
GYU (SHOVE)
ぎゅっ
GYU
SLAM
ぎっちり...
GICCHIRI (CRAMMED)
WE'VE SECURED THEM! LET'S GO!
......

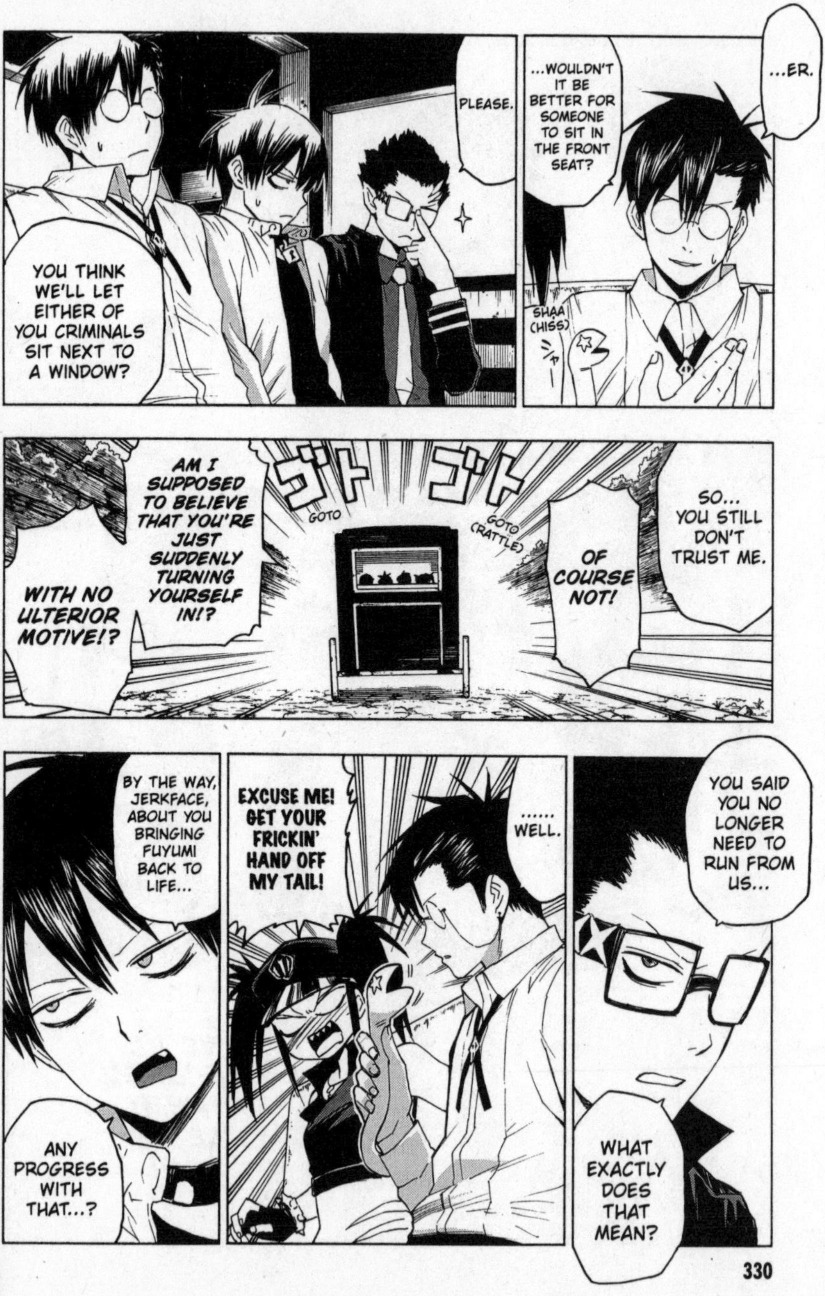
...ER.
...WOULDN'T IT BE BETTER FOR SOMEONE TO SIT IN THE FRONT SEAT?
SHAA (HISS)
PLEASE.
YOU THINK WE'LL LET EITHER OF YOU CRIMINALS SIT NEXT TO A WINDOW?
SO... YOU STILL DON'T TRUST ME.
OF COURSE NOT!
ゴト
GOTO (RATTLE)
ゴト
GOTO
AM I SUPPOSED TO BELIEVE THAT YOU'RE JUST SUDDENLY TURNING YOURSELF IN!?
WITH NO ULTERIOR MOTIVE!?
YOU SAID YOU NO LONGER NEED TO RUN FROM US...
WHAT EXACTLY DOES THAT MEAN?
......WELL.
EXCUSE ME! GET YOUR FRICKIN' HAND OFF MY TAIL!
BY THE WAY, JERKFACE, ABOUT YOU BRINGING FUYUMI BACK TO LIFE...
ANY PROGRESS WITH THAT...?

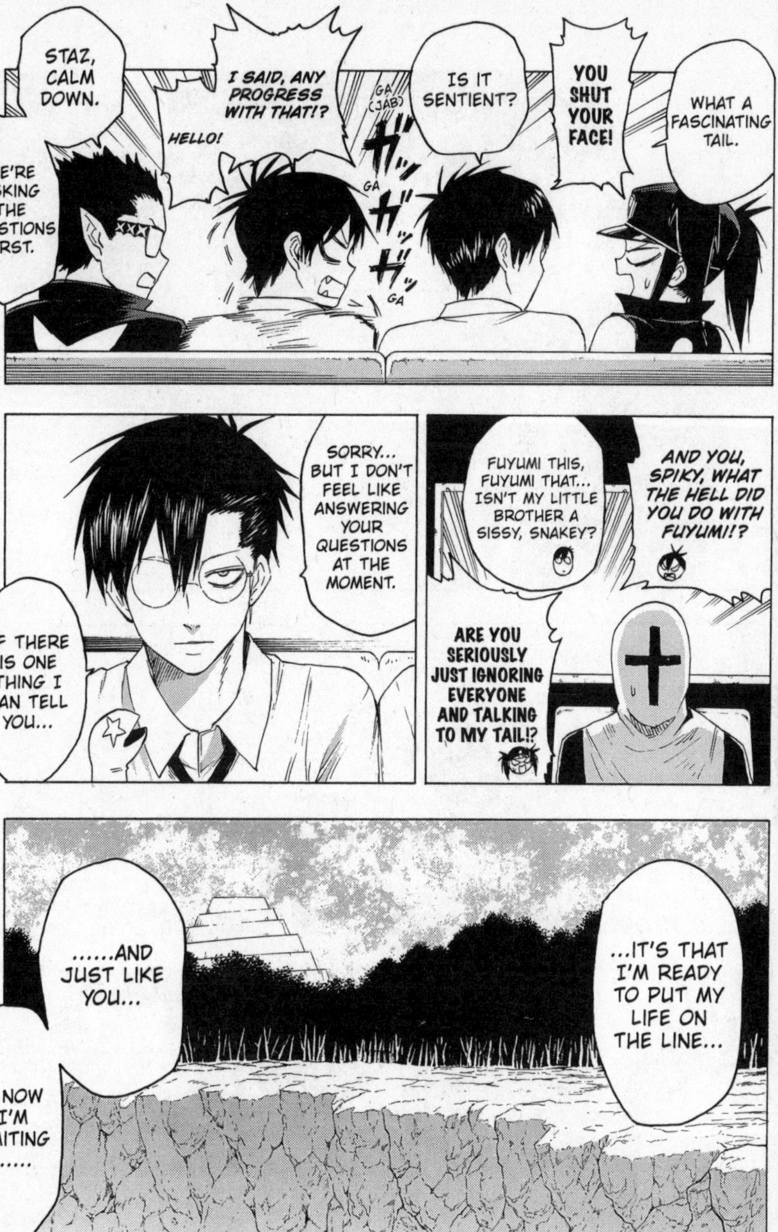
WHAT A FASCINATING TAIL.
YOU SHUT YOUR FACE!
IS IT SENTIENT?
GA (JAB)
GA
GA
I SAID, ANY PROGRESS WITH THAT!?
HELLO!
STAZ, CALM DOWN.
WE'RE ASKING THE QUESTIONS FIRST.
AND YOU, SPIKY, WHAT THE HELL DID YOU DO WITH FUYUMI!?
FUYUMI THIS, FUYUMI THAT... ISN'T MY LITTLE BROTHER A SISSY, SNAKEY?
ARE YOU SERIOUSLY JUST IGNORING EVERYONE AND TALKING TO MY TAIL!?
SORRY... BUT I DON'T FEEL LIKE ANSWERING YOUR QUESTIONS AT THE MOMENT.
IF THERE IS ONE THING I CAN TELL YOU...
...IT'S THAT I'M READY TO PUT MY LIFE ON THE LINE...
......AND JUST LIKE YOU...
...NOW I'M WAITING ......

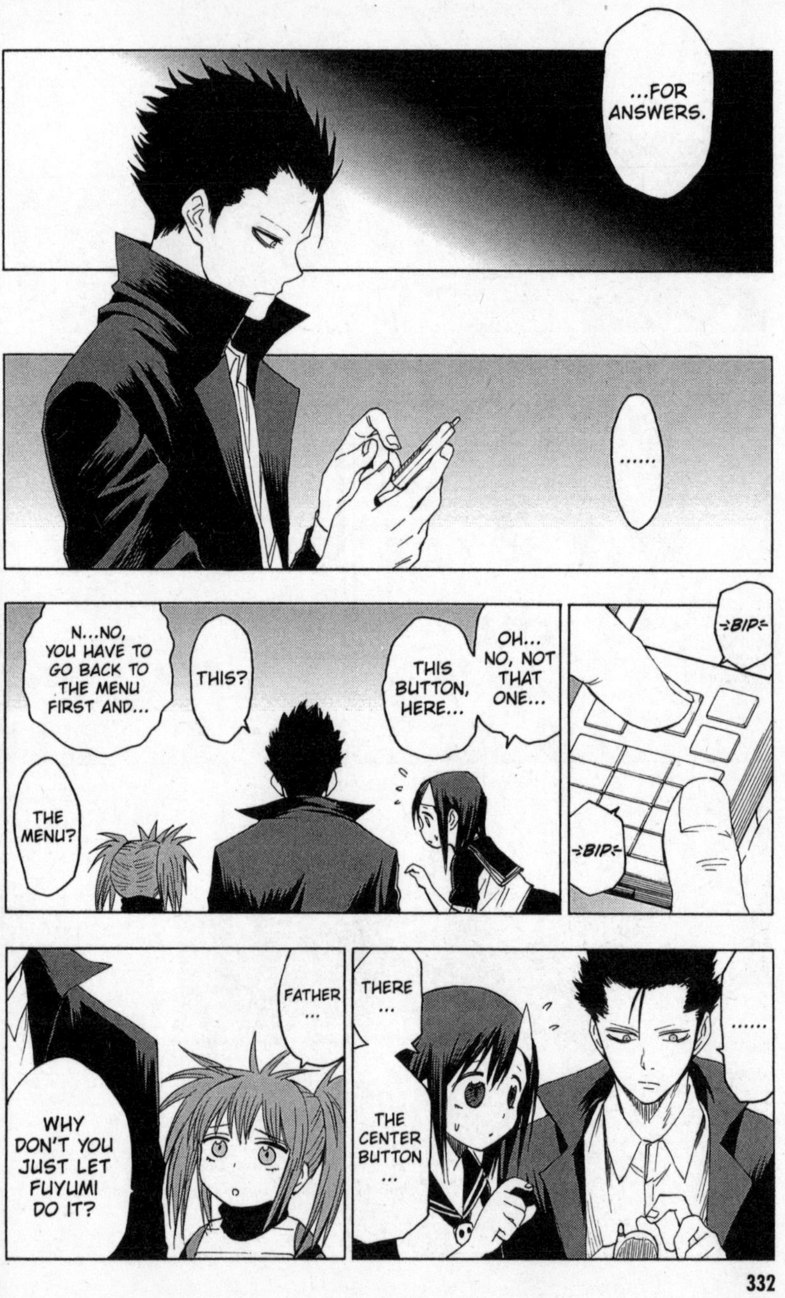
...FOR ANSWERS.
......
≈BIP≈
≈BIP≈
OH... NO, NOT THAT ONE...
THIS BUTTON, HERE...
THIS?
N...NO, YOU HAVE TO GO BACK TO THE MENU FIRST AND...
THE MENU?
......
THERE ...
THE CENTER BUTTON ...
FATHER ...
WHY DON'T YOU JUST LET FUYUMI DO IT?

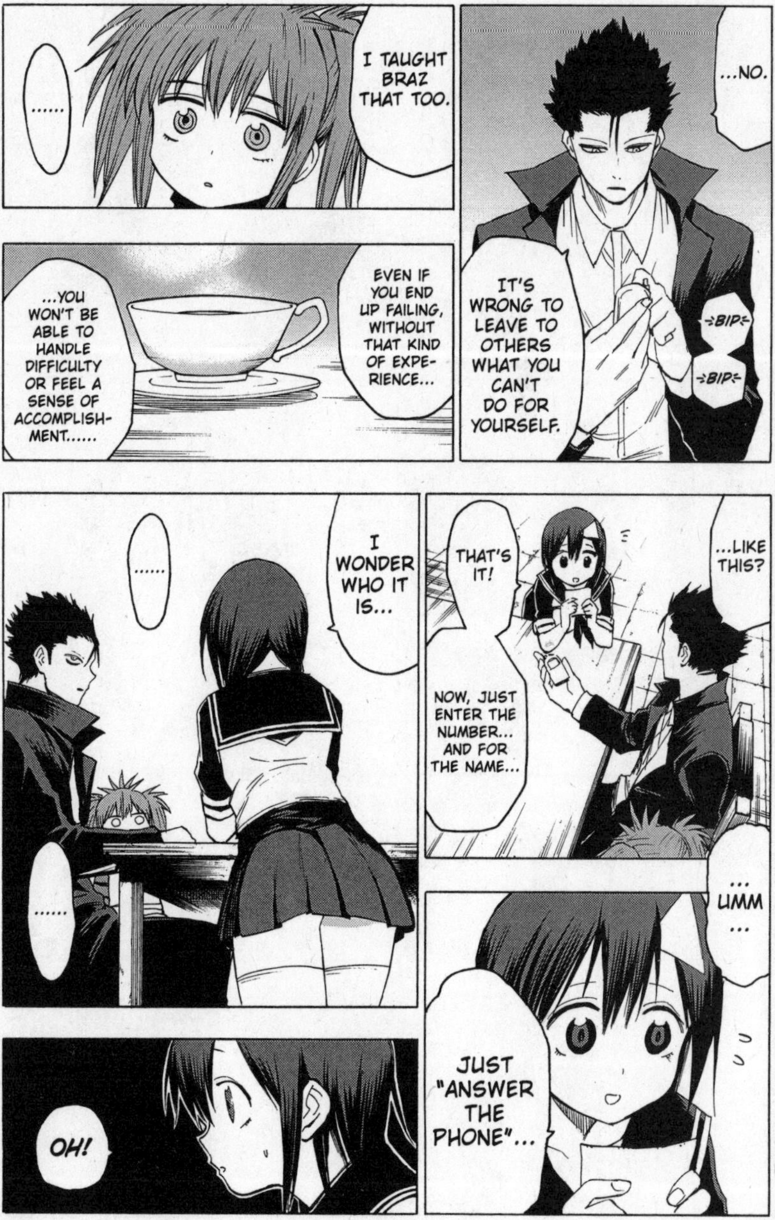
...NO.
IT'S WRONG TO LEAVE TO OTHERS WHAT YOU CAN'T DO FOR YOURSELF.
BIP
BIP
I TAUGHT BRAZ THAT TOO.
......
EVEN IF YOU END UP FAILING, WITHOUT THAT KIND OF EXPE-RIENCE...
...YOU WON'T BE ABLE TO HANDLE DIFFICULTY OR FEEL A SENSE OF ACCOMPLISH-MENT......
...LIKE THIS?
THAT'S IT!
NOW, JUST ENTER THE NUMBER... AND FOR THE NAME...
...UMM...
JUST "ANSWER THE PHONE"...
I WONDER WHO IT IS...
......
......
OH!

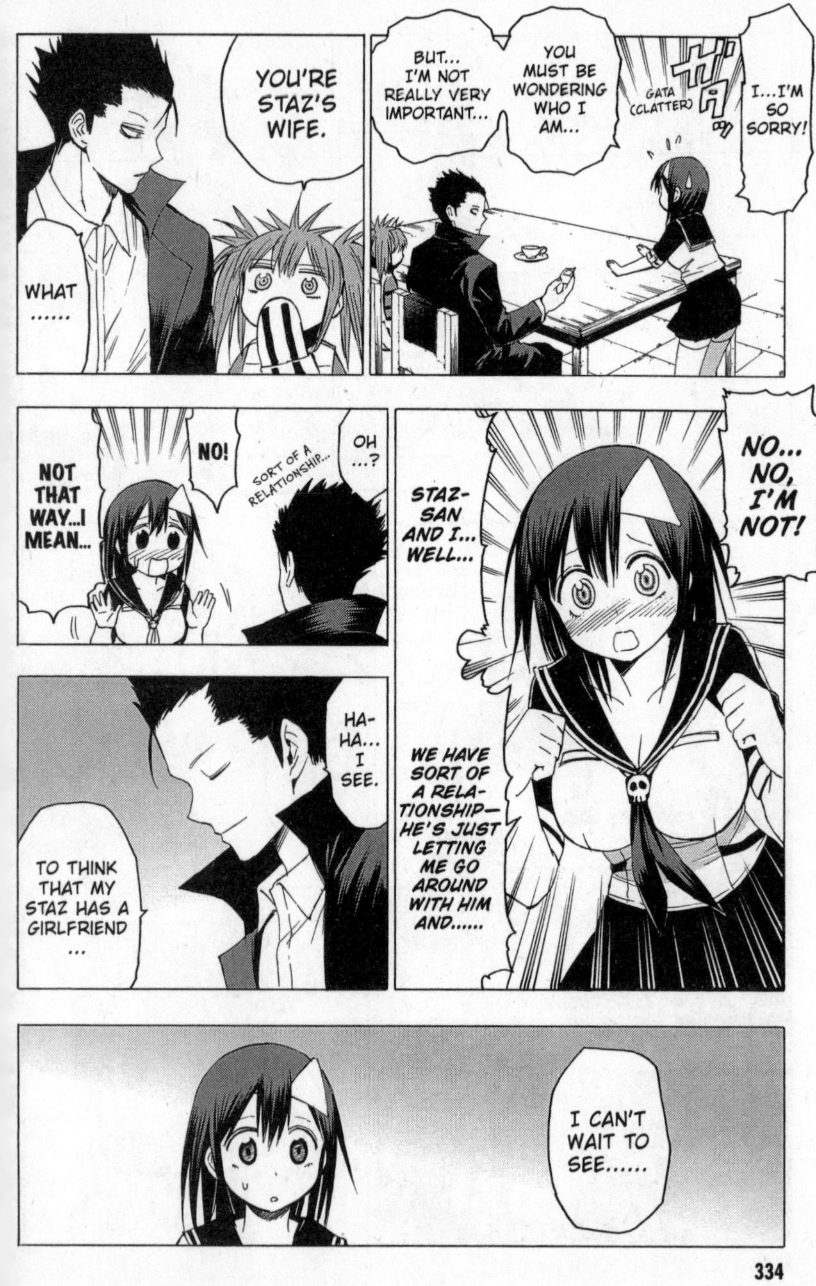
I...I'M SO SORRY!
GATA (CLATTER)
YOU MUST BE WONDERING WHO I AM...
BUT... I'M NOT REALLY VERY IMPORTANT...
YOU'RE STAZ'S WIFE.
WHAT ......
NO... NO, I'M NOT!
STAZ-SAN AND I... WELL...
WE HAVE SORT OF A RELATIONSHIP— HE'S JUST LETTING ME GO AROUND WITH HIM AND......
OH ...?
SORT OF A RELATIONSHIP...
NO!
NOT THAT WAY...I MEAN...
HA-HA... I SEE.
TO THINK THAT MY STAZ HAS A GIRLFRIEND ...
I CAN'T WAIT TO SEE......

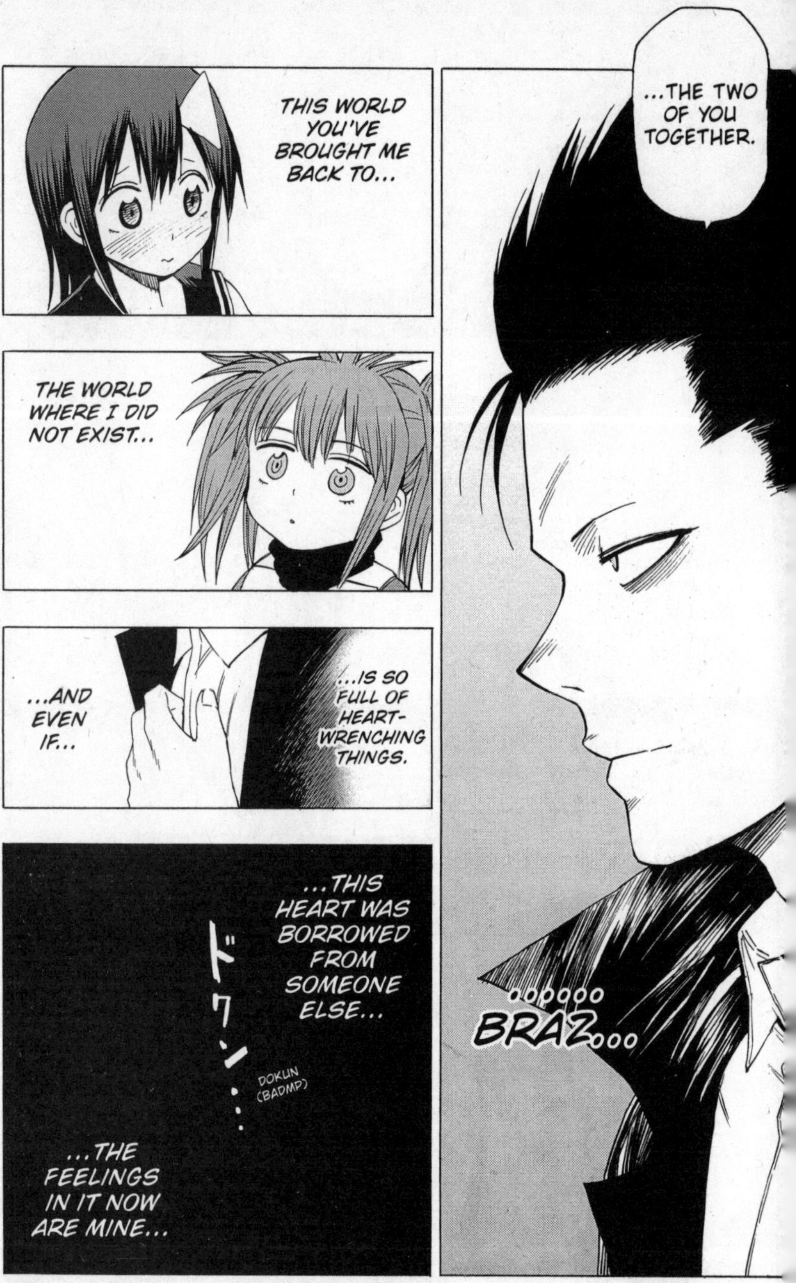
...THE TWO OF YOU TOGETHER.
......BRAZ...
THIS WORLD YOU'VE BROUGHT ME BACK TO...
THE WORLD WHERE I DID NOT EXIST...
...IS SO FULL OF HEART-WRENCHING THINGS.
...AND EVEN IF...
...THIS HEART WAS BORROWED FROM SOMEONE ELSE...
ドクン...
DOKUN (BADMP)
...THE FEELINGS IN IT NOW ARE MINE...

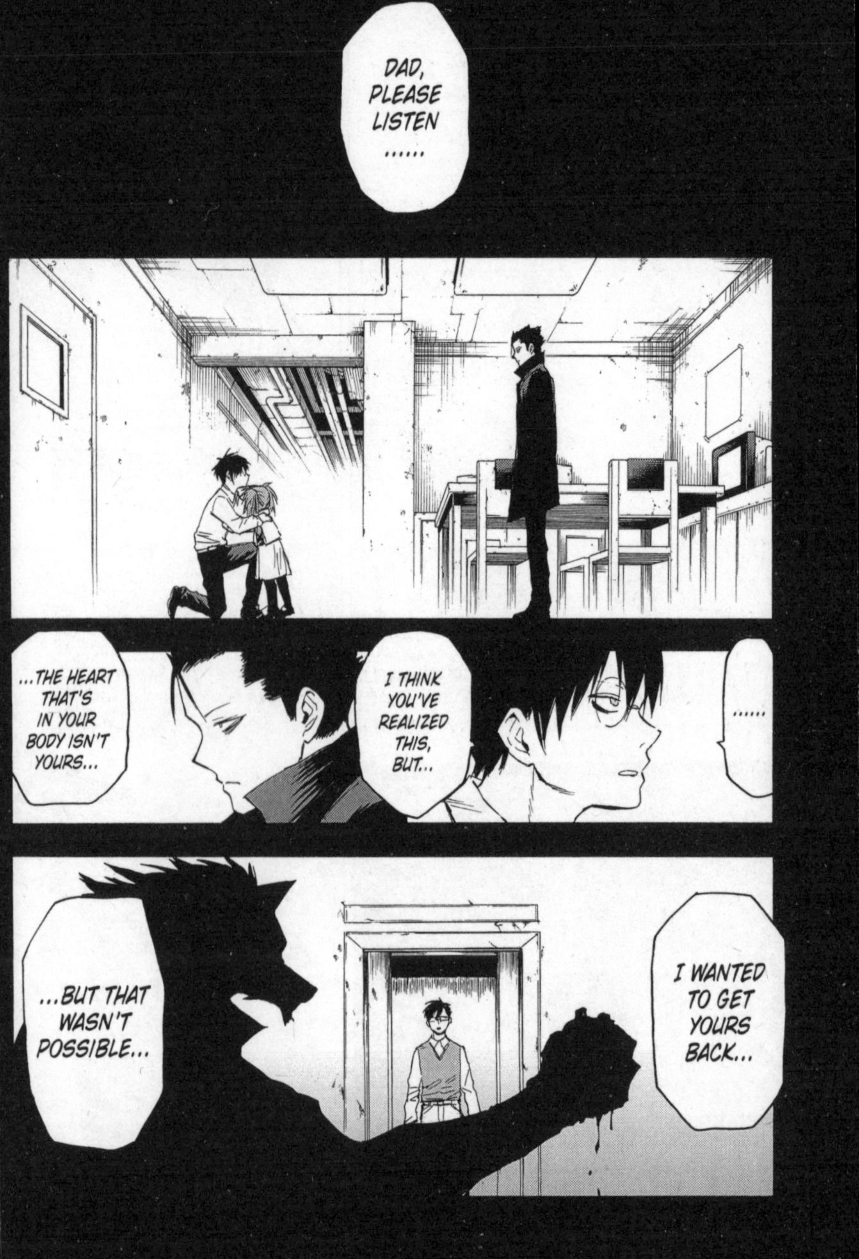
DAD, PLEASE LISTEN ......
......
I THINK YOU'VE REALIZED THIS, BUT...
...THE HEART THAT'S IN YOUR BODY ISN'T YOURS...
I WANTED TO GET YOURS BACK...
...BUT THAT WASN'T POSSIBLE...

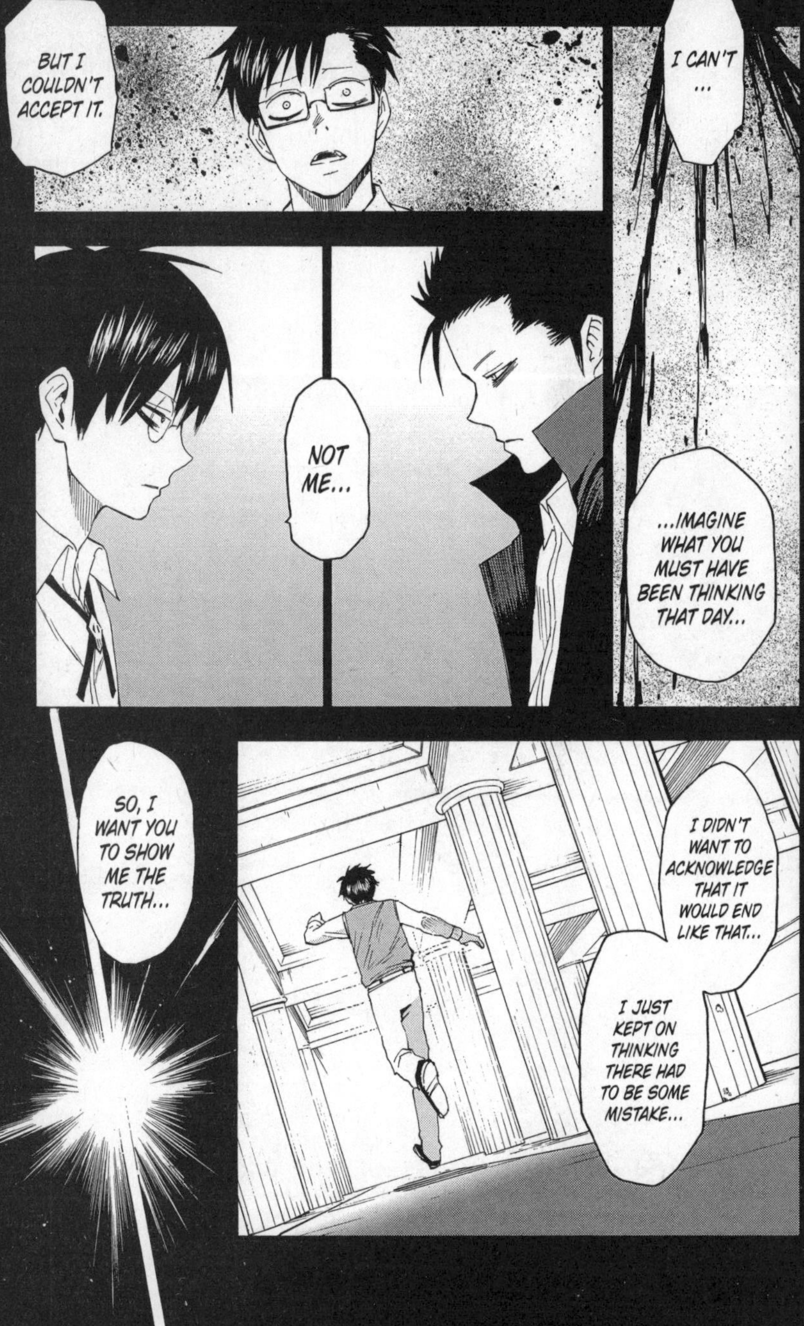
I CAN'T ...
...IMAGINE WHAT YOU MUST HAVE BEEN THINKING THAT DAY...
BUT I COULDN'T ACCEPT IT.
NOT ME...
I DIDN'T WANT TO ACKNOWLEDGE THAT IT WOULD END LIKE THAT...
I JUST KEPT ON THINKING THERE HAD TO BE SOME MISTAKE...
SO, I WANT YOU TO SHOW ME THE TRUTH...

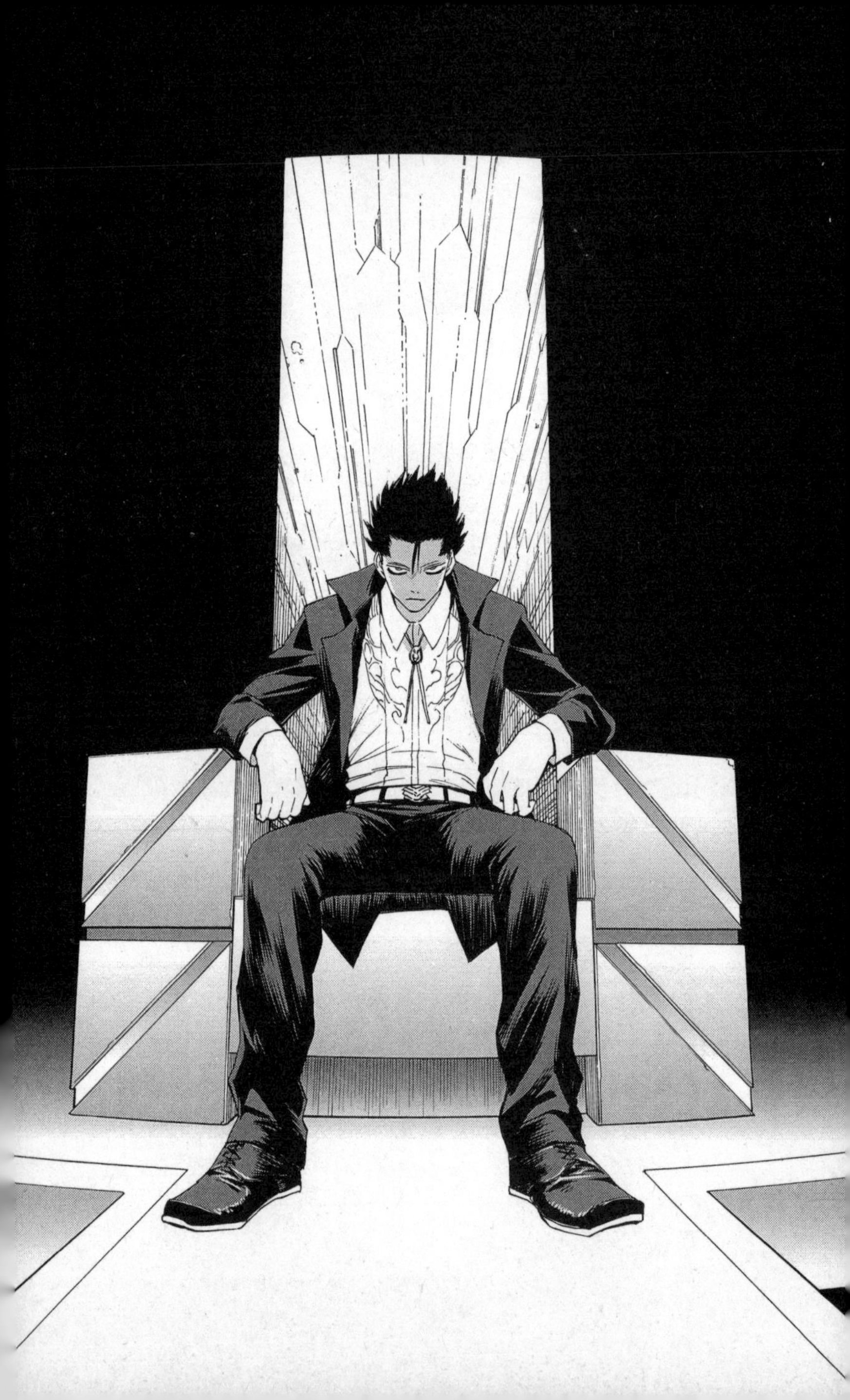

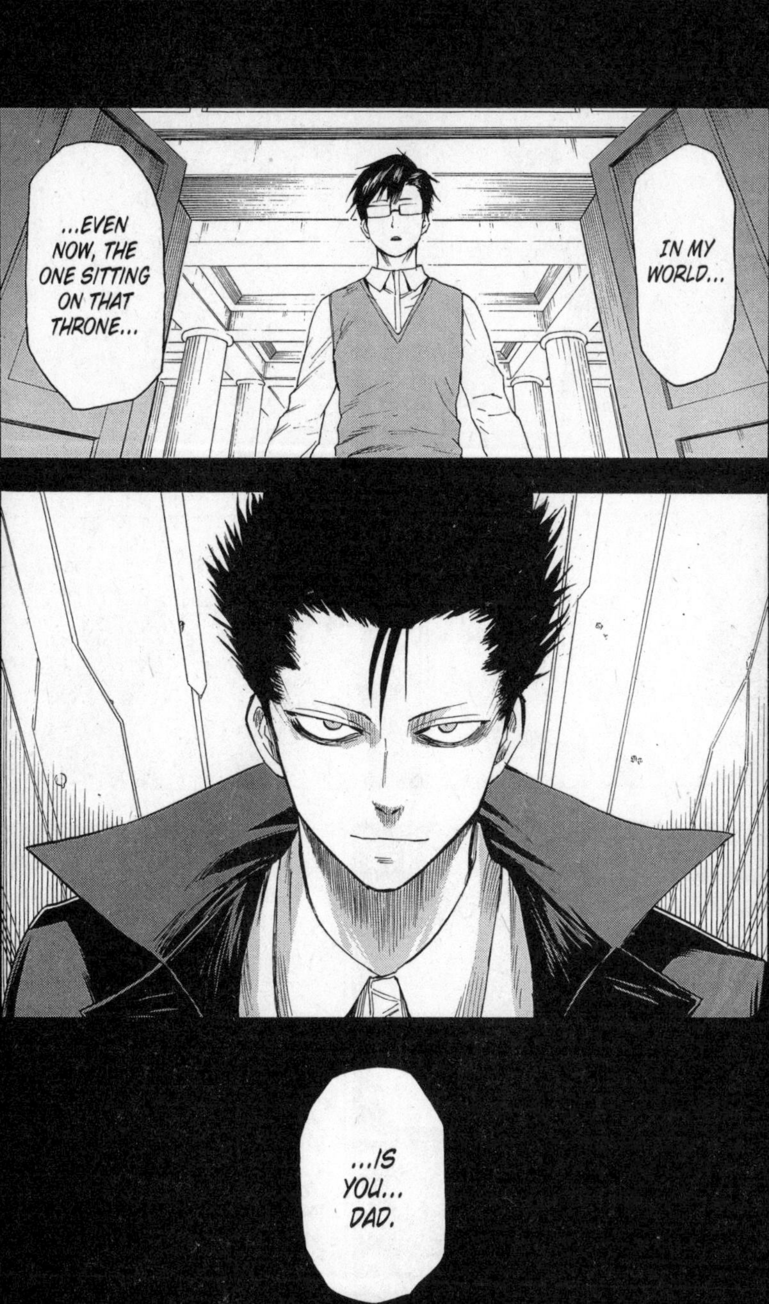
IN MY WORLD...
...EVEN NOW, THE ONE SITTING ON THAT THRONE...
...IS YOU... DAD.

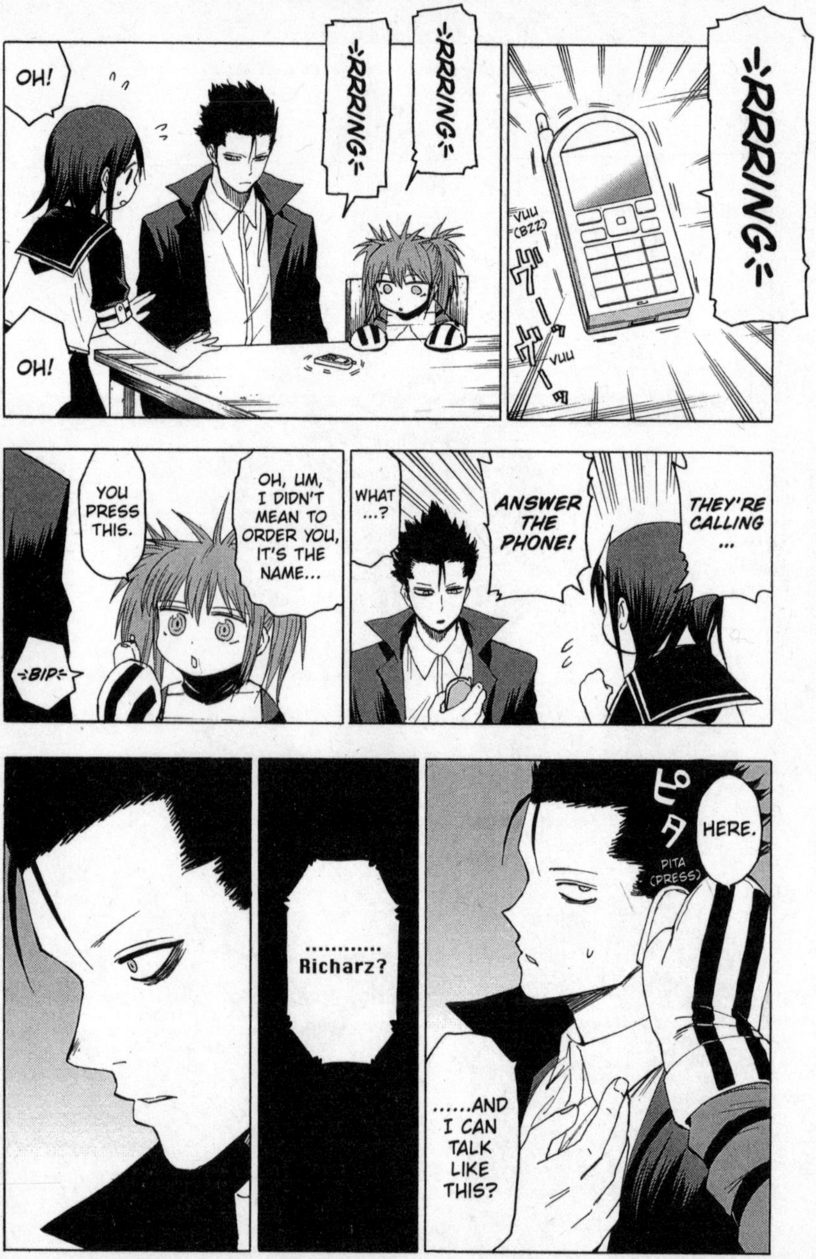
RRRING
VUU (BZZ)
VUU
RRRING
RRRING
OH!
OH!
THEY'RE CALLING ...
ANSWER THE PHONE!
WHAT ...?
OH, UM, I DIDN'T MEAN TO ORDER YOU, IT'S THE NAME...
YOU PRESS THIS.
BIP
HERE.
PITA (PRESS)
......AND I CAN TALK LIKE THIS?
.... Richarz?

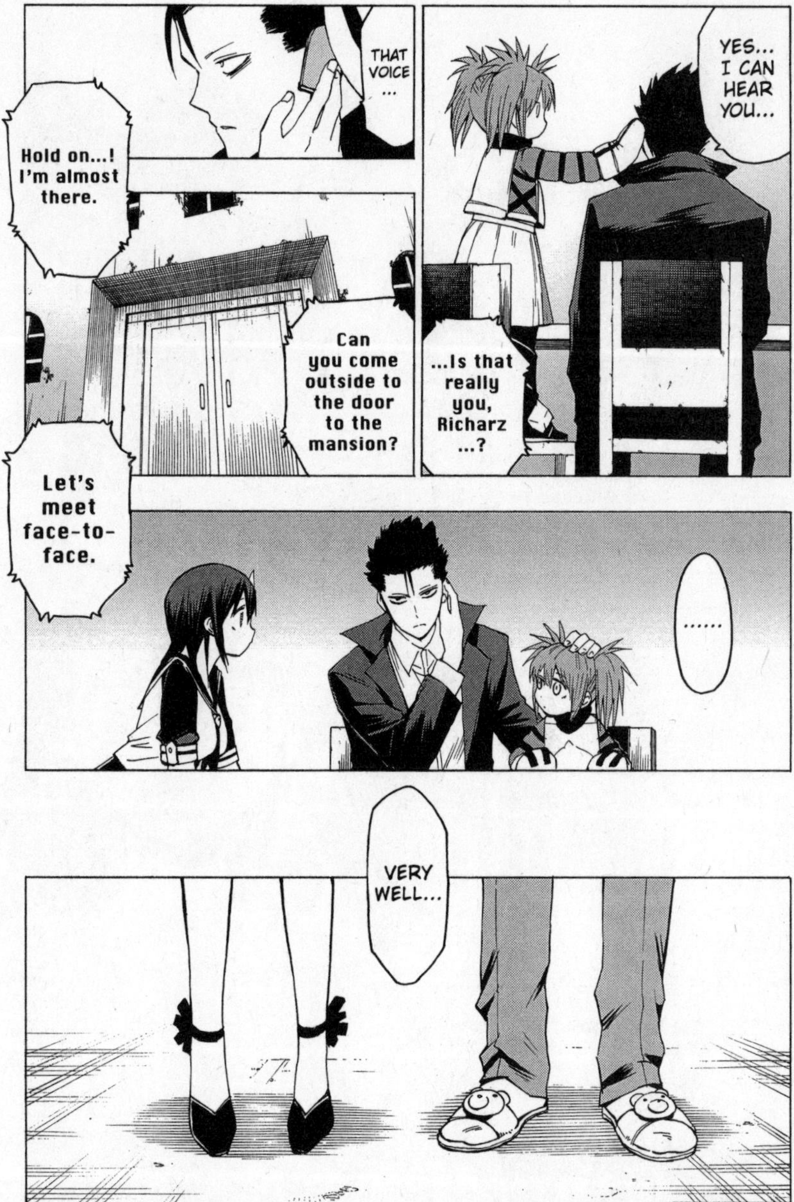
YES... I CAN HEAR YOU...
...Is that really you, Richarz ...?
THAT VOICE ...
Hold on...! I'm almost there.
Can you come outside to the door to the mansion?
Let's meet face-to-face.
......
VERY WELL...

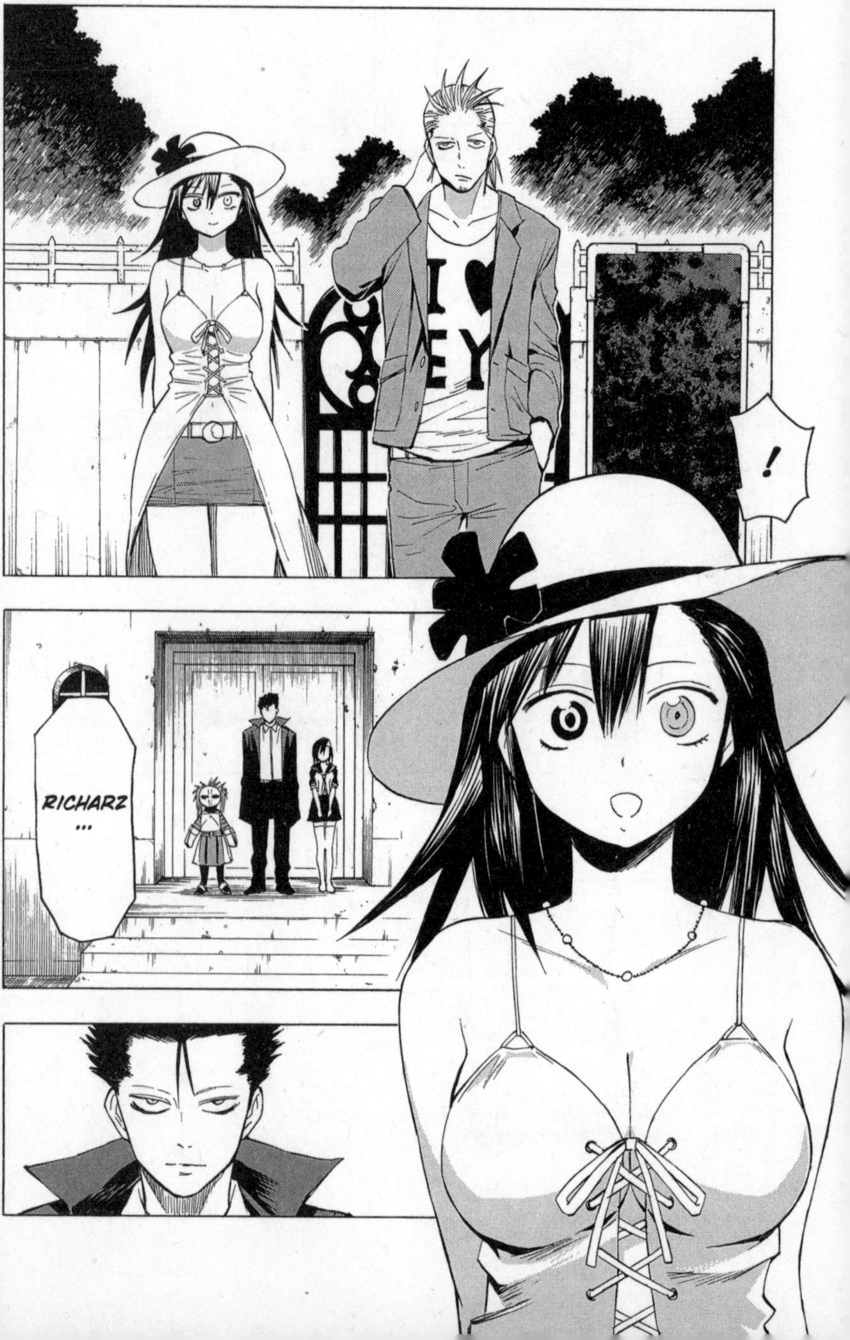
!
RICHARZ
...

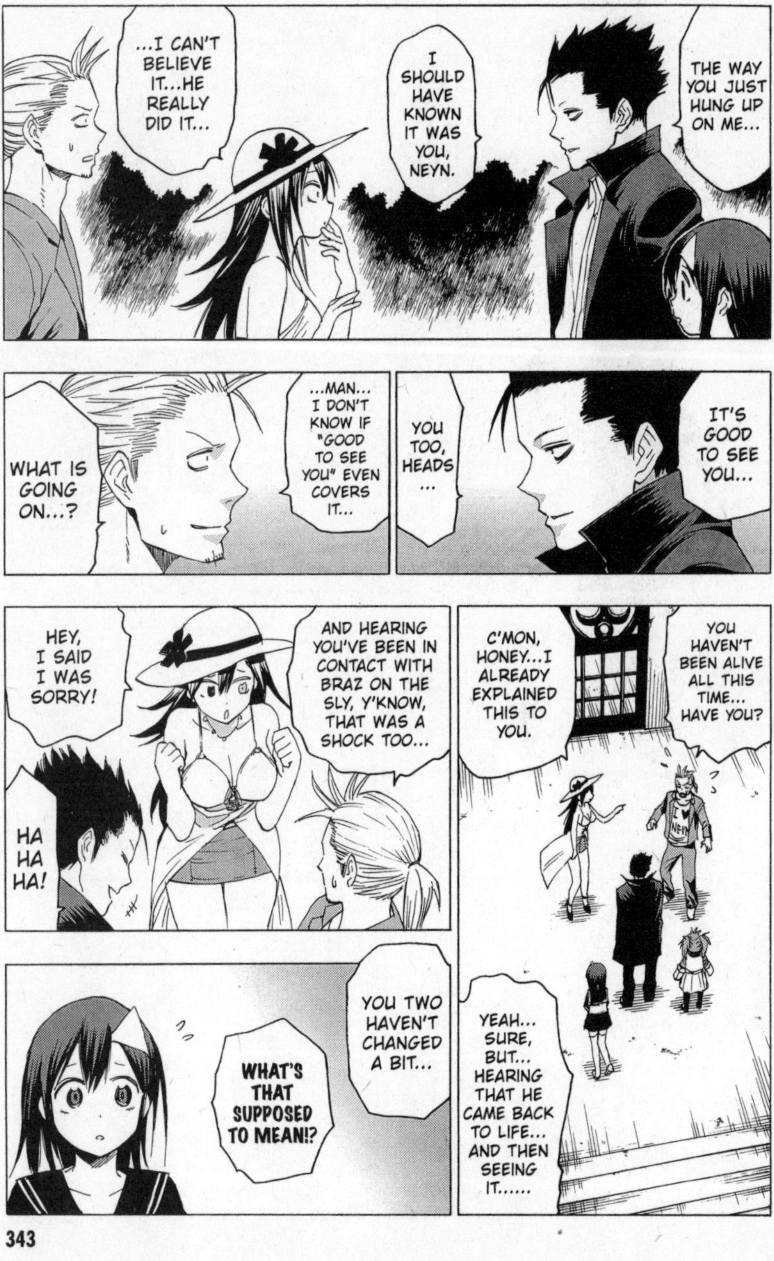
THE WAY YOU JUST HUNG UP ON ME...
I SHOULD HAVE KNOWN IT WAS YOU, NEYN.
...I CAN'T BELIEVE IT...HE REALLY DID IT...
IT'S GOOD TO SEE YOU...
YOU TOO, HEADS...
...MAN... I DON'T KNOW IF "GOOD TO SEE YOU" EVEN COVERS IT...
WHAT IS GOING ON...?
YOU HAVEN'T BEEN ALIVE ALL THIS TIME... HAVE YOU?
C'MON, HONEY...I ALREADY EXPLAINED THIS TO YOU.
YEAH... SURE, BUT... HEARING THAT HE CAME BACK TO LIFE... AND THEN SEEING IT......
AND HEARING YOU'VE BEEN IN CONTACT WITH BRAZ ON THE SLY, Y'KNOW, THAT WAS A SHOCK TOO...
HEY, I SAID I WAS SORRY!
HA HA HA!
YOU TWO HAVEN'T CHANGED A BIT...
WHAT'S THAT SUPPOSED TO MEAN!?

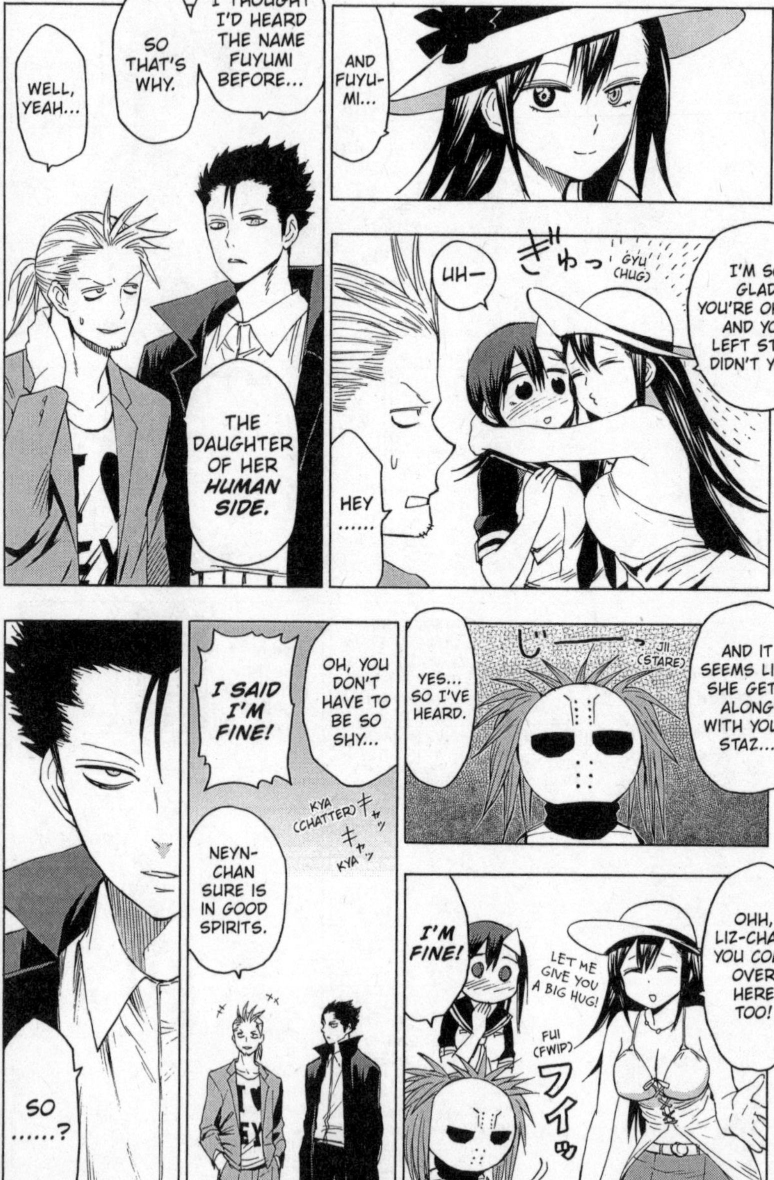
AND FUYUMI...
I'M SO GLAD YOU'RE OKAY... AND YOU LEFT STAZ, DIDN'T YOU!
ぎゅっ GYU (HUG)
UH—
HEY ......
I THOUGHT I'D HEARD THE NAME FUYUMI BEFORE...
SO THAT'S WHY.
WELL, YEAH...
THE DAUGHTER OF HER *HUMAN SIDE.*
AND IT SEEMS LIKE SHE GETS ALONG WITH YOUR STAZ...
じーっ JII (STARE)
YES... SO I'VE HEARD.
OHH, LIZ-CHAN, YOU COME OVER HERE TOO!
LET ME GIVE YOU A BIG HUG!
FUI (FWIP) フイッ
I'M FINE!
OH, YOU DON'T HAVE TO BE SO SHY...
I SAID I'M FINE!
KYA (CHATTER) キャッ
キャッ KYA
NEYN-CHAN SURE IS IN GOOD SPIRITS.
SO ......?

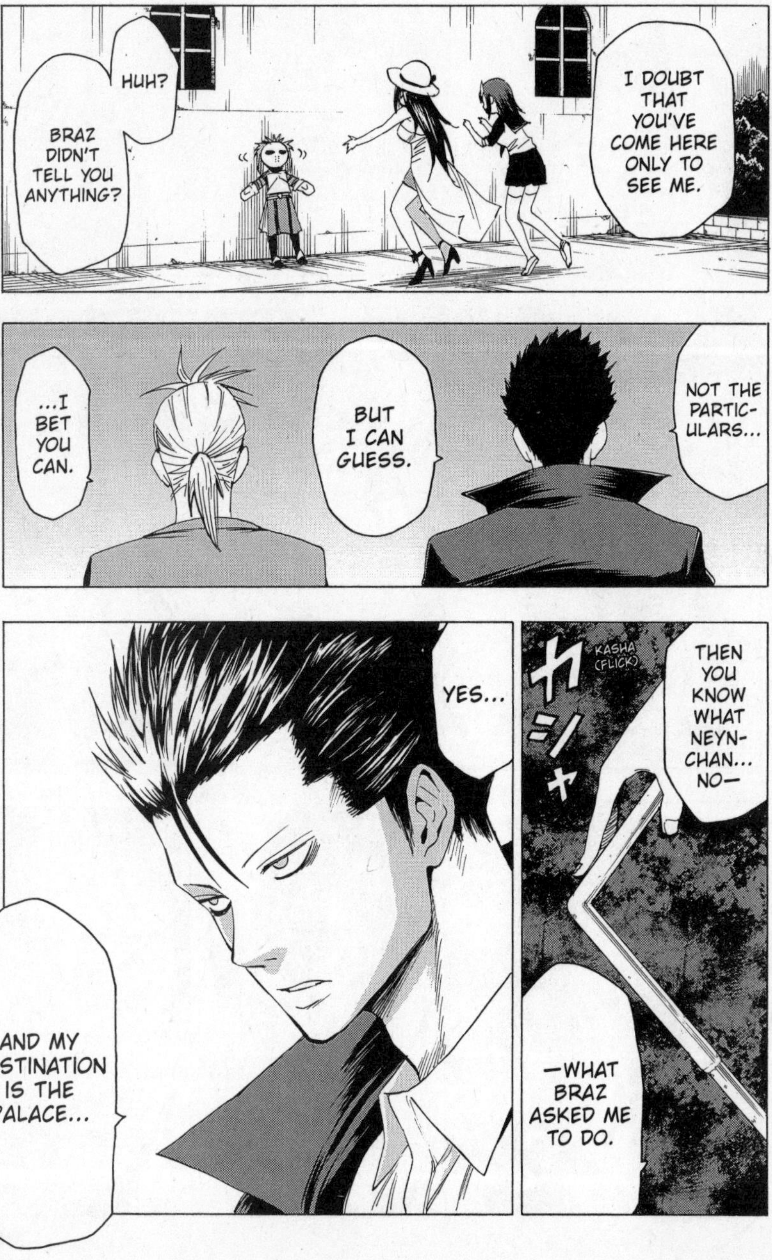
I DOUBT THAT YOU'VE COME HERE ONLY TO SEE ME.
HUH?
BRAZ DIDN'T TELL YOU ANYTHING?
NOT THE PARTICULARS...
BUT I CAN GUESS.
...I BET YOU CAN.
KASHA (FLICK)
THEN YOU KNOW WHAT NEYN-CHAN... NO—
—WHAT BRAZ ASKED ME TO DO.
YES...
AND MY DESTINATION IS THE PALACE...

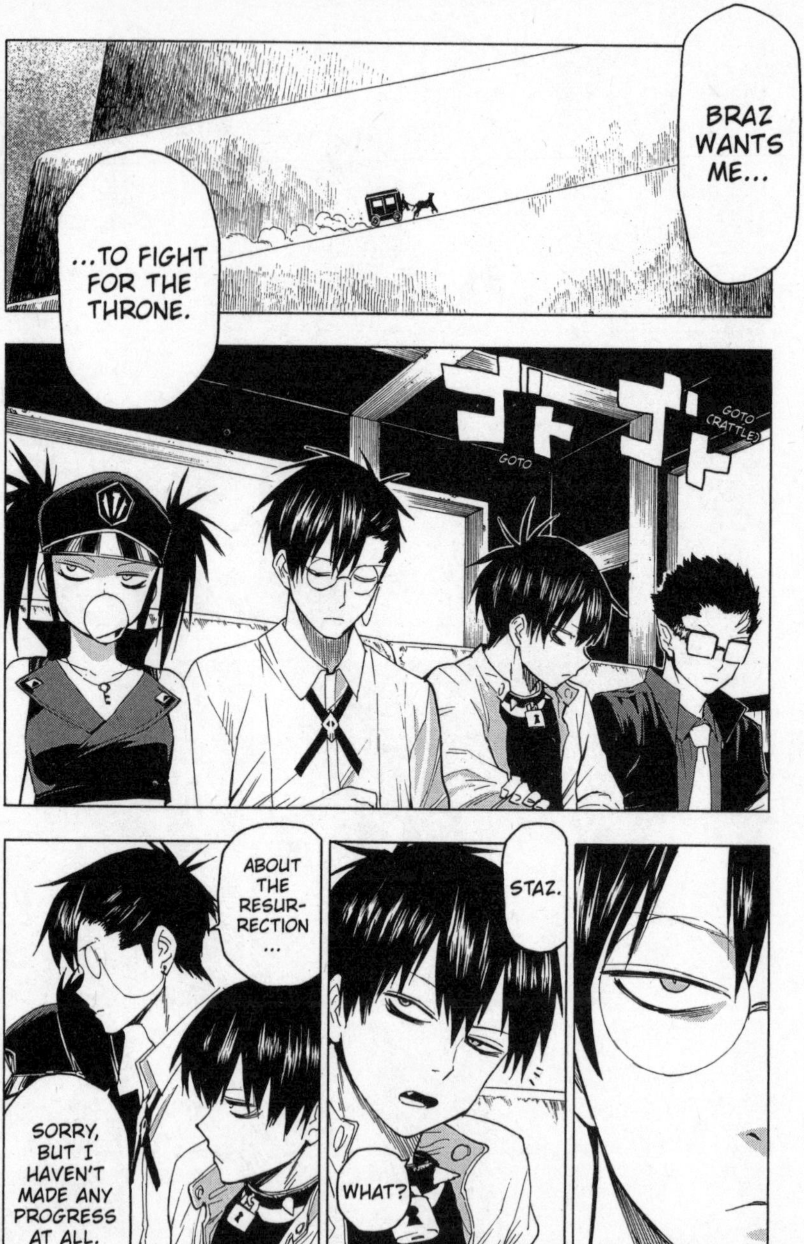
BRAZ WANTS ME...
...TO FIGHT FOR THE THRONE.
GOTO (RATTLE)
GOTO
STAZ.
WHAT?
ABOUT THE RESURRECTION...
SORRY, BUT I HAVEN'T MADE ANY PROGRESS AT ALL.

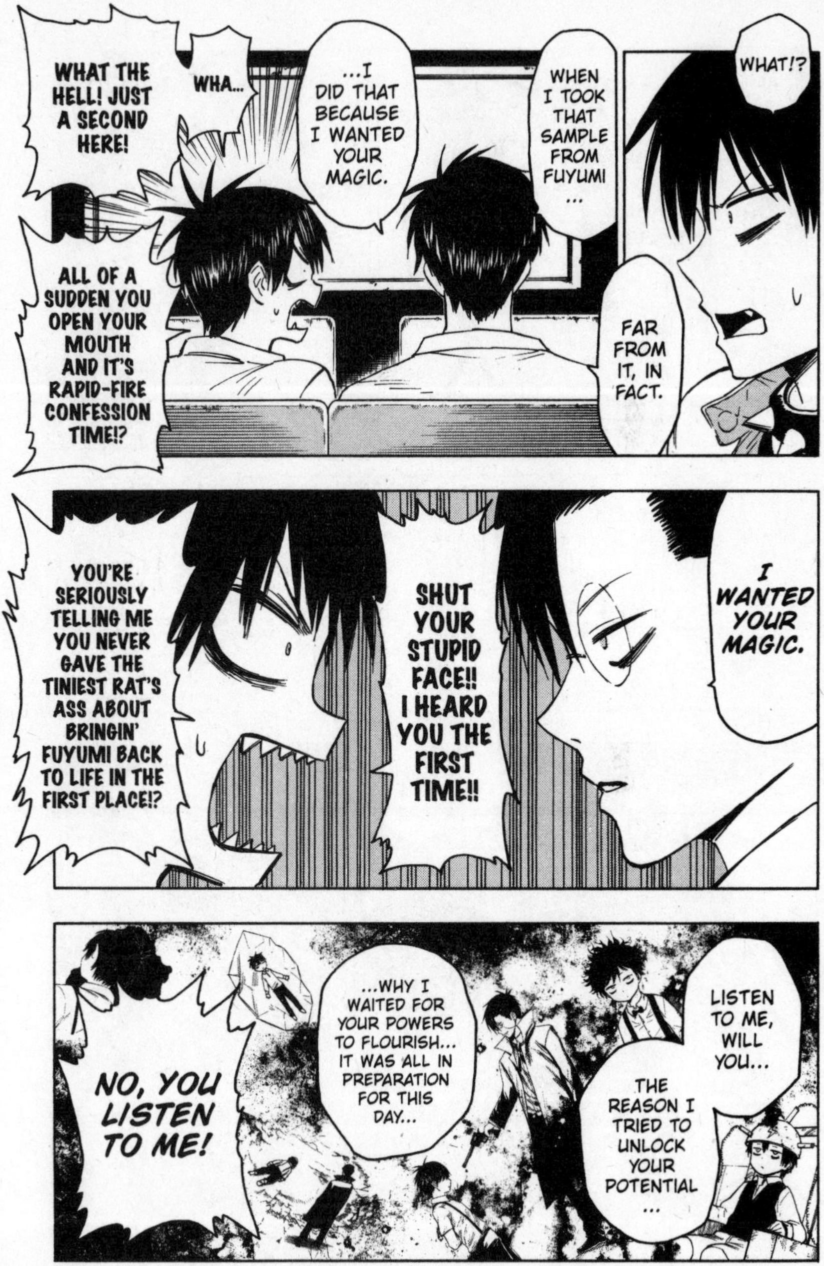
WHAT!?
FAR FROM IT, IN FACT.
WHEN I TOOK THAT SAMPLE FROM FUYUMI...
...I DID THAT BECAUSE I WANTED YOUR MAGIC.
WHA...
WHAT THE HELL! JUST A SECOND HERE!
ALL OF A SUDDEN YOU OPEN YOUR MOUTH AND IT'S RAPID-FIRE CONFESSION TIME!?
I WANTED YOUR MAGIC.
SHUT YOUR STUPID FACE!! I HEARD YOU THE FIRST TIME!!
YOU'RE SERIOUSLY TELLING ME YOU NEVER GAVE THE TINIEST RAT'S ASS ABOUT BRINGIN' FUYUMI BACK TO LIFE IN THE FIRST PLACE!?
LISTEN TO ME, WILL YOU...
THE REASON I TRIED TO UNLOCK YOUR POTENTIAL...
...WHY I WAITED FOR YOUR POWERS TO FLOURISH... IT WAS ALL IN PREPARATION FOR THIS DAY...
NO, YOU LISTEN TO ME!

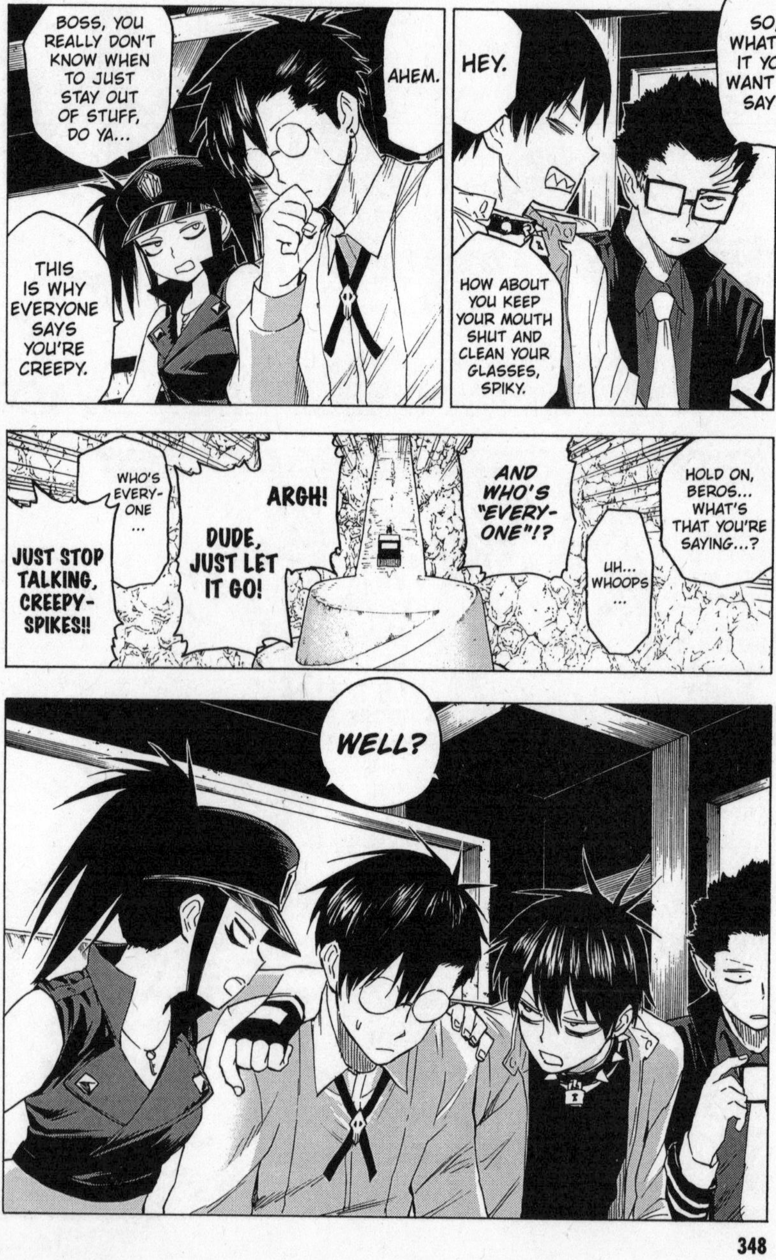

SO, WHAT IS IT YOU WANT TO SAY?
HEY.
HOW ABOUT YOU KEEP YOUR MOUTH SHUT AND CLEAN YOUR GLASSES, SPIKY.
AHEM.
BOSS, YOU REALLY DON'T KNOW WHEN TO JUST STAY OUT OF STUFF, DO YA...
THIS IS WHY EVERYONE SAYS YOU'RE CREEPY.
HOLD ON, BEROS... WHAT'S THAT YOU'RE SAYING...?
UH... WHOOPS...
AND WHO'S "EVERYONE"!?
ARGH!
DUDE, JUST LET IT GO!
WHO'S EVERYONE...
JUST STOP TALKING, CREEPY-SPIKES!!
WELL?

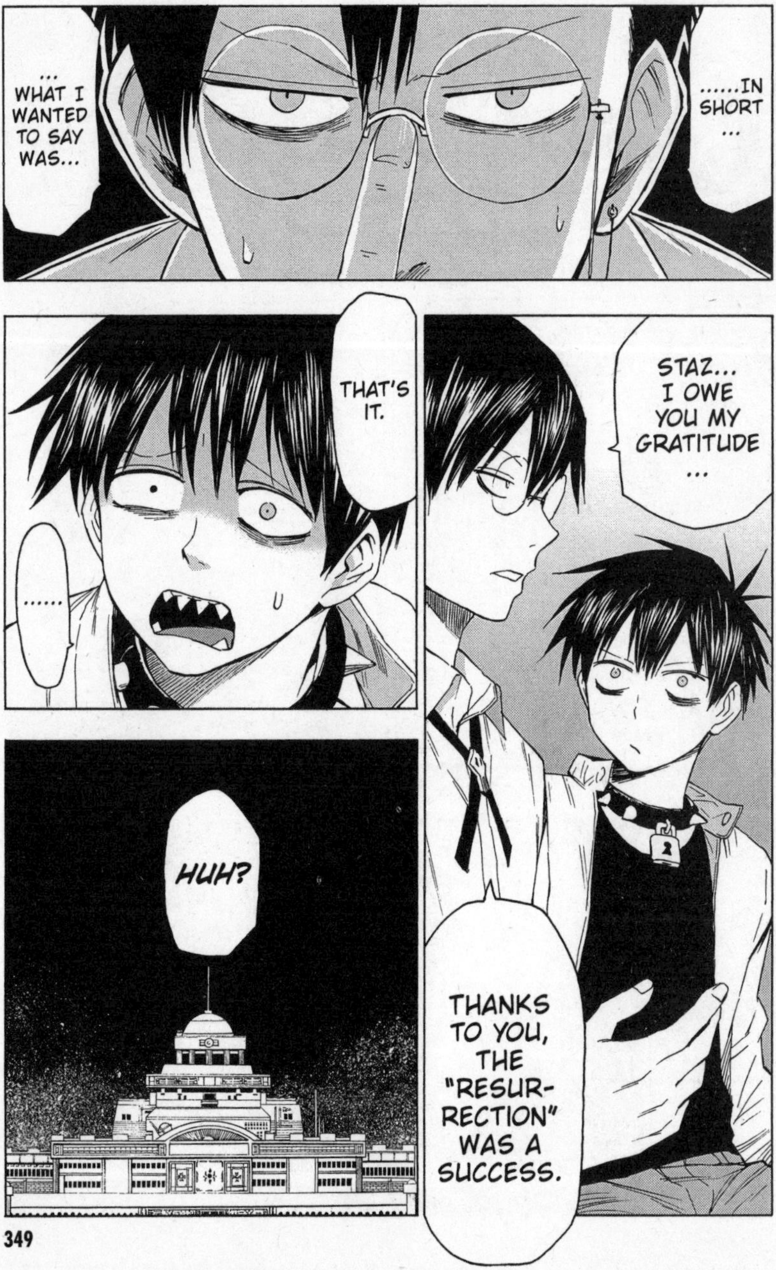
......IN SHORT ...
... WHAT I WANTED TO SAY WAS...
STAZ... I OWE YOU MY GRATITUDE ...
THANKS TO YOU, THE "RESURRECTION" WAS A SUCCESS.
THAT'S IT.
......
HUH?

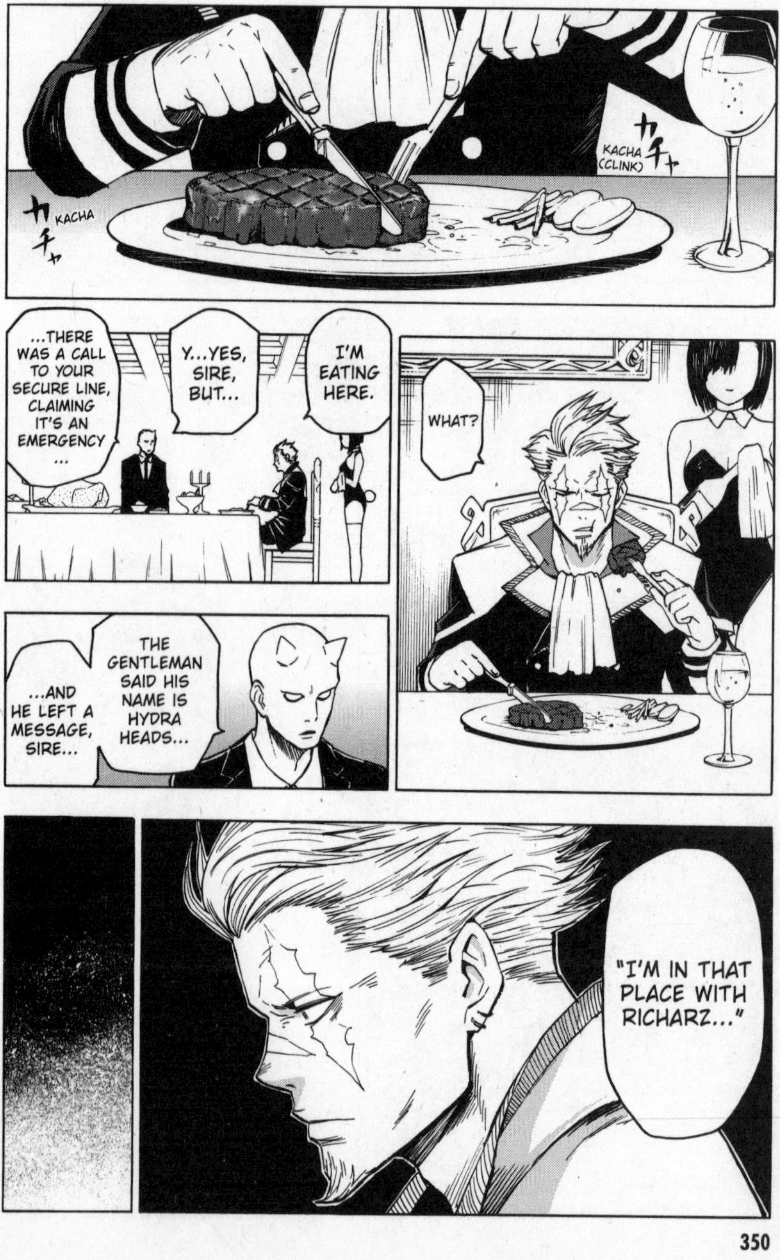
カチャ
KACHA (CLINK)
カチャ
KACHA
WHAT?
I'M EATING HERE.
Y...YES, SIRE, BUT...
...THERE WAS A CALL TO YOUR SECURE LINE, CLAIMING IT'S AN EMERGENCY...
THE GENTLEMAN SAID HIS NAME IS HYDRA HEADS...
...AND HE LEFT A MESSAGE, SIRE...
"I'M IN THAT PLACE WITH RICHARZ..."

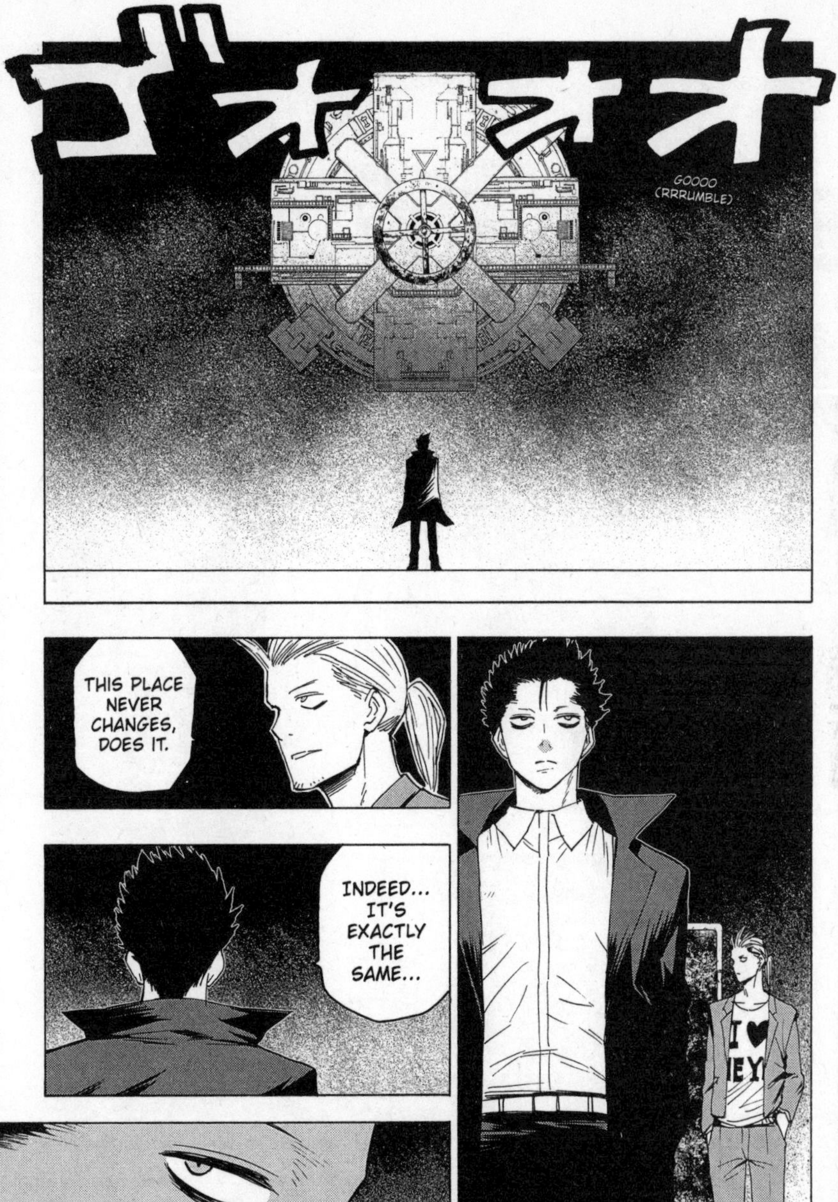
ゴオオオ
GOOOO (RRRUMBLE)
THIS PLACE NEVER CHANGES, DOES IT.
INDEED... IT'S EXACTLY THE SAME...

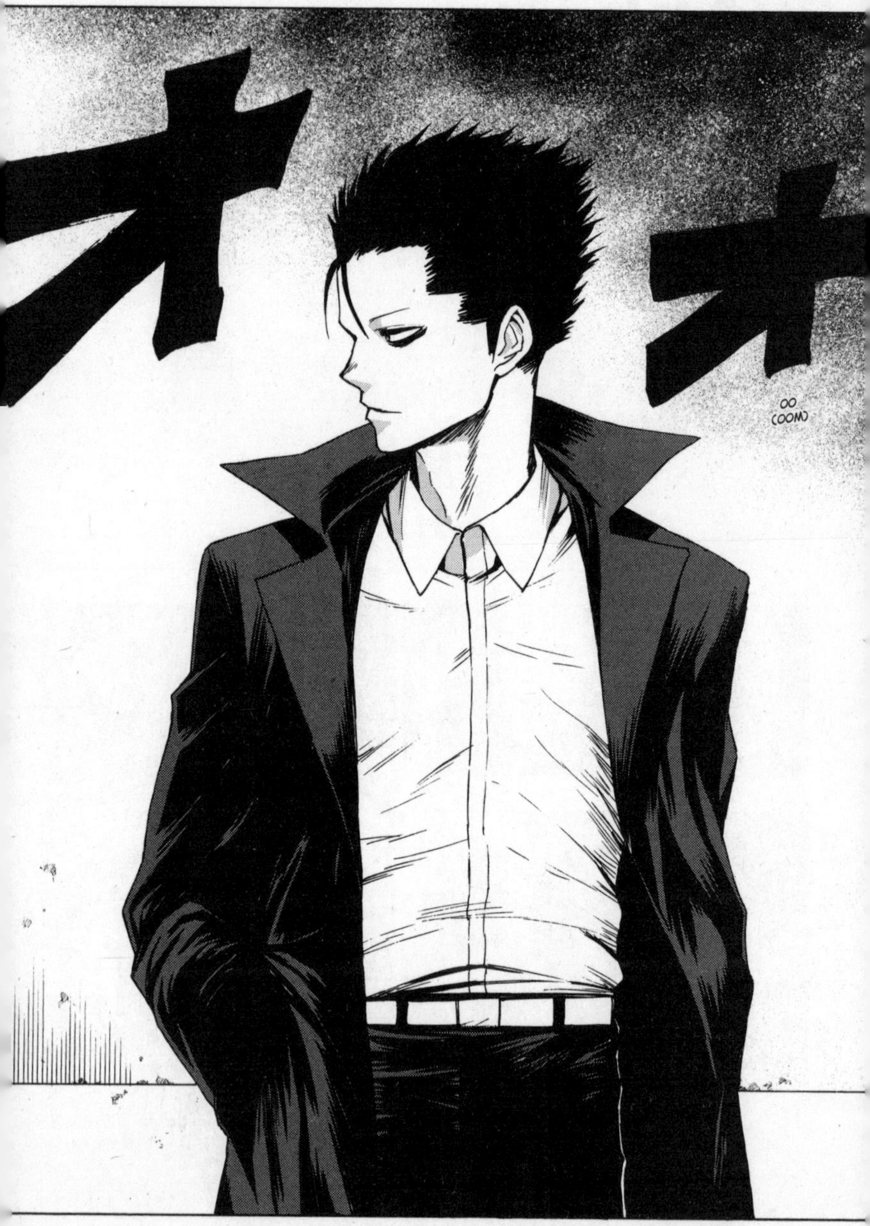
オオ
OO
(OOM)

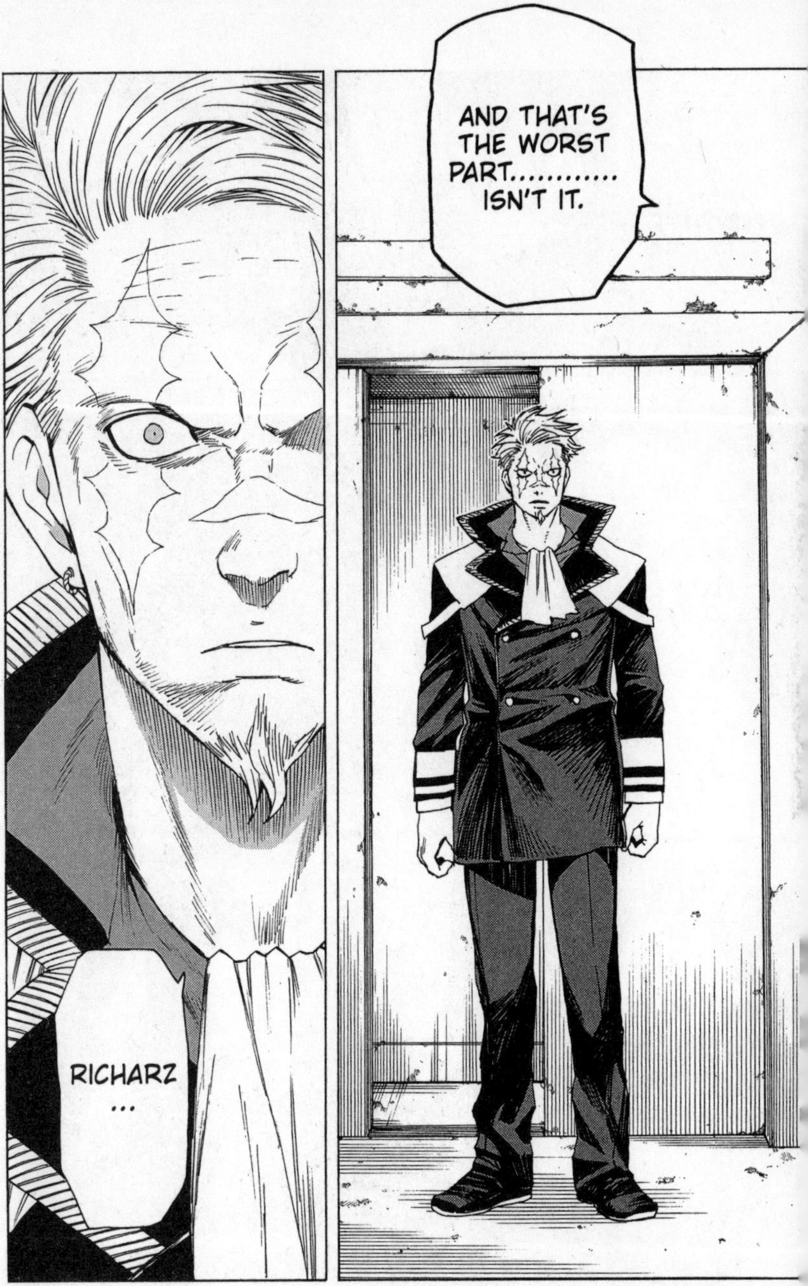
AND THAT'S THE WORST PART........... ISN'T IT.
RICHARZ ...

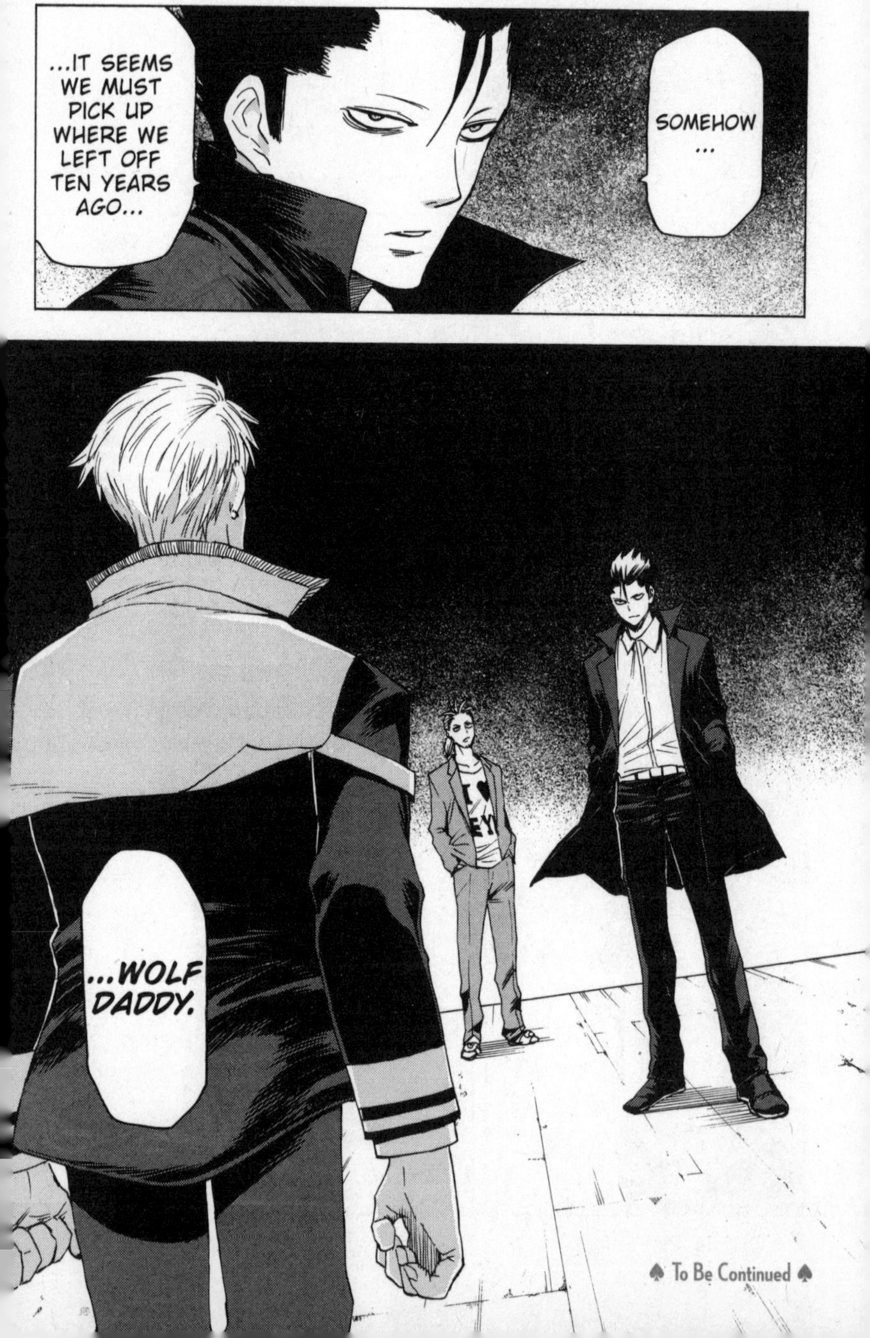
SOMEHOW ...
...IT SEEMS WE MUST PICK UP WHERE WE LEFT OFF TEN YEARS AGO...
...WOLF DADDY.
To Be Continued

To Be
Continued

BLOOD LAD

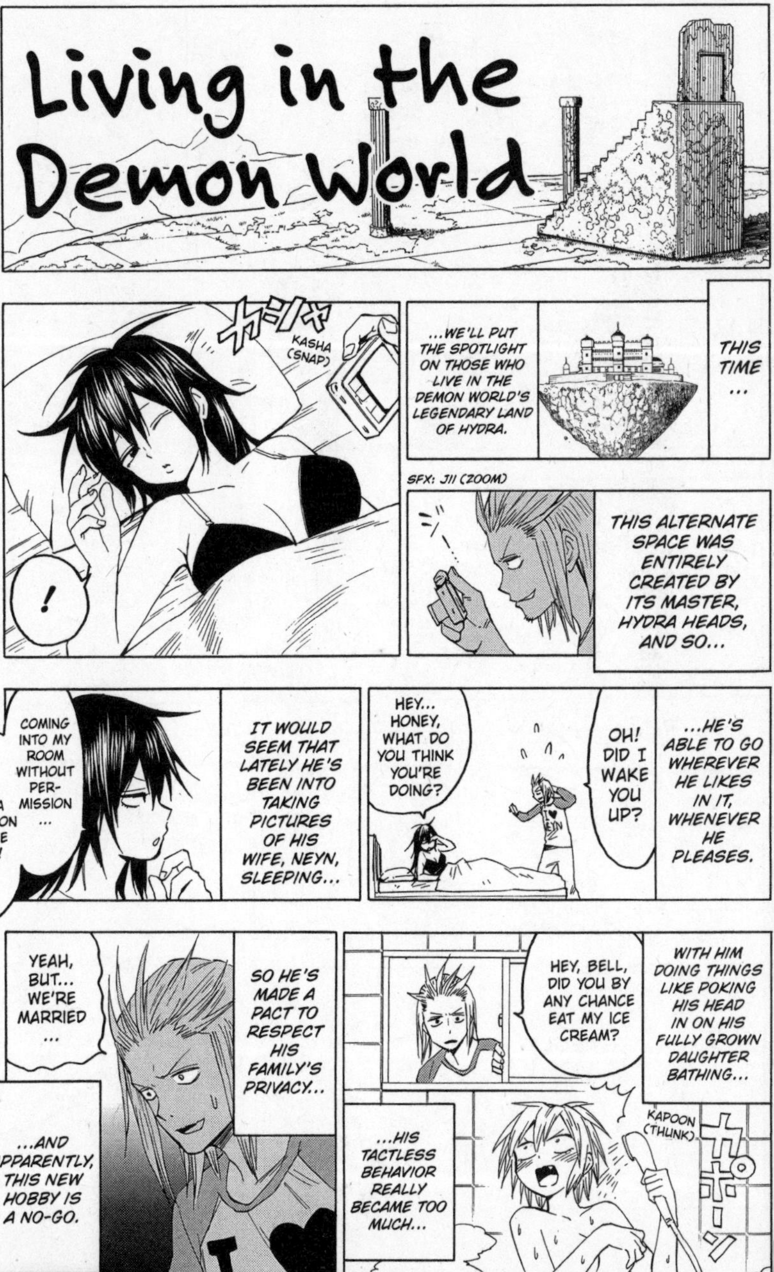
Living in the Demon World
THIS TIME ...
...WE'LL PUT THE SPOTLIGHT ON THOSE WHO LIVE IN THE DEMON WORLD'S LEGENDARY LAND OF HYDRA.
SFX: JII (ZOOM)
THIS ALTERNATE SPACE WAS ENTIRELY CREATED BY ITS MASTER, HYDRA HEADS, AND SO...
KASHA (SNAP)
!
...HE'S ABLE TO GO WHEREVER HE LIKES IN IT, WHENEVER HE PLEASES.
OH! DID I WAKE YOU UP?
HEY... HONEY, WHAT DO YOU THINK YOU'RE DOING?
IT WOULD SEEM THAT LATELY HE'S BEEN INTO TAKING PICTURES OF HIS WIFE, NEYN, SLEEPING...
COMING INTO MY ROOM WITHOUT PER-MISSION ...
...IS A VIOLATION OF THE PACT!
WITH HIM DOING THINGS LIKE POKING HIS HEAD IN ON HIS FULLY GROWN DAUGHTER BATHING...
HEY, BELL, DID YOU BY ANY CHANCE EAT MY ICE CREAM?
KAPOON (THUNK)
...HIS TACTLESS BEHAVIOR REALLY BECAME TOO MUCH...
SO HE'S MADE A PACT TO RESPECT HIS FAMILY'S PRIVACY...
YEAH, BUT... WE'RE MARRIED ...
...AND APPARENTLY, THIS NEW HOBBY IS A NO-GO.

FACE: PEEPING TOM

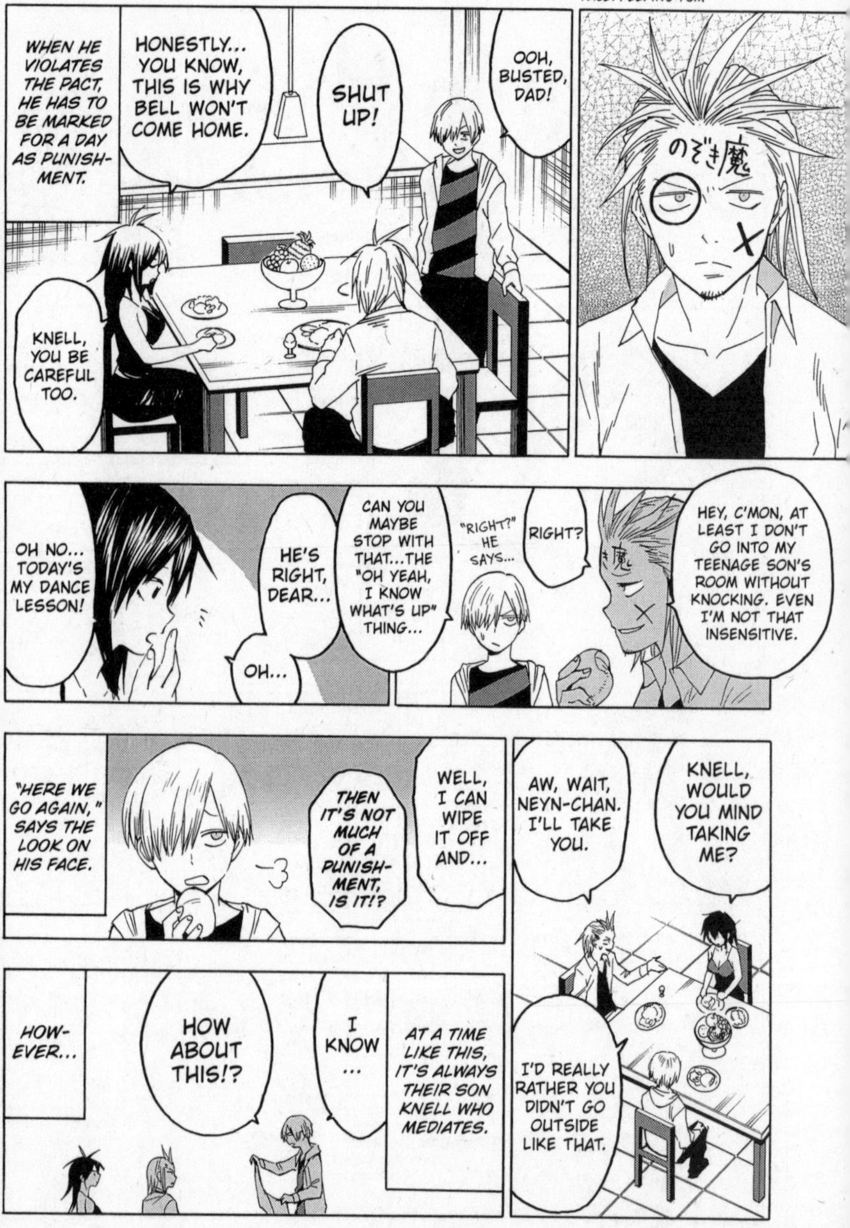
のぞき魔
OOH, BUSTED, DAD!
SHUT UP!
HONESTLY... YOU KNOW, THIS IS WHY BELL WON'T COME HOME.
WHEN HE VIOLATES THE PACT, HE HAS TO BE MARKED FOR A DAY AS PUNISHMENT.
KNELL, YOU BE CAREFUL TOO.
HEY, C'MON, AT LEAST I DON'T GO INTO MY TEENAGE SON'S ROOM WITHOUT KNOCKING. EVEN I'M NOT THAT INSENSITIVE.
RIGHT?
"RIGHT?" HE SAYS...
CAN YOU MAYBE STOP WITH THAT...THE "OH YEAH, I KNOW WHAT'S UP" THING...
HE'S RIGHT, DEAR...
OH...
OH NO... TODAY'S MY DANCE LESSON!
KNELL, WOULD YOU MIND TAKING ME?
AW, WAIT, NEYN-CHAN. I'LL TAKE YOU.
I'D REALLY RATHER YOU DIDN'T GO OUTSIDE LIKE THAT.
WELL, I CAN WIPE IT OFF AND...
THEN IT'S NOT MUCH OF A PUNISHMENT, IS IT!?
"HERE WE GO AGAIN," SAYS THE LOOK ON HIS FACE.
AT A TIME LIKE THIS, IT'S ALWAYS THEIR SON KNELL WHO MEDIATES.
I KNOW...
HOW ABOUT THIS!?
HOWEVER...

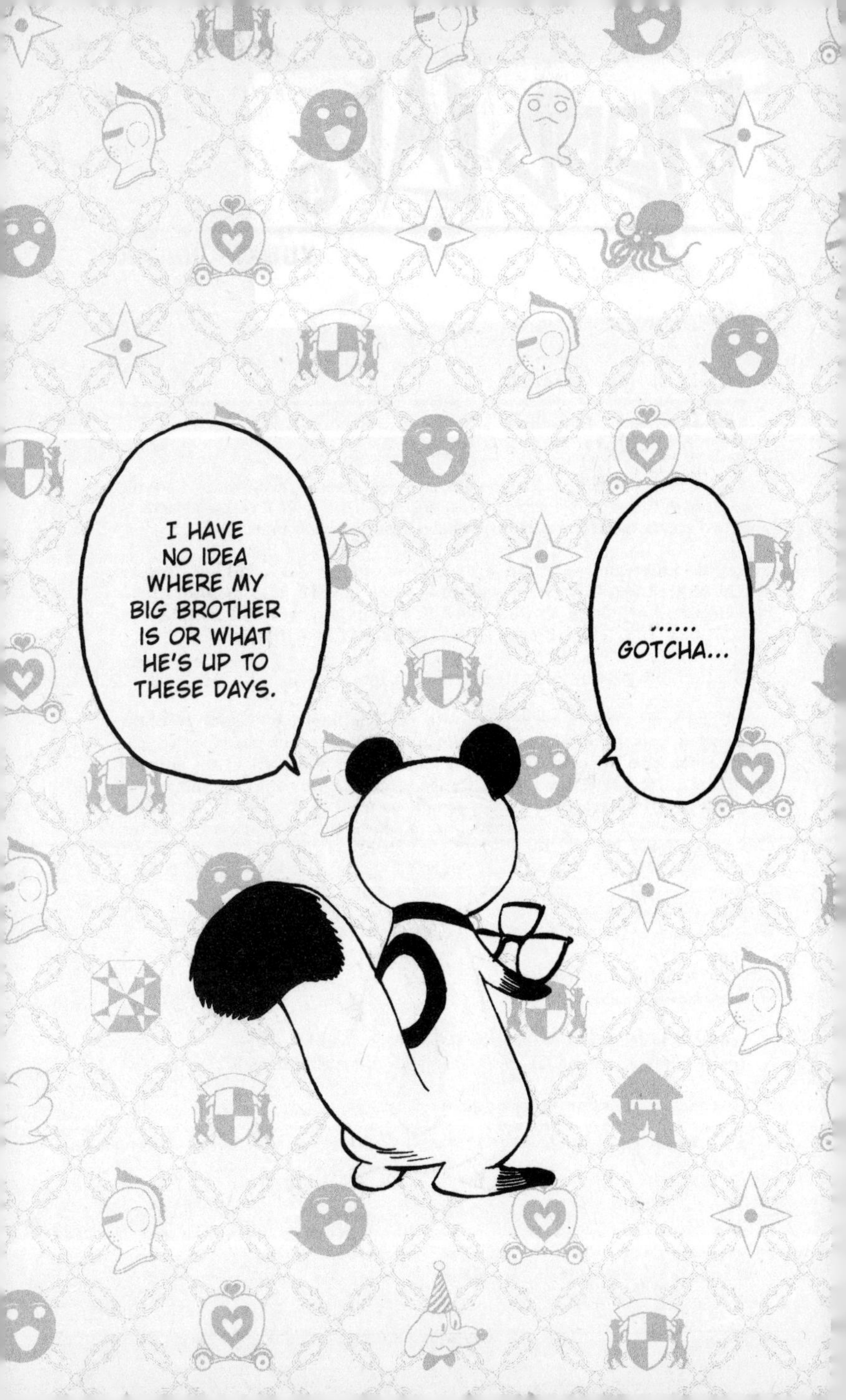

......
GOTCHA...
I HAVE NO IDEA WHERE MY BIG BROTHER IS OR WHAT HE'S UP TO THESE DAYS.

...KI KODAMA

Translation: Melissa Tanaka

Lettering: Alexis Eckerman

BLOOD LAD Volumes 7 and 8 © Yuuki KODAMA 2012, 2013. Edited by KADOKAWA SHOTEN. First published in Japan in 2012, 2013 by KADOKAWA CORPORATION, Tokyo. English translation rights arranged with KADOKAWA CORPORATION, Tokyo, through TUTTLE-MORI AGENCY, INC., Tokyo.

Translation © 2014 by Hachette Book Group, Inc.

Yen Press
Hachette Book Group
1290 Avenue of the Americas, New York, NY 10104

www.HachetteBookGroup.com
www.YenPress.com

Yen Press is an imprint of Hachette Book Group, Inc.
The Yen Press name and logo are trademarks of Hachette Book Group, Inc.

First Yen Press Edition: February 2014

ISBN: 978-0-316-36905-3

10 9 8 7

BVG

Printed in the United States of America